The Beach Boys of Sunset Beach

Part Two

by

Jacqueline DeGroot

©2023 by Jacqueline DeGroot

Published by October Publishing
Cover design: Zak Duff
Format and packaging: Peggy and Jim Grich

Printed in the United States of America

ISBN: 979-8-218-20538-6

This book is a work of fiction. All characters in this book have no existence outside the imagination of the author and have no relation whatsoever to anyone bearing the same name or names except where permission has been granted.

It takes a generous contribution of time to read and check a book for inconsistencies, grammar, and spelling errors. We don't ever get them all, but we get most of the errors, please forgive the ones we miss—as we always miss a few!

Shaw Berke
Bill DeGroot
Peggy Grich
Sandy Raymond

The Kindred Spirit Mailbox

The weathered "post office" by the sea has been operating for almost forty years now. What was started on a fragile sand spit near Tubbs Inlet, between Sunset Beach and Ocean Isle Beach, is now an established landmark that thousands of nature lovers visit annually on Bird Island. Hundreds of photographers and artists have trudged to the west end of Sunset Beach—to the nature preserve of Bird Island, and the mysterious mailbox tucked high into a sand dune. And many a beach walker has rested on the roughhewn driftwood bench that invites you to sit and slow down for a while. Yours truly has even penned a romantic murder mystery involving the Kindred Spirit Mailbox.

Before a sand-shifting storm in late 1997 filled in Mad Inlet near Little River Inlet, at Sunset Beach, caution was needed when venturing to the part of Bird Island that resides in South Carolina. Beachcombers have been stranded by the high tide because they were drawn to the Mailbox and the messages left inside, or were spurred on to leave an immortal message of their own. The inlet is no more, so you can walk to the Mailbox at any time. Watch the tides though; it's a brutal walk at high tide—a most pleasurable one at low or mid-tide.

Notebooks, pens and pencils are kept in the mailbox, replenished by a team of secret helpers, so that visitors are able to leave personal messages while they sit and enjoy the sights and sounds of the waves crashing on the shore. It is an unlikely post box, but over the years the exchange of thoughts and ideas has filled thousands of notebooks.

The messages often express the writer's utter contentment with the paradise found there, with the serene beauty of the place, and with the unspoiled wilderness they can count on finding, year after year. Others delve deep into feelings, sharing emotions that run from overwhelming grief to young, exuberant love. It is a favorite place for men to kneel and present their sweethearts with rings. It is a cathartic place to search your soul and purge your thoughts, or gather them together.

Claudia Sailor, from Hope Mills, North Carolina erected the mailbox in the sand at the edge of the ocean after seeing what she called a mirage. She didn't know the purpose of the recurring vision at the time, but many years later when petitions in the form of signed messages left in the notebooks were pivotal in saving Bird Island from development, and turning it into the coastal reserve that it is today, she finally got her answer. Over the years, the mailbox and its upkeep have been credited to Frank Nesmith. A long time local and the man who helped Claudia shore up the first Kindred Spirit Mailbox in 1981, Frank became her close friend and confidant. Several years later he helped move the mailbox to Bird Island to the North Carolina site. Soon after, he and Claudia ended their relationship, as Frank did not want to start another family. Claudia was younger and wanted children. She married a lawyer who worked for the Attorney General in Raleigh. Sadly, her husband died of a heart attack only a year after they were married. She lived the life of a grieving widow with her kindergarten students becoming her children, and in lonely moments, she read the Kindred Spirit notebooks graciously sent to her by Frank.

Claudia had only visited Sunset Beach, whereas Frank Nesmith has been a permanent resident since 1975. He's been active in the community and devoted to preserving the marshes and the coastline that he walked daily until just a few years ago. Frank, along with a handful of volunteers, has collected and replenished the journals for almost forty years. In 2016 Frank received the Order of the Long Leaf Pine, the Governor's highest honor, for his hard work and dedication to helping preserve Bird Island and making it the sanctuary and coastal preserve that it is today.

Claudia *was* the "Kindred Spirit," the mysterious person who put up the mailbox by the sea. Frank faithfully collected the notebooks and sent them to her, treasures, which she lovingly read and saved. Originally, the mailbox contained notepaper and stamped envelopes that she asked visitors to the mailbox to mail to a Shallotte, North Carolina post office box. She collected them on weekends when she came to the beach to visit Frank. Claudia felt that the anonymity going both ways made the Kindred Spirit universal and transcendent, and that it lent to its mystical otherworldly quality. Few people knew the true identity of the Kindred Spirit.

When Claudia died suddenly in January of 2013, the free-spirited kindergarten teacher left behind a legacy that continues to roll on just as the waves continue to roll in. Frank Nesmith is in his 90s, but he and his family diligently continue to keep the mailbox in the sand up and running. Claudia's mirage is now a famous landmark that many return to and many more discover every year.

People have asked what has become of the notebooks that have been collected over the years. Several have expressed the desire to read a book with a collection of the poignant notes and ramblings. I can tell you that, having read through many of the notebooks, it would be a daunting task to catalogue even a small percentage of the messages. Many different hands write them, and they are written in a vast array of languages. Some are barely legible. And of course, there is no continuity as each missive is either a letter of gratitude, a plea of surrender, a heartfelt prayer, a poem of love, thoughts of desolation, a tribute to a loved one, plaguing inner thoughts, or full blown stories that span page after page after page . . .

How do you get to the Kindred Spirit Mailbox? Due to the acceding nature of the beach and frequent storms, the mailbox is now located in the dunes about a mile and a quarter west of the last Sunset Beach public beach access at 40th Street. There are two benches, and sometimes an American flag on a pole is in evidence. Things are constantly changing at the beach, so the flagpole, the benches, or even the mailbox could be a victim of the next hurricane or washout. It is about an hour's walk from the pier. So put on your Nikes, grab a bottle of water and some sunscreen, and *Just do it!* You won't regret it.

The following book is my best attempt to write a few stories from letters left in the Kindred Spirit Mailbox.

Jacqueline DeGroot

The Beach Boys of Sunset Beach

Part Two

The Cockpit residents and the women who capture their hearts:

Chaz & Mags
Brent & Alyssa
Cam & Tamara
Dev & Gentry
Palo & Trixie
Kyle & Amy
Sean & Sandy
Rutger & Pauline
Alex & Emma
Deke & Shaw
Ryder & Kara

Dev & Gentry

Dev, after all his fraternity brothers had left The Cockpit
to go home after their two-week reunion

July 2019

I had clearly missed my shot with Kara. By the time I got
my courage up, Ryder had already glommed onto her. Next thing
I knew, they were engaged. But it's all right. I saw her wearing
two different sneakers one day and had to wonder about that.

Everybody thinks I'm a hard-ass, and that I'm difficult
to get along with. Okay, that part is true. But it wasn't always
that way.

While I was in Kandahar taking slimy showers and
peeing on my feet for some kind of relief from a pervasive
fungus, I discovered my wife was hooking up with the UPS guy.
The UPS guy for cryin' out loud!

But in retrospect, thinking about it now, it was probably
my own fault. I was always using the computer in the social
hall to order her something special, something I believed was
thoughtful that maybe she might need, using our Amazon Prime
account. Unknowingly, I was sending him to her door every
other day.

He made his move while I was overseas. And he took my
family from me—my wife and my two little girls. She'd been
carrying a boy when she divorced me, but it was his, not mine.

It makes a guy tough, you know? Working day and
night—mostly night for me—for your country and your family.
Learning your craft, honing your skills, and planning for a future
when you can sleep in a bed with your wife again.

I don't sleep with women now. I may take them to bed,

1

but then I'm out of there once the deed is done and we're both happy campers. I know, cliché, cliché. I never have an original thought these days. There really isn't much I care about except working to keep Jack Daniel's in business.

But then on the last day of our reunion at *The Cockpit,* something interesting happened. I met a woman named Gentry and my insides did that flippy thing they did so many years ago when I met my ex at a Stanford mixer. But this time it was in a wilder, more freeing way. I felt myself smiling all the time as I floated through the day, as if led by a bewitching siren—even when she wasn't around, I was happy. By that evening, it felt as if I'd been saved—redeemed by a clowder of cats, as it were.

Lying on my bed, hands behind my head, staring up at the ceiling fan making its slow, lazy revolutions, I remember the morning. Everyone left today. It was the last day of our ten-year reunion. Except for me, I opted to stay another day and fly home tomorrow. I have total recall so I am remembering the chaotic morning in great detail. It makes me grin. Muscles in my jaw that haven't worked for years are straining to come back to life.
As all my frat boys were packing up to leave and go home, I found the culprit that had been stealing everyone's power cords for their electronics.

I spotted the big cat in the upper hallway, coming out of a room, and then walking down the hallway, trailing a long white cord. Naturally I gave chase. Having just returned from the shooting range in Ash, I was climbing the steps to my room to put my gun away. Crouching into hunter mode, I ran after the cat, pointing the gun and shouting for the cat to stop. It didn't.

My shouts alerted my friends and everyone came running to see what the commotion was about, and we all gave chase.

Sean and I cornered the cat on the outside lower level. He was concerned that I had plans to shoot it, so he went into negotiator mode, telling me to, "Put the gun down." To which I responded, "Relax, you idiot. I'm not going to shoot the cat," my exasperation, that he thought I would, evident.

And maybe if he hadn't been around, I just might have. The thought kind of haunts me right now. If I had, everything would have turned out badly, and Gentry wouldn't have been in the picture. We'd have never met.

"Just put the gun down, it makes me nervous," Sean muttered.

I slipped the Glock into my waistband as the cat looked from one person to another, then nonchalantly put its paw on the Hardi-plank siding covering a small access panel. The door popped opened and the cat disappeared behind the opening.

We stood stunned as the rest of my alums arrived on the scene. Only Brent, as the architect of the house, knew that the spring-latched door was the access point to the elevator emergency switches and breakers, and that inside was an encapsulated crawl space that followed the steps up on each side.

Bending and looking inside led to the discovery of five kittens and a cache of all the tech cords that had gone missing over the last two weeks—mangled and chewed.

It was everyone's last day at the beach house and they were all in the process of packing up to leave. Since I had opted to catch a later flight and stay another day, it was decided that this was now my problem to fix.

Left to me to handle the situation, my solution might have been to get a bag and find a well and not bother to track down a rescue organization that would take the cats off my hands. I had not been happy to have this task foisted on me. I don't care for cats. I am a dog person. I actually shot a cat once—one of the big ones while on a hunting trip with my father. He owns a gun manufacturing company and is an avid hunter. And, as a former Army sniper, I admit now that it wasn't a fair competition.

Cam, who was very supportive of local animal rescue efforts, found the number of a shelter and I called it. Then I waited for the rescue people to show up. I expected a team of well-trained cat catchers. What I got was a young woman in a flannel shirt over a torn and taped up tank top wearing jeans, mucked up boots, and a broad brimmed hat.

The moment she removed the hat I was slayed. An abundance of springy chestnut curls fell around her face as she swiped at her damp forehead with her sleeve. She had beautiful cream-colored skin, lending an overall Irish lass appearance to her. Especially as her green eyes flashed in the late afternoon sun and small light copper freckles dusted her nose. I remember that her light coral lips quirked into a broad smile as she asked, "Got kittens?"

I stood and stared at the lovely, farm-fresh, girl that could have just stepped off a Hummel plate depicting a girl feeding chickens.

She'd had to repeat herself. "I was told you had kittens?"

I snapped out of my reverie and asked, "R.A.C.E.?"

"Mmm, actually no. I was there when you called though. They don't have the space for a momma and her kittens right now, so I offered to take them to the Brunswick shelter where I volunteer. My name's Gentry."

I nodded and led the lovely animal rescue lady named

Gentry to where Momma and all her kittens were. Then I helped her get them all into a carrier.

By then I was smitten. I knew what most people thought of me. They thought I was a troublemaker, a mischievous practical joker, a smart man with deadly aim, but also a fun guy to be with. They knew I cared about my friends, that I had been married and divorced and had two little girls, and that now I had rare, short relationships with women. But for some reason, I wanted to get to know this woman whose name meant wellborn—who loved animals, who protected animals—while I hunted them down and killed them to make trophies out of them. I wondered how this would go—if I could even get her to agree to go out on a date with me.

Well she had. And knowing her as I now do, I hadn't given her a choice. I basically paid her for a date. And I am not ashamed to admit that it had worked.

Yes, I had used money to get my way again. And I felt kinda bad about it. But a $5,000 donation to support the shelter got me the date, so I had my foot in the door. I just had to make sure after the evening was over that she didn't slam said door in my face.

She had agreed to dinner. Now it was up to me to find a vegetarian restaurant that was decent, close by, and not too noisy. It seemed to me that Gentry might be a few years younger than I was, but that might not be true. Women had so many ways to disguise their age these days. But if I was a betting man, which I definitely am—she hadn't had a bit of makeup on—maybe lip gloss, but I didn't even think she'd had that.

I Googled "vegetarian restaurants." In all my years coming to Sunset Beach, I never remembered seeing one. I knew there was a decent Thai restaurant with great vegetarian dishes in North Myrtle Beach, but I wasn't sure she'd be comfortable with me driving her that far.

Searching Sunset Beach, Ocean Isle Beach, Calabash,

and Shallotte, I could only find places with vegetarian or vegan options. One coffee café at OIB had specialty vegetarian dishes, but it looked to be geared toward carryout.

I wondered how she would feel about eating soba noodles next to someone who was chowing down on a rare steak? She had specifically said she ate vegetarian, not that it had to be a strictly vegetarian place. Then again, she might be offended if I didn't make the effort to accommodate that one thing for her.

As I strummed my fingers on the countertop with one hand while intermittently scrolling up and down and checking out restaurants with the other, I wondered what Kyle would do in this situation. Well, of course Kyle, a famous world-class chef would just whip up something for her himself.

I took a stroll around the kitchen opening cabinets, freezers, refrigerators . . . hmm. It was pretty obvious after thirty seconds that we were a meat-eating group. I did find a frozen Adobo protein bowl made with whole grains. But how was that going to impress a first date? And besides, there was only one. I would make no points with this woman if I did not eat veggie-based food with her.

I wondered if she would let me take her an hour south to Myrtle Beach proper where there were some great vegetarian options. It would give me more time to talk to her on the way down and back. Might be too far though. I Googled North Myrtle Beach as the location for vegetarian restaurants and found that many restaurants considered seafood, pancakes, and pizza vegetarian. The only restaurant claiming to be vegetarian/vegan closed at 4pm. Geez, wooing this woman with food was going to be hard!

I ended up calling Thai Season in North Myrtle. I had been there before and knew the quality of the food was good and that the service was exemplary. I verified that they had a selection of vegetarian and vegan dishes, asked about their hours, and then reserved a table where at least one seat did not face any other diners. I'd done about as well as I could for our area, unless she agreed to the hour-long drive into Myrtle Beach proper.

Chapter 1
Thai Me Up
Later that Evening

Gentry arrived on time in her little green Kia Soul, dressed in a very short, very cute, lacy red dress that zipped down the front, exposing a tiny bit of cleavage. Her lovely wild hair was tamed with cute red and black clips, her feet buckled into cute strappy sandals. A cute purse hung off her shoulders; it looked as if it was made out of recycled candy wrappers. In a word, she was cute.

"Hey," she said with a small wave when Dev opened the door for her.

"Hey yourself," he said as he opened the door wide so she could come in. He was glad he had opted for casual slacks and a button-down untucked shirt. The color, dark teal, was one a personal shopper for Nordstrom's had once said was his best color. Paired with slate gray slacks and what his friends called his shaggin' loafers, he knew he looked sharp.

He wasn't vain exactly, but he knew he was good looking. Women were always staring at him in restaurants and at airports. His close-cropped thick black hair and perpetual three-day beard enhanced his rugged bad boy look. His penetrating deep blue eyes, framed by inky dark lashes and set off by the shirt he was wearing, didn't hurt anything either.

"You want to have a drink first, before we go?" he gestured with his hand toward the inside of the house.

She looked him up and down and hesitated. Then pursed her lips, closed her eyes and shook her head slightly.

He got the picture. She didn't want to come inside.

Particularly as she knew he was alone now. While they had been busy with the cats she'd seen everyone leaving the house with luggage and calling out their good-byes to him.

He didn't acknowledge the issue. Just stepped out and closed the door behind him. Then he pressed a series of buttons in a metal panel by the door to set the alarm.

He led her to his Lexus SUV parked in the circular drive. "Okay if I drive?" he asked.

"Sure. That would be great."

He decided to address the elephant in the room. "Is it because you don't drink or that you don't know me well enough to drink alone in my house?"

"Oh, I drink."

"So just being cautious?"

She smiled over at him. "Well all I really know about you is that you don't particularly like cats, you have a lot of handsome male friends who sleep over, and apparently you have a lot of money at your disposal. You could be a drug dealer or maybe you run a male escort service. Those guys could be male strippers and you own the agency they work for. They could be pro athletes, for all I know. I don't really follow sports."

He laughed as he opened her door and waited for her to climb inside before closing it.

"My frat boys would be flattered." Once he was on the driver's side and belted in, his started the truck and began explaining about his Stanford days and how he and nine of his former college dorm mates had pooled their money to have the beach house built. And now they meet for a two-week reunion each July. He added that even though they didn't see each other often, they still kept in touch by phone text, and email throughout the year. "We're still very close. Several of us, the ones that can get away from jobs and families, go skiing during the winter."

"I don't have those types of friendships," she said. "My best friends are animals and they keep getting adopted out."

He turned to give her a raised eyebrow before turning

back to the road. "No human friends?"

"I have a few friends at school. We do labs and study together, sometimes we have drinks, but we're all very busy with our jobs and volunteer work."

"Where do you go to school?"

"I'm doing a program through North Carolina College of Veterinary Medicine, this summer. I've been working as a vet tech, and helping out at the shelters. I also help with several fund raising and adoption events. I'm a co-chair for a really big one that's in a few weeks. I'm way too busy to keep friendships going right now."

"So, no boyfriend either?"

"I had one back home last year but he's out of the picture now."

"Found a new girlfriend?"

"Nah. He's in the seminary now, decided to become a priest."

"Wow!"

"Yeah, it kinda does something to your ego when that happens." She turned in her seat and gave him a bemused self-deprecatory smile where her lips quirked down in a comical way. Then with a bewildered shrug she chuckled, "*Que será será,* as they say."

"Don't really know what to say to that. Except give him a big thank you from me."

She laughed and pulled down the visor as the sun streamed in when they pulled onto Route 17. "Where are we going?"

"Thai Season, if that's okay. It's the only place I could find where I could be sure the vegetarian dishes would be good ones."

"Oh, I like that place!"

"Good. Me too. Where else do you usually go for vegetarian food? There doesn't seem to be many places around here."

"Oh, lots of places have salads, and I'm good with

that. But usually I just get something premade from Lowe's or Publix. If I have time, I make a big batch of something from one of my cookbooks on the weekend. I freeze the leftovers in small containers, so there's always something I can pop in the microwave."

"My friend Kyle is a professional chef and although he's not a vegetarian, he makes some great vegetarian dishes. He just got married last year and he and his wife Amy have a bunch of kids they've adopted so he's working on a kid-friendly eat-your-veggies type of cookbook right now. Should be out in the fall. I can get you a copy."

She looked over at him, "Kyle? As in Kyle Merritt?"

"Yeah, he's one of my frat boys, he's one of the owners of *The Cockpit.*"

"Cockpit?"

"The name of our beach house."

"You're all pilots?"

"Nooo . . ." he dragged out the word then hesitated, "let's just say we all have a particular appendage in common."

She laughed, and then laughed even harder. When the chuckles bubbling out of her didn't seem to have an end to them, he said, "It's not that funny."

"Just imagining a group of women naming a beach house after their . . . umm . . . privates." She tilted her head up and thought some more. "Hmmm. Nope. Nothing works that would be legal. We're not that bold. We'd have to opt for something really tame, like *Hen House.*"

He gave her a sideways frown, "That's the best you can do?"

"*Chicks with Eggs?*"

He snorted. "None of you would ever get laid."

"Well, you come up with something better."

"How about *Pussy Galore?*"

She snickered, but ended up smiling. "Not bad. Might even be legal, not sure."

"Or even better—*Snatches*."

She lost it with that one and had to put her hand over her mouth to keep from laughing like a chimpanzee. When she stopped laughing she huffed, "How did we get off on this, we were talking about Kyle Merritt."

"Seriously," he looked at her, his eyebrows arching as he chided her, "Get off on this?"

She blushed, her smooth pale skin acquiring a soft rosy tinge. Along her hairline, her cheeks, her neck, and her modest cleavage it was like watching the glorious color of shame taint her in all the right places. He almost went out of his lane.

"I meant off topic," she said. "Kyle Merritt is one of the best TV chefs ever!"

"I know. You should see our kitchen—state of the art everything."

"I'll bet your spices are alphabetized."

"Yup, each in its own hand painted apothecary jar with a locking clasp. Handmade in Italy by a ceramics shop just for him."

"I bet he makes amazing meals for you guys."

"You would win that bet. It's always the highlight of our reunion having him cook for us. It's an amazing thing to watch, he's quite the showman."

Dev pulled into a parking spot in front of the restaurant. "Well, here we are! Now I have to ask, are you vegan or just vegetarian? And do you eat any seafood?"

"I'm vegetarian with a vegan bent."

"Well that makes it easy." His sarcasm not lost on her. He walked around and opened her door and she continued.

"I don't eat meat and I don't eat things that cause animals to be locked up and mistreated."

"So . . . free range eggs, and organic milk from a cow that's been home on the range as well?"

"Funny. But yes. Whatever the animals give freely to us without any stress put on them, I'm fine with."

"I'm guessing just catching a fish might be a tad stressful for them?"

"Yeah! They flop around hurting themselves trying to breathe and basically suffocate . . ."

"I won't mention lobster then . . ."

"Would you like to have your arms and legs rubber banded then dropped into a big pot of boiling water?"

He winced, "I knew I shouldn't have brought that up . . . so, fruits, vegetables, grains, and dairy." He opened the door to the restaurant for her.

"Mr. Dev!" a short Asian woman in a lovely silk embroidered jacket called out to him. "Welcome back!"

Gentry looked over at him her eyes wide, wondering about the familiarity.

"Restaurant owners tend to recognize you when you come with nine very hungry males who drink a lot and leave big tips."

"Where Mr. Merritt?" she asked and Gentry laughed.

"Or if you come in with a famous Top Chef."

They were ushered to the back, and when he pulled out a chair facing the wall for her, she tilted her head in question.

"I figured you'd want to face away from the room rather than watch someone desiccate a chicken."

"Well, that was thoughtful. But I'm not as bad as all that." Still she took the proffered seat and faced the beautifully decorated wall.

To his surprise she ordered a glass of white wine. He upped the order by changing it to a full bottle and they ordered. Neither needed a menu as they both had their favorite—and it turned out to be the same noodle dish—with a vegetarian variation for him.

When the bottle was opened and both glasses filled, they toasted, "To feral cats and their kittens, everywhere . . . and their rescuers," he added.

She smiled and sipped thoughtfully, then took another,

fuller sip.

"You do know that healthy grapes were squashed to death for that?"

She almost spit out her wine, getting her napkin to her mouth just in time to keep from embarrassing herself by disgorging wine all over her blouse.

"Are you always like this?" she asked as she swiped at her mouth and chin.

He noticed the napkin had no lipstick smear on it. It was just about the sexiest thing, knowing that her lips were naked.

"What, smart? Charming?"

"Annoying."

"Then yes. Ask my friends. They will tell you I can be very annoying. Also very witty, kind, and just generally fun to be with."

"So let's start with some negative traits. What's your worst?"

He thought about it for a moment and bit out, "Jealousy. I don't share well."

"Sounds as if you had a bad experience with that."

"Yeah, I'm divorced. My wife was unfaithful while I was fighting a brutal war in Afghanistan. I have two little girls, Sadie and Maggie."

"That's a shame. Do you see them often?"

"Yeah, for a week at least every other month or so during the school year and for a whole month during the summer. Plus, we Facetime a couple of times a week. But it's not just the kids that I miss."

"You still miss your wife?"

"No, hell no. I miss coming home to someone though, and them coming home to me."

"You need a dog."

"I had a dog. She took that too. Henley died a few years back."

"So, get another one. There are plenty of rescues that

13

need a good home."

"I travel too much."

Just then their food came, one dish at a time. First a small papaya salad with a summer roll, then a bowl of tofu and vegetable soup, and finally a veggie version of Drunken Noodles for both of them. She surprised him by using chopsticks to eat both the salad and noodle dish. Then she surprised him with the answer for her proficiency using them.

"When you don't eat meat, you get finished with your meal faster—no cutting off the bone, no cutting into smaller pieces, no prolonged chewing. To keep myself from finishing first all the time, I often use chopsticks." She had opened her candy wrapper purse and pulled out another paper wrapped package containing a set of disposable wooden chopsticks and offered it to him.

He declined by waving his fork and saying, "We'll be here all night if I use them." Then thought to himself, that would have actually been a fine idea. "You would have used them even if we were eating Italian?"

"Sure. People stare sometimes. But then, they always stare."

"I imagine so. It's because you're so beautiful."

"Thank you. But it's usually because of my hair. There's too much of it."

He smiled and shook his head. "Women who are truly beautiful always seem to have to find a flaw where there is none. Why is that?"

"We live in a society where it's hard not to compare yourself with others."

"Well, I find it hard to believe you would find yourself lacking when comparing yourself to anyone."

"I'm told men do it too."

"Yes, but we don't give a rat's ass." He threw his arms out wide. "Take me as I am or find a better version. I've learned not to defend my body."

She made a huffing sound. "Don't tell me you've accepted the body you were born with, because I see signs that you work out."

He gave her a smarmy smile. "Oh, you've been checking me out have you?"

"No more than you've been checking me out. Answer one question, honestly."

"Okay."

"How many times have you mentally pulled down this zipper?" She toyed with the little metal tab situated half an inch below where her breasts were being pushed together because of the form-fitting dress.

"Honestly?"

"Yes."

"I lost count." He glanced at his watch. "We've been here an hour, 60 minutes. Using my teeth to drag it all the way down to where it ends and your dress falls open would probably take 12 seconds or 5 times a minute, so 300 times, give or take."

"That's impressive."

"It's math. I'm good with numbers."

"Well, zip me back up please. I would like to use the ladies room."

"My pleasure." He made a show of clamping his teeth together and purposefully dragged his eyes up from where he could just see the zipper at her waist. His eyes tracked up, past her breasts to the neckline, then to her lips—where they remained until she stood and disappeared down the back hallway.

Their server came to clean away the dishes and to ask about dessert.

"I sure hope so," he said, completely confusing the server who went back to the kitchen and brought back two complimentary dishes of rolled ice cream drizzled with chocolate.

When Gentry came back to the table he would have sworn that the zipper had been lowered a quarter of an inch. There was a light freckle visible that he hadn't seen before. He would never have missed seeing that.

"Ooh, rolled ice cream! Thank you!"

In his opinion, her smile was worth the price of every scoop of ice cream served at Broadway at the Beach that night; an amount that he knew would be substantial.

When the bowls were empty and the bill paid, his mind raced for a way to postpone ending their date. She must have been thinking the same thoughts as she piped up, "Hey, if you're not in a hurry to get home, you wanna go by and check on the momma and her kittens?"

"Sure. But you're hardly dressed for visiting a kennel."

"I keep a change of clothes in my car. We could go back to your house and each of us could change first."

"You'll actually come in this time?"

"I want to see Kyle Merritt's kitchen."

He laughed. "It wouldn't be the first time Kyle seduced a woman with his saucepans."

He opened her door and watched her climb inside. Before he closed it, she put her open hand on his chest. "Just for the record, it's not Kyle I want to be seduced by."

He had to hold in his gasp. But he couldn't help his nose flaring and his eyes going wide. Did he really have a shot with this woman? It sounded like he might.

Chapter 2
A Cheeseball Lesson

He was not surprised that she had to run her fingers over every spice jar, touch every burner on the stove, open each oven door, look through every glass refrigerator panel door, stroke the faucets in the oversized farm-kitchen sink—the act of which almost stopped his heart from beating.

She opened and shut every cabinet, tsking when she discovered the cache of open snack packs and cereal bags in one cabinet. Granted most bags had clips, but some had just been folded over and left there.

"This is what draws mice and rats, which draw cats, who have a romantic field mouse, Doritos, and cheese ball meal together . . . and then have kittens. The cries of hungry kittens draw coyotes, foxes, and bobcats, and even cougars on some beaches. If you're not going to winter here, you need to get rid of this stuff. Or seal it in plastic totes."

"I'll take care of it before I leave. Promise."

"Good. Now where can I change?"

He walked a few paces and pointed past the big theater room that served as a gathering room, rec room, and game room. "Powder room is down there, first door on the right."

He watched her pick up the rucksack she'd taken from the Kia, and walk down to the bathroom. Heard her close the door and saw the light flick on under the door. He waited. Hmmm. No scream. Now that surprised him.

"Nice cat!" she called out. "I don't think you'll see any leopards on this beach though, no matter how many pretzels or Pringles you leave for them."

He smiled. To his knowledge, she was the only person, male or female, who had not screamed in fright at the realistic mural of a leopard ready to pounce in the first floor powder room. Bless Amy, the muralist and painter Brent had hired. Her realistic depictions of wildlife always looked uncannily real.

"Well, it's good to know that we will have the only leopard on Sunset," he called back.

She came out in an old gray t-shirt with duct tape covering her breasts in the area where her nipples would be. She had worn some similar tape stripes on her t-shirt this afternoon.

"What is that on your shirt?"

"Duct tape."

"I know that, but why?"

"Kittens have tiny sharp claws, and tiny sharp teeth. And they like to climb up onto your chest, digging in as they go. Then kneading whenever they find a soft place they like, usually on an upper swell of a tender breast. The duct tape is to protect my bra cups from getting torn and my breasts from getting all scratched up."

"Man, you think of everything." That's all he could think of to say as he was picturing his own hands kneading those firm mounds.

"Experience. Lacy bras and knit tops. Not good around cats. Ready to go?"

He looked down at himself. "This'll be fine."

"You sure?" she seemed dubious. "You're likely to be sitting on the floor or on the ground."

"It's okay." He looked down at his $100 Elastane Untuckit shirt and $500 Burberry chinos and knew he was down to his last clean outfit. He liked to travel light; counting out the exact amount of clothing he'd need for each trip. Since he was supposed to leave in the morning, and hadn't been planning on dinner out tonight, this was the last set of clothes unless he did laundry tonight. He'd never used the top-of-the-line, electronic monster machines in the laundry room. And figuring out how to use the ultra hi-tech electronic control boards seemed like a time consuming project.

He quickly reasoned that, at times, he'd spent more than $500 on a date. This date with Gentry was worth way more than that. So he'd sacrifice his stretchy, traveling pants and perfect fitting comfortable shirt if he had to, adding, "These have seen better days, any way." Mentally it flashed through his mind that he had just paid the credit card bill for them and that they were practically brand new.

"Alrighty then. You want to follow me?"

"Either that or I can bring you back then follow you home."

"I am not sleeping with you tonight, Dev. Not saying I wouldn't want to. But I like to get to know someone before that happens. And often, I don't always like what I see and it doesn't happen. You should know that. I am particular in that department."

"Glad to hear it. Me too." And he gave her a winning smile that belied that last part. "Still, I'll drive you."

"That's a lot of extra driving. Just follow me, okay?"

"Whatever you say. I aim to please."

"And I am sure that you do," she said with a sexy wink. Then she sashayed out the door in front of him, showing off her fabulous jean-clad butt.

He waited until he was in his truck to groan.

Chapter 3
Helter Skelter Shelter

When they got to the shelter, Gentry threw a coarse blanket in the corner of the cement pad and Dev settled himself on it. He was against the wall with his legs stretched out in front of him watching her coo to the kittens. Rounding one up, she dropped it into his lap and then handed him a tiny baby bottle. "See if you can get her to drink this. And maybe you can come up with a name for her."

As the tiny kitten kneaded his expensive slacks, digging sharp claws into the flesh of his thighs in the process, and barely avoiding crucial places, he forced himself to wrap his hand around the ball of fur and lift her up off of him. He had never held a cat or a kitten. He was surprised how soft she was. How clean. She did not have a bad smell about her as he'd expected. In fact, it reminded him of his youth, when he would wake up early at the lake house in Kentucky, see the mist rising and take in a deep breath—woods and moss blending with the smell of his grandmother's Ivory Soap smell still fresh on his face.

He lifted her higher and held her face up to his, saw how beautiful her tiny blue-green eyes were. And what a cute pink nose and mouth she had. She licked the side of his thumb. That was a surprise. The surface of her tongue felt like fine sandpaper. And apparently she liked his thumb, quite a lot.

"While she's licking you would be a good time to put the bottle in her mouth," Gentry said as she managed to feed two kittens at once.

With the kitten in one hand and the bottle in the other, he put the two together.

"Geez, haven't you ever fed a baby?"

"Actually no."

"Try to put her on her side a little, it'll be easier to feed her that way."

When that didn't work, Gentry stopped what she was doing and took the kitten from him, crooked his arm and moved it into his chest, then plopped the kitten down so she was facing up and was tucked into his body. She led his hand that held the miniature bottle to the kitten's mouth and the kitten began to greedily lick at it. Dev's body stiffened and his eyes widened, but he tried not to give away the fact that this simple act of feeding a kitten was unnerving him.

As the kitten continued to find ways to get some nourishment into her mouth, Dev had to marvel at how bizarre an experience this was for him. A funny thought occurred to him. If she only knew the lengths he was going to for what crassly boiled down to getting into her panties. And remembered the name he'd come up with for a beach house filled with women— *Snatches*. He fought back a hilarious burst of laughter, only managing to turn it into a choking fit at the last moment.

"You okay? You're not allergic are you?" The concern in her voice was touching, considering what he'd just been thinking.

"No, don't think so. I'm fine, just new to this."

"I find it relaxing. Makes you stop and appreciate the simpler things."

"And you don't get paid for this at all?" He found that odd and extremely interesting at the same time. In his world people didn't volunteer for things. There was always an angle that led to money somewhere. To cover up his thoughtlessness, he added, "I mean you've given up your whole day and night."

"Well, technically, I would not have had to give up my night. If I hadn't gone out to dinner with you, I might have just taken them all home for the night and put out some bowls for them to knock over."

"Can't the mother feed them?"

"Maybe in a few days. Right now she's in no condition

to. She's barely keeping herself alive. And by the time she's better, they will be used to getting their meals easier than nursing would be, so they may not take to it again. It is what it is. We'll do whatever we have to as long as we have to."

"Don't you have a real job? Sorry. I mean a paying job?"

"Oh yes. I'm a vet tech and a dog walker during the off-season. I am actually one exam away from my DVM. What is it you do?"

Fish or cut bait, he thought before answering honestly. Something told him it would be important for their future for him to be forthright with her. She didn't seem to be the kind of person who would stay in the social circle of anyone who would lie to her. "I'm an arms dealer."

"Artificial? Mechanical?" she said, her face scrunched up as she tried to make sense of his answer.

He lost it. His laughter peeled from the ceiling of their little kenneled area. He almost dislodged the kitten tucked into his side and had to secure her with his other hand. Again, he marveled at how soft and downy she was. Like a puffball that he used to watch his mother use to apply face powder when she sat in front of her mirrored vanity table.

When he could catch his breath and settle back to feeding the kitten, he said, "No. Guns actually."

Her eyes bugged wide and her eyebrows rose as if he'd said he sold heroin on the street corner to first graders. "You sell guns?"

"Don't look like that. I don't sell to the cartels. I am a legitimate gun dealer, my family manufactures them and I sell them—to the military, to the police, to sporting associations, to stores that sell to hunters and to people who have permits to have them."

He watched as she visibly drew in a deep breath, dragged her eyes over his entire body, then closed them for what seemed like an eternity. He knew he had to change the subject and fast.

"I have a name for my kitten. Puffball."

Her eyes popped open and she looked at the kitten that was now asleep in his crotch. She smiled. "Aww, that's sweet. I like that. Did you mean what you said?"

He was confused. "Mean what I said?"

"That she was your kitten."

"Oh, no no! Just that she was my *assigned* kitten. You know, to feed and to name."

Her smile became a sideways pout of unhappiness. "Oh, I just thought . . . well . . . one down."

"I couldn't possibly own a pet. I travel too much."

"Lots of people who travel have cats. In fact, they are the perfect pets to have if you travel."

"I mean *travel*, like to Europe, Japan, Canada, places I stay for weeks at a time."

"Oh, well that won't work then. Cats can be left alone for a few days but not weeks."

She had finished with all her kittens and was now lining them up alongside their mother in the large screened-in area. "Well, I think they're down for the night. I'll come back in the morning to check on them. I should go home now. I have early labs."

He handed over a resistant Puffball. She had dug her claws into his pants again, and in a critical area. "Umm, I think she's latched on."

"Here, let me help," she said and got up to lean over to help untangle the kitten's claws from the pants material. The mere act of having Gentry's fingers moving over his crotch area—the visual image or the tactical sensation—caused a reaction. One she hadn't been ready for.

"Oh!" She almost tumbled back from the squatting position she was in, but he reached out and caught her elbow in time and managed to steady her. He also managed to catch the kitten in the fist of his other hand, which he immediately loosened at her sharp cry of distress.

Embarrassed, but not shamed by his impressive reaction

to her hands fumbling around with the kitten stuck in his lap, he distracted her by handing over the kitten. "Good night, Puffball," he murmured, and was surprised he had an urge to press his lips to the fur on top of her head. He did not however, as he did not like cats.

They both stood up. His hard on had abated a bit so he was somewhat presentable. With the kittens secure in the caged area, he shoved his hands into his pockets and faced her. "Can I see you again?" he asked.

It occurred to him in that moment that he had never had to ask that of any women he had ever met. They all had wanted to go home with him or to take him home with them after a date. And until things got . . . complicated or off in some way, they had always wanted more.

He could tell before she answered that this one did not want to go home with him, or vice versa. He reached into his pocket for the check he had already made out for $5,000 and put it in her hand.

She looked down at it and stared, eyes unbelieving as she slowly shook her head. "I didn't think . . ."

"That I'd honor my word?"

"Well it is a lot of money . . ."

"It will get Puffball a good home."

"It will get many Puffballs a good home, many Rovers too."

"It's a good cause."

"Still, it's a lot of money for just one date . . ."

"Does that mean you'd consider another?" He'd grab at any chance to see her again. And he'd cancel his flight as many times as he had to so he could get to know her better.

She looked up and her eyes met his. He kept his face impassive, as if it didn't matter to him one way or the other, but he let his eyes tell her that that it did. That it mattered a lot.

"I have a class and labs in the morning, but I'm free tomorrow afternoon after I check back on these little fellas," she said, indicating the sleeping mother in her crate, separate from the others in the pen. "I think of them as my responsibility since I rescued them. I like to come and help take care of my animals, play with them and whatnot until they get adopted out."

He jumped at the opening, "I could meet you here and help you with them, then afterward I could take you for a gelato, or a banana split." Then as an afterthought he said, "That is if you eat gelato. Obviously, we won't know where the eggs came from."

"That sounds nice. And yes, I eat gelato. I'm not all the way vegan. I'm good with eggs and milk products. So yes, I would like to have an afternoon ice cream treat with you."

"Great! I have a place in mind that I think you'll like."

He walked her to her car, held the door, and then when she was inside, he pulled the seat belt out to hand to her. He watched as she turned in her seat to clip it and then he gently closed the door. He waved at her through the glass before walking to his truck, getting inside and following her out of the compound.

At the gate, he watched as she got out of her car, pulled one side of the gate toward the other and latched them together.

Then she surprised him by walking over to his opened window, gripping the sill with both hands and smiling up at him, "I think that a wonderful Thai meal with such good company, and a $5,000 donation deserves a goodnight kiss. And I have to admit to being curious about what it would be like to be kissed by you. I've never been kissed by an arms dealer, artificial, mechanical or weaponly, if that's even a word."

He was out of his truck and standing in front of her in a flash. He pulled her into his arms, leaned her back in an exaggerated theatrical manner, and covered her surprised mouth with his.

Chapter 4
This Kiss, This Kiss

She closed her eyes and felt the press of his mouth on hers. Then parted her lips when his tongue ran along the seam in a silent plea for entry.

She let him in and he lost himself in the sweet taste of vanilla, reminiscent of the decadent ice cream roll they'd had. He let everything fall away as he savored her, allowing his tongue to tangle with hers. He delved deeper, as she gave his lips and tongue tacit permission to explore.

When she moaned, he felt his body tighten and his heart speed up. The musical strain and the words *This Kiss, This Kiss* ran through his head. He wanted this woman and more of her kisses.

"Mmm," she moaned when he pulled back and their lips separated. He was utterly pleased with the dazed expression on her face. And when her eyes drifted opened, he fell into the abyss of a dewy-eyed blue cerulean sea. His hand cupped her jaw and he drew her close for another. This one was more about savoring her lips, feeling her softness, inhaling the spicy fragrance of her hair, and claiming her mouth. *Mine.*

"I think the word you were looking for was weaponry."

"What?" In her lust-filled daze, she had lost the thread of their conversation.

"The word is weaponry, not weaponly."

"Oh. Yes, of course. Arms dealer. "

Leave her wanting more, he said to himself. He made sure she was standing well, then walked her back to her car and said, "See you here tomorrow at two. Or I could follow you home now so I could pick you up there instead."

"I'll just meet you here."

"Still not comfortable with me?"

She shook her head, "It's not that. I live in an old broken down bungalow at the end of a gravel and dirt road. Unless you go 1 mile per hour, it will ruin the paint on your Lexus."

"It's a rental, but even if it weren't, I would chance it."

"I can't let you do that. My old 'Soul' has hundreds of paint chips from that pea gravel road. No way am I letting that happen to a new Lexus."

"Okay," he whispered as he stroked the side of her cheek with his fingertips.

He saw her safely inside her Kia, and then followed her until they reached the main road. He smiled when she honked goodbye, and they both turned in a different direction.

He pressed a button on his phone and asked Siri to use Pandora to play Faith Hill's *"This Kiss, This Kiss."*

When it was cued up and playing, he sang the song with her. Over and over again, until he drove over the Sunset Beach Bridge, and a little over a mile later, reached *The Cockpit.*

Chapter 5
Big Shot to Little Shot

Dev was on the phone the next morning rearranging plans and rescheduling appointments. He had planned to be on a plane home today, but meeting Gentry had changed those plans. Now all he wanted to do was to be with her. Talk with her. Feed and play with her and those darned kittens. Only this time, he was going to wear jeans. First thing this morning he'd unpacked his suitcase and washed some of the dirty clothes that he had been taking home for his housekeeper to either launder or take to the dry cleaners.

His phone rang as he was getting dressed to leave to meet Gentry. He saw it was his dad, who he had tried to call earlier, but had only been able to leave a message. "Hi Dad. Thanks for calling me back."

"Hey Li'l Shot." Since his dad had always been Big Shot, he'd been dubbed Little Shot as a toddler. The name had stuck, even through it was far from apropos now. "What's up?"

"Not comin' back today. Gonna do some work from here then leave on Wednesday instead."

"What about the Knoxville meeting?"

"I'm going to let Peter handle that one. He's coming along fine with his training. Some time getting out there and into the stores with the managers and buyers will boost his confidence. I even think he's going to be ready for the big show in September."

"I think that's a good plan. He's going to be a real asset to the company in the years to come. I love that he was an Olympic medalist in shooting. Buyers are impressed with that kinda shit."

"Yeah, I think so too."

"So . . . hmmm, what's keeping you there?"

"Mmmm. A girl."

"Well hallelujah! She pretty?"

"Pretty doesn't even begin to describe her, Dad. She's gorgeous."

His dad let out a loud sigh, "Not another empty-headed stunner, I hope."

"No Dad. This one's smart. And kind. She's studying to be a vet. In fact, she's taking some kind of big test right now. She volunteers at the local animal shelters."

"Well that's great!"

"She comes with some challenges though."

"Don't they all. What are her issues?"

"Well, due to her calling and her love of animals, she's a vegetarian."

There was silence on the other end of the line.

Dev took a deep breath and continued, "And you might as well know, she's not particularly enthralled with my occupation with regard to hunters killing animals."

Still silence.

"So, I won't be bringing her home anytime soon Dad."

His dad finally spoke. "I get that."

"Yeah. Your trophy wall will give her as Mom would say, 'apoplexy.'"

"You gonna be able to reconcile your differences? Li'l Shot, you like a good Rib-Eye better'n anyone I know."

"We'll have to see. Right now I'm not trying to reconcile our differences. I want to see where this can go first."

"You gonna give up meat, son?"

"I dunno, Dad. I suppose I can live without it for a while. And it wouldn't do me any harm to eat healthier. I'm not even sure she'd require it. I just want to see where this goes. And hell, you gave up smoking for Mom."

"Yeah . . . well, that was because I fell in love with her."

"That maybe the case here too, Dad."

Dev sighed as an acknowledging harrumph came over

the line and with unspoken agreement, they both disconnected.

A few minutes later, Dev's phone pinged with a text. It was from Big Shot. *Follow your heart boy. Ain't no cheeseburger better than the love of a good woman being in your bed come nighttime.*

Dev laughed out loud. Big Shot had the right of it.

He finished dressing and left the house. He had allowed himself extra time to stop at Pet Smart in Shallotte to get a few toys for the kittens to play with. Some women you wooed with flowers. He was betting that this woman would react better to a ball of yarn, a plush mouse on a string, a laser light, and a big ass bag of wholesome kibble.

Chapter 6
Batman, Puffball & The Shack

When Gentry got to the shelter she was shocked to see Dev already inside the enclosure along with one of the other volunteers, playing with the kittens as if he'd been around kittens all his life. Which she now knew, he definitely had not.

He sat on the concrete pad with his legs out in front of him with Puffball in his lap reaching up to grab at a tiny stuffed mouse dangling from a string. A long braided rope with bells attached to it was entertaining the other kittens.

Gentry unlatched the door and slipped inside. "Hey there. Where'd all this come from?" Then she laughed as Puffball swung at the mouse and missed and ended up doing a summersault into a water dish. The cat shook her head in surprise, trying to get her bearings as water dripped from her dazed face.

Dev thought it was pretty funny too, but took pity and reached for her. He dried her face against his t-shirt. It was the first time she'd seen him in a form-fitting shirt and his muscled chest and arms were quite impressive. This was a man who worked out in a very serious way. You didn't get that kind of definition without endlessly lifting weights.

"I stopped at the pet store. They had an enormous supply of cat toys. I had to rein myself in."

Lisa, one of the other volunteers added, "Yeah, he reined himself in on the toys, but take a look in the office. We have enough dog and cat food stacked in there for a month."

"Awww Dev, that was so sweet of you." She plopped down beside him and took the soggy-faced Puffball from him. She lifted her up with one hand and touched her nose to the cat's. "Are you trying to make this man your Daddy, little one?"

"Mmm, no." Dev said.

"I don't see you playing so much with the others . . ."

"She's special. She's the runt."

"She may be the smallest, but tomorrow she's scheduled for spaying. The others will get neutered, which is not quite as involved."

Dev was visibly shaken at the idea of that. "So young?"

"They heal faster that way. And they can't be adopted out until they have their surgery. I saw that there were a lot of online inquiries this morning. White kittens with blue eyes are hard to come by. A few more days of hand feeding them and they can be adopted out."

"Don't they get to be with their momma any longer than that? Where is she any way?""

Lisa spoke up, "Unfortunately, the momma is not doing very well, Dev. She has a urinary infection and some kidney issues. She's also had some parasite infestation for a while. Her numbers were not good this morning. She's on a drip right now and in isolation."

"Is she going to be okay?" The concern in Dev's voice was touching.

Sadly, Gentry had come up against these types of problems with feral cats all too often, so she knew better than to assure him that all would be well. It was more likely she would succumb to the infection and parasitic damage to her organs even with massive doses of antibiotics. A full recovery was not the norm in these cases. And the shelter could not afford to throw away a lot of money on a case like this.

Lisa had no qualms about relaying the facts and touching on the heartless truth though. "Probably not, Dev. According to the vet, this was not her first litter, probably her third or fourth. And being a feral cat, she's lived on whatever she could find. On the beaches, that usually means mice, birds, or if you're too old or pregnant to hunt efficiently—trash bins. People's garbage cans when they've been on vacation have very little in the way of nutrition—so she's deficient in many ways. And in the summer months the garbage itself could be rotten and full of hideous things like maggots. It's going to take some powerful drugs to rid her of intestinal parasites and her heart just might not be able to take it. To put it bluntly, she's a mess."

"So what's going to happen to the kittens? Doesn't she need to teach them things to get along in the world?"

Lisa was just warming up to the subject so Gentry let her have at it. It would spare her having to divulge the facts of life for the world of animal rescue. "These cats will go to homes where they'll become someone's pet, so likely indoor cats for the most part. They won't have to find food; it'll be in a bowl on the floor somewhere. They won't have to go outside to process the food; they'll have litter boxes. They won't have litters of their own to take care of as they'll be neutered or spayed before leaving the shelter. All they will have to do is clean themselves with their tongues so they will look cute and be soft and cuddly, and entertain their owners with their adorable antics. Oh, and to also annoy them with trying to trip them all the time, especially around steps."

Gentry nodded her affirmation. "In fact, today we're going to try to get them to lap up some milk instead of bottle feeding it to them. Once they're eating out of a bowl, the next step is kibble and occasionally some wet food, then they'll be ready for a new home."

Gentry opened the bag she was carrying and took out what looked to be five small empty margarine containers. She filled each one part way, just enough to coat the bottom, with a tannish liquid from a formula bottle. Then she grabbed one of the male kittens by the scruff of its neck and lifted him up. "C'mon Batman, show 'em how it's done."

She put his face into the milky mixture. The kitten balked and tried to step back. Gentry gently pushed his face in again. On the fourth try, the kitten finally got the idea and used his tongue to lap at the milky amalgam. He quickly became proficient at it and as his siblings wandered over to see what he was up to, they too were captured as Batman had been, and introduced to using their tongues to satisfy their hunger.

Dev marveled at how well they took to it. Even Puffball, who was the smallest, finally got the idea. On her first attempt she face planted, barely avoided falling in due to her two front paws catching her. The second time the front paws went in and she licked one. Deciding she liked it, she stepped all the way in, and tipped the bowl over. Finally, on the third try, she got the idea.

"So how old do they have to be before someone can adopt them?"

Again, Lisa jumped in, ready to impart her knowledge to this great looking guy with the broad chest and great hair—having no idea whatsoever that Gentry had first dibs. "Usually five or six weeks. When they're eating well, have had their shots, and someone applies for adoption, it happens pretty fast. They get scheduled for surgery, and often they leave here the day they get their sterilization procedure done. The sooner we can move them on, the sooner we make room for another rescue. There's always more. It's an unending cycle."

Dev smiled over at her and then looked up at Gentry. "Looks like they've all eaten, although more went on their fur than in their mouths. Is our job done here for today? You ready to go?"

Gentry smiled at him and nodded while Lisa visibly deflated, finally realizing that Dev was not merely a client interested in adopting, and possibly her as well, but a man with a connection to Gentry. She sighed. All the men looked at Gentry with interest. She didn't get it. Gentry dressed in strange farmhouse hick clothes, often had duct tape all over her shirts, had her wild hair in scruffy ponytails, braided in lopsided messy plaits, or had clips stuck all over her head, and she never wore a lick of makeup. While she, dressed to impress every single place she went. What was the deal?

Dev stood, impressively popping up from a kneeling

position, to standing upright. At 6-foot 3-inches he towered over Gentry's diminutive 5-foot-3. It was as if he was casting a shadow in the small screened-in area in the late morning sunlight.

He grabbed her hand in his as soon as he was standing and then turned back to Lisa to thank her for her explaining everything so well, and for letting him into the enclosure before Gentry had gotten there.

As he walked Gentry over to his truck he asked her how her lab classes went.

"Great! I passed the written part with a 98—only the lab and surgical part has to be graded. I might even hear something today. Then I'm certified—I'll be a vet!"

"That's wonderful! Do you know where you'll be doing your residency yet?" He hated the idea that she could be relocated anywhere in the country. But he was pretty sure he'd follow her wherever she landed.

"I've requested Brunswick County, New Hanover County, Pender County, or Horry County in South Carolina. There's a clinic in Ocean Isle that requested me and three Banfields!"

"Banfields?"

"Pet Smart's in-house hospitals. The experience would be pretty limiting though, only small animals. No cows, horses, or pigs. But plenty of cats, dogs, snakes, lizards, hamsters, birds, and fish.

"I'd really like to stay in the area though. I have this really cute little house I rented, and I kinda know my way around the area now. But I'll go wherever I'm needed."

"I would hate for you to go to Timbuktu."

"That's in Mali, isn't it?"

"Yup."

"Not likely. I will have passed the American Boards. Each country has their own, you know."

"Well, it's a good thing for me then, that the company has a jet."

"Your company has a jet?" Her eyebrows rose in disbelief.

"Two actually. Have I mentioned guns are big business?" he gave her smug smile.

"And I suppose the U.S. is your biggest market?"

"By far. Although our International Division is beginning to claim its fair share."

"So you're not in the International Division?"

"No, I run interference and close tight deals when I have to. But I still travel overseas about six times a year, not including pleasure trips."

They were standing by his truck. He could see her Kia parked a few spaces away. "You want to leave your car here? Or . . . I could follow you home and we could drop your car off there?"

She looked up at him. She could feel his hand holding hers. He squeezed it once.

She hesitated then said, "I suppose we could drop it off at my house. On the paved part before the road becomes gravel. But don't be expecting much. My parents think it's a dump, although I like it. And, it's all I can afford."

He smiled down at her. Ran his finger down her nose, and then tipped her chin up so he could look into her face. He marveled at how pretty she was with absolutely no trace of makeup.

"I lived in a tent for a year. Had to walk the length of three football fields to shower. Ate things I hardly recognized that always tasted of dust. Dump is a relative term."

She gave him a huge grin. "Well then, let me show you my Taj Mahal."

He opened her car door and lifted her onto the driver's seat—more to be able to touch her than anything else. She had a nice heft. From his years of carrying heavy duffle bags, he estimated her to be about 130 pounds—four or five of it easily being hair. She had a glorious mess of burnished curls. And it was long, mid-way down her back. He entertained thoughts of gathering it in one hand and leading her mouth . . . no, don't go there, he told himself. He was already having a hard enough time keeping a certain part of him suppressed.

He got into his truck and then followed her for twenty-five minutes, going south on Route 17, then turning onto Business 17 and driving through downtown Shallotte and its outskirts until they turned left onto Pigott Road, which he remembered driving on when he and the guys made trips to the Inlet View Restaurant. Two more right turns and two lefts, and then they were on a paved road for about a quarter of a mile. At the end of the paved part, she stopped and motioned for him to park his truck.

Then he got into hers and the road became dusty from the pea gravel mixed with oyster shell as the road wound around stands of trees. She'd had to steer hard left and then hard right. He felt a wash boarding action going on as the small truck bounced in and out of potholes. Then the road opened up into a clearing and they arrived at a shack on pylons with what seemed to be marshland behind it.

It *was* a dump, he thought, looking up at the tumbledown house on stilts, the weathered wood devoid of any paint whatsoever. The aging wood siding had turned a mottled gray. Somehow the accumulated crud it had collected over the years had managed to layer on and protect it.

He'd never seen anything quite like it. The wood looked petrified in places and streaked with windblown silt in others. The house must be ancient, he thought. The truly odd thing though, the thing that gave the house a cartoonish look, was that all the windows and window frames appeared to be brand new, oddly stark bright white against the aging charcoal-colored wood.

She parked her Kia on the patchy coquina driveway where tufts of grass were fighting to find the sun between broken pieces of oyster shells, chopped up pieces of cement, and mismatched river stone.

She smiled shyly over at him, then gathered her things

and got out. He got out on his side and she joined him on the path that led to the stairs that seemed to go right up through the middle of the house.

She tugged him by his t-shirt, indicating that he should follow her. "We have to go under the house to get inside. And the stairs leading up are not safe. The railings are loose and the steps are rotten in quite a few places. So be careful."

His eyebrows went up and his lips thinned as if he wanted to chastise her for living here. If it was that dangerous to even get inside the place, she should never have moved here.

But he bit his tongue and followed her over to the wooden steps. Each plank had three non-slip strips attached. He had no doubt that she had been the one to install them. They lead up under the center of the house to a wooden door.

After six steps, there was a roughed-in door that she opened by turning a corroded brass doorknob. He noted that there was no place to insert a key.

Then there were seven more steps, but without the abrasive strips for traction. This part of the stairway was finished off with bare sheetrock. The steps led up to a small six-paneled door. One of the bottom panels had a piece of aluminum sheeting riveted around the edges. It had obviously lost a panel somewhere, and this was the slap dash fix.

Across both top panels the words, **KEEP OUT IF YOU KNOW WHATS GOOD FOR YOU** were scratched into the wood and then filled in with dark blue marker as if written and colored in by a preschooler. They continued walking up the narrow passageway toward the door. At the top, they could not be on the same step at the same time. Bringing up a grocery bag would have necessitated carrying it in front of you and making you work for your balance the entire way.

Gentry opened the door at the top by flipping a handle down and pushing it in, and they walked into the interior of the house.

"No lock on any of the doors?" he asked with incredulity,

as she opened the second door without a key. He cursed himself for leaving his Glock in his truck.

"Nope. You can't get up without making a fair amount of clatter, and I suspect you'd have met a shotgun at the top when you opened the door when the owner was in residence."

"But *you* don't have a shotgun?" he asked, but he already knew the answer to that question.

"No. I've actually never had to open the door to anyone. You're my very first visitor. And I've been here for quite a while, close to two years."

"And if someone were to open the door on their own?"

"Well . . . there's a broom closet at the top of the steps, one good poke with the handle and down, down, down, they would go."

He shook his head and continued into the house behind her. Nothing could have prepared him for the sight that greeted him.

The screech of a loud bird assailed his ears and he grabbed Gentry and shoved her behind his body as he drew his secondary gun, a small Tarsus, from his ankle holster.

She screamed "No!" at the same time he saw that the big bird was inside a huge three-tiered cage, its wings flapping, its eyes red and wild. It had some kind of appendage attached where one of its legs should have been and stunted tail feathers that should have kept the big bird from being able to do anything but topple over.

Gentry pushed him aside and stood in front of the tall wrought iron birdcage as if she'd defend the bird from a bullet. The cage the bird was in, with its verdigris patina scrollwork, bespoke museum quality.

"I should have told you about her. This is Jillie. Now stop scaring her with that gun!"

He slowly bent and holstered it, and then looked between her and the bird. "You own an American Kestrel?"

Her eyes went wide with that observation. "I'm surprised

39

you know what it is."

He didn't want to tell her that he went hawk and falcon hunting all the time. "Yeah, I know my birds. This one is not usually a pet. You know that, right?"

"Yeah, I know that. She got hurt. Somehow she got her leg mangled and her tail feathers clipped and she can't fly until they grow back—*if* they grow back. We're not even sure that will happen. It looks as if her tail might have hit a live power line."

She pointed to a corner of the cage on the backside. He saw four white eggs with brown markings. "She laid them five days ago, so in about three weeks she'll have babies. She can't feed herself now; no way can she feed them when they arrive. So I volunteered to watch her and feed her until the babies hatch. Then they go to Topsail to fledge."

Gentry walked over to the counter, grabbed a big coffee can, jimmied off the lid, and using a scoop, deposited some of the freeze-dried nutrients into a pan that slid in and out from the bottom of the cage

"The bird sanctuary made up this concoction for her. Seems to be satisfying her for now. But I sure hope her feathers grow back soon. She doesn't like this cage one bit."

"No, I wouldn't think she would. She's a hunter of mice and snakes and small mammals and lives high up in trees."

"You *are* knowledgeable about birds."

He smiled. "You might as well know, it's the hunter in me."

"You and I," she pointed between her and him with the silver scoop, "should not even be friends."

He nodded silently. Yeah, this is insane, he said to himself. How was this ever going to work?

Then he turned around and took in the interior of the house. And couldn't help himself. "Whoa! This is not what I was expecting."

She gave him a huge grin. "Right? Pretty amazing huh?"

And it was. It was so out of character with the outside of

the house that he had to stop and take it all in.

While the outside was shanty ugly, the inside was . . . the best way to describe it was Danish modern. Every surface was sleek, new, uncluttered and not at all what you'd expect of a house at the end of a rutted road near a swamp.

He could see the new appliances from where he stood and they where all in the trendy style of matte slate. The French door refrigerator freezer with access to ice and water from the door, the dishwasher with recessed controls, the double ovens with unlit screens until you touched them, the gleaming double farmhouse sinks—notably empty—stainless steel dish drain atop the gleaming white quartz countertops. The floors, as far as he could see were high quality planking in a light ash gray. The wooden furniture in the family room, which he could just make out from here, was a light golden pecan. There was a three-cushioned sofa and an easy chair upholstered in light sage with colorful swirl accent cushions to match. Glass accent tables were tucked into several niches along the walls. They held books, vases with wildflowers, chrome-based lamps that doubled as charging stations with pleated shades, also sage. It was lovely, tasteful, and so incongruent with the outside of the house that it confounded him.

He shook his head, "I never would have believed this was how this house looked on the inside."

"Well . . . as the owner told me, there are two reasons for that. One, he's not here all that often and that the way it looks on the outside doesn't attract what he calls Looky-Loos. And two, he's a handyman, based out of Raleigh now, who works for several contractors. For years, he's bought up any extra supplies on the cheap. When he got enough of one thing to do a job, he'd haul it all here and install it. He said all the appliances were damaged goods or returned items that he refurbished. The furniture, he got when a place in Thomasville went out of business."

"So he got a good deal on the new custom windows . . .

they sure do show up against the old wood. They give the house a comical, quirky look."

She laughed, throwing her head back and it was everything he could do not to step over to where she stood and press his lips along the column of her throat.

"It's does that," she said and then continued with, "well, those windows are from his unsavory side. He said every time he installed windows for someone, he reported one broken or missing. When they sent a replacement to the place he specified," she circled her hand around to indicate the place as being there, "he installed it, until finally the whole house was done. If you look close, they don't really match, they're all different styles, but being all white, you don't really notice. He said the new windows saved him a shitload of money heating the place. He was able to chart the amount he spent on heating oil go down with each new window he installed. He's a funny guy. When I answered his ad and saw the place, I asked if he wanted proof of income from me so I could show I could afford to pay the rent. He said, "Naw, if you're takin' care of people's pets, that's good enough for me. Every one of my brothers and sisters spends a fortune taking care of their animals. Ya'll have a goldmine there."

"He sounds like a real character alright." He was still looking around and taking it all in. "And he did a great job with the house. Judging from the outside, I can only imagine what it had to have looked like on the inside before he started renovating it." He continued walking around, admiring the handiwork.

"Only thing he said was that I couldn't have a dog."

"That seems odd."

"Not if you knew the area. C'mere," she motioned to the other side of the house where there was a big bay window with a long padded window seat with cabinets under it.

When they were standing side-by-side she pointed, "See that big Hemlock tree over there?"

"Umhm, yeah?"

"Well, just behind it is the Sasspan Creek and its feeders. Every once in a while up comes a gator. And shortly thereafter, down goes a dog. He said he didn't want that for me, me being a dog lover 'n all."

Dev smiled. "Thoughtful guy. How long did you say you've been here?"

"Finishing my second year in September. It's a great little place. And he was absolutely right. No one ever comes here. Not even on Halloween despite how spooky it looks in the fog. You should see the bedroom, it's incredible."

He quirked a brow and looked over at her, "Is that an invitation?"

She smiled in chagrin. "I guess not. Although I imagine in time, that you'll probably get to see it."

He turned his body so he could face her. "Oh you do?" Again that eyebrow.

"Well, you don't seem to like cats, although Puffball seems to be edging into your dark side, you eat meat—we don't live anywhere near each other, we sit on totally opposite sides of the fence on gun control, in manner of dress, style of living, background . . . we have nothing in common. So I'm guessing it's a sexual spark we're both feeling."

He was standing in front of her now, his hands in the pockets of his dress slacks, taking her in. The t-shirt she was wearing with the picture of a sloth hanging over a tree limb embossed on it, the message underneath saying, NOT TO BRAG, BUT I TOTALLY GOT OUT OF BED TODAY, her form-fitting jeans had fashionable slashes across her thighs, exposing light skin, and her chunky no-nonsense, rubber boots that were horribly scuffed had rainbows and unicorns all over them. He looked down at his ultra-soft, fine linen shirt under the ultra-suede sport coat, the leather belt that alone cost $600, his Tommy Bahama jeans and kidskin loafers. Yeah, they were just about opposite in every way. But it didn't matter. He wanted her. And now she had pretty much told him that she wanted him, too.

He looked over and their eyes met. His lingered, then roamed her face, took in her supple lips, went lower and reread her t-shirt, noticing that the O in NOT and that the top circle of the G in BRAG were right over her nipples. They were showing as buds through what seemed to be a stretchy spandex-type bra.

"I think being without clothes on would equalize us some."

She laughed and it was such a delightful sound that he had to smile.

"Let me change out of my work boots, and then you can take me for that ice cream. Whether you're going to see my bedroom anytime soon is yet to be established. But honestly, it's everything I can do to keep my hands off you. Except for the fact that you're decked out in a multitude of animal hides."

He shot her a sideways smile. "I thought about that while I was dressing. But honestly? I had already packed pretty much everything except my traveling clothes when I met you."

"How long are you staying?"

"I was supposed to be home by now. But I've decided to stay a few more days."

She pursed her lips and quirked her head, "What changed your mind?"

He reached out to pull her close, wrapped his arms around her back and laced them together. "You. You changed my mind. I've never met anyone like you. You're so genuine. So caring." His lips lowered, "So damned sexy."

She thought about ducking, getting out of harm's way, but she wanted this, more than she would have thought possible. So she looked up and met his gaze. Let her gaze fall to his lips. She would have another one of his kisses. And she would find it did nothing—that it wasn't even good—that it didn't do a single thing for her. That it wasn't like the one last night that had made her remember her girl friends talking about panty-dropping kisses and not knowing what they were talking about. Last night the light bulb had gone off. But it wouldn't be the same today. That one had been a fluke. No way would it happen again.

Chapter 7
A $4,000,000 Parking Space

She couldn't have been more wrong. His hands came up to frame her face, and then he leaned in and gently placed his lips against hers. She felt his momentary hesitation, heard his gasp as he pulled her close and took her lips with his.

Like a master, he knew when to suck, lick, and then slip his tongue inside when she parted her lips to inhale. His lips captured hers while his tongue meandered and imprinted his quintessential maleness while he learned her essence intimately.

She was helpless against the onslaught of a masterful tongue that tantalized and teased and left her needy. Surrendering to the kiss, or to the man, she wasn't sure which, she opened her mouth to take him deeper. He groaned at her submission. He wanted more, so he took what she was offering.

The sound of his groan and its earnest plea for the pleasure of her participation, sent trills throughout her body. She flushed hot and then felt her panties dampen. Damn! This was exactly the way the girls had described it: flush hot; feel liquid pooling in her nether region; get lightheaded as every other thought vanished except for wanting something more . . . needing something more . . . longing to be carried off to a suitable horizontal surface.

She wanted something more all right, and with this man in particular. Only he didn't make a move to lift her into his arms so he could carry her to the bed or to the sofa. The kiss had begun expectantly, and now it ended the same way. His hands fell from her face to cup her elbows. Which was fortunate, as she felt a bit woozy and his subtle influence in that regard allowed her to concentrate on his face instead of remaining upright. He had a huge grin, which she slowly matched.

"I bet you thought that kiss was going to fall flat," he whispered.

She looked up at him and her eyes widened at the thought that he could read her mind so easily. She raised both brows and quirked her lips. "Yeah, I kinda did."

"Sorry," he breathed out, and then pressed his forehead against hers. "I think we're going to be spectacular together. But if there's going to be any ice cream today, we'd better get going."

She fought the feeling of disappointment. But he was right. It was too soon for them if they wanted this to be anything but superficial. He'd already sensed that she was a thoughtful person and not prone to rash decisions. And whether or not to have sex with a man she'd just met, who was older by several years, and way beyond her pay grade in life style, was a huge decision for her.

She'd been with two guys, both boys really—one in high school, one in college. Both times she'd found herself with a vibrator in hand afterward to sate the jittery feeling of missing out on something in the exchange. She was pretty sure Dev would not leave her unsatisfied in that way. He seemed world-worthy enough to have learned all the tricks to make sure she was more than satisfied.

But she couldn't stop thinking about how transient a liaison with him would be. He didn't live here, he didn't work here—he only vacationed here. The wham-bang adage came to mind. She didn't want to be somebody's hook up, someone to be entertainment for beach week. If he had an itch, it could be taken care of at a myriad of places in Myrtle Beach. And maybe already had been on this particular trip—he and his friends had already been here for a few weeks.

She looked up at him, took in his gorgeous eyes, saw the way they were totally focused on hers. She wanted a chance with this guy. But deep down, she knew that if they were going to have a shot at anything serious, they needed to slow down, find some common ground. Get to know each other better. Level the playing field a bit. Right now she felt her youth and inexperience working against her.

He took in every aspect of her face. He could tell she was being more cerebral than one would hope after a kiss of that caliber. He was totally into her, but was now having doubts as to whether she was feeling anything emotional at all. The vibe he was getting was that she had flipped the switch from emotional to intellectual. Never a good sign.

He looked down at her booted feet. "Go change out of your work boots and I'll take you for some ice cream at a fun place I discovered."

She flashed him a smile, grateful for the transition to something else so she could get out of her head for a while. "Won't take me but a minute."

"Oh, I've heard that before. You women are all alike. It'll be twenty minutes before I see you again, after you try on every pair of shoes in your closet."

"No seriously, I'll be right back." She walked down the short hallway and into the first doorway. He walked over to the living area to admire the artwork on the walls. It wasn't hers, he could tell, as it was old-timey local art—original oil paintings of marshes and estuaries, most of them focusing on people fishing with nets or collecting oysters in buckets.

"Ready!"

He hadn't had a chance to study the pictures. "That was fast. I'm impressed."

He looked down at her feet, now clad in lime-green plaid sneakers. She had also changed from her jeans into a pair of taupe colored bib overalls with a white mini-tee under it, leaving the area below her waist open, and showing off a fair amount of pale smooth skin. She had gathered her wild curls in a scrunched up piece of green fabric that matched her shoes.

"You are the cutest thing," he said, and then couldn't help himself. He ran his finger along one of the side openings, trailing it down from the bottom of her tiny white shirt to just above her hip. He smiled when she shivered.

She wore a little cross-body bag with a dragonfly embossed on the front. It was so her—small, delightfully whimsical, and not at all pricey if he was any judge. It certainly didn't say Hermès or Coach on it as those his former dates all carried did.

"How did your tests go this morning?"

She smiled over at him. "Great! I'm one hundred percent sure I passed. I might have even aced it. My dad says I'm brilliant!"

"Does he now?"

"He has no choice. He has to speak the truth since he's a preacher."

Oh, that was interesting, he thought, and tucked it away to chew on later. "I don't doubt your father. But what do your teachers say at this point in your schooling?"

"Well, one of my clinical teachers said if he had a pet that needed surgery, I would be the first one he called."

"Fine praise indeed. That's a pretty high opinion," he said as he nodded and led them to the center of the house and the small rickety staircase.

Once on the steps, he gingerly placed his large feet on each of the narrow slats in turn. He huffed out, "Boy, you sure wouldn't want to go down these steps in a hurry."

"Oh, I run down them all the time."

"Well, I wear size 12. You look like a size 6 at best, plus you don't have to keep ducking your head to avoid smacking your noggin," he said as he barely missed hitting an X-shaped cross panel.

"I'm a size 6 and a half, I'll have you know."

"Still, I'm almost twice your size."

"Not boding well for us if you're twice my size in everything."

He let out a laugh that was more of a guffaw. "I can't believe you just said that."

48

"What? No comeback?"

"Oh, I have a comeback alright," he said as he closed the door at the bottom of the stairway and steered her toward her truck.

"Oh yeah, and what's that?"

He leaned in close to her ear and whispered, "Some things are designed to stretch to accommodate."

He opened the driver door and wrapped his hands around her waist and lifted her up onto the seat of her SUV. "Just drive us back to my truck and I'll drive from there."

"Okay."

When he was settled in on the passenger side, she turned to look at him, "I don't think we're going to get there."

"To the ice cream place?"

"No, to us finding out if we're a fit."

"Do you mean physically or in some other way?"

"I think we might just be different in too many ways for this to work." She indicated them both by pointing at him and then pointing at herself, and then repeating the action.

"I don't think we're supposed to look for a mate who is the same as we are," he said as he watched her start the car and put it in gear to back up.

"Mate? Who said anything about mating?"

"I thought that's what we were talking about. You and I working our way toward a convivial coupling." He mimicked her hand gesture of pointing at her and then pointing back at him.

"That's not mating. Mating is propagating. I should know, I'm almost a vet. I am probably one right now since I know my test results are favorable."

"Ah, pardon me. You're right, no mating going on here then."

She pulled next to his truck and they switched vehicles. When they were on the paved road, at the four-way intersection with no cars in sight, he stopped the truck and moved his hand from the gearshift to the back of her seat, turning his body to face her. He looked into her eyes and didn't move a muscle, just took her in.

"Don't you think you should," she wangled her hand, "get through the intersection?"

"I want to know something first. And no beating around the bush."

"What's that?"

"Do you have any desire at all to be fucked by me? And I don't mean today, but one day . . . one day soon, hopefully."

He had taken her by surprise. So much so that he watched as she sucked in a huge breath that expanded her chest. Then she surprised him by slowly letting it out accompanied by a long drawn out "Yeeeessss."

"Okay!" he said, as he put the truck back in gear. "Ice cream."

"But no mating . . ." she whispered.

"Right. Definitely no mating."

He drove her to a little ice cream parlor run by two sisters—Two Ladies and A Scoop. When they pulled up and parked she said, "I didn't even know this was here."

"It's a small shop, filled with games to play while eating yummy ice cream. And they make their own pies and cakes if you feel like something more substantial . . . because I really can't vouch for how they treat their cows . . ."

She laughed and let him open the door for her. After much deliberation they decided on a banana split to share—a huge concoction piled high with lots of toppings, which they took to a table that had checkers set up on a small-fringed rug. He won. They moved to the Connect table. He won. Then to the Domino Race table. He won again. They ended with the beanbag Tic Tac Toe Toss. And of course, he won.

While she pouted he tried to console her, "Hey, I'm a gamesman, that's what I do. In high school I was on the football and archery teams. In the Army I honed my shooting skills with sniper duty. And now, I show people all over the world what our guns can do so that they will buy them. I am competitive—to the max. I see a game and I light up. What can I say? We all have our special talents." He patted her hand to reassure her, "But I can't operate on a llama or on a goat like you can. You would win hands down there."

She smiled and patted his hand. "I'm not so sure I can either, at least I never have. Dogs and cats, horses and cows? Now I think I might have you beat there. And also I can run down narrow, wobbly steps much faster than you can."

"There is that." He turned his hand over so that now he was holding her hand in his. He nodded to a stack of games over in the corner. "If you want to play a game of chess, I promise to lose."

She laughed and the sound was so beautiful he wanted to record it so he could play it over and over again. Even without the recording, he was sure it would be imprinted in his head for all time. It was that kind of moment.

"What say we take a walk on the beach?" He looked at his iWatch and pressed a series of buttons. "It's mid-tide now and the sun is just starting to set. Should be a pretty sunset . . .."

He didn't want this day to end. And although they had jokingly talked about eventually having copulating plans, he knew it was too soon to press for such a desired scenario. As much as he wanted her . . . he wanted her for more than one tumble in the sack. It shook him to realize that he just might want her for all his future tumbles. Such a thought, coming out of the blue, had him blinking—sitting upright in his seat.

But yeah? The thought of being with another woman after knowing her? Well, it wasn't a good one—it left him feeling empty. It felt like the worst kind of betrayal. And not having forever with her? It bothered him a lot, just to consider it.

These were crazy thoughts. They had only known each other two days. He tried to shake the strange thoughts out of his head. He was a love 'em and leave 'em kind of guy. The only time he hadn't been, had ended in disaster. He couldn't go through that again.

She watched his face; sure he was processing something other than an upcoming beach walk. He seemed thoughtful, but not in a good way. Did he think she'd turn him down just because he had an overdeveloped complex to losing?

"Sure. I rarely get to go to the beach—unless it's to help an animal. I thought when I first moved here that I would go to the beach all the time. But with school, work, and then volunteering, there just isn't enough time in the day."

He shook off his wayward thoughts and stood. Then he pulled her up from her chair and tucked her into his side as if it was the most natural for him to be doing. "Let's do it!"

"Then I have to go check on the kittens."

"I'll go with you."

"You just want to see Puffball again."

He smiled, "You know, I do. She's growing on me. What a scamp she is. While I was sitting on the mat with her, just before you got there, she managed to pull my handkerchief out of my pocket and then had the audacity to make me chase her to get it back." He laughed at the memory.

"She's growing on you," she said with a flirty smile. "You should adopt her."

"I can't have a cat."

"And just why can't you have a cat?" She was posing with a glower—her sweet lips were turned-in on themselves. He wanted to kiss the pout off her mouth.

"I travel. A lot. I'm never home. I don't like my clothes or my furniture shredded . . .."

"Cats don't mind being left alone. You can be gone for as long as a week or two if someone comes in to check on her. And they travel really well in a carrier." She scrunched her lips and tilted her head to one side, that wasn't necessarily true, and she wanted to be honest with him. "The ones that don't can be sedated so they sleep while on the road or in a plane."

"Then there's the smell." He scrunched up his nose. "I had the honor of changing the litter boxes this morning as I was apparently the first person there. Some lady corralled me and handed me a scoop, a plastic bag and pointed to a huge barrel of cat littler. She said the litter boxes needed cleaning, in a way that indicated she thought I worked for her."

Gentry laughed with that lovely trill she had. It slayed him. Every time. "That had to have been Donna. She's particular about having the litter changed first thing in the morning, before any clients arrive. No one likes the smell, Dev. There's good and bad in all relationships. But there are some amazing cat litters out there if you don't mind the added cost to take care of that. We use the cheap stuff at the shelter."

"I don't know. She's cute 'n all. But I think she can do better than me for an owner."

Gentry knew when to let it go. You couldn't force something like this. Someone had to really want a pet, not have one forced on them. The animals just got returned if they were unwanted and unloved. Or not wanted enough or loved enough. Because good pets required time and patience, and a fair amount of money—vet bills were not cheap. Although from what she'd seen, money to spend on food and vet bills would not be an issue for Dev.

He walked her back to the truck and after situating her, he got in and drove down 179 to the circle and from there, over the bridge to the island. It was high season so he knew that parking would be scarce at the gazebo and on Main Street, so he drove down to *The Cockpit* and parked in the circular drive.

"Nice that you have your own parking space."

He smiled over at her as they both got out of the Lexus. "Yeah, for four million give or take, and you too can have an excellent parking space at the beach."

"That's another reason I don't come here during high season. Unless you come here very early or very late, you can't count on getting a parking space close to the beach. Even street parking several blocks away is iffy. September and October are my favorite months—great weather, no traffic, plenty of parking. I often stick my kayak in the back of my car and go to the park here though. I enjoy going up and down the Intracoastal and wending through the marshes. On days when I have nothing to do, and nowhere I have to be, it's a very relaxing time."

"We'll have to do that sometime. We keep several kayaks stored under the house."

"I'd like that."

He took her hand and led her around the side to the back of the house. They walked across the terrace, and then up onto the steps leading to the wooden access.

They walked hand-in-hand down the long boardwalk that led to the beach. She commented on the impressive dunes that protected the houses and also provided a coastal habitat for the many birds and animals indigenous to the area.

He watched the sun glinting off her bright copper hair and silently marveled at the vibrant aquamarine color of her eyes. Once on the beach, she dug into her dragonfly purse and extracted a pair of sunglasses. The multicolored wonder of her stunning blue eyes disappeared behind whimsical mirrored glasses. He had to laugh as he saw himself reflected in the lenses.

"Don't laugh, they were free." She touched the bridge and pushed them up a bit as they were quite obviously too big for her face. He saw the logo and name for one of the local animal support groups, Paws-ability. He knew they did a lot of work for animals in the area. He had seen them represented at many of the festivals.

"Only cost me a day under a tent in the hot sun walking and watering dogs at an adoption fair."

They were dollar-store sunglasses at best. Again, he was reminded of the women in his life the last few years. The cases for their sunglasses were three hundred dollars, the glasses themselves eighteen hundred or more. And they often left them places or scratched them and had to replace them. He liked hers better. They suited her. But it would have been nice it they had fit. He'd get a rubber band and wrap it around the bridge so they'd at least stay on her nose better.

They talked about all the wildlife he'd seen on the island over the years, and she floored him with her extensive knowledge of the native animals.

"I treated someone's dog that got attacked by one of the bobcats. What a mess! But he survived. I stitched up his ear and the vet said I did a superb job, that it was good as new."

He smiled over at her as they walked along the shore. He loved how animated she got when she talked about her work.

"There used to be more wild animals here, even goats, but I think there's less of them with each coming year," he said.

"Sadly, that is true. I think that's everywhere now. We're taking away their habitat. Every year we clear more and more land for development, so they have no place to live. It's really bad out west, what with the forest fires and mudslides, and massive flooding. The clear cutting they're doing in the southeast is creating a lot more tornadoes, and that's affecting everyone, not just the wildlife," she genuinely seemed sad about that.

"Yeah, due to logging operations and mining and oil development, two million acres lost their federal protection over the last four years. That's had to have endangered a lot of animals," he shook his head as he remembered reading about it. "I'm a hunter, but I am also concerned with protecting the species."

"Oh, don't even get me started on that. The Endangered Species Act is always under attack." Then she proceeded to rattle off a list of animals and their current standing: "Wild Salmon, Grizzly Bears, Polar Bears, and Canada Lynx are *threatened*, and Bighorn Sheep, Jaguars, Monk Seals, Whooping Cranes, Black-footed Ferrets, Panthers, and even Kemp's Ridley Sea Turtles are *endangered*. And that's just some of them. We stand to lose so much . . . *forever* . . . if protections are not put in place now. It's sad. Really, really sad."

He thought she might be about to cry. Her voice had become wobbly after her spirited tirade. He grabbed her hand and spun her around to face him. He lifted her sunglasses up and then dropped them back on her nose. Sure enough, her eyes were filled with tears.

"I love how you care so much. You're going to make a great vet."

Her face lit up. "I almost forgot! They said I could log in and find out if I passed my certification after four o'clock." She grabbed his wrist to see his watch. "How do you turn this thing on?"

"Same way you turn me on. By touch." He tapped the side and the screen lit up. It was 4:13.

"I have to find a computer!" She had already turned to head up the beach to go back the way they had come.

He grabbed her hand and pulled her to him, held her tight to his chest and stared down at her beautiful face, all lit up, eyes shining, her hair flying out around her face and lifting with the breeze. She was bouncing up and down on her toes with excitement—vivacious and high-spirited, as if she had a lit fuse under her feet and was about to explode like a firecracker. God, this woman . . .

He gave her a quick kiss on her forehead and together they ran toward the access, hand-in-hand, stopping at the foot of the steps to pick up the shoes they had kicked off when they'd began their walk.

"There's a computer in the house you can use." He hesitated, and then added, "Unless you want to do this by yourself. I know this is a special moment, it must mean a lot to you."

"Oh no! I want you with me! And if the news is good, I want to buy the best bottle of champagne Food Lion has and celebrate!"

He laughed. "Well if the news is good, there's no need for that. We stock some of the best champagne in the world, mostly because Kyle is so particular, but also because he gets such good deals."

"Oh, I couldn't accept that."

"Of course you can. My treat." He paused again. "Even if you want to share it with someone else."

She stopped on the boardwalk, causing him to jerk back when their arms pulled tight.

"Hey . . . there isn't anyone else I'd want to share this moment with. Other than maybe my parents, but they're in Raleigh, and they don't drink."

He smiled down at her. "Well, let's go and see then, shall we? Although I have no doubt, that very soon I'm going to be calling you Doctor . . . hey what is your last name by the way?"

"Macrory."

"Well, *Miss* Macrory, come with me and we'll see about this new title of yours."

Hand-in-hand, they walked up the decking, coming off at the walkway that led to a short path that joined the terrace of *The Cockpit*. From there, Dev punched in a code on an access panel, and when the elevator came to the lower level and opened, they rode it to the main living area.

Coming off the elevator, Gentry's eyes went wide taking it all in. "Man, this is some place. Fancy schmancy."

"Well it's what ten of us could agree on. And it suits us all just fine."

"I love the kitchen that Kyle Merritt designed. And I'd like to see the rest of the house sometime."

"Of course. But first, those test results." He took her by the hand and led her into the TV/game room where there was a workstation with a computer set up for household use. "I think it would be better if you viewed the house from a more lofty job position."

"Are you saying you wouldn't be interested in me anymore if I remained a lowly vet tech."

He brought her hand to his lips and kissed it. "I would

still be interested in you if you were the pooper scooper for the elephant at the San Diego Zoo. I would insist on supervising very thorough showers though."

He kissed her hand again, and this time she felt his tongue drag alongside her thumb. A delightful shiver ran through her entire body.

He pulled out the roller chair and she slid onto the plush seat as he woke up the laptop on the desk.

Once he had the Safari screen up, her fingers flew over the keys. He watched as screen after screen lit up and led to another, until she landed on a page that lit up with gold script that began with: *Ms. Gentry G. Macrory,* and ended with *Congratulations on passing your Veterinarian Licensure Board Examination.* It was signed by the president of the North Carolina Veterinary Medical Board.

She rolled back the chair, spun it around and jumped into his arms, startling him in the process. Her legs were hugging him around his waist and her arms were wrapped around his neck.

"I did it! I did it! I did it! And I only missed one question!" Her words were huffed against his throat, and it made every hair on his body tingle and other parts harden and come alive.

He wasn't sure what he had liberty to do, but as she was slipping, he grabbed her linen overalls-clad butt and hefted her higher—rubbing the center of her body along the rapidly hardening ridge below his zipper.

He wanted this woman and he was not at all embarrassed to show her how much. "That is wonderful news, *Dr. Macrory.* I didn't know you before your years of schooling and training, but I know that you must have done a superb job on that test if you only missed one question."

"I'll have to find out which one. Maybe they have it wrong."

He laughed so hard he had to adjust his grip on her bottom and heft her up again, using his hardness to help leverage her higher. The crown of his penis was separating her folds. He groaned and she hissed. He looked for a convenient wall. But then thought, *no, my first time inside her is not going to be up against a wall.* He relaxed his hands and eased her down his legs. Her hands on his back, his waist, and his butt caressed him until her feet hit the floor. If she'd had any pickpocketing skills, he'd have been fleeced.

His body missed the connection of hers, so he stooped and lifted her again. This time her ankles crossed behind his back and anchored her to him. He was careful to hold her above his hips. This wasn't the time. Her mind was elsewhere. And he didn't have a condom handy.

"It's time for you to select a bottle of champagne from the wine cooler, and for me to uncork it."

"Oh, but first I have to call my parents, and then all my brothers and sisters, my boss, and my friends at the clinic, the volunteers at the shelters, all my teachers . . .."

He stopped her with a kiss as he carried her over to the four-cushioned sofa, dumped her on one end of it and followed her down until he was sprawled on top of her.

He lifted his head and met her eyes. She looked so happy. He couldn't steal this moment, one she had been looking forward to for many years. Complicating it with his attraction to her would do him no favors in the end. When they made love, he wanted her mind to be totally focused on him, and what he was doing to her.

He grinned down at her, and then kissed the tip of her nose. With one upward shove on hands that were aligned with her shoulders, he lifted off her.

"I'll tell you what, I'll pick out a bottle from Kyle's collection, grab an ice bucket and some glasses, and then fix up a plate of cheese and crackers while you make your calls. Then we'll celebrate how awesome you are. Deal?"

She had already grabbed her phone from the purse she had left on the computer desk and taken a quick picture of the computer screen with its congratulatory message. Now she was scrolling through her Favorites and tapping on the picture of her mom and dad. She looked up and gave him a 1,000-watt smile and a thumb's up gesture and nodded as the number she had selected was already ringing.

Of course, everyone was thrilled for her, and not at all surprised she had achieved her goal. It was an hour before she ran out of names on her phone list to call. During a break in the phone calls, he'd managed to uncork the bottle and pour two glasses and they had toasted to her career of, "Helping animals stay healthy all over the world!"

With each squeal of glee and run on babble of excitement over her accomplishment, he became a little more unbalanced. She was so genuine. There was nothing fake, no pretense about her at all. She was pure delight to watch as she bubbled over while giving her good news to family, friends, and coworkers.

As she made one call after another, he slowly tipped and then toppled, until he felt himself tumble off the edge of his ingrained mountain of detachment.

The words to one of Cinderella's songs began to run through his head. The animated Disney movie was one of his girls' favorites and he had watched it with them at least fifty times.

The words coming back to his mind right now, along with the tune being hummed from the back of his throat, should have been an anathema coming from a man's-man such as himself, but it wasn't. It was nice. *So this is love, mmm. So this is love. So this is what makes love divine.* He was giddy with an emotion so profound it amazed him. When had he ever felt like this before? The answer was never.

He'd been led into marriage in his mid-twenties just as all his friends had. The relationship had evolved until it was the next logical step. He'd cared for his wife deeply. Had professed his love over and over and been staunchly faithful to her. But he'd never had this sense of heady giddiness. Possessiveness yes, but not this delightful woozy lightheadedness that left no doubt how he felt about her—he was in love. Like two dogs sharing a spaghetti noodle kind of love. There was no duty in it—just pure joy.

When she had made the last call, he watched as she sat yoga-style on the carpet by the coffee table, where her twice-refilled champagne glass awaited her. She let out a long sigh and he watched her deflate from the massive high she'd been on. He had a twinge of guilt that he'd been repeatedly filling her glass—for a self-serving purpose. He'd only filled his once, as he wanted to be able to drive her home when it was time to take her back. But now, feeling these new and over-the-top exciting feelings about her, there was no way he was going to take advantage of her good news and good mood to seduce her.

She must've felt the same way; seduction by either party was not on her agenda tonight. Twirling the stem of her now empty champagne glass she said. "We need to check on the kittens." A long sigh followed, as if it was the last thing she wanted to run out and do right now.

"You look like you could use a nap."

"I'll be fine, but I should get home before I crash. Man what an adrenaline rush!"

"Me plying you with champagne didn't help any."

"Actually it did. I feel fabulous!" She ran her fingers though her thick head of hair, tousling it and letting the curls tumble freely. With her sleepy-eyed gaze, it made her look sexy as all get out. He wanted her. Wanted to lick and kiss every inch of her, settle his body in the cradle of her hips and see stars when he came inside her. It was his turn to sigh. Not gonna happen tonight, he told himself.

He reached a hand down and pulled her up. When she lost her balance and fell into his chest he groaned from the contact. Her hand splayed out on his chest, her pointer finger landing on his nipple. An unconscious action on her part had her rubbing it in tiny circles. She looked up into his face; her eyes were inviting him to kiss her. He hated to have to deny her. But one kiss and he'd be lost.

He covered her hand with his. "You're going to have to stop that, unless you want to be carried upstairs to my bedroom."

"Mmmm," she swung her arm around behind her as if looking for something. Then pointed, "Whaz wrong with that coush?"

He laughed. "Nothing. But you're not capable of making a decision like that right now. Much to my regret, since it appears it would be a favorable one. C'mon, let's check on those kittens, and then I'll get you home. You've had a very busy day."

"It's been amazing!"

He smiled and bussed her on her nose. He loved doing that. "Yes, it certainly has."

Chapter 8
Jillian, We're Home!

The sun was starting to set when they pulled up to the compound. He helped her out of his truck as she'd drifted off to sleep just as they'd reached Route 17, and had napped until they'd bumped onto the unpaved road.

"Sorry I fell asleep. Getting up at 5 and driving to Raleigh so early this morning for that test has wiped me out."

"I had no idea you'd had to do all that driving this morning, plus take such an important test."

"Yup. It's the only place they give the test."

"You should have gone home and taken a nap."

"I wanted to be with you today."

He smiled and brought her hand to his lips and kissed the back of it. "Ditto."

He helped her unlock the enclosure and before they could get all the way inside three kittens were crowding their feet and butting their heads against their ankles. "Where's the other two?" he asked.

"Oh, I forgot to tell you, they got adopted out. They were neutered this morning then taken to their new homes this afternoon."

"Wow, that was fast."

"If it's someone who's willing to manage the frequent feeding schedule, sometimes we let them go sooner. And often, once they're spayed or neutered they go home that day or the next. They were both males, so that's pretty much the norm here."

He had already bent to pick up Puffball and was holding her close to his chest and stroking her head. "Two females and one male to go."

"Yup," she said as she began tidying the litter box. "It goes in spurts as to which sex is more popular. Older women like the females best. But these kittens being all white, it kind of makes them unique. It's unusual for a cat not to have any markings."

"Which breeds are the most popular?"

"Tabbys and Calicos are the most popular, then the greys. Longhaired cats can be tough to place. The extreme shedding can be a problem for some people."

Dev stooped to pet all three and Puffball jumped from the ground to his shoulder. "Wow, look at that. Look how high she just jumped."

Gentry smiled over at him. "She seems to be possessive of you."

She put out the bowls of food and all three cats scampered to investigate. Gentry shook out and straightened the bedding and while the cats were eating they slipped out of the pen.

On the way back to the truck, Dev looked at the other cats through the screening of their enclosures. Most were full-sized. "Kittens go first I assume?"

"Oh yeah, especially with families that have small children. Older people like the sedate older cats, less scampering about and knocking things over—cuddle buddies more than anything else."

He looked over at her and grinned. "I think you'd make a good cuddle buddy tonight. You look exhausted."

"I must admit, I'm down for the count."

"We didn't eat dinner, just cheese and crackers. Are you hungry?"

"Yeah, but I'm too tired to eat. I'll just grab something from the fridge."

"You sure? We can stop and get something."

"Nah. I know I'll be ravenous in the morning, but it's my day off so I can sleep in and have a big breakfast."

The idea of sleeping in with her and having a leisurely

breakfast together in the morning had a great deal of appeal to him. But he didn't want to chance being shot down if he proposed he stay.

When they got to her road, he drove past her Kia parked at the top of the lane, through the turns in and out of the woods, and down to her bungalow by the river.

"We going to see the kittens tomorrow?" he asked, as a way to ensure he would see her the next day.

"Sure. I'm going to assist with their surgeries the day after so they'll be ready to be adopted out by the weekend. Tomorrow will be a good time for you to say goodbye since you're leaving on Friday. There's a big festival in Shallotte on Saturday where we're having an adoption day. With several thousand people walking by and checking them out, I'm sure those little cuties will find a home."

The thoughts of leaving, being away from her, and of Puffball being adopted made him a little melancholy. He pulled up into the drive and got out to walk her to the door.

Once they were under the house, at the bottom door, she turned to him. "Thank you for a wonderful day. I loved every bit of it."

He smiled wistfully and stroked the hair beside her face. As he tucked a piece behind her ear, he drew his finger down and around the shell of her ear. She shivered from his light touch and he laughed.

Then he cupped her face and bent to kiss her. He leisurely tasted her soft lips until she reached up and pulled him closer. Then he feasted on them—nibbled, licked, and sucked, until finally he breached her lips and let his tongue cavort with hers. A minute later when he pulled away and looked down at her, her eyes were closed and there was a look of ecstasy on her face. He groaned. The sight of her there, waiting for more was so compelling; he could have stared at her all night.

"God, what you're doing to me. I want you so much."

She whispered, "Ditto," using the single word he'd

expressed earlier. Then she said simply, "Come up."

"If I come up, I won't leave."

"Then by all means, come up."

"Are you sure?"

"I've had a very nice day today. Let's go for making it perfect."

He sighed and kissed her again. She took the key fob for his SUV from his hand and used it to lock the Lexus behind him. A small chirping sound followed, signifying the task was accomplished so she put the fob in the front pocket of his jacket and patted it to indicate that was were his key should stay. He reached behind her back and turned the doorknob, then pushed the door open.

They climbed the rickety mismatched steps to the upper floor, and he opened the door at the top for her. Once inside, she flicked on the light switch by the door and a loud flapping sound with several shrill shrieks followed.

"Hello Jillian. We're home," Dev said as he closed the door behind them.

And he meant it. This dilapidated-on-the-outside, spruced-up-on-the-inside little house off the branch of a tiny, marshy river felt more like a home than any he'd had in a very long time.

Chapter 9
Dev & Gentry—Quirky House

Settling in for the night, Gentry toed off her shoes, then walked around turning the lamps to their lowest settings. She got out a bowl of grapes and apple slices from the fridge and put them on the countertop, before popping into the bedroom to remove her purse and necklace. She washed up and changed into an old faded t-shirt and a pair of jersey pajama-type shorts.

Coming out to sit at the counter where Dev had already settled, checking his phone, she opened the fridge again and took out a pitcher of water with lemon and lime slices. She poured them each a glass while Dev took in her skimpy outfit. It allowed him to see her smooth velvety-looking legs, the skin so light he wondered if they'd ever seen sunlight. This must have been the way men in the Victorian era must have felt when seeing their new bride's bodies for the first time, he thought. Her well-defined legs were flawless, with tiny dimples on the sides of her knees—so sexy, so pure and chaste-looking. He felt as if he was worshiping a virgin goddess. The t-shirt, a soft slate gray, fell over full rounded breasts. Even though there was a shadowed valley between her joggling mounds, the words printed across the front were easy to read: **I DON'T CARE WHO DIES IN THE MOVIE AS LONG AS THE DOG LIVES.**

He read it and smiled. She was the whole package—brain, body, and heart. "You take my breath away. You are so beautiful. Sexy, yet innocent at the same time."

"Well, I am not innocent. But I am not terribly experienced either. I've only been with two guys, both for a little over a year, but nothing recent. I just haven't had the time to date during the last two years. Or the mindset to belong to anyone but myself."

"Sounds as if you've been hurt."

"Let's just say, I wanted exclusive and they both

wanted to play."

"I can do exclusive. In fact, I want exclusive myself. I can be whatever you need me to be. My playing around days are behind me. I want more."

He reached out, gripped her by the waist, and pulled her to stand between his spread thighs. "I want the whole deal—no war to tear me away this time." The heat in his eyes told her that she was the more he was referring to.

Neither said a word, just looked at each other, memorizing each detail in their faces. Then, as if cued by a conductor, they both slowly nodded. The moment was broken by the sound of Jillie fluffing her feathers and softly cooing as she settled onto her perch for the night.

"Do you mind if I take a quick shower? Being at the shelter and then on the beach has left me feeling a bit gritty."

She laughed. "Of course not. I always power down by reading a few chapters in my book before bedtime. Join me when you're finished, okay?"

"You sure you're good with me sleeping with you?"

"I am. But don't expect much more than a cuddle. I am beat."

He bent and kissed her on the forehead. "I was up late last night doing some work, so I am a bit flagged myself."

"Bathroom's on the other side of the bedroom. For some reason, the hot and cold taps are reversed. Don't ask why. I marked them with nail polish. Feel free to use anything you need, the towels on the rack are clean, and there's a blister pack of Dollar Store toothbrushes under the sink."

"Thanks. The quaintness and hospitality of this place is really amazing, so juxtaposed to the outside, which is quite frankly, more than a bit foreboding and rundown."

She laughed and he felt his insides clench with desire. He could not recall a single time before meeting her that a woman's laugh had turned him on like this.

"I almost didn't pull into the drive when I came to look

at the place. I think Jason, that's the owner's name, suspected I'd drive right by after seeing the front of the place, so he was standing by the mailbox and gestured me to drive up. I remember his exact words when I rolled down my window to tell him I didn't think this was the type of place I was looking for. He said, 'You are going to love this place. Trust me.'

"And I'm so glad I did. It's small, but it suits me just fine. It's the right blend of eccentric and quirky for me. And he gave me a good deal because he didn't have to empty out the shed of all his tools and kayaks and fishing gear."

He shook his head as he walked through the bedroom to the bathroom. "It's perfect for you and Jillie. Now, if you only had cable, it could be perfect for me, too."

Twenty minutes later, Dev walked into the bedroom drying his hair with a towel, while another was wrapped around his waist. Gentry was asleep on her tummy, her arm wrapped around a pillow, a book open on the colorful puffy quilt made up of cartoon animals.

He smiled, moved the book to the night table, dropped both towels to the braided rag rug, and climbed in beside her. He watched her sleep for a few minutes then closed his eyes. The night sounds from being so close to a fertile tidal river played out around him. Low background sounds of reeds rustling, insects buzzing, crickets chirping, frogs croaking, owls hooting, and the low drone of an engine of in the distance lulled him to sleep.

Chapter 10
Feeding the Kestrel

Gentry was a sprawler—her limp arms and legs were draped over him like a starfish when the sun came through the blinds and lit up the room. With one hand tucked behind his head, he quirked a brow as he realized that there were many things you could learn about a person the first time you slept with them: whether or not they steal the blankets, snore, pound down their pillow, toss and turn, talk in their sleep, laugh while dreaming, cry out from nightmares, kick you, or cuddle with you. Gentry owned the whole bed. And anyone in it did not get to have their own territory—you became her bed.

Her burnished curls were arrayed over his shoulder; one of her hands was splayed open on his pillow near his ear, the other was on his chest, her thumb just below a nipple, her hip resting just above his. As he looked down his body, he could see one of her legs spread out, her knee crooked as if she was running. This was a great way to wake up, he thought—a beautiful young woman draped across his body, her heart beating close to his—until the kestrel woke up as well, with a shrill screech that pitched higher with each succeeding squawk.

"Damn, I forgot to get grasshoppers," Gentry mumbled, her lips vibrating against his neck.

Dev laughed out loud. Of all the things she could have said upon waking, that was the most off the wall and least expected comment he could have imagined. He picked up her hand and kissed the palm

"Good morning, Sunshine. Shall I procure a delectable selection of orthopteras, and maybe some worms, and snails for your breakfast?"

"Not for me, you idiot, for Jillie. She needs more than that freeze-dried stuff."

"Well, I *am* a hunter. I can fetch her a few small squirrels."

"And you think I'm going to be okay with you killing baby squirrels?"

"Kestrels eat mice, too. I could trap a few. Interesting tidbit: Kestrels can see ultraviolet light. They actually track mice and other small animals by following their urine trail which glows bright yellow in the ultra violet light spectrum."

"My, this bedroom banter is getting me so turned on . . ."

He quickly rolled her over and while tickling her along her waist, he plastered wet kisses over her neck. "Oh, I've got some bedroom moves for you." He ran his hand under her t-shirt and smoothed it over her stomach and around her hip. Both hands met behind her back, slid down her backside, delved into her pajama bottoms and cupped her naked cheeks. They both groaned at the same time that Jillie commenced screeching again. This time she was more insistent, building her pitch until the long ear-piercing shrieks threatened to deafen them.

"Time to go hunting," he said. "Give me fifteen minutes and I'll satisfy that bird. Then I'm going to work on satisfying you."

He hopped out of bed, and having come straight from the shower last night with just a towel on, he was stark naked. He flashed her his butt, impressive back muscles, and long toned legs with well-developed calves as he ducked into the bathroom.

What a very fine butt he came with, she thought as she rolled over and put a pillow over her head to try to silence the loud bird's screeching sounds.

After her shower, Gentry stood at the window watching as Dev squatted near the water's edge in front of a stand of marsh grasses. He appeared to be running his hands along the reeds and collecting a lot of something that he slid into a glass jar on the ground.

A few minutes later, he returned to the house and presented her with a foggy Mason jar he'd found in the tool shed. Inside was a smorgasbord of marsh crabs, white spiders, snails, a highly agitated long-legged brown frog, three green grasshoppers, and a thin squiggly, still- moving-inside-the-jar nine-inch-long green snake, that was trying frantically to get out through one of the holes he'd punctured in the top.

When he saw her sideways grimace, he chuckled and said, "It's not unlike a bouquet of roses. I am presenting you with a gift you are in need of. Although even to you, knowledgeable as you are of a kestrel's eating habits, this must seem terribly gross. But pretend for a moment that this is a bottle of fine wine or a bouquet of cut flowers. It's all I got."

He put his other hand on his heart as he tendered the actively engaged jar toward her hesitant hand, adding, "*Please*, do not drop it."

Gentry took the jar in both hands, her eyes never leaving the darting movements of the snake writhing inside. "Um, thank you, my gallant suitor."

"You might need to hurry up and feed Jillie. The frog seems to be eating all her appetizers."

"Got it!" She spun on her heel, walked directly to the cage, unlocked the gated door, and having the kestrel's full attention now, unscrewed the lid and dropped the jar inside. "There ya go, Jillie. Eat up. And I do not want to see a single crab, snail, grasshopper, frog, or especially that snake, left on your plate."

Then she turned to face Dev. "Will you please watch and make sure she eats all her breakfast. I'd hate for anything to get loose in the house. I can't bear to watch."

He looked over her shoulder at the cage, "She went for the snake first. It's history. Her head's in the jar lapping up the crab spiders. The frog will be a toy for later if it doesn't have a heart attack first. The snails . . . mmm . . . maybe dessert. She seems real hungry. In any case, I don't think you need to worry about crabs in your bed."

She walked into the kitchen because the sounds Jillie

was making were distressing to say the least.

After a few minutes he joined her by the coffee pot. He ran a hand around her waist, pulled her against his chest, lifted her hair away from the side of her neck and kissed below her ear.

The satisfying sound of her deep sigh and the jump of her belly against his hand made him smile against her smooth skin.

She reached her hand up and stroked alongside his stubbled cheek. "Hmmm, good opener. While we're on the subject of crabs . . . maybe we should have the AIDS, herpes, STD, protection talk."

He put his hand in his front pants pocket and drew out his phone, flipped to a document screen and showed her a screen shot of his latest test results. Out of his other pocket he drew three round foil packages.

"I'm clean. How about you? Safe and on birth control?"

"Safe, but not on birth control. There just hasn't been any reason to be dealing with the bother and expense for quite some time. When was the last time you were with someone?"

"There's this cute secretary at one of the armories in Indiana. We hook up whenever I'm in town. That was in May. I used a condom, hmmm . . . actually two. The frat boys bought me a blowjob in Myrtle Beach the night we got here. Other than that, I've been *handy* in the shower."

"So you think I should take a chance on you?"

He pulled her to face him, this time with a hand on each of her hips. He looked down into her serious doctor face. "I most definitely do. I'm a safe bet."

"Have you washed your hands since procuring Jillie's food?"

"Yes. I used the hose attached to the house before I came in. And then I used hand sanitizer from my truck. When I came inside I washed them with the soap you keep beside the sink. I think it said it kills germs and bacteria."

"Well okay then." She removed his hands from her waist

and examined them. They were nice hands—long fingered with light hairs sprinkled on the knuckles. She saw several white scar lines against the tanned skin. These were hands that had done many things, some she would not have approved of. But still, she wanted these hands on her, touching her everywhere.

"Where's the first place you want to put them?" Her cheeky answer surprised him. But he didn't question it.

"Here." He took her face between both hands and dove in to taste her sweet soft lips. This morning they were a light mauve color. He did not think he'd ever kissed a woman who didn't have some kind of gloss, lipstick, or garnishment on her lips. Hers did not, and it was heaven. Soft, smooth, and now slick with the laps his tongue was making as he tried to devour them and consume her mouth. She tasted divine. The hazelnut of her coffee blended with the mint of her toothpaste and he could not get enough of the sensation of naked lips on naked lips, tongues delving in riotous search to discover nuances, teeth nipping for dominance.

He came up for air, looked at her glistening lower lip and bent again to take it between his own lips, tugged lightly—then allowed his tongue inside again to savor her silky inner cheeks. He used his teeth to gently scrape along her bottom inner lip. Not since junior high had he spent so much time on kissing. But by her soft moans and needy tugs on his hair to direct him, she told him that he was doing it right.

Behind them he could hear Jillie flapping her wings and chasing something inside her cage, but neither one cared if she caught it. It was time for them to satisfy their own urges.

Dev bent and wrapped his arm behind her knees and easily lifted her against his chest. Then he carried her down the short hall to her bedroom.

Placing her carefully in the center of the bed, he stood and unbuttoned the wrinkled linen shirt he'd hastily donned when he'd gone outside. He tossed it into the corner.

He watched as her eyes widened, taking in the abundant

pelt that covered his pecs. He worked out all the time, so he knew he had an enviable chest—women seemed to get off on it—so the time invested was well worth it. And he'd never been into manscaping, so the sprinkling of dark curling hair added to the intense virility of his maleness.

Watching Gentry's eyes widen and her face redden made him especially proud of his body. To please this woman with his body would be a dream come true. He could forget all the others now. From now on, his focus was all on her. It was all about using this well-honed body to please her. Only her.

"Your turn," he whispered, and she instantly complied as he watched each tiny button on her pajama top come undone and the opening grow wider, until with a quick fanfare she spread both lapels wide and her full breasts were revealed. Lying propped on a pile of pillows, she was a vision. Her wild curls were spread out around her head, her cheeks flushed from desire or maybe she was still blushing. This wasn't an everyday thing for her.

She was biting her lower lip, still red from his repeated kisses. But now, now that she was topless, he could see that her chest was also flushed. He was betting that the orgasm he planned to give her would reflect with a fan of passion over this beautiful, soft, enticing upper chest. He was eager to see the evidence of his lovemaking efforts.

But now his attention was focused on her coral nipples. Atop smooth white mounds that he could grip in each hand were hard pebbly peaks. Her pale breasts were perfect—the size, the porcelain unmarred beauty, and the pouty tips hardening in the cool breeze from the slow rotations of the overhead fan.

He was not going to wait to reveal more to her, or she to him. He needed to touch her now. He came around to the side of the bed and sat. Gently cupping her left breast, he slowly rotated his thumb to graze over the tip and heard her gasp of pleasure.

"You are gorgeous." He bent to kiss the tip.

He had allayed her fears with that statement. What woman didn't fear her breasts were going to be enough, shaped as desired, properly sized, all a man would dream of. But the look in Dev's eyes told her with all certainty that her breasts were exactly what he wanted. If things went well for them, maybe they would be all he'd ever want—because right now, in this moment, she loved him. And she wanted him to find pleasure in her body.

Looking at him, seeing how handsome he was, how sexy he looked, what woman wouldn't feel inadequate, she asked herself.

When his other hand cupped her right breast, then tweaked its nipple with his thumb and forefinger, she was gone to the pleasure. She gasped and closed her eyes as she felt the world tip. When he pinched both nipples at the same time and gently tugged, her universe flip-flopped.

The groan she emitted caused his cock to jerk in his pants at the exact same time her hand reached out to grip him. His groan echoed hers. Then he gently removed her hand and placed it open on the bedcover.

"You might as well settle in and enjoy. I plan on doing this for a while. These babies are going to be hard and needy. Then I'm going to let my tongue and teeth lose on them. I am going to drive you wild before I fuck you."

After his fingers had pinched and tugged and flicked her nipples mercilessly, his lips and tongue got into the act and created their own magical sensations. Her hands were fisted into the rumpled sheets because he had forbid her to do anything with them, telling her that her hands on him were not an option right now, that he was going to look his fill and touch her everywhere first. Only then would she get her turn to touch and learn his body.

When he was satisfied he had loved her breasts and made her nipples as hard as she could stand, he ran his hand over her exposed belly, stopping to own it with his large hand protectively claiming possession. "Mine," he whispered as he bent over her and peppered her belly and hip points with tiny kisses.

His hands gripped each side of her pajama bottoms, and slowly tugged them down, his eyes following the path as the satiny waistband slid lower and lower. He stopped when a tuft of chestnut curls became visible. The sight was so lovely, so enticing that he couldn't go any lower without paying homage. He bent and kissed her curls, drew his nose through the fine hairs, inhaled the heady sent building just a few inches lower, in her sweet pussy.

With one downward jerk of his hand her sex was revealed. Leaving her shorts bunched at the top of her thighs, he ran his fingers through her short curls. "You are glorious. What a cock stiffening sight."

And it was. He was tented in his chinos, straining at the zipper and moisture was dampening the material. He unzipped and gave his cock room to expand.

His hands on either side of her mound, at the juncture of her hips, he used his thumbs to fan away the damp curls, then bent and kissed the triangle of skin he had uncovered. Her sudden yelp and then the purring sound as he settled in made his cock jump. He was well pleased with her reaction.

With one hand he drew her soft pajama shorts further down and then off one leg. Then he wrapped his hand around her calf and stroked, lifting her leg and drawing it away from her body. He kept lifting it until he was able to hook it over his shoulder.

The action served to open her up to him as her labia spread, offering him a splendid view, and giving him full access to her. With his fingers splayed over her downy curls, his thumb stroked to learn her needs. He discovered her wetness and his cock jumped again. A gentle probing between the silky lips brought a gush of dampness. He smiled and looked up to gauge the pleasure on her face. Her creamy white throat was exposed, her head thrown back in pleasure, her eyes closed to take everything in more fully.

He shifted so he could allow his fingers to explore her,

letting his longest digit sink deep inside her. When her pearly dew coated his finger and her even more, he sighed. This was a woman who liked sex and knew how to welcome a man into her body.

Her channel was slick and tight—the answer to every man's basest desire. Her answering groan when he was three-knuckles deep made his cock leap, anxious to join in. He was fully hard now and could feel the first drops of precum coating the head of his penis and making him ready to enter her.

"So lovely . . . soft . . . smooth . . . silky, and *so* wet," he whispered. She answered him by moaning and placing her hand on his and encouraging him to continue. He added anther finger to the first, and with his palm facing upward, gently pushed them inside her in a slow rhythm. Soon she was lifting and he was thrusting harder.

He bent to lick her clit and to bestow tender kisses on her mound. When her soft mewling sounds told him she was close, he lapped along the length of her opening then wrapped his lips around her clit and softly drew it past his lips, his tongue flicking as his lips closed round the nub and gently sucked— not changing cadence, not increasing pressure—just letting her experience his ardent ministrations as her pleasure built. He would do this for as long as it took—when it came to eating pussy, he was marathon man.

The rewarding explosion came on fast and was more than he expected from her this first time. As she coated his tongue with a warm slickness and began to tremble beneath him, her fingers threaded into his hair and she clenched the short strands tight, holding his mouth to her as if to force him to still his actions, which he did. Yet experience had taught him to hold still and to keep his lips in place. He obliged her and held, letting her control the path this was going to take.

After a few seconds, where his tongue could feel the pulse of her body through her clit, she exploded again and the tiny nub throbbed fiercely against his tongue. A second later she shattered, and after that, her hands fell from his head to the bed. There was a series of unintelligible mumblings that sounded a little like a vinyl record being played jerkily backward.

He grinned, very pleased with himself, and with her. She was sated for the moment, and now his body was primed for him to achieve satisfaction. He was hard, so hard that he felt the softness of the mattress rebounding against him with each breath he took, as he lay prone on the bed, his upper half leaning over her. His cock was begging for some friction and was working harshly against the sheets. He could have gotten off that way, had in the past, even though it wasn't good for a man's penis to do so. But he wanted to be inside her, wanted to feel her silky heat stroking him. If he could make her come with him inside her, he would feel the walls of her vagina clamp down and hold him. And right now, he wanted that sensation more than anything in the world.

He lifted himself up onto his hands, reached over to the nightstand for a condom, and watched as she took it from him, tore it with her teeth, and drew the circle from the package. So sexy, so fucking sexy.

He sat back on his heels giving her access to him, and was full of pride that his cock was so prominently poised and ready to go. Angry-looking in its full glory, the erection he sported was tall and thick, with blue veins bulging along its length, the extended tip looking mottled with purple coloring it. His cock had a pulse of its own as it flexed and stood proud. Everything about it signified commanding, masterful, forceful. Yet right now, he knew it to be nothing if not the neediest thing ever, taking over his thoughts with its concern only for itself.

He groaned as she placed the condom on the tip and rolled it down—achingly slowly. Once covered, she gripped his penis with her hand and slid her wrapped fingers to the base and then slowly tugged them up.

He heard his gasp echo through the room. He got up onto his knees, gripped one of her ass cheeks in each hand and pulled her down the sheets until she was flat on the bed. He placed the crown of his penis at her opening and eased in, then shoved fully inside to seat himself. In the process, she slid several inches up the bed, and he had to pull her back to him to keep them joined. When he was all the way inside her, he took a moment to enjoy the sensation of being encased inside this woman, who he now knew he loved beyond all reasoning.

He took in the wonder on her face, her unfocused eyes and slack jaw. He knew he was at the center of her being and owned her womanhood like a Viking who plundered, but in this moment he was helpless to stop. He began in earnest to thrust. Selfishly, taking his pleasure by going deeply in and only thinking of hers while drawing himself out, as he looked down into her dazed eyes, her flushed cheeks, and her wildly panting open mouth.

He leaned over and took her lips with his, then breeched her mouth, thoroughly searching it with his tongue, lashing to taste all of her, and trying to seek out her thoughts, as if like him, she had any right now. Other than begging him to move her through her passion, urging him to help her find the secret place inside her that would give her the release she needed.

They established a rhythm of kissing, gasping, thrusting and retreating until he felt her legs cross behind his back and draw him in tighter. Her hands gripped his ass cheeks hard enough to force him to hold. And even though it went against everything his body wanted, he did. He bore down. And he held. He felt her as she bloomed, throbbed entirely independent of anything else, right there where they were joined, and she uttered sheer nonsense up to the ceiling. Then softly, her vagina fluttered and softly vibrated, like a butterfly leaving a flower. The beauty of the moment forced him to stop everything—to take the moment for what it was, and to stare at her beautiful, relaxed and peaceful face. To wait for her eyes to open so he could be witness to the miracle that had just gone on inside her body.

Her body shuddered and her eyes slowly opened. She

smiled up at him, a lazy, tremulous smile that brimmed with pleasure. "Wow," she murmured.

He was done for, totally defeated. And so in love with this woman his heart actually ached.

"Thank you," she whispered. "I really needed that."

He smiled back and said, "Not done yet. Let's try for another."

She shook her head. "You now. You whipped my ass."

"Well," he said with a huge grin, "that's an idea for another time."

She swatted his ass and he drew slowly out only to plunge back in with great fervor. The intensity built with each depression of the mattress rebounding, until the bookcase headboard, repeatedly slammed up against the wall. She matched him, staying with him for each stroke as her own enthusiasm intensified to the task, until he called out some very choice curse words, held to her tight, and spilled into her.

She felt him quiver inside, shake violently in his legs and then every muscle hardened and held. The act of him coming crushed his pelvis into hers. A distended part of him pressed against a conforming part of her, deep inside her vagina, a place she wasn't even aware of, a place that arched toward him on its on volition.

When they managed to just barely touch, a hard spasm went through her—full throttle for all of two seconds before tapering off and fading to little misfiring tremors. In those moments neither had control of anything in their universe. It was as if they existed for this magical moment to come upon them and then to hastily expire—without them having any say in the matter. It was as if they were taken to an alien place and then returned, with only the memory of something truly spectacular having happened to them.

He collapsed on top of her. She whispered as if afraid someone might hear, "What the hell was that?"

He laughed into her shoulder, bit it lightly. "It appears

you're multi-orgasmic, either that, or your g-spot is right out there and not hidden deep inside that marvelous little channel of yours." He kissed alongside her neck.

"I've never felt anything like that. It was a-maz-ing."

"If that's what it was, then you are a genuinely happy, and nice person."

"Hmmm?"

"Well, theory goes that the first time that little nut is cracked, it releases pent up emotions stored from angst, anguish, anxiety, and sorrow. It's like a garbage bin dumping intense feelings. Your past emotions must mostly be good ones for you to have had such a pleasant experience. Otherwise, you'd be bawling your eyes out."

"I think most of my past emotions have been good ones. I try to be positive and upbeat."

He pulled her close, into his side and turned her so they faced each other. "You are. And I can assure you, that you're positively good for me."

She started drawing tiny circles in his chest hair. She wanted to ask him if this had ever happened to him before. But, the next thing she knew, he was fast asleep. She looked up into his face. For the first time she could take it all in at her leisure, the rugged chin and jawline with its five-o'clock, and now ten o'clock shadow, the full sensuous lips that did a sneer so well, the nice straight nose, smooth cheeks, great long dark arching lashes over lids that held gorgeous light blue eyes. Nice full brows, one with a slight white scar toward the end. He had an intellect inside that handsome head that she already knew didn't miss much. She reached up and ran her fingers through his thick, cropped dark hair that had been styled to behave. Even after wild sex.

She smiled. Then she covered her eyes with her arm. She'd had her life all planned out. Now what? She didn't think she could let this man go. Her feelings were conflicted; they were nothing at all alike. But she wanted him. He made her happy and satisfied her in ways she'd never been. There was a thread of something running inside her now, something that had very positive feelings and emotions attached to it. Was this truly love?

She fell asleep in his arms wondering what was next. She'd always been a plotter and a planner. Had to always know the next step to take, the next place to be. Something told her that with Dev, she would never know the next thing. That everything would be chaotic and tumultuous. Not disorderly or frenzied, as he seemed to be neat and always in control. But with him, she suspected spontaneity was the key element of his make up. That he followed pleasure and looked for excitement everywhere he went. He was a man to be reckoned with that was for sure. She had never been with a man who was so . . . well manly. Part of her wanted to try and tame him. But the part of her that was still tingling from his attentions did not. No way!

Chapter 11
Seeing Stars & Eating Power Bowls

Dev's eyes opened to Gentry looking at him in confusion as if she was trying to figure out an equation written on his forehead.

"Hey there, sorry I zoned out."

She smiled. "I hear good sex does that."

He smiled back, "Then you should be in a coma."

"Rightfully so," she agreed, with a self-satisfied grin.

He pulled her close, looked into her gorgeous, sex-satisfied face. "You have the most amazing skin. It's unblemished, flawless, there's a sense of purity about it."

She laughed, "Oh, it's blemished all right," she pointed to a faint scar on the side of her neck, "roller skating and ran into a stop sign." Then she pulled up her knee, giving him a swift glance at her coppery bush, "Hit a rock when I fell off my bike." It was all he could do to take his eyes from the shadowy cleft she had just flashed him, to her knee, where she pointed to a small, slightly raised jagged line.

"Where can I go to exchange you, you *are* flawed!"

She gave him a little pout. "There will be no exchanging, I am a one-of-a-kind. Well, unless you go to Ireland, then there are thousands of me."

"No, I'm sure there's no one quite like you," he breathed out, as he ran his fingers down her arm. "When they call people white, you're what they're talking about. I have never seen or felt such soft, smooth skin. You are perfect." It was a statement said as fact.

"Well, now you sound like my dad."

He kissed along the length of her neck. "He doesn't know how perfect you taste, how sexy you look with your chest all flushed from coming, and these damp, dewy curls," he cupped her mound and groaned. "Feel what touching you does to me."

He took her hand and placed it on his penis, closed his eyes when she wrapped her fingers around it and lightly squeezed. Mewled when she began stroking his length and running her thumb around the head, catching the moisture and spreading it.

"Let's try something different this time," she said softly, then bent her head and took him between her lips. And sucked.

He'd never really got that seeing stars expression. But now he did. He not only saw stars, but he saw whole clusters of them expand, and then explode behind his eyes.

Gentry had never really felt confident servicing a man's penis in this fashion. Had never enjoyed it, and looked forward to the release as a means to an end. Because, really, you couldn't have a long-term relationship with a man without oral sex figuring into it—at least on the receiving end for the man. But for her to get her head into a man being down there, it always took longer then they had bargained for. Since her girlfriends had told her that type of orgasm couldn't be faked, she always tried to make intercourse the main act.

But this, this cock of his, it was magnificent. And she loved loving on it. His reactions to what she was doing, his gasps of delight, and his groans of down deep satisfaction fueled her to try new things. Little licks and lapping motions on the underside using her tongue flattened out, and then circles around the corona using the tip of her tongue that seemed to please him immensely.

His fingers shoved into her curls, and holding her in place as he guided her where he needed her. Then he hissed, "Suck, oh please, suck!"

She did, and was soon rewarded for her efforts. She had never swallowed before, always reaching for a wad of tissues from the nightstand. But this time she wanted to try it. And was sorry she did. She hid her reaction by coughing in her hand and running for the bathroom.

He had recovered by the time she returned, and made room for her beside him. Holding the sheet up so she could slide in next to him, he laughed. "That bad huh?"

She grimaced. "Damn, you're salty!"

He smiled. "I wouldn't know."

With fingers running through her hair to push back her curls, and then teasing her ear lobe, he whispered, "But thank you. That was truly special, really . . . on a whole other level. I don't want to sound corny, but I saw stars. Lots of 'em. I assure you, I'm well and truly spent. C'mere you, I need some cuddling."

He pulled her into his side, then adjusted her so her back was to his chest. Gently squeezing her tight, he kissed along the back of her neck. "I think I'm in love with you, Gentry. Wait. I *know* that I'm in love with you. There's not a doubt in my mind. I love you."

She turned to look over her shoulder at him. She didn't say anything, just met his eyes.

"I understand if you can't say it, too. But you will. That's my number one job now—to make you fall in love with me."

She didn't want to tell him she thought she already had. It just seemed too soon. Wasn't it? How long was it supposed to take? How did you know for sure? And anyway, she had her life planned out. She wasn't ready for all the changes coming at her as it was. This would affect every part of her life. Every day would change if they became a couple. But deep down, she already knew that if her days didn't include him, she would be devastated. She liked having him here. She liked nearly everything about him. The gun/hunter/carnivore part was something she was trying to reconcile. If he loved her, surely he would make some concessions for her beliefs? But a lifetime of loving and protecting animals could not be ignored. These differences could be game changers. It was why she couldn't say those three little words back to him right now.

Instead she said, "I'm hungry. How about you?"

"I could eat. A little refueling might serve my cause well right now. I don't have a lot of time to win you over before I have to leave on Friday. Tell me your heart's desire and I will procure it."

'Hmmm," she thought for a moment. "How about a power bowl? I think that would perfect1"

He smiled down at her as he covered her body with his. "Grains, greens, protein . . . I can do that. Too bad we don't have a Cava here. There's one in Wilmington though. It's the Mediterranean version of Chipotle. But a Mexican bowl would be good, the spicing is all that would be different and there's one of them in North Myrtle."

"Actually, I think I have most of the ingredients. Let me shower and get dressed and I'll see what I can throw together."

"Let's shower together and I'll help."

She turned and gave him a quick kiss. "That'll work. Then I have to go check on the kittens."

"I'll go too. See what trouble Puffball's getting into."

"Actually, we had an inquiry about her this morning. I think they've set up an appointment for someone to come check her out."

His lips pressed together, and a long "Hmmm," sounded through them.

"You don't sound like you're pleased."

"I'm not sure that I am." He turned and walked to the bathroom, his supreme maleness evident in his broad shoulders, muscled back, tapered waist, long toned legs, and most excellent ass.

Chapter 12
Death Trap Stairs & Wild Horses

Together they chopped vegetables, tore greens, cooked quinoa, roasted some fresh corn, mashed avocado, rinsed beans . . . made a harrissa sauce, and topped it all with feta cheese.

They sat at the small round table at the back of the kitchen that was under a big picture window. The view of the river and the marshes at high tide was stunning as the mid afternoon sun came over the trees.

"This view is worth climbing those death trap stairs for," he mumbled as he mixed everything in his bowl together, while she ate hers in sections.

"I know! The first time I came here though, I thought for sure I'd end up on Dateline."

He stopped eating and looked into her animated face. "Did you check out your landlord before you agreed to lease this place?"

"No, and he didn't check me out to see if I could afford it either. We just hit it off right away; the arrangement is perfect for us. If I need anything done he comes on the weekend. If he gets some new materials and needs to do anything to the house, he does it while I'm working. It's a great arrangement. And look at this view!" she pointed with her fork, indicating the live oak trees with dripping Spanish moss that framed the panoramic view of a wide, lazy river.

"It is a fabulous little place, tucked away from everything. So, he doesn't bother you at all? No coming on to you?"

"Oh no, he's got a partner in Raleigh. His husband runs an herb farm and has several booths at farmer's markets during the season. No worries there."

"Good. I'd hate to have to disembowel someone and

bury their remains in the marsh when I return."

"Wow, talk about Dateline. When do you think you'll be back? You're leaving day after tomorrow right?"

"Yeah, flight's at 10:15 in the morning. I think I can get back in about two weeks. Gotta tidy up some accounts and hand off some stuff to my latest apprentice. I have a good team. It's taken me years to get it set up, but they allow me the freedom to hunt, ski, travel, go to gun competitions, and . . . to return to you. That is, if you want me to."

Dev was not the type to force himself on anyone, or to beg a woman for her attentions. But this girl was different. He knew that he would change up everything—move across the country, live in a tent or an RV, a houseboat or a jitney bus, just to be with her.

"Of course, I want you to come back! I would be devastated if you didn't. Please tell me you will."

He reached over and covered her hand on the table. "Wild horses . . . couldn't keep me away."

"One of my favorite songs!" She grabbed her phone and made a few swipes on the screen, then the sound of Susan Boyle singing *Wild Horses* filled the tiny alcove.

They held hands and listened to the song as they took in the expansive view and each one let one pervasive thought after another tumble through their minds. It was inescapable the feelings they were generating. Despite their differences—and there were many—they felt drawn to each other.

When the song was finished, Dev picked up his phone, made the identical swipes that Gentry had made on her phone but chose a different selection, and then sat back, staring deeply into Gentry's eyes as *So This is Love*, sung by Ilene Woods played—a song from another of his Disney favorites, thanks to his girls.

After the kitchen was cleaned up they left for the shelter, both in their own vehicle so he could go back to *The Cockpit* to do some work and to start closing up the house. Palo had left to go back to Italy, and no one was expected to be back to the house until late fall. It was decided he would come back and stay at the *Scrapyard Bungalow* as he had dubbed it, if it was okay with her, as he had to be at ILM by 8 a.m. to make his flight, and where she lived in Shallotte was closer by about twenty minutes. Of course, there had been other considerations for him wanting to stay over. It had definitely been okay with her as she had those same considerations in mind.

Gentry was going to be driving to the Mad Boar Restaurant & Pub in Wallace to meet her parents for a congratulatory dinner. It had been their meet-in-the-middle place ever since she had moved to Shallotte to be able to work as a Vet Tech while studying for her degree. She hated the name of the place and all their meat specials, but they had delightful salads, fresh slaw, wilted spinach, and a chipotle lime quinoa pilaf with fresh roasted seasonal vegetables that she loved and always looked forward to having. It was about half way to Raleigh, so they each had a little over an hour's drive.

Sometimes, when she had special classes or exams at vet school, she would pop in to see her parents for lunch or to just share a bowl of ice cream. They understood her time constraints and did not guilt her out for not visiting them more often. So many of her friends were driving back and forth on Route 40 trying to meet family obligations that they had no interest in attending, just felt as if they had to. Her parents were the most understanding parents. They loved to see her, but they loved it more that she wasn't always harried and always driving interstate roads when she was dead tired.

She wondered what they would think of Dev. He was seven years older than she was. And a lot more worldly. And probably not at all the type of man they thought she'd be with. Heck, he was not the type of man *she* thought she'd be with. She laughed out loud as she drove her Kia Soul to the shelter with Dev traveling behind her.

Puffball was delighted when Dev opened the door to the kitten's enclosure. She was scheduled to have her sterilization procedure done tomorrow afternoon, so he was fairly certain that he and Gentry would be texting after he landed so he could check on how that went. He seemed more than fond of Puffball and if the situation had been different, she thought he could have probably been persuaded to adopt her.

But that might not have been a good thing. She knew he traveled a lot, but she didn't really know anything about his home life. She knew he visited his two girls a lot, and that he was even fond of their brother Anson, who often accompanied the girls on their outings, even though he was not Dev's son.

But she had no idea whether he lived in a luxury condo, a contemporary-style townhouse, a big travel bus, or in a Quonset hut on the property at one of the gun manufacturing plants— although Dev seemed more the old-fashioned farmhouse type than the high-rise type, in her opinion. She could picture him at home almost anywhere though. He struck her as the type of person who could fall asleep on a plane, flop on a couch at a friend's, doze while waiting for a dental appointment, fallout in a ski lodge in front of a roaring fire, or nap in the back of a taxi in an old city like Copenhagen.

She envied him that. She could only sleep if it was fairly quiet, if she was completely prone, covered up somehow, and in the dark. She blamed it on her mom, always tucking blankets around her when she was an infant in her crib, always turning off the light, and closing the door to household noises and not doing any loud chores.

The more she thought about her and Dev, the more she realized how very different they were. She hoped not too different though, she thought, as she cleaned up the area and changed out the litter.

"Hey," he nudged her elbow as she maneuvered out of the enclosure. "You okay? You look a little down."

She smiled over at him. "Yeah, I'm fine. Just overthinking things."

He raised an eyebrow at her, and damned if he wasn't the handsomest man ever. "Care to share?"

She shook her head, felt her curls caress her bare shoulders. She hadn't bound them as she usually did when coming here. "Just seeing some crossroads ahead. And I'm not fond of change. I like to see the big picture ahead of me, like that picture you see in the optometrist's machine of the big balloon way down that long road."

"Don't get upset over anything involving me. I'm used to change. So you don't have to be the one that adjusts. If it makes you feel better, I don't have to come over tonight."

"Oh, I want that, believe me! I just don't know what else I want anymore."

He turned her to face him. "Gentry, I am a patient man. No worries. We'll work through this . . . much slower if it needs to be. I'm a pragmatist. I know that just because I love you, doesn't mean you love me, or that you ever will. But I'm an optimist too, so I am hopeful that you will. You're at a very exciting time in your life, and maybe you need me to back off for a little while so you enjoy that phase of it without me. I want you to know I'm fine with that. I don't ever want you to be unhappy. And if I am distressing you in any way, I'll back off."

She ran her fingers through the hairs at the nape of his neck and drew him down for a kiss. Then they pressed their foreheads together. "I don't want you to back off Dev," she whispered. "Just give me some time to settle into this. I've been alone for a long time. It's just been me and whatever orphan animal needed specialized care. You're a chaotic whirlwind for sure. But one I'd rather have in my life than not. And although I know I need some downtime where I'm not answering to so many challenges, I don't want to stop seeing you. I don't want to give up on us, and what we might become to each other."

"Maybe while I'm away, you can walk on the beach,

spend a few days lazing in the sun. I'll text you the code for *The Cockpit*. There are beach chairs, surfboards, kayaks, and bikes galore in the bottom storage area. One code opens everything, even the elevator. At a minimum, please use the house for parking."

"Thank you. I think I'll like the premium parking package that comes with knowing you."

He smiled down at her, "Use whatever you want. Just don't drink all the champagne. Save some for me, for when I get back."

"Which bedroom is yours, in case I want to sleep in your bed?"

He laughed. "The one with the big gun safe." He tucked some curls behind her ear, "But if you do that, please send me a picture. Something provocative."

"I don't do sex texting."

"I know you don't. And I *never* want you to. Let's keep things simple, and just between us until you're more comfortable. Owww!"

He looked down, and Gentry's eyes followed. Puffball was climbing up his jeans-clad leg. She had reached his waist where the jersey of his shirt was not as sturdy as the denim. Her sharp little claws were digging into his skin.

Gentry laughed that delightful laugh she had that melted his heart and had him pining for her already.

He gently tugged Puffball away from his shirt and held her in the crook of his arm, stroking the top of her head. She chased his hand so she could lick on it. He smiled and then laughed when she jumped to his shoulder and pawed at his hair.

"She likes you."

"I like her, too. She's a sweet one."

"She'll probably be adopted out this afternoon. There are two client appointments later today and I just got a text that confirmed her surgery for tomorrow."

"That great news, she needs a good home. I want that for

her. I hope she gets a good one with some kids in it."

"Mmmm, children aren't always the best bets for cats, kittens might work though, if the kids aren't too rowdy."

Dev moved Puffball off his shoulder, held her close to his chest and scratched the top of her head.

"She's not a dog, Dev, cats don't like their heads rubbed like that."

Just to prove her wrong, Puffball stretched up and licked Dev's chin—his whiskered two-day beard. And apparently she liked the feel of it on her tongue, because she kept doing it.

"Hmm, maybe I don't need a girlfriend after all . . ."

Gentry laughed, "Oh yeah? Some of my worst injuries were from cats. They're particularly fond of swiping at things that dangle."

"Well, fortunately, I don't dangle much. At least not when you're around."

She thought that was hysterical. "Well, I've got to get going if I'm going to meet Mom and Dad on time."

"I'm going to hang around here and refill the litter totes from the bags in the office, then I'm going to leave some cash to replenish the supply. See you later at the scrapheap?"

"What happened to *Scrapyard Bungalow*? I like that name a little better. Anyway, unlike your place, you won't need a code to get in."

"Yeah, and sadly you don't need a key either. We should rectify that when I get back . . ."

"What's your solution, a steak-eating Doberman?"

"How about just a locksmith? My treat."

She stood on her tiptoes and gave him a kiss—a nice, sweet one. "Let's talk tonight, I gotta git."

He saluted her and watched as she ran to her Soul, her mass of hair flying out behind her.

He was done. So done. He might as well call the family jeweler. This one wouldn't want a diamond though. Hmmm . . . maybe a cat's-eye tourmaline

Chapter 13
His Back Story in Dev's Storytelling

Two weeks later, Dev was sprawled out on a gray-painted slab of concrete, helping Gentry inject a potent cocktail of antibiotics into the front leg of an anesthetized golden retriever. One they'd spent the better part of the afternoon and evening bathing, over and over again, until finally they got the stench of urine and feces out of the poor dog's fur, paws, and ears.

A month ago, if you'd told Dev that he'd be washing filthy dirty dogs, bottle feeding neglected puppies, and pulling clingy kittens with very sharp claws away from his expensive pants, shirts, sweaters, socks, and even his hair, he would have said you were Looney Tunes. Yet here he was, with a monster of a dog pinning him down with her weight draped across his thigh as if she belonged there—unwilling to budge even if she could—which she could not. So Dev was immobile for the time being. And he was just fine with that. He didn't mind it one bit, as Gentry was here. And he loved watching her work.

She knew her stuff, it was obvious that she was proficient at her job; capable of calming even the most agitated animal, and so capable and caring that it humbled him. He'd never known anyone like her. She was the most selfless, altruistic, kind-natured person he'd ever met. To be able to just watch her work settled him—calmed him in a way that he couldn't explain. He just knew when he was not with her that he wanted only to get back to her side. He had taken to praying—actually praying, that she felt the same way about him. He thought that would be a miracle if it turned out to be true, and so he prayed every morning and every night that it was, or that it could be. But even so, he was almost certain that he would always love her more than she loved him.

Gentry finished bandaging the dog's leg and then

plopped over from her squatting position to tumble down beside Dev. As she sat back up and leaned against his shoulder, her hand brushed against the holster that held his Glock—which in deference to her, was now in the door of his truck ever since she had said that guns terrified her.

"How did you get into the arms business?" she asked. "It seems a little against your nature to not always be carrying. Unless, you're showing me a nurturing side of you that you don't actually have."

"Oh, I have it alright, it just took you to bring it out in me." He looked at the golden asleep on his leg and knew the medicine would keep her knocked out for quite a while, and that until the dog woke, and she was doing better, Gentry wasn't about to leave her side. They likely had an hour or more, so he knew he had time to tell her the story of his history lesson of a lifetime.

"It's a long and involved story. You sure you want to hear it?"

She schooched in close to his side and grabbed some coarse blankets that were piled up by the wall and reclined next to him on the cement pad. They were inside the largest enclosure the rescue center had, but they were still sitting in a tight space.

She kissed him just below his ear and whispered, "Yes, all of it. And make it exciting! I can't nod off until I'm sure her numbers are getting better instead of worse."

"Then we can go home? Get in your horrible excuse for a bed?" The bed was too short for him. The bedsprings squeaked, and the headboard rattled due to the built-in bookcase with the sliding cabinet door that was loose on its glides.

"Yes." She snuggled closer and Dev wrapped his arm around her shoulders to pull her into his side, her head rested on his upper chest. Her wild curls, tamed by barrettes, tickled his neck.

"Okay you asked for it." He cleared his throat to make way for his best story telling voice. Storytelling around the campfire was one of the talents he had been known for while serving overseas.

"My drinking buddies touched on an idea one night in a smoky New Bedford bar. I was often there for business early in my career, so a gang of us met regularly. The idea was insane, but the longer we drank, the more it made perfect sense. By the time the night was over, none of us would ever be the same.

"I realize now, but didn't see it then, that there was an underlying significance to the fact that our ragtag group of regulars often chose this particular bar to gather in when the urge to swill copious amounts of alcohol came over us. Big Dan's was the bar that Jodie Foster made famous in the movie *Accused*. The scene of a pool table gang rape that occurred in the early 1980s seemed the perfect place to roil our emotions and to end up sending us all to the one place in the world that none of us had any business going to.

"Each of us was dealing with our own life crisis in those days. My wife was starting divorce proceedings. Mickey, a cop, was dealing with PTSD from a carjacking that went wrong. Charlie was tired of being stuck in one place all his life and was beginning to hate living in the city. Larry was dead broke after many years of carefully managing his finances, but due to having an affair and his wife hiring the better attorney, he was now all but homeless. Molly was an underappreciated barmaid, a real stunner who'd had her education on the docks but just couldn't seem to catch a break. Kevin, who couldn't outrun his nightmares and instead ran to booze. Chike was a crude dockworker that had it bad for Molly. And Tommy, well . . . we didn't know it at the time, but Tommy was dying from cancer.

"That night Aerosmith was blaring out over the slurring voices that were raised in defiant defense of the latest shock jock to be caught cheating on his wife, when Molly, our young harried barmaid, raised her voice in timid inquiry, "Um, who ordered a dozen hot pepper stuffed quahogs?'

"Tommy Wharton's hand went up in a nonchalant wave from the end of the bar and Molly held the pewter platter high above her head as she maneuvered herself between men of all shapes and sizes to bring them to him.

"'Thanks, doll, been waiting for these all day. This is the only place that bakes 'em in Portuguese red wine, ya know.'

"Tommy had to slap at Mickey's errant hand that was trying to steal around his shoulder to grab at one. With a low growl Tommy muttered, 'Get your own dinner, you damned mooch.' Then relenting as usual, he dumped three of the stuffed quahogs onto the saucer of his coffee cup and handed them over to Mickey Burns. The rest he offered around and then shrugged when there were no other takers. 'More for me,' he grumbled and then settled into stuffing them into his mouth. He gave me one to try, but they weren't for me.

"On the TV, mounted high above the shelves of the dusty liquor bottles along the back wall, a red banner was flashing under the CNN logo. The serious tone of the announcer drew many eyes as the image of a man kneeling, with a blindfold over his eyes came into view. Someone walked over to the jukebox and hit the power button to shut it down. Crackling static filled the space vacated by Aerosmith. The quality of the video feed was poor and the station broadcasting, Al-Jazeera, was using outdated equipment.

"Both staff and bar patrons watched as an older, bearded, dark-skinned man in flowing robes ranted and raved in a foreign tongue, his hands gesturing wildly with a long sword. Then in a heart-stopping moment, the kneeling man was brutally beheaded.

"Everyone in the bar gasped. On the screen, a gleeful soldier held up the severed head for the camera, gripping it by the hair and shaking it in triumph. Ayman Al-Zawahiri, Osama bin Laden's right-hand man, had performed his evil, sick justice once again.

"Photographs identifying the dead man flashed on the screen and soon it was clear to all that he was the American businessman that had been held hostage by the insurgents who were now overrunning the Pakistani government and sending out videos of their supremacy.

"When the CNN announcer's voice faded out, Tommy was the first to speak out in the now quiet bar. 'Fuckin' bastards!'

"Everyone nodded in agreement while picking up their drinks and downing the contents. It was impressive synchrony as heavy tumblers met the old wood of the long bar in a common man's salute to the now deceased American.

"Someone walked over to the jukebox, hit the power button, and dropped in coins to restart it. But as soon as the music began, the machine was kicked by someone else's hard, angry boot. The lead-in to a song by Leanne Rimes was abruptly stopped.

"'If I have to listen to that damned Bluoooewew song again I'm going to retch!'

"Two guys at the jukebox got into it and Kevin Murphy had to pull them apart. 'Cut it out, you two! I know you're angry but don't take it out on each other. That's what they want, that's what Al-Qaeda wants—us at each other's throats.'

"'Yeah,' Tommy sneered, 'that's exactly what they want.' Another drink had been perfunctorily shoved across the bar to him and he picked it up and tossed it back. Wiping his mouth with the back of his hand he added, 'You know, there's a hundred million dollar price tag on bin Laden's head. Why don't we put a team together and go over and get it? I don't have anything to live for anymore with my Kate and my dogs gone, and I'd dearly love to kill a couple Al-Qaeda before I die. It'd be a fitting way to end my life.'

"'Count me in,' said Mickey Burns, a retired city cop, as he slid onto the barstool beside him. 'I'm sittin' here drinking beer every night while that poor bastard done got his head lopped off. It's not right I tell ya.'

"'No, it's not right,' Charlie Giel mumbled, 'not right at all. How far's this Afghaneeestan anyway? I've never even been over the Mystic River Bridge, but maybe it's time. Maybe it's past time.' Charlie was a teamster and a hardworking truck driver. He drove the big construction rigs that often never saw a paved road. He pushed, towed, or hauled dirt from one place to another, grinding gears while listening to Bluegrass and cussin' at anyone who got in his way. His supervisors could never figure out why he was always in such a big ass hurry because there was always more dirt to move no matter how fast he drove. Boston's Big Dig had sure proved that.

"'You mean Pakeeestan you moron! And it's 7,702 miles from D.C. to the airport in Gwadar, Pakistan. It's a whole other world over there.' This was the voice of Lawrence Miller, known to most as No Balls Larry. He'd been a C.P.A. for Cantor Fitzgerald and had been home with a stomach virus on 9/11. His ailment had actually been his secretary, and because of not being in his office that fateful day, he'd been found out. He was now divorced and rather than work for his ex's house payment, he had turned in his Pilot automatic pencils and Hewlett Packard calculator for a red fireman's helmet, but only as a volunteer. He said he was not going to work just to hand the money over to his ex. He got in shape and ran the Boston Marathon the next year, and then every year after as a tribute to the men and women who'd gone down in the towers as a way of making amends that he hadn't joined them.

"In some parts of the country, 9/11 emotions were abating, but for those in New York, New Jersey, and Massachusetts, feelings were still raw. The victims had not been faceless to them. They had worked, played, ate, and drank with those people. Some of them had even slept with them, whether they were theirs to do that with or not. So the victims were very real and the insult was felt down to the core in that bar. Especially for guys like Mickey Burns and Kevin Murphy, both cops at the time, who were now divorced because they hadn't handled things all that well when the towers fell.

"Kevin had been a former Army Ranger and for months after 9/11, he slept so violently that his wife had to sleep in a separate bedroom, and once that started . . . well things rarely work out for the best in those situations.

"Mickey, the fourth in an Irish Boston generation of cops, continually walked around with a fist ready to smash into a wall. His wife had managed to get his Irish up a time or two and so had walked right into it, or at least that was his side of the story.

"Molly, the pretty, tousled-haired barmaid, walked over to collect the empty quahog platter, and Chike, sitting at the end of the bar, ran his fingers up her arm. Molly's skin, the color of cinnamon was always warm, while her hair, an exotic shade of black that often looked like midnight blue was cool to the touch like soft watered silk. Through a devastating political quirk of fate, many people now thought that the stunning Middle Eastern beauty was Muslim and therefore a terrorist. Paradoxically, Molly had spent her formative years among the wharf rats on the Dublin docks before seeking asylum in New York. It was an incongruity few could reconcile with after hearing her speak for the first time. The sassy brogue of a spirited

Irish woman coming out of what could easily have been an Iranian princess turned many a head in disbelief.

"Chike was a dockworker, competent and certified on all manner of cranes, especially the ones that often defined the skyline over Boston Harbor, the ones so high you could only see them moving and never the man inside who was operating them. Which was a shame, as Chike was a handsome man to look upon. With tawny golden hair and warm brown eyes he was the image of a Timberland model.

"Grabbing Molly's wrist and placing it on his denim-clad thigh, he leaned into her and with a devilishly smooth brogue whispered in her ear, 'The men here say you have an iron box with a lock on it, that you're cold as the arctic, but I say you're hot and that you're just waitin' for the right man to warm your bed. I fancy myself to be that vera man.'

"Without turning to face him, Molly gave him a backhanded slap to the side of his cheek, 'If it's my bed needs warmin' I'll get meself a hot water bottle before I let the likes of you under my quilts, Chike McDougal!'

"'Aw lassie,' he moaned as she moved out of his eager reach, 'have a heart, it's *my* quilts I'm havin' to wash ever'day from my wayward thoughts of you.'

"'That's real good, Chike, tell her that she's going to have to share you with your very first love—your fist!'

"Everyone hooted, and Chike had the good grace to blush to his ears. Despite his tan the red creeping up his neck was hard to hide.

"Tommy Wharton reached over and ruffled Chike's sandy brown locks, 'S'all right, you'll warm 'er up next time. Don't you be givin' up, I think she's beginnin' to cotton to you.'

"'Yeah, right. So what's this about goin' to Pakistan? You're not serious are you? The country's finest are over there and they canna find the lout, what makes you think you can?' Chike stood and braced himself against the wall, his booted feet crossed at the ankles while he looked down at Tommy who was fumbling for a cigarette. He already had one burning in the ashtray in front of him.

"'Hey, old man, you think maybe you had enough? As they say in the old country, you appear to be in your cups,' he chided as he pointed to the already lit cigarette.

"Sam, coming over to Tommy's other side, holding a pool cue, pushed the drink that was coming across the bar for him out of his reach.

"Tommy, so mellow now that he didn't even notice, lifted sad eyes to the Irish black man who came around and sat on the barstool Chike had just vacated.

"'I can't stand this pain, Sam. It hurts so badly. I just want to kill somebody and get this all over with, then lie down somewhere and be out of this misery. I lost everything that meant anything to me in one week. It's not like I'll ever be happy again, so I might as well do some good. Killing some *Tallybans* would do a world of good, don't 'cha think?'

"Sam nodded and helped Tommy light his cigarette as he was apparently determined to smoke this one rather than the other one. Sam Muldoon was the local UPS deliveryman and as even-tempered a man as you'd ever want to know. There was always a smile on his face and a good-natured joke on his lips. He had been playing pool with Lester most of the evening, so hadn't been immersed in the conversation, but the whole bar was now buzzing with the old engineer's challenge. 'Killin' ain't all it's cracked up to be. Take my word on it,' Sam said.

"As Tommy's head nodded toward his chest, Chike pushed off from the wall he'd been leaning against and helped Tommy up from the stool.

"'You ever lost someone you woulda died for; you ever carried this dread around with you all day, everyday?'

The words were slurred, but Chike had no trouble making them out.

"'Yeah, my mum and my da, all in one night, and mind you, I was just fifteen. C'mon, let me get you home, you need a bed and I could use some rest before the sun shows itself in the morn.' I got up and told Chike I'd come with him to help out.

"Half dragging, half carrying Tommy, Chike and I made our farewells to the regulars. Now that was surely a misnomer, I remember thinking that and chuckled as Chike led Tommy out of the bar and over to his beat up work truck. Not a one of us was anything close to being a regular kind of person back then.

"It wasn't the first time I'd had to help take Tommy home and I was pretty sure it wouldn't be the last. But it was the least I could do for the man who consciously or not, continued to pick up the tab for all his bar buddies week after week.

"Zawahiri's head's worth twenty-five million, ya know,' Tommy said as we rode through a sleeping city. 'I'd almost rather have that Egyptian's head instead of bin Laden's. He's a doctor, a surgeon, he shouldn't be killing people!'

"'You've a point there.' I remember saying.

"'He was last seen in Afghanistan, in Kost. Not too far from the Kyber Pass.'

"'Really, and you know this because . . .'

"'Been there. Built a bridge near there once. Never thought I'd go back though. Guess I'd better find my passport.'

"'I think you'd better find your keys, this is your street.'

"A month later, Tommy sat at the bar waving a cocktail straw as his cigarette. 'I'm tellin' ya, I did it. I did—

really. I sold the houses, cars, stocks—all my assets. And I quit smoking. If that doesn't prove I'm serious about this, I don't know what does.'

"'You sold the house, the one I drove you home to a few weeks back?' Chike asked.

"'Yeah, that one and the one in Florida. I got 6.8 million when everything was shook out and signed for. Sold every stick of furniture, every fancy Calphalon pot and pan, every piece of Wedgewood, Waterford, and Royal Doulton. Like to have killed me selling off Kate's angel collection, but what was I going to do with two hundred spun glass Christmas ornaments? I ain't never gonna have a tree again no how. Merry Christmas? Yeah right, that's never gonna happen again, at least not for me.'

"'So you're homeless now?' asked Mickey, the studied voice of a police officer doubting everything he was hearing.

"Tom shifted on his hip and pulled a gold American Express Card from his pocket along with a money clip that was straining to hold its bounty. 'Long as I got this I'm not homeless. I'm welcome at Hiltons, Hamptons, Holiday Inns . . . you name it. Islamabad Embassy Suites is my next stop.'

"He took an envelope out of his jacket pocket and threw it on the bar; his passport slid out along with a lot of foreign currency, it was a weird collection of assorted bills—an impressive stack of bank notes, all very colorful, all with pictures of old bearded men with some kind of headgear on them, and all having watermarks—most with an indecipherable script going up the sides and appearing as if written upside down.

"'You're serious? You're going to find Osama bin Laden and blow him up?' This from Larry.

"'Yup.' Tom put the straw in his mouth and started to mangle it up and down with his teeth. 'Just need to know how many plane tickets to buy.' He looked around at the gathered group. 'So, who's in?'

"After everything was said and done, we were all in, including Molly. Tommy got us all passports, Arab clothing, MREs, and a ton of military supplies. He had several ex-recon guys give us briefings and then he chartered a jet. He gave me a shitload of money for me to buy guns, but since my family owned a huge gun-manufacturing plant, I just grabbed what I thought we'd need—like two hundred of 'em—and put the money in an envelope with a note to my dad in the safe . . . in case I didn't come back.

"Then we all got on an old decommissioned military plane and we went to Pakistan. Tommy figured that if Pakistan didn't pan out, we'd go to Afghanistan from there. And eventually, we did. Everywhere we went Tommy hired trucks, drivers, translators and guides. It was tough going for a while trying to get our bearings in all the strange places, pretending to be civilian ex-pats. I had it easier than most as I'd already been to some of those places when I was in the Army.

"People stopped talking when we mentioned who we were looking for. There'd already been a slew of bounty hunters in and out of the country from all over the world due to the size of the reward. But the tyrants we were looking for were the worst kind of evil and people were afraid to cooperate. Retribution to the perpetrator as well as to their family and friends would be violent and quick if anyone in the regime even thought they were abetting the enemy. We were the enemy. No one liked us. No one wanted to help us. No one wanted us lurking around. They wanted us to leave. That's why we took our own food wherever we went—they would have poisoned us if they could.

"Then one of the guides we came across, a sheep herder, who stunk to high heaven, nodded at us when we mentioned bin Laden. Tommy gave him a wad of money and off we went—to Abbottabad—where we discovered we were too late. Two weeks earlier Seal Team Six had been there and had discovered bin Laden's hideout. They had killed him and one of his sons. It was all over. We were happy. Jubilant really. None of us had been counting on the money. We just wanted the bastard dead. To us this was a huge victory.

"By this time, the State Department and the military on both sides had gotten wind of us and we all ended up detained. Tommy had gotten real sick by then and he was taken to a military hospital where he died a few days later. And that's pretty much the end of the story."

Chapter 14
Vegetarians, Carnivores, & Dr. Katz

The dog that Gentry had named Heidi woke up and rolled off Dev's leg as she tried to get over to Gentry. Every animal I'd ever seen here had immediately fallen in love with this woman. I figured, I'd never had a chance of avoiding the same fate.

"Wait, what happened to all the guys? What happened to Molly?" Gentry asked, her eyes bright with curiosity.

Dev laughed. "You're really into this," he chucked her under the chin with his knuckles and grinned at her.

"Tell me!" she implored her light green eyes lovely coronas in a beautiful, sweet face. He constantly marveled at her flawless cream-colored skin, a striking contrast to her light coppery hair. He didn't see the tiny freckles sprinkled here and there as imperfections. To him, they were part of her beauty, exactly perfect in their random placement.

"Okay, okay. Sam the UPS man came home and retired and joined the choir of a Baptist church. Turns out he was a baritone and could sing opera with the best of them. Mike and Kevin bought a food truck and spent weekends feeding the hungry. Each week they earned enough to replenish the food given away by the paying business they had during the week.

"Larry went back to being a volunteer fireman and saved four children from a burning apartment the first day back. Charlie went to Las Vegas where he became a professional Texas hold 'em player. He also joined a bluegrass band and was having the time of his life last time I talked to him.

"And Molly met a wealthy Arabian prince and joined his caravan of camels that was heading back to his palace. His name was Aladdin, and he whisked her away right in front of our eyes on his magic carpet. Oh wait, that was Chike and it was an old Army Jeep covered with red dust as they bounced along the rutted roads crossing the desert. They had twins on Christmas day two years later.

"Awww, that's sweet."

"That was fate, honey. Those two were always meant for each other. Everyone knew it but them."

"What happened to all Tommy's money?"

"Well, there's the rub. Tommy was a generous soul. He used it all up bribing drivers, translators, innkeepers, hashish dealers and homemade hooch makers. You couldn't buy alcohol, and the homemade stuff you could find that you could buy illegally was god-awful and very pricey. But some really good pot could be had if you made the right connections. Tommy lived large in a place that had little to recommend it. He used some to bribe officials, and doled it out to us as we needed it. And he tipped every single person in the hospital that came into his room. He was a king until his last breath. What was left we used to ship him home and to bury him with his beloved Kate. And trust me, getting his body stateside cost a small fortune. Red tape only gets cut with the help of the military or a lot of American dollars. He'd had his grand adventure and he'd loved every single minute. Except maybe that week he'd had dysentery."

"And you, what happened to you?"

"Well, the State Department ran the numbers on all our guns and the search led to my family's business in Kentucky. My dad came to collect them, and me. He wasn't very happy that I'd taken the guns without his knowledge and he was furious about where I had taken them and for what purpose. He made me refurbish each one, and then I was sent around the country to all the different gun dealers to sell them, along with a slew of others he dug up from God knows where. It's how I became an arms dealer. Turns out I'm pretty good at it."

"I hate that guns are used to kill animals. And I hate the hunters even more every time we get an abandoned coon dog or bird dog that's been discarded because it's too old to hunt or retrieve anymore. A dog that was once treated like a best friend and given the best food gets old and is left to fend for itself by eating rotten carcasses and having maggots eat their bodies from the inside out. *They* are the ones that deserve to be shot."

After he helped her to stand, he wrapped his arm around her neck, pulling her close. He kissed her cheek. "I hate that part too, baby. And I'm going to help you do something about it."

He looked around, taking in all the occupied cages. "I want to help you with these animals. I know the county can't do it all." He waved his hand to encompass the shelter and its mishmash of kennels lined up throughout the compound. "I can make people more aware, help set up foundations, get corporate donors, sponsor marathons—whatever it takes."

She grabbed his hand and squeezed it. It was so much larger than hers. She loved that his hands were so strong, competent, yet gentle and loving to her, and to the animals.

"I know you do, and everyone is so grateful for all you've done already."

"And I want to marry you. Why won't you tell me yes?"

He'd asked her three times since he'd returned. Once with the ring he'd bought in her champagne glass at dinner, once while they were in the bathtub, her back reclined against his chest, and him floating the ring in a box balanced on a bar of soap, and once letting her discover it on her own in Jillie's cage hidden inside a porcelain hinged box depicting Noah's Ark.

"I told you, I'm not doing anything until I get my license in hand and find out where they're sending me for my residency."

"I understand that part. I'm willing to wait as long as it takes. I just want you to start wearing my ring, so everyone will know that you belong to me."

She tilted her head up at him and gave him a sideways look full of scorn. "Really? You want to own me? Like a house or a truck or a watch?"

"No, no no. I don't want to own you. I want to possess you, which is different. It means I want to enjoy you, have you, hold you keep you, take care of you."

"Well, that's better. There's another thing," she said as she began folding blankets while Dev tried to make Heidi comfortable for the night tucking one around her head.

She smiled at his caring, gentle manner as he stroked her nose and settled her floppy and frayed rabbit toy by her chest, where she could feel its presence and smell the familiarity of Gentry's scent on it.

"And what's that?"

"I don't believe in mixed marriages."

"What's mixed? We're both Anglo-American with a southern bent."

She gathered up all the bandages and disposable pads they'd used and put them into a trash bag. "I'm a vegetarian and you're not. That's going to be impossible to deal with. Me watching you eat burgers and chicken and steaks, while I chow down on bulgur and lentils and eggplant parm."

"Lots of vegetarians co-mingle with *car-ni-vores,*" he said, drawing out the word and making it sound downright evil. "We'll make it work. I promise not to eat rabbits or lamb or any animal you'd actually have to treat, like a dog or a cat or a horse."

"Veterinarians treat cows and pigs."

"Then I won't eat any animal you give a name to, and I promise to eat meat sparingly and to eat more salads and grains when I'm with you. I'll save the rib-eyes on the grills for when I'm with my frat boys."

She pursed her lips and thought about it. Then gave him the stink eye said, "And I won't shop for any meat. You'll have to do that on your own, and then keep it in a separate place. I don't want to look at it."

"I can do that."

"And our kids, if we have any . . . I'd want them to be . . . well . . . more like me in that regard."

"I agree. Until they are old enough to make that decision for themselves."

"That's fair."

"So . . . we're good?"

"That ring, it's too ostentatious. I can't work with animals with that monstrosity on my finger. I want a plain gold band."

"I can take care of that with one phone call. Anything else?"

"I want to honeymoon in Australia. I want to see kangaroos and wallabies, and koala bears. Maybe even a platypus if we can find one."

"Deal."

"Okay then. I'll marry you."

He gave her a sideways look. "That was almost too easy. When?"

"When the invitations can say and Dr. and Mr . . ." she hesitated, "what is your last name by the way? I can't believe I haven't known it all this time."

"Estating."

"Estating?"

"Yes. Dev Estating. Get it?"

"Nah, your mom wouldn't have done that."

"Yeah, but my dad would."

"Isn't your full name Devon?"

"Yes."

"What's your real last name?"

"Okay, it's Shire."

"Really . . . like Devonshire?"

"Yes."

"Why don't I believe you?"

"I don't know, why don't you believe me?"

She held out her hand. "Show me your license."

He put his hand to his back hip pocket and drew out his wallet, then flipped it open. Several impressive badges folded out first, then his license.

"Devon James Katz? Really? I'm going to be Dr. Katz?"

"I knew you wouldn't like that. Maybe I should change

my name instead and become Dev Macrory."

"You'd do that?"

He nodded. "I'd do anything for you, Gentry. You should know that by now."

She laughed at that. "Devon Macrory has a nice ring to it."

"Yeah, it kinda does."

"But I want to have my sheepskin on the wall someplace first. I want to settle into a practice someplace before all that wedded bliss happens."

He smiled down at her, ran his fingertips over her lips. Little did she know that he had plans for setting her up in her own practice anyplace she wanted after she finished her DVM residency. But he was not going to broach that now. She had said yes to marrying him. For now, that's all he wanted. "Let's go home and start practicing for the honeymoon."

She smiled back at him and stroked the side of his neck, ran her fingers through his hair, stroked alongside his ear. "I think you've already achieved expert status in that field. Let's go home and have a protein bowl and some guava juice."

"Can that be spiked with vodka?"

"I might be agreeable to some champagne, what with us celebrating another rescue saved."

"And us getting engaged . . ."

"Yeah, there is that." She pulled his head down and kissed him, her tongue liberally wandering, her fingertips doing amazing things in and round his ear while stroking the hairs on the back of his neck.

When the kiss had ended, he took the hand that had been caressing his neck and kissed her palm. "I'll help you lock up," he murmured, his eyes not leaving hers.

"Then you can follow me home," she said.

"How about we go together? I want to check in on Heidi in the morning. I can get my truck from here then." He wasn't ashamed to admit he was finding satisfaction helping her change the lives of animals for the better.

He had surprised her by adopting Puffball for his girls and then having one of his assistants who serviced Horry County shooting ranges deliver it to their house for him. She knew that his arranging the adoption with his ex was just a way to keep Puffball in his sphere. And of course, she didn't mind it a single bit. But he couldn't fall for every stray. Look who's talking, she chided herself.

"You can't get attached to every animal you help me with. You know we can't do our work or go anywhere if we have a menagerie at home to care for. We'll find a good home for Heidi, but it won't be ours."

"I know. I just want to make up for all the times I didn't help these creatures when I could have."

"You could help these creatures by not selling guns to people who kill them."

"You know I only sell to the military and law enforcement now, right?"

"Yeah, I have to remember that. You're out to save the world and I'm out to save the animals."

He swatted her on her butt as they walked down the path that led to the parking lot. "*We're* out to save the world, and *we're* out to save the animals."

She smiled over at him and then looked over at his Hummer, the paint done up in a camouflage pattern. He'd driven up this time instead of flying. "Isn't it time for you to consider a hybrid . . . something better for the environment?"

He laughed. "Life with you is going to be challenging."

"That's exactly what I was thinking about you."

"Are we going to have to live in an adobe house with a clay oven and chickens running around outside?"

She threw her head back laughed. He found it delightful the way she laughed with pure enjoyment, letting everything bubble up and burst out. God he loved this woman—her energy, her kind nature, her love for everything that lived. He could trade spirited barbs with this woman forever.

Her cell phone rang.

"Don't answer it! Don't answer it!" But he knew his words were wasted. No way would she not answer a call for help. It was one of the reasons he loved her.

He leaned against the side of his truck while she leaned against the side of her new Prius, a graduation present from her parents that had arrived while he was away.

"Uh huh, Uh uh, yes. Of course. I understand. Thanks for letting me know." He watched as she swiped her finger on the screen and disconnected.

"Let me guess, there's a cat, or a mouse, a fox or a coyote caught in a trap somewhere and we have to go help."

She quirked her lips to the side in a half smile. "Not exactly. There's been a fire. And we've lost our venue for our big fundraiser. The annual gala is only two weeks away and now we have no place to hold it."

"How many are you hosting?"

"About 150."

"Would a yacht moored on the Intracoastal Waterway with a full staff help?"

Her eyes bugged wide. "You have a yacht?"

"My *family* has a yacht." He was always trying to minimalize his wealth with her. It seemed to put her off to know he was rich— intimidated her in a way that made her anxious. He knew she wanted a simple life helping animals. And now so did he.

"It just docked in Wilmington yesterday. I can have it brought down to Little River and you can use it. The fore and aft decks can hold close to two hundred people."

"Wow. That would be amazing."

"You have a caterer?"

"Well . . . we have volunteers that cook."

"Our chef and his staff can help them with the food."

"You have a chef?"

"Honey," he gave up, she was going to find out sooner than later, "I have money. Lots of it."

"Then why are you living with me in my crappy little swamp cottage at the end of a dirt road?"

He wrapped each of his hands around her hips and pulled her to him. She could feel the length of his erection through the fabric of his jeans.

"Because that's where you are. And I want to be anyplace you choose to live. I have lived in huts, caves, tents, Jeeps, tanks, boats . . . in mansions, penthouse suites, on private islands, and on luxury yachts. But I've never been happier than I am with you in that little *junkalow*, eating your granola and nuts and befriending every single bird and snail. I *would* like to replace that excuse for a bed with a *real* bed that doesn't rattle every time I fuck you proper though. And get a bigger hot water heater."

She cupped her hand over her mouth to try to hide her reaction to his hilarious but true-to-rights comment about her bed, gave up, and laughed out loud again.

"I thought you were the black sheep of the family—disowned or something after your debacle overseas."

"Hardly. I get into scrapes now and again. But I'm the apple of my mom's eye, Dad's too. They keep my first paper targets in albums, bronzed my first bow and quiver, and have my military medals framed in boxes over their mantel. They like me quite a lot. And they're going to love you. Except for the animal thing. But they'll come around. Instead of lobster, it'll have to be ceviche with tofu. Instead of filet mignon it'll be pasta primavera. Ice cream's okay, right? Milk from a cow? Eggs from a chicken? Cheese and yogurt from a goat?"

"Mmm, not really. They don't exactly treat those animals very well in a lot of places. But you know I don't impose my beliefs on everyone else."

"Yes, I do know that. And that's one of the reasons I love you. Now let's go home and have some celery and pinto beans and drink some champagne. I'm starving."

She smiled up at him. "I have an amazing lentil salad I made this morning in the fridge."

"Bring it on! Just you me and that noisy kestrel of yours with the clipped wings, prosthetic leg, googly eyes, and eggs just about to hatch."

"Hey, that was my very first solo replacement limb surgery. She loves her new leg."

"Let's go home. I need a shower. I still smell Heidi the way she was when we first got her."

"Yeah, me too. Shame about the hot water situation—we don't have enough for two showers . . ."

"Hey, I have an idea."

She tilted her head and looked up at him through her dark lashes. "Wonder if it's the same one I'm having . . ."

"I am betting it is." He took the keys from her hand and opened the passenger door for her. "Also, I've been meaning to talk to you about your t-shirt."

Today she wore a white t-shirt with burgundy letters that said **Accidentally used the dog's shampoo today and I'm feeling like such a good girl.** There were paw prints all over it.

She looked down and held it out as if to remember what shirt she was wearing. "What about it?"

"It's too bad, as I happen to be looking for a very bad girl," he said in a husky voice.

"Oh, I can be bad."

"I was actually thinking naughty."

"I think I can do that too . . . with proper direction." The way she looked up at him, her head tilted as if ready to take step-by-step directions if need be, made his heart stutter.

"I'll drive. You go too slow. I find I am in desperate need of a shower."

Chapter 15

Palo & Trixie
Lemon Sherbert & a Leaping Leopard

The woman he had rear ended on Route 17 on his way to ILM, was arriving at the beach house in ten minutes. After settling up with her, he'd have to head back to Wilmington, turn in the rental car, catch a flight to Charlotte, and hightail it home. He had a whole list of things to do once he got back to Italy. The summer tour season would soon be in full swing, and the fall season, usually his busiest, was in the last stage of set up and planning.

And, just yesterday, his mother's doctor had informed him that his mama's health was declining and that he should seriously consider live-in medical help. The doctor said that without close supervision and nearly constant monitoring of her health issues, she would likely succumb within the year. No one was ready for Mama to go live with Jesus yet, certainly not him. As his mother's only son, it was his job to see that she had the care she needed. If she needed live-in help, he would find someone. There was no other option.

His mother was more than a beloved parent to him. She had been at his side, working with him through every single hardship since his father's death from a heart attack five years ago. She'd kept her job managing the villa's extensive orchards and vineyards while taking on the additional task of running his father's restaurant in town.

When Palo was fourteen, she'd arranged for him to get a student visa so he could travel to America as a high school foreign exchange student in California. She'd been supportive when he'd managed to get a scholarship to Stanford, essentially leaving her and Papa alone for six more years to handle things on their own, while he followed his dreams of getting an MBA from the prestigious university. At that time, she'd hidden it from him that he was needed at home to help care for things. She didn't tell him that Papa was slowing down.

Then a stroke of bad luck for his aunt, and ultimately good luck for his mama, occurred when his uncle died and his aunt asked if she could come live with them. She offered to run the restaurant, which took a big burden off the family and allowed him to stay in America for his education. After graduating with honors, he came home to Italy to fulfill his dreams of owning an elite tour company.

The first years back home had been a struggle, trying to get his business going. After several years, his father had died and it fell to him to oversee his sister's education and social life, while attending to both his mother's and aunt's many ailments.

The whirlwind of activity just to do the tours on hot summer days could be exhausting. Yet every day he piled on more and more to his to-do lists. Still, he managed to get it all done. It was helpful that he thrived on the constant state of activity. He went from one task to another, doing endless errands and micromanaging himself, and eventually so many others, that it was several years before he discovered that he was rich.

He remembered the day he'd sat in his accountant's office signing papers and checks and listening to payroll and investment advice. "Palo, you have outgrown me. I cannot manage this many agencies in so many places. You need an accounting firm, payroll management, better tax people than me, and a team of lawyers that is not just your cousin putting out fires. You need an investment team and you need it *now*.

Look at how much money you have just sitting in your bank account," he had shoved a hand written ledger over to him. "This much is not needed for operating expenses, it's surplus— totally unnecessary. This money should be making more money for you. You are wasting your money paying me. Your success is too much for me to handle now. You went to business school. You know this."

When Palo had looked down at the carefully penciled-in journal of debits and credits, and then been shown the last bank statement, he'd had to blink hard to be sure he'd read the balance number correctly. He thought he'd seen two more digits to the left of the period, and a comma in the wrong place.

"Whoa!" was all he'd remembered saying.

He watched the seventy-eight-year old man, who had been his father's best friend and business partner, nod and smile proudly at him. "Palo, I am full of pride in all you have accomplished. Your father would be so very proud of you. You are a very rich man, and not yet even 40. You've worked hard and you've done well for yourself. Now go find better people than me to manage this amazing company of yours.. And treat yourself a little as a reward; your father would expect that. Then go find a woman to give your mama grand babies before she is no longer with us."

Then Papa Giuseppe, as he was known to many, stood, shook his hand, and handed over a tall pile of ledgers. "I am retiring, you are my last account. I thank you for all the money you have paid me."

He handed him a business card. "See this man, he is a good financial advisor. He will see you are set up with the right companies. Now go, I must meet my wife for dinner. We are in the last stages of planning a trip to Greece."

Palo remembered shifting the journals in his arms to shake the man's hand and to ask what agency he was using to arrange his trip.

"Why yours of course, we want the very best."

"I will take care of arranging everything personally for you."

"No need. Alyssa took care of everything last week. She is a very hard worker. Palo. She knows what she is doing. She and my wife have been talking for several weeks. It has all been arranged. We leave in two weeks."

Palo smiled at the thought of his sister, and of how careful she was handling all the necessary paperwork and detailed itineraries.

"I would like to pay for your trip for all you have done for me."

Papa Giuseppe waved his hand as if dismissing the idea as preposterous, "You do not need to give me a free trip. You have provided me with a very good income these last several years. I have made more than I ever thought I would have earned in this business. You've paid me enough. Now go make some smart investments."

The first investment Palo made was a month later when Brent proposed the idea of his frat boys building a beach house in Sunset Beach, North Carolina with each man owning an equal share of the property.

And now, after a two-week summer reunion with his former Stanford dorm mates, he was going back to work, to his tour company and to Mama, who was still nagging him about giving her a few grandchildren before she went to join Papa.

He ran a hand over his face at the thought. His business was a social business; he met hundreds of women on a monthly basis. And he did date some, but no woman had appealed to him in that way. There was no "zing" as Papa had described feeling when he had met Mama, coming off the funicular on the isle of Capri, a little too fast. She had run right into his arms, smashing his cup of limone gelato between them.

They had shared many limone gelatos between them over the years—not on their clothing though like the first time. His mama still had one on each anniversary of their wedding day. Sitting alone, upright in the bed they'd shared, she took her time enjoying the delicious confection, and remembering.

He hoped that when he finally did meet that special person, that he'd be granted the many happy years that his parents had shared.

The sound of the doorbell woke him from his reverie. He got up from where he'd been sitting in the TV room and walked through to the foyer.

He opened the door to see the woman he had hit while driving his rental car to the airport. No one was hurt so he had opted not to involve the rental agency or his insurance company in Italy. Tomorrow at the airport he'd settle with the car rental company for the damages to the car he'd been driving. Her car had faired a lot worse than his. They had towed it to a body shop for an estimate of the damages.

He wanted to resolve this quickly as he needed to get back to Italy. The lady, Trixie, had agreed to the money he had offered her and said she would sign the necessary papers releasing him from any further claim. As it turned out, she'd just come from a job where she'd lost a patient after eight months of caring for her. She didn't want the hassle of dealing with an insurance company either.

He didn't remember much about her. Except that she'd been sad, her eyes red and her face pale and splotchy as she swiped at her red nose with a tissue. She been wearing navy scrubs that looked like she'd slept in them for weeks, Crocs that had seen better days, one of those paper head coverings that nurses wore to keep their hair away from their face, and had lips that she couldn't seem to stop biting on. It was obvious that she was distraught, and he was very sorry he'd caused her this distress on top of what she was already dealing with.

He'd apologized several times, but she'd waved it off. After he had negotiated a generous settlement for her twelve-year old car, and while they were exchanging contact information, she'd muttered, "It's actually for the best really."

The car was still drivable so she agreed to come to *The Cockpit* later that evening to get the cash they'd agreed on. She was happy with six thousand dollars, and he was fine with that number too. It was an older model Ford that had seen better days. He figured the amount of damage he'd done to a 12-year old car would total it so he offered to pay her what the car was worth. When she'd said it only had 84,600 miles on it, he upped the ante from $5,000 to $6,000.

She'd seemed happy with that and they'd agreed to meet after he went to the bank for cash. He didn't mention that they always had that much and more in the safe at *The Cockpit,* which he'd replenish with a check to Brent who handled the house accounts. Since it was Saturday, he knew that the banks in the area weren't even open.

And so here she was to collect. When Trixie heard the door open, she quickly turned from looking at her impatient UBER driver to greet the man who had totaled her car.

Palo flinched. Then tried to hide his shock. She was beautiful. Big blue eyes framed with dark fringed lashes sparkled in the sunshine. Lots of short blonde curls framed a heart-shaped face. Gone was the red, splotchy skin, replaced by smooth pale skin with a faint rosy blush on her cheeks. Tiny freckles dusted the top of her pert nose. She was holding a small cup of ice cream in her hand. The spoon had just touched her lips. She hurriedly sucked on the curved part of the upside down spoon, taking the dollop of ice cream between her lips and quickly swallowing it.

"Uh, hi. Trixie Sanderson. Sorry about the ice cream, I was parched so we stopped at the little trading company here on the island. They didn't have any drinks though . . . so, next best thing." She held up the cup. It looked like it held vanilla ice cream, but he couldn't be sure.

"I just realized that I hadn't eaten all day. What with . . . well, you know." She waved her hand between the two of them, indicating their little run in earlier in the day.

"Oh no problem. What flavor you'd get? They have a great Moose Tracks."

"Umm, not sure. I thought I was pointing at vanilla, but it tastes kinda lemony. Very yummy though."

Palos eyebrows rose to his hairline. "Really? I didn't think they had that flavor there. Come in." He opened the door wider.

She turned back and pointed with her spoon at the black Audi. "I've got an Uber waiting. Can you just give me the money and I'll get out of your hair?"

He noticed the color of her hair when she turned—light blonde-honey streaked with sunshine, the breeze gently lifting the feathery short ends like wheat swaying in the wind. Her eyes were blue. He envisioned the same blue as the water off Capri. Capri? What an odd thought, he mused; it had been years since he'd been to the isle of Capri, where his parents had met.

"Sure. It's on the kitchen counter. I'll be right back."

"Actually, if you don't mind, I could stand to use a bathroom before my ride to the airport."

"Sure, sure," he gestured her into the entryway and then used his arm to point down the hall, "Second door on the right."

He watched her walk down the hall, mesmerized by her shifting hips. She had a slight build. Toned as if she worked out often. She wore floral capris, a white sleeveless shell, and strappy sandals. No tan though, she was pale for this late in the summer, he thought.

She was very pretty though, in an understated way—no make-up, no earrings, no piercings or tattoos that he could see—a totally different look from earlier in the afternoon when she'd looked tired, distressed . . . defeated. He knew that worry and desperation could take over and ravage someone's face, and she had told him that she'd lost a very dear patient this morning.

Now she seemed refreshed, but still distracted and nervous. Maybe she didn't like having to do this today. Or maybe she just didn't like him, and was nervous being here. There was no reason she should like him though. However unintentionally it had been, he'd complicated her life.

A loud "Aaaahhh!" reverberated down the hall and the piercing sound had his eyes widening and his flight sense at full attention. Until he remembered the mural. That damned mural. One of these days it was going to cause someone to have a heart attack.

He yelled down the hall, "It's not real. Just a picture. Sorry, I forgot to mention it. Everyone reacts like that." Then in a tired voice, "I think we should have it painted over . . ."

A few minutes later when she came out and found him in the kitchen, she put her empty ice cream cup on the counter and whispered, "Don't paint over it. But a sign hanging on the doorknob might be helpful. "DANGER YOU'RE ENTERING THE JUNGLE NOW! That is a very realistic painting."

He smiled over at her as he trashed the cup and spoon in the compactor and slid the envelope filled with hundred dollar bills down the counter toward her.

"A local artist named Amy worked on it for a week. I don't remember whose idea it was, but it was a bad one in my opinion. Scares the hell out of everyone."

She gave him a quizzical look, "This isn't your house?"

"Technically yes. I own a tenth. My college buddies and I had it built. No one lives here fulltime though. We all come here to vacation in July every summer, and then on our own throughout the rest of the year."

She looked around the kitchen, took in the long granite countertops, the top-line appliances and the impressive grill and ceramic stovetop. The multi-tiered racks of spices, each spice in its own hand painted, hand labeled, ceramic jar, drew her eye. The vibrant red, blue, orange and yellow pattern that evoked thoughts of Tuscany made her smile. "Looks like some serious cooking goes on here."

"Oh, it does. Kyle Merritt is one of the guys who makes up our 'Beach Boys' group. Brent, our homeboy architect designed the house, but Kyle designed both the indoor and outdoor kitchens."

"Wow. I've heard of him. My last patient watched his cooking shows on cable for the first six months of my assignment here. She had been a cooking instructor at the community college."

"Patient? Assignment? You mentioned a patient dying earlier today?"

"I'm a traveling critical care nurse. I care for people in their homes, 24-7 mostly. Terminal cases, for those who want to stay home and can afford private care until the end. Lillian died this morning. I was pretty distraught while I was driving, so I'm sorry I hesitated at that stop sign causing you to run into me."

"No apologies necessary, I was distracted too. Flying back to Italy and going back to work after two weeks off, I had a lot on my mind, and not a lot pertained to driving."

"What do *you* do for a living?"

"I own several tour companies. We do elite small group tours to Italy, Germany, Switzerland, and Greece. But I was mostly thinking about my mama. She's having heart issues."

"Oh, I'm so sorry to hear that. Illness in the family can be very stressful."

"Tell me about it. I've been told I have to find a caregiver for her. She's going to need monitoring on a daily basis."

"Hmm. That's my specialty. My advice would be to find someone she shares some common interests with. Makes it not seem so clinical all the time."

"That is good advice. So where are you traveling to next? Where's home?"

"Well, that's the thing . . . with traveling nurses we rarely have a place we call home. Some have apartments or tiny houses, 'cause they're hardly ever there. I go one better. Between assignments I cruise. I'm on my way to Ft. Lauderdale where I'll get a last-minute cabin on a cruise ship."

"Going to where?"

"Don't know yet. It's a seat of the pants thing. Usually, I can get a cheap price on a nice cabin going to one of the Caribbean islands. Once, I got to go to Panama for $299 for eleven days. Another time, I got the last cabin available to Antarctica. That was a bit more, but well worth it."

"So you don't know where you're going . . . and after you're done with cruising, do you know where you'll be working?"

"Sometimes I do. But not this time. There are over three hundred in our group of critical care nurses who travel all over the country. Once you leave one job, it usually takes two or three weeks to work your way up the list to get a new assignment."

"So you live in private homes and on cruise ships?"

"I do. And right now I have an Uber driver waiting, so I have to go. Thank you for the money. It helps that I don't need to sell the car before I leave; the tow company is also a salvage yard and they said they'd take it. That means I can leave today instead of Monday."

Palo was leaning his tall, lanky frame against the counter, his Ferragamo loafers crossed at the ankles, his arms folded across his Parrino dress shirt.

His dark, shiny, almost-black hair was perfectly styled back from his forehead in a smooth wave. His equally dark defined brows were arched over brilliant green eyes; his sculpted beard was trimmed to appear as if perpetually two weeks old, which it actually was. Only Sean shaved while on vacation.

Trixie drank him in. Immaculate white cuffs peeked out of his dark blazer sleeves, a contrast that drew her eyes to his hands. Large capable hands with long fingers that were perfectly manicured drew her eye. They were a model's hands. They'd look good holding a tumbler with Gentleman Jack in it, flashing a Michael Kors watch, or stroking a woman's bare shoulder.

He looked every bit the Italian playboy standing in his over-the-top kitchen, she thought.

Palo was old school and believed travelers should dress up for the extraordinary occasion of getting on an airplane. So while he chose comfortable, wrinkle-free clothing, he was always GQ. It was important in his business to broadcast success and confidence. So when he walked down an airport corridor, he did that in spades, drawing the eyes of contemporary women like a magnet. And since he was always checking something or other on his cell phone, he rarely noticed the attraction—the force field of a wanton stare would inevitably break without him ever having known the connection.

Now he pushed up from the counter where he'd been leaning and stood to show her to the door. He was again unaware of approving eyes. But this time his own eyes were involved in a quiet perusal, as he checked out the back of her bobbed blonde hair, her slim neck, the lacy bra straps showing through her silky top. He scanned her swaying hips, took in her tight backside, drew his eyes down from the back of her thighs to her dainty feet tucked into white barely-there sandals.

She was a nice package. And apparently she had it in spades in the brains department. From his mother's hospitalizations, he knew that critical care nurses were aces in chemistry, mathematics, science, pharmacology, medical procedures for the body's many ailments and diseases, and all the legal matters pertaining to patients' rights and their advocacy, and so much more. And because of her extensive travel, he was pretty sure she was interested in history and the arts.

She turned at the landing to face him and offer her hand. "Thank you again."

He met her eyes. Felt something waiver . . . connect . . . entice . . . like the attraction that moved between the moon and the tides, he felt something draw tight, deep inside his chest.

Without thinking it through, he blurted out, "Send the driver away. I'll get you to the airport tomorrow. Let's have dinner together tonight. I want to talk to you about a business opportunity. I think I might have your next assignment lined up, if you'll consider it."

She arched a brow and held it high for a few seconds, debating. "Where's the patient?"

"Italy."

"Hmmm. My registry is not international."

"Take a sabbatical."

"Not licensed there either."

"It's a private home. We'll work around that. She will still have her doctor. He lives only two kilometers away."

She met his eyes again. Saw he was sincere. And felt her interest in him bloom. He was very handsome. And apparently well to-do—tall, tanned, with thick dark brown hair that was almost black and Aegean-sea green eyes that missed nothing. Now they were assessing her eyes, looking for a matching spark to ignite.

Why not, she thought. It had been over a year since she'd had a good tumble. And she'd bet her nurse's cap (now in long-term storage), that he would be worth her delaying her cruise.

"Okay. Dinner. We'll talk. This job I have is a dream job, so I can't just up and leave the registry. And I can't afford to start over again to get back on the roster—it took three months last time."

"No problem. Dinner," he smiled down at her and winked, then touched her elbow, "and it doesn't have to be business related at all. I would still want to spend time with you even if you weren't a very much needed angel of mercy."

The wink caused a ripple through her belly. The words conveyed the very same thought she'd just had. That this could be a very therapeutic dinner. Beneficial in so many ways if she was reading his subtle signals correctly.

He moved her aside with a gentle touch and grabbed his phone from the granite countertop. "I'll settle up with the driver and get your bags."

"Oh you don't have to do that. It's a business expense that I can deduct. And I only have one bag."

"One bag? Are you sure you're a woman from this planet?"

She laughed. "I mostly wear scrubs and since I use an online uniform rental service, it's just bras, panties, and pjs—they don't take up much space. On cruises it's a bikini and a cover-up. I travel light. No makeup, no hair products, just a phone, charger, wallet, and a Kindle."

"I think I'm in love," he said as he held up his solitary leather carry-on that was leaning against the wall. "I travel light too."

She took her phone from her back pocket and typed in a tip for the driver. "You fall fast for someone with a minimalist life-style, while you live like this?" She waved her arm back toward the interior of the house, clearly the most luxurious on the island.

He laughed. He liked this woman. He added witty to the list of her credentials.

Chapter 16
Superlative Men

Palo ended up having the Uber driver drop him and Trixie off at the Ocean Isle Beach Airport where he and Trixie took Chaz's rust bucket of a Jeep out of storage. They were happy to have it as Trixie's car was on its way to a salvage yard to be sold piecemeal, and Palo's rental car, although it fared far better than Trixie's secondhand sedan had in the crash, was soon to be towed back to the rental car company to be repaired. He'd managed to limp it along and get it back to *The Cockpit*, but it wasn't safe to drive.

He apologized to Trixie for the less than pristine ride. "I think it's called Rusty Busty or Trusty Busty, or something like that. It doesn't look like much, but it's pretty reliable."

"I'm used to cars that don't look like much. I've never had a car with less than 70,000 miles on it. As long as it's reasonably clean inside, legitimately owned, and I think I can get two years out of it, it works for me."

"Well, I'm the snob there then. Stateside I usually rent a BMW. At home I drive an Alfa Romeo or I ride a vintage Indian motorbike. I don't usually have accidents; I'm actually a pretty safe driver. But today? I think I got distracted by everything coming at me so fast. It's like someone rang a bell announcing Palo was off vacation. I have to admit, this business with my mom is weighing heavy on my mind."

He got her situated in the passenger seat and went around to the driver's side. His plan was to have dinner, then go back to the house for their luggage, and by some miracle, have her end up on the same plane as his in the morning, winging their way toward Italy.

"How does The Isles Restaurant sound to you?"

"I've never been there. But then I haven't been to most places around here. My job requires me to be on hand for pretty much anything that can happen to the patient, so I rarely wander farther than the nearest park or gym. Sometimes there's a pool or workout room in-house, so that's a bonus. Eating out? Hardly ever."

"Until it's time to cruise?"

"Correct. Until it's time to cruise. Then I make up for all the bag salads and frozen protein bowls."

He started the Jeep, let it warm up for a minute then shifted it into gear. "So, no boyfriend?"

"Not usually. But there often seems to be a ne'er-do-well male relative hanging around who thinks me sleeping with him would be a perk of the job."

He threw his head back and laughed as he pulled into the traffic circle.

"It's funny to you . . . not so much when you're holding a syringe in your hand and you get goosed."

He laughed again.

She loved how his laugh sounded—throaty and full of genuine good humor even if it was at her expense.

"So . . . what *do* you do for a social life?" he asked.

She shot him a flirty side smile and batted her eyelashes. He was surprised when the sight made his abdominal muscles jump.

"I have enchanted evenings on exotic islands . . . every now and then. If the mood's right, the itch is there, and the man's . . . superlative."

"Superlative?"

"Yes. It means exceptional, incomparable, unparalleled, peerless, consummate, unmatched . . . shall I go on?"

"I get it. Only the best for those most excellent evenings on tropical beaches when the moon is bathing you with what-if possibilities."

"Very well said."

"You should try it in an ice cave, it's pretty outstanding too."

This time she threw her head back and laughed. He admired the long column of her throat, and for the first time he noted that she wore no jewelry—no earrings, no necklace. He looked down at her hands that were fumbling with the edge of her blousy top—no rings either.

"I try not go anywhere where the temperature can dip below 60."

Palo downshifted as he pulled into The Isle's parking lot and after selecting a spot, allowed the clutch to stall out the engine. "Tricky beast as I recall," he murmured, "have to do that or she tends to flood out."

Everything was silent except for the soft ticking sound of the engine cooling and the faint riff of the waves crashing less than three hundred feet away. He turned to look at her at the same moment she turned her face up to look at him. The moment was suspended, heavy between them as they assessed each other. He thought her clean, fresh, no-makeup look refreshing and had a visceral desire to lick the skin along her chin leading up to her ear and to sample, maybe for the first time in his adult life, dewy-looking lips that had absolutely nothing artificial on them.

She took in his deep tan and several days beard. He was a little swarthy looking, dark-complexioned with a distinct European aspect to his profile—with his dark green eyes, he could be Greek, Spanish, Portuguese, or Italian—from this century or any of the last five. And apart from the fact that he smelled exceptional, he could be a farmer, a shepherd, or a seaman. But the spicy, woodsy scent with lemony overtones and bergamot layered with a mixture of bourbon, cedar wood, patchouli, and musk, spoke of money. It drew her nose to precarious places and made her mind wander. Then her eyes settled on his lips. When her eyes lifted, it was to see that his eyes were intently focused on *her* lips.

"One of my girlfriends just got back from Rome, she

says all the men are gay, either that or metrosexual."

He chuckled. "Not gay. Not that I have anything against it. I might cop to being metrosexual for the refined taste in clothing part . . . maybe for the liberal views, as well." He leaned toward her. "If there's a question in your mind though, the answer is that I only like women."

The tremor that ran through her wasn't something new. She'd felt it before. That kind of jolt zinging through a woman's body was a warning that something deliciously sinful was on the horizon. And that she should run for her life if she didn't want to get destroyed by it. The first time she'd felt it, she hadn't heeded the alarm. Nor the subsequent times since. She liked sex. And she missed having it. A lot.

His hand came up to cup her cheek and she realized that this time she wasn't going to heed it either.

When their lips met, it was not so much a spark as a hum. A low hum coursing through her veins, more of a vibrant homecoming, a welcome home sigh emitting past her lips to his . . . and the word *finally* rushing through her mind and parking agreeably in her brain. The sweet humming along her nerve endings practically sang, *where have you been all my life?*

He felt it too. She knew it by the way he held her face between his hands and searched her eyes with an astonished look widening his own eyes.

Finally, he was the brave one, "You feel that?"

She thought about shaking her head and denying it, but with her lips still tingling she whispered, "Mmmm hmmm."

"What do you suppose it means?" he asked a huge grin on his face. "That I'm not gay?"

She smiled back. "If I were to venture a guess, it means I'm going to Italy."

"Damn straight." He said, then blinked as if coming out of a trance.

Her eyes met his and they both grinned. He caught her hand in his and gripped it. Something had happened here.

Nothing they'd been able to control even if they'd wanted to. It was like a nudge from the universe. Which was exactly how he'd felt about their accident earlier today—a cosmic shove that drew two wanderers home.

"Dinner first. We can discuss logistics over some good seafood." He opened his door then walked around the front of the Jeep to open hers.

"How's this going to work if I'm working for you and we get "friendly?""

"Oh, we're definitely going to get friendly. But let's not rush things. I want to savor every moment of getting to know you. And if you do take the job, you're going to be working for my mama, not me. Her heart may be failing her, but her mind is as sharp as ever. "

He took her hand in his again and laced their fingers, then led her up the stairs and into the restaurant where they shared calamari and enjoyed Caesar salads while he told her about his hometown and the villa that had been in his family for six generations.

"The villa sits at the end of a country lane, yet it is close to the city. There is a formal portico on the front of the villa, but you have to open the scrollwork gate and then pull open these huge twelve-foot doors that meet in the middle. An iron bar stretches through the family crest, so nobody uses the front door. Everyone uses the kitchen door which is reached though a low, creaky back gate.

"It is a very old house on the outside, mostly stone and cedar, an odd combination of terracotta and slate on the roof, but it has been modernized throughout on the inside. Outside is Old World, inside is completely updated—all the conveniences. The villa has been added on to over the years, there are six more bedrooms now, a much larger kitchen, several expansive terraces, and just last year we updated the pool and added a hot tub. There used to be a limestone wall all around the house, but with each new addition, the wall had to be moved or taken down, so it's not the walled fortress that it once was. The first thing you will notice when coming down the drive is that there are gardens and arbors everywhere. It is very beautiful."

She could see the wistfulness in his voice, and knew he was looking forward to going home.

"To me it is home. To you, it will seem antiquated and chock full of curiosities. To mama every item is a memento, a treasure from a friend or a loved one. We have a housekeeper, her name is Gabriella—and she is tasked with dusting them all."

Trixie laughed. "It sounds delightful. What's your mom's day like? Is she able to get up and walk around?"

"Yes, though she no longer goes to town. She is living on the main level and uses a walker throughout the house. She takes naps during the day and spends her time writing letters and sending out cards, talking to her girlfriends on the phone and micro managing the estate workers.

We lease out the olive vineyards and grape vineyards now, but she's still hands-on with the gardeners and the kitchen help. She is not able to cook or tend to her flower or vegetable gardens anymore, as she is not to do any heavy lifting, but she is still able to tell others what to do and how to do it—*esattemente*, exactly." He laughed as if remembering specific incidences.

"She can be a tyrant, but in a nice cajoling way. Everyone who knows her loves her and tries to please her. She has a way about her that endears everyone to her, as she is so kind, always gentle and caring . . . but always outspoken. She is what you call . . . opinionated, for sure."

"Well, that would be a change from what I am used to. My last two patients were on the crotchety side . . . just so tired of dealing with all the pain. And the one before them was angry at God because He wouldn't heal her. A kind and gentle patient would be a nice departure for a change, even if she is forthright and blunt. But I get attached to them all. When you know about their lives, how hard they've worked, all they've lived through, how they've sacrificed, you have to admire them."

"There is much to admire about Mama. But I don't want to sugarcoat this. She is kind. But she is very much stuck to the old ways of doing things. And she can be demanding. She looked out her window one day and saw rabbits eating her flowers. She pressed the buzzer beside her bed and kept her finger on it until the whole household was in her room. We all had to go outside and chase rabbits away from her garden. Then she insisted the hunters be called to trap them for dinner. We didn't do that though."

Trixie laughed, "She sounds amusing."

"Oh, she is that." He closed his eyes and his face changed, became pained for a moment. "She is my mama, and she is genuinely a good person, to everyone, even if she has been spoiled like a princess by my papa. I am not ready to let her go. I will do whatever must be done to keep her longer.

So, you, as you are qualified to do that, will also be treated as a princess in our home, and you will be paid well. You and I will become good friends, and maybe even lovers—that will be all good. If not, it is also all good. I am a kind and caring man, as my father was, and I will want you to be happy above all else in our home. You will not be required to do anything you do not wish to do. Yes, you will be providing us a service, but you will also be our guest."

She reached out and placed her hand over his on the table. "Palo, I can see that you are an exceptional family. "Let's go to Italy so I can meet your mother and talk to her doctor. If I can help her, and she likes me, I will stay."

"There is one thing . . ."

"And that is?"

"She doesn't speak much English."

"Hmmm. That could be challenging."

"I'll get you the translator app for your phone. I'll pay for lessons, hell . . . I'll hire you a translator. I am desperate. I run a big company, we're going into the high season. Mama can't stay in the house alone and she refuses to leave her home. Rear ending you is the best thing I ever did."

She was sipping her water through the paper straw when she heard him say that. Water went everywhere. The straw came out of the glass and flew to the other side of the table, flinging ice water in a wild arc and hitting Palo on the nose before dropping to his plate. Trixie managed to get her hand to her face before she snorted water onto the table. The glass she was drinking from teetered and threatened to fall over but she managed to catch it in time.

Palo laughed hysterically. Then she joined in. When the waitress drew up alongside the table, her brows arched, they were both sopping up the tablecloth with their napkins.

"Uh . . . everything okay?"

"Yeah, just talking about our car crash this morning," Palo said.

"Oh, I'm sorry about that," the waitress replied.

"Oh don't be. God provides. And he provided me this woman," he used his hand to indicate Trixie, "she is the answer to my prayers." He winked at Trixie, "She's not doing too well with water, how about we try some prosecco?" To Trixie he added, "We can toast to our trip across the pond, your upcoming adventure at *Villa Stelle Cadente*, and your new patient."

Their server left to go to the bar and Trixie asked, "*Villa Stelle Cadente*?"

"House of shooting stars."

"Oh, that's lovely." She smiled over at him. "Okay to the prosecco, but let's just have one glass, since we're flying tomorrow."

He gave her a crooked grimace. "Are you always so health conscious?"

"Yes. It's my job. And I have to set a good example."

He quirked his mouth again and raised an eyebrow. "We don't even get there until late Monday night, and you don't have to start working right away. You just started your vacation," he looked at his watch, "in fact, I might be able to get you on the

138

Sicily tour leaving on Thursday."

"Oh, I don't need a vacation."

"Sure you do, everybody does. It's how I earn my living."

"Seriously, I don't need a vacation. Going on a cruise was just my way of having a place to stay until I got another assignment. And now I have another assignment—working at an Italian villa! By the way, don't I need to be interviewed?"

"Don't worry. Mama will interview you. She'll ask you a thousand questions. She'll know more about you than your own mama."

Trixie's face went pale, her chin drooped, her eyes closed. He watched as she put her hands in her lap and clasped them together.

"Oh, I'm sorry. I said something wrong."

"It's okay. It's a long story, but I never had a mother. Or a father," she added. "I grew up as a ward of the state."

"Wow. That's very sad." He let out a deep sigh. For a moment she thought he could actually feel a little of the desolation and rejection she'd dealt with all her life. He seemed to be a very caring person.

"Well, come home with me. I promise you, you'll get smothered with mothering."

She frowned as if mulling something over, then raised both eyebrows as if considering what she wanted, no needed, to say. "Umm. Can I literally come home with you?"

He looked confused. "I thought that's what we were talking about."

"I mean tonight. I have no home to go to."

"Oh . . . that's right."

"Or I can just go to a hotel."

"No, no! Of course not. No way. You'll stay at *The Cockpit*. I hadn't even considered tonight, and that you were homeless."

"The Cockpit? You're pilots?"

"No, although one is." He shrugged his shoulders.

"It was the best name we could come up with . . . ten guys, one thing in common."

She smiled and shook her head.

"Are you sure it's okay if I stay there tonight? I don't want to impose. Especially if you were planning to go out later, or have someone over."

It was his turn to shake his head. "No. No to both of those things. Just going home to get a good night's sleep before tomorrow's long day. You are more than welcome to pick from ten different bedrooms . . . well nine, as one's mine."

"Well, that would be great. It's been a long day and I could use a good night's sleep, too."

He downed the rest of his prosecco and signaled for the check. When the leather folder came he opened it and quickly scanned the bill, then inserted a black American Express Centurion card.

She knew from her experiences with several of her well-to-do clients that this was a very elite card to have. Two men, one the son of a terminal patient, and the other a husband, had tried to use the card to pay her salary so they could get points to redeem. But it wasn't an equitable situation for her, as she would have had to become an American Express merchant and then pay a hefty fee associated with each transaction. In doing her research, she noted that to be considered for the card, the cardholder had to have impeccable credit and a verifiable income of at least a million dollars a year. She made good money for what she did, but she only made about a sixth of that.

They drove back to Sunset Beach. At the top of the bridge he turned to her and said, "I'm going to take a walk on the beach before turning in. It's likely to be a year before I get back. You want to join me?"

She pursed her lips, thinking it over. "No. I'm really beat. I think I'll just turn in if that's okay."

"Sure. There are bedrooms on two floors. Look around and feel free to pick out whichever one you want. Mine's the one with all the Italian art on the walls."

"Thanks. Just a bed is all I need."

"Well they all have that, as well as a bathroom."

"You live well."

He chuckled. "No reason not to."

Chapter 17
All the Women Love Alex's Room

"So which bedroom did you sleep in last night?" he asked as they sat at the counter drinking coffee and pulling apart two of Kyle's Morning Glory muffins fresh from the freezer. The combination spice cake-carrot cake-hummingbird cake muffins were perfect after ten minutes on the counter and one minute in the microwave. The instructions Kyle had printed on the label attached to the seal-a-meal bag they were in had been very specific. The light fluffy carrot and pineapple nut muffins were perfect for a light meal before a flight.

"I don't know, do they all have names? It had white and gold furniture and beautiful paintings."

"That's Alex's room. All the women love that room. The furniture was from his first wife's childhood bedroom. Her name was Mallory. She died giving birth to twin girls."

"Oh, how sad! That poor man."

"That sure was the case for several years. But then he found Emma this summer. Gosh, what a soap opera that was until just a few days ago when they got everything sorted out."

He got up and starting cleaning up the kitchen. "You have everything out of the room?"

"Yup!"

"Bed unmade and towels on the floor so the housekeeper can see to remake it?"

"Check!"

"Suitcase on the landing?"

"Check! Boy, you really are a drill sergeant."

"You're just one person. Try this with thirty sometime."

"No thank you. I like my job of jabbing people, collecting bodily fluids, and emptying bed pans."

"And people call me perverted and dystopian."

"They do?" she looked alarmed.

"Yeah. I like books and films where society has gone wrong for some reason—usually due to a major tyrant—and then the hero comes along and musters forces to make everything right and just again—usually by blowing everything up first."

"Oh, that's not so bad. Where does the perverted part come in?"

"There's always got to be sex involved in those kind of plots."

"Yeah, I can see that. It's Mel Gibson's claim to fame."

He laughed. "Well, now you see what I'm talking about."

"You like to blow up things while kissing the girl?"

"Well, let's just say that my romantic life is rarely conventional."

"I'm going to need to hear more bout that."

"Later. We need to get a move on. The car just pulled up."

"What about Trusty Busty?"

"The housekeeper's husband will get it back to the airport for us."

"Wow, are you guys rich or something?"

"Yes, we are the something. Now get your ass in gear, we have a schedule to meet!"

"You must be the Simon Legree of the tour guides."

"Don't doubt it."

Once the house was locked up, their luggage stowed in the trunk of the hired car, and they were settled in the back seat of the Lexus SUV, Trixie took in a deep breath and sighed, "I think I already need a nap."

Palo looked over at her and smiled. "Well, we did get up at five and the sun is just now rising. We've got a long day ahead of us—Wilmington to Charlotte to JFK, then to Frankfurt. Go ahead and close your eyes for a while."

She already had. He had a chance to drink her in. She was naturally lovely. Not a speck of makeup on her, yet she was gorgeous. He studied her bone structure, her hair coloring, her perfect nude nails, clipped short and a natural pale pink. She looked almost Swedish, but usually Swedes weren't quite so small or petite, not that she was short. She was a good height. Her eyes were a very nice blue that sometimes looked light gray. Her lips, now dream-smiling, were a natural light peach color. He stopped himself. What was he doing? Shopping? Comparing? Putting her on a shelf and assessing her as to whether or not he'd have her? Damn it. Yes, that was exactly what he was doing! And why *was* that, exactly?"

The driver asked him a question and he looked away from the lovely woman sleeping next to him as they rode north on Route 17.

For the rest of the ride he chatted with the driver about Wilmington restaurants that they both favored.

Chapter 18
First Class to Europe

"I can't believe you were able to change everything and make the new arrangements so quickly." Trixie said as they sat across from each other in the VIP lounge at JFK waiting for their flight.

He looked up from his phone and over at her and winked. "It's what I do." He waggled his phone at her. "It's the connections and favors you build up over the years. Wait 'til you see where we're staying in Frankfurt tomorrow night. Very posh—*Elegante*, as my mom would say."

"We're not flying direct?"

He shot her a look, his eyes focusing on her over the top of his reading glasses. "I add in an overnight flight at the last minute, upgrade it to a pod, factor in your TSA pre-approval, get you mileage points, and pay for it. No, you're not getting direct—a layover in Frankfurt, then Florence the next day. Take it or leave it. Besides, from Wilmington or Myrtle Beach, it's never direct. "

She flashed him a brilliant smile, "Of course I'll take it! I've never been to Frankfurt *or* Florence. I can't miss this chance."

"Good." He shook his head, "You cruise line junkies, no class whatsoever." He typed a text out on his phone, and then looked up again. "We've only got the day and one night, but I'll show you a little of Frankfurt, if you like. It's one of my favorite cities. Florence though?" He put his hand over his heart. "I predict I will spend my entire life showing you my beloved city. From the Duomo to the Uffizi to the Ponte de Vecchio, you will see it all!"

"And will I love it?"

"You most definitely will. But mostly, you will love the

food, and the wine." He waggled his brows up and down. "It is the hook that will get you back—year after year—no one leaves Florence for good." He touched his heart with the palm of his hand again. "It says here."

She laughed. "You sound like a tour guide."

"It is how I started when I was just 14. Giving tours during the summer months. The rules are quite different now though, now everyone must pass many tests to be a tour guide in each city. But I was always the best tour guide, in every city. Ask anyone."

She laughed, "You don't come from humble roots, do you?" She tilted her head as if sizing him up, squinting her eyes as if she could see him as a youth and the thoughts he must've had running around inside his head back then. "But that wasn't enough for you, was it? You wanted more."

He shrugged. "I became an international transfer student. I applied to go to a California high school and I was accepted. It was a very different world there. Not so old as Europe." He smiled as if remembering those long ago days.

"Excitement was everywhere. America was filled with new delights. I had a wonderful host family every year, and companionship with a group of students that I had not expected to ever have. As the only son of a farmer, living on a large farm outside the city, we had no neighbors close by. I had no friends, really.

"I hadn't known I was lonely until I made friends—good friends. And these friends begged me to return each year. And so I did.

"After graduating, they urged me to apply to Stanford, the university they were all going to the following year. So I did. When I was accepted and I did not have to pay for anything except for books and incidentals, my parents gave their approval and agreed to house a student from the United States to be reciprocal.

"So off I went to University for four years, which ended

up to be six. I became a 'frat boy' after the first mixer. Suddenly I had a lot of brothers, whereas I had never had any before. It was a new experience for me to be part of a group like that. It was amazing how well we all bonded and did things as a team. We are as close now as if we had shared the same mother. You saw the house we built. It is so we can be together at least once a year—so we can stay close throughout our lives."

"That's a lot of money just to assure time together every year."

"Friendship is everything. Your family is your family—you are stuck with them. But you choose your friends. They chose me when I had to carry around a Barron's Italian to English guide just to understand them. Plus, the house is an investment—with tax benefits."

She nodded. "Unconditional friendship, it's hard to imagine. I never had that," she said, and you could hear the wistful tone weaving through her words. "Even living within a family for a whole year or more, I never had that."

He cocked his head and stared at her, "You had no family? You were an orphan? You said you were a ward of the state, is that what you meant?"

She closed her eyes and moved her head from side to side, a subtle shake of the head that Palo would have missed if he had blinked.

She didn't like to dredge up her past, but sometimes it was necessary. "Not exactly, but I might as well have been one though. I was taken from my parents when I was an infant. They were both abusing drugs."

"Oh, I am so sorry that you had no family that was close."

"Oh, they were close . . . in proximity. But they were always tripping . . . way out into the universe. In the end, they just couldn't give up the drugs to get me back. So I was put into a foster program. I was passed around to several different families for a while, and then as I got older I was taken to a group home for girls my age.

"Things dragged through the courts for many years because my birth parents refused to sign the adoption papers that would have allowed me to be sent to a good home.

"By the time I *could* be legally adopted, I was too old to be considered by anyone. In the home, I didn't have many long-term relationships as the girls were taken away as soon as they were placed with a family. But I *did* have some wonderful adults who cared about me. Some very honorable people who said they would help me, and they did.

"Although I was in the system, I was one of those rare kids that didn't pine for adoption. I was a smart cookie. I knew I had it better than most kids. On supervised visits, I saw how my parents lived and I didn't like it. Where I was, I had a clean bed, plenty of good food, unlimited books and videos, warm clean clothes and toys—lots of toys. And if I was sick, there was always someone to hold my head and get me to a doctor if I was really bad off.

"I loved going to school and I loved all of my teachers. It really didn't matter to me that I didn't have parents at the pageants, or at the basketball games, or at graduation. I always had six or seven nuns cheering me on. The applauding for me was usually the loudest."

He watched as she smiled at the memory. What a brave little girl she was, he thought as she continued.

"I was fairly happy. And then one day out of the blue, they told me that now that I had my diploma, I had to leave. *Unless,* I applied to the local community college and could get a scholarship to attend. So I applied and got a full ride—books and tuition. Then I was told there was also a stipend for housing at an apartment complex that was within walking distance of the school. I later found out that there was no such stipend, that the nuns had pooled their money to pay for the little studio apartment.

"I graduated with top honors in science and chemistry. By then some of the sisters had retired and the apartment was no longer available to me, so it was time to get a job.

"*Unless,* I went to nursing school. So off I went to nursing school, with housing provided on campus. When I graduated with a Masters in Nursing, the school administrator said that was as much schooling as they could help me with. It was time to find a job."

Trixie sat quietly, jiggling her sandaled foot back and forth. She didn't seem inclined to continue. He noticed her toenails were unpolished, not that they needed to be. Her feet were actually quite pretty; trim ankles, pale unblemished skin, the nails trimmed and natural.

After a quick perusal of her other features he realized that she had no embellishments—no piercings, not even holes in her earlobes—and no tattoos either. At least none he could see. But that made sense didn't it? It was peer pressure that led to those types of decisions. And she'd had no peers.

"I'm assuming you got a nursing job, as you're still in that field, right?"

"I worked as a clinical nurse in the hospital for two years. Then one day as a patient was being released, her daughter approached me. We were taking the elevator down to the main level to wait for her mother, who was coming down in a larger elevator to accommodate her gurney and IV drip poles.

"She said her mom really liked me, and that now that she needed in-home care, she wondered . . . would I consider living with them and taking care of her?"

"All these years, I'd been looking for a home where people cared about me, and these people did. They wanted me to live with them, in their home—be a part of their family. I said yes.

"I worked for the daughter who was an attorney for the Justice Department until her sweet mom died, almost two years later.

"She gave me a glowing reference and recommended an agency where I could apply. And as they say, the rest is history. I've been with the agency for eight years now, helping eleven people stay at home during their final days instead of having to be institutionalized. And then yesterday, you ran into me, literally. And now *you* have a patient for me to consider. It seems this profession I've chosen has no end to jobs available for someone like me."

Palo had been staring at her, drinking in each word, learning about her past, her education, her job history, and her sad life with no family. He felt he had to lighten the moment, "I *did* run into you. And I apologize for referring to it as rear ending you to my friend Dev when I got back here that day— just in case you meet him one day and he mentions it."

"Your friend must've thought that was funny."

He harrumphed. "Dev thinks everything is funny. We all wonder about that guy."

"Why is that?"

"Well, we had all deserted him yesterday morning. We left him with the chore of dispatching a mama cat and her five kittens that we discovered living under the house . . . just as we were all getting ready to leave to go back to our regular homes. He hates cats, so he was not at his best when the rescue lady was trying to gather up all the cats. And then I came back pissed off about the accident and ended up embarrassing him in front of her when she overheard us talking. He puts up a gruff front, but once you get to know him he's kind of melty inside."

She laughed. "I don't know any man who would like being described as "melty."

"We can all be melty at times. Anyway, it was a pleasant experience meeting you, despite the fashion. And getting to know you continues to be delightful. He winked at her, "And maybe there will be another 'run-in' . . . of some kind . . . down the road."

She chuckled. "Really? That's the worst line of all time."

"Yeah. That *was* pretty bad."

She shrugged. "Happens to me all the time. People are

not themselves when they're in the hospital. There's a lot of fending off advances, from both the patients, *and* their spouses."

"Doctors and administrators too, I imagine."

"Sometimes. It's better now due to strict HR regulations. But nary a day goes by that I'm not asking some jerk if has something in his eye that I can flush out with saline."

He gave her a quizzical look, "I don't get it."

"They get this lecherous wink thing going on. It's revolting." She tried to mimic it for him.

He laughed. "In Italy, the men have a reputation for pinching women's asses. But I don't know anyone who actually does that."

"Well, that's good to hear. I'd have to lay a man out flat if he did that to me. I practice MMA. I would have no mercy, not this angel of mercy, no siree."

He smiled and shook his head from side to side, "You sure are quirky. With so many hidden talents. And quite the natural beauty. You're fun to be with—stimulating, if you get my drift. But yes, I really do need a nurse."

"I get your drift. But I have to ask myself: does this need for a nurse amount to a come-on? Or is there really a patient?"

He grinned at her. Then a rueful expression quirked his lips, "Yeah, worst pick up line ever: Come home with me to help with my mama who is in her declining years. She has frequent bowel issues and often requires either an enema or anal stimulation to get her going, and due to her rather large size, she can't reach back there to do it herself. It's either that, or she simply can't stop going because of the dizzying array of pills required to keep her heart pumping and her other systems functioning. And that's just a small part of the overall care she needs."

She matched his look with her own wry countenance. "Yeah. Not a good pick-up line. So it must be true. You do need a nurse. I get it."

He nodded. "I *do* need a nurse."

There was a moment of silence between them before he opted to take the curse off the conversation. He cleared his throat. When he was sure he had her attention, he gave his very own version of a smarmy wink. "I could easily do you though. The Mile-high Club still needs members. . . ."

With flawless timing, the call for first-class boarding was announced. "Sadly, we will have separate pods, and they are not even on the same side of the plane."

"What happened to your most excellent connections, can't you get them shoved together or have someone yanked out of their seat?" She was teasing him now, her smile wide and saucy.

He quirked his lips sideways. "Well if I'd been in my right mind, I'd have booked us as honeymooners or at least husband and wife. Sadly, I think I might have checked the business partners box instead. There's no hope for this Mile-High Lothario."

She laughed. "So once we get on the plane, I won't see you again until the morning, in Germany?"

He stood and gave her a sad moue. "I believe so. We should probably shake hands and call it a night."

She laughed and put out her hand for him to help her up. He, still with a dejected look on his face, gingerly shook it up and down before slowly and tantalizingly releasing it.

"Good night, fair Trixie. Have a safe flight."

He pulled her in close and kissed her on the cheek. "Don't eat too many nuts, they make your feet swell," he whispered in her ear.

Then he followed her down the ramp and they were preloaded, him on one side of the plane, her on the other. They couldn't even see each other due to the pods having such high partitions around them.

Trixie settled herself into her seat and organized her area. Reading glasses tucked into the console, reading light around her neck, eye mask and ear pods in a side pocket, iPhone in airplane mode, a lone stick of gum preloaded in her pants pocket, seat tilted slightly back until time for takeoff.

She leaned her head against the seatback, closed her eyes and sighed. What was she doing? She was on a plane for Europe for God's sake. She should be in Ft. Lauderdale booking a Caribbean cruise. Not on a plane with a handsome stranger who made her insides jump around.

A hand touched hers ever so slightly. She opened her eyes to find a young woman smiling down at her. She eased Trixie's fingers around a cold champagne flute. "Welcome to First Class."

Her phone dinged and she saw it was a message from Palo.

Get some rest and look forward to our night in Frankfurt. Oh, The Places You'll go! With me . . . Palo!

She leaned up and looked over to her right, in what she thought was the general direction of his seat. She saw him leaning over the back of his seat, in a front row, so that he could get a glimpse of her.

He lifted his own flute in salute and graced her with a full on smile. *Salute*, he mouthed.

She lifted hers as well and joined him in the toast, acknowledging him with an arch of her brow and an amused smile. He disappeared from view as he sat down. She leaned back and slowly shook her head back and forth. What was she getting herself into?

As Palo and Trixie sipped the golden bubbly while the rest of the passengers boarded, they both wondered about the accident that had occurred that morning, and all that had happened since.

Chapter 19
Zucchero Mama

Trixie was dozing, her ear pods in, as her playlist shuffled songs by Il Divo, Susan Boyle, The Boston Pops, Patsy Cline, and Harry Belafonte, when she felt a slight touch on her hand. The sensation jerked her fully awake, as she was used to slight nudges for her attention from her patients. Thinking it was the attendant with more champagne, she mumbled, "No more champagne, thank you."

A voice near her ear whispered, "That's not something I hear from women very often. In fact, maybe never."

Her eyelids fluttered open and she looked down at her hand where she saw a man's long fingers entwining with hers. Then she raised her eyes and saw Palo, standing there smiling down at her. She took out one of her ear pods.

"Hi," she whispered. It was late; most of the passengers were asleep, so she just peered through the semi-darkness with eyebrows arched in question.

He leaned over and whispered, "I traded a discounted tour to Amsterdam for a pod-swap. I couldn't stand you being so far away from me. I'm right behind you now."

She smiled, dimples appearing at the bottom edges of her cheeks, extending her smile and emphasizing her pleasure. It gave an air of genuine happiness to her features that often caused the recipient to smile as well. Palo was a victim of this phenomenon and was grinning life a buffoon back at her.

He squeezed her hand. "Go back to sleep." He pantomimed sleep with his folded hands resting under his tilted head.

In consideration of the other passengers, she removed her phone from her pocket and opened the last text box from him and typed Not really all that sleepy. Tell me about my new patient.

She didn't send the message, instead she simply handed him the phone to type his reply.

She's 74. She had four miscarriages before having me, then she had my sister Alyssa eight years later. As all Italian mothers, she is an amazing cook. But now it is difficult for her to walk or stand around in the kitchen so she sits at the table and directs everyone. He handed her back her phone and she read the message. Then she replied:

What else does she like to do? And what am I to call her?

Most people call her Zucchero Mama. Zucchero is sugar in Italian. Papa gave her that name after Alyssa was born when she often quieted Alyssa with sugar water sucked from her finger. You can just call her Mama if you want, many people do.

Will she like me?

She will adore you.

And Alyssa?

Alyssa is not home much. She works for me. She is a tour guide and she also travels the world promoting the tours. She has a boy friend named Giancarlo she spends too much time with as well. You'll meet her for sure, as she lives in the house with us, but she is always out and about.

You sound as if you don't care for her boyfriend.

I do not. He is a player. And she is all in. Not a good match if you ask me. But she is old enough that I cannot interfere, so I just advise and she ignores me.

What else does Zucchero Mama like to do?

She reads, she has visits from friends, sometimes she goes to church, sometimes one of the priests brings the Eucharist to her. She used to garden. A lot. Most of what you will see around the villa was planted by her or by her and Papa. Now she looks through catalogues, circles what she wants the gardener to order and shows him on an intricate diagram where she wants things planted. She leaves him a list of things she wants done and when he sends her a picture from her phone, she checks it off her list. She is merciless. But Alessandro is patient with her. He is grateful for the job and for the chance to learn her secrets. She calls him Ale, and he calls her Zuma, both abbreviations of their names. She treats him like a son. A son she works to death. Just like me. Lol

Sounds like a busy household.

It can be. Or it can be silent like a tomb. Everyone knows when Mama is having a bad day. And we all hate it.

When did her heart problems start?

Childbirth was not easy for her, and with each child she lost, her heart suffered. Her own Mama and Papa died from heart conditions, and so did my Papa. Her doctor has taken her beloved pasta and bread off the menu, and she is only allowed one small glass of wine. But she sneaks or outright ignores his orders. Also her blood pressure and salt intake are supposed to be monitored. I don't believe that they are. Her pills are a trial, as they have to be taken at certain times with certain things. But without them, she would not be with us today.

I do agree with her doctor that it is time for her to be managed by someone who is knowledgeable in these things.

Any surgeries or procedures over the years?

Her heart stopped once and we were able to keep it going until the hospital team arrived. She has had catheterizations, stents, and a bypass. Her doctor says her heart should not be operated on again—something about the veins. If she were younger, she would be on the transplant list, but she is not healthy in other ways as well, so she is not a good candidate.

Let me guess. Overweight with elevated liver enzymes?

Yes. You know your patient well already. She has other issues that she will tell you about herself. Gastrointestinal problems that she needs help with and anxiety can be an issue. As if she doesn't have enough problems of her own, she often borrows other people's troubles too. It's just her way. You'll see.

I can see already that this is not going to be one of those hammock-by-the-pool jobs.

Sadly, no. But I will need you to be all in if you decide to take the job of her care, because I travel a lot. You will have plenty of people to help you though. There are always people in and out during the day, and we have a live-in housekeeper, gardener, and chef. You will need to be her primary caregiver until full-time hospice care is necessary, which she is reluctant to allow, or you ask to be replaced. There will be no hospital for her. She does not want to leave her home. So her care falls to family, friends, and someone professional.

She is my mama, she has lived a hard life and she deserves to have things as she wants now. And also, she can afford it. She and Papa hold many patents and they have owned many successful businesses, which thankfully have all been sold now. So meet Mama and name your price. You will find we are very generous when it concerns her care.

And if I decline?

I will cry. I will gnash my teeth and tear my clothes. And I will hire a helicopter to airlift you to a cruise ship full of wanna-be tap-dancing-child-pageant contestants. There will be no men under the age of seventy on board, so nary an enchanted evening will be in store for your heartless soul.

Hmmm. I feel the venom. Unless she vetoes me, I feel certain I am your woman—er nurse.

Be still my heart.

He leaned toward her and handed her back her phone. Kissed her softly on the cheek, and whispered, "Sleep now. I'll need you well-rested for tonight's night on the town."

She turned off her phone and tucked it way. Then she pressed the button that lowered the back of the pod until it went from a lounger to a bed. She found her eye mask and put it on.

Behind her, in his own pod, he did the same, closing his eyes and finally allowing sleep to take over and silence his chaotic thoughts. He was fairly certain he had a critical care nurse for Mama. So maybe now Alyssa could rejoin the tour roster as he'd promised her.

Whenever he was home, he would spend his time getting to know Trixie better. For now, he had all day tomorrow with her. He planned to make the most of their layover in Frankfurt.

When they got to the villa it would be chaotic, as the height of the fall touring season would be only weeks away. In the middle of that would be the harvest season. And while he wasn't directly involved in that anymore, he still needed to oversee things and as a courtesy, in Mama's absence, participate in several special events the family had attended for years.

Yesterdays accident was one of those God-sent, life-altering occurrences his mama was always talking about. He was sure of it. She always called it *occhiolino*. God's answer to prayer. Someone had been praying very hard for them to have been graced with such a sweet woman . . . with such a sad past.

He vowed in that moment to make things as good, as fun, and as happy as he possibly could, at least while she was in his family's home.

Chapter 20
A Perfect Pod & Two A Personalities

Neither was bright-eyed the next morning when they were deplaning. But by the time they were ensconced in the lounge waiting for the limo that would take them into the city, they'd used some eye drops, stretched their backs and legs, and chugged some bottled water.

It was Trixie's habit to sleep in a chair or bedside when her patients were terminal so that she could ease any distress they were experiencing as they passed, so she was used to sleeping in weird positions. Being in the pod had been lovely, but deep sleep had been elusive.

She was not an A personality, she was an AAA personality. She liked, not only knowing what the next step would be, but also what the next six steps would be. Today she knew she'd be sleeping in Germany, and that tomorrow she'd be in Italy. The rest was up in the air for now. For many people the not knowing would not be an issue. For her, it set her nerves jangling. A little chant of what's next-what's-next-what's-next would be playing through her head all day, like a song worm with no end.

She was grateful for the job opportunity Palo was offering her though. Since her patients never got the opportunity to send out a positive survey on the extra care and loving concern she provided them for their final journey, he had no benchmark to rate her quality of care. Rarely did family members return assessment sheets. Sometimes thank you cards showed up. Every once in a while someone took the time to go online. There were so many things going on during and after her patients' finals days to distract them that she couldn't fault them for not returning a multi-page survey.

Yet here he was, willing to trust her with the care of his cherished mother. And while she knew she was up for the task, she did have some reservations. For one, it sounded as if she would be left alone for unspecified amounts of time in a strange country, with people she wouldn't know, who spoke a language she didn't understand or speak—including his mother. How was this supposed to work?

Still, no positive surveys aside, he was willing to trust her, so maybe she should trust him. She was nothing if not patient and caring. She had ample experience with getting people through their final days and handling the details thereafter. It was, after all, her field of expertise.

But it sounded as if this woman could be around for quite some time, so she'd either feel stuck in place or she'd work her way into becoming part of the family. She was thirty-six. How much longer could she do this? It took its toll. It kept her confined. It did however pay the bills. Scratch that, it allowed her to have no bills.

The money she earned provided a hefty savings account, brokerage accounts with four companies, and a maxed out retirement account each year. A few more years and she'd be set for life, secure in a way she'd never been before. Being raised in the foster system was the antithesis of feeling protected and sheltered. Living in a home, no matter how nice, had no permanence about it—at any moment you could be yanked away, taken someplace else and dumped on anther doorstep—vulnerable to bad people and helpless to your own unfortunate fate. But she'd found the key to feeling secure, to being secure—education. Education had led her to this career, which she really did love.

The trade off was no social life, and no home life other than being in someone else's home. And vacations only after funerals. Part of her wanted to take this position solely to help Palo out. Part of her was intrigued about living in Italy. Part of her was terrified of the language barrier. Hell, she thought . . . would there even be a cable series or TV show she'd be able to understand? TVs were an indispensable benefit for this type of nursing—both for the dying person and for the caretaking person—each needed it for distraction. How would that even work in a foreign country? And oh God, what if her passport expired before her patient did? How would she ever get back home?

She was starting to panic when the limo pulled up to the curb and her lone suitcase was wheeled over and loaded into the trunk. Suddenly she was petrified. The words NO GOING BACK flashed and then raced through her mind. She reached out and put her hand on Palo's arm. He had put his sport coat back on. It was the softest ultra suede she'd ever felt.

His hand came up and covered hers. It was as if he could read her mind. "It's going to be okay. Everything's fine. We're just going to enjoy the day. I know we still have a lot to talk about, so nothing's final. It will never be final; you can *always* change your mind. If I only get to keep you at the villa for a month, that will be one month I will have less to worry about, okay?" He used his other hand to lift her chin up so she could look him in the eyes. They were such a vivid green in the bright sunlight, that she was momentarily mesmerized.

"One day at a time. Today is just about having fun and seeing the city of Frankfurt. Relax. We'll talk later. You'll see everything is going to work out, I promise. And if you want to go home— *whenever* you want to go home—planes fly back to the U.S. every single day. Remember that."

"Thank you. That actually helps."

"I know you have a lot on your mind. This is all new to you. Focus on one thing: do you want a bratwurst on a hard roll for lunch? Or a bockwurst, weisswurst, frankfurter, some braunschlanger or a wiener schnitzel?"

As he assisted her inside the car, he kept her mind busy. "Do you drink beer? They have excellent pilsners here, and of course crisp fruity Mosel wines with no sulfites. This is the home of Liebfraumilch after all!"

She had to smile. He was so into this. She could see why his tour companies did so well. If they had half his enthusiasm . . . and then her mind strayed to the bedroom, and to what that type of enthusiasm could mean . . .

Chapter 21
Frankfurt in 100 Minutes

They were whisked away from the airport, the driver nimbly managing the wheel while steering from lane to lane, joining and separating from circles, and then speeding through the busy streets. Being "managed" by someone who knew the airports—which Custom lines to get in, which bathrooms were less frequented, which lounge belonged to which airline, which mini-cafes had the best coffee . . . well, it really made a huge difference, Trixie thought as she settled into the back seat of the Mercedes sedan.

She couldn't remember traveling under such pleasant conditions. She felt more refreshed this morning, after a full night on a plane, than she usually felt after just going from the United States to the Bahamas.

She could see how being on a tour with specialized attention to the little details could make a trip a lot more pleasant. Up to now, her touring experiences had been limited to day excursions offered on the cruise ships, where you were taken on a catamaran where a cooler of booze awaited you, dropped off on a private island for the day, or led to a taxi line where a driver would point out tourist attractions as you passed by them, then take you to the shopping district where he introduced you to his *friends* who supplied you with trinkets to take home for ridiculously high prices.

Yes, she could certainly see why a high-end tour guide could make things go a lot smoother and provide for a more interesting experience.

She was surprised when instead of pulling up to a hotel, they pulled up a to a busy riverfront. She couldn't read the main sign leading to the landing area, as it was in German, but an enterprising soul had provided a hand-written translation in

English below the heading: *Frankfurt 100-Minute Sightseeing Tour.*

"Wow, what is this?" Her eyes were wide as she took in the impressive boat with the long gangway that was rocking lightly with the current of the river.

"We have a few hours before checking into our hotel, so I thought you'd like to see the city of Frankfurt from the Main River. We can sit back and relax on the deck, take in some sunshine and enjoy the breeze with a superb bottle of Riesling while we cruise along and see some of the historic sights. The tour is in both German and English so you'll be able to understand everything the guide is saying. My clients love this tour. It's just the right length of time, with the exact amount of commentary, and there's always something to see. Are you up for this?" He held his hand out to indicate the skyline of the city they could see from the car's window.

"Sure! I would love the boat ride if nothing else. I love being on the water, it's why I love to cruise so much."

He opened the door and reached back for her hand. "Well, come on then, they're waiting for us."

"They're holding the boat for you?"

"Well, I do spend a lot of money with them, but they won't hold it much longer . . ."

She slid across the seat to his side of the car and took his hand. It felt warm and firm in hers. He used their joined hands to effortlessly draw her up beside him, then pulled her along as they jogged up the gangway.

A man in uniform who saluted and bowed, then said something in German, met them at the top. The only word she recognized was *fraulein,* so she knew he was referring to her.

"What did he say?"

"He said I kept them waiting, but that he didn't mind as you are very *ziemlich* to look at."

"*Ziemlich?*"

He smiled down at her. "Pretty."

They were led to a private table on the riverfront side. All eyes were on them as they were ushered to their seats at a pre-set table. As soon as they were seated, she heard and felt the engines rumbling. Within moments, they were pushing away from the pier and heading out into the middle of the river.

It was a stunning day, the sky a crisp soft blue with fluffy clouds flitting by high above them. Trixie looked around at all the people standing by the railings and seated at the tables that were bolted to the deck. Everyone was smiling or laughing, pointing out things of interest, jabbering in a variety of languages, or toasting to the good day and the journey ahead.

A man in uniform brought a chilled bottle tucked into an ice bucket and wrapped with a linen napkin to their table, along with two wine glasses. Palo nodded to him and they spoke a few words as if cordially bantering. They seemed to know each other, and at Palo's nod, the man poured out two glasses. Then it was their turn to toast each other and the voyage as so many others on the ship were doing.

"To you, *Ziemlich* Trixie. My answer to prayer."

She met his glass with hers and heard the soft chime of crystal. She looked around at all the other couples and at the groups of friends gathered at tables. Most had pilsner glasses, some had steins, a few had bottles. "I'm surprised they're using glass onboard ship."

He gave her a haughty look, his brows indented, his nose pinched. "This is a classy boat, they're setting the mood here. You can't rebuff that lovely skyline with paper cups."

He used the glass he was holding to indicate the view behind her. She turned and gasped as the bank of tall buildings shone against the sun and were reflected off the water. So majestic and brilliant against the blue sky. With their mirrored and chromed finishes, they dwarfed the expansive bridge they were motoring under.

She sipped her wine. "Oh, this is lovely," she breathed out.

"The wine or the view?"

"Both." She took another sip. "So lovely."

He smiled over at her and she smiled back, a little shyly at first, but then she gifted him with a full-on grin.

A voice came over the speakers and she listened as the guide explained what they were seeing and the history of the tall buildings they were passing. There were many cathedrals, office buildings, factories, and shipping companies, most built after WWII. It was very informative and Trixie listened intently as the boat cruised along and they sipped their wine.

Palo watched her expressions as she took in the sights and idly stroked the stem of her wine glass. Slim fingers, slowly caressing and toying with the tall glass stem, then her palm cupping the bowl and caressing it—it gave him ideas—salacious ones. He sipped his wine and took in the view of both the scenery on the shore, and of her profile as he followed each thing that garnered her attention. He refilled her glass and topped his off. She looked over at him and with the sun now behind her, it seemed she glowed with happiness.

"Thank you. This is wonderful. I am having such a good time!"

He covered her other hand that was resting flat on the table. "I am too. I'm delighted you're enjoying yourself."

When the cruise was over and they had returned to their starting point, he spoke to several of the people that came up to their table in German. He shook hands with the men, and stood to hug several of the women. She had not been aware that he knew any of the other people on the boat.

When they all left and they were alone on the deck at their table, he stood to help her pull out her chair. "I had no idea you knew any of these people," Trixie said.

"I don't really. They are on one of my tours. This was one of their excursions today. At the end, the captain came over the speaker and informed them that I had paid for all of their drinks. They were just showing their appreciation is all."

"That was very generous of you."

"You do these unexpected things on a tour, that's what makes my company so successful. Always do more than they expect you to do and they will come back—over and over again. It makes the difference that sets us apart. It's a very competitive business. We have to do more. We have to be better than the rest. Make it more personal."

"It's why you are so busy, wearing yourself out all the time."

He smiled. "It's why I need *you* Ziemlich Trixie, to help me out with Mama."

She laughed. "Do you always get your way?"

He bent and kissed her on the cheek beside her ear. The contact caused her to shiver. "Always. It's because I do more. You will see. I will meet your every expectation. It is what I do." His voice was husky toward the end. The verbal signals he was sending caused tiny tremors to go through her. The thrill of the day and the timbre of his voice were euphoric. She hadn't been this happy in a long time.

She stepped back and looked up into his face, trying to read his expression, but couldn't. "Are we still talking about the job, the tour, or something else?"

He smiled, but said nothing. He just took her by the arm and led her off the boat and back to the car, where the driver was holding the door open for them.

Waiting for them in the back seat was a picnic basket with a platter of cheeses and another with a selection of wursts with three different kinds of mustards—coarse, Dijon, and American—red and green relishes, warm sauerkraut, and some hard rolls.

"Wow. Someone's been busy."

"Thought you might be getting hungry, especially after the wine."

"I am actually. Thank you."

Together they destroyed both platters.

Chapter 22
A Sweet Suite

The hotel was impressive—sleek and modern with upscale furnishings and intriguing lighting. There was no art to give a hint of the city they were in, but instead, pleasing textures covered the walls and attractive carved panels drew the eye to welcoming gathering places. It was all very calming.

Except for the fact that he'd booked a suite instead of two rooms. She was a bit unnerved at first, but then he explained why.

"I do a lot of business here, and I send everyone who asks for a hotel recommendation in this city to them. So when I am in the city overnight, which is not all that often, they comp me a suite. I didn't think you'd mind as it has two bedrooms and two en suites. I figured once we're in Florence, we'll be living in the same house anyway. But if it's a problem, I'll call downstairs. I'm sure they'd be amenable to switching out a suite for two singles."

"No, this is fine. Knowing it was a happenstance, rather than a contrivance, makes all the difference in the world."

As he sat, emptying everything from his pockets onto the coffee table, he looked over at her. "So no contrived seductions. Got it."

She sat down in the armchair opposite him and removed her sandals. Then she lifted one foot up from the floor and folded her leg in front of her, she did the same with the other one, her ankle resting on the opposite knee. It was impressive the way she did it so effortlessly. He wouldn't have been able to sit that way if he'd been given a week to practice unless he broke something.

She folded her hands as if cupping an invisible treasure in each then closed her eyes and took in several deep breaths. He shook his head, stymied that there was any way she could conceivably be relaxed and comfortable in that position. But it seemed that she was.

He sat on the sofa in front of the coffee table and took his time sorting out receipts, business cards, and bills and coins of different currencies. Then reloaded his wallet and filed the receipts in his laptop bag. He put the coins on the dresser in his room, along with some bills as a tip for housekeeping.

He slipped off his shoes and washed up. Then he returned to the salon where Trixie sat prim and proper, her back straight and tall, her eyes closed as if asleep. He marveled that she wasn't using any part of the chair to support her back. As if waking from a trance, her eyes popped open as he stood drinking her in. Gorgeous eyes, he thought, and well-defined brows . . . that now lifted in inquiry at his intrusion.

"I can't believe you can sit like that for so long."

"If you get into the pose just right, you can actually hold this pose for hours. But it's hell to pay getting out of it sometimes. It's good for working out the kinks in my back and stretching my legs out."

He laughed. "If you say so. I guess we all have our regimens. I'm about to go down to the indoor pool and do some laps to work out my 'kinks.' You want to join me?"

He watched her as she unfolded her legs and stood. This woman was missing her calling, he thought. She should be teaching yoga.

"That is, if you've got a bathing suit in there," he indicated her suitcase, still parked with the handle extended by the door to the suite. "I imagine since you were originally going on a cruise to the Caribbean, that you packed a bathing suit or two."

"Yeah, I have two swim suits. Swimming a few laps sounds good, but a hot tub sounds even better. You think they have one here?"

"They have a full service spa with a sauna, so I would expect they do. Let's get dressed and go see." He put two knuckles under the side of his chin and tilted his head, thinking. "Hmmm, last time I was here I do recall seeing some teenagers in one. I remember I thought it odd that they were all using their cell phones in the pool. One was even streaming music."

"That doesn't sound relaxing to me."

"Well hopefully, they're not still there."

Trixie made her way over to the door to get her suitcase. "This looks like a pretty classy place. Both of my suits are for maximizing my tan. You think anyone will mind that they're more the Riviera type than the San Tropez style? They're teeny tiny bikinis."

He laughed. "I won't mind, I can assure you that. There should be a robe on the back of the door in your bathroom along with some slippers to get you down there. They'll have towels for us at the pool. Five minutes enough for you to get ready?"

She flashed him a smile and strolled down the hall toward her room, "You betcha!"

Four minutes later she was waiting for him by the door in the hotel's thermal weave robe and terry cloth slippers.

"Did you put your wallet and passport in the closet safe?" he asked.

"I did. You?"

"Yup."

"Then we're good." She reached into her pocket and produced her room card and flashed it at him. Got your card?" she asked, knowing full well she'd never trip him up on something as simple as that.

His hand slid up from the deep pocket of his robe and he waved his room card at her. "Make sure you put your room card in the locker in the changing room. Someone taking one of these cards could charge a Presidential Rolex in the boutique store."

She put a hand on her hip and touched her pointer finger to her chin. "Hmmm. I don't need Rolex. But I could use a new Fendi purse . . ."

"Well this would not be the place to buy one of those. *Italy* is the place for something like that."

As they left the room and the door closed behind them, she sauntered down the hall, exaggerating her movements like a stripper by gyrating her hips and twirling the sash on her robe. "Does this position come with a Christmas bonus? Because my last job came with a box of chocolates—the good stuff— Whitman's."

He laughed as he caught her by the belt and tugged her into his side. An arm wrapped over her shoulder, he led her down the hall toward the elevators. "You won't believe your Christmas bonus. All of my employees get a huge basket full of wine and cheese, and the best chocolate in Italy—Slitti."

"A-rated hotels with spas, day cruises with wine, a boss who's easy on the eyes . . . I think I'm going to like this job."

"Easy on the eyes, huh?"

"Oh, don't tell me you don't know that. Don't you have a girl waiting for you back home? Surely, Zucchero Mama is begging for grandbabies."

He nodded as they pulled up to the elevators and he pressed the button. "She is at that. She's been on me for some time about that. But no, no girlfriend, at least not the type I'd want to settle down with and raise a family—just the kind to take to a party or out dancing. The girls I know are flighty and fickle; they are not ready to give up the nightlife for the home life yet. Life for them is not about work and family. It is about having fun."

Once on the spa level, they each made their way to the gender designated locker rooms and changing salons. Trixie had been in many posh hotels during her travels, but this one was over-the-top clean, was decorated with impeccable taste, and had concierge staff around every corner.

The fact that everyone they met greeted Palo as Herr Palo and smiled genuinely at them both, made her feel as if she was one of the privileged elite. If there was ever a moment in her life when she could sit back and acknowledge that she had achieved the success she had always been working so hard at, this had to be it. Not only did Palo make her feel special, everyone he associated with did as well. Not bad for a kid who grew up as the ward of The Department of Social Services.

As she worked the lock of her combination mini-safe on the locker door she'd been assigned, she let her mind flit back for the ten thousandth time to her humble beginnings.

The child of parents who were alcoholics and drug abusers, she was taken from what she was told was an old conversion van her parents were living in. Her mom had given birth to her between the parking lot and the emergency room double doors—a fireman having caught her wriggling red body in his arms as her mom had slumped to her knees eight-feet before the door.

There had been a whole lot of commotion and even some press reports on the news about it. Which had led to donations on behalf of the young couple and their new baby.

The surplus money had allowed the couple to rent an apartment and to celebrate the baby's homecoming with some primo drugs. Due to drugs having been in the baby's system at delivery, DSS was assigned to check on her welfare. At a random drop-in, both parents were high on meth. Little Trixie, whose name was spelled Tricksy at the time due to her mother's sporadic occupation, was crying in her crib. She was dehydrated and had a severe diaper rash that was infected. The baby, whose paperwork from then on reflected the name Trixie, was taken and admitted to a Catholic hospital. Her parents did not visit her. Nor did they ever go to court to try to get her back.

Only a month old, Trixie had to be monitored by a team of doctors as she was considered to have fetal alcohol syndrome and drug dependence due to her mother's addiction—words which would follow her for years—words which would keep her from being adopted through regular channels. Words, which when disclosed as required, would scare off potential parents until she was no longer a desirable age for adoptive parents.

As a newborn, no amount of testing could assure

prospective parents that Trixie would be a normal, healthy, intelligent child. Later, when Trixie had delayed speech, inquiring couples had even more doubts.

All the while, doctors, nurses, nuns, and teachers, were charged with her care. As a team, they all loved on her, read and sang to her, and repeatedly, they told her how special she was. When she was between the ages of 9 and 10, it was discovered that she was smart, very smart.

She began scoring higher than the rest of her classmates on standardized tests. Then she was tested above her grade level and beat out every child at that level, too. She was reading books several grade levels above what was normally expected. She continued to test well advanced of her grade level. At age 14, she tested even with most high school seniors.

Within the confines of the local social services agency there was no place they had to place her. But they had access to funds, limited for cases such as hers, from the federal government, which had been untapped for many years. It was decided to send her to an elite boarding school within the county. From there, due to scholarship money provided by an International woman's group known as P.E.O. or Philanthropic Educational Organization, she was accepted at the all-girls Cottey College in Nevada, Missouri. She studied Nursing, received her Bachelor's Degree, easily passed her nursing board exam to become an R.N., then she went on to get her Masters in Nursing, specializing in Geriatric and Critical Care at the State College.

During those years she was hungry for knowledge and driven by the conversations she'd overheard all her life—that due to her mother abusing drugs during gestation, she had no chance to be on par with others her age. It had steeled her for always beating everyone's expectations and excelling despite the odds against her.

As she stuffed her blonde curls into her bathing cap, she smiled. The nuns had been the first to tell her about her parents, her traumatic delivery on the hospital steps, and the circumstances thereafter that had left her an orphan. Every specialist along the way had confirmed her unusual happenstance by their concern and caring attitude while performing endless tests. It was all the testing that finally spurred her on. It was because of her background and all those tests she was subjected to, that she had set some long-term goals. Determined to prove everyone wrong, to prove she was normal, that she didn't have an addiction to drugs or any syndrome making her an alcoholic, she began studying harder, reading more, quizzing librarians as to what subjects she should be working on next. It turned out she was well beyond normal—toward the end, she was considered gifted.

She smiled into the mirror. And then she'd found her passion . . . nursing. Which shouldn't have surprised anyone—least of all the nuns who had cared for her. Caring for others as others had cared for her became her focus. And it still was. It gave her purpose. It validated her, made her count for something in a community where everyone had written her off as uneducable from birth. Except for the nuns. They believed in prayer and they believed in miracles. And they had always believed in her.

And now, this man Palo was going to pay her more money than she'd ever been paid before. And not only house her, but house her in a villa in Italy. She actually took her thumb and forefinger and pinched the skin on her arm. Yup, she was Trixie now, a Critical Care Nurse with a Masters Degree in Geriatrics, not Tricksy, daughter of a junkie whore. She had conquered her worst fears. She wasn't of below normal intelligence, she wasn't lacking in any physical capacity. She didn't have a learning issue or a speech impediment, or any type of neurological problem. At this point in her life she felt she was as good as it got. She was on top of the world, making her mark and overcoming the odds.

Suddenly, there was the most amazing sense of satisfaction that rained over her and it left her feeling as if she'd been clothed in a sumptuous royal velvet robe, like a princess being crowned. She was not only good enough; she was the perfect embodiment of herself. And because she knew all the self-affirming words in the dictionary, she leaned over the sink, and whispered one, "*Quintessence*. That's *me*!"

And because she had needed this validation for so long—all her life really—she needed to affirm it one more time. She leaned in closer to the mirror, her nose almost touching, looked herself in the eyes and said, "I am the personification of the ideal woman, the *epitome* of heart, soul and mind. Today, I am *perfect* in every way."

She gave herself a big kiss where her lips lined up with her image on the mirror. "Mmwwwa!"

Then she turned and bounced away, a spring in her step, a smile on her face, and joy for her future. She was worthy, despite her parentage.

A lady in her fifties came out of a lavatory stall situated behind the vanity area where Trixie had just been standing and talking to herself while putting her swim cap on.

"I want what that woman has. What confidence! And God, what a stunner."

The matron, who was serving as the concierge, came around the corner and leaned against the tiled wall at that very moment. "Wait 'til you see the guy she's with." She used her hand to fan her face. "He's gorgeous. And Holgar, my boss, says he's one of our best customers."

"Well, he'd better watch out, she's gonna be a tigress tonight."

The matron smiled, "Oh, to be young like that. And to be able to wear a bathing suit like that!"

The woman dropped some money in the tip plate. "I'm going to see if I can get myself an eyeful. Sounds like he could be the man in my dreams tonight."

The matron laughed heartily as the woman left to go into the pool area.

Chapter 23
Itsy Bitsy Teeny-Weenie Mismatched Bikini

Trixie had to laugh out loud when she saw the expression on Palo's face when she dropped the towel she was carrying onto one of the lounge chairs near him. When artists draw cartoons depicting someone's eyes popping out of their head with disbelief or shock, they draw three sets of eyeballs, one in front of the other in graduating sizes, all of the eyeballs goggled wide. Palo's face looked like that right now. His eyes, opened as wide as could be, his brows raised to his hairline, and his mouth agape, did even more for her ego than her pep talk. She was confident, boisterous, and sassy.

"Never seen a bikini before?"

"Not one filled out like that one, with very little hiding the good stuff." The top was a thin strip of stretchy sequined material in coral, the itsy bitsy bottom was aqua, and there was no doubt in his mind that it exposed a good deal of her ass checks.

She smiled as she came alongside him and ran her finger along one of his biceps. "Zucchero Palo, it's all good stuff."

When she turned and walked toward the pool, he saw that her ass cheeks were indeed bare, except for the thin thong of aqua material running up the center. She was toned and tanned a golden bronze from the tiny waistband tied at her hips down to her slim smooth heels. He felt his blood drain, rushing to his penis. In order not to embarrass himself, he said, "I'm going to do some laps."

He walked over to the edge of the pool where she was now standing, adjusting her cap. He did a shallow dive into the deep section. She followed right after him, jumping in while holding her top in place.

Together they did twenty laps, then she got out and sat on the side and watched, as he did twenty more.

His strokes were powerful, his muscular arms pulling the water back and away with smooth strokes. It was like watching a choreographed dance in the water, graceful as each arm left the water to curve overhead and pull back. She could have watched his beautiful body moving through the water for hours, but too soon he used his feet to push off the side of the pool, reversed, and swam underwater toward her.

She felt his hands cup her knees and when he surfaced, he had a devilish smile on his face. Before she knew what was up, he'd gripped her by the waist, lifted her from the ledge, and took her down into the water with him.

She'd had just enough time to take in a breath before he'd pulled her to the bottom of the pool, where he pointed out the intricate mosaic work depicting a ruined Atlantis. It was beautiful—a hidden treasure known only to those who ventured down three meters.

She took in as much of the sight as her breath allowed, then removed her hand from his and pushed off the bottom, bursting up through he surface seconds before he did.

"That's amazing!" she said.

He smiled over at her as he used his fingers to rake the hair from his eyes. His hair wasn't long, but the front was longer than the sides. Now his dark brown hair looked almost black. She tilted her head. She could see his Italian heritage now that his beard had grown in some and shadowed his face. She took in his sculpted chest as he put his palms on the edge of the pool and effortlessly lifted himself out.

"That's why you need a good tour guide. Otherwise you miss all the neat stuff." He put his hand out to her as a way of offering to lift her up and out of the pool.

"Uh, no thanks. You'll either pull my arm out of the socket or lift me out so fast my bathing suit bottom will be left behind."

He laughed. He had straight beautiful white teeth. Not a lot of European men did, as many smoked.

"I would dive right in to fetch it for you," he offered, and then added, "but I might take my time . . ."

It was her turn to laugh. Then she had to cover her mouth with her hand as the laugh turned into a huge yawn.

"Uh oh, someone needs a nap before dinner," he said as they both sat on their loungers.

"Yeah, it's been a long day, what with the overnight flight, the river cruise and now swimming. To be honest, I'm not sure I'm going to be up to going out for dinner." She gave him a pouty moue to soften the news then muttered, "Sorry."

"Hey, no problem. There is a restaurant on the main level here or we can order room service in. Or if you want, I'll go out and bring back whatever you'd like."

"You know, I think I might just want a sandwich, a salad, a wrap or some soup—something small. I'm still full from lunch."

"You're in Frankfurt. They make the best Wiener Schnitzel here."

"Did you like my ass?"

He cocked his head at the abrupt change in subject. "Mmm, yeah . . ."

"Well, if you keep feeding me rich foods, it will be twice the size."

He chuckled. "You win. We'll order something from room service."

She smiled over at him and quirked her lips. "I'll get Wiener Schnitzel when I'm on my way back next week when I find out that there's really no Zucchero Mama for me to take care of. Or that she's a virago of a fishwife who doesn't deserve the Zucchero name at all."

He laughed again. "Oh there's a mama alright. And she can be a bit of a beldame if things don't go her way, but for the most part, she's . . ." Trixie watched his face go soft with adoration. "Well, she's kind . . . caring . . . concerned . . . interesting . . . thoughtful . . . forgiving." Then he broke into a grin and added, "Nosy, opinionated, stubborn, *unforgiving*."

"Wait, she can't be both, forgiving and unforgiving."

He chucked her on the chin. "Depends on who you are and what you did and who you did it to. You do not want to do anything bad to Number One Son," he said, pointing his thumb toward his chest.

"I'll remember that. Don't poison, shoot, knife, drive into, or push Palo off a bridge."

"Or break his heart, that would be worse."

"Anyone ever done that and lived?" she joked.

"Yes, Angelina. When I was eleven and she was ten. She turned me down on Confirmation Day. I asked her if she would show me her new underpants. I'd heard her talking to her girlfriends about her first pair of lacy grownup pants that she was wearing that day."

Trixie's eyes went wide and she sat stock-still. "Wow. Times sure have changed."

"You mean because I and every man here has already seen your bare ass without benefit of even a first date? Mind, I'm not complaining."

"Well, yeah, something like that. Gee, the changes in just, what? Twenty-two or twenty-three years?"

"Um hmm. Yes, just twenty-three years ago, I couldn't even *see* a girl's panties. Now, I get to see what's under them all the time."

"Well. Not *everything* that's under them."

"Let's see what happens in another twenty-three years. I think I'm going to stop investing in Victoria's Secret. You girls won't be wearing any underpants in the year 2045."

She laughed. "I will be 55 then. I don't think anyone's going to want to see me without panties."

"Dirty old men will. And that's exactly what I'll be."

"How in the world did we get on this topic?"

"Mama being unforgiving. Me being turned down on Confirmation Day. Lacy panties to thongs to no panties. What we're going to be doing in 23 years when everyone is walking around naked."

She laughed and stood up. "I think you might be right, I do need a nap." She began to walk backward, toward the changing rooms, "And to stop showing my ass to my new boss!"

He got up and stalked after her. "Don't you dare cover that fine ass."

She jerked a towel up off a pile in a small alcove and wrapped it around her waist. "Too late!"

He mashed his lips tightly together forming a straight line to show he was not happy with that. But actually he was. Somehow over the last hour of them frolicking around the pool and bantering back and forth, he'd become possessive. Yes, he'd like to see that fine ass again. But he didn't want another man to see it, ever again.

Chapter 24
Charcuterie, Champagne, & Jet Lag

When Trixie woke from her nap, the sun was setting, limning the city with a golden light that reflected off the wall-to-wall glass in the salon. "Oh, how beautiful," she whispered as she tiptoed into the room before she saw him sitting in a wingchair reading a book.

He slid a bookmark in place and closed the book as she made her way into the room, suddenly self-conscious of being in her lounging pajamas as he was in a dress shirt and slacks.

On a side table that had not been there before was a table set with a white cloth, a charcuterie board full of cheeses and meats, crackers and breads, olives, relishes, a full regalia of condiments, fruits and nuts, and a tall silver bucket with an open champagne bottle in it.

On his end table sat a partially full flute.

"I'm sorry I didn't wait." He picked up his flute and took a hefty sip.

She focused on his lips as he sipped. They were full, generous lips, perfect for forming all those musical Italian words she heard him speaking into his phone all day. She wondered what they would feel like if they covered hers and had their way.

"It's a good bottle though," he stood. "I'm enjoying it. Let me pour you a glass."

"Sure. I mean *Grazie*."

He smiled over at her as he lifted the bottle from the bucket and waited until the condensation had stopped dripping off the bottom. "I like the sound of that . . . you speaking *Italiano*."

"I've never been good with languages, but I will make the effort to learn if I take the position."

He nodded as he poured champagne into a clean flute. "I will provide a tutor. It will be easy, you'll see."

She popped a grape into her mouth and took the glass he handed her and then walked over to the window that was gradually darkening as the city slipped into shadow. Only in this part of downtown, she suspected that things never really became pitch black as there were so many buildings lit with neon signs.

She saw him reflected in the window, as he came to stand behind her to share the light show with her as the sun went down. It was reflecting off the glass panels on the building across from them and giving everything a magical glow.

She sipped. He rimmed his glass with his middle finger. It was sexy, she thought, the way he was so tactile with his fingers.

The grief of losing a patient, now combined with the anticipation of having time to herself to unwind and get back to a semi-normal sleep cycle, made her antsy—a combination of being kind of sad, a bit horny, and simply needing a validation of life.

Looking up at the glass and seeing the reflection of his eyes on her as he drank her in—as she was doing to him—made her force the words out. "Well, I'm beat. If it's okay with you, I'll fix a plate and turn in. I've got a few things I want to repack. Thank you for dinner. I'll set my alarm and see you in the morning. I'm anxious to meet your mama."

The thought of his mother brought a smile to his face. He turned to face her. "*Buona notte bellissima*," he whispered. Then he turned and placed his glass on the coffee table. "I'll turn in soon as well. Just have a few emails to get off first. I hope you sleep like a baby."

She smiled over at him. "Ironically, babies don't actually sleep all that well. I'd rather sleep like a bear."

He laughed. "They sleep too long. Don't do that."

She made a plate and topped off her flute then retreated into her room to reorganize her things for tomorrow's flight to Florence.

When she got up two hours later to get a bottle of water from the mini-fridge she saw the bar of light under his door.

The man must have the weight of the world on his shoulders, she thought. His mother, his sister, his business . . . all of them needing to be managed.

It struck her that his perfectionist tendencies must make things frenzied at times. From her experience, she knew that travel arrangements often didn't go as planned. But Palo seemed to thrive on the activity, every text or phone call a new challenge to solve. She'd not seen his energy wane, not a bit. Nary a yawn from him, while she had hardly been able to keep her eyes open just to make her way to her room. After eating while packing, she didn't even wash her face or brush her teeth, just stripped, pulled back the ridiculously soft duvet, and fell in.

Chapter 25
Going Caveman

Business Class. It sounded like a college course or a way to dress for dinner at a convention. Who knew it was an elite pampering service for apparently, the wealthy. Beck and call stuff and all that.

As if the basket of to-die-for-muffins that had been waiting on the sofa table when she woke up and ventured out of her room weren't enough. Seriously? He'd still been up after she'd gotten up at 2am for some water. Was he a werewolf? Was he some sort of reincarnated Renaissance man? What was the deal here?

She'd stuffed two muffins in her face while trying to find the cap for her toothbrush in her travel kit. This man was supercharged. Like running on some kind of adrenalin pump. Where did he get his energy?

Then he'd come into the salon when she'd been rolling her case to the door, smiled at her, and she'd lost all thought. The man had gotten handsomer overnight—while traveling. That didn't happen to anybody. And that jaw that was chewing on an English muffin? It was firmer, squarer. It looked like he'd trimmed his mustache and beard, maybe that was it.

He lifted his hand with the muffin in it in her direction as if approving her dress choice. Which was what? She had to look down to remember. Oh yeah, her go-to white Capris, multi-colored top depicting a busy tropical beach scene, and braided leather thong flip-flops. As she had packed for the islands, and not for Tuscany, she didn't have the proper wardrobe, but still it kind of worked. And she appreciated his nod saying so.

But now, an hour into this flight seated in Business Class? Fine leather. Ample room. Two of her could fit in it—maybe. It had an electric footrest, controlled by a button and enough room in front of her that she could actually use it. Their breakfast had come on real dishes, with actual silver, and a cloth napkin. If Palo taught her nothing else, it was worth running into him to learn that it paid to upgrade. Amend that, it was worth it, him running into her.

She'd never been one to keep track of air miles, or to be particularly loyal to one airline. But now . . . she wasn't going back to economy. She wanted the perks now. He'd spoiled her for life.

"What is going through that mind of yours?" he asked as a steward refilled his coffee cup—coffee cup as in a real cup, with a saucer, not a Styrofoam imitation.

"That this is a whole other level of flying that I never knew about."

"If you were strictly booking for price, as most people do, you probably never considered what the next level got you."

"Well . . . it got me space. And, um, courtesy. And . . ."

"And?" he prompted.

"These amazing croissants," she breathed out as she took a big bite out of a chocolate-filled pastry. "Why are these so damned good?" she asked.

He smiled over at her. "Because they are flown in from Paris every morning."

Her eyes popped wide. "You flew these over from France?" The incredulity in her face was priceless.

He shook his head and quirked his lips, "*I* didn't. The airline did. I think Air France has some sort of a food arrangement with Lufthansa. I think they get the Wiener schnitzel to serve for lunch in return. Remember the lunch that I couldn't get you to try?"

She smiled over at him, dark chocolate covering one dimple. He wanted so much to lean over and lick along her chin and sample both her and the croissant. He knew they'd both be primo. She was primo. And he had to admit, was falling for her. He loved the open joy on her face—the brilliant twinkle in her blue eyes that told him she was enjoying herself. She was living in the moment, a thing he spent a lot of time encouraging his employees and clients to do.

He was known for reminding everyone on a regular basis to: "Forget about back home and the job that keeps tugging you away from the magical moments. When you stand in front of Trevi Fountain and toss a few Euros in, be there and nowhere else."

He always encouraged his clients to dwell in the moment, drink in the history, see the architecture, feel the centuries-old square under their feet, and hear the sounds of the city all around them.

He told them, "Visualize what it was like 600 hundred years ago, when Michelangelo was here, when Da Vinci was just a few miles down the road. When the city was full of artists trying to prove their worth and to make a name for themselves. When Florence's Duomo was being built, the metal plates being hammered into place and polished until they gleamed more than the sun."

"I think you are spoiling me because this mama is going to be a lot of trouble."

He laughed. "Oh, she will be that. I can just about guarantee it. Papa spoiled her in grand fashion. He treated her like a princess. And there is no going back, I'm afraid."

She wrinkled her nose at him. "She isn't like Cinderella's stepmother or Sleeping Beauty's old hag?"

He laughed again. "No. Not so bad as that. But exacting."

"What *exactly* does that mean?" She laughed. "Like the way I did that?"

He shook his head at her play on words, and gave her a sideways smile. "For instance, Mama will not ask for a drink. She will say, 'I think I would like a glass of the 2005 Sagrantino Di Montefalco warmed in the sun for five minutes and not the usual pour, a smidge more, in one of the large bowl glasses that matches the decanter from my wedding set—and some crackers, the cheese ones from that little shop in Montepulciano. And maybe a sliced pear with some Asiago."

"So you run around for thirty minutes getting all that ready and you take it in to her and she's asleep, right?"

He smiled. "No . . . she is not. She is impatient. But once she sees you and all you have done for her, you have earned a big wide smile. And when you watch her taste all you have brought you get to hear her sighs of appreciation. And you are another who has fallen under her queenly spell. Living to please."

"She sounds spoiled."

"Yes. With Mama, because of all she has done for everyone else, we indulge her. As we are all very aware that she may not be with us much longer. It is wrong I know, but we all do. You shall see. And I predict you will spoil her some, too."

Trixie pursed her lips and made a humming sound. She had her own thoughts on this, but better to wait and assess, not assume what she suspected. Best to move on. "Well, I can't wait to meet her."

He smiled, giving her one of those boyish grins that made her heart skip. God, he was impossibly handsome.

And just like that, as if she wasn't the only one in his sphere, a flight attendant appeared and offered him a mimosa. Not her. Just him.

He smiled, nodded and said yes, he'd love one, and she went to get it. When she brought it to him he thanked her and then as soon as she turned away, he handed it to Trixie, saying. "Enjoy. If there's one thing we *metrosexual Italian* men know, it's how to please women."

On her next pass, when the attendant saw Trixie drinking Palo's champagne while Palo worked on his laptop on the small tray table, Trixie couldn't help but notice that the attendant momentarily stiffened, then smiled with distaste.

He must get this a lot, she thought. Women flirting, and him pretending to be oblivious. She knew him enough by now to know that he was well aware of what was going on as his fingers continued tapping the keys, typing out answers to a slew of emails.

Meanwhile, Trixie managed a wide-eyed and innocent

mien as she looked all around the coach trying not to meet the young woman's penetrating glare.

"Do you know that attendant?" she whispered in Palo's ear.

"No," he answered as he kept on typing.

"So why is she acting like this?"

"Like what?"

"Groveling to you and shooting daggers at me."

"She thinks you're not good enough for me."

"How can you know that? How can *she* know that?"

"She doesn't. She just knows that she would be better for me."

"Do you know her?"

"No. I just know her kind."

"Does this happen all the time?"

"Yes. Do you not see I am busy here?"

"Just trying to get the lay of the land. Should I toss the rest of my drink on you and say we're through, even though we haven't even started, so you can seduce her?"

"I do not want to seduce her. And don't you dare throw that sticky orange juice on me."

"I want to tell her we're not a couple."

"Why?"

"So she will stop being mad at me."

He laughed. Then he looked up and caught the attendant's eye, and raised a finger to summon her. She smiled full on at him and hurried over. "Yes, sir."

"My sister would like another mimosa, please."

If Trixie thought the woman had been smiling before, she was mega-watt smiling now. "Yes, sir!" She spun around and dashed to the galley.

"Now look what you've done," Trixie muttered.

"Yeah, well . . . now she likes you, and you're getting another drink. Now let me finish this letter."

"Sure." Now that they'd screwed around with the flight

attendant, Trixie was bored.

She thought back to Palo's not-gay kiss. She could recall every nuance and was surprised when just thinking about it conjured up the same wild sensations in her lower belly. She actually felt her vagina clench.

Her head back on the padded headrest, her eyes closed, she became aware of his change in breathing, felt him tense, if that was at all possible since they weren't touching. She turned her head toward him and slowly opened her eyes.

He had stopped typing and was staring down at her, a smoldering look in his eyes, his nostrils flared. From physiology classes, she knew about the power of pheromones and other come-hither provocative scents a woman gave off when aroused. She had never experienced being "scented" though. But from the look in his eyes, the connection was undeniable. He knew that she wanted him. Now he was figuring out what to do about it.

"You keep doing that and I'm going to go caveman on you," he murmured just loud enough for her to hear before he turned back to the lit screen of his laptop.

There was no need to reply, or to deny she knew what he meant. So she sat there trying not to think about kissing and all the other things her body was craving. The stewardess, as she preferred to call her, returned with her other mimosa.

She sipped at it slowly, trying to settle her mind. Finally, she settled on doing metric conversions in her head. She'd need to know them forward and backward. She should arrange to speak to a pharmacist who spoke English about the medicines Palo's mother was taking and the proper dosing amounts just to be sure. And were they measuring fluid volumes? Watching her intakes and outputs?

She knew Italy's biggest health issues were with the aging population, which was her specialty. So she doubted she'd come across a problem she'd never seen or heard of, but translating any issues to Mama's doctors was going to be challenging. Unconsciously, she began to nod her head several times. She'd take Palo up on an Italian tutor.

"Yes, to what?" he asked. She hadn't noticed that he'd stowed his laptop.

She looked over at him. God, he was good looking. It took a moment to understand his question. "Oh! Yes, to taking Italian lessons from that tutor you mentioned."

He nodded as well. "They're already arranged. Signora Sofia Ricci will be coming by the villa tomorrow afternoon to get you started. She used to teach at the American Academy in Rome. You will like her."

"Wow, you work fast."

"I will only have today and tomorrow with you and Mama. Alyssa will be leaving to join a tour in Venice next week. So you must know the basics, as I will not be back for two weeks. Although Anna will still be there to help out, she is my cousin, Mama's niece. She has agreed to help you for a little while, she speaks both languages."

Trixie nodded dumbly, trying to take it all in. Her and his mama, one-on-one, alone and speaking two different languages. Her in a foreign country, having to not only get along, but get along to the extent that Mama would listen to her and do what she said. "Will this Sofia come every day?"

He laughed. "Do you want her to?"

She smiled back at him. "Yes, I think so."

"Are you a fast learner?"

"Well, I've never learned another language, although I do know a fair amount of Latin due to it being the root of most medical terms. But I was thought to have savant qualities once, including recall. I guess we'll have to see how quickly I can pick it up."

"Hand me your phone." They had just landed and were pulling up to the gate. All around them you could hear people prematurely unclicking their seatbelts, at the same time the attendant was reminding them over the intercom to keep them on until they were at the gate, and the pilot gave permission.

She dug in her purse, brought up the screen and used her forefinger on the button to unlock it, then she handed her iPhone to him.

His fingers slid expertly over the screen, swiping and taping and then grabbing her hand, separating her fingers and pressing her forefinger to the home key to accept the app.

"We'll let you cheat for a while. I just downloaded Google Translate. All you'll have to do is speak a word, in either language and Google will translate. You can also send a picture of a sign or a menu or a note and it will translate that for you as well. That should get you by for the time being."

"Wow, thank you. How much did that cost?"

"Nothing. It's free. And it's pretty amazing. Here, let's try a few things."

Their heads were together, oblivious to the passengers around them deplaning, until the attendant tapped Palo on the shoulder and said, "The cleaning crew is waiting to board. You two planning on staying aboard much longer?"

Palo smiled up at her and said something in rapid Italian. The woman beamed at him and stepped aside for them to exit the plane.

"What did you say to her? It sure improved her attitude."

He laughed as he looked down at her. He was so tall that once standing, he towered over her. "I told her I was just showing my gay sister a new App I installed on her phone."

She smacked him on the arm. "Gay! And do I seriously look like I could be your sister?"

He shook his head. "No, you look nothing like Alyssa. You are both beautiful. Just in different ways."

"That's better," she said as she gathered her things and preceded him off the plane. She noticed he stopped to talk to the attendant and she said something that made him laugh.

She was not going to ask him what he said. She decided she was not going to be that kind of woman.

But by the time they cleared the gate and walked out the exit, she couldn't stand it. "So you two are friends again?"

"Who?"

"You and the flight attendant."

He hooted. "I knew you wouldn't let that go."

"So . . .?"

"I gave her a tip, which she isn't supposed to accept, and then told her how happy I was to be back in Italy as I was marrying my boyfriend Roberto next week."

"You didn't!"

"I did. I think the new metrosexual side that you discovered in me fits rather well, don't you think?"

She shoved against his arm. "What a waste to womankind that would be."

He pinched her bottom. "Glad you think that."

"What was that for?"

"You're in Italy. Every woman deserves to get her ass pinched while in Italy. Trust me, every woman thinks that. It's the number one complaint on surveys, that they didn't get pinched while they were here."

He looked up and saw his driver and called out to him, "Enzo!"

After that, it was the two of them and a seemingly endless stream of Italian spoken incredibly fast. She shook her head. She doubted she would ever be able to translate or speak the Italian language that fast.

She pulled out her phone and opened the translator app then sidled closer. She smiled. Enzo was saying how pretty she was, and Palo was readily agreeing—and demanding hands off.

They both turned as they became aware of a digital voice translating their words. When Palo saw the phone in her hand he threw his head back and laughed.

"There are no secrets anymore, Enzo. The tourists and those new to Italia can understand all our words now." He put his arm around Trixie and drew her close so he could introduce her.

Then Enzo loaded their cases into the trunk and off they sped.

Chapter 26
Piazzale Michelangelo & The Duomo

"Sped," being the absolutely correct word. She had never been in a car that was being driven so fast, or so erratically. Enzo expertly dodged buses, vans, motorbikes, scooters, mini-cars and bicycles, as well as many elongated sedans like the one they were in.

Trixie could not believe how fast everyone drove, it was as if all the drivers were aiming at one another, and then by some stroke of luck, or some mysterious signal, one or the other veered off at the last possible second to avoid a collision. It was the largest and longest game of chicken she'd ever seen. Certainly the lengthiest she'd ever been in as a player.

Palo kept smiling at her and patting her knee to reassure her.

"Is this normal or is it just because we are close to the airport?" she asked.

"This is pretty much normal anywhere in Italy, on the communal roads and regular highways, or what we call *strade*. We are on the *autostrada* now, the toll roads where everyone goes super fast. There will not be as much darting in and out on this type of expressway, as everyone is going very, very fast."

"I'm afraid to close my eyes, yet I am terrified by what I am seeing. Aren't there a lot of accidents?"

"Not anymore than any other large city. Everyone is hyper vigilant, just always in a hurry here. Relax, Enzo is a good driver—he's one of the best."

Palo pointed out the sites as they drove, and when they entered the city proper, he named the various churches and bridges while relating some of the history.

"We are going to make a quick stop before going to the

villa. I want to show you my city, all laid out in front of you like a *mantile,* a tablecloth. We are going to Piazzale Michelangelo, where you can see the whole city. It is a panoramic view of the town proper and the surrounding hills. It is a splendid view.

"You will see the dome of the Cathedral Santa Maria del Fiore—referred to as the *Duomo.* The idea of building such a grand cathedral was conceived in 1293. At that time, there was no technology that existed to build the dome as it was designed, but they began building the cathedral anyway. After the cathedral was built, parts of the dome's roof were left open for many years. It was 140 years more before the cathedral was completed. It is a fascinating story—and one of my favorites, which you will hear once you see the magnificent dome that was designed by Fillippo Brunelleschi.

"Brunelleschi was only 23-years old at the time. Florence had to wait for this genius to be born and then grow up before they could have their beloved dome constructed. The dome is truly amazing. Over four million bricks, weighing over 40,000 tons were used just for the dome, which is suspended over 10 stories high. It is the largest masonry structure in the world—still a very big deal today. You can just imagine what it must've been like living in the city back then and looking up at it. Before the technology existed to build something so grand, they were doing it!"

Trixie marveled at the pride of his hometown so entrenched in his voice. He was like a kid, over-the-moon excited to share the story of one of its first churches with her. There was no telling how many hundreds of times he'd already shared the story with others. She couldn't wait to hear the rest of it. The man had a charismatic energy that drew people along with him.

She smiled up at him. Here was a man who had truly found his calling. He genuinely loved sharing the culture and the history of his country. And he lived in an area of the world where there was no end to the exploits of the past. He'd already shared some of the history of the Etruscans who had lived in

Italy during the 8th to 3rd centuries BC. He'd promised to take her to see many artifacts from that time.

She knew what it was like to truly love your job. And here was someone who truly loved his as well—but apparently, his paid light-years better than hers.

He would have made a good teacher. In fact, he was a good teacher. He just chose to do field trips every day instead of remain in a classroom.

After Enzo parked the car in a very chaotic and crowded lot, Palo got out, walked around the car and offered Trixie his hand. He pulled her up, but then kept hold of her hand—twined his fingers through hers—and led her toward the Piazzale. Together with many groups of people streaming off of huge tour buses, they made their way from the south side of the Arno up to the huge panoramic terrace that honored Michelangelo.

It was a bit of a trek getting up to the square that had a large bronze statue of Michelangelo dominating its center. And she was out of breath when they got there. But it was well worth it to see the city of Florence spread out before you, just as Palo had said, like a multi-colored tablecloth; only this view had 3-D bridges and buildings alongside an expansive flowing river.

Trixie stood and took it all in from the vantage point Palo had pulled her eagerly toward. In an excited voice, he pointed out the churches, the gates, the baptistries, the bell towers, the palaces and the piazzas, the museums, all the bridges leading into the city, and then the famed Uffizi Gallery, adding. "I will take you there one day, maybe in the fall when the tourists are less. We will spend the entire day there. You will be amazed at everything you will see, but especially the art. It is magnificent!"

"You make the city come alive, Palo. What a truly beautiful place. I can practically feel the history bubbling out of you." And so could many others. She noticed a circle of avid tourists gathered around them, eavesdropping as Palo gestured and described his jewel of a city.

"I will finish the story of the dome and then we will leave.

But of course, we will come back. Always we will come back."

She smiled and nodded, encouraging him to continue. Several people grouped around them nodded for him to go on as well.

"Santa Maria del Fiore, referred to the world over as simply the *Duomo*, is the most prominent feature of the Florentine skyline. Known for its size and beauty, it is a masterpiece of architectural design . . . so far ahead of its time. So far advanced, it almost did not happen at all.

"As the construction continued, the cathedral grew larger and more grand than even originally depicted. Yet, they still had no design for the domed roof. Even the artists who had conceived the grand cathedral had no idea how to finish it. But the Florentines were determined. This would be the most magnificent cathedral in all of Tuscany, no matter how long it took.

"But it ended up taking so long that they were beginning to be made fun of. Florence was becoming the butt of many jokes. After well over a hundred years, they finally put the problem out as a challenge to all the designers and architects. They needed a solution that was inventive, but also cost effective. Up until then, everything proposed required a wooden structure, requiring over 400 trees and untold manpower. Fillippo Brunelleschi entered the competition and as he was the only one with an idea that did not involve wood, the judges listened to him with an eager ear.

"Several years earlier Brunelleschi had lost the competition for the design of the east Baptistery doors to Lorenzo Ghiberti, as the judges preferred Lorenzo's classical style to Fillippo's humanist depiction, though many felt Brunelleschi's entry was years ahead of his time in showcasing the Renaissance period. His ideas had merit then, so this time the judges gave him his due and listened to his idea with an open mind.

"Also, they were desperate at this point. Brunelleschi won the competition without ever showing the judges a single plan. Forward thinking had lost him the earlier contest with the doors, but this time it was what persuaded the judges to accept his idea. A simple egg was what finally convinced them. He said if anyone could make an egg stand upright on a table he would reveal his plans. No one could meet the challenge. When they had all failed, he took the egg and smashed the bottom of it on the surface of the table, thereby causing the top part, the dome, to stand upright.

"They were amazed. They hired the man even though he refused to reveal his plans. And he had no experience whatsoever to move the project forward. Despite having secret plans and no references, the project began with Brunelleschi in charge. He asked his former rival Ghiberti to join him, and together they started in April of 1420."

Palo moved his hand expansively in front of him, with a flourish at the end that encompassed the cathedral in the foreground. "The dome was completed in only sixteen years. In an era when most designers never got to see their completed work, Brunelleschi was able to finish his project and see the reaction of the people to his amazing feat. Sixteen years was unheard of for such an amazing project, especially this one, a fantastical cathedral that sat stagnant for so many years with no promise of ever being started.

"When it was completed in the 15th century, it was the largest cathedral in the world. It is now the third largest, second only to St. Peter's in Rome, and St. Paul's in London.

"And not only did Brunelleschi design the dome, he invented the technology he needed to build it. He came up with an ingenious idea for a freestanding brick structure using curved walls without the assistance of a frame, and he invented the tools that he needed as well.

"He used oxen, walking in circles to create the mechanism for a cogged wheel system to control lifting and lowering the heavy loads of bricks. It was unprecedented.

"He was a genius. And unlike many others, such as Da Vinci and Alberti, he left no notebooks or drawings behind. Such a secretive person, he didn't leave a single plan or document to tell how he managed his designs. Scholars worked for years to find the missing pieces as to how he got things to work. There were many theories on how he built the dome. After many years of scholars studying his methods, the secret was finally discovered by a document that was originally meant to discredit Brunelleschi.

"A man from the University of Florence found an extremely detailed drawing that showed the rope patterns he used to guide the structure's brick layout. It illustrated the secret to the successful building of the dome. It was the herringbone brick pattern, and ironically, it had been a flower that had been used to guide him.

"Again, it was something never tried before. So once more, Brunelleschi, who had had to convince his critics, even had to convince his building team to trust him—these men who were working 170 feet up in the air on a structure that seemed doomed to cave in at any second. Yet there they were, adding more and more mass to the structure—layering a series of inverted arches, as the walls grew higher and higher.

"At the base, on the interior of the dome, was the secret it all relied upon—the shape of a flower. As there were no lasers or levels at the time, an ingenious rope system was employed. It was all they had to guide them. Starting at the base, the design guided the ropes, forcing the bricks to create a series of inverted arches, which were the key to the reason why the structure has lasted through the years.

"Instead of gravity pulling the heavy bricks down, causing them to cave in on each other from the top, as nearly everyone assumed they would, the herringbone layout combined with the inverted arches, used gravity to reinforce the whole structure. It is absolutely genius.

"The name of the cathedral translates to Saint Mary of the Flower. Ironically, there is no connection to the flower design Brunelleschi used as his pattern for building the dome, but it is serendipitous, as the cathedral gets its name from the symbol of Florence—the lily.

"So there you have it," he pointed his finger at the faraway dome, "Brunelleschi's magnificent miracle, *The Duomo*." There was a volley of clapping from the eavesdroppers.

Trixie sighed. "You are amazing. What a storyteller. And you keep all that in your head. No notes, whatsoever."

He smiled and ran his finger down her nose. "Do you have any idea how many times I have told the history of *The Duomo*? A thousand? Maybe more? I have no idea myself."

She laughed. "Well, you still tell it like it fascinates you."

His green eyes flashed in the sunlight and he laughed. "It does still fascinate me." He shook his head, "I wish Brunelleschi had left notebooks, drawings, something. I would have loved to read them. He was brilliant."

She looped her arm in his and let him lead her back down the steps and then the hill, to the car park. Behind them the small crowd they had gathered began dispersing. Several had tried to put folded Euros into his hand, but he had waived them off saying, "*No no nessun disturbo sul serio.*"

"You are brilliant. And thank you. I think I will enjoy learning about your city."

"You most definitely will. I will see to it!"

He had a child's enthusiasm wrapped up in a very handsome and confident package, she mused to herself. "Where to next?" she asked.

"We stop to pick up some components of the afternoon meal, then we go home to see Mama. Are you ready for this?"

"I am."

When he was within sight of the many rows of cars, he lifted his hand, and within a few moments, Enzo pulled up to the curb they were standing on.

"We will stop at my favorite restaurant, they will have everything ready. When we dine at the villa, we will dine *al fresco*."

"Sounds wonderful. Thank you. You make every moment

so special."

He patted her hand, still wrapped over his arm. "You will find that just being in *Italia*, makes everything special. It is why people always come back."

Enzo steered them through the crowded city streets until they were back on the highway, where cars, like racing horses that had been held back, continuously shot forward and commanded their lane, the drivers maintaining distances that were mere inches from the bumpers of the cars in front of them.

Trixie had to look away. It was unnerving to see the daredevil antics playing out all around them. Instead, she lifted her head and focused on the rustic hill towns that rose ridiculously high, nearly touching the low-lying clouds. She took in the endless fields of sunflowers, the tidy rows of olive groves, and the gnarly low hedges of grapevines that covered anything that wasn't asphalt. It was truly a beautiful setting everywhere she looked—broken only by the expansive petrol auto parks that popped up without warning that seemed to be a welcome oasis for the nicotine and caffeine deprived race car drivers, as well as for the tour buses and their gelato-seeking passengers. Palo had asked her several times if she needed to stop for anything, but she simply shook her head. She was anxious to get to Palo's home and meet his mother.

Along the way, Palo mentioned that Frances Mayes, author of "Under the Tuscan Sun" lived off of this very highway, in the hilltop town of Cortona, which was an important Etruscan history center.

He told her about the country's architectural covenants encompassing all the hill town communities. How one town resembled the next as buildings of ecru, buff, tan, and sandstone colored the houses that dotted the steppes around the Tuscan towns—only earth-toned colors that blended into the surrounding countryside were allowed. Subtle nuances of light tan and lemon-colored stuccoed walls shone in the afternoon sun, most with roofs layered with the traditional curved terracotta tiles. The conformity of the houses gave the villages a quaint ageless appearance. The light colors were practical. They didn't absorb the heat of the sun as much as dark colors, and they were easier to maintain as the sun-bleached and weathered look left a soft patina that created an ancient timelessness to the homes. New homes looked much like the older ones, their notable size difference and impressive blue-water pools with multi-leveled terraces were the only difference.

Bright spots of color were sprinkled liberally by the profusion of flowers, most in huge ceramic pots, or in box planters on windowsills. The varied bushes and trees used to landscape around the houses and fill the beds often had colorful blooms, their petals reaching for the sun..

This was the way it had always been for the hill towns. Only newcomers objected to the muted traditions—the old ways. So, every once in a while, there would be blue, pink, or purple shutters or a garage door painted in garish primary colors. Instead of an old-timey mural painted with matte colors, the side of a house would have a Day-Glo faux art fountain spewing fluorescent lime green water from a flashing neon waterfall. A wooden fence would boast tasteless posters, or a clothesline waving to the blue sky and white clouds would flaunt a long row of a rival team's bright-colored soccer shirts.

There were always renegades, non-conformists who wanted to flaunt their novelty, or promote their private agenda. The rest toed the line, and the landscape was simply stunning, every single vista.

"It's idyllic," she whispered.

He reached for her hand and entwined his fingers, then lightly squeezed hers. "It's home."

A few moments later, Enzo turned off the paved road onto a wide lane that had been tamped smooth by many years of tractors, trucks, cars, carts, wagons, horses, cows, and pigs trampling it.

The lane meandered left then right as it wound upward until Trixie could see the road they had just left behind them, out the window, way below them. There was sparse traffic now, only the occasional hay wagon, a putt-putting motorbike, or a threshing tractor. There were no more whooshing sounds droning in her ears. After the motorbike made its way down to the bottom of the hill and out to the highway, it was eerily quiet.

She turned from her window in time to see a large house come into view through the window on the other side. At first it looked immense. A closer look revealed that it was an intricate complex of houses that had been arranged next to each other and made from different types of materials. They were connected by arbors and pergolas, and in one place an intricately tiled portico with an arch bearing fancy lettering. *Villa Stelle Cadente* stood out in glossy black script against a colorful pattern of blue, red, and yellow swirls—all against a white tile background. Even from here, she could see cracks in some of the tiles and small chunks of the design missing.

There were slight variations to the lemon and manila colors of the stucco for all the different additions. It was easy to see the newer additions, as the windows were larger and the lines sleeker, the doors more substantial and wider.

There was a low wall that encompassed the entire area, allowing only a partial view of the first level of the buildings and gardens, but as her eyes drew upward, she could see that the next two levels of stucco were covered with colorful red flowers against shiny green climbing vines that rose high enough to touch the roof tiles.

The low walls had rustic wooden gates in several places, but now, where Enzo was pulling off the road, there was a tall wrought iron gate that was opening in the middle on its own accord. The words *Villa Stelle Cadente* were separating in the middle, half going to the left and half going to the right, breaking between the double *l*s.

The gate opened electronically, widening until there was enough room for Enzo to drive inside, and for her to see the lower levels and the spacious lawn. Large colorful patio tiles bordered the house as walkways connecting the terraces. All along the front veranda with its many ceramic planters of lemon and lime trees, was a tidy row of white painted rocking chairs, all with thick, floral print chair pads.

"Wow, this is beautiful."

Palo smiled. "Yes, this is the best view to come home to." Then he frowned. "But, be aware, the house is old. And it has been added on to many times. Not always in the best manner. Mama will not let me renovate, so things are . . . what you say . . . getting a bit tawdry. Her focus has always been on the gardens and the terraces. My mama, she is a good cook, but housekeeping . . . not so much. You will need to watch your step as the tiles are cracked and not level in many places."

Trixie tried to take it all in. It did look a little tumbled together here and there. But it was still very grand, especially to her. Convents tended to be unadorned—embellished only by standard Catholic icons: crosses with folded palms tucked under them or rosaries draped over them; pictures of Jesus praying by a large rock in the Garden of Gethsemane, or the Virgin Mary with the baby Jesus in her lap with him holding a crucible with a cross on top. This looked . . . well, homey.

He pointed to a building in the back, slightly to the left and behind the front porch. "That is the original house. Two levels. The barn was on the first floor and the family lived on the second floor. There was no heat or air conditioning back then. Not even a fireplace. The heat of the cows and the horses huddled together and their warm breath escaping into the confined space carried up to the second floor. That's how primitive this house was when my grandfather first bought the property. Both he and my father, along with other family members, built everything you see."

"Well, they certainly fixed it up quite a bit." She was

impressed at what must have been a lot of resourcefulness and ingenuity—and for his grandmother and mother, untold patience.

"Yes, every spare lira went into planting the orchards, the olive groves, the vineyards, and to adding on to the main structure to make it more of a home. Now it is all a mish-mash of what they call shabby chic décor and nouveau riche décor. My nonno and my papa scrounged around for materials and took whatever people threw out, so it is a bit of both. Often there was some pretty good stuff to be had, but they still had to haul things here. Even if something wasn't of good use then, it was saved for later. They wasted nothing. They eventually found a purpose for everything. I call them the fathers of recycling."

He patted her knee. "But take heart. There is indoor plumbing and heat and air conditioning now. You will not have to use the outhouse or wash by the well as my grandmother and grandfather did."

She looked over at him, and smiled, "Did you?"

He laughed. "No. And neither did Mama. By the time they married, Nonna and Papa had fabricated a bathroom of sorts. However . . . there was this huge tank attached to the wall that someone had to climb up to fill. As soon as I was old enough to climb a ladder, it became my chore. I think was age five or six. It took six buckets of water to fill the tank to the top every day—twelve for me, as the buckets were smaller. When you pulled on a long chain, everything washed down through a hole in the floor."

She shook her head. "I can only imagine how much work that was for you."

"It was nothing compared to the amount of work my nonna and papa did for us." He got out of the car and offered her his hand. "Come, let's go see Mama."

She let him pull her up and into his side.

He kissed the side of her head, close to her hairline, and inhaled the heady scent of her. He knew how she smelled now. Fresh out of the shower she was spicy sweet. After a long plane ride she was floral fragrant. You could capture her scent in her hair or behind her ear. After freshening up at a petrol station, she was lemony fresh, as if she'd just reapplied hand cream or spritzed something akin to 4711 all over her neck. He couldn't get enough of her smell. It was intoxicating.

"I will show you around in the moonlight tonight. Everything looks magical then. Not quite so old."

He looked up then and saw his mother on the front porch and solemnly whispered "Mama" with such reverence that Trixie had to turn to seek her out.

How could any woman not love a man who adored his mother so? Oops! Did she say love? No, surely not. It was too soon for anything like that. Waaaay too soon.

There was Mama, standing in front of one of the porch rockers, her hands twisting together in front of her. All at once she looked shy and somewhat ashamed. Mama was huge. Trixie knew with one glance exactly what all her health issues were, and what their cause was.

The woman was maybe 4'6" or 4'7"—and likely close to 200 pounds. She had definitely been a spoiled princess and given everything she wanted in terms of food and drink for many, many years. Trixie held back a sigh. She would have her work cut out for her. This woman, sweet as she looked in her colorful apron and clog-type shoes, was going to have to lose weight—a lot of it.

Seeing *Mama* smile full on at the sight of Palo, then quirk her lips sideways with disparagement at the sight of her, Trixie could already see she was in for a battle of wills. This woman did not appreciate her son's efforts in finding her a new care companion. She had no idea of the extensive training Trixie had in the care of over-indulged geriatrics. Neither did Palo. She was the Nurse Ratched for the corpulent geriatric set.

She took in a deep breath. Tomorrow, she thought. Today, she would try to make a friend, attempt to earn this woman's trust. Try to make Palo happy. But after Palo left . . . .

Chapter 27
The Villa Stelle Cadente

Trixie stood behind Palo feeling awkward as he and his mom prattled off in the lyrical, romantic language of Tuscany. She understood two words that were being said over and over again by Palo: Trixie and America.

Then when all seemed lost in their apparent argument, he said "*Ospedale*," with a few other words between. Then repeated them, over and over, while flailing his arms all around, indicating the villa and its many additions.

She knew he was repeating the word hospital and indicating she would have to leave her home. Finally, that seemed to take the wind out of his mom's sails, and she seemed to deflate even lower into her squatty, uneven healed clogs.

Trixie noted that her ankles and feet were unacceptably swollen; so much so that she felt sure her toes would be tinged with bluish-purple blotches. Often there was loss of feeling due to veins being unable to return the blood to the heart, a condition called venous insufficiency. This woman needed to be off her feet, yet at the same time, she needed a daily exercise regimen that included walking—a dichotomy she'd had to deal with before.

There were going to be so many lifestyle changes for this woman within the next few days . . . and Trixie was going to be the unwelcome initiator of all of them.

But for today, today she would smile and be accepting even if she had to watch the woman chow down on cheesy manicotti, creamy linguini, buttery rolls and sugary cannolis. Palo deserved a happy reunion. And she needed to figure out a way to help this woman without causing a family feud. So, first things first . . . her job was to smile and be genial, try to pick up some of the nuances of the language, get the lay of the land and make friends with the staff. No way was she concerned with being pals-y with Mama at this point. No doubt she was going to end up being her nemesis as soon as Palo left to join the tour he was leading.

Palo introduced her, and she was sure he was saying flattering things about her, but from the expression on Mama's frozen face, she'd had no idea he was bringing home a live-in caregiver, none whatsoever.

"She says she's happy to have you here, absolutely delighted, and welcomes you to our home," Palo said.

Trixie shot him a sideways look, one eyebrow dramatically raised. "Does she really? Just reading her body language, it doesn't appear to square with someone at all pleased that I am here."

He pulled her around the corner and into a large room that seemed to be a sitting room, a den, and a study, all in one. It was a room with much memorabilia on display.

"Well . . . this is somewhat of a surprise to her. I did not prepare her exactly for your role."

"Really? I hadn't guessed."

He pinched the bridge of his nose and rubbed in tiny circles as his mother, behind them on the terrace, said something to two young women approaching from a side gate. Palo lifted his head and saw them through the glass door.

"Lydia and Sofia will show you to your room. Why don't you wash up and join us in about half an hour. We'll have *aperitivo*, *antipasto,* and *primo piatto* on the back terrace. Then *secondo, contorni, insalata, formaggi e frutta,* and *dolce* in the dining room. Meanwhile, I will explain things to Mama so she will be more receptive."

He took her by the elbow, "You know, I thought about introducing you as my girlfriend, in which case she would have been over the moon to have you here. But as I am leaving in two days, I thought she and I should have our battles now so it will go easier for you when I leave. You must understand, she knows you will be going against her wishes in many ways after I leave.

It is always that way with her caregivers."

You have no idea how 'against her wishes' this is going to be . . . she said to herself. Out loud she said, "It's best to be upfront when dealing with health matters as serious as hers are. And I am not your girlfriend."

He shot her a sad moue, "Do you not want to be my girlfriend?"

"It's not that. Maybe that will work out for us, who knows? But that is not the issue now. You are leaving me here to care for her and it doesn't appear that she wants that. Also, there will be no way for her and I to bond as I don't speak Italian."

"Your interpreter will be here for dinner. You will like her. But the important thing is that Mama adores her. So she will not want to disappoint her or cause her to lose her first job ever."

Trixie squinted both eyes and drew her eyebrows into a deep frown. "Boy, you've really planned this out, haven't you? So who's this super-duper interpreter?"

"Anna, her best friend's daughter . . . and Mama's goddaughter. She dotes on her and won't want to be the reason Anna loses her first job. Anna is saving her money for her first year at university in the fall."

"Oh, so . . . when first we practice to deceive . . ."

"What makes you think this is my first time deceiving, or that I need any practice?" he said with a grin.

Then he bent and kissed her—a quick kiss, full on the lips, but one that he drew out by running his tongue along the seam of her lips as he pulled away—in full view of his mother. She shivered and was sure he felt the tremble move up her arm to his.

He laughed. Then whispered, "Someone will come to collect you in half an hour. And you *are* my girlfriend. Don't doubt it."

Chapter 28
Aperol Aperitifs, Antipasto & More

Trixie had never seen so much food for one meal in her whole life. Aperitifs were first, an Aperol spritz with slices of blood orange and a spike of fresh mint, served with tiny baked pieces of thinly shaven Parmesan cheese. She could have popped those amazing things into her mouth all day long.

Next, was what was called antipasto, which could have been the meal by itself—should have been the meal by itself—at least for Mama. Farm fresh black and green olives, bite-sized pieces of marinated cauliflower, pickled veggies, grilled eggplant, pepperoncini, cherry peppers, marinated mushrooms, beans, and artichoke hearts, roasted tomatoes with red and green peppers, crudités such as celery, cucumber, cherry tomatoes, and carrots. Then the meats: salami, pepperoni, coppa, capicola, and sopressata. The cheeses: gorgonzola, parmigiano reggiano, asiago, fontina, and mozzarella balls marinated in olive oil, herbs, and red pepper flakes. Five types of breads: baguettes, ciabatta slices, hard and crunchy breadsticks, crostini, and flatbread. Almonds, hard-boiled eggs, figs and fresh berries completed the platter. It was a feast all in itself.

The second course was Minestrone, chock full of vegetables and orzo with hard rolls . . . *and,* linguini in a clam sauce. Then came the entrée of roasted pork loin with sautéed asparagus, zucchini, and mushrooms with mango chutney. By then they'd all been eating and chatting for an hour and a half.

Fortunately, Palo had thought to sit Trixie next to Anna, so she was able to translate and "talk" for her. Anna told her about her studies and the classes she hoped to take at the university. And about her boyfriend who was doing his mandatory two-year government service driving an ambulance while working on a degree in law.

Insalata, or salad was next. Trixie thought they'd all had

plenty of veggies up to this point, but no, this was a full-blown Caesar salad, down to the homemade dressing using a coddled egg and anchovy slices with freshly fried bread croutons.

Despite taking small portions of everything, she was up to her ears with food. She was beginning to understand the ancient Romans' need for vomittoriums.

Next was a fruit and cheese platter. This time the fruits were tropical: slices of pineapple, melon, kiwi, mango, pear, and jicama. The cheeses were soft, similar to a Boursin or Neufchatel.

And finally dessert: Panetone with dried fruit, and next to it, a white cake with a thin layer of raspberry cream icing, and beside that, a rainbow layered gelatin dish with smooth as glass layers of orange, lime, and lemon, sandwiched between creamy layers of pannecotta.

Chocolate fudge with sea salt sprinkles and a bowl of pistachios served with coffee were the climax of the meal. Trixie was so full she thought the zipper on her jeans was going to pop its teeth out onto the tiled floor at any moment. It had been two and a half hours since they'd sat down at the table. And they'd been eating the whole time.

Surreptitious glances at Mama showed she was chowing down with the best of them, and to Trixie's astonishment she actually went back for seconds of the linguini in clam sauce after they'd had the fruit and cheese platter. This was not a healthy way to eat.

Trixie asked Anna if this is the way they ate all the time here and was told that this kind of feast was mostly for weekends and celebrations. But then she admitted with chagrin, that everything was pretty much a cause of celebration in Italy.

Softening the statement, she added that during the week the dinner meal usually consisted of only meat or fish, salad, soup, two or three kinds of vegetables, and a simple dessert such as gelato or a treat from the local bakery such as a Napoleon. Aperitifs and after dinner drinks were always offered though, as you were not thought to be a good host if you did not keep the liquor pouring. Wine was served throughout the meal with everyone's glass replenished frequently. Custom dictated that an empty glass meant the host was out of wine.

Hmmmm. Trixie had an internal debate with herself. Talk to Palo now and outline her game plan and get opposition from the start, or wait until he was gone and implement what would be a stringent diet plan for his mama compared to what she was used to. She opted for a middle ground, a bit of both strategies.

After a *digestive,* which was yet another form of alcohol, on the back terrace watching the sun go down, Trixie tapped Palo on the shoulder and asked to have a word with him. He took her by the hand and walked her down toward the rows of olive trees softly silhouetted by the encroaching twilight.

The heat of the day was dissipating as they made their way down one of the rows. She felt a chill go through her and was glad Palo had grabbed his sweater, which he now draped over her shoulders.

"Please don't tell me you want me to arrange a flight home for you."

"No. Unless you tell me you're not on board with what I have planned."

He looked over at her, curious. "What do you have planned?"

"Your mother eats too much. She's *very* overweight. So is most of the household. Too much food is served. The whole house needs to go on a diet."

He shook his head and laughed. "Do you have any idea how many people have tried to get her to lose weight?"

"Well, I know why it's not working."

"Why?"

"I'm betting that everyone sabotages the person who's making her go on a diet. I can almost guarantee that while one person is making her eat egg whites and dry toast, another is bringing her a bag of donuts and croissants."

"You could be right. In fact, you probably are. Papa

instilled a dictum before he died. He expressed his wish that everyone should keep Mama happy. Food makes her happy."

"If she could lose 30-50 pounds, or whatever your equivalent of that is, her blood pressure and heart issues could be more easily managed. She wouldn't have to be on so many drugs that are causing other health issues. Have you looked at her feet? She is a stroke waiting to happen."

"I don't disagree with anything you've said. What can I do to help you? Name it and I will."

"Talk to the staff, the workers in the field, her friends—anyone who could undermine my efforts. Explain that I am here to help her, not to make her miserable or to starve her. But mostly talk to her. Tell her to give me a chance. I'm good at what I do. I know I can help her if she'll work with me."

"What will that entail? From the perspective of her cooperation."

"Food I prepare for her or that I have her staff prepare for her, nothing provided secretly by friends or a hidden stash in her room. Two glasses of wine in the evening—and I pick the glass. And some exercise—outside."

"She can't exercise outside. She can barely make it from room to room inside the house."

"We'll start small. I saw the pool. It has walk in steps and two areas where the water is the perfect depth for exercising. I'll do water aerobics with her. We'll work up to getting her more stamina. Ultimately, she should be able to walk one to two miles a day."

"I don't see that happening."

"Why not?"

"I don't think she has a suit that will fit her."

"That's truly sad, don't you think? That gorgeous pool . . . and she can't get in it."

He nodded, his hands in his pockets as they walked and he thought things through.

"Although, I am pretty sure that if she had a suit she

could wear, she would not want anyone to see her in it."

"I can certainly understand that. But we're talking about her health. What time do the workers start showing up in the morning?"

"Different times. As early as five-thirty, as late as nine or ten o'clock."

"Is the pool heated?"

"Yes."

"Then we can start at 6:00 or 6:30. It will just barely be light outside. I doubt she'll go a full thirty minutes at first, so she'll be in by seven."

He laughed and the sound carried. She was sure everyone in the house had heard it.

"Mama is not an early riser. Ten is early for her."

"Well, things are going to have to change. I think the pool is the best option to get her exercising. How fast can we get her a suit?"

"Alyssa can make one, she has amazing sewing skills. I will ask her to make something Mama can swim in."

"And can I have Anna full-time for the first week? That way I can at least be understood and I can show your mother what I expect."

"Anna does not have to go back to school until mid-September, so you have the rest of August and part of September. She has said she will make herself available for you. But I don't know about six in the morning."

"6:30 then, and that's my best offer. And that's from someone whose body clock is already seven hours ahead of theirs. It's the middle of the night to me right now. But I don't think we should wait any longer. Her arteries are getting blocked more and more with each unhealthy meal. She's in danger of a heart attack, and I think you know that. You seem to be in denial though. Trust me, time is not on her side."

His lips pursed and he broke away to pace for a few moments. Walking back and forth in front of some tall cedars, he appeared to be talking to someone. It was as if he was praying.

Then he stopped, sighed, and turned back to her. "Okay. I will go find Alyssa and get her to fashion something she can wear in the pool tomorrow morning. You go to bed and get some rest. I will talk to the staff, the workers, her friends, and Mama herself. And I will tell Anna that she has to attend your water aerobics class tomorrow morning at 6:30 to translate for Mama."

"Perfect! By this time tomorrow I'll know whether I'll need you to arrange a flight back to the States for me before you go join your tour. I'm not staying if she's not going to do her part."

His hands tucked into his pockets, he sighed, then nodded with the air of someone who'd just received solemn news and was forcing himself to accept it. Feeling that he'd settled the argument to her satisfaction, he reached for her and murmured, "Come here."

When she did, he walked her over to a majestic blackthorn tree; its branches reached high over a wall and toward the waning moon. A purple cast was over everything. Soon there would be nothing but darkness.

He leaned her back against the wide trunk of the tree. Then stepped between her spread legs and pressed his body into hers. He cupped her cheek as he looked down into her bright shiny eyes. "You are so beautiful. I'm going to hate leaving you."

He lowered his mouth to hers, his large hand wrapping around her neck. He captured her lips with his, savoring the first taste and wanting so much more. His tongue breeched her lips, swept inside and found traces of the Limoncello she'd chosen as her digestive.

"Mmmm," he moaned. "You chose well. I don't like Sambucca very much."

She laughed as they separated. Then she wrapped her hand around the back of his neck and pulled him back to her. It was her turn for her tongue to learn his mouth. When their lips parted this time, she whispered, "I will also be unhappy to see you go—in more ways than one. I will miss you."

"I will miss you as well. But I don't think you will have to worry about Mama's cooperation anymore."

"Really? How come?"

He smiled down at her—a smile that broke into a wide grin. "This tree is just fifty feet from her window. And she's standing at the window."

She jerked back as if to move away, but he grabbed her before she could and pulled her back into his chest.

"Shhh. Mama wants grandchildren more than anything in the world. Which means one of her two children needs to fall in love and marry. Right now, we are giving her hope. Feed this notion, and I predict that while I am gone, you will have no problem getting her to work with your plan."

She looked up into his face and grinned, "My aren't you devious."

"Yes. And what's more, I get to kiss you a few more times to seal the deal."

His hands smoothed over her jean-clad ass. He gripped her butt cheeks tightly, then lowered his hand behind the back of her thigh, and brought her leg up and over his hip. He let her feel how hard he was for her.

She met his eyes with hers, dove the fingers from both hands into his hair and brought his face down to hers. "How am I doing?" she asked in a husky voice, just before she took his lips and began enticing his tongue to dance with hers.

She felt him throb where they were joined. He didn't bother to answer her, he let his mouth do the talking and it told her all she needed to know. He'd be back.

Chapter 29
The Time Change & Breaking Bad at 4AM

The time change had her up and prowling around the house at 4 a.m. No longer able to stay in the guestroom she had been shown to in the main house, she began to wander. There were others available on the upper level but Palo thought she should be closer to his mama, and she was on the main floor.

Last night he'd walked her to her room, asking along the way if she liked dolls. She remembered she'd looked up at him and said, "Not particularly, why?"

Then he'd opened the door and she'd seen all the dolls. Dolls from all over the world, in intricate costumes, most with porcelain faces, hands, and feet. With very few exceptions, they all appeared to be looking right at her.

"Oh, this is creepy," she had said.

He and Alyssa had gathered them, eighty in all, and put them into the closet with a promise that someone would clear them out in the morning. He had given her a special look and a wink, as no way could he kiss her goodnight in front of his sister.

She had showered in the surprisingly modern bathroom and then fallen into the pristine bed linens on the big brass bed, falling asleep within moments of her head landing on the lacy eyelet-covered pillow. But now, having risen refreshed, she was eager to be up and about.

She was careful to stay away from Alyssa's room and Mama's room. She wanted to explore . . . to learn more about Palo's home, the house he had grown up in. But she did not want to disturb anyone's sleep.

Palo had told her that over the years his father and his grandfather had built many additions to the original thirteenth century house, which had been a mere barn in the mid-1400s.

As livestock was more valuable than people to a farmer

in those days, cattle had been provided the first shelter. A farmer could manage without a son, a daughter, or even a wife. But one needed horses, donkeys, cows, chickens, and pigs to survive. You couldn't work the land without a team; and you couldn't get protein into your body without eggs and milk, ham and bacon. A body needed nutrition for the rigors of farm work. The animals were the key to a successful farm—reliable labor was what made the farmer's life easier. That often came with sons.

The farm had been handed down from generation to generation until there was only an old widow with no children to leave the farm to. When she died, Palo's father paid to bury the widow and bought the farm for the unpaid taxes. Then he moved his bride into the small house and together they worked the land, planted the trees and vines, and fashioned a useable house.

Each farmhand or sharecropper added, along with his or her family, became additional workers, and allowed for more expansion—more olive trees, more fruit trees, and more grapevines.

From the very beginning, *Villa Stelle Cadente* had been blessed. The weather had been splendid, the crops abundant, and the workers had been plentiful. Neither Palo nor Alyssa, when they had arrived on the scene, had ever had to work the fields, the vineyards, or the orchards.

When Palo had given her the tour before walking her to her room last night, he told her that the former barn floor was now the grand entryway and the formal receiving room for guests. The beautiful blue-gray slate was the same floor the cows, pigs, and horses had stood on, slept on, pawed at, and well . . . done many other things on.

To that, a large front terrace with outdoor seating had been added. Parts of the original slate flooring could be found in wide paths that meandered all around the house. At every turn, there was seating of some kind where one could plop either into a chair, onto a sofa, or stretch full out onto a lounger to read or nap. Unless you had your cellphone, there was an implied assurance of not being found unless you asked to be. It was like a welcoming hostel where everyone became a part of the home.

Palo had told her that as Mama and Papa had their babies, a sewing room was added, then a parlor, four more bedrooms, and finally two playrooms. By this time, bathrooms were acceptable inside the house, so Papa had gone crazy figuring out the piping and drainage systems. The house had slowly evolved into a home—and a very nice one by community standards, as Papa had always strived to give Mama the best. And she had loved showing off all his inventions and improvements as expressions of his love toward her.

One spring, when relatives had come to celebrate Palo's confirmation, it had been time to add two new guestrooms, both with their own salon. After that renovation, Mama had boasted that they now owned the largest villa in town.

Then vast prosperity came to the family annually, due to the bountiful grape and olive harvests. Soon there was more money for inside servants so an upper level was installed. That level had four bedrooms and two bathrooms, and a huge sitting room for people to use to play cards, or to listen to the brand new phonograph . . . to even roll up the rug and dance to the lively big band albums Papa scoured the stores for.

Walking through each room now, Trixie marveled at Palo's papa's skill, to have accomplished all this on his own, to have even dreamed up the plans for a house as grand as this now was, was an amazing feat.

As she traveled the hallways and climbed the staircases, she ducked into rooms where doors were open to find an odd mix of memorabilia. Each room had lovely art on the walls, a mish-mash of homemade and antique furniture, and an untold number of handmade doilies under mementoes that had to have been collected over many years.

It was a lot to dust, she mused. But then she was not connected to each event or each occasion that had merited a gift. She could only imagine the people who had scrimped so as not to arrive at this villa empty-handed, without a little trinket for Mama.

No doubt Mama cherished each one, could probably tell you the event and person contributing to the vast collection of what contemporary crossword puzzles would deem appropriately as bric-a-brac or tchotchkes.

So much stuff, over so many years—it was actually a little overwhelming. There was no coffee table, end table, or bookshelf not adorned with some figurine, porcelain flower, or small devotional or prayer book. Photo albums and picture frames of all sizes and shapes were displayed everywhere—the pictures were either black and white, or garishly showy, as they'd had color added to them after the fact.

Trixie's years in both foster homes and universities, and then in guestrooms in other people's homes, had not allowed for a collection of memorabilia of any kind. Something small such as coins or stamps possibly, but they had never interested her. She would have loved collecting cookbooks though. They had always intrigued her, with pictures of families and friends sharing meals together, opening a window to things she had never had, and making her yearn for those special meal times.

Now, as she looked around at all the memorabilia, odd bits of things given out of obligation or love, she had to acknowledge that Mama'd had the kind of life she would have loved . . . would have thrived in. Family everywhere, friends who remained true year after year, a community that worked together and prospered—and had for hundreds of years. This was as stable as life got. These people, in this small Italian hill town, knew their grandparents . . . their great grandparents . . . all their aunts and uncles, while she knew no one that she was related to. Only the people she stayed with, and later, the people she cared for . . . who all died.

Palo found her as she sat in a tufted, straight-backed chair that she thought might have looked just fine in a sitting room at Buckingham Palace. She was thumbing through a small photo album. The pictures showed riders on a funicular on the

Isle of Capri. The people were too far away to recognize, but they were all happy and smiling, waving at the camera as if they knew the photographer.

"My first tour to Sicily. The summer I was twenty."

She closed the book and looked over at him. "You always knew what you wanted to do. I envy you that."

"You didn't?"

"No. The only thing I knew was that I had to be really good or I'd be sent away."

He walked over and pulled Trixie up, brought her up tight against his body. His chest was muscular and impossibly firm—toned like an athlete who weight-trained. "What if I told you that you needed to be really *bad* to get to stay here?"

He nuzzled his nose into the side of her neck, which made all kinds of little jolts run through her body. Some down low, where her insides melted and liquid began to pool.

She laughed and it freed up her heart. She felt all the hard things she had been feeling splinter away. "How *bad* do I have to be?"

He bent and kissed all along her neck. She felt his wet tongue licking behind her ear. "Very, very bad."

"I think I can do that."

He pulled back and set her away so he could look down into her face, met her bright shiny eyes with his surprised ones, "So you want to stay?"

She thought about his question before answering. "I think I do. But mostly because I know this is the place where you're going to be coming back to."

He flashed her a satisfied smile. "I will miss you," he murmured as his fingers dug into her hips and gently massaged the smooth flesh there. She felt him harden. Encased in the crease alongside her hip, he thrust once . . . and sighed, twice . . . and groaned.

She reached down and cupped his balls. His eyes went wide and he drew in a long, shaky breath through his nose.

"I am going to make sure that you do. I don't want to be forgotten with no one coming back to claim me ever again."

She unbuttoned and unzipped his jeans, then pushed them down, past his ass. His pockets were full so they made a soft thudding sound on the braided wool rug.

There was a cushioned footstool, stitched in needlepoint, right beside the chair she'd been sitting in. She'd had to push the stool with its colorful floral bouquet away to be able to get into the chair a few minutes ago. Now she knelt on it as his jeans bunched around his ankles. His boxer briefs followed as she pushed them past his knees. Her hand gripped his erection and she smiled as a low hiss was sucked in through his clenched teeth and then allowed to slowly escape through his parted lips when she eased up and flattened her palm against his length.

His cock was so tall that it grazed his midriff, obscuring his navel. Impressive, she thought. Now . . . let me do it justice. Her thumb slicked the tip, gathering the moisture she found there and spreading it. She looked up and met his eyes, slumberous and dark with need.

He watched as her thumb transferred some of his slickness to her bottom lip. A shiver went through her as his eyes widened, then stayed locked on hers. The heat in his dark pupils was want personified. His hand found her jaw and cupped it in a tender, encouraging caress.

She curled her tongue under and licked her bottom lip as he watched her. She felt the burning heat on the back of his thigh as her hand gripped it to steady her while she leaned forward.

He groaned when her lips covered the head of his penis in an ardent kiss, damned near howled when she took the head into her mouth and sucked.

Her best efforts were rewarded as she circled, licked, stroked and sucked. She felt his muscles tighten, heard his breath become ragged and escape in harsh gasps. She heard the steady tick-tock of the blue and gold Ormolu clock ticking on the mantel. She counted each second as it passed, taking him as deep as she dared. After one minute and nine seconds, she felt his thighs lock and his body shudder. He groaned and came. She managed to softly purr at her accomplishment because she knew his male ego needed to hear her appreciation . . . while secretly searching the room for a tissue.

Before she could pull away and stand, a light blue handkerchief with dark blue lettering was pressed into her hand. The emotion she felt from Palo's intimate gesture stunned her. Never had anyone cared to this degree. She was astounded at his gallantry. His action was more than politeness or courtesy, it was consideration. She felt the area around her heart warm and her head went fuzzy with pure joy as she wiped her mouth.

During her last year at college, she had run with a pretty wild group of women. Friday and Saturday nights were spent barhopping and showcasing their young, toned bodies by doing lewd dances. Looking back on those nights, she'd been stupid and naïve.

She'd thought she could earn her way into a man's heart, and that due to the superb lovemaking skills she'd honed that year, one lucky man would offer her his home to stay in forever. She'd quickly learned that it didn't work that way. Too many women were willing to offer the same favors with absolutely no conditions—most of them being her own circle of friends.

The possibility of ever being taken to their home was nil, as they always seemed to prefer going to her place or using someone's car. She'd finally wised up and realized that most of the men at the bars already had a woman they were attached to, that they'd offered a home to. They did want to return to her place though, or meet in the back of their SUV . . . because of her newly perfected skills.

In that moment, when Palo had offered his soft, monogramed handkerchief to her, she realized that she hadn't thought of sex in terms of using it to secure a home for a very long time. This house she was in definitely wasn't the home she wanted, but she was beginning to realize that he was the man she wanted.

She was surprised at her first thought as he caught her by the elbows and drew her up for a kiss that blazed like a banner through her brain. *This man is my home.* Her next thought was, never before had a man wanted to kiss her after fellatio. Something about them tasting their own cum was apparently a huge turn off.

"You are a vixen," he murmured against her cheek, his warm breath coating her ear. "I wasn't ready for that."

"You appeared quite ready," she said with a sideways smile and a glance at the handkerchief that was balled up in her hand.

"I don't mean like that. I meant I wanted to go slow with you. Romance you more. I want you to stay."

"I will stay," she whispered, meeting his eyes.

"Because of me or the job?"

She burst out with a delightful chuckle. "Not the job. There is no end to the available well-paying eldercare opportunities in the United States. I do not have to travel this far for a job. If you hadn't hit me, I'd be on my way to one of them soon."

"So you didn't fly overseas to take care of Mama?"

"No. I can admit it now; I flew 2,000 miles to be with you. Being with you is exciting. Mama's a job. There are lots of jobs. You're the bonus. The enticement I needed. Plus . . . you said there was a pool. And I have a very thirsty bikini . . ."

He stroked alongside her arm. "Um, er about that . . . you can't wear that bikini here."

She gave him a sullen, put-on pouty look, "I can't?"

"For God's sake, Trixie, no. There are men all over this place. Men using power tools, climbing ladders, up in trees. You could kill somebody flashing that gorgeous ass. I will get you a new suit. I'll bring one home tonight."

"I could wear it with shorts in the pool, but then when I tan . . ."

"No! That ass is mine. You hear? No one else gets to see

your ass."

"Hmmm." She pursed her lips. "If that's the way you feel, I'm going to need you to claim it before you leave for two weeks. Just to be sure."

His long, guttural groan would have been comical if she wasn't trying to get the advantage and establish possession and proprietorship before he ran off to all points Italian with beautiful versions of a young Claudia Cardinale on every single sidewalk.

He felt his blood pumping—draining every single drop from every cell and redirecting it. He had never recovered this fast. He actually felt faint from his brain emptying itself out so fast. His penis jumped, stroked the silky material of her tunic top . . . searched for an eager entry point. This had never happened so fast before.

"You are a bold one," he murmured as he reached down and began putting himself back together. Outside he could hear the sound of barn doors bring opened, chickens squawking at the intrusion, and the low murmur of tractors off in the distance.

"What exactly do you mean by claim it, spell it out for me."

"Ummm . . . rear end me, like for real this time?"

He looked at her quizzically, "Why do you want to start with that?"

She blushed. "I just went back on birth control. I won't be protected for two more days."

He tilted his head. "There are other things . . ."

"I know. But I just feel like . . . like I need the possession, you know?"

He groaned and brought his forehead down until it met hers. His eyes tightly shut. "I would love claiming your ass."

"Thank you," she whispered, kind of ashamed she'd been bold enough to ask for something she truly wanted, craved actually . . . especially as it was so perverted, but thrilled beyond belief that he'd accepted.

They broke apart and he looked down into her face, "You're sure? I too, can offer oral services . . ."

"I'm sure. I can't explain why I like it . . ."

"You don't have to. I'm honored you're offering."

They could both hear the sounds, inside and outside, as the household woke up and the workers began arriving along the road.

She used her forefinger to trace circles in the chest hairs that poked out of the vee in his Polo shirt. "Maybe you could draw me a map to your room? This place is immense. Your father was a very busy man."

"He was."

Then thinking about his father, where they were—and the possibility of someone walking down the hall and into this room made him back away. His pants were up, but not fastened, his shirt untucked.

All those thoughts came into play, trying to quell the desire burgeoning and building up inside him. He made an attempt to right his thoughts by forcing himself to take yoga breaths. He wanted this woman so much. He took a deep breath in. Held it. Let it out and hollowed his chest out. Repeated it twice.

His erection was abating. But only because he was squeezing his toes tightly together inside his shoes, painfully trying to curl them under to send a message to his brain: *there's trouble here. Need help. Man on fire. I want this woman so badly. I think I'm finally in love.*

He opened his mouth to talk, having no idea what he was about to say. Then he surprised himself by inviting her to his sanctuary. He never allowed anyone there.

"Tonight, after dinner. Walk out past the pool to the back gate. Follow alongside the gravel cart path; keep the twelve tall cedars on your left. After the twelfth one, you'll see a beaten-down grass path veer off to the right into a wooded glen. There will be fireflies to light your way, lots of them. They won't bother you, just walk through them. You'll go through a natural arbor and come out into a lit clearing. That's where you'll find me. I no longer live in the house unless there's a reason that I have to be there. I have my own space set apart from the main house. So, if you want to see my room . . . that's how you get there."

She pushed her finger into his side and tickled him. "I'll be there, right after all eighteen dinner courses are served."

He laughed and felt like himself again. Not the love-starved man that he really was. And no longer a rutting bull ready to climb this woman's haunches and enter the cavity most sacrosanct. "We don't do that every day. Just on Sundays and special occasions."

"Special occasions? Like welcoming the new help?" she teased, smiling up at him

"I don't want to disillusion you, sweetheart. You are certainly welcome here and we're all glad to have you here. And I hope that you feel that way. But it was more about the favored son returning home. That was the special occasion. Plus I was the one who secured most of the food," he added with a huge grin.

"You've got a bit of an ego, you know that?" she began singing the words to, *You're so Vain*, the song by Carly Simon. *"You're so vain, I bet you think this song is about you, don't you, don't you?"* She had a clear, sweet voice, thanks to the nuns and all the hymn singing.

He laughed again. "No, it isn't vanity. It's reality—my reality. Momma doesn't like it when I'm gone. She never has. Not since Papa died anyway. She's always over the moon when I come home. It's one of the reasons I need my own space. She can be smothering with her attentions, and her need to know every single thing I've been doing and every place I've been. For me, she's exhausting. But I go along with her wishes when I can.

"You may not get to see that side of her; she may be standoffish to you. If she is, count yourself lucky. It's not so wonderful being one of her *adored* ones. My sister is famous for shutting off her mobile and running away from home all the time. We call her *disperso in azione,* or missing in action. Mostly we find her with her boyfriend Giancarlo."

Trixie pulled her hand away from where she'd been stroking the area around his neck.

It surprised him how much he missed it after her hand was gone. "I never had a family. I think I would love being one of her *adored* ones." Her lips were pressed together and she had a look of condemnation on her face.

His lips formed their own pressed-in look of regret. "I keep forgetting that. I'm sorry for the childhood you had. It sucks that you had no family. Maybe you will win Mama's favor and be the coveted sojourner and take the onus off of me and my sister for a while." He brushed her cheek with the back of his fingers. "You can have all of her fawning in my place. I will decree it before I leave."

It was her turn to laugh. "As if that will make it happen. I've seen enough to know that your mom doesn't do as she's told."

He nodded his solemn agreement, "Hardly ever."

"A lifetime of being coddled doesn't disappear overnight . . ."

"Well, lucky for you, tomorrow I will be gone for two weeks."

She groaned. "What have I gotten myself into?"

He pulled her into his chest, and then shifted her so she was under his arm as he worked to right his clothing. 'C'mon, let's get some coffee, or as we say in Italy, café. By the way, I have a surprise for you."

"Oh, I love surprises!"

"I put a bathing suit outside Mama's door. Alyssa's going to help Mama get into it."

"How did you get a suit for her so fast?'

"Alyssa made it. She took apart three of her old suits and sewed parts of them together. All three were black, so it looks really nice."

"Three?"

"Well, she hasn't been in the pool for many years. These

227

are from before Papa died. She was not so big then. Large . . . still, but not *so* large."

"That's wonderful!"

"And . . . she will meet you at the pool at 6:30."

Trixie disengaged from his arms, stood back and put her hands on her hips. "And just how did you manage that?"

He let out such a boyish laugh that she had to smile. "It was so easy. I laugh just thinking about it." He was still laughing.

She smacked his arm. "What did you do?"

"It was child's play really. I am kind of ashamed of myself."

"Tell me."

"Walking her to her room last night, I bent to kiss her cheek, then asked, 'Do you know, is Nonna's engagement ring still in the office safe?' Nonna was my grandmother, and I inherited her ring to pass on to my bride. I watched her eyes go wide and her mouth drop open as she nodded. Then I left and made my way back up the hall as if I was going to go to the office."

"You didn't," she hissed.

He nodded, "I did. And it worked. She's meeting you at the pool in her new bathing suit at 6:30 this morning, isn't she?"

"I don't know, is she?"

He smiled and chucked her under her chin. "I would bet my grandfather's vintage bottle of Grappa on it."

She shook her head, but she too was smiling. "You play dirty."

He waggled his eyebrows up and down then bent to her ear and whispered, "Later tonight, we will play dirty *together*."

Chapter 30
An Agreement of Sorts . . .

In her opinion, it had been a very good day. Mama surely had a different opinion. However, she'd been cooperative, first getting into the pool, with a considerable amount of help, then actually exercising a bit before having her breakfast outside on the terrace, in the most colorful caftan Trixie had ever seen.

It was a meal Trixie had ordered special for Mama, and Gina, the cook had fretted the whole time Anna translated the paper for her and even more so while she had worked to prepare it: melon slices, wheat toast with a tablespoon of jam, a poached egg, and two thin slices of ham, as Gina said they didn't have any of the requested turkey bacon. A big glass of water with lemon was served with black coffee. Mama was allowed one stevia package for sweetener—not her usual four teaspoons of sugar, and skim milk instead of cream.

Mama asked for real milk in her coffee. She asked for a pastry. She asked for oatmeal with butter, brown sugar and walnuts. She asked for more jam. She was permitted the oatmeal, the steel–cut kind, with walnuts and stevia.

Anna accompanied Trixie and Mama for a short mid-morning walk through one of the orchards and Anna translated Mama's questions for Trixie and then Trixie's answers to her:

Mama: Have you ever been married?

Trixie: No.

Mama: Palo said he hit your car.

Trixie: Yes.

Mama: You have no family? He said that you did not.

Trixie: He's correct. I was an orphan. I was raised by nuns.

Mama, clearly delighted with that news: Oh, so you are Catholic?

Trixie: Yes, I was baptized and confirmed in the church.

Mama: Palo likes you. Do you like him?

Trixie: Of course, otherwise I wouldn't be here.

Mama: Is he paying you well?

Trixie: You should ask him that, but I am happy with our agreement.

Mama: Do you like your job?

Trixie: Yes, . . . and I am good at it. I will save your life if you let me.

There was a long silence pause, then. Mama said: I might let you. However, I insist on wine with dinner.

Trixie: One glass. That I will pour.

Mama scrunched her face up and made slits of her eyes as she glared at Trixie. It was so comical that both Trixie and Anna had to laugh.

Their little walk together had set the nature of the relationship they would build on—cordial, curious, and considerate—but still combative.

When Palo got back to the villa in the late afternoon, he was surprised to see the three of them walking back and forth on the back terrace, Mama pumping her arms up and down as she walked, using two water bottles, all three talking at once. He had to smile—what a relief that they were at least getting along. Mama could be difficult when she didn't get her way.

He focused on Trixie, walking beside Mama in a sleeveless knit top and capris, her hair gathered in a knot at the nape of her neck. Not a speck of makeup on, yet so beautiful she nearly stopped his heart. When she looked over and spotted him, she smiled and waved. His heart threatened to fly out of his chest.

Mama spotted him too, and he knew at once that she was going to plead her case for leniency if he got close enough to listen, so he decided to just wave and call out to her that he'd see them all at dinner. He made his way around the house to the twelve cedars and followed the path up to his tree house.

While he had been in deep grief over his father passing, his friend, frat boy, and former college dorm mate Chaz, had flown to Italy with one of his building crews and built him a sanctuary to live in. A place where he could take his mind of his deep concerns for his mother and sister, work out the many estate matters, and handle his own business affairs . . . as well as grieve the loss of a father he had adored. Chaz had spent a month at the villa ordering in supplies and directing his crew of five. And when he'd left, Palo had not only a state-of-the-art refuge, but also a home.

He stopped when he got to the last cedar and walked up a small rise and just stared. Stared at the manifestation of love one of his best friends had given him—a two-level tree house with a wrap-around deck, complete modern fixtures, and bamboo and marble floors.

When he'd first seen it being built he had no idea what it was. He'd come around the corner and seen what looked like an open shoebox turned on its side, made of what looked like teak panels, stuck up high in a tree. He later learned it was a cementitious set of panels that had been painted with latex paint and embedded with iron grit, then oxidized to form a natural weathering layer. He had learned not to ask Chaz too many questions after that particular dissertation.

Chaz was one of his fraternity brothers that he owned the Sunset Beach house with, and a world-renowned tiny house and tree house builder, so he trusted him to come up with something not only unique, but perfect for his needs.

When it was finished, his modern sanctuary was beautiful. Contemporary and sleek, it appeared as if it had been built into the arms of a mature tree, but it was actually held up by steel framework covered by masonry and painted to look like part of the tree.

The long open edge had a wall of glass doors that slid open to a wrap around deck. Inside there was a large sitting area with modular, moveable furniture and a huge flat-screen mounted to the wall, a nook with two moveable benches in hand-polished maple, a bedroom with a queen–sized platform bed with two floating nightstands attached, and a bathroom with a walk-in shower whose entire interior was sheathed with marble in muted tones of gray.

The floors were tiled to match with no separation, so that the entire room could be reached by one of the two ceiling-mounted rain forest showerheads or the handhelds on each wall. There were anti-fog mirrors and a graduated towel rack that was heated and tucked into an alcove that was the only place where the water couldn't reach.

If you really wanted to, you could sit on the composting toilet while shampooing your hair. Or you could just use one of the teak drop-down seats that were built-in on each of the four sides. It was an awesome bathroom—a masterpiece really, as Chaz had dubbed it.

All the windows throughout the tiny house slid back into the walls to allow for cross ventilation when the weather permitted. But there was heat and air-conditioning for when it didn't.

Douglas fir paneling was in the living area, used straight from the mill and coarsely sanded to give it a rustic look along with the aroma of fresh-cut timber. IKEA cabinets were attached above the counters and the sink area for storage, and transparent Lucite bookcases were used in the bedroom to keep the spacious feeling. Under the bed was rolling storage. Otherwise, there were niches and ledges built right into the walls for doodads, whatnots, thingamabobs, doohickeys and gismos. It was perfect for Palo's needs. Down to the work desk and filing drawers on rollers that nested into each other.

Everywhere you looked, it was state-of-the-art and ultra modern. The upstairs deck that was accessed by a spiral staircase from a back wall, held a two-person hot tub, loungers, a table and chair set, a mini-fridge, a small bar, and pots overflowing with herbs. It was lovely and had a view of the beautiful Tuscan valley below.

Palo had been humbled by Chaz' gesture, and his unwillingness to take a single penny for labor or materials. He did however agree to allow a film crew inside for a special tree-house documentary that promoted Chaz' company and pictures for two different style magazines.

Then it was all his. And the word sanctuary hadn't done it justice. It was his retreat, his refuge, and his time away from work that caressed him and gave him a private place to let his grief play out without anyone intruding. It was a piece of heaven that had gotten him through the worst of the last five years. Now it was a place he rested. Where he planned. Where he prayed and where he read. He had never had a woman here, so it was not a place where he dallied.

He was surprised that he had invited Trixie to what he thought of now as his home. He was the owner of a huge estate, the villa that began as a barn was now many acres and housed several compounds where workers lived. Yet he was most at home in less than 900 square feet.

He was proud of it. And he never forgot how it came to be. How it had been Chaz's idea, but that all his frat-boy friends had a hand in it. Some had helped the crew, others had taken orders from Chaz after he'd had measurements and found the necessary supplies. The rest had stocked the house with the best linens, even a purple mattress, and top shelf booze. Cam had sent the softest and most luxurious bathrobe ever. He'd said it would hug him when he couldn't be there to do it himself. And he'd had donned it many a time and felt it doing just that.

He walked to the house, patted the masonry wall that was painted to make the house appear like part of the tree, and ducked under to climb the series of steps that lead up to the wrap around deck.

Once upstairs, he made a few phone calls so he wouldn't have to later, and tossed off his clothes so he could take a nice long shower.

He would take the dirty clothes bag with him when he went down for dinner, as he did not have a washer and dryer. Mama had several women helping her at the house, so he just added his laundry to hers.

Everyone at the villa knew that the tree house was Palo's private domain, which no one was allowed to climb up to, unless there was an emergency. He kept it clean himself and took care of whatever problems arose. Trixie coming up tonight would be the first time a woman had ever been in his sanctuary. Even Mama had never been there. Not being able to climb up the stairs had been the reason for that. But everyone had seen the magazine pictures and oohed and aahed over his place when it was finished.

As he was shampooing his hair and listening to the music from his Bluetooth speakers, he thought about Trixie—wondered how her day had gone. How she'd gotten along with Momma, if Anna had been helpful translating for her, if she liked it here, if she was picking up any Italian. He was surprised by how much he wanted her to like living here, and to feel as if she belonged.

He needn't have worried. Trixie was in her own bathroom showering and marveling at how well the day had gone. Mama had been far more cooperative than she had expected. And Anna was a true gem, so helpful, so polite, so obviously caring about everything that concerned Mama. This was a wonderful place, with great people. She really thought she could like it here. And that scared her. She never got to stay in any of the places where she felt at home. There was always a reason why she had to leave.

All the money she made, all the money she'd saved—she could have bought almost any home she wanted in practically any city in the world. But a home was a home because of the people in it.

While she was blow-drying her hair, she vowed to just take it one day at a time. To enjoy each moment she was here, and her time with all the people she met here. Especially Palo. She smiled. Yes, especially Palo. She wanted to enjoy a lot of time with him. And tonight, she would. After dinner she would follow that path and find him, in the place where he would be waiting for her.

She was eager to be held by him and hungry for his kisses. She had a big smile on her face when she walked down to dinner.

Chapter 31
Dinner, No Longer An Unending Affair

Dinner was indeed a significantly smaller affair. There was salad, of course. Palo said there was always salad. The gardens were too bountiful for there not to be. But she didn't mind, as the sliced tomatoes with basil, olive oil, and the real-deal Parmesan, the *Reggiano* kind, were the best she'd ever tasted. The *Panzanella*, that accompanied it, had a lot of healthy elements, except for the coarse day-old bread that was pretty much the main ingredient.

The main dish was *LaGallina Ripiena*, or Stuffed Chicken. Gina, the cook, had been chopping the chicken giblets and the Mortadella sausage, along with making long strips of ham from thin slices, when Trixie had gone into the kitchen for a glass of pomegranate juice after her run while Mama had been napping this afternoon.

She'd seen the slices of bread soaking, the pile of grated Pecorino cheese, and the ground veal and eggs getting ready to be added to make the stuffing mixture that would go *inside* the chicken. She had vowed to wait until Palo had left for two weeks before approaching her about cutting back on fat.

Now, as the threads holding the stuffing inside the chicken were being cut, she wished she hadn't waited. Even if Mama took a small helping, which was not likely, this could easily be a 1200-calorie entree. She was not going to be very popular around here after Palo left for his tour. These types of meals couldn't keep happening.

The Tuscan Beans, made with white *fagioli* or cannelloni beans, fresh sage leaves and garlic, dressed in olive oil, were amazing, and the *Fiori Fritti*, or Zucchini Flower Fritters were also delicious.

When Mama's plate was put in front of her, fixed by Gina, who had liberally piled it high, Trixie had to turn her head and shield her eyes. When she faced forward again, she met Palo's eyes. The guilt on his face for having allowed this kind of gluttony to go on for so long was the only thing that kept her from leaving the table and going to pack her bags.

She bit her lip and then asked Gina, through Anna, about her name, saying she liked the name Gina and wanted to know if it was spelled with two ee's or i-n-a. Gina, on her way back toward the kitchen, smiled and said "i-n-a."

Mama, who was preparing to dig into the large scoop of dressing, coated with gravy, stilled her fork. Then meeting Trixie's gaze, she scraped off the gravy and lifted the sliced ham and any meat that wasn't chicken off to the side. It was a start. This woman was smart. She knew what was good for her and what was *not*.

With the *Panne Cotta*—a delicate cream custard that was the best dessert anyone ever put in their mouth—Mama made the grand gesture. She met Trixie's gaze and cut it exactly in half and then ate the first half. Then, maybe thinking better of it, and getting Trixie's eye again, she defiantly stuck her spoon into the second half and slipped the full spoonful into her mouth before putting the empty spoon on the tablecloth beside her plate—her way of signaling she was finished eating—for now.

Trixie had to laugh. As grand gestures went, that was a good start. Maybe after Palo left, she could sort this all out. Have a nice talk with Gina, while occasionally hinting at the possibility of a grandchild somewhere down the road to Mama. She knew it was mean. But so was letting her die from overeating.

Chapter 32
A Tiny House Tree House!

After dinner, Trixie excused herself, saying she had some emails to attend to. Then she replied to the pharmacist who had been so kind as to return her message from this morning. She had introduced herself as Mama's new caregiver, attached photos of her credentials, and asked about all the medicines she'd found on Mama's bedside table.

He'd sent her a translation of sorts to the English version of each drug, adding the generic equivalent, explaining the dosages, and the specifics for each drug's use and his recommendation for her to get in touch with her doctor, whom she had already called and made an appointment to see.

Then she took a long bubble bath and washed her hair and dried it straight before dressing in a Spandex crisscross push-up bra dress with a built-in shelf that emphasized her breasts. It came to mid-thigh, so it also emphasized her legs. It was a bright lime green color and was the dress she favored when she was going barhopping and on the hunt for an amorous adventure. It had never failed her. So she wasn't taking any chances. She always dry-cleaned it.

Bending down and fluffing her hair up before she flipped her head back up, she scrutinized the look. Without the curls, it was a poufy razor cut that said *don't mess with me, or else.* It worked. She looked hot, but approachable—knowledgeable, but Ellie Mae senseless and reckless as well.

She slipped out the back door and tiptoed across the terrace instead of clicking across it in her heels. Then she counted the cedar trees and walked toward the fireflies. Hopefully, Palo was there and ready for her. They hadn't spoken since she'd given him the evil eye that accused him of having permitted his mother's atrocious eating habits.

Nine-ten-eleven-twelve, a few more paces and there they were—a cloud of random sparks of lights, jetting back and forth as short dashes before burning out and another taking its place. There had to be hundreds of them. It was beautiful to watch. She almost didn't hear him as he called out to her from an overhead deck, so lost was she in the fairyland of darting lights.

She looked up and saw him leaning on a deck rail, a shock of hair over one brow and a wicked smile on his lips. He was the sexiest looking man she'd ever known. Did all Italians know how to quirk their lips that way? Eyes assessing in a way that spoke of yearning . . . and then joy at finally finding exactly what they'd been looking for? She felt very desirable. Was it the man? Was it the night? Was it her lucky dress . . . or the fact that her quick self-waxing had left her all tingly under her tiny VS thong panties?

"Hey Bella," he called down to her.

She grinned up at him as she continued walking up the grassy rise until she was almost directly under him. "Hey yourself."

Trixie threw him a puzzled look, "How does one get up into that magnificent tree house? And please don't throw a rope over and tell me I have to shimmy up."

He shook his head while smirking, "Oh, I don't want any rope burns on those gorgeous thighs." Then he straightened. "The steps are on the backside. I'll meet you."

He turned and walked behind the house, which to her, looked like two elongated wooden boxes stacked slightly off-center. The bottom one had a glass front that she couldn't see through. The top floor had a series of diagonally placed wooden planks in a herringbone pattern. In the corner was a series of clear cubes stacked in tall multiple rows—likely the bathroom, she thought.

She walked under the tree, which wasn't really holding up the house. It just appeared that way from a distance. Instead, sturdy rods jutted out here and there, camouflaged to be hidden yet it was obvious what they were when you were up close.

She used one to pull herself up and around and onto the first floating teak step. He was holding the door open at the top. He flipped a switch and the underside of a smooth teak handrail lit up. She held tightly on to the railing as she climbed up. She was not all that used to wearing heels, but the dress she had on called for them. When she got to the top step, he wrapped his arm around her waist and lifted her up and over the threshold until she was inside. He gave her a quick hard kiss that told her how much he'd missed her.

"Welcome to my home. My little aerie."

"Oh, are you an eagle?" she asked.

"No! I am a hawk. A very hungry hawk."

"I saw you eat, about an hour ago. So I doubt you could be very hungry."

"Well I am. I am hungry for flesh. Your flesh." He bent and snuffled her neck, drew in the essence of lemon, sandalwood, and heady roses. "Mmmm, you smell good enough to eat."

She tilted her head and looked up at him and smiled. "I was actually hoping to be on the menu tonight."

He took her by the hand and tugged her into the main part of the house. "Well, I think I can accommodate you quite nicely. Come, see my little nest, and then I want to see yours." He waggled his eyebrows at her.

"I think you'll be pleased. I tidied it up a bit."

The heat in his eyes was a visceral thing. Like the primitive being she felt tonight, she felt a rush of liquid heat coat her labia in response.

He drew her into the living area and walked her up to the full-length picture window. He pulled her in front of him, and with each hand flat against the glass beside her head, he leaned in and kissed the side of her neck.

She flushed with heat and slickness dampened her panties. She moaned as his lips traveled up to her ear, his tongue curling around the rim and lashing the whorls. He took the lobe between his lips and sucked. His teeth nipped. Her knees buckled.

His left hand left the glass and splayed open over her womb. "You look lovely in this dress, but can I take it off now?"

"The window . . ."

"It's one-way. No one can see in."

"Really?"

"Mmmhmm," his hand wandered down, inching the dress up and the panties down until he had uncovered her mons. "Yup, no one can see this sweet pussy but me."

He removed her panties, letting them fall onto the area rug. With his longest digit he slicked his finger along her labial lips and entered her, plunging deep. A stream of Italian burst from him. She heard it both in her ear, and felt it against her neck. She had no idea what he had just said, but it sounded beautiful and somehow she knew that he was pleased with what his fingers were now discovering.

As he thrust and circled he carried moisture to her clit. And she, helpless in a world of sated with pleasure, moaned. "Ooohh Palo, mmmmm. More, more please."

He knelt and spun her around at the same time. "More, you'll get, my lovely." He spread her legs, pushed her dress to her waist and kissed her belly. Then he took his time reaching his target—too much time.

"Palo!"

"Shhh, I am a hawk enjoying your flesh, remember?"

"I need you to enjoy it lower."

"Oh, I will," he murmured, his lips against her belly, his tongue licking in a tight circle around her navel. He used the scruff on his chin from two days of not shaving to roughen up the tiny patch of hair guarding her entrance. "Now where is this special little nub that needs my attention?"

Then he purposely lashed out and touched every part of her but that burgeoning, pulsing nubbin of flesh.

She cried out her anguish, "Please. Just touch it please."

"One minute." He sat back on his heals and gently blew

on it, while his thumbs parted her cleft, allowing him to see her swollen, angry-looking clit better. He watched it pulse, and then he touched it with the barest tip of his tongue.

"I . . . need . . . you . . . to . . ." She never got to finish her harsh demand.

His lips closed around her and he sucked. She shattered. She screamed. She fell into his arms.

He soothed her with tiny kisses along her hairline, and then whispered into her ear. "You have delicious flesh."

She moaned and drew in a deep breath, then looked up under her hair at him and smiled. "Wow. Just wow."

A few more deep sighs followed. "I needed that. You can't know how much I needed that."

He took her hand and placed it between his legs. He was still in a squatting position. She had to marvel at how long he could hold that pose, but more than that, she had to marvel at the length and breadth of the bulge her hand caressed. It was his turn to groan. "I think I might know how much you needed that," he whispered. "I'm kind of in the same predicament here."

"You want some relief?" she teased, looking up at him with her tongue curled over her bottom lip.

"If you wouldn't mind . . ."

"I have to do an inspection first."

"Uh . . . what does that entail?"

She smiled. It was wicked. "Well, first I have to unwrap the package . . . you know, unzip that looong zipper, tooth by tooth, then I have to haul that huge thing out. Put my eyes all over it. Admire every . . . inch. Let my fingers roam, pressing, stroking, rubbing along the stretched skin, circling the tip, finding the precum, coating the whooole head with it, fingering the whooole length, making sure it's standing up tall and throbbing to get my full attention. Then I'll lick my lips and lean in. I'll have to figure out if I want to lick the tip first or shove the whooole head in my mouth all at once."

His groan was almost comical. "Please . . . just do *something.*"

"We'll work on that zipper first."

She dug for the tab, lifted it and eased it down, truly, one tooth at a time. He finally removed her hand, tugged it all the way down and brought out his penis. It was tall, the skin stretched and tight along the length, the tip swollen and red, and the slit wet with one huge pearly drop. He wrapped his hand around it and pumped it with his fist.

She stopped him. "No, no, no. That's my job." She uncurled his fingers with one hand while tugging down the top of her dress. After baring her breasts, she grabbed his hand and used it to cover her left breast. "Here, this is your new job."

He went right to it, pinching her nipple and making it hard. She threw back her head and whimpered.

"Hey, none of that. Get back to work."

"Yes, sir."

Her head ducked and she took his penis between her lips and sucked. More wild Italian words were unleashed. She loved hearing him talk Italian in such a slumberous, hoarse voice. So needy, so much enthralled. She had no mercy. She licked and sucked and used her hand to grip him, being the perfect velvet glove he needed as she coated him first with his own wetness, and then with hers. He gave her a one-word warning, "Coming." And then he did.

She sucked and gripped him, feeling him pulse, throb, and then erupt. She took everything to the back of her mouth and held it. Then, when she could catch her breath, she managed to swallow and loosen her grip.

Her eyes went up to meet his, but they were closed in bliss. She smiled. Looked down to where his hand still cupped her breast. His fingers began lazily trailing around her nipple as she looked back at him. He had a big smile on his face.

"I am so *relieved*," he whispered.

She flashed him her own smile. "That makes two of us."

"I am relieved. But not completely satisfied. I need more."

"You can have more. The only thing you can't do is take my virginity."

His eyes squinted and his lips quirked as his head tilted to study her. From the look on his face he was definitely perplexed. "Virginity? You're a virgin?" This didn't make any sense to him.

"Technically, yes."

"You have never been fucked?" He could not believe what he was hearing. "How can this be? You go on these cruises, you hook up with men . . ."

"I do. But I don't let them put anything in my vagina. My mouth yes, my ass yes, my vagina no."

He blinked his eyes wide. "Why?" It was as if she had told him she'd never breathed, eaten, or driven a car.

"Simple answer . . . the nuns."

"The nuns?"

"Yes, the nuns who raised me. They said I must be a virgin when I marry. No ifs, ands, or buts about it. It was sacrosanct. I could do other things . . . and they gave me books explaining them . . . but I could not lose my hymen. Not until I married. My husband deserved to have that, they said, no one else could have it. And they made me promise."

He sat back against the glass. "Wow. I've never met a virgin. At least one who was an adult."

"There are a few of us," she said with a smirk.

"Well, that's . . . that's . . ."

"Finish your sentence."

"It's uh. Good. It's good."

"Yes. It is," she affirmed.

"So this is why the anal sex . . .and the ass showing?"

She nodded. "Yes. With the right man, I allow anal sex. But only with a condom."

"And you give head."

"Again, only with the right man. I'm very cautious. I have to feel that I'm being respected . . . if that makes any sense." She laughed. "That's kinda funny. 'Fuck me in the ass.

But you'd better respect me.'"

He sniggered. "Yeah, that is kinda funny."

"I have to be convinced that they won't take something I'm not willing to give."

"I get that. It's important to you. And you promised."

"You're the only one who gets that part."

"Do men think you're trying to trap them into marriage?"

"Some do. But that's not it at all. I actually haven't found a man that I would even consider marrying."

"So, aren't you . . . curious?"

"Oh yeah. I am. But I figure it'll happen one day."

"Hmm. So . . . a shower before . . ."

"Before what?"

"Before I take your ass."

She laughed. "Sure."

He stood, tucked his penis away, and pulled her up, taking her dress off at the same time. Then he leaned her back against the glass. One hand went up to cup each breast and he gently squeezed them together. His thumbs grazed the nipples. "But first. I want to taste these. That's allowed, right?" he teased.

"It's not only allowed. It's mandatory."

"These are a very nice size. Can I use these to fuck you with as well?"

She laughed. "Yes. But you have to clean up any mess you make."

It was his turn to laugh. "As long as I can smear it around a little first."

His head ducked and he took first one nipple, and then the other between his lips. He licked, sucked and gently ran his teeth over them.

His hand cupped her between her legs. His fingers stroked her, separating her slick lips, rewetting her clit with her moisture, rotating his thumb over and around it. "Finger fucking allowed here?" he rasped into her ear.

"Yessss," she hissed. "No fisting."

"Who the hell does that?" He asked as he reached down and put his arm behind her knees and picked her up.

She shrugged her shoulders, it made her breasts jounce. Her nipples were swollen from his kisses and the hard peaks jutted out, grazing his chest. She was gorgeous, he thought. Perfect really. Except for the virgin part. He so wanted to be inside her taking her like a rutting primate.

He started walking toward the spiral staircase that led to the second level and to his bathroom. She motioned with her hand toward the floor. "I need my panties."

"I can assure you that you do not need your panties."

"I need something that's in them." She waggled her fingers and he dipped her so she could snag them off the floor.

"Those panties are microscopic, what could you possibly have inside them?"

She held them up as he continued walking up the spiral steps with her still in his arms. Her slim fingers dove into a hidden pocket sewn into the miniscule front vee panel. Then she smiled and held up her treasure—a condom at the ready—the pre-lubed kind.

"Oh, you are ready aren't you? How clever. Did you design that?"

"Yes. I just sewed on a tiny pocket to the front panel. Part of my job is to stitch people up. And old people tend to fall a lot. So I've gotten pretty good at making tiny stitches in thin material."

"You're taking the mood away."

"Sorry."

"Besides, even though I haven't had a woman here, I do have condoms."

"Well that's good, because I only brought one. And I am not about to ask your Mama's *farmacia* to include a box in their next prescription order."

He laughed and then set her down at the top of the stairs. She didn't have a chance to do more than register the huge bed against one wall before she was being pulled into the open bathroom where the walls and the flooring were completely covered with tiles in muted shades of gray.

"Oh, this is nice," she whispered with a touch of reverence in her voice.

"Having you in here with me is nice."

He started turning on faucets and adjusting streams of water. "My buddy, Chase, remembered from our college days how much I loved a good, long vigorous shower. So he put two huge rain forest showerheads in the walk-in shower, plus a hand-held attached to each wall. And thankfully, he included two super-duty hot water heaters mounted on the roof to give me the water pressure I would need for them to work for long, hot showers.

"This shower is so many things to me: medicinal, therapeutic to my body and mind, a relief from the stifling heat or the freezing cold on tour days, and in many ways—my sex partner. During touring season there is no time to date, and by evening I am too exhausted to do anybody any good, including me. If I need to rub the carnal longings away, I can dispatch myself in the shower. It's unemotional, but it gets the job done. But now, just looking at you, I can hardly believe my good fortune."

He saw a gorgeous woman who had her head tilted back and was lifting her hair off her neck to let the pelting water pound on her. He felt he'd found a soul mate—or at least a water mate. "I want you so much."

He removed his clothes. He used one of the handhelds to test the temperature, then adjusted the dial on it to make it pulse. He knelt in front of her and used both the pressure of the water and his fingers to stimulate her clit. He stopped just before she could come.

She looked down at him kneeling in front of her and gave him a pouty face.

He chuckled. "You don't get to come that way. We're

going to come together, remember?"

"And just how are you going to make that happen?"

"My cock in your ass, my fingers in your pussy. You'll see. I was just letting the water do some of the advance work."

He abruptly stood. Looked down into her face and marveled at how beautiful she was—fresh and luminous without any makeup, her eyes pools of brilliant cerulean.

"But first, kissing. We have not done very much of what I consider my favorite part of lovemaking. I think they should not have named it after the French. As it is the Italians who do it best."

"Show me."

"I am about to." He leaned into her, his breath smelled of the Galliano he'd had after dinner, citrusy and tart. The stubble of his days-old beard defined his jawline. The smooth, sexy curve of his lips as he smiled in anticipation of the upcoming kiss caused a shiver to run through her. He was so masculine, so powerful. And with the press of his lips to hers, and his hand coming around to support the small of her back and pull her in close, she felt his protective side. This was a man who cared for what was his. And now more than at any time in her life, she desired to be someone's. Not just a part of their family, but a girlfriend, a fiancé . . . maybe even a wife.

Oh this was not good, she thought as he engaged her tongue to dance with his. *I've done some stupid things, but this could turn out to be the worst.*

Yet, her hands went to his shoulders and pulled him closer, felt the pelt of his wet chest hair graze her nipples. Felt them tighten, heard her own moan as his fingers began to pluck and tug at them. She felt her heart racing. His tongue was learning her mouth and she remembered her textbook knowledge of why kissing was so important to primitive man. He was passing on hormones that would entice her to let him go further, dampen her in secret places, and make her know and trust him through his tenderness. Even knowing that his well-thought out intentions to seduce her had happened time and time again with other women, she allowed him to explore and seek out her secrets—the contours, the textures, the taste. She stood under the waterfall and let him ravage her mouth, knowing what he was up to but helpless to stop him.

Her hands felt his chest, gripped the muscles she found firm and smooth. Ran her thumbs over his nipples, giving him some of the torture she was enduring when she rolled and tugged on them.

She broke away from the kiss and kissed his nipples. Hearing his moan, she upped the ante and sucked on them, then lightly bit and tugged until she was getting too much water in her mouth.

As the shower blanketed them both in steamy clouds of warmth, the smells of her drove him crazy. He wanted her so badly. And now she'd gripped his cock and was pumping it. He felt the ooze of the tip getting lubricated. He wanted this woman in every carnal way he could have her. And right now, she was wagging a condom in front of his face and smiling.

He took it from her and rolled it on. Then stepped back to sit on the teak bench. He spread his legs and patted them. "C'mere you, walk backward and sit on my cock. Give me that ass."

She walked back until he held a hip in both hands then he lifted her. "We're going to go slow, reach back and put me where you need me to be."

She gripped him and he thought he'd lose it right then. Just the thought of her, of where his cock was going threatened to unman him. He needed to get inside before the lubricant washed away, so he helped her place the tip at her opening. Then he held her hips and worked the head inside.

"You cannot know how good this feels," he said, his forehead resting against her shoulders.

With his help she stood between his legs and bent forward until her hands were splayed on the floor and she was bent in half. The sight was unbelievable. He could see where he had entered her. He was almost in to where the condom was rolled down. He wrapped his hand under her bottom and began stroking her, entering her with long digits.

"This is fucking amazing," he moaned. "I don't think I can last."

"Just do what you need to. I'm okay, but it's slippery in here, so don't lose me. I don't want to fall flat on my face."

"Don't worry baby, I am not going to lose you." He gripped her hips and thrust. She responded by pushing back. At the same time his middle finger began circling her plumped up clit. My heavens, but she was wet. He wanted to plunder this sweet hole she was offering him. But he didn't want to hurt her. And he knew he was sizeable considering the area with its tight rim.

He held her as tight to him as he could without hurting her as he withdrew and reentered her, still toying with her with his other hand. After about a dozen thrusts, he shouted her name and then his brain splintered into prisms every color of the rainbow. His heart was beating so hard he thought it would burst. Vaguely, he felt something happening with the fingers of his other hand, fingers that were deeply embedded inside her. He felt contractions shuddering through her while at the same time he burst through the wall of colors and was thrown into a splintering black void. His body was convulsing, his mind all but shut down. He was in the throes of the longest orgasm he'd ever had. As he had lost all semblance of control over his body, he ceded to it and fell into the abyss. When he came out of it, it took a few moments for him to gather his wits.

"I've never . . .. That was . . .. You are one incredible woman. I'm not going to ask how it was for you, I think my hand fell away." Then he looked down and noticed that she was still hanging upside down, her hands on the wet tiles, her arms locked and holding her up. She was spluttering out water. He saw then, that the hand-held sprayer had fallen and was now spraying a stream of water right into her face.

He quickly pulled her up, a much easier feat now that

he was flaccid and no longer attached to her. He sat back on the bench and pulled her onto his lap and cradled her head with his big hand, while kissing her face everywhere. "Are you okay?"

"I'm fine. Just need to clean up a bit." She reached behind her and pulled out the condom that was still inside her. She examined it to make sure it was not torn before knotting it and tossing it into the toilet and then flushing it.

"That's a composting toilet."

"Oh, well. Sorry. I am used to flushing them. Did you know that a man's semen can still be used to impregnate women one to two days after ejaculation? You're better off to dispose of your used condoms in a more permanent manner, rather than tossing them into a trash can."

"Well . . . as I don't plan on using any condoms unless you're involved, I won't worry about it. But I will keep that in mind. It's a good thing to know."

"Yeah, you don't want babies with your DNA running around all over the place. And even worse, being made to pay for their support."

He shut off all the water and then pulled her back onto his lap. It was eerily quiet after the sound of the water flowing from all the showerheads had ceased.

He held her sideways, close to his chest with her legs draped over his thighs. "Speaking of kids . . . are we going a little overboard with tugging on Mama's heart strings about the possibility of a grandchild on the horizon?"

"I actually settled that question with myself today. My reasoning is, isn't it better that Mama lose weight and get in better shape so that she can live longer, for surely there will be a grandchild eventually. Or is it better to take away the carrot now and then she refuses to lose any weight or to exercise, and dies in a year or two? Because if things don't change, her heart won't be able handle it. Her blood pressure is already worrisome even with meds. You do know that she could have a stroke at any time, right?"

"I know."

She quirked her lips, "Facts of life. I see it over and over again. You can't change it without changing diet and adding exercise."

"Yeah. And I know you're right. You're really doing great with her. Better than anyone has done so far."

She stood and got them each a towel. He started drying his hair first and she had a few moments to admire his impressive chest without him noticing.

He turned back to her and stared at her intently.

"What? Am I drooling?" she asked, afraid she'd been caught staring at him.

"What? No, why? What were you doing?"

"Admiring you. You are one fine specimen. As far as thirty-something males go, your body is in superb condition."

"I work out when I can, but I do walk *a lot*—almost everyday. Uphill. That's what most of these tours are."

"Well it shows."

"And speaking of tours, the season begins tomorrow. I will be gone and so will Alyssa. It will just be you with Mama at night. During the day there are always people around to help with anything you need. But at night, you will be on your own. And then there is the language thing. Do you think you are going to be able to manage?"

"I am picking up your Italian language. Anna says I am a fast learner. Google Translator and I are becoming fast friends. And Mama seems to understand more than you give her credit for."

He smiled and grabbed her hand to pull her in close. His eyes met hers. He smoothed some wet hair away from her face and tucked it behind her ear. "I'm developing feelings for you Trixie. Is that okay?"

"What do you mean, is that okay?"

"I mean, do you want me to? Would there be a future in it? Do *you* want to have kids someday down the road?"

She moved away, her hands suddenly fidgety. She turned

to the mirror and fluffed her hair a bit. Then turning her head from side to side, she preened like a peacock with a bath towel wrapped around her.

"I do want you to. "Be-caw-se," she drew out the word while searching for the next words, "I might be developing some feelings for you, too. But you know as well as I do, that the future can't be planned, things just happen as they are meant to. And sure, I'd like a couple of kids. One day . . . down the road."

"How long is this road? Even with the best conditions possible, I'm not naïve. Mama has only a few years, five at best."

"The road can be long or short. It depends on many things. My most fertile years will likely be within the next five, so our timetables could intersect. But there are many other factors. I can't just have a baby because it's what your mama wishes."

He had his hands clasped between his thighs. He looked over at her, and simply nodded. That conversation over and put away for now, he asked, "Are you hungry?"

"I can get something back at the house."

"That's not what I asked," he chided. "And what makes you think I'm going to let you go back to the house tonight?"

"Mama . . ."

"Alyssa is there. She has a monitor. Everyone knows where to find me. We should take advantage of this time together. We won't have many nights like this until late fall. "

"Are you asking me to sleep with you, Mr. Palo?"

"That is *Signor* Palo. And yes I am. It's about time this fabulous bed had a woman in it. It's the only thing that could possibly make it more perfect."

"Wow, you do know how to turn a phrase. Yes. I will sleep with you."

"Good. Now . . . food?"

"Some cheese and crackers? Maybe some wine?"

He stood, nodded, and put his hands together while bowing, "Your wish is my command."

"Then I wish the nuns hadn't made me promise."

He laughter boomed through the tiny house. "That's funny, you and I have the same exact wish."

It was her turn to laugh. "Do you have something I can sleep in?"

"Yes, my bed."

"I mean to wear."

"I know what you mean. And no. It's our only night together for two weeks. I want to hold you in my arms with no barriers."

"Okay, then." She looked around, conscious of only the towel covering her. And then going to bed totally naked. What if she had to get up and turn on the light? "Are you sure no one can see anything up here?"

"I am positive."

"How can you be sure if no one else is allowed up here but you?"

"Do you want to go outside and look up? I will stand here naked and spread eagled for you to see."

"But you said I wouldn't be able to see you."

"Exactly."

"Ooohh, you are so frustrating!"

"Trust me. Always, just trust me," he said as he walked past her on the way down to the kitchen to get something for them to snack on.

Chapter 33
Panties as Payment

Five o'clock in the morning came fast. Trixie felt she had just laid her head on the pillow and Palo had slid in behind her, his legs overlapping hers, his hand protective on her shoulder. And then the loud crow of a rooster echoed over and over throughout the room.

"I should change that alarm to something soothing," he muttered. "But then, I'm afraid I would not get up!" As he said that, he sat up and stretched. Then patted Trixie's sheet-clad bottom.

"Rise and shine Florence Nightingale. Time to sneak back into the house before Mama wakes up and has us walking down the aisle and pushing baby carriages."

The arm that was wrapped around her pillow arched into the air and plopped down into the space between them with a thud. "I can't believe you have to go—and for two weeks. We had such a good time last night."

He jumped out of bed and patted her ass again. "That we did. I am going to miss you, seriously miss you. You make my days whole somehow . . . nothing missing. Before they were just . . ." he grabbed her and began tickling her until she begged him to stop, "looonng." He made his voice sound like a slow record. "Emmmppty." He made an echoing sound through his cupped hands.

"Yeah, well . . ." she said finally sitting up and thrusting her fingers through her unruly hair. "Mine will likely be looong," she mimicked his slow record sound he'd made, but they won't be empty, unless it's to empty bedpans, and I sincerely hope Mama never gets to that point."

She got up and shimmied into her dress then looked around for her underwear. "Where's my thong?"

"In my suitcase."

"What's it doing there?"

"It's traveling with me. It will sleep with me on my pillow."

She pouted. "I made that pair special, with the condom pouch and all."

He turned to her, tilted his head and shot her a penetrating glare. "Are you going to need them before I get back?"

"No! Of course not."

His eyebrows rose as if defining his point. "So then . . ."

She acquiesced, "Okay. You keep them."

"I will trade you this for them." From his backpack he produced a small white gift bag with gold lettering on the outside and light blue tissue paper poofing out of it.

"Oh, a present!"

"Just something I promised to get for you."

She gave him a quizzical look, then pulled out the tissue and looked into the bag and smiled. "Oh, the bathing suit you said you'd get that does not show off my derriere." She pulled it up and out of the bag, dangling it in front of her face. It was a sleek one-piece that had a convertible halter-top, in emerald green. "Oh, this is nice! It straps at the neck or around the back. This will be great for swimming and for tanning. Thank you," she whispered.

"You are very welcome. I will take your panties as payment though."

She turned the suit around and smiled. One piece, very stylish, by a famous Italian designer, and ample coverage in the tush area. Okay. But remember I haven't patented that special pouch yet."

He shook his head and smiled. "I am not planning on showing them to anyone. Although . . . that design could be useful for many other things. Your panty design could be globally marketable and therefore highly profitable."

She turned and looked at him, the question clear in her

eyes. "Like for what?"

"Oh, I don't know. One of those mini-pads you women keep in those tiny clutches, emergency money folded up, a wedding band."

"A wedding band?"

"Yeah, for dallying," he said as he ran his finger down her nose and shifted by her to get to the bathroom. "Which you are not going to do while I am away. And no dilly-dallying with yourself either."

"What?"

"You heard me. I want to taste your next orgasm with my tongue." He bent and gave her a quick kiss. "I'll see you when I get back. I already said good-bye to Mama last night, and I'll be talking to Alyssa multiple times every day because there are always things going wrong on the tours: people falling; getting sick; losing their luggage; having emergency calls from home; having their pockets picked; credit cards being refused; getting drunk and then getting lost. I will have too much of talking to Alyssa. This I already know." He stopped and stared at her, then touched his heart with his fingers. "Take care of you."

Then as he moved past her, he swatted her backside lightly and used the remote to turn on all the showerheads.

With her sandals in her hand, she stole down the outside stairs, careful not to make any noise. It was still dark. There was the faintest line just starting to appear on the horizon. Before she got to the bottom she heard a real rooster crow. She had to smile. She knew that whenever she heard that sound in the future, she'd think of Palo.

As she tiptoed around the terrace, she could hear the sounds of the workers walking along the fields on their way to the villa. She wished her dress was not such a bright neon blue. But no one seemed to notice as she slipped in through the back kitchen door, which Palo had told her was always unlocked, as the key had been lost for many years.

Once in her room, she too stepped into the shower. Palo

would be a busy man for two weeks, but she would be busy as well. She would work on learning this lyrical language he spoke, talk to doctors and pharmacists, help Mama to exercise and have a few cooking sessions with Gina. It would go well. She would not let Palo down.

As Palo dressed, then grabbed his suitcase and the backpack he used as a briefcase, he heard the car coming for him come up the drive. He smiled. Enzo was always prompt. He was one of his best workers. Alyssa was the other. But he would never tell her that.

He put his suitcase in the trunk and slipped into the passenger seat. *Ciao Enzo, andiamo,* he said in a resigned voice. Ciao, the greeting for hello, good-bye, see you later, and andiamo meaning, let's go. Usually he said it with more enthusiasm. But today, he was for the first time reluctant to leave.

Sure, he was always glad to come home. But after a few days of mama, all the questions from workers, and his own duties at the villa, he was happy to see the gates close behind him for a week or two. Not so today. Today he was leaving Trixie. And he absolutely did not want to. Part of him was afraid to say exactly why that was. The other part was doing cartwheels, because it knew exactly why that was. He was falling in love. As he put his head back against the headrest to get a few more minutes of sleep, all those mushy Italian songs began to run through his head. They had never made a lot of sense to him before. Now they speared his heart with all the words he wanted to say to her.

"*That's Amore.*" Enzo's voice called out from the driver's seat.

"What?" Palo asked, looking over at the grin blooming on his driver's face as he fought his way out of a deep sleep. A quick look around showed that they arrived at the Florence airport and that it was time for him to greet his arriving tour group.

"You were singing in your sleep."

"Really?"

"*That's Amore*. You are in love, no?"

Palo shrugged and quirked his lips as if to deny it then changed his mind. "I am in love. Yes."

Chapter 34
A Pact & A Problem

The next two weeks both fled, and crawled. The days were full of getting Mama to exercise, to actually encourage her to have a hand in preparing her own meals as Gina could not seem to break herself of the tradition of serving bread, ladling on syrup, spreading butter, and adding risotto or pasta to what might have otherwise been a healthy sauce or meal.

They'd had several talks via Google Translator on Trixie's phone. The gist was that Gina only knew one way to cook. If she deviated from a recipe, it became unpalatable. Who knew gnocchi with pesto sauce made with a lower fat version of ricotta and Parmesan, and an egg substitute for the yolks would turn out gummy and an unappetizing shade of green?

After a few days of water aerobics Mama was able to stand at the kitchen counter long enough to give Gina some advice about safe substitutions. Growing up during the war when many foods were rationed, including cream, butter, eggs, and cheeses, gave her vast experience in creating a sumptuous meal without those extra items.

A lighter fare eventually evolved after the first few tries to make cherished Italian family recipes more heart healthy resulted in disaster. Finally, things started working out on some chicken and veal dishes.

Adding freshly grilled veggies instead of the typical platters loaded with deli meats, many types of cheeses, every kind of olive known to man, and marinated artichokes, turned out to be easier than she'd thought. "The blackened vegetables are delicious," Mama crowed.

Then, mixing fresh, pureed pineapple with sugar-free gelatin to a tub of the Italian version of Cool-Whip Zero finished the meal. Everyone loved the easy-to-make dietetic dessert. And right away, it became Mama's job to make it each night. She was partial to using fresh peaches or sweet cherries, picked from the farm's own trees, chopped fine with lemon-flavored gelatin.

By the end of the first week, they had conquered the food feuds and Mama was even suggesting other vegetables they should try grilling. A week after the morning that both Palo and Alyssa had left, Trixie held her breath while Mama weighed herself. She had lost eight pounds! The day before Palo and Alyssa were due back, Mama weighed herself again, with Trixie looking over her shoulder as the needle on the ancient scale settled. Mama had lost a total of seventeen pounds! Everyone was jubilant. They were all excited for Palo to get back so they could give him the good news.

For Trixie, Mama had been a worthy adversary—scrunching her eyes up or pursing her lips and initially refusing to try new things. As the days progressed, they developed a friendship. The meals that had been a time of anxiety and uncertainty for both of them, turned out to be pleasant gatherings. Each dinner event became something to look forward to, as both Mama and Trixie were exceptionally good cooks. Each lent their expertise, and together they made meals that were both tasty and healthy.

Every day, early mornings were spent in the pool. Trixie was able to work Mama up to doing twenty minutes of cardio in the water. Then breakfast was served on one of the terraces, where Mama, with Anna's help, would regale Trixie with stories of her youth and her early days on the farm after marrying the love of her life.

Then it would be time for medications and a shower, which Trixie would help her with, then a short nap in her bed. Mama hated to be awakened from those afternoon naps, but Trixie insisted an hour's nap during the day was plenty. She knew that Mama needed a regular schedule and that going to bed in the evening at a reasonable hour would provide for a more beneficial sleep than multiple naps taken in chairs during the day. Plus, Mama really did need to keep her feet up to help with the swelling. Every time she could force Mama to use a footstool or to prop her feet up, was a victory

After lunch, which was a palm-sized amount of protein, usually fish or chicken, accompanied by a side salad and Balsamic dressing. A special treat would be served in the afternoon that Gina made from recipes Trixie had adapted from one of Mama's many cookbooks.

A walk around outside, with her arm linked through Trixie's, developed into a special time for both of them. Anna walked behind translating as needed, and Mama talked about the villa and when each thing was updated or changed. It was a nice time of reminiscing for Mama and a time for Trixie to glean things from Palo's early years of growing up on the farm and following his father and uncles around as they did their chores.

Nearing the end of the two-week period, Trixie had to acknowledge that, although Mama was one of her worthiest adversaries in the eating-for-health department, she, without a lot of fuss, had dutifully complied with nearly every demand she'd made of her.

They'd had some frank talks from the very beginning. Trixie made it known that she would not stay, would not take a penny of Palo's money, if she were not accomplishing her goal of getting his mama better.

Through Anna, she'd told Mama, "You and I know that you are very sick. And it's much worse than you let on. Without even seeing your medical chart I could tell that you have high blood pressure, high cholesterol, recurring infections that are very dangerous, and quite possibly congestive heart failure. Colitis, and gout are in your future if you don't already have them."

Mama had replied, "How can you know all this? Just by looking at me?"

She nodded, and then answered, "I observe, I listen, and

I smell. You have an underlying stench, it's faint, but I have a lot of experience in these matters. You are on the road to dying; your body is beginning to decay from the inside out. I know this. But we can turn this around. You can get better; you can get your health back. You might even be able to get on the rug and play with your grandchildren one day if you choose to do the work and lose some weight and become more active."

Mama had stared her down, then finally she asked her the question that no one could know the answer to at this point, "*Will* their be grandchildren?"

Trixie decided to do one better than Palo's hints to her, since there was probably not going to be a way to keep their dalliances a secret in this house anyway.

"I don't see why not. He seems to have all the proper equipment."

Mama's eyes widened and then she positively beamed, a smile so broad that Anna had to laugh along with Trixie.

"I will do my part if you do your part," Mama said.

"It's a deal," Trixie had said. Then they had smacked hands in mid-air and laughed. That afternoon, as Mama was being put down for her nap, she hugged Trixie and said something softly and lyrical in Italian by her ear. It sounded very much as if she was saying a prayer.

Trixie felt bad for leading Mama on—a baby would not be forthcoming anytime soon, if ever. But she knew how important it was to have hope. Palo loved his mother. But unless she turned her life around now, she probably wouldn't be here in two years. He had wanted to give his mama hope. So she would, too.

And who knew what the future would bring? She wasn't opposed to children. Just opposed to bringing children into a world where they were not wanted . . . wouldn't be cherished or taken care of.

The evening before Palo was due to come home, Anna and Mama and Trixie sat on the long front porch watching the stars came out and fill the sky.

Just before bedtime, Trixie noticed that Mama's temperature was up. And that she seemed achy, and complained of needing to pass gas. It was hard to get her settled into bed. She decided not to give her anything to help with the fever, instead opting to see if there was a reason for it. Her Italian was getting better, and Mama was picking up some of Trixie's English so she joked with her that if she didn't pass her gas by morning Trixie was going to have to put something up there to work on it. Mama had frowned at that and then said she thought she was going to throw up instead.

Trixie quickly dumped a plastic bin that she used to keep supplies in and put it in place. Then felt her head again. She was spiking. She pulled the covers back and pulled her gown up and palpated around her abdomen. When Mama had rebound pain in the lower right quad, she knew what the problem was.

Gina and Anna had gone home for the night so she and Mama were all alone. She took a deep breath and told herself not to panic. Then she picked up her phone and punched in the emergency number for the nearest ambulance service that Palo had programed into her phone.

The male voice that answered inquired as to the trouble in a long jumble of Italian. She didn't know if he spoke English or not, so she just gave him the specifics. "Mama. *Villa Stelle Cadente.* Appendix. Please hurry!"

"Si. On our way."

She disconnected the phone and looked at the time. 11:48. If she was remembering correctly, Palo would be returning from Venice on the Euro train early in the morning. Nothing would be gained by waking him at this hour. He wouldn't be able to get her any sooner. And Alyssa was in Rome due to fly back in the morning. She would wait until Mama was in the hospital and seen by a surgeon. For she was pretty sure that Mama's appendix needed to come out right away.

She ran to unlock the door and to open the gate. Then

she helped Mama who was moaning and holding her side, vomit into the basin. Her temperature was now 103 and her face and hands were getting clammy as blood was leaving her extremities to battle the raging infection.

Trixie was beginning to get anxious when she finally heard the wail of the siren coming off the main road. She grabbed her phone and purse and Mama's medical file, then sat beside the bed and tried to calm Mama, whose face was stricken with fear. She held her hands and rubbed them so Mama could feel she was there and began saying The Hail Mary prayer, knowing the cadence of her saying it in English would get Mama repeating it in Italian. It worked. They prayed together as the sounds of the siren drew closer.

As Trixie fought to keep Mama cognizant, she tried to assure her that everything would be all right. Then she ran to the door to show the ambulance crew the way into Mama's room, and stood out of the way as the EMTs rushed into the room with a stretcher.

Within ten minutes they were on the way to the hospital, sirens wailing all the way. Technically, she outranked the EMTs. As a nurse with a masters degree, she had more clinical knowledge than they did, but they had skills to handle a life-threatening event in a crisis situation, so while she insisted on riding with her, she let them do their thing, all the while communicating with the hospital they were taking her to.

Trixie hoped they had a good surgeon on duty. With Mama's history, this was not going to be a cakewalk. Blood pressure and heart issues were already evident in Mama's color and her breathing, and Trixie had to acknowledge that this could go either way. She was dreading making the call to Palo. But as soon as they took her into surgery, she'd call him.

Fortunately, this was the hospital that Mama had been taken to many times so they had all her information in their system. The doctor, a middle-aged man with salt and pepper hair and big owlish glasses met them in the ER suite Mama had been rushed to. He spoke English so Trixie was able to tell him about her symptoms, the fever, achiness, abdominal pain, her need to pass gas but her inability to do so, the bouts of vomiting, and the rebound pain Mama had when she had palpated her.

A quick scan was done and then Mama was prepped for surgery. Trixie held her hand and reassured her everything would be fine—that an appendectomy was a fairly routine surgery. But Mama knew a few people who had died during her youth from this very things, so she was distraught and panicked. She called out for Palo and Alyssa as she tried to comfort her, and kissed her on the forehead until she slowly succumbed to sedation. Trixie watched as Mama was rolled down the hall and the automatic doors opened and then closed behind her.

Trixie looked at her phone to note the time—2:13. This type of surgery could go several hours. It would be better to wait and have good news to report, she reasoned. There was nothing to be gained by waking Mama's family in the middle of the night and making everyone as anxious as she was. She would pray and wait this out on her own.

She turned and saw a woman behind a surgical mask approach at a fast clip. She held a Styrofoam coffee cup out to her. "Here, take this, it's a mocha latte. I just got it from the canteen. But it seems I'm being called in to assist. Don't worry, we have a really good team."

"You're English?"

"From Manchester. There's a lounge around the corner. Get some rest."

"Thank you," Trixie called out to her as the doors opened and then closed again.

Chapter 35
Ospedale

Palo woke up at 4:30. It was an hour before his alarm was due to go off, but that didn't surprise him. This whole last week he'd been waking up horny as hell, nothing but thoughts of putting his penis into Trixie's pussy running through his mind.

He grabbed one of the pillows and tucked it under him. Then plowed into it over and over again, grunting and moaning until he came.

Then he rolled over and stared at the dimly lit ceiling. Damn it, he wanted to be her first. As he thought about it, turning thoughts of her over in his mind, he realized, that quite possibly, he wanted to be her last as well. He wasn't quite sure what that meant. But after a few minutes, he accepted the fact that he was dead set on being her first. He blinked his eyes closed and tried to go back to sleep. But sleep wouldn't return.

He wondered what she was doing right now. Was she having dreams of him? Was she waking up horny and diddling herself? What was the deal here? He had never felt this way about a woman before. Never wanted one so completely as he wanted Trixie.

When the phone rang, he was surprised when he saw the caller ID. Well, well . . . she was thinking about him. He wondered if they could talk dirty to each other and make each other come over the phone.

The second he heard her voice, he knew that phone sex was not going to be an option.

"Palo?"

"Yes? Is it Mama?"

"Yes. We're at the hospital. She's just now coming out of surgery."

"Surgery?"

"Yes. She had her appendix removed. It was infected. However, they got it in time, and they were able to do a laparoscopic procedure rather than an open one, so she should heal pretty fast. She will only need to be here for a day or two if all goes well with her recovery."

"Wow. I don't even think I ever knew whether she still had one or not."

"Well, apparently she did." Then she told him how it all came about, ending with, "By the time you get back this morning, you should be able to see her."

"Thank you Trixie. Thank you for saving Mama's life. For being there when no one else was. You are a lifesaver, literally."

She smiled, though he couldn't see it. "It's what I do."

"I miss you."

"I miss you, too. I'm glad you're coming back today. After I see her, I'm going to go back to the villa to clean up the mess, and then get some sleep. She'll probably sleep all morning. I'll go back to the hospital in the afternoon. What's the easiest way to get back? Do they have a bus from here?"

"I'll call Enzo to come get you and take you home. He only lives a few miles from there. He's coming to get me from the train station at eleven thirty. Then he can bring you back this afternoon. You can arrange it with him. I'll have him drop me off at the hospital and I'll stay until you get there."

"Oh, that would be great."

"I'll call him now. Give Mama my love. Tell her I'll see her soon."

"I will."

"Trixie?"

"Mmmhmm?"

"We have something we need to talk about."

"What?"

"I'll get into it more later. But it has do to with a promise you made."

"Sounds like an interesting conversation."

He smiled, and this time, she couldn't see it. "I guarantee you, it will be. I'll send Enzo your contact information. He'll text you when he gets there. Ciao Bella."

"Ciao Palo."

Chapter 36
Trixie Finds A Home

When Trixie arrived back at the hospital, she was hugged warmly by Alyssa, Gina, Anna, Anna's mom, Mama's priest, several friends, and workers who had heard the news of Mama's middle of the night emergency appendectomy.

She accepted everyone's thanks for saving Mama's life while she looked around for Palo. He was nowhere to be found, but many people mentioned he was here. She was a little pleased that she was picking up some of the nuances of the language and even understanding some of the men, who tended to be gruff or to mumble all the time.

She figured he was with Mama so she worked her way around the crowd and headed down the hall. When she got to the room right before Mama's, a man's hand reached out, gripped her by the arm and pulled her into the room.

She cried out, making a tiny shriek, but cut it short when she realized it was Palo. His unusually tall stature and his unmistakable scent gave him away. He smelled . . . well, Italian. It was hard to describe but it was a rich smell, as if he'd just eaten fresh gingerbread with a spicy, nutty, bourbon-laced icing, and then walked through a stand of fir trees picking clary sage. It was heady and it was *him*.

He closed the door and leaned her into it, then kissed off every bit of the lip-gloss she'd just reapplied before getting out of the car.

"I have missed you so much. I dream about you. I wake up with a hard-on. Lord knows how many pillow cases I've ruined these past two weeks."

She did some kissing of her own, moving down his neck and taking in more of his scent as if she was a hound dog with his nose to the ground. "I've missed you too. But why could I not dally if you were jerking off?"

She pulled away and looked up into his face. "I don't think that's fair."

"I will make it up to you. Tonight. But first . . ."

He dropped to one knee and took his hand from his jacket pocket. He flipped open the lid. "Trixie. I love you. I think I have from the very first day. You make my heart tumble with joy. I wish for you to marry me. Will you do me the honor of marrying me?"

She stared down at the lovely woven gold ring with small diamonds at the juncture of each knot. It was stunning.

"This was my grandmother's ring, she left it to me to place on my bride. Would you honor me by wearing it?"

This was so sudden and so unexpected, she was sure her eyes were popping out of her sockets.

"And before you answer no, think about this. I come with a home, several in fact, in different places, and a family who already loves you. You would not only belong to me, but to an adoring family who would never want you to leave them. You would have a mama, a sister, aunts and uncles, and more cousins than you could count."

"You had me at, 'I love you,' and 'I come with a home.'"

He stood and drew her into his arms and kissed her long and hard. She knew she would savor this moment forever. This moment of belonging—of being accepted for who she was—a child born to parents who abused drugs, who overcame the odds and became someone people needed . . . someone they could even love.

"I want to get married today, right now," Palo said.

"What?"

"Mama's priest is here. There is a chapel. We will make it official with a license later at the Duomo in Florence."

He bent his knees so he could look into her face. His eyes were bright, crinkled in the corners with happiness. "Tonight, I want you to keep your promise to the nuns who raised you. In

270

the eyes of God, I want you to be my wife."

This was sudden—and a lot to take in. But she knew she loved him. And she knew there was no way they would go without making love tonight. She smiled and said, "Great! Now I have to get all my quirky t-shirts with the funny sayings translated to Italian."

She nodded and watched as he slipped the ring on her finger. It was a perfect fit and it felt surprisingly light and freeing, not like a symbol of ownership. More of a signet of being accepted into a loving family, a seal of pride . . . that the family had in each other, and now in her. She felt like she was home. Finally.

She would be a virgin for her bridegroom. After all, a promise was a promise. And she'd promised that to the nuns who had raised her.

With his hands on her cheeks, cupping her face and holding it up for him to see, he vowed, "I will spend my life making you happy. You will want for nothing. And together we will make beautiful babies."

"For Mama."

"No! Well yes . . . but for us, too." His face closed up a bit, and he looked sad. "You gave us more time with Mama today, there's no denying that. But if we are both honest she will not watch our kids grow up. She may only know them as babies. And that's all right. We'll have each other, and we will become the next Mama and Papa of *Villa Stelle Cadente.*"

"I hope we can have kids."

"No worries. I am a bull. I will show you tonight." He waggled his eyebrows and grinned, "C'mon, let's go tell Mama and the others, they will be over the moon."

"Do you know the first thing Mama asked the doctor when she woke from surgery?" she asked.

"There's no telling with her," he replied.

"She wanted to know how much the appendix he took out weighed. She said she was going to take it off this week's goal for her weight loss."

He threw back his head and laughed, then pulled her into his side as he walked her into Mama's room.

"Zucchero Mama," he said in Italian, as she and Gina and Anna and her mom looked on, "Trixie has agreed to marry me!"

"I know."

"How could you know?"

"I checked the safe, Nonna's ring was missing."

"Well, how did you know she'd say yes?" he asked her.

"Who would say no to my son?" she waved her hand in front of her face as if the was the most ridiculous thing anyone could imagine.

"Well, I'll bet you don't know this. We're getting married today, right now, here in the hospital chapel."

That she hadn't known. But she recovered quickly. "*Bueno*. You can start making my grandchild tonight!"

Everyone in the room laughed, even Trixie. She hadn't understood every word, but she got the essence of the conversation.

Chapter 37
Trixie Finds A Family

And so they were married. Trixie had never seen such a flurry of activity within a family. It was as if everything was choreographed, had already been planned, or had been repeated many times. Everyone called out something and then left, suddenly having a special job to do, excited to be a part of such a special event..

Within half an hour she was dressed in an elegant but simple white dress. A garland of fresh flowers, created from several of the many flower arrangements that had been sent to Mama's room, was fashioned into a beautiful Roman wreath for her head. One of the cousins happened to be her exact shoe size, although the number was a much higher EU number.

The priest, Father Antonio, used his connections at Town Hall to get a permit delivered, and then he called two of his altar boys to fetch his wedding vestments. Two cousins ran home to get their cameras, and one of Palo's uncles called a jeweler who brought a selection of rings from which Trixie chose a ring for Palo.

By the time everyone made it to the chapel the small salon was full to bursting. Mama, having been wheeled in and propped up in her bed, was smiling like the sun itself was radiating out of her.

Trixie raised an eyebrow at her from across the room and then laughed out loud. There was absolutely no way anyone could fake a soon-to-be-bursting appendix, but Mama seemed to delight in taking the credit for the hasty nuptials due to her emergency.

Mama was a pistol, but she going to love having her as a mother-in-law. But of course, she was still going to manage her care, so she'd have plenty of time to get one over on her. And together, they would eke out as much time as God would allow for her to be with them.

When Palo came into the chapel with one of his cousins as best man, he was properly dressed, no surprise as he always traveled as if being on a plane or a train was a special event.

He made for a very handsome groom. And all the women in the room made sure he knew it. Their clasped hands and loud sighs done in unison were almost comical.

Joy coursed through her. This man was going to be her husband. There had never been a man in her life that she could say made her happy. But Palo did, in all the ways that there were. That day, in that small chapel in a small community hospital, she could say that her joy was complete.

The ceremony was beautiful. Everybody cried, even the men. Mama was the queen of the day, believing that she was the one to have orchestrated this grand romance from the very beginning, and Trixie was not of a mind to deny it. The vows the priest read were repeated as both the bride and the groom grinned unabashedly. No one but them knew how monumental this wedding night was going to be.

Palo looked around the room. Except for his eight-and-nine year-old second cousins, he doubted there was a virgin in the room, other than his beautiful wife, who had been so devoted to the nuns who raised her that, she had been saved just for him. He felt like the luckiest man alive. He could not wait to introduce her to his "brothers" across the "pond."

The frat boys were going to adore this woman. Then he remembered that Dev had briefly met her. He was going to be floored by this news. Italy was seven hours ahead of the east coast. Some of his Stanford buddies were on the west coast though, and Rutger, geez, where was he this week? He'd have to shoot an email out to all of them. Next year he'd take her to the reunion in July. Most of his classmates were getting paired up too; there had been a few marriages already this year, with some babies on the way. They were going to have to have a big gathering to celebrate their good fortune and to introduce their wives to their best friends. He looked over at Trixie who was hugging Alyssa.

His brows rose when he saw the man standing beside her. Giancarlo. Ugh. He watched him ogling his female cousins while Trixie and Alyssa chatted and laughed about something. He was going to have to do something to separate those two. He was sure if she did, that Giancarlo would show his true colors. He thought for a moment, then made a mental note to get her trained to work the expo shows. There was one in New York during March that she would be perfect for. It would get her away from that sleazebag for two or three weeks at least. He'd talk to her about it and start setting it up.

Gina announced that there would be an impromptu reception at one of the local restaurants. She had taken it on herself to arrange an informal wedding dinner for the couple. Mama would not be able to attend, but she did not mind. She was dreaming of babies and planning on doing some shopping for cribs and playpens, and maybe one of those new padded rockers with a rocking footstool. She loved rocking babies to sleep.

Chapter 38
So This Is Love

It was nine o'clock before Trixie and Palo got home that night. It was eerily quiet as they were the only ones at the villa.

"Your place or mine?" Palo said as they watched Enzo pull around and go back out through the gates after he'd dropped them off.

She smiled up at him. "If I say yours, does that mean you have to carry me all the way up those back stairs, then up the inside ones as well?"

Leaving his luggage under the portico that led into the main house, he turned to her, bent, and picked her up by wrapping his arms around the back of her thighs. With one quick maneuver, he threw her over his shoulder. "Up we go."

Her tiny purse, which had been over her shoulder, bumped the back of his calves as he carried her up, up, up, into their sanctuary within the expansive tree.

In the bedroom, he gently brought her upright and stood her up. His hand swept the hair from her eyes as his lips lowered. Gentle kisses followed passionate ones, until his lips were licking and kissing alongside the column of her neck.

"You have made me the happiest man in the universe." His hands worked the buttons on the back of her dress.

"I can't help but think that your mom's illness rushed you into this." Her hands were tugging at his belt and working at the button and zipper on his slacks.

"If Mama hadn't made it through the surgery, I still would have wanted this. Us together," he breathed as he pulled her dress off her shoulders. "I love you, Trixie. I have from the first day. You had already been crying when I ran into you, your eyes were pools of color as you dabbed at them and handed me your license and insurance card. I wanted so much to kiss away your unhappiness. I knew deep down that you didn't deserve to be so sad."

She wore a strapless bra and rather than unclip the back, he pulled each cup down, baring diminutive mounds with long hard nipples, the areolae soft and puffed like small crowns until his lips took them and made them hard . . . achy . . . needy.

She moaned. "It's always devastating to me to lose a patient. I get too close; I kind of adopt them, making them my family. I'm so glad your mama's okay."

"Thanks to you," he murmured against the underside of her breast. "I love your breasts. They are the perfect size."

"They are small."

"They are perfect. I like them small, round bubbles instead of big pillows." He thumbed both nipples. Her knees buckled from the intense sensation zinging through her. He caught her with an arm around her waist, then stripped her of her gown, the tight band that was the strapless bra one of the cousins had loaned her, and her strappy thong with the tiny front pocket sewn on.

"What's in the pocket?" he asked as he fingered the enclosure?

"Some guys phone number."

"What?"

"Kidding. It's something blue and borrowed. Anna's mom gave it to me. It's a little enameled medallion of the Madonna and child."

"Everyone adores you." He placed her on the bed, then stood to remove his clothes.

"Oh, I am just a means to an end. *Everyone* wants a *bambino* for Mama. I cannot tell you how many times I heard that word mixed into people's conversations."

He chuckled. "She's kept it no secret."

As his pants hit the floor and his erection sprang free, she smiled up at him. "I am pretty sure that if I had a doctor call in a prescription for birth control to the local *farmacia*, that they wouldn't have filled it for me."

He laughed. Then placed his knee on the bed between her legs and covered her with his body.

"We can use protection if you want, we don't have to honor Mama's wishes. This is our life we're starting together. I will understand if you are not ready to have a child."

She looked up into his face, brushed a lock of hair back off his brow, "I don't know if I'm ready for a baby. I guess that's why God gives mothers nine months to prepare. But I know that I'm ready to have a family. And I'm definitely ready to get fucked good and proper."

"Oh, I doubt it's going to be proper. But I will do everything in my power to ensure it's good." He slid down her body and began to prepare her for him.

While his tongue gamboled over and around every part of her labia, his fingers danced their magic on her clit—a light airy touch at first, working toward an erratic staccato and ending with a grand timpani as he sucked and brought her to an explosion of ecstasy. His words coaxed her as his fingers, lips and tongue delved and teased until he felt her shiver, heard her keen, and tasted her on his tongue.

Then he climbed up her body, placed the tip of his penis at her opening, and brought her leg over his hip to open her up for him. "Ready?" he whispered.

Her eyes were still closed to the colorful explosions in her head, but she gave him the tiniest nod of acquiescence.

He looked down and mentally set this moment in his memory. Then he took the gift she had been saving just for him. With one forceful shove he was fully seated. He heard her gasp at the same instant he felt resistance to him give. Acceptance greeted his cock as her body gave him access, and then clenched around him in welcome.

"Okay?" he asked, searching her face for signs of distress. "Better than okay. Now what?"

"Now, I fuck you until one or both of us comes. But honestly, this feels so good, I doubt if I'm going to be able to last long enough to take you with me." He began moving in and out. Slowly at first, trying to make complete strokes instead of short jabs. Throwing his head back as he felt each thrust fully seat, then pull incrementally back. He slicked his thumb in her dampness then found her clit and circled it, slowly flicking, grazing, skimming, tapping, all the while easing his penis inside her in long even strokes.

He watched her face for signs of mounting pleasure. Smiled when he was rewarded with long drawn out groans, short gasps, and her head lolling back on the bed, exposing her throat as she closed her eyes to the building bliss.

He saw when her eyelids scrunched as she was fighting the pleasure, then saw them release when she decided to let go and accept it. He thrust to bury himself as completely as possible inside her and held as his thumb pressed. He was rewarded with the tiny nub going into a wild spasm while the walls of her vagina contracted around him. He closed his eyes and let go, feeling his balls draw tight before he was rocked out into the universe while inside her, he was emptying his essence of life deep into her clenching channel.

His moans joined hers as they both lived inside their heads, fully accepting the immense pleasure the universe had bestowed on them.

Ten seconds later, Palo was lying on the bed beside her, drawing her body close into his side. Then he dropped off a ledge into a chasm of slumber so deep the back of his eyelids only saw a black void.

Trixie, blinking, and fighting her way back to consciousness, examined every inch of her new husband's face. Vulnerable in ways men didn't usually allow, his face was slack with sated passion, relaxed in the deepest levels of sleep the body could surrender to.

Looking over at him, then allowing her eyes to scan the

beautiful marquis bedroom ceiling with its inset canister light rings, then going to the rows of dormer-style windows that reflected eerily-lit branches swaying in the gentle breeze, she smiled.

As wedding nights went, she was pretty sure hers was one of the better ones that women throughout the ages had dealt with. She accepted the weighty reckoning that she was a married woman now . . . possibly her body was even already working on becoming a mother. The song from Cinderella, *So this is Love*, began running through her head—a brain worm that she knew would not end with her humming it only tonight. It would be her mantra every time she laid her head on her husband's chest and felt it rise with each of his deep breaths.

So much had changed in just a few short weeks. But the main thing that had changed was that now she was happy. A hunger deep inside her had been assuaged. She was part of a family. She had a home. She had people who loved her. Especially Palo, who was now lightly snoring, in their hawk's nest, high in a stately old tree.

Something caught her eye in one of the windows and she watched with reverence as a golden moon slowly rose against the inky night sky.

She didn't make it to see the moon move up and over the house, as she fell asleep, more content than she could ever remember being.

Chapter 39
A Childhood Promise Kept

In the morning, they woke to the sound of a delivery van pulling up to the main house. Seconds later Palo's phone dinged, and he sat up in bed, looking like one truly satisfied man. He reached for his phone and pulled up his email. Then he laughed.

"Guess what they just delivered?" he called out to Trixie who was just coming out of the bathroom, drying her hair.

"If it's for Mama, it's a crib."

"No, it's something for us. Something I ordered while I was in Florence."

"What?"

"A box of 48 KY ultra-lubricated condoms. You told me I couldn't use the local *farmacia* so I ordered them online."

She laughed. "If memory serves, we did not use one last night."

He smiled and looked over at her, "No, we did not."

"I guess using them now would be like putting the cart before the horse."

He chuckled his agreement.

She plopped down beside him on the bed and purred, "You were superlative last night."

He patted her thigh. "My thoughts exactly about you," he whispered as he kissed along her neck until he got to her ear lobe. Then he jerked the towel she was wearing off. "And I think that together we can be *superlative* again this morning."

"I am so glad you did not have to break your promise to the nuns."

"Me too."

"Sorry about the rushed ceremony in the hospital. I feel I must make things up to you for the way that came about. Do you think you could forgive me if I arranged to marry you again in one of the biggest Catholic churches in all of Italy?

"The Vatican?" she whispered.

He laughed. "I notice you're more concerned with the church than answering my question."

"Can people really get married there?"

"Of course. There are many chapels. And I have, shall we say, friends in high places."

"You know the pope?"

He laughed again. "He is not actually the one to make those arrangements. But I do know the people who do. But I was actually thinking of the Duomo in Florence. I do not think it best for Mama to travel as far as Rome."

"Oh yeah, you're right. I don't even know what kind of gown you'd have to wear to get married there, something ancient and gothic?"

He chucked her under her chin, then looked into her eyes. "I think you must be buttoned up from your chin to your toes. Nothing sexy or at all provocative, and you must be barefoot."

"Barefoot? Why barefoot?"

"You must show you are subservient to your husband. That you will obey your master as a slave obeys his master."

"You must be kidding."

"Yes, I am kidding. I do not think you even have to agree to be obedient anymore."

"Well, that's a good thing."

"Does this mean you will marry me again?"

She moved her head back and forth as if considering. "I'm really fine with the ceremony we already had. But if it's important to you . . ."

He shrugged. "We'll see. Meanwhile, we must decide where we will live."

"Can't we live in the tree house?"

He laughed. "Yes, if you want to—until a baby comes along. It wouldn't be safe to live this high up with an infant."

"Well, he or she would have to be close to Zucchero

Mama, that's for sure."

"Speaking of Zucchero Mama, you have to keep paying me as I am an independent woman. I will have to have my own money."

He laughed. "A woman who doesn't want my money? You would be the first one. Don't worry; I will pay you well, many many rubies. The Bible says a woman of virtue is worth many rubies."

"I lost my virtue. You took it last night."

"I am not sure I did a thorough enough job though. Let's give it another go, shall we?" He pulled her over and slid her naked body under his. "No one expects us anywhere until it's time to bring Zucchero Mama home. I want you to look well-loved by then."

Chapter 40

Sean & Sandy
The Lost Book Turns Up

Sean had been back from his annual reunion vacation since Monday. Now it was Friday evening, and Sandy had an unsettled feeling. Her boss had been looking at her a little oddly all week. A few times she'd caught him staring at her with his brows creased as if looking at a rare creature he'd never seen before.

She'd gone to the restroom several times to see if her makeup was smeared, or if a strand of hair had come out of its Tippi Hedren-styled French twist. She checked her crisply ironed, white pleated-front blouse to see if it was buttoned properly, scanned her hose for runs.

And then this morning, out of the blue, Sean—her stick-to-the-Day-Timer-boss—had asked her to work late—tonight. That was odd because it was so rare not to have a few day's notice, but not unheard of during their five years of working together.

Twice, he'd entertained Japanese clients who were on a strict timetable and they'd had last minute dinner meetings in his office so his clients could take the ferry and go sightseeing in Southport during the day. But to her knowledge there were no sightseers waiting in the wings. She would know, as she always booked their flights.

Stunned, she'd looked up from her work, blinked at him, and simply nodded. Then she returned to her computer and the document she'd been working on. She'd had to retype the same paragraph over three times as she couldn't keep her mind on what she was doing.

At five-thirty, her phone set chimed and she touched

the sensor in her ear to answer the call. Of course it was Sean. Everyone else had left half an hour ago. "Sandy, are you free to take some dictation now?"

"Yes. I'll be right there."

She stood, straightened her black pencil skirt, checked to make sure her white silk blouse was properly tucked in, and ran a hand under her French twist to make sure it was still tidy. She picked up her steno pad and pen, then walked the fifteen feet of ultra plush carpeting leading to the tall mahogany doors that granted access to Sean's inner sanctum.

She gave two quick taps on the right-hand door and then pushed against the brass plate, entering the "Leopard's Den." Sean was not a lion, fearsome as he might be sometimes, he never roared. And he was not a tiger; he didn't stalk his prey and then pounce. He reminded her of a leopard—black haired, sleek, cunning, and able to stand perfectly still while getting the lay of the land. Then waiting until it was time to tear out someone's throat. In his case, he did this by using words—mincing words that clearly defined his client's case and tore apart his opponent's.

Many feared entering the Leopard's Den. She had seen how he could use those penetrating dark green eyes to send a malevolent stare in someone's direction if they displeased him. She tried very hard not to be on the receiving end of one of his derisive scowls. She pictured herself kicking off her high heels and running down the elegant hallway, her sable black hair unraveling behind her as she tried to avoid the *Leopard's* sharp teeth sinking into the side of her neck. The thought of his mouth anywhere near her neck caused her to quiver. She quietly closed the door behind her. The soft snick announced her presence in the room.

He was pacing in front of the wall of windows when she walked up to the set of chairs facing his rosewood desk. That was unusual for Sean, not so much for a leopard. So off the mark, that she didn't know whether to sit or to stand once she had approached the grouping. He sensed it and waved with his hand for her to take one of the chairs in front of his desk. Funny, that just by the wave of his hand she knew that he was irked—yet not in carnivore mode, thank God.

She sat and waited, watching as he returned to stand behind his desk. He didn't pull out his chair and sit. He just stood, staring down at the surface of his vintage Wanscher desk that he never allowed to be cluttered.

This was odd. And it unnerved her—mostly because she could not read his mood when usually she could. What could be wrong? She didn't know of anything business-related that could have occurred without her being aware of it. Had he received an upsetting phone call on his cell? All his other calls went through her first. Had they lost an important client? Was someone is his family ill? He didn't seem sad, or anxious, or mad really. He seemed . . . predatory.

His head lifted and he looked over at her, his dark olive eyes boring into hers, seemingly asking a battery of questions with them. None that she could divine though. It was as if, all of a sudden, he didn't know who she was. His brows creased together as if he was trying to ferret out where she'd come from.

His eyes darkened and then held a strange, curious glint that she'd never seen focused on her before. If she didn't know better, she'd have thought her being there puzzled him, intrigued him—made him curiously interested. She'd been at conferences with him when she'd seen him glance at a woman and appear to be attracted to her. But in the moment, whether or not a woman captivated him—he was always professional. And as far as she knew, while he was working, he had never acted on the attraction.

Yet she was seeing some noticeable awareness in his expression right now. And he had called her in here to discuss something—something that had to wait until after hours. But at this moment, it seemed he didn't know how to proceed now that she was sitting in front of him.

The Sean she knew was never at a loss in any situation. He researched a project until he could anticipate any question, knew every facet, and was familiar with every detail that could become an issue he'd have to tame, reinvent, or circumvent if it came up. He was an amazingly good corporate attorney, with an enviable track record for chalking up wins. But now, something was off.

He tapped his fingers on the desk, something he often did when he was gathering his thoughts. She watched his long, tanned fingers with their perfectly trimmed nails gallop in a strumming sequence, doing a kind of drum roll as little finger riffled to the longer, pointer finger—once . . . twice . . . three times . . . then they stopped and held.

"I know we agreed two years ago that you would do some personal shopping for me from time to time after I lost my longtime personal shopper. You told me then that you knew me better than a stranger would and offered to take over those duties. I thought about it and it made sense, so I offered to compensate you for the extra time involved."

"You didn't like the swim suit," she murmured. She was crushed. She thought the board shorts perfect for him, conservative in dark blue, yet with just the right touch of a tropical embellishment in the form of a white flowering hibiscus over one knee.

"No, the swim suit was fine. Perfect in fact."

Still standing, he reached down and opened the long center drawer. "But when did I ask you to select my reading material?"

He took out a book and tossed it onto the perfectly centered blotter. And as the workday was over, there was nothing else to detract from the shamelessly brazen cover of the book.

As soon as she saw the bold stylized cover, she recognized the book as the one she had been reading—the book she had frantically searched for before giving it up as permanently lost.

She felt her face flush hot while every other part of her body froze. *Oh dear God. He had seen what she had been reading, her go-to recreational reading—the smuttiest erotica about secretaries and bosses she could find on the Internet.*

She was mortified. Beyond mortified. She was shamed, humiliated, embarrassed—disgraced in so many ways that her brain couldn't put it all together. Just like the characters in her books, she found herself in a predicament she didn't know how to handle. She sat there numb, eyes wide with fear and trying to take it all in—how to breathe all but forgotten. She had no idea what to say to this man who was her boss . . . her very staid, conservative boss.

He seemed to be giving her a few moments to absorb the enormity of this . . . this singular revelation. From her reaction, he had to know with certainty that this was her book. And that she hadn't meant for him to see it.

He cleared his throat, and giving her an opening to explain, said, "I don't know if it was intentional or not, but I found this in my suitcase." He lifted the book up and brandished it, questioning her as if there was still a doubt in his mind that it could be hers. The cover screamed *His Submissive Secretary* in deep scarlet against a black background.

Her mind flashed back to when she'd added the swimsuit to his already packed suitcase. The suitcase had been open on the sofa in his office, waiting for her to add the things he had requested her to buy during her lunch hour. Last minute items he'd forgotten he'd need for the annual reunion trip to his beach house in Sunset Beach.

She'd already added the new shorts and tropical beach shirts the previous day. The swimsuit had been ordered and she was going to pick it up on her lunch break, as it would be the last day he would be working before leaving for his two-week reunion with his friends at Sunset Beach.

On the way back from the store, she had stopped to read her book at the park before returning to the office. It had been such a glorious, sunny day with a fine gentle breeze keeping the humidity at bay.

Now she remembered that she had slipped the book into

the shopping bag alongside the swimsuit that was wrapped in tissue for the walk back to work. The handles on the bag had made it easier for her to carry her book, her purchases, her purse, and her latte back to the office. Once there, she had put the bag right into the suitcase. She cringed at the memory.

That night and the following night, she had looked everywhere for her book. She had finally accepted the fact that she had left it on the park bench and bought another copy.

"You're fired."

"What?" Her head jerked up and she looked over at him. Surely, he couldn't do that? Wasn't she entitled to read whatever she wanted on her own time?

"I said, you're fired."

She sat there blinking. She had no idea what to say to that. Could he do that, with no warning whatsoever in her file? No black mark ever?

"Whaaa . . . t?"

"Until Monday. When you can ask for your job back again."

"What!" she sounded like a parrot with a one-word vocabulary.

He walked around his desk and leaned back against the front of it, his feet crossed at the ankles—his oxfords gleaming as if dust moved out of the way for him to pass by.

"This weekend I'm tying you up and giving you the longest tongue lashing you've ever had. And I want to make sure you know that it's not a job requirement that you *submit* to it. Because this weekend, you have no job—while we play at being boss and submissive secretary. As of this moment, you are unemployed."

She felt herself flush all over. Weird sensations fluttered through her belly. Her head began to pound as blood was redirected. She knew her cheeks had to be turning scarlet. "But, but . . ."

"You will call me Sir, and I will call you Beth, the name

of the secretary in that book."

He used his thumb hiked over his shoulder to indicate the book still in the middle of his blotter. "You will do my bidding, and I will see to it that you come. Over. And over. And over again."

She managed to lift her head. Forced herself to look at him, her eyes so wide she feared she might look owlish as she blinked to make sense of all this. She met his hard gaze and dark no-nonsense expression with a blank stare as her lips parted in a small "o" of surprise.

She registered the heat in his eyes as he took in her parted lips and her heaving chest. She blinked hard, as if that would set things right again—or at least, transport her back to her desk, back to a time when she had been transcribing a deposition.

Then, as if her body had translated his intent far faster than her brain, she felt wetness pool in her panties. Dear God, what was going on?

His right eyebrow rose in inquiry and his lips quirked as if mocking her. He firmed his mouth and drew in a long breath. She could see his nostrils flare. For one outlandish moment she thought he might be scenting her. Was that even possible?

Could he tell that she had just flooded her panties? That thoughts of him making her do his bidding and then making her come were flashing through her mind like a naughty picture show? She sensed that he did know. And because of that book, he knew exactly what she wanted—what Beth had wanted.

Oh my God, he'd read that book! The scenes from the book flipped out like cards being dealt from a deck: exposure, spanking, bondage . . . oooh, that scene with the nipple clamps. She'd underlined it. Yikes! Her eyes flew wide.

He chuckled. "Having second thoughts? Maybe this wasn't even your book?" Without his eyes leaving her face, he reached behind him and picked up the book, brought it around to the front where he gestured with it. "Let's see," he opened the book where a bookmark had been placed.

She cringed as she recognized it. The bookmark was personalized with her name. In gold metallic thread, *Sandy* was emblazoned against a blue sky. Her sister had cross-stitched it for her for her birthday. She'd forgotten she'd left it in the book.

He paused long enough to be certain she'd seen it before he continued, "Whoever was reading this book was at a particularly interesting part. Seems this secretary kept making typos so her boss decided she needed to be taught a lesson. In this scene she's across his lap with her panties down around her ankles. You don't find out until the next page, what happened. I can imagine that whoever misplaced this book, was anxious to know what came next. Or should I say, *who* came next?"

She was too mortified to comment.

He walked back around his desk until he was standing behind his chair. He reached over and opened the right-hand drawer, took out a piece of paper that had printing on both sides. He placed it on her side of the desk, face-up, in front of her.

"You'll need to read this. If this type of involvement with your boss is what you want, you'll need to sign it. If it's not, this conversation never happened and we will go back to our normal business relationship on Monday morning."

She was speechless, but at least she had closed her mouth. She had no idea what to say, how to respond to this proposition. "I-I-I . . ."

He pushed the page closer. "Read," he instructed. "Then we'll see if you have any questions."

She took a deep breath, picked up the page and read, all the while wondering who had typed it for him, as it surely hadn't been her.

Chapter 41
The Contract

During the time she was reading, she had a chance to gather her thoughts. And to debate with herself if this was what she truly wanted. He was offering her what Beth had. No questions asked domination. Sex with him, Sean . . . the man she fantasized being with when she toyed with herself.

She turned the page over and read the back, all the while aware of him staring at her. This was surreal. Could they really do this? Did she want to do this? What was he thinking? Was he seeing how nervous she was as she followed each line with the tip of her pen? Was he watching her chew on her bottom lip? Had he noticed her pumping her foot up and down so erratically while her legs were crossed that now her high heel was in danger of dropping off her toe and thudding to the carpet? She was aware that he hadn't taken his eyes off of her. Not once.

She read the last line over twice, and surrendered to the moment. She would surrender to him and she would surrender to her desires. She wanted to know what it would be like to have Sean touch her . . . to have him kiss her . . . to have him do wicked things to her—things she had dreamed about for years. She wanted to know how it would feel when Sean covered her body with his and entered her. She was tired of imagining him with other women. This time she wanted to be the woman he undressed and made love to.

She signed on the line at the bottom and placed the paper on the desk facing him. She looked up to see that his eyes were intent on her. She had no doubt that they'd remained that way the whole time she'd been reading the pseudo-legal document. Because, could you really spell all this out? Then take it to court as a defense?

She decided not to attack that angle. Signed or not,

whether it would stand up in court was not the issue. But clearly, whether she wanted to cross the boss-employee relationship lines with him was. And she did. She always had. The montage of dreams she'd had over the years, where he had taken her in every conceivable way, flashed through her mind.

She could always get another job. If she didn't do this now, she would always wonder. And likely regret not taking this chance to be with him in a physical sense. She put down the pen.

"Questions? Surely, you have a few."

She slowly shook her head. "No, not really. Everything is pretty clear. Non-disclosure. No fault. This is a mutual decision. No penalties, no rewards to either party. This is an agreement either party can break at any time. No repercussions whatsoever to either party. We both sign mutual consent and agree to hold no one liable for any consequences coming out of this shared venture. We both sign we have no transmittable diseases. And I sign I am on birth control. It's pretty straightforward for a sexual assignation. Almost like a no-fault pre-nup, without the marital part—except that the conjugal rights are spelled out. In great detail, I might add. Every opening can be breeched with the exception of my nose and my ears."

He smiled at her. It was the smile he used when he was proud of her for the things she grasped so easily, or for something she taught herself and surprised him with.

"A very concise brief précis. I'm impressed. But we both know there are ways around every legal issue. Connubial or conjugal rights are not usually spelled out in such detail contractually for even marital celebrants, nonetheless those just planning a tryst. But if we're going to do this, I want to be very straightforward. It is not required. I would love to train you as my submissive, just as I have enjoyed training you as my secretary. But they are not mutual and never have to be. You do understand that?"

"I do."

He laughed. "Then I pronounce us Dom and Sub."

He walked around the desk and pulled her up from the chair by her forearms. His eyes met and held with hers, then fell to her lips. "May I kiss my sub?"

She couldn't help it, she grinned up at him, "Yes. Please."

He lifted her chin with his fingertips, bent his head, and took her lips with his. They both let out a satisfied sigh at the tentative connection. He allowed his lips to move over hers, savoring the silky feel of them meshing and opening against his, before he plundered the depths and explored her mouth with his tongue. It was a very thorough exploration as his tongue learned her depths and textures. It was several long moments before they parted and he pulled away. She was dizzy with lust and had to grip his forearms to steady herself.

"You seem shorter."

"I seem to have lost my shoes."

He laughed. "You're going to lose a lot more than that tonight."

She smiled up at him shyly. The blush that rose up her neck and covered her cheeks stole his breath away. She was gorgeous. And she was going to be his.

He looked down at her, his face growing serious. "Are we really going to do this? This isn't just a fantasy I've dreamed up?"

It was her turn to laugh. "Well if it is, then it's my fantasy too. I've wondered for a long time . . . what it would be like to be with you."

"I have fought my desire with regard to you for a long time as well. It's going to be wonderful to let my imagination reign and do all the things I've thought about doing to you."

"I hope I don't disappoint."

"I don't think that's possible."

He bent and kissed her again, then pulled back, holding her by her elbows. "Pack a bag of necessities. You won't need much—a toothbrush and something for your hair as I plan on taking it down. You won't need any extra clothing. I plan to keep you very close to naked most of the time. I'll send my driver for you at eight."

She shivered in his arms and he chuckled. Then he led her out of his office, waited while she got her things from her desk, and walked her to the elevator. Knowing the guards downstairs would see her to her car, he kissed her on the forehead and watched her enter the elevator.

As the elevator doors began to close, he looked her in the eyes, and with the same commanding voice he often used to say, "Type this up," he said, "Shave your pussy."

Her eyes flew wide open and her face flushed scarlet just as the doors closed.

Chapter 42
Less is More

At home, sitting on her sofa, she could not remember what she had signed. But snippets came back to her later as she bathed, groomed herself down there, fed her goldfish, watered her plants, and packed an overnight bag. No clothing—only cosmetics and necessities, those were his instructions. She would normally have packed a book to read. The one he still had that was hers—the one she'd reordered—she'd finished last night. But she had a hunch she'd be far too busy this weekend to read.

She had agreed to oral sex, vaginal sex, anal sex, and different forms of coercion, including being bound and chastised with spankings. She had signed papers to the effect that she was disease-free and on birth control. All things, she would never have discussed with her boss . . . until he had called her hand—and offered her the role of the lead character in the erotic book she had misplaced—in his suitcase!

She had thought to refuse his offer—but only for the merest second. She wanted this. She really did. After Sean had walked around his desk, stood her up, took her chin in his hand, and then bent to kiss her, she had become undone. No longer her own person, she wanted to be his.

At first, it had been a chaste kiss, but even then she had felt the heat travel from his lips to hers and then go directly to her clenching woman parts. For the second time, she knew she had given off the aromatic scent of a woman aroused as she had seen his nostrils flare when he inhaled. As if a hunter in a great forest, he had scented her and was primed for the hunt. The lion aroused—or in his case the leopard—had invited her into his den. And she had agreed to go there. She would be his quarry, the prey he had enticed to his multi-million-dollar mansion, the neophyte that would play sex games with him for three days and then go back to being just his secretary on Monday.

She had signed the papers saying she would do his bidding. That she would be his from 8:00 this evening, until Monday morning at 6:00.

On the way to the elevator he had said they would discuss hard limits when she arrived at his house that evening. She knew enough from reading BD/sm books to discuss all that intelligently, but she worried that he might have the wrong idea about her. Despite her being incredibly well read in the romance and erotica genres, she was still technically a virgin. She had no real carnal experience, only what she read through reams of literature describing the different forms of decadent pleasure. The sex act had been described in many scandalous and inventive positions. Yet, she herself had never had a man go all the way with her. Despite a few being well intentioned, and her being open to it, it just had never happened.

When was she supposed to tell him *that*?

Chapter 43
The Drive to Figure-Eight Island

A Mercedes sedan came for her at eight. She looked out the window at the scenery passing by as they drove through the Mayfaire area. When she realized the driver had left the city she began to get nervous. It gave her pause to see the lights lessen as they left Wilmington. They turned onto Porter's Neck Road, and then they were in the traffic circle that led to Edgewater Club Road. From there it was Bridge Road, and then finally Beach Road North. She drew in her breath as they drove past the magnificent houses that dotted Figure Eight Island.

She knew Sean had money. His parents were mega-wealthy and he was an only child. Through typing his correspondence, it would have been hard to miss the fact that he was one of the elite upper class. The portfolio gifted to him in his twenties was only a small part of the fortune he had amassed for himself as one of the most gifted lawyers in the city. But still . . . Figure Eight Island? It was legendary.

Kim Bassinger and Alec Baldwin had a home on the island in the 90s. It had been a vacation destination for Jennifer Anniston, Dustin Hoffman, Robert Downey Jr., Andy Griffith, Paul Newman, Richard Gere, Al Gore, Susan Sarandon, and many other celebrities, along with many noted politicians and businessmen. It was aptly nicknamed The Hamptons of the South.

In the years that she'd been Sean's secretary, she had never had cause to visit him at any of his homes or to even mail a letter to his residence. Everything was done by email, except when it required a notarized signature, and even that could often be done by email now.

It was a shock to see the place he drove his Jaguar XF Sedan to every evening after the office closed. She was familiar with the car he drove, as she had to pay for his parking spot every month and the parking agency for the building was very particular about knowing everything about the cars it housed. Once, she'd had to go down to look at the license tag, as he said he couldn't remember his tag number. She had come back up in the elevator fuming. "Really, you couldn't remember JAG-U-ARE?"

He'd laughed. "Made you look."

To which she responded, "You dirty crook."

"You're going to have to do a lot better than that to insult me. Remember, I'm a lawyer."

To which she had added, "A corporate environmental one to boot, you bottom feeder."

He had laughed full out at that. They often had fun bantering, both of them being smart and competitive, and eager to one-up the other.

When the driver made the turn onto a crunchy circular drive, she initially thought they had mistakenly pulled up in front of a hotel. But when she saw no signage or other cars in the vicinity, she realized that the sprawling manor house was an enormous private residence.

The main part of the house had four levels; the wings had two, and balconies or terraces were everywhere. The garage had five bays, one of which was open. The JAG-U-ARE tag gleamed in the reflected light from the front porch carriage lights. She had to smile when she saw the car and remembered their wordplay that day.

Off to the left, was a fenced–in tennis court. She couldn't see a pool, but didn't doubt that there was one somewhere.

The driver parked the car at the top of the drive and got out to open her door. She stepped out onto the oyster shell path and drew in the heady fragrance of oleander riding on the gentle breeze. There were no sounds other than that of waves crashing onto the shore a short distance away. And no other lights beyond the lit circular drive and the welcoming portico of the front entrance. Security lights for the tennis court had come on as they had turned onto the lane, but by the time she stepped out of the car, they had already gone off.

Wow. This was the boonies, but the really nice boonies. She'd never been inside a mansion, apart from the Bellamy Mansion in Downtown Wilmington. But this one dwarfed that one by a full city block, and she had no doubt it was one of the nicer ones in all of New Hanover County. It appeared brand new, but then as she got closer she realized it might just be that it was impeccably maintained. Stately places like this were timeless as new owners refurbished and redecorated to their own eccentric tastes.

Forty sets of windows and eight sets of glassed-in doors faced the front drive. Lights from a massive chandelier, high up and behind a huge wall of tall windows, lit the entrance hall and a staircase that curved up alongside a far wall. A water feature in the center lawn lit up plumes of rainbow-colored lights as water cascaded down a multicolored trough before running into a mini Bellagio-styled dancing fountain. Every new thing she saw reinforced her initial impression that she was way out of her league here. She was a Cottey College graduate from Missouri, on a P.E.O. scholarship. What in the world was she doing here? And why had she signed that paper?

Before she had a chance to answer her own questions or to get back in the car and tell the driver to pull the rest of the way around the drive and leave the way they had come in, Sean was there, at her side.

She turned to face him, ready to renege. Then she looked up into his face, and took in his gorgeous emerald eyes—his too handsome face, and his sexy wide grin. It was more than apparent that he was thrilled to see her. Had he thought she might not come?

"Welcome to Egret's Roost," he leaned down to her ear and whispered, "and to my sexy secretary's storybook retreat."

She blushed full on, but because it was dusk, only he

could see it.

He took her by the hand, squeezed it, and walked her away from the car. When they were at the steps leading to the portico, he turned her to face him and pulled her close. She was up against his chest. Her breasts, in an open lace work demi-bra, grazed against the silk of her blouse. The action drew her nipples into tight buds.

He looked down as if he somehow detected her arousal. Then sensing her trepidation, he said, "Don't be intimidated. It's just a house. And it's just me. You know me—better than most people do."

He added, "And I am just a man. A man who is delighted you came."

She blushed, her cheeks reddening under her lashes, and now visible to him as the fountain lights danced behind them and lit up the area.

"I almost didn't," she admitted.

"I feared as much."

"But then . . ."

"I know . . . me too. Let's just see where this leads."

She nodded.

He picked up her bag from the top step where the driver had placed it, and took her by the elbow. He walked her to the front door. She had been tottering on her heels while walking along the path, now she stomped them to get the dust off them on the doormat.

"Oyster shells are hell on heels," he said, "but it's imperative to have pervious driveways and pathways on an island like this so the storm water has a place to go." The way he said it, she knew he'd said it precisely that very same way many times. She wondered how many women he'd brought here.

She knew from the letters she typed that he was a genuinely serious environmentalist, always supporting various coastal groups and contributing to anything ecological relating to the local beaches. He had won many court cases against companies found violating regulations that were in place to protect the coast. It didn't surprise her that he practiced what he preached.

She heard the crunch of the limo's tires rounding the circle and then the quiet swish as they gripped the asphalt of the road and the sedan sped up. She shivered. She had been left alone here—with him.

He chuckled. "Don't worry. You know the three words that will bring him back to take you home if you so desire."

She looked up into his strikingly attractive face, with the well-defined brows and dark fringed lashes, now outlined in sharp detail by the twilight in tones of silver, and she smiled. "Yes, the last three months of the year."

She'd had to pen them in on the document she had signed. He had called them safe words. In the books she read, they only used one word, if any. He had said he wanted both parties to be absolutely sure if things had to be called off.

"I am hoping you will not need them. Come inside. Have you had dinner?"

"Yes, I already ate."

He gave her a wolfish smile. "You will be *my* dinner. I cannot wait to have you . . .."

Her eyes went wide and he laughed out loud. It was a delightful sound and she welcomed it. It took the edge off. He didn't laugh often, but when he did it was full on and with genuine joy.

She wondered when she should tell him of her inexperience. Maybe mention that his lips and teeth touching her down there would be a novel experience for her as well . . . if he did in fact, eat her.

He opened the door for her. "In you go, let's get you a drink so you can relax a little. But just one—I don't want to dull your senses. I want you to have the full effect of my tongue lashing."

Her insides heated up at his words. She could hardly

believe that tonight would the night. Finally. Tonight, she would become a woman. That she would have an orgasm that she didn't cause to happen.

He placed her small case on a table as he closed the door, and with his hand on the small of her back, led her through the foyer and into the first room off to the right.

She had never been in a house this large. The ceiling was very high up, with trays inset around ornate fans that had huge woven bamboo blades. Each tray had a series of recessed lights giving the room a soft glow. She took in the rest of the room.

Like the lobby of a fine hotel, there were several distinct seating areas, that were so diverse, so opulent, so refined, and with such attention to detail. Everything screamed quality. This was how celebrities, politicians, and rock stars lived.

She could hardly take it all in, but then she realized she had to stop gawking and pay attention to what he was asking her.

"Wine?" he repeated.

"Yes, please."

"White, red, rose, bubbly?"

"Whatever you have open," she murmured. "I'm not particular." And she wasn't. Wine had been a rarity during her college days and she hadn't had the luxury of giving allegiance to any brand, nonetheless color or type. Whatever was the house wine was her wine.

He threw back his head and laughed, delighted at her answer. She admired his long neck, the tendons corded there, and the action of his Adam's apple.

"We only serve fresh wine here, we don't recap the bottles so you might as well choose your favorite." He pointed to a long bar where wine bottles were in x-shaped niches along the back wall. "Reds." Then he pointed down and over, where against the wall, under the counter, was three sets of glassed-in doors. "White, rosé, prosecco and champagne."

Remembering that red wine could be chalky and often gave her bad breath in the morning, and having no experience but a bad one with champagne having given her a debilitating headache, she walked over and opened the first glass door and chose a pinot grigio.

He took the bottle from her and read the label. "An excellent choice." He walked over to the end of the bar and to a tall brass contraption that was attached to the counter. The word *Legacy* was engraved on a long silver lever. Sean used it to uncork the bottle. It took all of two seconds.

"My, that's a handy thing to have. It usually takes me ten minutes of tugging with my cork screw."

He patted the top of the handle. "This was my grandfather's. It was on his bar in his house in Rhode Island. I inherited it. It's part of my legacy, get it?" he said with a grin. "I've moved it four times. Although, I originally bought this house as an investment, I now plan to keep it, at least for a few years. So I think my *Legacy* has found a home for a while."

She accepted the stemmed glass that he'd filled halfway up into the beautiful crystal-cut design of the bowl. It was the largest wine glass she'd ever held. He'd handed it to her by the long thin stem, but she felt safer holding it with her fingers threaded around the bowl. He offered up a toast with a glass he'd filled to the same level for himself. "To misplaced books," he said as he clinked his glass with hers.

She smiled over the rim of her glass then sipped. She gave him a shy smile, "To stupid blunders that hopefully turn out all right." She took another sip. "My, this is good."

He nodded his agreement and took another sip. Then he moved closer to her, took her free hand in his, lifted it, and turned it over. He bent and placed a kiss in the center of her palm. "Tonight will be memorable."

She quirked her lips sideways and made a small chuckling sound that had negative undertones. "Memorable could mean either good or bad."

He tilted his head at her and sipped his wine again. After he swallowed, he asked, "You have doubts?"

She let out a deep sigh. "Of course I have doubts. I lost my book. You happened to be the one who found it. And now I'm pretty sure you think this is something I do all the time, like it's a normal thing for me."

"Normal?" he asked, confused by what she was saying.

"Like I've done this before."

He frowned. "No, I *definitely* do *not* think you've done this before."

Now that irritated. She tilted her head, and bordering on indignant, she bit out, "Hmmm, and just why *not*?"

He looked her up and down and smiled again. "I— just— don't—think so. You don't have that air of experience about you. I could be wrong though. We'll see though, won't we?"

Chapter 44
A Hampton's-styled Beach House in NC

He took her wineglass and walked both his and hers over to the bar where he placed them side by side, next to the bottle he had slipped into a stainless steel sleeve.

Then he walked back to where she stood carefully watching him. He eased off the little jacket that was part of her suit and draped it over the back of one of the barstools, leaving her in her white silk blouse and the short skirt that matched the now discarded navy blue jacket.

He took her hand in his and walked her over to a grouping of wheeled barrel chairs that were set around a low bar table. He pulled out a chair and sat down in it. With his hands on her hips, he pulled her close and stood her in front of him between his splayed knees.

His eyes met hers and didn't waver as he looked up into her face and said, "Okay, my sexy secretary. Let's get you undressed. Untie the knot that's at your neck and unbutton your blouse. I want to see what kind of bra is cupping those lovely breasts of yours."

She gulped noticeably, forcing the lump in her throat to go down . . ."Mmmm."

"Not enough wine yet?" he chided.

She looked back over her shoulder to where her glass sat on the edge of the bar. She was surprised that she had drunk more than half. More than she had intended to.

He snickered. "No? Yes?"

She took a deep breath in. Let a slow shallow breath out. "A few more gulps of wine aren't going to make any difference."

She looked down at the bulge in his pants. As she stared, it grew more prominent. The sight gave her a shot of confidence. Looking at what she had done to him and knowing that he desired her boosted her ego. It made her want to see what else she could do to arouse him even more.

She reached up and began untying the knot she had so carefully fashioned and pinned in place from the underside.

His eyes were focused on her fingers as she removed a small pin from the back of the knot, pinned it to the underside of one of the ties, then watched as she pulled the long ends through her fingers. The bow unraveled.

He noticed her fingers were a little unsteady—not the usual sure and efficient touch she normally had. He'd often watched her with pad and pen, letters and envelopes; she was precise, purpose-minded, to the point of being robotic sometimes.

Now she hesitated, as if unsure what was next. He motioned with his hand. "Now the buttons."

She appeared timid now, not the confident woman he knew her to be. That surprised him. He hadn't expected her to be the brazen type, but this skittish shy colt was confusing . . . and yet endearing—and damn, so cock-warming. Majorly. He felt his penis jump . . . lengthen . . . begin to throb.

She flicked the top button through the buttonhole and met his gaze.

Was that uncertainty? Trepidation? Was she going to change her mind? God, he hoped not.

He tilted his head and simply nodded for her to continue, encouraging her with a lift of his eyebrows and a tiny smirk.

Her hand moved down to the next button and she released it. He heard her draw in a breath as if gathering courage for the next one. It caused him to draw in deeply, too. He could scent her now. She was getting wet. He had always been able to do that. He knew a lot of men who couldn't distinguish such subtle nuances in a woman's fragrance. But there was something about a woman's natural musky bouquet—when it heated and rushed to dampen and invite that beckoned to him and drew him in. Hers, even more so.

She looked at his face, memorizing the look of lust that

was blooming there. Saw him inhale deeply through his nose. Listened as he moaned softly. It did wonders for her ego. She felt her panties dampen.

This time, he moaned as he waved his hand for her to continue.

Her knees were going soft and she felt her insides quiver somewhere under her belly. It seemed her body liked the sound of his approval. Another button was slipped free.

She was brash with this one, flicking it open nonchalantly as if this wasn't affecting her in the least. Oh, but it was.

The long bulge that was straining against his zipper forced him to shift in his seat to accommodate it. His hand tugged on his pants to force the material to allow more space for his cock to grow. There was only one button left. Then she'd have to pull her blouse up from where it was tucked into her skirt. More buttons likely awaited.

She toyed with the small white button, teasing him until he growled, "Beth," in a stern voice. She quickly unhooked the button. The placket gaped now, but was still not revealing much.

"Go on," he stated in a harsh reprimand. When she hesitated again, both of his hands reached out and tugged her closer so his fingers could begin massaging the smooth skin on back of her thighs. His thumbs toyed with the hem of her skirt, brushing it up and smoothing the soft skin on her legs. He was grateful that southern women rarely wore hose, even when wearing heels.

Using both hands now, she tugged her blouse free from the skirt's waistband. One button on the shirt came free of its mooring with the action—only one button was left to free.

His eyes met hers and held. He didn't need to use words to tell her what he wanted. She fingered the very last button, shoved it through the hole and removed her hands from the blouse. The silky shirt fell off her left shoulder revealing her bra strap and the demi-cup straining to keep her left breast covered.

The sight made his cock jump and he felt precum

coat the tip.

She had often wished her breasts weren't so large, but until this moment she hadn't realized how much fuller they could get just by having a man gaze at them. They were plump inside the cups, the lace straining to contain the hardening tips. Her nipples, tight and jutting out against the lacy cups were needy, as if begging to be displayed and allowing this man to see them . . . and touch them.

He leaned forward and tugged lightly on her right sleeve. The blouse slid to the floor. The whisper as it caressed her skirt on the way down was an audible thing. She felt it brush her ankles then flutter to the carpet.

She stood before him in her best demi-bra, its lacy scalloped half circles covering the undersides of her breasts while underwire held them up high. The upper swells were exposed and had a faint blush to them. Her nipples, having become impossibly hard peaks, were poking through the lace.

She could hear Sean's harsh breathing. His breath was a living thing, escalating and relaxing as he shifted in his chair. The way he was drawing each breath fully in, told her he liked her fragrance and was trying to savor it and take it deep inside him.

"Reach behind you and unclasp the hook." His throaty, harsh-sounding whisper was foreign to her. She'd never heard him needy before—never heard him want . . . for anything.

She stood stock-still, her eyes wide as she debated going further. This was it. She'd dreamed of a scenario exactly like this--many, many times. So why was she so scared?

"Do it!" he commanded. His voice was soft in timbre, but gruff with command.

His tone made her jump—it brought her out of her reverie. His words, once issued, brooked no refusal. She reminded herself that this was something she wanted as well. She knew she'd never forgive herself if she opted out now.

Her hand stole behind her back, and in a much-practiced move with thumb and forefinger, she flipped the clasp and released the tension. The lacy cups slid forward. One nipple was bared, then the other. She gasped and let her head fall back as the headiness of the moment overwhelmed her senses.

He made a guttural sound that signaled his approval. She felt wetness slick her panties—a gush of wetness that she would not be surprised to feel running down the inside of her thigh soon. This man did incredible things to her. Every nerve felt alive.

"Roll your right shoulder forward."

She did as he commanded and the bra fell to the floor. She was topless—both breasts on full display—in front of her boss. Her *boss!* The thought sent thrills through her veins and pebbled her skin with goose bumps. She had never been so turned on in her life.

Sean could not take his eyes from her bared chest. The smooth skin of her chest was blooming with a very fine blush. And her breasts, they were amazing. Perfect in every way. They were generously plump, the milky white globes cast with light blue shadows where veins could be seen under the pale skin. Her nipples, a dusky rose color, were darkening with her desire, the tips long and hard . . . as if a man had just pinched them. Dear Lord, she was perfection.

Her breathing grew ragged as she watched him taking her in. Long moments passed as she focused solely on him. Watched him as he stared at her breasts as if studying them . . . memorizing them. She saw his chest heaving and knew hers was doing likewise.

Her knees were getting wobbly from some heightened sensation that was heating her core and tightening her tips. She wondered if that sensation was due to her feeling of shame, or if the feeling of shame was the reason for the heightened sensation. At any rate, her nipples had drawn tight and were hard, and so very needy.

"Touch them."

"Wwhaat?"

"Your breasts. Caress them for me, one hand on each, from the underside. Plump them and hold them up for me."

She moved her hands up from her sides. Drew each palm up to cup a breast. Then she lifted them high on her chest while pushing them together. He groaned and she felt more wetness pool in her panties.

"Use your thumbs and forefingers and pinch those nipples—hard."

She dragged in a deep breath and did as he asked. She moaned, keened really. The sound was not totally foreign to her. She'd done this, alone in a darkened room, many times. But this was in front of a man, and not just any man—this was her boss. Sean. The lights were on full and bright. And he was staring at her as if memorizing the wanton image she made.

"More. Do it more."

She did it more. She pinched, she tugged, and she moaned. She thought her legs would give out. She thought her vagina was leaking and sending rivulets down the inside of her legs.

"Harder," he rasped. She watched as he rubbed his cock through his trousers. Saw the ridge of his penis rise up to meet his hand. And when he removed it, his pants were tented with an impressive erection.

"Pinch and tug on them the way you want me to."

She pinched and tugged harder and had to close her eyes to the sensation. She breathed out a long, "Aaaahhhhh."

"Keep tugging on them. And don't stop until I say so."

She threw her head back, and using her thumbs and forefingers she pulled on her elongated nipples. They were almost painful in their engorged state. But still, it felt exquisite. The added knowledge that he was watching her increased her desire exponentially.

He stood and unzipped his pants. Put his hand inside the opening and released his cock. Her eyes bugged wide when she saw his penis in his hand and him working it. He was more than ample and she was fascinated with what he was doing to the rigid pole he was holding in his hand. He tugged on it, wrapped his hand around it, and then jerked it up and down inside his clenched fist. When he slicked his palm with the moisture oozing from the head and used it to lubricate his hand, she groaned at the sight.

He stood and pulled her skirt up. Then stuck his hand into her panties. Then groaned when he found her slick opening. His longest finger entered her and she almost collapsed from the sensation of him penetrating her. Another finger joined the first. His head dipped and he took a nipple into his mouth. She hadn't realized she had dropped her hands and was now holding her skirt up and her panties down for him.

"Push your panties down to your thighs," he hissed, his lips still against her breast.

Still holding her skirt up with one hand, she used the other one to tug her panties down to the tops of her thighs.

His fingers worked frantically on both his cock and on her. They were both breathing as if they were on the last mile of a marathon. His lips were latched to her left breast and he was sucking on the nipple, his hand jerking his cock and the fingers of his other hand stroking her clit.

She was trying not to topple over from the sensations affecting her legs. Her thighs began to tremble. The tip of his middle finger circled her clit, flicked it on the underside twice and then two of his fingers entered her while his thumb took over stroking her clit at the top of her opening. With each thrust of his fingers, and tap of his thumb against her burgeoning nub, it bloomed more . . . until it burst with her orgasm. Her whole body bucked forward, her vagina clenched around his fingers and the tight walls of her vagina milked his fingers as she keened her release.

He let out a litany of obscenities and came all over her thighs while his fingers were still inside her feeling the aftershocks from her coming.

She felt the heat of his ejaculate as each spurt found its mark on her inner and outer thighs. Where they were connected, his hand still gripping her between her legs, and her hands now resting on his shoulders, they both felt the after tremors shudder and then exit their bodies.

For the better part of a minute they stood there, him holding her up by his hands on her hips, her with a death grip on his bunched up shirt as they caught their breath. Sometime during their passion, his pants had fallen to the floor. She took in his flaccid penis, still impressive in size, his hard thighs and his long legs covered with dark curling hair. His pants were at his ankles.

Her mind not focused on passion matters now, she realized with sudden clarity exactly who this was. She looked up into his face. My God, this was Sean, her *boss*. And he'd had his fingers *inside* her. *Way* up inside her.

She needn't have worried though as he was sporting a huge grin. He watched as all the different reactions ran across her face. The sight of her realizing her predicament and trying to come to terms with it, made him laugh out loud. A second later, he collapsed against the back of the bucket chair, pulling her down on top of him and settling her sideways across his lap.

They were both a sticky mess from their thighs down. Half on and half off his lap, her slick skin had her sliding away. He pulled her higher onto his lap when he felt her slipping down. Within moments, where they were skin-to-skin, or skin-to-hair, they became glued together.

A full minute later, after much heavy breathing, a few more soft curse words emitted from him, and several long deep sighs escaping from between her lips, she turned to look up into his face at the exact same moment he looked down into hers. Their eyes met and held for several beats.

Not knowing what to say or do, but picturing all that had happened and now seeing how they had ended up, she began laughing. And then so did he. He sat more upright, still holding her tight to him to keep her from slipping further down, while she continued to grip his shoulders. Then their eyes met and they simply grinned at each other.

"That was one amazing orgasm," he murmured.

"So that was what that was," she said. "I wondered. So much more than the ones I give myself."

He pulled away to look down at her face, shock registering on his. Then he laughed, a great belly laugh. "Yes. That's exactly what that was. I am shocked that you didn't know for sure."

She shrugged. "What can I say? It was my first that wasn't self-induced. And apparently, I have been doing it aaalllll wrong, aaalllll this time."

"All this time?" Now he was truly shocked. "You've never had an orgasm induced by a man before?"

Chapter 45
She's Really Not All That Sure About This

"Nope. Just the ones I've given myself. And . . .well, they're not like that. They are tiny trills of pleasure and a quick shudder, nothing at all like that one was, which was great huge waves of ecstasy rolling through me accompanied by uncontrollable spasms. It was like being swamped by the ocean over and over again while the whole earth was shaking and everything inside me was convulsing and quivering with total abandon while my brain was flashing *Delight! Happiness! Joy! Glee!*"

He pressed his forehead to hers. "I think that is the best description of an orgasm I've ever heard."

She smiled back at him. Swiped her fingers over his abs and collected the sticky slickness she found there. Then she examined it. "And to think I did all that to you."

"Umm, pardon me. But I think I did that to me."

"It wouldn't have worked without me there. I think you liked the visual."

"Now that is true. You have a very good point. The visual . . . ummm, wow," he said as he managed to stand, adjust his pants and zip them.

"Oh . . . do I go home now?"

"Oh no, you do not. Why would you think that? We've just gotten started. We're going to do a lot more of this," he motioned with his hand between the two of them, down low to indicate his sex organ connecting with hers. "And we're going to keep doing it until we get it right."

"We didn't get it right?" she gave him a soft moue.

He laughed at her chagrin. "Yes. Yes, we did it right. But don't you want to see what happens when I'm inside you when we do it? When I'm putting my cock inside you and fucking you into Monday morning?"

"I admit, I am curious. But I don't see how it can get much better."

Curious? He wondered at her choice of word. What an odd thing to say. He closed his eyes, smiled, put his hand over his heart, and nodded like a knight accepting a quest. "I love a good challenge. I will show you how much better it can get."

Then he opened his eyes and let out a long sigh as he saw her breasts, still flushed and full. He reached out and caressed her left breast. Thumbed the nipple tenderly, as he knew she'd been a bit rough with them due to his demands during those final moments of passion.

"Let's get cleaned up and we'll move on to your next lesson in being a submissive. Or should I say, being *my* submissive. Although, I don't know how much instruction you need. You don't seem to need much tutoring for an ingénue. Am I assuming wrong, that this is new to you?"

"No, no. You're not assuming anything wrong. This is *very* new to me."

He bent, clasped his hands behind her knees, and lifted her into his arms. Her skirt was bunched below her hips. Her panties had long since dropped, ending up over by the chair.

"Wow, nice strength move."

"You're hardly a burden, what do you weight, 115?"

"126."

"I bench press 300, and jerk 230. You are no burden. Not in any way. Off to the shower we go. I want to wash you. Then we're going to talk about why you've never had an orgasm by a man before."

Chapter 46
One Cold Cucumber

He carried her through the house to the first floor master bathroom. Seating her on the edge of the freestanding tub, he picked up a remote from a tiled-in shelf and turned on all the showerheads in the walk-in shower. Then he set the water temperature to 102.

She sat balancing herself on the rim of the tub as she took in the most opulent bathroom she'd ever seen. It was a monster of a bathroom, with three long marble vanities along one side, each with a tall ebony framed mirror over the three Asian bowl sinks. The sculptured marble bowls had lapis lazuli metamorphic rock imbedded in streaks going up the sides.

There were two private water closets; both doors were open now so she could see toilets with matching bidets in each. She saw two multi-tiered heated towel racks just outside the shower enclosure, next to the stand of heat lamps.

There was another vanity table at the ready at the opposite end of the room with a padded azure blue suede boudoir chair tucked under the countertop. It was a palatial room with the most up-to-date conveniences. The showerheads, faucets, drawer pulls, handles, and knobs were ebony. The whole room with tile and all, reminded her of the pictures she'd seen of the water off the Seychelles. Soft whites, light greens, and a hint of light tan, with vivid sapphire blue accents made for a gender-neutral appeal. Who didn't like deep blue paired with white and sea grass greens?

"I love the beautiful tile work, it's like a living sea," she murmured.

He smiled. "The master bathroom was one of the reasons I bought this house—it was functional, beautiful, spacious, and over-the-top gorgeous." He waved the remote at her. "And I love being able to regulate everything."

She laughed. "Don't I know it!"

He looked at her and drank in her soft, gently beauty. Her dark hair complemented her fair skin. And her eyes . . . in this room they looked like the color of blue irises. He saw her shoulders tremble.

"You're shivering. Are you cold?" There was concern spreading across his face as he walked over and switched on the towel warming rack and the heat lamps.

"Nnno. I can't be. It's August," ever the efficient secretary answering practically.

"Maybe the air conditioning is set too low?" he asked.

"I don't know what it's set to," she replied.

He chuckled at the absurdity of her answer and got up to kneel in front of her. He ran his hands up her thighs and down her arms. He used the opportunity to turn her skirt so that he could zip her out of it. He slid the zipper down then began to tug the skirt down her legs. He noticed that her skin wasn't cold—still, she was trembling, but with no goose bumps.

"You know, neither do I. It's set by the housekeeper. Regardless, you're shivering. Are you frightened?"

"Petrified of what might be coming next might be the better word."

He frowned. "Why?"

"I've never done this before."

"We've established that. This is all new to you."

"No, I mean, I have never done *this* before." She gestured with her hand, indicating her nudity. He had just removed her skirt and now both of her hands were clasped and held together in her lap.

"You've never been naked in front of a man?" He couldn't keep the incredulity from his voice.

She picked up on his shocked tone and jerked back, and then shrank into her body, folding her arms in front of her chest to shield her breasts from him. Her crossed arms left the area between her legs vulnerable, so she crossed her legs over each other as well. She shielded as much of her body as possible, trying to hide the fact that she was naked in this very brightly lit bathroom.

His head jerked back. "How is that even possible?"

He got up to get a towel, then came back to kneel beside her. She was rocking back and forth, staring at the ceramic tiles on the floor.

With his hand on her knee to stop her from rocking, he touched the side of her face. "You are so beautiful," he said. "You never need to hide your body from me."

Then, seeing that his words of praise didn't ease her distress one bit, he got up and grabbed his silk dressing gown from the hook on the back of the dressing room door that led to his walk-in closet. He slipped it over her shoulders and wrapped it around her. Then went to turn off the water running from all the different showerheads.

The room, now steamy from the hot water, was definitely not cold. He lifted her, bundled as she was in his robe, and sat with her in his lap on one of the overstuffed dressing chairs at the end of the room opposite the other walk-in closet.

"Sandy, please tell me what's going on. We can't have secrets in this type of relationship. None." His voice was brusque, but not unkind. It was his lawyer voice. It was obvious he was piqued, but his concern for her was apparent in his manner and in the way he stroked the side of her cheek before turning her head so that he could look into her eyes.

They were wide, but there were no tears. She looked skittish, as if she might bolt at any second. He felt that if he had not been encircling her body within his arms, she might have gotten up to leave.

"I thought I was to be Beth . . . from the book."

"I've changed my mind for the moment. To me you've always been Sandy. And I like Sandy better. It's a lovely name . . . makes me think of the beach."

He had gathered her up, robe and all, his hands moving

from being around her hips to holding her under her knees and around her back, with her legs dangling sideways across his. His muscular arms held her body close to his chest. He had removed his shirt when he set the showerheads; her eyes were now focused on his bulging biceps and his well-developed chest. "Tell me what's going on. Why has no man ever seen you naked?"

His fingers ran up and down where the robe had separated and exposed her shin. She visibly swallowed then took a deep breath . . . toyed with the satin sash of the robe—knotting it loosely and then untying it, over and over again.

"Well, we owned a farm out in the boonies and I was homeschooled by my aunt and my mother, and then I went to an all-girls college. I ended up on every committee and got so involved in so many groups that I had no free time. Plus, I had a part-time job helping an invalid get to all her classes and also helping her with her studies and correspondence. On Saturdays, I had to study and do housework, and on Sundays I had to attend church and help with civic projects. I was too busy to date like the other girls who had full-rides. Besides, I was hardly ever in places where I would meet any boys. I didn't have a car. Not even a bike.

"I went on a few dates during the holidays, as I didn't have a way to get home. But I still needed to be the caretaker for my friend in the wheelchair, as she didn't get to go home either. So I always had to get back to the dorm early.

"After a while, it seemed pointless to go out with guys when all they wanted to discuss on the first date, over burgers and fries, was my method of contraception. One guy was so mad that I wasn't on birth control that he just up and left me at the table. I had to pay for both our dinners and then take a bus back to the dorm. He was a guy I met working at the drug store one day when I was picking up my friend's prescriptions. I couldn't stand to go in there anymore. I thought he'd be there and laugh at me.

"During my last year at Cottey, there was this one boy I

liked who lived on a nearby farm. He delivered milk and eggs to the college. His name was Paul. He'd driven us to town in his pick-up truck and his father caught us making out in the back of the movie theater. His Pa took one look at me and said I wasn't breeding stock and he wouldn't let Paul see me again. He made a big scene. Said I was a scrawny heifer with no meat on my bones. I was mortified. I hadn't enjoyed Paul's slobbery kisses, and his hands when he held mine were clammy, so I hadn't really been into it. So that experience kind of killed the idea of dating for me for a while.

"Then an agency I'd applied to called and offered me the job with you the week I graduated, so I got on a train and I've been working for you ever since.

"Now, don't take this the wrong way, but I'm pretty doggone tired by the time I get home most days, so I'm really not up for going out at night. And weekends are the times I get my chores done—shopping, cleaning, laundry . . . cleaning out Goldie's bowl."

"Goldie?"

"My goldfish."

"I see."

He got up, gently dumped her in the seat he had just vacated, and began to pace. He ran his fingers through the front of his hair, leaving it mussed and sticking up in several places. It made him look boyish, when he was anything but. That back, his chest . . . he was no boy. He was the most masculine man she'd ever seen . . . in the flesh. Because yes, she watched movies with Chris Hemsworth, Henry Cavill, Jamie Dornan, Chris Pine, Channing Tatum, and Jason Momoa. Lordy, she'd re-rented *Aquaman* from Redbox so many times she should have just bought it at the onset.

Sean came back and knelt on one knee beside her chair.

She jumped when he placed his hand on the inside of her thigh. "Mmm, sorry," she mumbled. "I didn't mean to jump. I'm a little nervous. You make me nervous. No other man has ever made me so jumpy. I'm usually so . . . well . . . let's see, I've been called: stern, unyielding, prim, a prude, standoffish, unsocial, sanctimonious, and a cocktease."

He smiled. He had often thought her rather prim. Then he looked at her, truly looked at her. He took in every feature of her face. Her perfectly sculptured winged brows, her sooty lashes framing vibrant blue eyes, her pert nose with three tiny freckles on mid-bridge, her bowed lips that were the soft pink color of a conch shell's lining. His own deep green eyes were sincere as he drew in a deep breath.

"So . . . what you're telling me is that you're a virgin?"

He didn't make it sound like a bad thing as so many other men had. He didn't say it with a sneer—just mild skepticism.

"I've used a dildo."

He quirked a brow at her.

"It didn't do anything. I couldn't get it to work for me. I just put it in some."

He smiled and rubbed circles on her knee with his thumb. "Did you turn it on?"

"It wasn't that kind."

"What kind was it?"

"It was a long cucumber, an English one, still in the wrapper. Of course, I washed it first."

He couldn't hold it in, he laughed. After a few seconds he caught himself. "Mmm. Sorry. Just picturing that. No luck though huh?"

"It was cold—very cold. I couldn't get it to warm up. Wetting it with hot water didn't last past getting away from the sink, and the microwave made it soft."

He totally lost it then. He had to duck his head under his arm where he was still holding onto her knees. He tried clamping his lips together then biting his tongue. It was no use. He knew she could see his shoulders shaking from laughter.

He stood and walked a few feet away. He was a proper business man, still in half of his weekday attire—creased slacks, leather belt, socks, dress shoes . . . pacing in front of a semi-naked woman who was wearing his bathrobe while sitting in a boudoir chair in his bathroom. The woman was making him laugh. She was a gem, and he knew it. What was wrong with the men who had dated her? How could they not see beyond their own needs?

How was he going to get her to relax? He had to put her at ease if he wanted to be the one to unburden her of her maidenhead. If indeed, she still had one . . . due to the English cucumber, which he knew could be quite long, although usually they were on the thin side. Knowing her choice of reading material, he knew she must be more than ready to be relieved of her virginity so she could for once, finally experience carnal pleasure.

When he felt he had his composure back from imagining her propped up in bed with a long green vegetable in her hand, he turned to face her again.

"You're not joking about any of this, right? You are really and truly a virgin, although maybe not technically due to the . . ." he couldn't even say the word, so he just waved his hand and rolled it forward a few times and then used both hands cupped as if typing from the center of keyboard then drawing them out to the sides and back, to mimic something elongated.

"I am not joking." She did not have even the hint of a smile. If anything she seemed offended. And then he realized that she'd probably had this type of conversation a few other times when things hadn't gone well afterward.

"You're what 27?"

"28. I had to do farm work for six months to earn travel and spending money before going to Cottey College."

He put his tongue behind his front teeth, quirked his lips, and made a slight sucking sound as he paced and thought things through.

She had seen him do this at work when he was pondering something. He usually wasn't in a great mood while working on a problem and she knew it annoyed him to have anyone present while he was working out a problem out in in his head. A woman who was shivering in his silk robe, sitting on his tufted satin bathroom chair, who had just professed to having an intact hymen, was probably not a problem he had to encounter often.

After several passes, he stopped. Then he left the room and came back with a chenille sofa throw. He took her by the elbows, stood her up, and removed the robe she was wearing. Then he wrapped the throw around her shoulders and tucked the ends into the crevices of the chair.

Was his aim to secure her to the chair or swaddle her? Or just get her out of his favorite over-the-top silk bathrobe? The soft plush throw had the feel of cashmere, yet there was weight to it. The fabric felt heavenly against her skin. She felt infinitely better covered up and was now actually getting warm. And being bound so securely to the chair comforted her somehow.

She hadn't realized that the silk of his robe actually had more of a cooling effect, than a warming one, until she felt the difference. The fabrics, their weight and texture, made a huge difference.

He must have realized that it would be hard to have the upcoming conversation with her naked, in his robe, shivering, with him still dressed for the boardroom. Well except for those muscled arms and that magnificent chest.

He went back to the bar and grabbed two bottles of water from the mini-fridge, downed the rest of his wine from the glass he'd left on the bar, thought better of it, and took her glass to her as well.

"Thank you," she said when she saw him offering her the wineglass. Her arms were bound by the throw, but she managed to wiggle a hand out so she could clasp the bowl in her fingers. She downed the wine in two healthy sips.

She watched him as he spun her chair so that she sat across from him as he now sat propped on the lip of the tub. He separated his knees and steepled his fingers under his chin, resting them on his thighs. She'd seen him in that pose at work also, and knew better than to disturb whatever thought process was running like a ticker tape through his head.

Finally, he said. "I'd like to start over."

"How far back?" she asked. She was wondering if she needed to go back to the time she got off the train in Grand Central Station to look for another job instead of taking this one.

"To when you arrived here this evening."

"Okay."

"Knowledge is a great thing."

"I agree."

"Knowing you're a virgin changes everything."

"Does it have to?"

He stood up abruptly and began pacing again, "Yes, yes it does. We can't approach this the same way I had planned."

"We can't?"

"No. We can't."

"Enlighten me. I'm the one sitting here semi-naked with an empty wine glass, heady with arousal after having been diddled by my boss."

He turned to face her. He'd been pacing away, now he turned back. He was a good ten feet away, but her words had arrested him in place. His wide grin was infectious, so she flashed him hers, too.

"You liked me *diddling* you?"

"I loved you *diddling* me."

"Good to know. But now I know that I shouldn't have started with that. Exactly what have you done before? Have you done a lot of kissing? Petting? That sort of thing?"

She slowly shook her head no, then added, "No, not really. The kissing I've had hasn't really been all that great."

"Hang on. I'll be right back."

She watched him leave the room, heard him walking briskly through the tiled foyer and then running up the stairs. Moments later she heard him running back down, entering the bar area again, then coming back into the bedroom and through to the bathroom.

He had a plush bathrobe in his hand. It was a deep sable brown. A velvet so thick and sumptuous the dark hollows of the folds looked like ermine. It was the most elegant men's dressing gown she had ever seen. There was a regal quality to it. She knew that it had to have come from Dior, Armani, Marc Jacobs, or Ralph Lauren. She'd shopped for him for two years, but she hadn't bought this. It had to have been a gift. And from what she knew of the stores he and his family favored, this robe would have cost her at least two week's salary.

"Here, stand up," he said as he came closer. When he was standing beside where she was sitting, he reached out and helped her to her feet.

Before she knew what was happening, he had stripped off the throw. She had a moment to realize that she was naked in front of him again, before he enveloped her within the folds of the robe. "Mmmm, this is as soft and as cuddly as a cloud," she moaned.

"Mom got it for me for Christmas last year. Honestly, I hardly ever wear it. It makes me too hot. I start sweating moments after I put it on..."

The thought that he had sweat in this robe should have disgusted her, but for some reason that she wasn't going to question right now, it had the opposite effect on her. She drew the luxurious folds of the lapels close together and hugged her elbows. "This is the softest thing I've ever worn. I feel like a royal princess. It's so nice and warm."

"Well, enjoy. We need to talk and I can't do it with you naked and huddling in that sofa throw."

"If we're just going to talk, may I have some more wine?"

"Of course."

Ever the gentleman, he returned to the bar area to get the bottle, then came back and refilled her glass. She'd seen him serve many clients from his office, often even bowing to the

Japanese businessmen when he handed over their tea, but she had never had him serve her. It was odd; it should have been the other way around. But he did not seem to notice the juxtaposition of duties as he handed over a glass of the chilled white wine in the fragile-looking cut glass crystal.

He took her by the other hand and led her out of the bathroom and to a sitting room off the master bedroom. He used a remote to dim the lighting and ushered her over to a large curved sectional with a gorgeous polished burled wood coffee table in front of it.

"Let's sit in here and talk for a few minutes. See if we can get this train back on track."

He helped her get situated, covering her feet with the robe when she opted to curl up into the corner with her feet tucked under her.

He took a sip of his water, placed the bottle on the table and faced her. "Virgins are rare these days. I am pretty sure I've never had one. In theory, I know what to do, but in practice I do not. But I guess the first thing we should discuss is are you sure you want to give your virginity to me, whether there is a physical barrier or not?"

"Yes. There really are no other candidates. And I don't hold it sacred, it's just never happened due to weird circumstances."

"You don't have needs? You don't feel sexual arousal?"

"Oh yes! I do! Sometimes I get so horny I feel like climbing the walls. I get itchy and bitchy and sometimes I just want to go to a bar and drag the first man I come across home with me."

"So, why haven't you?"

He was sitting forward again, his knees spread with his hands knitted in front of him. A very familiar pose in her mind, but usually, she wasn't the problem he was working on.

"Because I work for you."

"What does that mean exactly? Surely you don't think I

would hold you to a higher standard than any of the other women who work for me. Look at Janey, she has a new boyfriend every week."

"It is because I work for you that I can't settle for less. You are, well, sexy . . . commanding, extremely attractive, and I think over the years that I have developed a bit of a crush on you."

He turned to look at her, cocked his head and then smiled. "You think I'm sexy, huh?"

She smiled back. "You are that. But you already know it. *Many* women have told you that. I've heard some of them even call you that. "Heeeey Seeexxxxy," she mimicked one of his past girlfriends and the way she always came into his office tapping along on spiked stilettos.

He laughed. "Heeeey, you mean Jaaaanice. She reaaallly was all about superlatives, wasn't she?"

Sandy laughed. "Yeah, everything had to be over the top for her. I never knew what you saw in her. She seemed so flighty."

"Yeah, but she liked to ski and scuba dive. She was fun at a party. And she gave great head."

"But just another girlfriend to you."

"Yeah. I guess you've seen most of them."

"42."

"Wow, you know the exact number?"

"Umhmm. Their birthdays, favorite flowers, restaurants, bars."

"You make me sound awful."

"No, not awful. Just not committed. To be honest, I think there was only one I could see you with."

"Oh yeah, which one was that?"

"Whitney."

He laughed. "Yeah, we didn't see that coming did we?"

Sandy laughed too. "Nope." She jabbed her foot into his side, "It's gotta do something to your ego when your girlfriend tosses you over for a girl she met at your cousin's wedding. Did *anyone* see that coming?"

"Nope." He took another sip of his water.

"Had she been good in bed?"

"Yeah. Nothing spectacular. But now that you mention it, she was always kind of holding back. The only orgasms she had with me were from my hands."

"Oooh. Those magic fingers."

He took one of his hands away from his water bottle, stared at it as he moved it front to back, and then waggled his fingers at her. "Maybe you should try them out again." It wasn't a question.

"Maybe. So . . . where do we go with this? Are you going to shy away from me because I'm inexperienced?"

He put his bottle on the table and turned his body so that he faced her fully. His eyes met hers. He studied her face to assess if she might be lying to him.

Instead, she looked vulnerable under his scrutiny. He was fairly certain she was telling him the truth. He'd never had reason to doubt her before . . . why start now?

"Nope. I'm going to teach you. I'm going to give you the experience you lack. We'll start with what you missed out on in middle school, work our way through high school, then college. By the time I get you to your career days, I might just be able to ease you into being my submissive."

She felt a thrill go through her and she shivered. "I think I like the sound of that. That was a good shiver, by the way—a really good shiver. The excited kind, not because I'm cold."

She took a big gulp of her wine and stood. He had caught her off guard. Until a few minutes ago, she thought he might just send her home. But no, they were going to do this after all. All the things she had read about in so many books. The spankings, tying up, displaying, . . . maybe sharing. She was suddenly unsure of herself. Could she really go through with this?

Under his fierce, intensive observation, she was feeling rather awkward. Knowing that he had sharp observation skills, she tried to mask her anxiety. She had worried that he might not want to do this with her after knowing about her past.

Now that she knew he was still committed to making her his sub, she was apprehensive—yet oddly excited. Could she be a wicked vamp with no scruples somewhere down the line? Be arm candy for him with his mates watching? She acknowledged that she had a long way to go before becoming Beth of the book.

Baby steps she reminded herself. Her becoming a genuine submissive to Sean as her master and dominant would take some time to accomplish. She promised herself that she'd have a good attitude and let Sean led the way.

She strolled slowly around the room, the long hem of his robe trailing behind her on the gorgeous striated rug. "So, how do we do this? *Are* we going to do this? Are there rules to go by?"

He stood and invaded her space. She took a step back to avoid his nearness. He advanced again and stepped right in front of her. This time she found herself backed up against a tall wing-backed chair. He tipped her head back to force her to look up at him. He wanted her to see the expression in his eyes.

He looked stern. Was he mad at her?

Then he let his lips form into a tiny smile. "Oh, we're *definitely* going to do this." He took her hand and led it to his crotch.

Oh my God, he was aroused—majorly.

"First rule: No one touches your sexy bits except me. No one. Not even yourself. And no more cucumbers. Do you understand?"

"Yes, sir."

"Second: You stay here every weekend until we get this worked out. We should know within a month how we're getting along and if we can fulfill each other's needs. Make this work somehow. During the week, we are business as usual."

"Gotcha."

"Third: "This is just between us. No one knows our

business. No one. Any questions?"

"Will you be exclusive as well?"

"Yes."

He smiled over at her. "I think I will have my hands full with just you. For me to even think of another woman after seeing those magnificent tits of yours would be a sacrilege."

She flushed from the praise.

"So, when do these lessons begin?"

"Now. Tonight. I would like you to go back to the bathroom we were in, and for you to take a nice hot shower. Afterward, put on your bra, blouse, skirt, and heels—and your panties. After I find where we left them. I'll meet you in the bar after I have showered in one of the other bathrooms and we'll have our first date."

"Where are we going?"

"To the movies."

"We're going out in public?"

"No. I have a theater here."

She laughed. "Of course you do."

"I think my panties, when you find them, are going to be quite damp." She flashed him a pouty moue.

He laughed at her chagrinned face. "Don't worry. It won't be long before I'll be taking them off. And they're sure to be even wetter."

She smiled. It was a sexy, satisfied smile.

He laughed. "Now say, *Yes Sir*, and go take a shower. You'll find everything you need either in the shower or under one of the vanities. 102 on the remote for the temperature should be ideal for cleansing you and pinking your skin for me."

He lifted his chin toward her and waited expectantly.

She blinked and said, "Yes, sir."

Then she turned and went to go take a hot shower and to get re-dressed for her master.

Chapter 47
Giving Over to Passion or Sating Curiosity?

While in the shower, she was tempted to touch herself, especially her nipples, as they were begging for more mistreatment. But she remembered Sean's words and figured that if she wasn't supposed to touch her pussy, she probably wasn't supposed to touch her tits either. What were "sexy bits" anyway?

When she was ready, she walked into the bar area and found him waiting for her. His hair was damp and lying curled on his collar. He looked exactly as he did each morning at work—pressed white shirt, suit and tie—except for his shoes. Instead of his typical laced up Oxfords, he wore polished cordovan loafers. So this was what he wore to the movies? For her, it had always been holey jeans and a baggy sweatshirt, no-brand tennis shoes with chicken feed stuck in the treads and mismatched laces.

He crooked his elbow as if to escort her away. "Ready?"

"Yup," she threaded her arm through his. "As I'll ever be. Squeaky clean except for my thoughts."

He gave her huge grin. "Then follow me. I've got just the movie to dirty you up again."

He led her to an open elevator. They stepped inside and he pushed the button for the lower level. Once there, he indicated for her to precede him out of the elevator and then down a carpeted hall. It was dim, but recessed lighting along the baseboards led the way.

"Since we're going back in time so you can catch up, I thought for our first date should be a movie date to erase the memory of that first one. We're going to banish that movie date with Paul from your mind forever. And since I happen to have a movie theater right here, I thought why not?"

He held one of the double doors open for her and she

walked inside. In the semi-darkness she could see that it was actually a real theater. With four rows of tiered seats, five in each row, it could accommodate a decent crowd. The seats were the rocker-recliner style with padded armrests inset with cup holders. The supple burgundy leather matched the velvety low-nap carpet that was embossed with gold fleur-de-lis every few feet. It was old timey corny, and yet elegant at the same time.

A large screen was in the front, dominating the small stage. Behind them, in a dark alcove there was a refreshment area with a glassed-in mini-bar, a gypsy-styled popcorn wagon, and a revolving carousel with vintage candy bars displayed. Everything lit with low lighting when Sean pressed a switch on the wall.

"I use it mostly for football games and World Series and March Madness play-off games. There is an extensive list of movies to choose from, but while you were getting ready, I selected one I think you'll like and appropriate to the occasion. So pick your seat and tell me what you want from the concession stand and I'll get it for you."

"Mmm, popcorn, light butter, and a Diet Pepsi?"

"Of course. Make yourself comfortable. Up front or in the back, wherever you like."

The lights were already down low, but her eyes had become adjusted to the dim lighting. She picked a seat in the middle of the second row while he popped fresh popcorn and poured their drinks. It *was* just like going to the movies, she thought. Even the waxy paper cups had straws and lids. The hot popcorn smelled heavenly and was in red and white striped bags.

They sat close together with the armrests between them pushed up, their drinks in the armrests on either side of them. Sean pushed some buttons on the little remote he took from his shirt pocket and within seconds they were watching the screen light up with the beginning credits. She marveled that the popcorn tasted liked authentic theater popcorn. So did the soda, having come from a tap just as his beer had, so it was nice and fizzy.

When the title for the movie flashed on the screen she laughed out loud. *Secretary* with Maggie Gyllenhaal and James Spader.

"I don't expect we'll watch the whole movie as it's late, but maybe you'll get an idea of the submissive life from both perspectives."

He didn't add that he would too, as he'd never watched it before. But Rutger had recommended it in a text after their phone call, so he'd downloaded it to the theater system.

The movie began and then twenty minutes in, much like an adolescent boy introducing his girlfriend to the idea of making out under the cloak of darkness that the theater provided, Sean began a slow and patient seduction. On his agenda for the night was kissing, necking, and heavy petting—which they had called running the bases when he was a teenager.

He began by wrapping his arm around her shoulders. Rubbing the area where her neck met her shoulder and then moving his way lower, toward her chest. When the screen went dark for a scene, he turned her face to his and kissed along the seam of her lips, meshing his lips with hers before parting them and slipping his tongue inside. He let his tongue wander, tangling it with hers before delving deeper and learning her soft palate and smooth inner cheeks. It was magical how their kisses led to more of the same . . . with an element of greed and doubling down on the pace added in.

Soon, their dueling tongues were learning all there was to know about each other's mouths. His tongue swept along her inner lips, lashed out at her teeth, delved behind them, all the while melding his breath with hers and discovering her unique taste. Tonight it was sweet and salty from the popcorn. He wanted to kiss her like this all night.

But the scene changed and with the sound of a boisterous slap their faces were both jerked back to the screen. After a few minutes, they both looked at each other and the kissing began again where they had left off.

While they listened to the dialogue and were aware of the changing scenes from the flashing of more or less light, he fed on the salty taste and the slickness from the butter coating her tongue. He encouraged her to take his tongue into her mouth so she could learn about him. He loved her tentative forays . . . and reveled in it when she went frantic to get more of his taste on her tongue.

She adored the yeasty malt taste from his beer. Combined with the chocolate and peanuts from his Snicker's bar, it was a vinegary-savory combination that she loved.

She became woozy from the heady onslaught of his mouth on hers. It was his turn to learn beyond her teeth to her inner cheeks and soft palate and he was ravenous. When they separated, both were panting. Their eyes met in the semi-darkness and he smiled down at her, liking everything he saw in her glassy eyes.

"I love the taste of you," he whispered. He bent his head and kissed alongside her jaw, sucked lightly on her neck, and huffed warm air into the whorls of her ear.

In the background they could hear the dialogue of the main characters as they bantered back and forth. He stopped kissing her for the first spanking scene, and they both watched with rapt attention. After the scene, he resumed his foray along her neck and ear.

As he licked and kissed, and breathed out with raspy warm huffs, the fingers of one hand dug into her hair, messing up her tidy chignon and sending her long hair cascading down. He caressed the rims of both ears with his fingertips, while his tongue sucked on the lobe closest to him.

His goal was to drive her crazy with passionate attention while she heard the heroine being chastised, reprimanded and punished. From the sounds she was making into his mouth and along his lips, he was successful.

He let up for the scenes where the boss was reprimanding

and castigating his inefficient secretary. He let her watch the scenes as the secretary paid the price for her incompetence with her boss's hand on her bottom.

Then his lips moved back to savor hers and to stoke her up again. His tongue dueled with hers, and he loved the way they were able to tease each other tirelessly. He knew he was going to enjoy her using her lips and tongue on his cock. And he couldn't wait until he had the chance to use his lips and tongue on her. He could picture it in his mind, and it made him incredibly hard.

Each time he broke away to refocus their attention on the screen and to the secretary's penalties for her disobedience; he took liberties undoing her clothing.

So engrossed in the action, she didn't notice that he had slipped three buttons lose at the bottom of her blouse. But she felt it when his hand slipped inside and begin caressing her breasts over her bra. She groaned at his touch, and audibly begged him for more of the same, whimpering, "Pinch them please, Sir."

Could his cock get any harder? He used his fingertips to pluck at her nipples through the soft fabric. Her low moans and long drawn out sighs urged him on—soon, he had to feel her sex, had to know how wet she was getting for him.

His fingers stole down, stealthily lifting the hem of her skirt and gently pushing it up to bunch in her lap. His hand slid up past her knee as he pushed her thighs apart.

His fingertips moved higher, stroking, teasing, conquering more territory with each upward movement until his fingertips were under the leg opening of her panties and stroking along her slit.

She gasped and wantonly opened her legs wider to accommodate his probing fingers. His circling thumb earned him cries of, "Oh, oh, ooooh . . . don't stop, don't stop." Her soft moans and harsh gasps were tinder to his already burgeoning passion.

Heat coursed through him and everything lit up inside his groin. He was hard, depraved with desire to the point of being malevolent with his need to rub up against something. His need to enter a tight channel that would clamp him and squeeze him—milk him . . . and satisfy this need to rut was making him single-minded with lust.

The sounds and sights on the screen didn't help matters as things were heating up for Edward who was spanking Lee, and he wasn't letting up. He was brutally smacking his secretary's ass, over and over again. No, the visual, when he managed to glance at the scene, didn't help matters . . . not at all.

Sean couldn't stop himself. He was way ahead of his planned agenda, but he didn't care. He jerked Sandy's panties down and slid them off her legs, dropping them to carpet. With two fingers, he entered her. Then went back to kissing her delectable mouth.

As he thrust his fingers up inside her over and over again, with his other hand, he worked on lowering his zipper. Each time she came up off her seat and met his hand, the action had him coming up off his seat to thrust into his fist. His palm slapping against her sex brought more sensation to her clit, but it was obvious she was trying to get even more contact. He added another finger, driving her delirious with want as he changed the angle where they connected. He shoved deep, used his thumb to flick against her clit. She rode his hand, coming up off the seat and jerking her body in rhythmic thrusts against his hand, almost standing as she begged for more.

All the while he was kissing her, and nipping her on the inside of her lip when she got too frenzied. She was trying to rush him to her orgasm. Bit he wasn't having any of that. He wanted her needy for him—so very needy.

She cried out once in frustration, and he tasted the acrid taint of blood on his tongue. He was upset in that moment that he had caused her real pain. He soothed and circled the tiny cut under the rim of her lip with his tongue, then sucked on it, once more drawing her lip out, and letting her know he'd do it again if she tried to take away his control.

He went back to kissing and dueling with her tongue in fierce stabs so she'd know his authority in this. He was determined to show her that he was boss of her, and her passions. She would come when he let her come, not a second sooner.

He swallowed her cries of frustration. She was being indoctrinated to his supremacy. She hated it. And he loved it. She would have to learn that he could manhandle her in any way that he desired, and that he could abuse her for his pleasure, while holding hers back until he was ready to let her come. She would have to learn to surrender her body to his. And learn, that for her act of total submission, he would reward her generously.

His fingers stopped working inside her and he slowly withdrew his hand from between her thighs. She keened her outrage at his denial. Then purred when he knelt in front of her and used his fingers to separate her lips to take in the sight of her slick arousal, and to examine her as thoroughly as possible with the light available.

She had surrendered her forthcoming orgasm to him by going still and by opening her legs while lifting her hips off the seat for his full view of her drenched sex. She was now offering herself to him—completely. And he could not have been more pleased.

His fingers pressed against her lips to open her even more. He leaned in and licked her clit, flicked it back and forth. Then wrapped his tongue over and around it. As his thumb languidly entered and withdrew from her vagina, his tongue lapped at her clit. He slid his tongue along her seam and jabbed it into the hot beckoning tunnel he so wanted to fuck right now. He kept his tongue coated with her slickness before going back to circle the tangle of nerves at the top and gently leaning in to suck on it.

She hooked her leg over the opposite armrest to make herself even more available to him. He pulled back several times just to look at her, to take her in at her most vulnerable while she was deep into her passion and offering herself to him. He could have her now. Any way he wanted her. He knew this to his core.

He hesitated long enough for her to know that he was looking at her. Examining her in the light, meager as it was, yet still able to see her glistening for him. As the light changed on the screen, and there was more of it, he could see that her lips were pink and that her tight little opening at the bottom was now gaping and beckoning him in with small, gentle, pulsing actions. If she could have sucked either his tongue or his penis inside, he knew she would have gripped it for all it was worth and wrangled her orgasm from it.

He had never wanted a woman more. He wanted to reward her, and himself. But he wasn't ready to fuck her yet. Although he wanted more than anything to ram his cock inside her and plow her until she screamed her pleasure to the rafters, he knew it wasn't time for that yet.

For his purposes, he knew she needed to be eased into the submissive lifestyle. She needed to be trained properly— needed to learn to hold back her climax until he granted it.

Plus, he wanted her first time to be when he was inside her and she was tied to his bed, totally at his mercy. Right now, he would kiss her senseless between her legs. He would claim her pussy with his mouth. He would drive her senseless.

Before he could dive in, her hand fell to his crotch. He swatted it away, but she fought to keep her fingers on him. He had managed to lower his zipper before, and the extra space had allowed his cock the freedom to grow and throb outside his pants while he toyed with her.

Now, she found him hard and pulsing. She gripped the heavy shaft that was no longer encased within the confines of his zipper. She had begun stroking him through the material of his pants with her open palm, pressing and learning the length of him, and gripping him with her fingers while he had been working on her. Now, now she was flesh to flesh with his cock in her hand and she was impressed with both the length and the girth. She didn't know that a man's part got this big.

She grabbed him firmly, trying to fist her hand around his

hard, needy shaft. When she had established a grip, she moved her hand up and down the length. He groaned and allowed her to play for a moment before reaching down and taking his cock out of her hand and denying her permission to touch him.

But then she pleaded, "Please Sir, may I touch it? Kiss and lick it? I have always wanted to suck on your cock." She said it in such a needy tiny voice that it slayed him.

"Yes, yes you may," he whispered and led her fingers not to his cock, but down to his balls. "Be gentle here. My sac likes to be stroked and licked. My cock enjoys a firmer touch and likes to be jerked and sucked."

Touch him she did, first with gentle, exploring caresses, then with that firm grip that he loved so much. As she learned his length and the smooth texture of the skin that was stretched tight, as well as the wrinkled skin that encased his testicles, she marveled that he kept all this hidden in his pants. She had no idea how a man walked with all this going on between his legs.

She could feel the heat coming off of his very needy cock. It was jumping and nudging her to get her attention as she caressed and stroked his balls. In the meager light she could see moisture beading on the tip, coming from a tiny slit. Rubbing along the crest with her thumb, she gathered and spread the moisture she found oozing from the engorged head. He was so hard, the skin stretched tight and was jumping against her hand. She loved each sound of appreciation he made. His words of encouragement allowed her to fondle and caress him everywhere along his length. She wanted so much to lead him to her opening, to feel this massive harness probing her, entering her. . . fucking her senseless.

This was her first time touching a man like this. She should have been more tentative, she should have been timid and awkward at this, but his sounds of pleasure and his own unassailable and masterful treatment of her overtook her reticent nature and made her bold. There was power in making a man so out of his head with pleasure, and she relished it. But then his fingers got busy on her again.

As she brought him close to the edge, he brought her closer to her own gratification. Her ass was on the edge of her seat, her body angled up as her legs were splayed over the opposite seats. He had a supreme view, and access to every part of her. He was leaning against the seat in front of hers, his fully engorged cock in her hand as she gripped him, learned his impressive girth, stretched him tall, rewet the tip with moisture from the crown and then added her own saliva brought with her fingers from her mouth. She was jerking his length mercilessly. The sight was incredible.

Facing each other, her legs were spread with one of his hands between them holding her open as he toyed with her with the other. It would have taken very little for him to position himself and plunge into her. But the little bit of sanity he held onto would not allow that. The image of her tied to his bed and him gripping her wrists as he fucked her was inviolable. The first time he entered her, he would have her in his bed, helpless to stop him.

He bent and leaned in to service her with his tongue while she continued to jerk him off.

The theater was filled with sounds of their raspy breathing and the wet slicing and sucking sounds coming from his licking, kissing, and sucking on her—and from Edward and Lee groaning from whatever they were now doing to each other on screen.

Their own sounds were interspersed with her cries of "Yes!" His flagrant use of crazy mixed-up curse words, a habit developed from masturbating with his head buried into a pillow as a teen, now spewed from his lips as what she was doing drovehim insane.

The movie droned on, the sound lost in the background as lights flickered from the screen all around them. It was heady to be able to catch glimpses of what they were doing to each other as the lights from the screen highlighted their sex play. She could look down and see him devouring her pussy.

He could look up and see her head thrown back, face flushed with pleasure from his attentions. Her hand was still gripping him and working him. She was beautiful in her passion. And he was delighted with her diligence, as she seemed obsessed with learning all there was to know about his penis and its preferences.

Several times she licked along her palm and used the slick moisture to coat him. Satisfied when it helped her slide him through her fist faster, she wet him more and pumped him harder.

Sean used her own slickness to bathe her clit each time he ran his tongue along the length of her slit. Gathering her wetness from her tiny hole he drew it up and circled and teased her clit, feeling her tiny nub swell to three times its size under the finger that was lightly tapping on it. They both kept up the blissful torture until she cried out and he saw her thigh muscles tighten. Her clit began a series of rhythmic spasms against his tongue and he gently drew it between his lips to lightly suck. Her legs convulsed and her vagina slickened with even more dew as she came. By then his fingers were inside her and he felt the delightful pulsing and throbbing as her vagina clenched around them. It was a lovely reward for his efforts, feeling her body give into the pleasure he had orchestrated in such a magnificent way.

When she was fully into her after-bliss, he gently cupped her pussy possessively—felt her wetting his palm as her last spasms played out. He looked into her face, saw her eyes drift closed as her head fell back against the seat. She was lovely. Her hand was gripping his penis a bit too tightly and he had to gently pry her fingers away.

When she opened her dazed eyes and smiled up at him, he was awash with a sense of pride. She looked at him as if he'd just given her the moon and the stars. And in a way, he knew that he had.

"You now," she whispered. "Can I taste you? I've seen how it's done in movies, can I suck you off?"

"No better words have ever been spoken," he said with a

grin. "I would love to watch you do that."

She squirmed off the seat, righted her skirt, and knelt before him. She looked up at him with her soft, doleful eyes. "Any special instructions?" she asked. He could see that she was nervous, and it was endearing.

He smiled his encouragement, and then barked, "Only one. Don't bite."

She flashed him a shy smile. "I read you're supposed to wrap your lips over your teeth. I practiced with a zucchini."

He laughed. "Well let's see how good you are at zucchini sucking, my sweet little ingénue, my delectable little secretary."

She smiled a little bashfully at his praise, and then slowly bent forward. She wrapped her fingers around the base and began by kissing the head, and then she licked all around the head, finally taking the whole corona into her mouth. The sight alone was enough to get him all the way hard again and throbbing for more. She did not disappoint. Her lessons with a zucchini were paying off for him in a big way. He placed his hand lightly on her head to encourage her and to show his approval of the job she was doing—a very fine job indeed.

He watched as she took her time, stopped to lick and blow, suck and kiss. When she took him deep and began to make long draws up and slow draws back, he took her other hand and led it to his balls. She tilted her head and her eyes narrowed in question.

"Caress them, *lightly*. They are very sensitive right now. You can even lick them if you want, and gently suck on them, but what you're doing right now with my dick in your mouth is marvelous, don't stop doing that."

She fondled his balls, marveling to herself over the texture, the shape, the way they had gone from soft skinned pouches to firm tight knots. And all the while she sucked, licked, and made sure to keep her lips over her teeth, while he lightly guided her head with his hand.

Then suddenly, on a downslide where she had almost all of him in her mouth, he held her tight to his groin—really, her nose was buried in his pubes—with what seemed like all of him inside her mouth. She tried not to gag, tried to mimic swallowing him as his ejaculate hit the back of her throat. She'd read she was supposed to try to keep the tip in place at the back of her throat, but she just couldn't do it. She needed to breathe. She fought against the hand holding her head in place and he quickly lifted his hand away. She came up off of him and managed to draw in a deep breath and then had a coughing spasm.

"I'm sorry. I'm sorry, I'm sorry. I'll do better next time."

"Shhh, shh," he murmured. "It's okay. You did great for your first time."

"But you didn't come," she wailed.

"There are other ways to accomplish that. I am close, very close. Let me show you what the sight of your tits does to me."

He tore her shirt open and jerked down her bra so that both breasts were bared over the cincher. He grabbed his cock and pumped it several times. Then he closed his eyes and let out a long groan as he came all over her chest. The sounds he made were guttural and plaintive—almost as if he was in pain. And then he cursed. Using vile language that made absolutely no sense. Words she had heard separately but had never heard anyone string together in such expressive phrases. For a moment she thought he was mad at her.

After the last spurt landed on one of her nipples, with even more coating his hand, he reached out and smeared his ejaculate on her chest, taking great care to spread it over both her breasts, and painting the nipples with his thumb.

When he was satisfied with his artwork, he bent, took her chin in his sticky fingers, lifted it, and kissed her softly on the lips. It was like a sweet benediction. "Thank you," he whispered.

She basked in his approval. Then watched as he stood and walked out of the room.

Had he just left? She was confused. Was their time over? Was he done with her now?

Chapter 48
Time to Hydrate, Rest, and Replenish

Alone in the theater, she looked down at her chest. Pasty, sticky whitish-gray goo was all over her breasts. Her bra straps were hanging from her crooked elbows. The chest strap was twisted facing out, the empty cups hanging down above her waist.

In her mind, this was not a sexy look at all. She used the seat to ease the weight off her knees as she slowly got to her feet. Her legs felt a little wobbly. She wasn't used to being on her knees for that length of time.

She reached back and unclasped the back strap, letting the bra fall to the floor. She was looking for a button to use to fasten her blouse together so she could go find a shower when Sean reappeared. He had a wet washcloth, a thick fluffy towel, and a cold bottle of water.

With his large hand encased in the warm washcloth, he knelt and began washing her chest with long, thorough swipes. She couldn't help the slight tremble to her voice or the hurt she was feeling as she whispered, "You left me here alone, without a word. I thought we were . . . done."

"You destroyed my brain with that orgasm. I could not have put two words together after what you did to me. But I had to get some things together to take care of you." He smiled over at her. "I don't think we're ever going to be done."

It was then that he registered the sadness in her eyes and it unnerved him. "I was coming *back*. You should know that I will always take care of you. You are my sub. My possession. I take care of what is mine. I will see to your every need when you're with me. You should never worry about that."

He finished up and stood. Wrapped his hand around the side of her neck and jaw, thumbed her lips, then bent and kissed them softly as he whispered, "You are mine. And I take care of what is mine."

"Oh," she said in a low contrite voice. It made her feel better to know he hadn't left due to any fault on her part. And she was more than pleased to know that she had passed whatever test he had divined, and by doing so, had won the right to be his submissive. Submissive-in-training of course, because she still didn't know what this was all about, aside from what she'd read in books. She just knew that she wanted to be with him. And she wanted him to keep kissing her and touching her the way he had. And now, more than ever, she wanted him to be the first man inside her.

After he was done cleaning her up, still admiring her, and not at all interested in re-buttoning her blouse with the two buttons left intact, he held up the bottle of water.

"Now, you will drink this water. All of it." He unscrewed the cap and handed her the bottle.

He watched as she took it and tipped it to her lips.

"Good sex can be very dehydrating."

"So, we had good sex?" she asked. "I don't know enough to rate it as a joint experience. I only know that I had an amazing movie date with you."

He laughed. "We had *great* sex. You were wonderful. And you pleased me very, very much. When you are finished drinking the water—all of it—I will bathe you. Then I will learn the rest of your body's secrets."

She shivered at his words as she slowly removed the bottle from her lips. She let a shy smile cross her lips. Inside her belly, gentle fluttering blips of something thrilling and magical were bouncing around. For the space of a few seconds she was in a dreamlike state. A calming peace took over her thoughts and in that moment she was happier than she had ever been in her entire life.

He had spoken in a deep and dark manner, as if promising her that she would be made to be uncomfortable with his thorough inspection of her. He'd been very thorough with his examinations of her so far; she couldn't imagine that he did not know all of her body's secrets at this point. But she would surrender everything. She wanted to please this man and be his forever.

When she had forced all 10 ounces down, he stood, put his hand down to grip hers and pulled her up. Once they were both on their feet again, facing each other, he drew the plackets of her shirt together and fastened one of the pearl buttons on her silk blouse.

"We've progressed rather rapidly tonight."

"Yes, we've done the kissing, necking, petting, and groping thing rather splendidly," she said with a wary smile.

"Yes, I fear it's been a bit more than you can assimilate in one evening. After your bath, I think we'll call it a night. Your indoctrination to the basics of submission went rather well though. You might be ready for an advanced class tomorrow. But for now, it's getting late and you must be tired. I know I am."

She nodded her agreement.

He shut everything down in the theater then wrapped her in the large towel he had brought, and lifted her into his arms. He carried her into the elevator and used his voice to command the floor he wanted. When it opened on the next level, he carried her down the hall and into the master suite, setting her on the bed while he went into the bathroom to fill the tub.

There was the huge walk-in shower that would be more efficient for them both, but this time, he wanted her to relax in hot fragrant water while he soaped her and learned more of her body. He wanted to know every delectable inch of his secretary's young body.

He came back into the bedroom and striped off his clothes while standing in front of her. He knew he had a nice body. He worked very hard to keep it in shape. He had broad shoulders, a tapered waist, strong arms and legs, all covered with straight, soft dark hair—it was not enough hair to be considered hirsute, but virile nonetheless. He was a manly man and women seemed to love playing with the furry pelt on his chest.

He wanted her to become as familiar with his body as he intended to become with hers. He wanted her to be comfortable with him being naked around her, and he wanted her to be naked around him without trying to shield herself from him.

"I'm going to jump into the shower to get myself clean, and then I am going to put you in the tub and wash you. Afterward, we'll have a light snack—some fruit with cheese and crackers. Then it'll be off to bed."

He bent to kiss her neck, and then tugged her blouse down so that he could kiss her bare shoulder.

"Most submissives do not sleep with their Doms. It changes the relationship. However, I will require you to sleep with me. As we will only have the weekends to be together, I want to spend as much time with you as possible. And I think sleeping together builds trust."

She looked up into his handsome face, shadowed by his beard that was dark against his light tan. It was sexy seeing him scruffy like this. With a thoughtful expression on his face, he was still Sean, but more approachable somehow. And his body . . . wow. Just wow.

"I trust you already," she said in a small voice.

"Are you sure?" he chided. "Mmmm, I don't think so. You're not quite there yet. You'll need to be able to trust me when you're tied up. While I'm wielding a paddle and smacking your ass. Maybe using a flogger to whip you. Allowing another man to leer at you."

Her eyes bugged wide. "Yikes!"

He laughed. "See? You're not all that trusting yet. Exhibiting you to other men could be a possibility down the road. After all, those things did happen to Beth in your book. But for now, I am not inclined to share you with anyone. That's a whole other scenario. You are nowhere near ready for that."

She nodded her head in agreement. Stunned with the idea

of being naked in front of Sean when other men were present, she shrank back and wrapped her arms over her chest. She needed to rethink this. Maybe she should get out while she still could.

He saw her reaction and laughed. "We'll go over your hard limits again in the morning. Don't worry. There will be no exhibitionism this weekend. And maybe there will never be. I haven't made up my mind about that. Just understand, that as my sub your body is mine to do with as I please. Tomorrow, I am definitely going to spank your sweet little ass. That will please me very much, as my hand is itching to smack that pert little bottom and make it pink. And you deserve a good spanking."

The look of confusion on her face was precious. "Why? I've been good haven't I?""

He flashed her a slow smirk. "Why? To assure that you swallow my cum next time, instead of spitting it into your hand, that's why."

"Oh." She hadn't been expecting that. She thought things were somehow different now that they'd been kissing and being romantic. All-in-all, she thought she'd done well, that she had pleased him. That he was happy with her. The idea that he was punishing her because he was displeased with her made her uneasy and a little depressed. Maybe this wasn't what she wanted after all.

Yes, he'd chastised her for not giving him a proper blowjob and at the time, she'd been a little miffed at herself for not being able to do it properly. But she didn't feel she deserved to be punished, still . . . along with the angst, the idea of being spanked by him *was* somewhat exciting. When had she become this depraved? His next words brought her back to the present.

"I'll be right back. Don't go anywhere," he said brusquely. Then he walked into the bathroom. After a few moments she could hear the showers running.

She closed her eyes envisioning his muscled arms, long legs, broad shoulders, and strong back bunching with his movements. She could picture his tanned body, the short black hairs that were now lying flat and straight against his skin from the pressure of the water sluicing off his skin. His long, strong arms that reached high as he washed his hair and his armpits, then delved low to wash the area behind his balls and between his legs. The soapy water coating the many folds in the skin of his long, flaccid cock.

She must have dozed off because she didn't hear the water shutting off, him toweling himself off, or him walking back into the bedroom. The thing that woke her from her reverie of the compilation of mental pictures of this magnificence man showering—the man that was her boss, and now the person in charge of her sexual being—was the heady scent of minty soap. The smell of a man scrubbed clean, who was no doubt mere inches away.

Her eyes popped open. He was standing right in front of her. A light green towel was wrapped around his hips—the hairs on his chest now springy and dry from a brisk rubbing. His eyes were greener than she'd ever seen them as they latched onto hers and held. "Were you sleeping?"

"Uh, maybe. I'm not sure. Has it been long?"

"I was only gone for five minutes. You should have been able to wait for me." If she wasn't mistaken, he sounded a little miffed with her.

"I'm sorry. I think I was daydreaming. I was thinking of you and what you looked like while showering."

He tilted his head and like a parent scolding a wayward child, he admonished her. "I told you I'd be right back. I did not tell you that you could go to sleep."

"I'm sorry."

"Lay across the bed, on your stomach."

He watched as she sat back and then flipped over onto the bed covers. Her skirt rose a little in the process. He pulled it all the way up so that it bunched at her waist. Her bottom was bare and vulnerably exposed. He raised his hand and spanked each cheek, angling upward and smacking her hard where each butt cheek joined with her thighs.

He only did it once, as it was meant to be a reprimand. But as soon as he saw the redness blooming, he felt the primitive primeval feeling of possession wash over him. He felt like a caveman claiming his mate. As soon as he saw the red imprint of his hand on her ass, her felt a wild overbearing sense of possession . . . and the idea of owning this woman flashed though his body. He had never wanted to own another person—ever. He was shocked to look down and see how hard he was. His cock was juddering in mid-air, primed for action. But, oh he wanted this woman.

For her part, the intense stinging sensation was such a surprise that she cried out. A long drawn out, "Oooww!" that sounded like a recalcitrant schoolgirl getting pulled by her cheek to the principal's office.

As the pain bloomed through her tender cheeks, she felt her body heat up, her hearing dim, and her flesh prickle from her body's reaction to the assault on her flesh. It was an odd sensation in that it woke every nerve fiber to full and complete attention.

Intrinsically, she knew that any other touch would be amplified due to this penal treatment of her. She shouldn't have enjoyed this. And she wasn't quite sure that she had. But she had to admit . . . that she had needed it.

She avoided looking up at him as she reached back to rub the sting away. She knew the expression on her face was insolent. She was conflicted in that moment. She'd wanted this. So why was she mad that he had actually done it?

He grabbed her hand to still it. Then bent so that his face was inches from hers, their eyes meeting, his lips firm, hers in a pout.

"I did not tell you that you could soothe where I spanked you. And what is that impertinent look for? You are supposed to my *docile* submissive. You are not to show your displeasure at my treatment of you. You're job is to take it. And be pleased because it pleases me."

"Yes, sir!" There was little obedience in the way her words were delivered—more insolence than the respect the words called for.

He had to chuckle at her cheekiness. Who knew that his efficient and obedient little secretary could be such a spitfire?

"I am your master, remember that," he scolded, but if was half hearted. He was finding the playacting of being a tyrant hard to manage with her being so cute and impudent.

Because her brazen manner was so daring and delightful, and in direct conflict with the naughty image of her naked on his bed with his handprint blooming on her bottom. And because he was losing control of the scene, he barked out his next words. "Go to the *master* bathroom, and get into the *master* bathtub. You need to obey me. Or there will be more of the same." He punctuated his words by pinching her on her ass.

"I'm going!" she grumbled as she lifted from the bed.

"I'm going what?"

I'm going, *Maaassster."*

"Good girl. Leave your clothes here. All of them."

She gulped. Looked him in the eyes and saw he meant business. His eyes were hard, his lips firm, his voice harsh. It was the first time she had serious doubts about this arrangement. Would he turn mean now? Would he actually harm her? Had he liked the punishing contact his hand had with her flesh? From her research into BDSM, she knew that more men were into spanking their brides than one would think. It had been the way men out west kept their women in line. Even mild-mannered preachers were known to have disciplined their wives with weekly spanking sessions. And who knew who liked it more?

She decided it was not the time to test him. She removed what was left of her blouse from her shoulders and let it drop to the floor. Her bra followed. She reached behind her and unzipped her skirt. It fell to the floor with a swish down her legs. Her panties were somewhere in this house, but again, she wasn't quite sure where.

She remembered him dragging them down her legs to get her open and available to his fingers. But she hadn't paid attention to what he'd done with them. But it hardly mattered, as he wanted her naked—standing in front of him.

Once she was undressed and standing with no clothes on in the master bathroom, her image duplicated or triplicated by all the mirrors, she shivered from the flash of shame that overtook her.

He chuckled as if mocking her, and then smiled and looked his fill. He motioned with his finger for her to turn around. Then he had her parade back and forth in front of him.

When she was able to catch his eyes and see the appreciation in them, she thrilled to the heat she saw reflected back to her. She had a nice body; she knew that, as men were always giving her appreciative glances and some saying lewd things. But it was something else to see the gleam of lust lighting up Sean's eyes as they traveled over her exposed body.

She wondered what he thought of her birthmark—a scarlet blotch on her left butt cheek that resembled a tiny closed rose. To him, it could easily be used as a target. She didn't have to wait long to find out what he thought about it.

"Nice birthmark. It will be a nice place to aim in the future."

He took her by the hand, pulled her behind him as he walked into the master bath, and helped her climb up into the tub. As she cleared the rim, with one leg in and one leg out of the tub, he caressed her ass and then lightly pinched her birthmark.

She slid into the hot water that was mounded with fragrant bubbles floating on the surface. As she settled her back against the tub, he drizzled jasmine-scented body soap all over her chest. It felt delightful to submerge herself into the hot water and to let the aromatic steam envelope her.

He gave her a moment to enjoy the calming warmth, and

to relax before he proceeded to wash her. With makeup remover wipes, he washed her face. Using gentle swipes and dabbing pats, he removed all traces of her makeup. "I want you totally naked. Everywhere. God, you are so beautiful."

He soaped her breasts, reverently at first with his open palms, and then more briskly with a cloth. "You have nice, firm tits—plump, with lovely rosy pink nipples. I have admired your breasts for years. Tucked into your crisp ironed blouses, they tantalized me and sometimes made it hard for me to focus on business. And the Japanese businessmen . . . they were always very complimentary about your *special assets*."

She was reminded of several times when doling out papers or pens or cups of tea, that both Sean and the Japanese businessmen often had secret smiles when they stared at her, that they tried ineffectually to hide. "I often felt more like a geisha girl in that office than a secretary."

"Every one of them would have paid a fortune to have you for one night," he said as he gently pinched the tips of her breasts, letting the slippery action of the soap slide them smoothly through his fingertips, over and over again.

The heady sensation caused her head to loll back against the rim of the tub. She exhaled as her shoulders were gently massaged by the water lapping over them. Her body began to relax. She sighed with surrender and let her arms fall off to the sides. Her legs released their tension and fell open.

No longer on edge, and no longer unnerved by his eyes on her naked body, she allowed him to take whatever liberties he desired. In that moment, she gave herself to him with no reservation, allowed his gaze to roam wherever he pleased. She was finally a good sub, she thought. She had surrendered her body to her master.

It was such a feeling of freedom that she felt weightless, unsure of whether she was floating or stationary. For all she knew she could have been high up in the clouds, or floating down a lazy river. She was buoyant and ethereal, floating away and peaceful in the moment.

She was nearly asleep as he trailed a bath sponge along her limbs, squeezed water out between her breasts, filled her navel to overflowing and aimed drops of water to plop where he imagined her clit to be, under the mound of bubbles. Then he leaned over the tub, bent, and took one nipple between his teeth and lightly bit.

Her eyes popped open. "Ow!"

"Your nipples are sensitive now, new to all this attention. But I'll toughen them up over time. I'll clamp them with nipple clips. I want to see those tips as hard and as tight as pebbles—and impossibly long.

"I'll dress you in some nice jeweled clips that will set off those sweet tits of yours. You are beautiful now; you'll be glorious in your surrender when you let me show you off with diamonds and emeralds attached to your nipples. Yes, you'll be stunning with your nipples encircled with tiny little gems. A cock teasing sight for all my friends to see."

His erotic words, spoken softly in his gravely, lust-filed voice were sending high voltage jolts through her heavy body. Her sex, now warm and throbbing, though underwater, pulsed and arched as she strained for some type of connection—a finger, a tongue, a clamping hand, or a hard and ready penis. She needed to be touched—there . . . and now.

He continued his low spoken words, sexy in tone, and sexy in meaning. "We'll go someplace where nobody knows us, one of those sex clubs in the Virgin Islands, where I can show off your body—especially these gorgeous tits. You'll be topless from the moment we check into the resort. Everyone will get to see them, even all the men working there. It just wouldn't be fair to keep these beauties all to myself."

He cupped both breasts and brought them together for a kiss between them. "You need to show these off. Let lots of men gaze longingly at them. Over the years, I've seen many men try to get a glimpse of your lovely cleavage during the winter, when you wore those soft cashmere V-necked sweaters to work.

"You might remember that a few times I dropped my pen and then watched you when you bent to retrieve it for me. My cock jerked to see that dark mysterious hollow. I can hardly believe that now I'm looking at you while your breasts are bared to me. And that soon you will bare your chest to other men while I sit back and watch them admire you. They will ogle your chest, and desire to put their cock between your tits the way I have desired to for years. Seeing your breasts like this, feeling them, and hefting the lovely weight of them, makes me so hard. I want to fuck you—between your breasts, in your pussy—and in your perfect little ass. I want to have you every way there is."

His words melted her. She loved that he was so pleased with her breasts. With her eyes still closed, she whispered, "I want that, too. So much."

He told her to get on her hands and knees in the tub. Then he helped her to turn over. When she was on all fours, he groaned out loud. "Oh, I like this view."

He reached under her and cupped her swaying globes, gathering as much flesh as he could in his hands and squeezing. "What are you? A 38 with C cups?"

"My, you *have* been studying my breasts."

He chuckled. "Intensively. So am I right?" He thumbed her nipples, flicking them back and forth. Then he turned his thumb down against his forefinger and tugged on her nipples as if he was a farmer milking teats on a cow.

"Ye-ye-ssss," she hissed.

He smiled and slid a soapy finger down the crack of her ass. Then he breeched the tight opening before she knew what he was up to. He was ready for her reaction and held her steady when her knees slipped out from under her.

"Easy. It's all right. Shhh, stay still. Let me feel you here. Ah, your sweet tight little bum hole. You are so tight. Mmmm. Can't wait to take this."

"Mmmm, no," she mumbled.

He laughed and slid his finger in a little further. "Oh yeah. I am definitely going to own this."

He made a few slow circuits, rimming her anus with his fingertip while all the while she tried to wiggle away. He lifted his other hand, reached over her back, and smacked her bottom.

"Hold still. Let me feel you. And count yourself lucky; some Doms live to shove their fist up there. I just want my finger inside you. For now."

She froze at his words. Then forced herself to stop squirming. She allowed him to explore a bit, but all the while, she whimpered. He gave her a reprieve and withdrew his finger. Then he wrapped his finger into the wet washcloth and wiped it off.

"A project for another day. Don't worry about it now. We have a lot of groundwork to do before I'll be able to squeeze my cock between those sweet cheeks of yours."

He gave each cheek a love pat then told her to "Flip back over and lie back, I haven't washed your legs yet."

He helped her turn over onto her back, and then pushed down on the lever to drain the tub. Water began emptying, and with each swirl and gurgle of water more of the suds went down the drain, and more of her was exposed.

She let out a sound of protest as he spread her knees. Then bent over the tub so that his face was between her splayed legs. His eyes were focused intently on her sex as he murmured, "I want to learn everything about your body, memorize every inch of it. When I walk past you while you're typing, I want to be able to close my eyes and visualize your breasts. When you're sitting across from me taking dictation, I want to imagine that sweet cunt of yours glistening with need.

A shiver ran through her and it wasn't due to the cooling temperature as the hot water drained out of the tub. She tried to cover herself with her hands between her thighs.

"We'll have none of that. Besides, you know you want me to look at you and to tell you how beautiful you are. Every woman needs that affirmation."

His hand moved hers away. Then his fingers grazed through the sparse tuft of pubic hair. He tugged lightly on the tiny dark thatch that stood guard to her opening. "You have some wayward curls here. I'm going to have to do a little trimming, shave this mons and the area just below it below for an unobstructed view of you."

"I did shave it," she said in a pouty voice.

"Not completely."

"I read online that men like to have a little landing patch to rub their chin on."

"Not this man. I want you completely bare down here."

She let out a soft mewl of protest as she saw him reach for the shaving cream.

"Now, none of that. You're going to love the feel of being absolutely smooth between yours legs."

He shook the can, removed the cap and pushed down on the nozzle. He stopped when there was a huge pile of shaving cream mounded in the center of his palm.

Before she could protest further, he placed his hand between her parted legs and laboriously smeared the foam over every part of her womanhood. Even going so far as to coat the area of her perineum.

Then he removed a new razor from a blister pack, and knelt beside the tub. He began by taking long smooth strokes with the 5-bladed razor. After several long swipes, he seemed satisfied. She thought he was done.

But then he detached the inflated pillow from the back of the tub, and slid it under her bottom. Then he hooked one of her legs over the edge of the tub. With his fingers holding the skin taut, he removed all the hair with two downward strokes. He replaced her leg back inside the tub and got up to walk around to lift her other leg over. After two swipes on that side and he said, "Okay, now you'll need to flip over onto your hands and knees for the rest."

"The rest?" she asked, but he ignored her and simply

helped her into the position he wanted her in.

When she was on her hands and knees with him standing facing her backside, he reached down and parted her ass cheeks and ran a forefinger along her crack, then rimmed the tiny hole he found there.

She gasped at the intrusion. "There is no hair there!"

"Yes, there is in fact. There are tiny little curling hairs, guarding your puckered little opening. You just can see them."

"This is beyond mortifying! Stop it!"

"Are you ready to use your words?"

She hesitated. "This is so humiliating!" she wailed.

"Wait until you feel my fingers inside, and my tongue tickling you here. You'll beg for more."

She whimpered.

He laughed and then stood. "I can see you're not quite ready for that." He smacked her on her buttocks and stood up to clean the razor.

"You have a cute little ass and a very sweet little anus. And after I get it stretched out a bit, I'm going to enjoy fucking it. Now, roll back over. I want to see that sweet shaved pussy."

She tried to sit up and in the process she closed her legs together.

He smacked her on her thigh and growled, "Don't hide yourself from me. Or I swear, I'll tie you up and take pictures."

Her eyes popped wide.

He laughed at her reaction. Then he added in a low serious voice, "I will you know. You won't be able to stop me unless you use your words."

It was the first time she had been scared of him. Truly intimidated by his lewd demands. She worried that she had made a bad decision by coming here . . . and agreeing to all this. It kind of sounded crazy now, all the things she had actually contracted to do with him.

He stared her down, his brow quirked in a defiant manner, brooking no denials on her part.

"You are going to need to do this. I must have absolute control, outside of you using your safe words and stopping everything. It's your choice."

She took in every feature of his face. He didn't look mean, he didn't look mad. He looked like a man in control who simply wanted his way. And wasn't that the part about him that she liked the most? Admired in every facet of his work tenet? He was the man who was always in control, even when things were not going as expected. She liked that about him. He was the reasonable, ethical force that everyone bowed to. So why not her?

She took her time lying back down, and then little by little, she parted her knees until her legs were splayed open again. Then, with his hands on her knees, he pushed them up and back toward her chest, and opened her even more to his gaze.

In her mind, she ran the safe words through her head, over and over again, before telling herself that she had wanted this. Had been turned on by the thought of him doing these things to her. And now . . . now she was allowing this. She was letting him do anything he wanted to her.

She felt shame washing over her. And was surprised to realize that she was highly aroused. The part of her that was deep inside her, a dark place she didn't even know that she had, now desperately wanted him to find her worthy, to think her lovely, to desire her beyond all reason. And because he did, she was blooming and becoming very wet. Because he was finding her worthy and desirable, she was drenched.

So . . . the end justified the means, huh? Who knew? That surprised her. But it made a weird kind of sense. Because apparently the reason she was allowing him such liberties, surrendering her body to him, to do with as he pleased, was because he knew that she had fantasized about a man, a very domineering and dictatorial man, doing all this to her.

She hoped that what he was seeing pleased him. In this moment, she was living for his praise—craved it above all else, because she wanted him to be completely enamored with her.

She was not ready when he shoved the bath pillow under her bottom, which essentially lifted and angled her so that she was completely open to his gaze. From this angle she could see where his focus was, knew from her awkward position that he was seeing her as only her gynecologist saw her. She tried to pull her knees in, but he was holding onto them, keeping her open to his steady gaze.

"Uh uh uh, I want to see you, Beth. All of you. Let me see all the things no one else gets to see. Ever."

His meaning hit home and she felt a huge rush of relief. His threats had been empty. He did not want anyone else to see her like this. Hearing his words and realizing that he had been baiting her caused a sense of joy and also a flood of moisture. Moisture he had to see. Had to scent.

His hands moved from her knees to her inner thighs where he clamped them firmly in his hands while he looked his fill. He could feel her thighs trembling under his fingers. "You are dewing up for me. I can see it," he murmured.

She felt his thumbs move down until he was able to part the inner lips of her labia and put his thumb inside the gaping void.

"There it is," he whispered in a husky voice, a tone of reverence in his words. "The holy grail of a woman's body."

He rubbed his thumb at her opening. "Look how wet you are for me." He ran his thumb over her clit. "Just look at how plump your little nubbin is getting."

She let out a soft sob. He was shaming her on purpose, trying to see how far he could go with this very thorough examination. She knew he was testing her. Trying to see if she would cry off, beg him to stop, or use her safe words to undo this. But she was beyond reason now, aroused to the max and on the verge of coming.

Sean had never seen a woman as responsive as she was. Her entire pussy was coated with vaginal lubrication. Without any hair to hide anything from his gaze, he could see the sheen covering her, slicking her, readying her to accept his cock inside. And her clit, it was blooming and tripling in size. He could feel it pulsing against the edge of his thumb. He was heady with the knowledge of what he was able to do to her body. He was fully in command of her orgasm. The power he had over her right now was intoxicating. He was king of the universe in that moment.

Chapter 49
Prized & Appreciated

Rutger had told him that humiliation was not every woman's hot button. But that if it was, which it appeared to be with Sandy, he could count on two things from his sub: explosive orgasms, and devoted loyalty. He could not have been more pleased.

Sandy's body was reacting very favorably to her being shamed. He knew all her dirty secrets. He had the key to his submissive. The way to her bliss that he'd been hoping to find, had been fully revealed to him.

God bless Rutger. Her body reacted just as he had said it would. Her arousal was evident in the way she had creamed up for him. She was one aroused woman right now. But that aside, her mind protested this abusive treatment. Despite her being so obviously turned on, her psyche was forcing her to fight back with protestations, condemning words, and actions. Because really, what woman would want this type of treatment? He almost snickered at the thought: *His, it seemed.*

A woman like Sandy, who had a sharp mind and a well-developed sense of independence, simply could not just take being abused without objecting to it. That would make her a bad girl—a very bad girl. And every good submissive wanted to be a good girl.

Getting off by doing bad things, things she was being forced to do, allowed her the freedom to succumb to his will. Whether it was being displayed; tied up; spanked; beaten, or humiliated. Whatever kink he was into, was sanctioned now because the decision had been taken away from her, it was out of her control. By being tied down, chained up, punished to submission by pain, she was free to wallow in her secret desires, shameful as they might be. This woman, who wanted a man to have his way with her, but only if he took her, could not agree to the denigration, could not ask for it . . . he had to be the one to *take* it. Like a caveman, dragging a woman back to his lair, the secret was to take away her choice in the matter. And this woman—his woman—was desperately hoping her caveman was the demeaning, degrading, belittling type . . . as he ravaged her body and fucked her savagely. He was proud of himself for grasping the nature of the Dom/sub relationship so quickly. What had not made sense before was now crystal clear.

By Sandy's soft yearning sobs, her head flailing back and forth against the back of the tub in mock protest to what he was doing to her, his submissive was telling him to appease the good girl in her, and spare her some dignity.

So unless he was ready to fuck her right this minute, which he was not—that was on tomorrow's agenda—he felt he had to slow things down.

He removed his hands from her thighs, lowered her legs to the tub, and covered her with the warm washcloth.

He touched the side of her face and made her look over at him as he crooned to her, "It's okay, Baby, shhh. You are every bit as lovely as I knew you'd be—your body is gorgeous." He used his hand to cup her over the washcloth. "I can't wait to fuck this. I can't wait to eat this. I can't wait to stick my tongue all the way up inside you and make you scream with pleasure."

He felt a different kind of shudder go through her. He brought his hand up to her face, thumbed along her parted bottom lip, looked into her brilliant violet-blue eyes. "Sweet," he murmured, " you are so very sweet. And I am so very proud of you. I think you deserve a reward."

He moved the washcloth aside, parted her legs, and inserted his middle finger into her while his thumb found her clit. He gently began tapping. He flicked and circled the slick bead as it bloomed again. As one finger frigged her and carried her moisture back up to slick her clit, the fingers of his other hand plucked her nipples. He added another finger while his thumb continued its torturous play.

Her chest flushed and he felt her recoating his finger with every circuit. He could smell the musk of her arousal, an intoxicating aroma he was quickly becoming familiar with as it wafted up to his nose. He thrust into her a little harder. Then he removed his drenched fingers and used them to do a little tap dance to flick her clit from the underside, and watched as she arched up to meet his fingers. He felt the telltale erratic pulse of a woman tumbling into her passion. He heard her cry out as she came as his fingers felt the wild spastic jolts of her fully engorged nub and watched as her thighs quivered.

He'd never seen anything more sensual. Never seen a woman succumb to her body so fully. She was lovely in her passion and her submission was a beautiful thing. Her body was amazing. And his erection was becoming downright painful.

As he gave her a moment to recover, he thought why not? He stood and jerked himself off, coating her thighs and allowing one of the long hot spurts to fill her navel. It was a depraved thing to do, but he couldn't help himself. This Dom stuff was taking over his brain and bringing out a perverse side he'd never experienced before.

She opened her eyes and met his. He stood looking down at her, taking in her smile of pure joy and felt his breath hitch. What a delight she was. He was oddly content in that moment, with no other thoughts forcing their way into his brain other than that of taking care of her.

He gently helped her to stand and then used the hand sprayer to wash and rinse her. Smiling when she laughed at him when he knelt to spray between her legs. "Do I need to be sterile?" she quipped.

"You need to be prized and appreciated." He lifted her out of the tub then stood her up and began drying her with two of the pre-warmed towels.

"That feels nice," she murmured.

"I wish it wasn't so late. I have so many things I want to

do with you."

She smiled up at him, her eyes still a little glazed over. As he wrapped her in another warm towel and walked her over the heated tiles to the bedroom, he added, "But tomorrow is another day, and I am looking forward to spending every minute with you."

"I have to admit, I'm more relaxed now that I know how caring you are . . . and how pleasurable this is."

"I know you've given yourself orgasms . . ."

"I have. But they are *nothing* like the ones you give me. Mine are baby firecrackers. The ones you give me are huge *rockets*."

"Well, we'll have to work on getting you some even bigger explosions tomorrow. You think you can get up for that?"

She smiled up at him and ran her hand down his cheek. "Yes. I'm ready for whatever you have planned. I want you to possess me . . . and to make me your carnally immoral woman."

Her dreams of being with a man who would cover her body with his and take her to sensual heights were finally coming true. She was looking forward to tomorrow like a bride looked forward to her wedding night.

"So you trust me, now?" he asked as he gave her a soft kiss.

"Yes. I always have."

He looked down into her beautiful face and took her lips again. He groaned when her lips parted to give him access.

His tongue took a slow foray around the inside of her mouth. He was still learning all the different tastes of her mouth as he traced, sucked and then drew her tongue back into his.

Between languorously learning her lips, and coaxing her to learn his, he realized that he had never really and truly enjoyed kissing until he'd kissed her. Her mouth was so sweet, so giving, so beautiful. And his. For now, her mouth was his. He'd table that thought for tomorrow. Thinking of anyone else ever kissing her like this was firing up a hot feeling of jealousy that he couldn't deal with now.

He pulled away and looked into her eyes. She covered her mouth with her hand as she tried to stifle a long yawn and failed. She was so drowsy he knew she'd soon be sound asleep.

"Time for bed." He walked her into the bedroom and over to his bed. "Which side do you prefer?" he asked.

She pointed to right side. He walked around with her and helped her in, taking time to cover her up to her shoulder with the soft linens and the sumptuous comforter.

"This feels incredible," she breathed as she gathered the soft weight of the covers under her chin and rolled to her side.

He walked to the other side of the bed, stripped off the towel he'd had tucked around his waist, and climbed in next to her. He gathered her into his arms and kissed the tip of her nose. "Good night, Angel."

Her lips quirked to the side, "I don't know anyone who would think my behavior tonight was angelic."

He chuckled. "No, I suppose not."

Chapter 50
Rutger's Advice Pays Off

Sean was a little unsettled as he lay beside Sandy, watching her sleep. This was all so new to him. He wondered what she would think if she knew that this was his first foray into being a Dom. How laughable was that?

He wanted to give Sandy what she desired, but he'd never done anything like this before. He'd never been with a woman who wanted to be submissive to him in any way. In fact, most of the women he'd dated he would have placed on the opposite end of the spectrum. The women he had slept with tended to be on the aggressive side, self-assured, raised by upper echelon parents, experienced in the art of lovemaking, and demanding equal satisfaction in bed. He had never really been all that dominate with any of them.

In fact, though he would have said that he had been acquiescent to their needs, he had probably been more arrogant and condescending about putting his own needs before theirs. And since they were mostly social climbers on the hunt for a moneyed husband with status in the community, he hadn't been all that concerned when things didn't work out.

But this woman . . . this woman he wanted to please. Ironically, he wanted to do her bidding, instead of it being the other way around—totally opposite of what a Dom/sub relationship was supposed to be.

What little he knew of the BD/sm lifestyle he'd learned from reading Sandy's book, and then afterward, talking to Rutger. Rutger had laughed his head off at the thought of Sean breaking in a sub. "This isn't going to work bro, you're not the demanding, punishing type. Hell, I can't even imagine you hitting a woman."

"How hard can this be? You act mean, take what you

want first, and give her some love taps along the way to keep her in line."

"That is not it at all. It's carefully searching out borders, knowing how sexual pleasure can be enhanced, without ever crossing the line where panic and fear take over. It's a mutual give and take. And don't think it's not emotional; it is emotional to the max. You can really mess someone up if you aren't careful. I wish I had time to send you some books or DVDS, but I'll email you some links to some websites that might help."

He'd given him some tips on several household things he could use as sex toys, since Sean didn't have time to go to the Adam and Eve sex shop on Market Street.

"I doubt you know where the clothespins are in your house, if you even have any, as you probably have a laundry service. But clothespins work well as nipple clips, especially the old-fashioned wooden ones. Most of the plastic ones are sprung too tight. Also large paperclips—the bendy plastic kind, not the metal ones. Sometimes you can find old-timey clip or screw-type earrings women used to wear at pawn or thrift shops; they work well for nipple clips in a pinch. Ha ha, in a pinch, get it?" he had laughed heartily at his own joke.

"I get it. In fact, I have some of my grandmother's old earring sets in the safe."

"Good! As long as you don't get flashbacks of your grandmother wearing them while you're in a scene. That might dangle your dong. And make sure you remember that nipple clips of any kind hurt worse coming off than going on. The blood flow gets restricted while they're on, and it hurts like hell rushing back. Twenty minutes is the max you should ever have them on. I'd go ten or fifteen for a newbie.

"Now, for a clit clip, you can use bag clips, like the ones we use at the beach house for chips and pretzels. Just make sure you clip the area above the clit, *never* right on it. You won't ever see her back again if you pinch that little jewel by mistake.

"Also, I think a little spanking is all you should attempt

on the first go 'round. Add in a little nudity to shame her, some gentle fondling or even a massage, some gratifying oral stimulation, and a really good fuck, and that should start things off right between the two of you."

"All this is a lot to process. And it sounds like work."

"Trust me, Bro. It is work. But it definitely has its rewards."

"Hey, I just remembered. I bought a Rabbit vibrator for Chaz' wife Mags for a Christmas present—a gag gift, sort of a way to mock him. You know how he's always acting like he's the most satisfying of husbands . . .. But then before I could gift it to her, she turned up preggers . . . so it seemed inappropriate."

"You still have it?"

"Yup, still in the box."

"She'll love that. That is one amazing little toy. Hell, Pauline uses it on me sometimes. It simulates the tip of a tongue moving like no body's business. We have a good time with the Rabbit. Every time we use it, I tell her I think we should invest in Duracell."

"I think most rabbits prefer Energizer batteries," he quipped.

"You know, you're not that funny."

Rutger had shocked him then by saying that he and Pauline were quickly becoming an item. They had decided to be exclusive and they were going to see where their relationship could go. He said he thought he might be falling in love, said he wasn't sure yet, but that he had feelings he'd never had before. He had laughed and said they had even asked each other about whether or not they might ever want to have kids someday. "This could be the one," he had added toward the end of their call.

Sean had been shocked at that news. He did not know all that much about Rutger's lifestyle, but he knew that in the D/s world, parading a woman around once she had a belly bump was weird, for everyone. Exhibiting a woman who had underage children was in very bad form, as what kid wanted to find out that his mom was doing things like that? Having her on film or on video would be a no-no if kids were ever going to be in the picture.

He and Rutger had talked about these things over the years, as they always seemed to be paired up for driving to events together.

That Rutger was even thinking about settling down had surprised Sean, as he'd never known Rutger to talk about the future with regard to a woman. And the thought that Rutger might commit to any woman—in a permanent way—was a totally foreign idea to him.

In college Rutger had hooked up with a lot of women, but Sean had never known him to actually go out on a "date" with one. His hook-ups had been about the sex, period.

But then Sean had met Pauline. He'd been with Rutger when she'd landed her plane at the Ocean Isle Beach Airport and walked down the steps to meet Rutger. Right from the start, Sean had liked her. She'd been shy. And she knew how to laugh. Sean had known right from the beginning that she was a special woman, well suited to Rutger's active lifestyle—both sexual and physical.

Maybe they'd have a shot at being together for the long haul. It was too soon to tell, as he knew they'd only met a few weeks ago. But a lot could happen in a few weeks if you met the right woman. He'd seen it happen with Chaz, Deke, Kyle, Alex, Ryder, and Cam, and now it seemed it was happening to Rutger.

Sean had thanked Rutger for his advice and then spent the time before Sandy was due to arrive checking out the links Rutger had sent and rounding up some of things he'd need.

But now, after having had their first evening together, he had to admit, it had been a bit awkward humiliating and talking dirty to her. At the same time, it had been quite scintillating being fully in charge and having a woman eager to acquiesce to his every demand.

His woman, who was asleep now, lying beside him and

371

so beautiful he could not believe that he was considering hurting her, reddening that gorgeous pale skin on her beautiful ass. How much pain would she want? Just how much of a spanking was she expecting?

After reading her book, and checking out some websites, he knew the different types of sex toys Doms often used to help their subs achieve satisfaction: paddles, floggers, whips, even canes to beat them with, and ropes, sashes, chains, and leather straps to restrain them while they administered the blows.

What the hell had he gotten himself into? It had been a rash idea to challenge her and invite her here without knowing more about this. Because he was pretty sure if she needed extensive treatment . . . which in his mind, wouldn't be anything more than his hand on her bottom . . . he was not going to be the man for her.

And yet, as he looked over at her now, he really wanted to be the man for her—for whatever she needed. Her dark hair was fanned across the pillow. Her eyelids were closed and relaxed, hiding her expressive blue eyes from him. Her coral-colored lips were soft and slightly bowed into a sexy little quirk to the side, as if dreaming of her upcoming adventures tomorrow. Her clasped hands were resting on the bed. Her long trim fingers with their pink manicured tips laced together and tucked close to her ear. Her sweet little trim body was perfect. Absolutely perfect—for him.

He did not want to let her down in this. He wanted to be the one to give her pleasure. He would try to be what she needed—mostly because he did not want her looking for anyone else to satisfy these sexual fantasies of hers. He wanted her happy. And he wanted to be the one to make her happy. Rutger was right. This was emotional to the max.

Chapter 51
Robe of Many Colors

Sean didn't remember falling asleep, but he must have. And it felt as if he'd slept like the dead. The sun coming in through the high transoms lit the opposite wall and brightened the whole room. He could have put up sunshades to prevent that event from happening each morning, but he loved waking up with the first rays of the sun as it came up over the ocean and shone on the back of his house.

There was something different about this morning though. As soon as he opened his eyes, he saw a very beautiful woman, her hand propping up her cheek as she leaned on her elbow and looked down into his face. She was smiling. He felt his heart trip at the sight of her.

"Morning handsome. You look like a god the way the sun is lighting up your face."

"You look like a tousled angel with a lovely morning blush on your face and a halo behind you. Are you always this beautiful when you first wake up?"

She laughed. "Not hardly. The blush is probably due to the wine."

He reached up and ran a finger down her nose, "Did you sleep well?"

"I suppose I did. I don't remember zonking out. We were talking about today . . . and you kissed me."

"The last thing you said was that you trusted me."

"And I do. I wouldn't be doing this otherwise."

"As much as I would love to start your next lesson now, nature calls. How about I meet you in the kitchen? The coffee maker should have clicked on by now."

"I have no clothes in here. Is it okay if I take the sheet with me?"

He chuckled. "By all means. However, there's another

bathroom at the end of the hall. It's fully stocked with toiletries and women's what-nots. There's also a robe behind the door that I bought with you in mind several months ago."

"Several months ago?" she asked, clearly intrigued by that pronouncement.

"For Christmas. Remember? I'm notorious for buying ahead."

"Yes, I do know that," she said as she rolled off the bed, pulling the top sheet with her.

He'd seen the one-off lounging gown in a catalogue and knew it would be the perfect Christmas present for his fastidious secretary the moment he'd turned the page. Rather than pull the page out of the book, he'd pulled out his phone and ordered it right then, from his dentist's waiting room.

When the package arrived at his house, he'd put it in the closet he used for gifts to family and friends. He was not a last-minute shopper. Never had been. He hated the last-minute pressure. So he bought thoughtful presents for people he wanted to gift things to all year long and stashed them away until the appropriate time to give them out.

This particular dressing gown was made from many different squares of silk, each swatch unique in its design, but holding to an oriental floral theme. The myriad of colors and fabric textures made the robe a stunning work of art.

He watched as she dragged the pale gray sheet along the floor until she was down the hall and ensconced in the guest bathroom. He heard her gasp, followed by a long drawn out sigh of pleasure at discovering the opulent dressing gown. He smiled. Nailed it.

As soon as he heard the snick of the door as she closed it, he got out of bed and went to his own bathroom to get ready for the day he had planned for them. A little man-scaping was called for if he was going to push her face into his balls and tell her to "Lick, until I say stop."

Chapter 52
Accident or Providence?

They sat at the counter sipping coffee. Sandy often fixed his coffee at work, so she knew how he liked it—black like his heart, as he had joked with her during that first week.

Sean was a little annoyed with himself that he had no idea how she took hers though. He leaned over and saw that the coffee in her mug was light with cream. Then he spotted the sugar bowl.

She apparently had a delicate taste for coffee, while he liked his harsh and robust, almost bitter.

"One, two, or three sugars?" he asked.

"Four. It's gotta be sweet or I can't get it down."

"Then why have it at all?"

"I need the jolt of caffeine some mornings to get me going. I'm not especially a morning person, unless morning can start at ten."

He looked over at the digital clock on the oven. 7:15.

"So you would normally be asleep right now if you were home on a Saturday morning?" he asked.

"Yup. This time of the year, I'm usually up by 9 or 9:30. During the winter? I've been known to sleep until eleven."

"How did I not know that about you?"

"Well, we've never been together before . . ." she said, waving her hand between the two of them while offering him a shy smile.

"Interesting how that came about," he murmured around the lip of his mug. "You slipping that book into my luggage."

"It was an accident you know. I spent days looking for that book before ordering another copy."

"You really had no idea where it was?"

"I thought I'd left it on the park bench where I'd been

reading it. You think I would have been able to work with you for a full week without being beet red in the face and mortified if I'd known you had it?"

He chuckled, "No, I suppose not. But it hadn't occurred to me that it was in my case by accident. I thought you were trying to tell me something."

She slowly shook her head back and forth. "I would never have wanted you to know what kind of weird kinky stuff I was into reading. In a way, I still don't."

"Obviously, we can't unwind this, can we?" he asked.

She jerked back as if she'd been slapped. "Would you want to?"

"Oh no! No. Certainly not. I just meant . . . well, what's done is done. Hell, that didn't come out right either. I don't know what I meant."

"We don't have to do this. I can go home right now. It'll be weird, but we'll find a way to work things out at the office." She was not put out by what he had said, so much as confused as to why he'd said it. Had she gotten this all wrong? Was this crazy feeling of desire, mixed with the intense sexual passion that she was experiencing, one-sided? Was he not feeling the allure along with the fantasy?

"Well, that's just it. I don't want to unwind this. Not one bit. I'm excited for us to play some more. But on another level, a more personal one, I also want us to get to know each other better while we're doing it."

"You sound tentative now. Different from last night."

"I didn't know you were a virgin last night. Except for the zucchini invasion, of course."

She sighed, a long deflating sound of complaint, ending with a low lament, as if the saga of her innocence was getting to be an oft-told thorn in her side.

"My virginity is not something I'm attached to in any way. I just wanted you to know, in case there's a barrier, or I bleed. I was just too . . . well . . . busy, in my late teens and early twenties. The right opportunity just didn't present itself. I got close once, but he was a doctor and got an emergency call from the hospital. Then another time I was with a police detective. And he got called out to a hostage situation. We had actually been in my bed at the time with him putting on a condom. So really, it's not a big thing. It should have been done a long time ago. It just wasn't."

She sighed and then let out a self-deprecating chuckle. "I would like to see what having a man inside me is like before I'm old and gray and my teeth fall out. Don't treat it special. To me, it's a hindrance."

He spun on his barstool so that he was facing her. Met her eyes with his. She saw something there. An assessing spark that morphed into clarity of the situation, and then his lips firmed in determination. She'd seen that look on him after he'd read briefs from companies who were trying to outrun blame when they were clearly in the wrong. His eyes got hard, his lips firmed and she could see the resolve to right the wrong. A lambasting letter typed up by her would be the next step with a full out courtroom challenge, which he almost always won.

She saw the same determination in his eyes right now—as if he was going to right this terrible wrong.

He put his hand on her neck, drew her close, softly brushed his lips over hers, and tasted the flavor of her sweet caramel coffee. He let his tongue wander along the seam of her lips, parted them and delved inside. He tangled his tongue with hers, moaning with delight, before pulling back.

"I want you," he breathed. "Let me be certain that I am conveying my intent about having you . . . and taking you. I will be plundering you in a predatory, aggressive despoliation. I will let no barrier stand in my way. You will not be a virgin when this day is over."

He kissed her on the forehead and whispered, "You will be mine. I will own your maidenhead."

His hand gripped her chin and he leaned in. With a hard

press of his lips to hers, he ravaged her mouth. His lips were short of bruising hers as he allowed his tongue to become a marauding, pillaging, plundering weapon, with its sole agenda being to own her.

In this poker game they had been playing, he had just thrown all his chips in, and now she had two choices—surrender or fight back. She didn't want to fight anymore. She wanted to let go and fall into these dark sensations, and into the even darker abyss they were leading her to.

She let her tongue go lax; let him suck on it as he drew it back inside his mouth. Her tongue mated with his, curling and learning the texture along its length. Until he wanted to be back inside her mouth again.

"I could get addicted to tasting your caramel-flavored coffee this way."

He dueled with her tongue, delivered harsh stabbing jabs, forced his tongue beyond her teeth where he took deep forays to lap at the soft palate he found there. All the while he was enticing her tongue to make its own assault inside his mouth.

He encouraged her with soft moans when her tongue ran along the backside of his teeth and ran along his gum line. His hands gripped the side of her face as he launched another assault on her mouth, holding her in place as he took and took and took.

Then he pulled away. Both of them were gasping for breath. He leaned his forehead against hers and whispered, "Let's make it happen this time. You and me fucking until we exhaust ourselves making you come."

She smiled, her face going from tentative to triumphantly radiant in the process.

He said he was going to make her come. It delighted her that he didn't want it to be just about him. No man had ever said he'd make it just about her. Even when that police officer had been putting on a condom, preparing to enter her, she'd known from everything he'd done and said up to that point that fucking her was going to be more about him getting off than him pleasuring her. But yet, she'd still been eager to accomplish the deed—curious as to what all the hullaballoo was about more than anything else. Now, it was finally going to happen for her.

Sean picked her up and carried her to a nearby armchair. He placed her on his lap and lifted her chin to gaze deeply into her sparkling light blue eyes. His face was serious, his manner intent with purpose. "But first, I think I want to spank you. Then when your ass is warm from my hand, I want to savor you with my tongue. Kiss and lick you everywhere. I'll wrap my lips around your clit and tug on it and suck on it until I make you come. And then, when you are wet beyond imagining, I will slide inside you and plow into you until you come again. Afterward, because I might be feeling some remorse, I'll probably need to spank you again for being such a bad girl and letting me fuck you."

"That sounds hot. Everything you just said sounds incredibly hot. Do you think you will need me to kneel between your legs Sir, to get you hard?"

He closed his eyes, and with cynical scorn at himself, he huffed out a long groan. He was trying to make things easier for her . . . better for her, while she was determined to be objectified. As if it was a drug she needed, she seemed to need some form of abuse to get aroused.

He could mock himself; say he didn't want her surrender because of harsh words or his ill treatment of her. But honestly, the thought of punishing her, demanding she submit to him, *was* hot—as she had said, *incredibly hot*. What she was suggesting sounded so perfectly marvelous, that he simply didn't care anymore if it meant he was treating her badly. He was treating her the way she wanted to be treated. He had to remember that.

"Yes," he whispered. "Get on your knees and suck my cock. Make me hard. So hard I can impale you and have you ride my dick while I walk you into the bedroom and keep you there for hours."

With his hand on her head, he eased her to the floor and then opened his robe. She dutifully closed her eyes and opened her mouth. And he, harder than he could ever remember being, placed the tip of his penis inside it. Her lips wrapped around the crown and her tongue licked at the moisture she found at the slit.

He closed his eyes and let his head fall back when she began taking more of him into her mouth and lightly sucking on him. He enjoyed her servicing him.

Holy shit! This was Sandy, his secretary, who was on her knees in front of him with his cock in her mouth. And she was moaning with pleasure and sucking on him and drawing him in just right. Yes, this was hot. So incredibly fucking hot.

After many minutes of divine torture, he untied her robe and pushed it off her shoulders. He withdrew himself from her mouth and picked her up, then carried her back to the counter and lifted her up onto a barstool. It was his turn to service her.

He spread her legs wide, hooking her feet on a wooden rung on each side of the chair. Then he pulled her forward on the seat and opened her with his fingers, enjoying the view as the full sun streamed in from the glass doors behind him. "So lovely," he murmured. "And so very wet."

He stood and cleared their dishes off to the right, then gripped her around the waist and lifted her up onto the countertop.

"A fitting place to eat this sweet, juicy pussy. I can't believe that you sucking on my cock got *you* this wet. Your thighs are coated with your slickness."

"Sucking on you is a huge turn on," she breathed as he kissed her nipples, her belly, her hips and then the top of her opening. She bucked forward at the touch of his mouth on her. He stood and leaned her back onto her elbows, then spread her thighs wide. Then he dove in. He left nothing unkissed, unlicked or unsucked as he circled and loved her warm flesh with his lips, mouth, tongue, and teeth.

Her thighs started to tremble and he could hear her gasps turning to whimpers, followed by a torrent of nonsensical babblings as her tongue circled her dry lips. He wrapped his lips around the pulsing nub he'd lavished and nursed to twice its size, and gently sucked on it. All the while his tongue flicked a frantic cadence against it.

While she keened and arched her neck, her head lolling back almost to the countertop he stayed with her. Softly milking the throbbing nub with barely-there lips he felt each pulse, each shiver, and each erratic throb as she came and her little nub did a little jig over and over again, before settling, shriveling, and going still.

He had never felt a woman's clit spasm so sporadically . . . and for so long. She tried to use her arms to sit up, but as she was right on the edge of the counter, and since her thighs and legs were of little use right now, she slid forward. He managed to catch her in his arms and made it to the floor with her. With one leg out in front of her, and the other crooked at her knee he was granted the view to see just how slick her thighs were.

He was not surprised to find her glistening with her dampness. Her upper thighs were coated with her arousal, or her orgasm—he wasn't sure which. He was learning that this woman had powerful and sensationally wet orgasms.

He was still hard from the blowjob he'd caused her to abandon, not to mention aroused to the max from having had his head between her legs and hearing how wild she was getting over everything he was doing to her. Now, he reasoned, with her being so very wet, and him so very hard, would be a good time to teach her how to fuck.

He stripped her of her robe while doffing his, and then carried her back to his bedroom. He placed her spread–eagled in the center of his king bed, grabbed a condom from his nightstand, and crawled up the length of her body.

"Do you want this, Baby?" he asked as he drew his long member alongside her thigh, coating it with her wetness. Then he rubbed the tip up and down her labia, transferring the dampness he found there to the head of his penis.

"Yes," she huffed out. "Yes. I want you. Inside me. Now. Please, Sir."

It was the *Please Sir* that did it. He couldn't say why, but something wild happened with those words. He rolled down the condom, placed the tip of his penis at her opening, and gently eased his way in. Partway in, he drew out and began to enter her again. He did that a few more times. Then he leaned up, kissed her lips, angled his hips down, and thrust home.

He saw her eyes pop open and stay full wide. Heard a quick intake of breath, and watched as her face settled into a state of bliss, her eyelids slowly closing. "Ooooh, that feels marrrrvelous. I feel so full of you."

"You are full of me. Every inch I've got is inside you now. But I can thrust deeper if you want me to, if you want to feel more. Tell me what you need."

"Not yet. Let me enjoy this sensation first. Then you can do whatever you want. I promise I won't mind."

He grinned. "You have a way of turning innocent words into the sexiest thoughts a man could ever wish to hear. Let me know when you're ready for me to do things that 'you won't mind.' I don't mind waiting, as I intend to fuck you good and proper."

"Not proper. I want you to be very improper."

Ten seconds later she whispered, "There's something inside me that needs touching, can you find it and touch it for me please?"

He groaned. "Sweetheart, I will do my very best to find that spot and touch it for you. You just tell me if I'm getting close."

She looked up at him and simply nodded, leaving her pleasure up to him. That was the moment he knew he was in love. The rush of emotion he felt moving through him made him heady and dizzy with lust.

He began thrusting into her, circling his hips when they were fully connected, then drawing out slowly. Speeding up and then slowing down while thrusting and gyrating. He watched her for signs, cues from her body and from her breathing to tell him whether he was giving her pleasure or pain.

So far, so good he thought, although her face had morphed into a grimace, her lips curling out as she sucked in air. Then all of a sudden, she grabbed at him. With hands tightly clenching his ass, she jerked his hips down to hers, drew her legs up and behind his back, and locked them in. Her knees were holding him tight to her in a death grip.

He was surprised at the strength she had in her thighs—she was gripping him hard and holding him in place as if her life depended on it. He felt her vaginal walls begin to convulse. Then his cock was gripped tight as if held in a fist. Where they were connected, deep inside her body, he could feel her orgasm building . . . and then releasing. He knew not to move, not even an iota.

It was clear that where he was, was exactly where she needed him to be. He froze and held, feeling all of their points of contact heating up and swelling. Then he felt a cinching, throbbing, pulling action begin inside himself as her vagina began milking him.

She threw her head back and cried out. As her legs trapped him in a vice-like grip, he felt her whole body shudder.

It was the most amazing and wondrous thing, feeling her orgasm build and then experiencing her release while he was inside her. The profoundness of the moment sent him over the edge. The sensation of coming inside her as she squeezed along his length was of hot lava spewing from deep within him. Each intoxicating spurt that violently exited his body triggered the most amazing feeling of well being and then the most pleasurable explosion of ecstasy. He was in a heightened state of bliss, one he had never achieved before.

A few moments later, coming up out of a cloud of darkness, he would have sworn that he had lost consciousness for a few seconds.

He doubted he'd ever had a woman sheathe him so completely. And now, it was as if she never wanted his cock to leave her. *He* never wanted to leave her.

This was by far, the best fuck he'd ever had. And it was all because of her. Without a doubt, this had been one huge explosive orgasm for her. And he had felt it growing and then happening inside of her.

He flushed with pride. He had managed to send her to the moon the very first time she'd ever been fucked. In his world, that never happened. It took time to learn a woman's nuances. And he knew from research that some women *never* managed to achieve a vaginal climax.

He caught his breath as Sandy began to settle. Like Snow White she seemed to awaken from a long deep sleep. He slowly rolled them both onto their sides. Facing each other, they each had huge grins.

"Wow," she breathed. "Just woooow."

He smiled while untangling her hair from around her face. "You were fabulous. I can't believe how hard you came. And that I felt it when you did."

"Neither can I! Did you have fun, too?"

He laughed at her choice of words. "Yes. I did. I definitely had fun, too. More fun than ever."

"Me too! So, how long before we can do it again?"

He smiled and shook his head. "I don't know. Maybe next year."

"Next year!" She swatted him on the arm.

"Hey, I'm the one who gets to do the flogging."

"Is that next?"

"Sweetheart. I think the next step is going to be a nap. Then maybe a shower and some food."

"Then you'll spank me?"

"You didn't do anything that merits a spanking."

"What do I have to do to get one?"

He chuckled and mussed her hair. "Usually you have to be bad."

"I can be bad."

"I'll just bet you can. Can we go a little slower? Not do everything in one day."

"You mean like Rome?"

"Not being built in a day? Yes. You have no idea how much that kind of lovemaking takes out of a man. When we come, we are truly spent. Trust me, there are many pleasures in store for you later. But we're going to have to work up to them over time."

"So I can come back here again?"

"Sweetheart, you can move your things in and stay. I don't want you out of my sight, or where another man can scent you and think that he can have you."

"I thought you wanted to share me?"

"I never really meant that. I may have mentioned showing you off. That was more playacting than anything else. But that's off the table now. You're mine. You belong to me."

"So you are my Dom and I am your sub?"

"You call it whatever you like. Whether you are Sandy, or Beth—or my submissive secretary—whatever you want to call yourself, you are mine."

He pulled her head down onto his shoulder. Now I need a nap. I suggest you take one too, as I have plans for you this afternoon and this evening."

"Spanking?"

He raised his hand and brought it down on her butt cheek.

"Ow!"

"Just tell me how many you need before you'll let me take a nap."

She put her head down and let his shoulder be her pillow. Then she began making soft snoring sounds.

He laughed and pulled her in close to his chest. And they slept.

Chapter 53
Band-Aids in the Pool

Sean woke an hour later, she had moved away from him and was hugging a pillow under her head, her face partially obscured. Her dark hair was fanned across one shoulder, away from her face. Her hair was longer than he had thought, shoulder-length with some waves in it. She wore it in an elegant twist on the back of her head at work. He couldn't remember ever seeing her outside of the office with it down either.

He had to admit that he'd found her attractive from the very beginning, but had forced himself to be professional and refused to acknowledge her as anything other than his secretary—until that day at the beach house when he'd found that book in the bag with his new swimsuit. He had spent the majority of his vacation time at *The Cockpit* with his hand on his cock reading that book. And then orchestrating that Dom scene with Rutger when they'd picked Pauline up at the Ocean Isle Beach Airport had made matters worse. He'd managed to chafe himself and had to go to the local Walgreens for some K-Y lube.

Now that he was free to touch Sandy, he had the desire to run his fingers through her lustrous tresses. But he knew it would wake her if he did, and he wanted these quiet, private moments to just drink her in, to marvel at her smooth unblemished skin, and to admire her soft full lips and the cheeks that now were tinged with a soft rosy glow.

He knew that soon they would be flushed scarlet with embarrassment when he took her outside to his pool—naked. And then later, when he clipped her nipples and tied her to the Mission-styled bed in the guestroom.

She was beautiful in her slumber. She would be beautiful when he tied her to the wooden bedposts tonight.

He slipped out of bed and prepared a light luncheon

for them. A charcuterie board was already wrapped and in the refrigerator for the proteins and carbs they would need later in the day. Fresh fruit with cranberry juice would provide the energy for her to swim with him, and then to lie naked under the sun canopy together, and then later . . . to make love with him. Love . . . now that was a strange word to bring into this unusual mix of things. What was this they were doing? Was it a date, an assignation, a rendezvous, or simply an encounter? Would it end up being a one-off thing? Or would they have Trysting Thursdays and Fucking Fridays? He had to shake his head at the unintentional course his thoughts were taking.

Anxious thoughts popped into his head that maybe this would be all she'd want. One weekend. Get the novelty of it out of her system. Move on from there and date other guys . . . who would then think her experienced in the love arts.

The idea of her not coming back concerned him. Then, like an errant hit to the solar plexus during a touch football game that took him down, pain and jealousy did a quick double whammy to his ego. Misery and fury sent him spiraling down into a black chasm. If she were to see other men, it would make things near impossible for them at the office. To continue working together after all this, he'd have to be more focused than ever on his work. And she'd have to up her professional game and grow warts.

This was a bad idea. He should have thought this through, considered all the potential scenarios—run through the pitfalls for their future working arrangement. Damn! He hated the idea that he'd have to replace her. She was a phenomenal secretary. But then she was a phenomenal sex partner, too.

He heard her moving around in the bedroom and forced himself back to the task of getting lunch ready.

Sandy walked into the kitchen just as he was setting out a large pitcher of ice water with lemon slices floating in it. He knew keeping them both hydrated was important, especially as hot as it was outside. And good sex called forth fluids that need to be replenished.

She was wearing her new robe, belted tight at the waist, her fingers trying to comb out her tousled hair.

"You should have woken me. I could have helped."

"I didn't need any help, and I wanted you to finish your nap."

He walked over, lifted her hair from one shoulder, and tucked it behind her ear. Then he leaned in to kiss along her neck and shoulder.

She felt the thrill of his kisses all the way down to the backs of her knees, which now felt jiggly. A warm feeling spread throughout her lower torso as tiny electric jolts ran up and down, zinging every erotic zone like a pinball machine lighting up.

"You are gorgeous when you're all slumbery and mussed."

She smiled. "Is slumbery even a word?"

"You're the secretary, you tell me."

"Honestly, I can't think of a single reason I would ever have to type that word in the course of a business day."

He leaned in to kiss her lightly on the lips, a smile on his own. "No, I don't suppose that you would. Come, let's have a bite to eat, then we'll take a dip in the pool."

"I didn't bring a swim suit."

"No worries. I have something you can wear." He picked up a baggie from the counter. Inside were four medium-sized Band-Aids, the type one would use for an area the size of their palm.

"Band-Aids?"

He opened the bag and dumped out the rectangular two-inch wide Band-Aids. "One to cover each nipple, the other two will get taped together to cover just below your mons and the area between your legs. But it's not like you need anything at all. The pool can only be seen from the air. Only private planes fly over the island, but even that's a rare thing."

"So why bother with the little pasties?"

"Remember Beth in your book? Her Dom liked to dress her in clothes way to small for her, skirts way too short . . . with no panties underneath."

"Yes," she breathed out on a long sigh. "Tantalizing him, while humiliating her, yet allowing her the praise and satisfaction of others that she so desperately needed to validate her as a woman, because she thought herself ugly."

"Yes, taking her out in public like that, not only fed her ego, but showed her off, and it fed his ego, too."

"Are you planning on showing me off like that? Because I don't think I'm ready for that."

He quirked his lips and tilted his head as he thought about it. "No, I don't think so. I'm a very possessive man. What's mine is mine. So you're off the hook, as I already know from past experiences that I don't share well."

When she didn't object to his bold declaration that he considered her his, he shuffled the Band-Aids around on the countertop, arranging them in front of him. Then he picked up the pineapple from the center of the fruit bowl that was a few feet away, and set it on the counter in front of him. "Two Band-Aids go horizontally across your nipples, just like this as your bikini top."

He opened the other two Band-Aids and overlapped them end-to-end. "This strip will be your bikini bottom. Start it just above your cleft on the front side and it should be long enough to cover your tiny little bum hole on the backside. They're waterproof so they should stay on in the pool. Later, when I yank them off, you'll experience the sweet stinging sensation that will wake up every nerve underneath the skin. While you're all tingly, it will be a good time for a spanking, and then some bondage. How does that sound for Saturday afternoon entertainment?"

She laughed. "Well . . . it beats doing laundry and

vacuuming my apartment."

They ate their fill of ham, salami, and turkey, along with several different kinds of cheeses, some pickled vegetables and olives, and a variety of nuts, crackers and fruit. He forced her to drink both a small glass of cranberry juice and a large glass of ice water, saying, "The way you dew up down there, you're going to need some extra fluids this afternoon. Especially as it's going to be pretty hot out there today, although even in August, we do enjoy a nice breeze on the island."

After they cleaned up the kitchen, they went to separate bathrooms to put on their "swim suits."

They met on the back terrace and she looked him over as he stood opening the umbrellas. Impressive in his Speedo, she was once again awestruck by his body. There was nothing hidden in the bright sunlight. His arms legs, and torso were muscular; there was definite evidence that he worked out regularly. And despite the current trend, he was covered with a wide pelt of dark brown curling hair on his chest. His well-defined legs were also covered in dark hair. She was reminded of Sean Connery in one of the Bond movies, when he was on a beach in a scene with Claudia Cardinale.

Sean was a very sexy man. He was definitely well put together. At six-four he had impressive height, a full head of cropped dark hair that despite looking easily manageable was very well trimmed by a very exclusive stylist. She'd seen the bills from the prestigious salon downtown in the Waterfront area. She could pay her monthly grocery bill with what he paid for a haircut.

The shadow of dark facial hair that was just below the skin could be seen on his cheeks, around his mouth, and above his upper lip. The sculptured outline that defined the shape of his beard-to-come was quite virile looking. Up to now, she'd only seen him clean-shaven. This look was swoon-worthy.

But then she focused on his bright blue eyes, which were now lasered on her and to the tiny and embarrassingly little scraps of adhesive tape that covered only her nipples and her down-under lady bits. She was too busy trying to find some way to shield herself while flushing red from his intense gaze on her to notice that his cock was straining against the thin material of his Speedo.

He had absolutely no qualms about staring at her and taking in every nuance of her appearance.

"Nice," he murmured. "You are in-cred-i-bly sexy looking. Very, very hot. I actually get it now, why a man would want to show his woman off like this. It's like owning a Picasso and keeping it in your closet. Is it weird that I kind of want to show you off right now?"

Her eyes went wide and she nodded, hoping he didn't really want to invite anyone over. She thought she looked ridiculous, not at all sexy. The thought that he was considering entertaining someone here with her looking like this was way more than weird. It was terrifying!

She looked down and saw how the meager front pouch of his Speedo had grown and lengthened as the tiny scrap of spandex tried to keep his penis corralled. She watched as he reached down, cupped himself and adjusted his balls.

"I could look at you like this all day," he said, his voice soft, yet unbelievably husky. "You are so sexy."

This time she flushed with pride. She loved it when she pleased him. And just like that, she realized why women did these humiliating and crazy things. She had never felt this sexy or desirable in her whole life. And he wanted her in a very big way; there was no denying the proof of it. The validation she got from being acknowledged as a desirable woman from this amazing man was making her dizzy with arousal.

She could tell that he saw her breathing change and her eyes go slumberous with desire. His nostrils flared. She knew that his desire to have her matched her desire for him to take her.

He came close to her and cupped her between her legs. His thumb stroked her clit over the adhesive part of the Band-

Aid. She wished there was no barrier, that nothing covered her but his hand. She wanted to feel his palm possessing her sex. And she wanted to feel his fingers entering her. She couldn't speak as his thumb circled, tapped, pressed. His eyes met hers, took in every nuance of her face as her breath came out in a long stutter. She'd never been this turned on before. She forced herself to admit that there really was something to this shaming stuff.

"Let's swim. Then I want to spank you for making me this damn hard."

He dropped his hand, walked over to the edge of the pool and dove in.

For an hour they frolicked together in the pool. He swam laps as she dove deep, sat on the pool bottom and watched from underneath as he methodically kicked his powerful legs and lifted one muscular arm after the other in a perfect crawl, each powerful stroke propelling him forward until he reached the end where he flipped, used his feet against the side to push off, and then began another lap.

Over and over he swam, over and over, she surfaced and then returned to the pool bottom. His graceful, yet masterful body mesmerized her. She wanted him. She wanted this handsome, virile, and commanding man to take her in primal ways—caveman ways.

She wanted to be pummeled by him as he took her—him incensed beyond reason because he wanted her so much. She imagined his hands gripping her ass cheeks tightly as he spilled his essence inside her. She shook her head in confusion as she sat on the bottom of the pool watching him. For the life of her, she could not figure out why she had this desire to be manhandled and forcefully taken, but she did.

With every fiber of her being, she wanted to be the repository for this man's passions. Was this what primitive women had felt as they were being tossed over a man's shoulders and carried back to their lair? She had never before wanted a man to ravage her . . . for him to be focused solely on his own needs—satisfying her needs in the process merely a secondary consideration. What was the appeal here, she asked herself. But she didn't have the experience to answer her own question. Had she erroneously pigeonholed herself as a submissive? Maybe she was actually a sadist instead?

He climbed out of the pool and she followed. Wherever he was going, she was going. Being horney was making her dingbat crazy.

They reclined on mesh loungers drying in the sun, taking in the sights high up in the sky as pelicans and gulls flew overhead.

He looked over at her. "I see you're still wearing your swim suit."

She smiled back at him. "Yeah, you should patent this idea. Covers the essentials, easy to pack, cheap, disposable. The tan lines are going to be a little weird though."

"Come over here."

The command in his voice brooked no disobedience. Intrinsically, she knew that this was not the time to tease or defer, but to just get up and obey. So she did.

When she was standing beside him, he turned his head, and using his teeth he took the turned up edge of the bandage that covered her womanhood. Then jerking his head to the side, he yanked both parts of the joined bandage completely off and then dropped it to the pool deck.

"Owww!" she hollered. Then, "Shit! That hurt!" she muttered.

His open palm quickly covered the abraded skin, his long fingers attaching the area between her legs. The second his palm and fingers made contact with her skin, the pain dissipated. She was amazed at how quickly his skin, in contact with hers, soothed the tender area.

"There, there," he whispered. Then he gently blew on the offended area. "It's okay now. You'll be fine in a minute when the blood stops rushing to the insult. But right now, I'm going to make it rush someplace else."

She was fine. Better than fine, she was majorly turned on.

He sat up and turned sideways on the chaise, then pulled her to him by her bare bottom until she was situated between his parted knees. Then his lips latched onto her, kissing, licking and soothing the offended area while his tongue sought out her clit.

When he had the tiny nub between his lips he began to lightly kiss and suck on it. Then he rolled his tongue over it. Flicked it. Lapped at it. Blew on it. Then he sucked it some more.

He felt her start to tremble, heard her cry out. But he already knew she was coming as he tasted her salty dew and felt the engorged nubbin throb against his lips.

He was ready to catch her when her legs gave way. With surprisingly little effort, he lifted her onto his lap where his cock, tenting his Speedo, was eager for her cleft to rub along the stiff ridge of his hard on.

Using his hands on her hips, he maneuvered her to where he needed her, while pushing his swimsuit down to his thighs. He used the notch of her pelvis to rub against his eager cock, angling her up, and then pressing her down—firmer than she would have thought comfortable for the pulsing ridge of steely flesh.

But he was unbelievably hard against her, and now, moving against her sex totally for his benefit. Like a rutting animal, he was lost to reason, ignoring how sensitive she might be in that area as he chased his own pleasure.

After having just come, she was tender but her only concern was for him and his pleasure. She didn't care that he was manhandling her. She sensed he was too far-gone with his own release to focus on her now anyway. Her only thought was to be his catalyst for a satisfying orgasm, as he'd just been for her. But this was new to her. She needed direction.

For his part, he just needed her to, "Sta-a-ay ri-ight the-e-re . . ..

So she did.

He thrust up, gripping her hips and rubbing her slick folds against his erection.

"Arrgh, raba shaddy dadit prig!" he yelled out.

Then he mashed her down onto him one last time and held her tight—his cock niched into her pubic bone. He moved her soft parts back and forth over the head of his penis—bearing down when the crown of his penis was captured between their two bodies, the purple angry tip the only thing visible when she looked down. His hips strained up as he gave one last thrust against her and the sound he made was one of torturous ecstasy. Long drawn out hisses escaped grimaced lips that locked his jaws. Vile curse words and harsh sounds spewed from him as his ejaculate discharged, splattering up and over onto his abs, coating the hand she was using to balance herself.

She had been looking down, and fascinated, watched as semen shot out from him in three long, arching, pulsing streams, his shallow navel catching the last remnants.

It was her supreme delight to be able to turn the tables on him by smearing it all over his belly, groin, and hips.

"Fuck, fuck, fuck. Man, that was sweet . . . sweet . . . sweet," he murmured. Then his eyes opened and he saw her expression. Full of wonder and pride, she wore a full-on grin.

"Wow, you had a lot of stuff coming out of you! Like a volcano."

He grinned. "It was one hell of an eruption, that's for sure."

He pulled her down onto him, heedless of the sticky mess between them. He held her tight to him as he caught his breath and his body began to let loose and relax.

After a few minutes, she felt the tips of one finger work their way under one of the Band-Aids covering her nipples. He flicked the tip of her nipple and teased the tip until it was hard and tight and she was moaning. He gave the other one the same treatment. Then he sat her up again.

With no warning, he yanked off both adhesive strips at the same time. She cried out and both of her hands went up to her breasts to grip them. She almost tumbled off of him from the sudden unbalancing of her body, but he caught her.

"That hurt!" She shot him an angry look.

"I know. And I'm sorry. But that was the best way to get them off."

With the fingers of each hand, he pinched her already hard nipples. "There now, I'll bet the skin around these nips doesn't hurt at all anymore."

He rolled and tugged on her nipples, then sat her lower so he could sit up and suckle them.

"All better," he pronounced as he managed to stand with her still wrapped in his arms. He walked over to the edge of the pool at the deep end and jumped in, with her still in his arms. Together, they sank to the bottom. He took her mouth with his, her lips tight to his, as he forced his tongue inside.

By the time they surfaced, all was forgiven. He managed to get his Speedo off and tossed it up onto the deck. Then they swam together, holding on to each other, kissing and talking, both totally naked and loving the freedom it gave them. When they got tired, they sat half on and half off the steps at the shallow end, each with their heads resting on their folded arms, smiling and staring at each other.

The angle of the sun told him it was after three—time for a short rest. Half of their time together was already gone. And there was so much more he wanted to do with her, and to her.

"C'mon, time for a quick shower and another nap."

Chapter 54
Plantation Windowsills & Vintage Jewelry

She woke to the sound of gulls screeching as they flew past the large bay window on their way to the beach for their final meal of the day. She opened her eyes in time to see the last in line tip its wings and veer off toward the sand and the promise of food at the end of a long glide.

She looked over her shoulder to see that Sean was still asleep, the sheet down around his hips giving her a view of his muscular chest with its generous pelt of dark curling hairs. His pecs were rising with each deep inhalation. So manly—he was such a splendid specimen that she had to take a few moments to admire him while he was unaware of how captivated she was. All male, so virile . . . a magnificent sight.

She wished she had placed her cell phone on the night table instead of leaving it in her purse. This would have made a drool-worthy picture, she mused as she simply shook her head at her current circumstances. In bed. With a gorgeous man, who knew how to satisfy a woman. She shivered with the thrill of anticipation of what was still to come.

Lifting her side of the sheet, she slid to the edge of the bed until she could put her legs over and feel the rug on the floor. She made her way over to the turret-style bump-out where a series of six floor-to-ceiling windows made a semi-circle you could walk into to get closer to the spectacular view.

Along the way, she pulled a throw from one of the chairs in the cozy grouping facing the window. She wrapped it around her naked body and stood in the alcove. The view was stunning.

It had been too late to see what lay beyond the minimally lit pool last night, but now in the late afternoon sun, she could see the aquamarine water, so still now that she could see the dark tiles marking off the lap lanes at the bottom and the steps leading up to the covered hot tub.

All around the pool were loungers and tables with colorful umbrellas. The loungers they had used were now askew, marring what should have been a picture-perfect setting. Off to the right was a louvered pergola with slats that could be adjusted to provide protection from the sun. Beyond that was a built–in stone fire pit surrounded by Adirondack chairs on a beautiful slate platform. It was a spacious backyard that was perfect for large scale entertaining. She doubted that he'd ever had a party here though, as she would have been the one to have sent out the invitations.

Cattycorner, and off to the far side of the yard, was another deck with series of steps leading down to a wooden walkway. Shielding her eyes from the brilliant sunlight, she could see rows of sand dunes that a long line of gulls was flying over. A thin sliver of blue on the horizon shimmered with glints of silver as waves moved closer to the shore.

She felt Sean's lips on the side of her neck. She angled her head to give him better access. "Mmmm," she moaned. She loved it when he kissed her there.

He continued to kiss her neck until he reached her ear, then laving it with his tongue, he huffed into it and whispered, "You're overdressed."

With one tug, the throw was sent to the floor.

"Uh, the window?"

"No one can see us. We're two football fields from the dunes. It's another hundred yards to the beach. Even if someone was on a boat and had binoculars trained on this window, it would be hard for them to see in unless it was nighttime and we were backlit. So just enjoy the view in front of you, while I enjoy the view in front of me."

His hand felt along her bottom, squeezed an ass cheek, and then slid up for a possessive hold over her belly, before cupping and lifting her right breast from the underside.

His other hand came around and gave her left breast the

same treatment. He pushed her breasts together and thumbed both nipples. Then he pinched the tips and tugged on them, sending tiny fireballs moving throughout her body, igniting every nerve ending. She felt moisture pooling between her legs at the same time she felt his cock nudging her bottom.

He bent her over the wide plantation windowsill that served as a low shelf for books and picture frames that ran the length of the alcove. Encompassing all six windows, it became the resting place for her hands as he pulled her body tight against his and walked her legs back until he could push down on her lower back and bend her how he wanted her. "Keep your hands flat on the shelf. I want to take you from behind. Hold on tight, you may have to grip the edge."

She did as she was told and felt the fingers of his left hand readying her and smoothing the slickness along her labia. His right hand went back to plucking at her nipples.

She cried out when he pinched them, hard.

"If you don't like that, then you're probably not going to like this."

He took the lid off of a decorative ceramic jewelry box that was on the shelf close to her right hand. He tipped the box and two earrings fell out onto the shelf. He picked one up and using both hands, opened the back and clipped it over her right nipple.

"Aaaah!" she cried out.

Before she could protest further, he treated her left nipple to the same torture by attaching the matching clip earring.

"Owww! That hurts!"

"I know, baby," he crooned. "But it's just for a little while."

He ran his fingertips over her pussy, making sure she was creamed up for him. Looking over her shoulder, he could see her nipples encircled within the diamond clusters that glinted in the sun. It was the hottest thing he'd ever seen.

Using his finger, he gathered some of her moisture and

brought it to the tip of his penis. It mixed with the slickness oozing from the tiny slit. He could not remember ever having this much natural lube come from the head of his penis. They were both so wet, and so needy. This was arousal times twenty, he thought as he closed his eyes and placed his cock at her opening. Then he shoved inside her hard enough that the top of her head hit the windowpane. "Ouch," she murmured. Then a moment later, "Mmmm. That feels good."

"Sorry about your head. Use your arms on the shelf to steady yourself and splay your feet out for balance. And be sure to enjoy the million-dollar view as I fuck you mindless."

He drew out slowly, hissing from the exquisite sensation of feeling her muscles gripping him to keep him inside.

"Now would be a good time to say, 'Yes, Sir.'"

He plunged back in, this time she managed to stay in place. "Yes, Sir!"

The barrage of in and out salvos progressed with him taking deeper thrusts and long drawn-out retreats, eventually forcing her to her tiptoes to keep her footing . . . and to keep her head from hitting the windowpane again.

His hand stole around to her front, and using two fingers he stroked her clit, gently flicking it from the underside, then circling it. Capturing her dew and rewetting it from the slick coating where they were connected, he kept going back to torture the tiny knot of nerve endings again until he felt it pulse, thicken, flower.

He quickly thumbed the spring releases and removed the clips from her tits and let the earrings drop to the rug.

He smiled to himself when he heard her suck in her breath from the flow of blood reversing. It was time.

He thrust hard to seat himself fully inside her.

He heard her gasping, trying to draw air into her lungs, knew her nipples were engorging themselves with blood again and sending strong currents of pain-pleasure to her nether regions. Everything was blooming within her body to bring her pleasure.

He fingered her clit with quick rhythmic taps and felt it begin to quiver beneath his fingers. Both hands were ready when her legs began to tremble and give out. He was able to keep her steady as a long series of "Ah-ah-ahs," escaped through her lips, followed by a drawn-out moan. It filled the room, then petered out as a quiet sucked-in hiss replaced it.

Holding her tight to his groin as her body collapsed onto his forearms, he felt the orgasm firing through her, felt the erratic spasms run through her body as her limbs jerked in an offbeat disjointed dance—he sensed her vagina gripping him, clenching and unclenching, then clenching once more before going slack.

Like tidewater flooding onto marshland, she had let loose her boundaries. Confident that he'd catch her and keep her upright, she had dropped her head onto her forearms on the shelf.

With her satisfied, he felt his own orgasm build again as he kept his groin pushed tight to her ass, his penis as deep inside her vagina as he could get it. Two thrusts were all it took.

He cried out with his release and fought to stay standing while his knees buckled. The blackness on the inside of his eyelids careened with kaleidoscope images and colors shooting through his brain. His head was thrown back and vile guttural noises spewed forth and were ground out between clenched teeth, "Mother fucking, cunt waggin', aaaargh! Blip blap dam shat bangin' pangin' prick me!"

She couldn't help it. She laughed—full out.

He felt it through his hand on her belly as her mirth reverberated throughout her body. It almost caused them to uncouple.

He didn't want them to come apart yet so he thrust back, but he was no longer hard enough to stay inside her. She stayed doubled over with her arms folded on top of the shelf—the rest of her in a disordered version of down-dog as she continued to laugh.

He remained connected to her by his penis—but just

barely—by his arms wrapped around her middle. As the aftershocks of both his orgasm and her laughing jag caused by his odd roster of profanities died down, she began to feel something dribbling down her thigh. Felt it run past the side of her knee toward her ankle. Goodness, how much of that stuff had been in there?

Then she realized that they hadn't used a condom.

Her own profanity reigned supreme as she lifted her head and said, "Shit, shit, shit!"

Out the window she saw seven storks fly by in a single line. She almost passed out on the spot, but then saw that they were actually pelicans . . . not storks.

"What? What?" he asked, stunned by her sudden distress and the sound of her cursing. He had never heard her use any cuss words—ever.

"No condom," she huffed out.

"Shit!"

Despite the situation, she chuckled. "I think that is the only cuss word you haven't used yet."

"I'm sorry. So damned sorry." He pulled all the way out and helped her up from her awkward position.

"C'mon. Let's get in the shower. I've got a wand attachment on one of the showerheads. Let's see if we can get the inside of you rinsed out."

He bent and picked her up, cradling her tight to his chest as he walked her into the master bath.

Chapter 55
Massage Heaven

"Well, we either rinsed all those little spermy things out, or we scalded them to death," she said. "I'm not sure, but I think I might be a little burned up there."

"I'm sorry. I don't know what I was thinking. I saw you'd had some bleeding . . . and I wanted to get you clean. And these on-demand hot water systems really fluctuate the temperature sometimes. But I should not have had it turned that high to begin with."

"I'm sure I'll be fine. I have to be. Because I can hardly go to the E.R. with a third-degree burn way up there. But . . . on the bright side, I am pretty sure none of those little buggers lived to find my little egg, should there have been one anywhere near that vicinity to begin with."

He chuckled as he was drying her off. "I could spray some Bactine up there . . ."

"I think you've done enough for today."

"How about a massage?"

"Oh, okay . . . " her lips went into a full-on smile, "maybe you haven't done enough for today after all."

And of course, he had his own massage table. In a massage room—with bottles of oils and jars of creams lined up on a bamboo shelf above the turquoise glass vessel sink.

"Who has their own massage room?"

"A man who likes massages."

"Do you often massage women here?"

"You are the very first."

"Wow. I am honored."

"But then, I've only had the house for eight months . . . "

"Oh yeah. I remember typing up some of the paperwork."

Her reminding him of their professional relationship gave him a moment of pause. What the hell was he doing?

Then she dropped the towel she'd wrapped around her herself after showering. My God, she was gorgeous. Her skin, usually pale, was now pinked from both the hot shower and yesterday's time in the sun. Her waist was trim, her breasts high and full, her nipples a dusky rose color that matched the inside of her recessed belly button. And as he'd denuded her of all pubic hair, he could see the beginning of her cleft. Her slim thighs, shapely legs, dimpled knees, and toned calves, ended at tiny feet whose toenails were devoid of polish. He didn't think he'd ever seen a woman who didn't have her toenails polished. And there wasn't anything pierced, not even her ears.

Her hair, normally up and out of the way on the back of her head in a twist of some kind, was now a mass of curly tendrils held up on the very top of her head by a claw clip. She was Venus from her head to her toes.

He answered the question he'd just asked himself a few moments ago about what the hell was he doing? He was finally satisfying every need she'd evoked in him over the last five years.

He was giving in to all the sexual urges that had crossed his mind over the many thousands of times she'd sat across from him. When she'd tapped her pen against smooth glossy red lips as he tried to keep his thoughts on whatever case he was working on. When she'd crossed her legs at the knee and let her high heel dangle from her toes. When he'd come across her bending over a file drawer, or reaching over her desk to reboot her computer. When she reached up to a high shelf in the storage closet and exposed her trim waist. And lord, that time she'd dropped her pen on the carpet in front of his desk and hadn't noticed that the vee neck of her sweater had fallen forward, exposing the upper mounds of her breasts encased in a very sexy lace bra. He'd always thought she was lovely. But he'd had to fight against his thoughts all the time. Now he didn't have to fight his thoughts at all. Or his body for that matter.

"You are the most beautiful woman I have ever seen. Your body is so natural. It's soft and malleable where it's supposed to be, not ridiculously firm and hard."

Her eyes went wide and it appeared to him that she took affront at that. He could see it in her raised brow and the lift of her chin.

"I should explain. Breasts should be soft and pliable—implants are hard. Butts should be firm, yet yielding. Butt implants yield about as much as a fully inflated soccer ball. You, on the other hand, feel just perfect . . . everywhere. And I love that your toenails are not lime green or pumpkin orange, or bright fuchsia. I love how natural you are." He kissed her on her shoulder. "You embody everything I think a woman should be."

He held out his hand and she took it.

"Thank you," she murmured, not knowing what to say to that pronouncement. All these years, she'd thought he liked the dolled-up, made-up, surgically enhanced women who paraded in and out of the office.

"No tattoos, no piercings, no nail polish . . . you don't even dye your hair."

"I don't like needles, I am lucky to have strong nails, and I don't believe in putting chemicals on my hair that will damage it. I suppose when I start to go gray, that I may change my mind about coloring my hair, but for now, I think it suits me fine."

"Everything about you, suits *me* fine," he said as he helped her up onto the table. Having decided to massage her while she was lying on her back first, he settled her in by covering her with a large white sheet that he took from a warming drawer that came on with the lights when the door to the room was opened.

"Oh my, this feels lovely."

He smiled. Then cleared his throat. "Now, I have no technical knowledge of massage. But I have had a lot of them, and I do profess to know a little about the way women like to be touched."

"Like, say . . . wearing earrings with huge Asscher-shaped diamonds, surrounded by brilliant-cut chocolate diamonds with clip-on spring-loaded backs clamped to their nipples?"

"Touché," he said with a smirk while warming a puddle of jojoba oil between his palms. "So . . . you know your jewelry." He walked over and used his elbow to press down on the slide button to dim the lights.

"I troll the LeVian, Mejuri, Ross-Simons, Etsy, and QVC websites. I know enough to say that those clip-ons are vintage and that they did not come from JC Penney's."

He began by massaging oil into the skin on her left arm. "No, they did not. They were my grandmother's, given to her by my grandfather on their 50th anniversary. They were designed by Van Cleef & Arpels. I just got them out of the safe last night for this little adventure."

She gave him a questioning look as he moved up her arm to her shoulder. "Why?"

"I was told by a friend that old-fashioned clip-type earrings make a good substitute for nipple clips. As our . . . assignation . . . was spur-of-the moment, I didn't have any nipple clips lying around."

"Rutger," she stated.

He stopped what he doing to the side of her neck, surprised that she knew of Rutger, and of his connection to the world of kink.

"How do you know Rutger?"

"Oh, I don't know him."

He relaxed, trying to keep from being obvious about it by letting out a long, slow, silent sigh.

"You know *of* him then?" Rutger was a well-known sports enthusiast, a charitable organization founder, and popular in BD/sm circles as somewhat of an authority. He wasn't famous like Kyle was—a master chef with restaurants all over the world and designer cookware with his name on it, available online and in big box and department stores. No Rutger was not famous—unless you were into the world of kink.

"Yes, I know who he is. He was on the list of owners for the beach house at Sunset Beach. Remember? You had me type up most of the paperwork for you."

"Yeah. So why would you connect him to nipple clips?"

She was silent for a few moments, then quirked her lips to the side.

"I um . . . Googled all your friends. I had kind of had a crush on you back then. I wanted to know more about you. What better way to learn about you than to learn about your friends? Rutger is all over the place online. There are a lot of stories about his sexual exploits. It's rumored that the clubs in the Virgin Islands comp him to fly in and do bondage demonstrations for men who want to learn more about the lifestyle. Or those who want to see their women on stage with another man."

"Wow, you're a lot more knowledgeable about this than I thought."

"No, not really. You can't access his stuff online, he's very private, no filming is allowed when he's at a club, especially now that he's been seen with this new woman named Pauline."

Sean drew in a big breath. He was not going to tell her that he knew all about Pauline, that he'd actually met her when he was at the beach house this last time. On the very same day Rutger had met her in fact. And that she'd been topless by the time he'd driven them back to *The Cockpit*. He'd played the part of Rutger's driver so that together they could reenact the scene when the real *Pauline*, the one she'd been named after, had arrived at an estate outside of Paris named *Roissy*. The scene had come from the book and the film, *The Story of O*.

He was also not going to tell her that he'd been there when Rutger had showed off Pauline's tits to all the frat boys that had been at the beach house that afternoon. Or that he had seen her on her knees out on the terrace as she knelt beside Rutger and he'd fed her lunch with his fingers, while she'd still been topless. Just how much did Sandy know about Rutger? This little affair they were having could get complicated if it turned out that she knew more about Rutger and Pauline's world of sex play that he did.

Was this an affair they were starting? Or more of a secret tryst? A date that had gone all the way . . . and then miles beyond? A one-off assignation? Or was it the start of a relationship?

He covered her shoulder, arm, and the hand he had just finished, then patted everything down over the sheet and moved to the bottom of the table to start on her left leg. His hands were itching to touch more of her but his brain was a bit angsty. What did she know about Rutger, Pauline, and their lifestyle?

He oiled his hands again and uncovered her left leg. Then he began massaging the entire length, in long even strokes, stopping just before her hip joint. Doing it several more times before concentrating on her ankle and foot.

She was softly sighing with pleasure and then humming with delight at what he was doing to the bottom of her foot, to her toes, and to each toe individually. He knew from experience, that it was pure heaven to have a foot massage like this.

He finished and moved to the other side to do her right arm and then her leg. They didn't talk for a few minutes as he massaged her and tried to sort things out in his head.

"Rutger is pretty deep into the lifestyle. That's for sure. I'm a little concerned that you might know more about him than you do about me . . ."

"Oh no! There's not much you can find out about him without being in a club he's at, or having passwords into the organizations he runs. A lot of what I read is just rumors or people making up stuff because there's no real dirt to be had."

"Well, that's good to know. He's my friend, has been for many years. But even I don't know where he goes or what he gets in to. I did call him for some advice. As . . . believe it or not, you are my first sub."

Her hand went to her mouth as she covered her laugh.

"I did know that. Shortly after I arrived here. But then, it's new to me too, except for what I've read. And now that move you showed me."

He was miffed for a moment, and then he laughed too. "How long have you been reading up on this bondage, shaming, beating stuff?"

She had to laugh at the way he posed the question. "A couple of years. I think I've read everything out there about secretaries and bosses. Those are my favorites."

"I kinda got that idea. Flip over, you. It's time to massage that gorgeous ass of yours."

He held the sheet up as she turned over.

"I don't know why you're covering me up again after each body part. It's not like you haven't seen every thing I've got."

"It's just a courtesy. My masseur does it for me. And he's seen everything *I've* got. Plus, I'm trying to remember exactly how he does everything, so I can do it right for you."

"Training for a new profession?"

"Not hardly. It's not lucrative enough."

"So if you're parroting your masseur, chances are you aren't going to be kissing my ass, then? Unless you have a special relationship with your masseur . . ."

"I do not. He arrives every other week, beats me up pretty good, and I pay him to go away for two weeks. He's pretty brutal There is no kissing involved. Trust me. He's a former wrestler—a big bruiser with dreadlocks and warts."

"Really? That surprises me. I would have bet you'd have a woman instead of a man attending you."

He shook his head. "Not unless he had a sex change since I last saw him . . . or before I ever met him."

She laughed. Then she jerked upright so that she was resting on her forearms. Holy shit. He *was* kissing her bottom!

Now he was using his teeth to nip at her. And now, his tiny little nips and nibbles were doing amazing things to her nether regions. He slapped her on her ass, and then used both hands to push her shoulders down so that she was prone again.

She slumped back down onto the table. She could feel herself getting wet . . . needy. Damn, she was horny again. He had a way of turning her on that made her throw caution aside. She spread her legs to let him see what he was doing to her.

His long drawn-out groan was delightful to hear. The next thing she knew, he had pushed her up onto her knees and pulled her down to the edge of the table until she was right on the edge.

His mouth latched onto her just below her perineum. His left hand was under her, two fingers circling her clit. The pointer finger of his right hand was up to the first knuckle inside her puckered opening, gently probing the rim and the tiny knot of nerves he found there.

She loved that they were so in tune to each other's needs. He was doing every naughty thing to her that she'd read about in books—he was rimming her ass, and at the same time, massaging her clit.

She came fast and hard, her whole body shuddering as she collapsed down to the table.

"Well that was hardly any work at all," he murmured as he bent over her naked body and adjusted the sheet, this time, covering up her splendid ass.

"Now for my legendary back massage. I bet you'll be asleep before I'm finished."

"What makes it legendary?"

"No one remembers, they always fall asleep."

"How many people have you massaged?"

"You're the first. So you'll need to start the legend."

She turned her head to the side and smiled so he could see. "It's the warm up to the massage that's going to put me to sleep. If you offer that service to every woman, you're going to be in demand for your *dex-ter-ity.*"

He laughed at her play on words. "I have it on good

authority that I am already high in demand."

"What authority?"

"That magazine that did the profiles on the most eligible bachelors in New Hanover County last year. They said I was 'Most Sought After.'"

"Ah yes, I remember that article. The phones were ringing for weeks. 'Can I please speak with Sought-after Sean?'"

"It was mean of you to put those calls through."

"How was I to know whether or not they needed legal help?"

"Legal help concerning the environment?"

"Well, one did have a problem with Ramshorn snails in her millpond."

He laughed out loud. "Well, that didn't bode well for her now, did it?"

"Nope. You got an injunction on behalf of The Center for Biological Diversity against her destroying the eggs under the leaves of her Spatterdock water lilies by throwing salt on them."

"I am impressed you remember all that. But yeah, that didn't work out for her. If she'd fought it though, she'd have won. Even though the magnificent Ramshorn Snail is endangered, we still don't have laws in place to protect them. Sadly, landowners are still actually allowed to have them removed from populated ponds. In fact, the United States Fish and Wildlife Service would have come and removed them for her. If she'd only done a little research, she would have solved her problem and saved a ton of money."

"Well, she was blonde."

"Only on the top."

"What? Did you date her?"

He realized his mistake, grimaced and said, "Mmm . . . maybe."

"You're not sure you dated her, but you're sure she wasn't a true blonde?"

"It might have been a one-time thing."

"You mean a one-night stand?"

"Fine. Have it your way. In fact, that might have been when I noticed the Ramshorn snails . . ."

"Hmmph," she was obviously put out that he'd fucked a woman, and then sued her.

"Now would you mind if I got back to my legendary massage, since we've established that I *am* high in demand."

"Fine." She plopped back down to the table. "Do your damndest."

He laughed and swatted her butt. "I'm going to be nice to you, just for this massage, but then I am going to spank your ass for your impudence."

"Talk, talk, talk."

He swatted her butt again. Harder this time.

"Ooww!" She reached back to rub the sore spot. But he grabbed her hand before she could.

"You don't get to ease the pain."

He kissed her palm instead. Then placed her arms to her side and began massaging her back and shoulders. She was sound asleep within two minutes.

He smiled down at her, kissed her on her cheek, and went to get things ready for her introduction to spanking.

Well . . . actually his introduction to it, too.

Chapter 56
The Intricate Anatomy of a Woman

When she woke up twenty minutes later, he was talking to her as if she'd never been asleep.

"Did you know that the clitoris has 8,000 feet of nerve endings? That the roots go down five inches on either side of the labia minora?"

She was used to him spouting off pertinent data for any situation: one oyster filters 50 gallons of water a day; the scent gland of the male Siberian musk deer is the source of musk, the most expensive animal product in the world, selling for as much as $45,000 per kilogram; it takes a sloth a month to digest a meal, the United States still has debt from the Revolutionary War. Still, this clitoris trivia was over the top.

He stroked along the top of her slit. "It's hard to find that magic button unless it's engorged, and then it's fairly easy. It's very responsive though, as I'm sure you know by now."

"I do, in fact, have some experience in that arena," she quipped.

With quirked lips in acknowledgment of that, he continued, "I read that pudenda means shame in Latin. That little shaming nerve is in this area."

He ran his finger down her perineum. She jumped from the intimate contact. "It's pretty sensitive. Hence, it's potential for pleasure." She jumped again.

He laughed and stroked it again, this time with a little firmer touch. "Shame is a very powerful feeling. It tells us that we should not want to be seen as we are being seen, in that moment."

She jerked against his finger and hissed. He snickered, and then announced, "Pudenda!" He said the word as one would say Eureka! Not the discovery of gold, but something far more prized if one was into the art of lovemaking.

"Our minds treat shame as any other evolutionary adaptive feeling. So unless we surrender to the threat of shame, in all likelihood . . . our needs will not be met. This very special nerve carries the sensation for both sexes from the back of the genitalia—the scrotum for me, the back opening of the labia majoria for you—to the anus. It does other things, too, mostly muscle motor things for the pelvis and the anal sphincter.

"When pressed like this," he pushed just inside the lower rim of her anus, "it can change an otherwise so-so orgasm into a fierce one. So, you might feel me pressing back here just at about the time I think you're going to be coming. It's the reason a lot of people, both men and women use butt plugs or anal toys that vibrate while having intercourse.

"I might ask you to suck me off when I have one in sometime. But mostly, I will be the one using one inside *you*. That's why the explanation, so you will understand that I am doing something that will enhance your orgasm. Got it? You okay with all that?"

"Geez, you'd need to be an anatomy major to know and understand all that," she said.

"If you like women, it makes sense to learn the things that please them. And I am all about giving women pleasure. Never forget that—even if it has to start with pain. Or in this case, shame."

He squeezed her butt cheeks together. Then made a slow deliberate show of separating them, his thumbs delving into her crack and parting her wide.

She froze and her eyes went wide, knowing where his eyes were now focused.

"When shame is inflicted it's mostly mental. Sex is actually a highly mental game. Humiliation and shame figure prominently in the heads of a lot of women. Especially novices, with everything being so new and embarrassing for them anyway, shame plays into their experience in a very big way."

He rubbed the edge of one thumb up and down her

puckered opening, pressing and pulling out the puckered skin as if to see inside her.

"To mortify or dishonor a woman is different from embarrassing her. Sadists seek to disgrace and degrade as well as to do physical harm to their subjects. I will never intentionally physically or mentally harm you. You should know that. It's not who I am, it's not what I am into. I want to give you pleasure, in the most maximum way that I can. So sometimes, I will try something new to see what happens, and sometimes it will not work out as I think it will. If it distresses you, and you let me know, I'll stop right away."

He pushed his pointer finger inside, up to the first knuckle. Gently circled.

She moaned loud and long.

"Until we get to know each other, in *every* intimate way, we'll be experimenting. I like to try new things. But I'll admit, I haven't been big on sex toys or inflicting pain. But if that's what you need, I'm willing to try most anything if you are."

He played with jabbing the tip of his finger in and out of her tight opening. "You have a very sexy ass. I can't wait to put my cock inside here."

With that, he swatted her on her butt and then pulled up the sheet to cover her.

"You seem more adventurous than most. Most of the women I know are not into butt play."

"Well, that's the thing," she said. "I really don't know myself if I'm into it. But I can tell you this, I've liked everything you've done so far . . . well, except for the annihilation of sperm by hot water up my vajayjay."

He turned her over and pulled her up and into his chest and held her. "I am so sorry for that. Are you feeling any discomfort up there now?"

"Oh no, I'm fine. Ready for Round Two, with a condom this time."

"Yes, I'll see to it." He put his forehead to hers.

"This is how rabbits apologize. My niece said she learned that in *The Peter Rabbit* movie. Here, I am apologizing for scalding your vagina."

She smiled but he couldn't see it. This man . . . this man was doing things inside her, making everything jump around and heat up. "I feel . . . sanitized."

"Up to trying it out again?"

"You bet."

Chapter 57
Lessons With Toys

He took her by the hand and walked her into a guestroom that had a queen-sized Mission bed against the back wall. The bed linens had been removed and only one pillow in a satiny case and the matching fitted bottom sheet remained.

They were both fresh from the shower and wearing robes—his was black silk with a red satin lining and belt; hers was the robe he'd given her, her early, already cherished, Christmas present. "I know it looks a bit scary in here. But let's talk for a few minutes. I need you to not be worried—about anything."

"I'm not worried."

"That's good. But I still want to show you what everything is and what it's used for."

"Okay."

He tried to gauge her, but she had her secretary face on, attentive and curious, afraid to miss an explanation she'd need to recall later. This was the inquisitive side of her that he loved to see. Over the years she'd surprised him often by seeing a solution to a problem that he had not.

The wooden bed had twenty slats on both the headboard and on the footboard, and long rails that things could be attached to. Right now, each of the four corners had two of Sean's silk ties knotted together at the ends and fastened to the wooden posts.

On a long dresser, on top of a folded towel, were four wooden clothespins, two sizes of plastic chip bag clips, and two sets of Sean's grandmother's earrings—the clip-backed ones he'd already used on her nipples, and a different set that had lovely diamond clusters that had screw-type backs. Those she hadn't worn yet. They looked quite a bit heavier than the first pair.

On the other end of the towel, placed side by side like

surgeon's implements, were four wooden spoons of varying sizes, six coiled belts—two leather, two woven cloth, and two nylon mesh, a Ping-Pong paddle, two knotted men's socks, the nylon dress type, each with something lumpy in it—and each distinctly different. She picked one up and hefted it. Some kind of glass or metal beads shifted inside it.

"Marbles. To be inserted inside you to give you a feeling of fullness," he supplied when her brow lifted and her head tilted in question.

She replaced it and picked up the other elongated sock. This one felt squishy. "Rice?" she asked.

"Yes. Heated for thirty seconds, you can enjoy the warmth inside you."

"I think you've already covered the bases on that one."

"Or put in the freezer for twenty minutes it can be a cooling compress," he offered. "On your forehead for a headache. Across your ass to ease the burn of a spanking."

"I think you're going to need a larger sock for that. Maybe a Christmas stocking."

He laughed, took it from her and replaced it back on the towel. "It's brown rice, so it's healthy."

She laughed at that. Then picked up two braided ropes with tassels on the ends. There were four of them. "Tie-backs for drapes?"

"Yes. They used to be. Now they will be used to tie your hands together or your feet together. Incapacitating you frees you from guilt. The idea is, that if you can't stop me from doing something, then you can't feel guilt at the pleasure it gives you. It's sort of permission to be a bad girl. Not that you need any permission from me."

He picked up three different types of eye masks; two obviously provided by an airline, one with flax seed designed to give weight and able to be heated or iced to help with a headache.

"Same principle here. If you can't see what's happening, you can't prevent it. And it heightens the sensation and creates suspense."

An odd assortment of wooden dowels, handles that had been removed from kitchen implements, and even a short squatty screwdriver, the kind with interchangeable nibs, lay at the end of the towel.

"Are we going to use all this?" she asked, with a mixture of both intrigue and trepidation, as she picked up the screwdriver and examined its length and gripped its black and red rubber handle.

He shrugged. "Maybe. It depends on you. What do you want to start with?"

"You're the Dom, aren't you supposed to orchestrate this?"

He turned to look at her, tilted his head and met her eyes with his. His eyebrows lifted and he nodded. "Yes. Yes, I am. I am the Dom. Indeed I am."

He took her by the hand and walked her over to the side of the bed. She noted that the nightstands had their own sets of supplies lined up beside the touch lamps. Lotions, oils, wipes, condoms, a silicon hand mitt, a little silk bag with the draw-string tie cinched at the top, and thoughtfully a scrunchie hair tie.

"What's in the bag?" she asked.

He smiled. "Things for me *and* for you—little silicon sleeves with nubby things on them. They fit over my penis and stimulate nerve endings along the vagina."

"You had these on hand?"

He grinned at her. "Turned inside out, they stimulate along the length of a penis. Namely mine. I use them when I jerk off sometimes. So I already had them. They're my go-to when I'm horny."

She laughed at that. She couldn't imagine him not being able to find a woman to service him, but she knew from experience, that some urges came on fast . . . and often in the middle of the night.

He found her laugh delightful . . . and uplifting. She

made him happy. Carefree in a way he usually never was.

"You of course, washed all these?"

"Of course," he quipped. "In the dishwasher."

"What!"

"Just joking. I was actually in the bath tub at the time, so they got washed with bubble bath."

"Then, let the games begin!" she announced as she let her robe fall to the floor.

Chapter 58
Nice Visuals & a Few Wallops

"Although you are stunning when you're naked, I want the visual to be right for this part. So put your bra, panties, and skirt back on, but not your shirt."

She had to go around collecting the items and then went into the bathroom to put them on. When she came back out, he handed her the long bobby pins she'd left on his dresser. "The look I'm going for is 'my secretary needs punishment.' Do that thing you do with your hair every morning before you come to work."

He watched as she gathered her hair to the side. With the skill of trained fingers, she held the hair she gathered high and rolled the ends, then secured the French twist in place, high on the back of her head. And just like that, she looked professional, efficient and businesslike, yet also beautiful and elegant. With her high cheekbones, kiss-swollen lips, and long smooth neckline, she was the perfect debauched secretary.

"You do that so expertly," he commented.

"I've had many years of practice."

He smiled. "Until this weekend, I've never seen it down."

"That was intentional. When I interviewed for the job I was told by the agency that you had a professional image in mind for your secretary. As this was how I had interviewed, when I got the job I decided I had to keep my appearance in line with your desires."

He ran a hand down her arm, gripped her fingers, and leaned in to kiss her. "Well my desires are certainly being fulfilled now—every one of them. Some I hadn't even known I'd had until I read that book of yours."

She gave him a sideways smile. "I keep thinking . . . what if I hadn't misplaced the book. This weekend would never have happened."

"My mother always says that things happen for a reason," he said.

"She surely didn't have this in mind."

He laughed. "No, I think she meant when I got accepted to Stanford instead of Chaminade. I really wanted to go to Honolulu and *surf* through college and law school. Instead, I went to Stanford.

"After I got out of law school, I became friends with a man who was the Dean of Admissions at Chaminade. I asked him to check the records to see why I didn't make it in. Turns out they were on a big push for several years to get criminal justice applicants. They weren't interested in someone interested in pursing an environmental law degree. I thought that odd for an islands in the South Pacific that is all about the ecosystem."

"Are you unhappy with the way things turned out?"

"Oh no! I can't imagine my life without my frat boys. I look forward to the reunions in July more than anything. And, there's a good chance if I'd gone to Hawaii, I'd have ended up staying there. And then I wouldn't have met you . . ."

Emboldened by his declaration, she leaned in and kissed him on the lips. "And I would have missed this incredible weekend with you."

He felt something warm flush throughout his body. He felt like a giddy teenager. Then his eyes focused on all the sex toys . "Enough stalling. Our weekend is getting away from us."

She saw where he was looking and raised her eyebrows. "Always the task master. Are we going to use all those today?"

"No. Exposure to three or four things at a time will be enough for one day. Too much stimulation is not advisable at first."

He sat on the edge of the bed, took her hand in his, and then spun her around and landed her across his lap as if he'd done this a hundred times. He gave a satisfied smile at her startled yelp.

"Now for the visual," he murmured as he pulled her skirt

up so that her panty-clad backside was right where he wanted it. Then he dragged her panties down until they were just below the creases where her legs joined her ass. The white globes of her bottom contrasted with his tanned hand. With her bunched panties in view it was a heady sight.

"This is a very nice visual," he said, as he placed his hand over one cheek and then used his palm to rub in ever-widening circles. "Nice tactile feeling, too." He stroked the backs of her thighs with his fingertips, saw her shiver from his gentle touch.

"Now . . . we need to discuss your punishment—the reason and the penalty. Do you know what you did wrong?"

"Mmm . . . I didn't swallow your cum?"

"Good. Very good. That is correct. You deprived me of the pleasure of feeling my cock at the back of your throat while you sucked me off . . . feeling you suck on my penis until the last possible moment before swallowing my cum. I'm thinking ten good wallops should take care of that for any future blow jobs."

She gulped. "Ten? Wallops? What exactly is a wallop?"

"A heavy blow. Sort of like a thwack."

She had to laugh, but it was a nervous laugh. "Oo-okay."

He drew his fingertips back and forth over both ass cheeks, then parted them with the fingers of one hand while he let his fingers trail down her crack and slowly circle the tiny puckered hole he found there.

His thumb slid down to play with the slick lips he found further down. He lightly grazed her with the side of his thumb then probed her with the tip. The dewy lips, now thoroughly coated, opened for him and he rimmed her opening. Circling with his thumb, he inserted it deeper until it was inside her. She moaned at the same instant that he groaned.

He didn't really want to smack her, but he knew that was what she wanted, maybe even needed. So he had to get on with it. "Ten will be the count," he announced, "as you need to be adequately punished for displeasing me."

Then his open hand lifted and came down, hard.

The loud smacking sound made her jump almost as much as the pain from the blow. A part of her could hardly believe that he'd actually hit her. But he had—and harder than she would have thought. Her boss. Sean. He had just spanked her! And damn, it hurt!

The pain bloomed across her bottom in waves. It stung. It burned. It throbbed. It ran through her mind that this was turn of the last century stuff—Dickensian or Edwardian treatment of women. Not modern day behavior. Why was she allowing this to happen?

Before she could process the outlandish thought that she was really across his knees and that he was really spanking her, she heard, "One!" called out. And then he did it again.

Another blow was landed—it seemed harder this time. Maybe because while it was painful in its own right, she had not yet processed the smarting pain from the first blow. It felt like her ass was on fire. "Two!"

She squirmed on his lap. Damn, she was surprised by how much this hurt!

The sting of his hand connected with her skin and the sharp, intense pain made her eyes water as number three was landed. She clenched her eyes tightly shut as her face contorted from the next abrupt sensation.

"Four!"

Dear God, had he really said she was getting ten of these?

She was unprepared for the loud crack as his wide palm met the rounded part of her ass—grazing her on the top of her thigh. The fifth blow sounded like a thunder crack and it felt as if lighting struck the tender skin of her thigh. She saw the color red behind her eyes as she held them closed against the pain. She thought about using her safe words. Because, damn it! This hurt! "Six!" echoed in her ears.

All she could register was four *wallops* to go as the pain ran through her like electric currents gone haywire. She didn't think she could take much more, was opening her mouth to tell him so when the seventh blow landed, this time encompassing part of her lower butt cheek and the back of her upper thigh again. As if it had been a glancing blow that missed its mark, it hadn't felt quite as bad as the others.

The pain that had been gathering was now slowly abating and leaving her body. It was easing up so she took in a deep breath. Maybe she could go on.

She heard the sound before she felt the pain as *Eight!* was called out. She felt as if her bottom was being branded. As if watching a horror picture inside her head, she heard someone scream.

There was no nine or ten to be announced as her upper body that had been hanging over his knees was now being hauled up and wrapped into the embrace of his strong arms.

She was still hearing the echo of her own voice screaming as it reverberated around the room, and tasting blood where she had bitten into her lip when she felt him kissing her all over her face.

Chapter 59
Learning What Works—And What Doesn't

He had been watching the skin turn pink on her smooth white bottom, listening to his hand connect, and counting. He'd been aware of his hand smarting after delivering each spanking. And he had watched as red splotches bloomed on the pale skin before fading to a lighter blush before he continued. He had just noticed the red blooms turning scarlet when he heard her scream.

He froze momentarily before quickly hauling her up, turning her over in his arms and seeing the flow of tears coming from her eyes. He cradled her in his arms as tears streamed down her face. There was a bit of blood on her bottom lip. Suddenly, he was terrified. Afraid he ruined things between them for good. He began kissing her all over her face.

"I'm sorry! I'm sorry! I must have been too rough and spanked you too hard. Oh my God, you're hurt."

He moved the strands of hair aside and caressed her cheek. "I am so sorry. Why didn't you use your safe words? I had no idea this was hurting you so much."

She swiped at the tears on her cheek. "I thought that was the idea. Spanking me and making me cry . . . am I not supposed to feel pain from the blows? Isn't punishment supposed to hurt?"

"If it's going to make you cry out and tear up like this, I don't want to do it anymore. I don't want to see you like this. I don't want you to be in that kind of pain. And I certainly don't want to be the cause of it."

He dried her cheeks with a tissue from the nightstand, then dabbed her lip where it had bled. Can you ever forgive me?"

"There's nothing to forgive. We were playing at sex, trying something new. It wasn't anything you did wrong. It just hurt more than I thought it would."

He put his forehead to hers. "This did not seem the

slightest bit erotic to me. Did it to you?"

She gave him a watery smile. "No, not really. The first part with your fingers on me was kind of nice though. It felt wonderful to have your fingertips exploring."

He pulled away and looked down into her face. Focused his eyes on hers. Then his hand slowly snaked between her legs and he felt her.

An expression of wonder crossed his face as he used his fingers on her. "Holy shit, you are drenched!"

His eyes met and held hers as he explored their depths, seeing things he hadn't noticed before as his fingers delved deep inside her. His middle finger was inside her up to the last knuckle and straining to go deeper.

"On some level, this must have appealed to you. You are so wet," he murmured. "But I am so sorry I did that to you."

"Don't be. I wanted you to do it. And I'm still glad we tried it. At least it satisfied my curiosity. But it seems spanking is not something I'm going to be into. My brain says no, even though my body seemed to respond with a wet juicy yes." Then she laughed. "Maybe we can try it again sometime with a velvet glove and less force."

He was in awe of her forgiving attitude. Entranced by her desire to try new things. And pleased with her practical reasoning to just forget something and discard it when it didn't work out. She was his levelheaded secretary after all, and generous enough not to blame or put this on anyone else's plate.

And despite everything, she was still eager to have him touch her, even after he'd brutally hurt her. And by all that was sacred, he had never felt a woman who was so wet.

He bent and kissed her. She allowed his lips to softly claim her mouth, to gently move over hers as a way of apology. The tip of his tongue laved and soothed the small cut on the inside of her bottom lip before breeching her lips to tangle with her tongue.

He couldn't hold back. He wanted her so much in that

moment. He captured and possessed her mouth with daring insistent jabs while moaning her name—her real name. "Sandy. Sandy. Mmmm, damn, you taste so good. I can't get enough of you. I need you right now. Need to be inside you so badly."

His hand snaked into her bra and he scooped out one breast, bent and took the nipple between his lips. He tugged on it lightly with his teeth. Sucked hard on it. Baring the other breast, he shoved them both together—licking back and forth between them and teasing her nipples to tight peaks with his lips and teeth.

"I want to fuck you. I need to make amends for my mistreatment of you. I intend to spend the rest of the day groveling at your feet. Or maybe, you'll let me pay homage to your pussy with my mouth and tongue on you instead?"

"Those words have a delightful ring to them. Grovel . . . homage . . . your mouth and tongue . . . down there . . ."

"Something tells me I've lost the upper hand here. Am I to be you're submissive now?"

She laughed. "No, I still want you to be the one in charge."

He picked her up and carried her around to the side of the bed and then dumped her in the middle of it.

"I need to be inside you right now more than I need to breathe." He unzipped the slacks he had put on and let them fall to the floor, took a condom off the nightstand and rolled it onto his very erect, jouncing up and down cock. He climbed onto the bed and straddled her body. With his hands on her hips he angled her, led his cock to her opening and entered her.

The sigh of her surrender as she sank into the mattress matched his sigh of wonderment and delight. Then he began to punish her in a way that held no pain. Using his cock as a ramrod he shoved and thrust while holding tight to her hips to get the best penetration.

She stopped him with a hand on his chest and a shy little smile, "Wait."

Then she lifted her legs so that she was bent in half with

her legs over his shoulders.

He growled his pleasure and pumped furiously into her. In this position, he was able to toy with her clit. With just a few strokes it doubled in size and began to pulse against his thumb. When he felt her start to come, he held and watched as she spent wildly, her musical sighs building until they reached a crescendo and all the air escaped between her lips in a long drawn out, "Ooohhhhh."

His orgasm followed hers as he held her sex tight to the root of his cock. His last words before he dropped into a coma on top of her were, "Sandy, you gaba mena figa du, abba me. Lip lap, cock dabba wish me love me."

They lay like that for quite some time, his chest half on and half off her torso, her hand stroking along his broad back as she tried to figure out what he had been trying to tell her as he came inside her. He was idly threading his hand through her hair that had come undone after her spanking.

She had been out of her head with pleasure, but she was pretty sure she had heard the word love.

Chapter 60
Being Spoiled

They each took a quick shower, then returned to the bed to rest against pillows propped against the headboard. Sitting in their robes and snacking on peanut butter and jelly crackers and bottles of vitamin water they discussed they day and laughed at the way things had turned out. The sun would be going down in about an hour, and he'd said that he wanted them to watch it together outside on the veranda.

"But first, I want to try something with you that I think I've become fairly proficient at."

"What's that?" she asked, as she licked the last of the jelly off her fingers.

He watched her tongue and thought another blowjob might be called for later on tonight.

He got up from the bed and rearranged the pillows that they'd been using to prop themselves up with. He stacked two together at the top of the bed in the center and patted the top one with his hand. "This will require you being tied up. Take off your robe and lie down with your head here."

She did as he asked and then he went around the bed securing the ties again, being careful not to make the knots too tight.

He stood back and admired how she looked. "You are so beautiful. It almost stops my heart to look at you."

"Well, we wouldn't want that," she said with a smile as he dropped his own robe onto a chair. "Looking at you does the opposite to me. My heart speeds up and I can feel my blood rushing everywhere."

"You're going to feel something like that right now," he said as he opened a nightstand drawer and took out two long white candles, the blackened wicks evidence that they had already been used before.

"Candling," he said as he put one down on top of the nightstand and fished in the drawer for a lighter. "I learned how to do this with Janine. Do you remember her?"

"Yes, petite blonde with big boobs. Always wore a high ponytail."

"That's the one. She loved having hot wax dripped on those boobs. And on other places . . . let's see if you like it."

He flicked the lighter on and put the taper to the flame. Instantly it caught and burned bright.

Her eyes followed his every moment as he came around to the side of the bed, bent, and kissed a nipple. "First, let's test this. I'm going to drip some wax into your navel. You tell me how it feels." He moved the candle and lightly tipped it. Hot wax splashed into her belly button.

It burned at first, the sensation of extreme heat firing through her and making her eyes go wide with the pain before it settled into a very pleasant soothing warmth.

"How was that?" he asked.

She quirked a brow at him. "Okay, I guess."

"Try this." He moved the candle, tipped it and let a splash of wax cover the tip of her nipple.

She hissed through her teeth at the hot contact, then slowly let the air blow out through her lips.

"Okay?" he asked.

She nodded and he moved to the other breast and coated that nipple too. Again, she drew in a quick breath . . . and then let it out very slowly.

"You okay?" he asked.

"Mmmm, yeah."

"Do you like it?"

"I'm not quite sure. Kinda weird feeling."

He dribbled a thin little stream over one of her breasts. She wasn't ready for it so he watched her flinch while her hands jerked and pulled on the ties.

He looked down at her face, trying to judge her level of discomfort. "More?"

She thought for a moment then nodded.

He tilted the candle over the other breast and let a stream of wax drip in a circle around the underside of her breast. Watched her eyes as she closed them to the pain. Then opened them again as it subsided.

"Will this leave marks?" she asked.

"For a while. Nothing permanent though. I'll rub some ointment on them when we're finished. One or two more?"

"Where?"

"Where do you think?"

"My clit?"

He smiled. "Yup. You ready?"

"What's my other option?"

"The crack of your ass."

"In for a penny . . ." she murmured.

He blew out the candle and placed it on one of their lunch plates. Then laughed when she looked disappointed.

"I have to use the other one. They burn differently. Something about the way the wax is made." He picked up the other candle and lit it. Held it and watched the flame until there was a tiny puddle of wax around the wick.

Then he walked to the other side of the bed. Her legs were already spread due to the ties holding them in place. He used the fingers of his other hand to spread her labia lips, ran them up and found her clit.

His eyes met hers, checking to see if she'd changed her mind. She hadn't. God, she was so trusting. Something in his heart flared that she could entrust her body so fully to him. And that she was so willing to submit to sex play to please him.

He moved the candle slightly and dripped two small drops onto her clit.

Her body arched off the bed at the same time she shrieked. He quickly cupped her sex and let her settle before blowing out the candle and placing it alongside the other one on the dish. Then he ducked his head between her spread legs and took her clit between his lips. He sucked on it while two fingers entered her. He frigged her and sucked on her until he brought her to her release—with an orgasm that went through her body so violently that she shook the bed.

With his hands splayed on either side of the pillow where her head rested, he leaned over her and watched as her eyelids slowly lifted. Their eyes met and they each smiled.

"Wow," she whispered, adding, "Just wow."

He grinned full on and gently kissed her on the lips. "I was hoping it would be good for you."

He grabbed the tube of ointment from the nightstand and began massaging all the red spots, working the wax off onto a handkerchief and then rubbing the soothing salve into her skin.

"That was amazing."

"You are amazing," he said. "So sweet, so trusting. You are a great submissive."

"Well . . . you are a fabulous Dom. I've never had such fierce orgasms. You are spoiling me."

"It's what we Doms do," he said with a chuckle, adding, "We take care of our subs."

"Where did you learn how to do all that?"

"This was Janine's thing. She was really into it."

"Whatever happened to you two?"

He shook his head sadly at the thought of one of his old girlfriends and at how their relationship had ended. "She cheated on me while I was out of town. And according to the guy involved, more than once."

"How did you find that out?"

He laughed. "In a very prophetic way. I was going to this gym and one day this guy who worked there was spotting for me while I lifted weights. He commented on my ability to lift so easily. He said, 'I am totally flagged this week. This chic I'm seeing is so hot, she literally sucks the strength right out of me. She's into some weird shit though. Likes me to drip hot wax onto her tits and twat.'"

"I looked at him and said, 'Janine?' And he said, "Yeah! You know her?'"

Sandy covered her mouth with her hand. "Oh no!"

"Oh no, is right."

"What did you say to her?"

"I met her for lunch and slid the card for the trainer across the table and I said, 'You ought to go to this gym. I hear this guy is into hot wax treatments.' Her face got red and her hand shook as she read his name on the card. I tossed down some cash for the meal and left. Haven't seen her since."

"Wow. I don't get it. How could anyone cheat on you? You're like the best boyfriend a girl could ever have."

He looked over at her and grinned. "You think that do you?"

Realizing what she'd just blurted out, her hand covered her mouth again. "Well, I guess it's no secret now that I have a crush on you."

He finished rubbing the ointment on the red marks on her nipples and breasts and belly button. Now his hand moved between her legs with a generous dab that he used to soothe her clit. "I think we'd better give this outstanding performer a little rest for a while." He made sure it was thoroughly coated with the unguent then patted it gently.

He got up and reached for her robe. "Let's put our robes on and get a glass of wine and go out to enjoy the sunset, then I'll make dinner for you."

"You're going to cook?"

"No, I already did cook. I like to freeze my leftovers. I have some Beef Stroganoff I made in my Insta-pot. Thought we'd have that with some salad."

"Sounds great. I can't believe I didn't know that you liked to cook."

"You don't know all my secrets," he quipped.

She laughed. "Yeah, but I'm pretty sure you know all of mine!"

He nuzzled her neck. "I love all your secret *places* that's for damned sure."

He helped her into her robe, donned his, and then walked her into the bar area where he opened a bottle of champagne. He put the bottle into a bucket with ice, and then he carried it out to the poolside table that was in a corner niche that faced the backside of the house, while she carried the glasses and a cheese tray.

Together they toasted the day and watched the sun go down against a glowing red sky.

"I love having you here," he said as the last slivers of gold disappeared behind the house.

"I love being here."

"How do you think things are going compared to what you read in your book?"

She thought for a few moments before speaking. "Maybe this D/s stuff is not all it's cracked up to be. But then again, maybe it is. I like some parts of it. Really like others. A few other things . . . not so much though. I'm thinking that we just need to be ourselves, and take what we want from it. Do what we enjoy and what we like to do for each other without some of the harsh pain."

"It's a good thing we have one more night, and one more day to get it right. Let's go have some dinner. Then we'll each take a soothing bath or shower to get cleaned up. I have a few more things I want to do to you tonight." He reached over, picked up her hand and kissed the back of it.

Chapter 61
Hard Limits and Mental Pictures

After a fabulous dinner, that in her mind, was just about one of the best she'd ever had, they cleaned up together and then they each went to separate bathrooms—him for a long hot shower, her for a long hot soak in the tub.

They met back in the guest bedroom where he removed her robe then took her hand and helped her up onto the bed. He positioned her so that she was facing up, spread-eagled. He took great care to tie each wrist and each ankle to a bed slat, leaving her ample room to shift her weight, as needed.

He gathered her hair up onto the top of her head and secured it with one of the hair ties he found in the guest bath. He was pretty sure it was one of his niece's, as Sandy was the first woman he'd had at this house. He used slipknots and placed the ends in her palms. "You can pull the knots out anytime you want."

He leaned over and kissed her on the lips. Then covered her eyes with a soft flaxseed-filled eye mask. He secured the Velcro strap behind her head.

"Everything okay, so far?" he asked.

"Yes. I am fine. Naked, splayed open, blindfolded, bound to the bed posts . . . but not at all nervous."

He chuckled. "You can't fool me. I've got your number now. You're lovin' this."

She smiled. "Yes. It's because I trust you."

"Well, you shouldn't. I botched your first and likely last spanking experience—in a really big way."

"Hey, we're in this together. I'll let you know if something's bothering me. I remember my three words. I'll use them if I need to."

"You should have used them before . . ."

He walked over to the dresser, picked up something, then turned to look at her. She looked hot—so incredibly sexy he almost couldn't stand it. The robe he wore was parted by his erection. He was hot, hard, and heavy. He felt his penis lifting and throbbing, eager for action. He shrugged the robe off his shoulders and let it fall to the floor in front of the dresser.

He had hoped he could give her the pain/pleasure combination she craved. Now, worried that he might have hurt her and damaged their relationship, he was more tentative about their next step. She seemed to sense this.

"I trust you. I'll be more open with you from now on. I promise."

He smiled to himself. Ever the efficient one, she was now settling him down. Bringing him back into the game like she often did at work.

"Okay, I'll need some feed back on this. Especially when I spank you . . . with a velvet paddle and a cotton candy flogger."

She laughed and it made her breasts jounce. So enticing.

He walked to the foot of he bed, stared at her body, drinking in all the nuances of her loveliness. He focused on the apex between her legs. He saw the lips of her labia clench, watched as moisture pooled. This woman was so responsive. He hoped he could satisfy her; make her forget her earlier experience with him as her inept Dom. He was beginning to suspect that she knew he was more of an ingénue at this Dom/sub stuff than she was.

He walked back to the bed with two wooden clothespins in his hands. He bent over her and took a nipple between his fingers, played with it, then stretched it out and clamped it well under the tip. He felt his penis jump when she drew in a harsh gasp. Looked at her face to see if she was registering more than a modicum of pain. She wasn't. If anything, he could see by the flare of her nose that this woman was pleased with this slow and sensual seduction of her. He clipped the other nipple the same way. Then stood back and admired the view.

"You are so damned sexy. So very hot. You look incredible.

With your nipples clamped and your breasts plumped up and begging for more mistreatment. I could cum just from looking at you like this."

He sat on the edge of the bed and ran his palm over her belly, working his hand lower until it was over her mons. His fingers strayed to the little bit of scruff he had allowed to remain there, then he toyed with the dampness he found at her opening.

"I'd love to take a picture of you like this. One we could look at together and then delete. Would you let me do that?"

Her face flushed. Her eyes, behind the eye pillow, must be clenched tight, he thought, as he could see faint lines radiating out at the sides. "Umm. No. No pictures."

"That would be a hard limit for you, wouldn't it? That's good. You should not feel uncomfortable about doing anything. Don't be afraid to say no to something if it is not for you. It's admirable that you've set limits. You should have boundaries that you don't want crossed when we're playing."

"Pictures taken in private always seem to find their way to the Internet," she said with a moue curving her mouth as her way of saying it's not happening.

He smiled and continued his supposition, "Well, the picture would definitely have to be deleted right away. If not, anything could happen to prevent the picture from being deleted. It would have to be done immediately. Seconds after it's taken, in the event there was a sudden earthquake, tornado or flood. Because, if the camera got lost in the rubble, anyone could find it later. Then poof!" he made an exploding gesture with his fingertips that she couldn't even see, "the photo would go viral!"

He used his open hands pulling apart from each other to indicate a headline banner. "Woman dies in horrific avalanche. The only way the authorities can identify her is by this picture taken just moments before her death. Anyone recognizing this pussy please call the police."

She turned her head and shot him a condescending look from where her head rested on the pillow. Unfortunatly, he couldn't see her eyes through the blindfold. "Or someone could take a picture and *stealthily* manage to text it or email it to themselves before deleting it. Someone sneaky, using some kind of slight-of-hand magic thing. Then I'd have that awful moment when my friends call or text . . . letting me know that I've been . . . well . . . compromised—in a very bad, life-changing way."

"Well first, you have to really know the person taking the picture. You'd have to trust them, know about their character. Know that even if things ended badly between you, that no amount of anger would make them do something so despicable. I hope you know that I would never harm you. If you walked out the door right now, and I never saw you again, I would be happy we had this time together and not feel the need to be vindicated because you left me."

"What if I left with your grandmother's million-dollar earrings?"

"Then I would hope you'd have the occasion to wear them again—even if it was with another man. Who would photograph you when they were clipped to your sweet nipples. And then send the picture to all your friends. Where eventually the police would see them. Who would then bring the earrings back to me. You would go to jail where you would be known as the Thwarted Topless Typist Tittie-clip Thief."

She laughed so hard the bed shook. "Another reason not to pose for a naughty picture. Besides these are just old wooden clothespins. Who would want to see these?"

He looked down at where her legs were still splayed, and he cupped her womanhood. "There is nothing naughty about what we're doing. You are beautiful—whether you're wearing expensive jewelry or old clothespins."

He removed her eye pillow so she could see him. Then he opened his eyes wide and closed them with a fast downward jerk of his head. He did this twice. Then he opened his eyes again and gave her a huge smile.

"What was that all about?"

"I took a picture—a mental picture. Two of them in fact. They're in my head—for all time. I will be able to recall how lovely you look right this minute, at any time I want."

She pulled on the cord in one of her hands and the knot came undone. She reached up and gripped his hot and heavy erection. She did the same eyes-closed and head-jerking motion he'd just done. Twice. Then opened her eyes and smiled up at him. "Now, I too, have a forever memory of this moment and of how hard and needy you can be for me."

"Yes. For you." He climbed onto the bed, reached over her for a condom and tore the package open. She watched as he covered the crown of his penis with the condom and then rolled it down. Then he reached under her and lifted her by her bottom, dragged her close, and entered her.

"Now, carefully remove the clothespins by opening them wide. Don't jerk them off. They've been on for a while so you're going to feel the bite when they come off. Don't make it worse for yourself by jerking them off."

They both groaned when she had slowly plucked them both off. Her, from the sensation of blood rushing back to the poor, denigrated areas. Him, from watching her areolas plump up and become engorged, the tips impossibly long.

He leaned down and took one of her sore nipples into his mouth and gently sucked on it, letting his tongue swirl around the tip to gently soothe it. The other received the same treatment. Her eyes were going crossed from the mind-numbing pleasure.

As her body arched up to meet his, he ground his pelvis into hers. Holding her by her hips, he repeatedly retreated and entered her. He slowly withdrew, then thrust back fast. He plunged into her over and over again, seating himself fully with each stroke and riding her pubic ridge while using his thumb to tease her.

He watched her face as her pleasure built. Saw when her eyes fluttered closed and her mouth fell open to a surprised gasp. Felt her body shudder as she fell over the edge into her bliss.

His head thrown back and his eyes tightly closed, he grimaced against the force of the intensely gratifying pleasure leaving his body and pumping into hers.

Kaleidoscope images swirled at top speed inside her head, hurling her through the black void while the rest of her body stayed pinned under him. She was vaguely aware that he had followed her to completion, perverse cussing aside; she had felt his erratic contractions reverberating inside her body.

He all but collapsed over her. A few moments later, when his penis slid out of her, he removed the condom and managed to drop it onto the nightstand before darkness engulfed him and he lost all thought.

She heard his steady, slow breathing. Knew he was asleep, and allowed herself to drift off as well. It had been an exhausting day, emotionally and physically. She wondered if he'd ever invite her back or if this was to be a one-off thing, with him moving on to the next girl that crossed his path at some social event.

She opened her eyes to the weight of him holding her in place. His face was turned to the side on the pillow beside her. His breathing was even and regular. He seemed to be asleep, but he wasn't snoring. An arm that was wrapped around her was resting on her shoulder and holding the upper portion of her body close to his.

Her weekend of BD/sm play was coming to an end. She'd had no expectations other than hoping that she didn't embarrass herself—and that he wasn't a closet sadist. She had little to gage this experience against. Had it gone well? Would *he* think it had gone well? He seemed pretty exhausted right now. That had to be a good thing.

He chose that moment to open his eyes. She had always loved his eyes, deep blue and always attentive to everything going on around him. "Hi beautiful."

She couldn't help but smile. "Hi yourself handsome." The hand that was not trapped by the weight of his body reached up and stroked the side of his neck. Her fingers toyed with the short wavy curls that were sweat-damp from his efforts at pleasuring her.

As if he had been thinking the very same thoughts about their time together, he murmured, "Are you having fun? Is this what you expected?"

"I am having fun. It is nothing like what I expected."

He rolled off of her so he could lean up on one elbow and look down at her. He stroked her cheek using the backs of his fingers.

"Better? Worse?"

She thought for a few moments and huffed out, "Well . . . I've learned a lot about myself. I'm really surprised by how quickly I was able to toss aside years of ingrained inhibitions. I never would have thought I would have allowed myself to be paraded around naked, and stared at while I had sex toys attached to body parts or inserted into private places."

"Why do you think that's so?" he asked as his fingertips trailed down her neck to her chest where he cupped her left breast and traced her nipple before gently plucking at it.

Instantly, she felt heat zinging her core and something liquid inside catching fire and sending a spasm to clench her vagina. Each time he plucked at her nipple, she responded with that wicked tightening down there.

She felt wetness dampening her. Places she was hardly ever aware of were now paramount in her realm of sensations. The longer he tugged on her nipple, the more her mind was attentive to what he was doing. After a while, nothing else seemed to matter, except that he not stop. But he did. Then switched to the other one.

She gathered her courage and answered his question. "It's because of the pleasure you give me. You make me want more of the same. You heat everything up inside me. Desire becomes stronger than modesty. The yearning for more . . . well it just doesn't leave. Until you do something to make it go away."

"And how do I make that desire leave?" he prompted.

"By making me come."

"And how do I make you come?"

"By teasing me, touching me, shaming me. Sucking. Licking. Kissing me. In all my secret places."

"I love kissing your secret places. I think of it as worshipping you. I love your body. Every part is perfect." His hand smoothed down her midriff, splayed open over her womb, and then cupped her sex. "I'm going to want more of this. More of you."

He left his hand in place but turned his head so he could meet her eyes with his. "Are you going to want to do this again?"

Looking down at her, his face serious, his eyes intense with the question he was asking, he never looked more handsome . . . or more intent on the answer to a question.

"Do you mean now, or later?"

"Both." His eyes were locked with hers. As if he could search their depths, stare into the wonderment of her glazed blue irises and find the reply he wanted. And glazed over they were as his middle finger entered her and his thumb nudged her little bud awake.

As if to make things clear, he said, "I want you now. And I will want you again later."

From the very first day she had met him, she'd been drawn to him. As he sat behind his desk assessing her and firing off questions, she had fought her attraction to him. Every encounter since had heighted her fascination but she'd learned to temper it—to put thoughts of him aside and get the work done. He was her boss and she did not want to lose her job. She often thanked the Lord that he kept her busy during the week—too busy to dwell on her attraction to him. Until the weekend when she made him the hero in every book she read.

He could be charming when he wanted to be, alluring, magnetic with a luminary presence due to his high-caliber job, and captivating with his intelligence and highbrow manners. She'd had plenty of evidence over the years that he appealed to a wide variety of women, and not just beautiful fortune hunters. Secretly, she had envied each and every one of them for their nights with him.

But he could also be sardonic, condescending, scornful, quick- to-anger, vindictive, and merciless, especially to those unprepared in a courtroom.

This weekend, she added voracious, sexy, sensual, scandalous, brazen, erotic, demanding, and downright naughty to his list of characteristics.

She'd seen all aspects of his personality. Had probably known from the very beginning that no man she would ever meet would compare to him, would ever come out on top. She'd accepted that, because she'd had to. But now things were different. He was hinting at more. But how much more?

She decided she didn't care; she would take whatever he was offering. That was the real shame that she should be feeling, not the shame of humiliation due to being naked, or for allowing herself to be abused by him . . . but for being available to him, for catering to him, for being eager to take whatever scraps he was willing to give her instead of focusing on her own needs. But the dichotomy in a Dom/sub relationship was; his needs demanded he satisfy hers. So maybe the true submissive in this type of relationship was actually the Dom.

He dove under the covers and began a slow seduction that began with her inner thighs and led to them being in the classic 69 position. He pleasured her with intimate kisses and a very thorough tongue lashing while she learned that lying sideways on the bed with him in her mouth gave her better control in bringing him to his climax, with her being able to suck down each drop of his ejaculate without gagging on his impressive size. Afterward, they both fell asleep—this time for the rest of the night—in the classic spooning position as if it was a normal, natural thing for them to do.

Chapter 62
October, November, December

It was late Sunday morning when Sean woke to golden glints of sunshine bouncing off the walls. He zeroed in on the woman lying beside him, already awake and drinking him in. God, she was lovely.

Her cheek was resting on folded hands as if praying. Her eyes wide open as she stared at him. They were moist as if she'd been crying, and were such beautiful pools of blue that it made his heart swell.

He saw her rose-colored lips move. He watched them slowly form words as his brain readied to interpret the sounds.

"October, November, December," she quietly breathed out.

It took him a moment to decipher the meaning of her words. Then his brows lifted and shock registered in his eyes. He couldn't stop the sound that escaped his lips. Like a dog howling, he bellowed, "Noooo!"

He drew in a long breath and held it, his lips firming as he forced them tight together. As soon as his brain translated the listing of the last three months of the year into their designated meaning, chills ran through his body and everything inside him screamed *No! No! No! This was not what he wanted to happen!*

It took several long moments to consider his thoughts and to put them together before he spoke. His words sounded shaky both inside and outside of his head as he spoke them, "You're using your safe words . . . you're calling everything off."

He sighed and took the sadness deep into his chest. This was over. He couldn't believe it. And he couldn't believe the pain he felt.

With sadness in her eyes and her head still on the pillow, she nodded. Then affirmed her choice of words . . . and their meaning. "Yes. I'm using my safe words. I've decided that I don't want to do this anymore. It's not working for me. It's not how I thought things would be."

His hand reached out, touched her shoulder, and gently rubbed. "We still have a day to go. It's only Sunday. I thought you were having a good time. I know I gave you pleasure."

"You did." She smiled. "You did," she repeated sadly.

"Then, why?"

"Ummm. I was curious. I thought it might be something I would like. But I don't really. The pain part is . . . not enjoyable. To me, anyway."

"Did I hurt you badly?"

"Not terribly badly, but bad enough. Each time, I just wanted it to be over with. So I thought, what was the point? Maybe it was more about the feeling of shame it brought on. I don't know. But the thought of doing it again is not a good one for me. I'd just as soon not do it again."

The empty feeling in his chest grew tighter. He felt like his heart could stop pumping at any minute. "Saying those words stops everything. Is that what you want? Is that why you said them?"

"No, silly. I don't want everything to stop. I just don't want to be your biddable submissive anymore."

"You don't?" Now he was confused.

"I don't mind you dominating me in some ways. I just don't think the spankings and hard swats are for me. I didn't really know what I was getting into. Reading the scenes in a book is nothing like experiencing them for real. I guess I don't really want brutal blows administered to my body after all. I'm glad we tried it though. But it's a little weird—the pain, the harm, the marking of my skin, and the actual meanness of it. I feel that if we really got into it, the beatings would have to keep escalating to bring the same level of satisfaction. And then where would it end? I don't think I need the pain or the humiliation to achieve orgasm—at least not with you. I think just being touched by you, and you just being you . . . does it for me."

"So that's the only part you want to change?"

"Well, I don't like to think about you sharing me either."

He gathered her up into his arms. "Oh Baby, I would never do that. You are mine. I don't want anyone else to have you."

She looked up at him. "Really? You're sure about that? You sounded like it was something you wanted."

"Oh, I am definitely sure about that. I think I would kill any man who tried to have you."

Her face brightened at that. "Really?"

"Really."

"And how about flaunting me . . . showing me off? Taking pictures?"

"They were just words. I was trying to appeal to your naughty side . . . and mine too. Nothing more. I was playacting to get you turned on. Apparently that didn't work out as planned."

"Hmmm. Maybe. In the moment the idea of it was kind of hot. But when I really thought you'd actually want to do it, it didn't turn me on anymore. It actually frightened me."

He gathered her into his arms and pulled her tight into his chest. "I was trying to appeal to the naughty girl that is supposedly inside every woman. But then you acted as if you actually might like to do some of those things, like be naked around other men so I played it up a little more. I never really meant for you to think that I'd actually allow it."

"But . . . Rutger . . . Pauline . . . they did it. And still do. And you were even a part of their scene."

"Well, that's them. They're both into that lifestyle. I was only doing a favor for a friend. I was a single and unattached male at the time. What straight man wouldn't want to watch one of his best friends show off his girlfriend's tits? And drive her around while she was topless? It was a lark. It didn't mean I wanted to do the same thing with any of my girlfriends."

"So you don't?"

"No, I do not. In fact, I don't want anyone to see your body but me. Ever."

"Will you still threaten me with it?"

"I feel like this is a trick question. Do you want me to?"

She thought for a minute. "Well, in the heat of passion . . . maybe."

He laughed. "Okay. I can go with that. Anything else we need to discuss?"

"I like the being tied down part. And being blindfolded was nice, too. As long as I knew it was just you . . . there in the room with me."

He smiled. "You know what? So did I. I liked that part a lot. So . . . you don't want to stop being with me?"

"No. No, I don't."

"You just want . . . what?"

"Normal, regular sex?"

"Ahhh. In the D/s world they call it vanilla sex."

She frowned. "So there are flavors to this? If so, I like butter pecan best."

He smiled and ran a fingertip down her nose. "That's you, nutty as a fruitcake. So . . . are you saying you want a normal relationship, not a BD/sm one?"

She nodded. "I've been halfway in love with you, from the very beginning. So I always want to please you. A little spanking is okay, but I don't want to progress to the flogging and caning stuff."

He took a strand of hair from below her chin and tucked it back behind her ear. He had a big grin on his face. "You love me?"

She gave him a crooked smile. "Yeah. I'm surprised you never suspected it. I have for quite a long while." She waved a hand indicating his muscular torso with the soft, springy covering of chest hair. "What's not to love?"

He chuckled. "Apparently my method of lovemaking?"

"What we've been doing is not lovemaking."

"No, you're right. We've been playacting. And I must admit I haven't been doing it very well. Not having had any experience in this particular type of sex, I was at a complete loss as to what to do with you. "

"What?" She scrunched her face up in disbelief.

He grimaced and shrugged his shoulders. "I don't know why I wanted you to think I had any experience with this. I don't. You are my very first attempt at trying to get into the lifestyle."

"Well, that actually makes me feel a bit better. So we're both inept at the Fifty Shades stuff."

He laughed and pulled her close.

She snuggled a bit then let out a resigned sigh, "We will have to table this discussion for later. I should get up and get going. We both have to get to work early tomorrow morning and I have to go home first as I don't have any clothes here."

He rolled over taking her with him. When she was underneath him, he dug his fingers into her hair and held her face in his hands, forcing her to meet his gaze. He lowered his face to hers and his lips moved over hers in a tender kiss. When he ended it, he pulled away and smiled down at her.

"Let's take tomorrow off. Both call in sick."

"Won't that be a bit obvious? Neither of us is ever sick."

"Actually, I closed the office. I emailed everyone but you late Friday afternoon that we'd be closed on Monday. I had a feeling I'd need more time with you."

"What? We aren't going to work tomorrow? No one is?"

"It's World Elephant Day."

"It is?"

"Yes, it really is. And I plan to keep you in bed for most of it."

"I did not know that. And I pride myself on keeping up on all the holidays."

"Well, Tuesday is International Left-handers Day, Wednesday is World Lizard Day, Thursday is national Relaxation Day, and Friday is National Roller Coaster Day. Do you want

449

me to tell you about the following week?"

"You're closing the office for two weeks?"

"No, just for tomorrow. But you and I? We still have some work to do."

"We do?"

"Um hmm," he murmured as he kissed along her ear and then took the lobe between his teeth and nibbled on it. "We have some contracts to draw up."

"What kind of contracts?"

"Ones where we spell out exactly what we want from each other—in great detail. So we're on the same page. No more giving me a heart attack that you're leaving me for what I've done or haven't done. For instance . . . what I want to do next is to take a long hot shower with you. Where I take you from the rear while you're in one of those yoga positions you have on that desk calendar of yours."

"Which one?"

"Down dog. Afterward, to be forever known on your flip calendar as Dirty Down Dog."

"What if I don't want to get my hair wet?"

He laughed. "Sweetheart, everything about you is going to be wet in a few minutes. Including this." He reached his hand down, wriggled his hand between her thighs, and began stroking her.

She began purring almost right away.

"I cannot believe how fast you cream up down here," he murmured. "You are one slick lady," he teased.

"Says the attorney who is using World Elephant Day to seduce his secretary."

He removed his hand from her, and then used his other hand to prop his head up as he looked down at her. The fingers that had been inside her, were now trolling along the outer edge of her arm. "We have to talk. I don't want to lose you."

Her face took on a serious mien as her eyes opened wide.

He looked troubled.

"Okay . . ." she whispered, then added, "Talk."

Trepidation moved through her body and alarms went off inside her head. This was it. She was sure of it. This was the let down. He'd have his fill of her soon and it would be time to move on. She'd have to be ready for that. Accept that this was fun and games for as long as it lasted—then to each his own. She'd seen it over and over again with him. Hundreds of gorgeous women had taken their turn with him. Now it was her turn. But that didn't mean there wouldn't be others after her.

"I can't believe I wasted so much time when you were thirty steps away all along."

"What?"

"You. You were the one—all that time. I cannot believe that I wasted years going from woman to woman . . . when I could have been with you from the very beginning."

She froze trying to take in his words and to sort out their meaning.

There was a long silence as he drew in a deep breath and then slowly let it out. "Or maybe, deep down, something inside me did know that it would always be you . . . and I simply fought against it."

"What are you saying?"

"I'm saying that I've been falling in love with you this whole time. And that I'm sorry that I didn't allow myself to see that. It's as if I refused to see you as anything but my efficient secretary, because I didn't want to lose my wonderful personal assistant. My stupid, proper, appropriate-behavior-always attitude just wouldn't allow me see you as the beautiful, sexy woman you are. I only allowed myself to see the capable woman you were at work: smart, efficient, hardworking, and occasionally, hilariously funny.

"I closed my eyes to your beauty and to your sexy body. The curious, flirty nature you kept hidden was because I never gave you an in—a chance to connect with me in a more personal way. I only saw you as Sandy—my assistant extraordinaire. I wouldn't let myself see you as anything else."

He barked out a laugh then. "Certainly not sensual, submissive Beth."

Then he snickered. "But now? Now, I will always want to pull you onto my lap when you walk behind my desk to get papers from my printer."

She smiled. "You know, at first I wasn't very happy that I'd lost that book. But now I'm glad that I did."

He smiled down at her. "I am too. It opened the door for us. It made me you see you as a woman—a very sensual woman. Not just someone I work with. That book gave me permission to get to know the real you. The beautiful, sexy you."

Tears were running down the side of her face now. He used his fingertip to catch a tear before it ran into her ear.

"Don't cry. There's no reason to cry."

"Yes, yes there is. You said you've been falling in love me all this time. I feel as if I've loved you forever, but I never thought it could ever be returned. I didn't acknowledge it, even to myself. I had to keep it hidden inside . . . because I really needed this job. It is *such* a relief now to tell you how I feel."

More tears sprang from her eyes as he bent to take her lips with his. He kissed her deeply, savoring the taste of her . . . even the tangy salt of her fresh tears. He kept on kissing her and letting his fingers tangle in her hair.

This time, when he covered her body with his, they did make love. With gentle, passionate, slow-burning strokes they did a sweet, chaste, tenderly choreographed dance—until he entered her.

"You might have noticed that there is no condom," he whispered into her ear as he shoved deeper inside. Once, twice, three times, he pumped his hips. Then held.

She looked up at him and getting his meaning, she simply nodded.

"That's because it's not going to be necessary anymore. I'm clean, you're clean. And I love you. And you love me.

Neither of us will be seeing anybody else. As my assertive, yet compliant submissive, you'll still want to do my bidding, won't you? And you'll still be my sexy secretary as well?"

She nodded again, this time more emphatically.

"Then say you'll marry me."

Her eyes bugged wide but she nodded again; her head going up and down like a bobble head doll in a classic car's back window.

"Say it," he demanded, "I need to hear your answer."

"Yes, I'll marry you," she whispered, the reverence of the moment conveyed by her gasping breath. Well, that and the fact that he was still shoving himself up inside her.

He nodded his approval as he partially withdrew. "And if . . . during the course of screwing ourselves silly, we produce a baby, we'll cherish it, right?" He thrust deep into her again to emphasize his point. Her head nudged the bed slats as the force of his thrust sent her sliding on the sheet.

She couldn't stem the flow of tears now, or the flow from other areas. She returned his thrust with one of her own, lifting her hips up to meet his.

"I would like to have a baby," she whispered, her lips close to his ear. "Your baby."

That was all he needed to hear. They frantically went at it, him setting the tempo with his hips pumping, her reaching behind him to grip his buttocks and to pull him in even closer. He bent to kiss her breasts and to take her nipples to task with his lips when they slowed down to circle, grind, and hold close.

"I love you," he whispered into her ear, just before he gripped her hips to his and emptied himself into her pulsing channel. "Daggit, shabgrith, matophobic, abteritic, ffuuuuccck!"

She felt her clitoris throb, ache, and explode as he held her close for the last several pumps.

Her orgasms always took so much out of her, but she managed to breathe out, "I love you. I love you. I love you. I have always loved you," before she mumbled, "ahhh, shibildeedick, frag a magga, yong yub yug,"

Using their own strange language they serenaded each other as they fell to an unconscious oblivion and slowly came back to themselves. They opened their eyes to catch each other's return to sanity.

The scared moment lingered until Sean asked, "It is okay if we don't use protection, isn't it?" as gravity separated their bodies. "I assumed it would be okay . . ."

She nodded. "It's okay. I'll have to stop birth control when we decide we want to have a baby."

"We should do that whenever you feel ready. I feel as if we've already lost so much time while I was stupidly trying to find a wife . . . when she was right under my nose."

She laughed and he pulled her in close.

"Does that mean that you'll marry me?"

"Are you really asking?"

He pulled away from her, frowned, and then looked toward the ceiling as if he was reconsidering.

Then he leapt out of bed and ran down the hall naked, while she scooted up against the headboard with a frown ceasing her face. She closed her eyes tightly and chastised herself. Why had she put him in such an awkward position? Why couldn't she just have left well enough alone and answered with a resounding, "Yes!"

She heard electronic beeping and the low hum of a rumbling motor. Then running footsteps coming back down the hall as Sean ran into the room, took a flying leap, and plopped down onto the bed beside her. He moved some pillows around and scooted up next her.

Then he flipped opened the lid of a black velvet box and showed her what was inside. Before she could allow her feelings to swamp her with disappointment, she murmured, "Oh, another pair of your grandmother's earrings."

"Yes!" he said excitedly. Then he carefully put the jewel-encrusted earrings on her, pulling each nipple until it was long and taut, and carefully snapping the spring clip around the tip.

When he was done, he sat back and admired her. "Gorgeous. You are one gorgeous woman in Harry Winston emeralds and diamonds."

She looked down and saw her breasts adorned with multimillion dollar jeweled clips. She didn't know what to say. Was he giving these to her? Because, no way could she accept them.

She had to acknowledge that she was disappointed—big time. Everything had changed as soon as she had asked him if he was serious about asking her to marry him. She was so mad at herself.

"Do you like them? Because I sure do!"

"Yeah, they're very nice." She could feel them start to do the tingly thing to her nipples, now drawn tight and beginning to get achy.

"I wanted you dressed up for this." He reached behind his back and brought out another black velvet box, this one slightly smaller and a little taller.

When he flicked open that box she saw the most beautiful ring. A brilliant cut diamond encircled by two rows of smaller diamonds in a platinum setting.

"Sandy, will you do me the honor of becoming my wife?"

Gobsmacked. That's what she was. She couldn't form her mouth around any single word. He immediately sensed her distress.

"I am so glad you're speechless and naked in my bed, dressed only in gemstones as I propose to you. I love you, Sandy—everything about you. And I would love to adorn you with jewelry like this for the rest of our lives. Will you please marry me?"

She simply nodded, uncertain what would come out of her mouth if she spoke.

He took the ring from the box and placed it on her finger. Then kissed her finger. Then kissed the tips of each breast.

"You're killing me here. Can't you say the words?" He touched her lips with the tip of his finger.

"Yes. Yes. Yes!"

"And when our kids ask how I proposed to you, will you tell them the truth?"

"No. No, no, no!"

Down they went onto the bed as he kissed her, wrapped his arms around her and admired her enticing breasts.

"I can't believe you're mine."

She laughed, finally able to make a sound. "I can't believe we're naked in bed, me wearing only your grandmother's over-the-top jewelry on my tits. Her jewelry is very nice. I'm sure it was quite opulent for the time, but it sure doesn't cover much."

He bent and began licking the very tips of her nipples, which were now very sensitive. "These have to come off soon. These clips are tighter than the other ones were. Looking at you with these on has made me incredibly hard. Again. I want to be inside you when they come off. See if I can feel your body react from the inside."

He quickly straddled her, positioned himself at her opening, and entered her. Then he gently opened first one clip then the other, before tossing them both aside onto the bed covering.

"Aaahhh. Damn, that hurts!" she cried out.

"Shhh. It's gonna feel real good now, Baby. Just give it a few more seconds."

He bent and gently suckled each nipple, drawing it out and teasing it with his tongue. Her breasts grew heavy as her areolas plumped up again and her chest flushed red. His thumb began massaging her clit as he rode her.

He saw when the pain was replaced with pleasure. Saw when her eyes closed with the intense rapture closing in. He felt her convulse, going from pain to pleasure and back to pain again as an intense expression come over her face. It was as if she was focusing her whole being on reaching something . . . getting somewhere. Then he felt her detonating.

She milked his cock with her vagina, then the tight muscles that had been building up to her orgasm let loose and opened the floodgates.

Her bliss was phenomenal. He had never felt a woman surrender to her body so completely. It made him feel whole— filled with the sense of being invincible making him one with the universe as he dropped over the edge and found his own release.

The sounds that filled the room were of long drawn out groans and indecipherable gibberish. To them, it was music. Love in action—as great sex was taken to the next level because of true love.

He absolutely loved this woman. And the miracle was, that she loved him, too—and now they would get married. She would be his wife, and he her husband. They would have kinky, imaginative sex . . . that might even lead to babies. If they didn't, it sure wouldn't be for lack of trying. As a bonus, his mother would finally stop badgering him to settle down and give her grandbabies. He hoped he could give her a dozen.

As he held Sandy in his arms, moving her sweat-dampened hair aside and kissing her temple, he murmured, "Is it okay that we don't use protection now?"

She looked up at him as he leaned over her, her brows winged up in confusion. "We kind of haven't been . . ."

"I know. I'm just asking it you're fine with that. And with stopping whatever you're on, as well."

"I am."

He kissed her deeply, sampling the taste of his new fiancé and marveling how all this had come about in such a short amount of time. Well . . . no. It had actually taken five years to get to this point.

When he ended the kiss he stared into her eyes, then smiled. "I don't want to wait a year or better for an over-the-top wedding. What can you pull together within six months?"

"Destination wedding in Vegas next week?"

"My mom won't go for that, she'll want some kind of spectacle."

"What do you suggest?"

"How about the Figure Eight Island Yacht Club?"

"Oh, yeah. The place I write that huge dues check to every year. Where you have those posh seminars. Don't you have to book that place years in advance?"

"Most people do. Mother won't have any problem though. If she can't get the actual venue, we can always use their yacht."

"It's going to take me a long time to get used to the idea of doing everything so upscale. I live in a 900-square-foot condo. I shop at Wal-Mart and the Dollar Store. I drive an old Honda Civic. You're going to have to be patient with me. This is a lot to take in."

"Don't worry. Mother will hire a wedding planner and I'll sign the checks. You won't even have to know how much everything costs."

"Good. Because I'm not sure I could handle dealing with a wedding costing more than my annual salary."

He smiled as he kissed her on the lips. If he knew his mother, it would be at least ten times that amount.

"Hey, how about using your beach house at Sunset Beach? I've seen pictures of it, it should be plenty big enough. We can get married on the beach and have the reception on the lawn and terrace."

"That's an excellent suggestion! That would be the perfect place for us to get married. And a sure-fire way to make sure all my frat boys show up for it."

Sandy sighed deeply and relaxed into his embrace. She was glad Sean had arranged the day off for them tomorrow. It seemed that now they had a whole lot more to talk about.

Tuesday, she would go back to work as his secretary, wearing his ring. She would not have to watch women, who nearly always alluded to the fact that they were having amazing sex with him, parade in and out of his office any more. She was, she was sure, the happiest woman in love that there had ever been.

Chapter 63

Alyssa
Stuck at JFK—4,400 Miles From Home

"They won't let me get on the flight!" Alyssa sobbed as she fought for space along the wall by the ticket counter. "They say global air travel is restricted now, and that Italy won't let anyone back in who's leaving from New York."

"Did you tell them you live here?" Palo asked.

"Yes. Many times. They don't care!" she wailed. "New York is a hot spot for the Corona Virus now, and Alitalia won't let anyone coming from New York on their planes."

"Did you tell them you were just there for business?"

"Palo, they don't care! The U.S. President has declared a public health emergency, and everything is *pazzo* here! *Pazzo*, I tell you. Craziness. I have tried. I cannot get on a plane! What am I supposed to do?"

Alyssa started in on her third crying jag since she'd first tried to check in for her flight over two hours ago. Ten minutes ago, the plane had departed from the gate, without her, for Frankfurt, Germany, enroute to Florence, Italy.

"I don't understand why they wouldn't they let you fly into Frankfurt? You could have driven home from there."

"I know! I told them that. It was something about them not being able to secure the final destination that I could not get on the plane. I think maybe they gave someone else my seat!"

Alyssa lived on the outskirts of Florence. She worked for her brother's tour company, taking tourists around the hill towns of Tuscany. She had been in New York City for two weeks working their tour booth at the Javits Convention Center, promoting next year's fall tours. She had never had to deal with the chaos that was JFK in this moment. Palo had always seen to the travel arrangements—every . . . single . . . detail.

"I-I- want-t- t-t-o-come home!"

"Shh, little one," Paulo cooed, "We'll fix this."

"H-h-how? No one here knows what to tell the thousands of stranded people. Everywhere you look, people are camped out on the floor. There's no place to g-g-o! *Passesco* does not begin to explain the madness here." Then the dreaded hiccups began and she cursed, in Italian. Vilely.

"Hey, watch your tongue. I don't want to hear that trash coming out of your mouth. And you should know, Mama just picked up on the other line."

"Mama! I'm stuck here in America!" Alyssa howled.

Mama's soft voice came on the line. Her quick words of comfort, spoken in a long lyrical stream of Italian instantly soothed Alyssa and had her swiping at her nose with a tissue, and using the back of her hand to curtail the tears running down her cheeks. They spoke in rapid-fire Italian, trading expressions of shock and dismay, with Alyssa's words conveying only worry and despair—and Mama's words offering comfort and encouragement to her beautiful young daughter.

Then Palo broke in with his serious business voice, the urgency in his voice conveying some of his own fear for the direness of her situation.

"Go out the main arrival door in twenty minutes. There will be a man in a business suit with a placard saying *Alyssa Peregrini*. His name is Carl Reynolds. He will drive you to my house in North Carolina. Even if you could get a rental car, you have never driven in the states. You certainly do *not* want to start with New York City.

"Carl drives executives for big corporations. I have used him before for special clients. He will drive you to my house in North Carolina. You know, the one I have with my Stanford brothers—I showed you some pictures of it a few years back. It is very nice. You will like it there. I will send you the code for the door. You can stay there in that house until this crisis is over. Do you understand me, *piccola*?"

"I cannot come home? I want to come home, Palo. Pleeease!" The desperation in her voice was palpable. Her high-pitched whine was broken up with new sobs of distress.

"No. I do not want you here." There was finality in his voice as he added, "It is not good here in *Italia*, 'Lyssa. It is very very bad. Some say worse than in New York. Plus, I cannot get you here."

He sighed, long and low, "And I have more than I can handle with Trixie and Mama. The virus is very bad here already. Many are sick with it. Trixie went against my wishes to work for the *osepedale* with Alessandro, who is driving the *ambulanza*. I am not happy with this, the way she can be exposed to the virus. But she will not relent. She says she must help. So I do not need you to resist me as well. Stay in the beach house. I know you cannot drive, so I will send you links to places that will deliver food and *necessità*. You must do as they say on TV—shelter in place they call it. It is a nice house—a very nice house on the ocean. You will like it. Just go there and stay. *Capisce?*"
"Palo, I just want to come home!"

"It is not possible now, *angela*. I need you to help me. I cannot manage everything—the business, Mama, and now Trixie who will not listen to me. *You*, you must listen to me and be safe. And give me one less person to worry about."

"Please Palo, please . . .." There was so much sadness in her cracked, woeful voice.

"No!" His voice was stern now. "America is safer, especially in my home in North Carolina. You go there. You will be safe. This is what I am asking. Do you understand me?" His voice had hardened, and for the first time Alyssa saw this crisis from Palo's point of view—75-year-old Mama with heart issues, a global business with hundreds of employees, having to shut down with this pandemic, and then, the love of his life—sweet, kind Trixie, ignoring him to keep her medical pledge to help others in need while putting herself in extreme jeopardy.

"Si, Palo, my father-brother. I understand. I do." She sighed, resigned with it all. "I will go to your home in North Carolina and wait there until it is safe for me to come home. Do not forget me though, as I am sure I will be very lonely in that big house by the sea. It is still winter, and no one will be there but me."

"That is true, dear one. It will be cold and bitter outside, but the house is warm and comfortable inside. The freezers and pantries are full. Find something to do. Watch TV all day. Work on your blogs. I do not care. But be safe from this horrible COVID. Call me when you get there."

"*Si.*"

"The driver is texting. He says he is waiting by the front door. Go there now. And be sure to check his I.D. before getting into the car—Carl Reynolds. He drives for Elite Transport. Do this for me, *Piccola.*"

She sighed. "*Allora.*"

Allora. The ubiquitous Italian word that meant so many things—now, well then . . . so . . . hey . . . let's see . . . in that case. It reverberated through her head as she made her way to the exit. While trundling her wheeled suitcase through the crowded aisles of the airport—past so many people with no options—she exhaled hard enough to blow a long strand of hair up into the air and away from her face.

Thanks to her brother, she had options. Not ones she was happy about, but at least she wasn't homeless on the streets of New York City, when the city was being overrun with a deadly virus. What a chaotic time. This was a mess—a *pasticcio, pasticcio, pasticcio!*

She had only recently learned to drive in Italy, so her brother was right, she certainly could not drive in America, nonetheless in New York City. So she was grateful for her brother and his influence in America . . . and for his money. She knew he had lots of it due to the success of his touring businesses and car leasing companies. But if his companies could not survive this pandemic . . . things could get tough for them all.

She mentally put herself in his leather Ferragamo shoes for a moment. Mama, 106 employees who counted on him, plus Trixie—his new bride, whom he adored, and her, his little sister—now stuck on the other side of the ocean—for who knew how long. They were all counting on him. Poor Palo.

She straightened her shoulders. She was not a little girl anymore. Her brother had enough on his plate. She would see this crisis through on her own. He would not have to worry about her. She would get to this beach house in North Carolina and she would, what was that phrase they were using on the American TV now? Oh yes, she would shelter in place.

How bad could it be, a few months in a nice beach house? No convention sales, no walking tours to make her feet sore, no tourists getting drunk on too much wine and getting lost at midnight in Positano or Venice? Yes, she would be on her own. Although Lord knew, she was a social person, not a social-distancing person, as they were now requiring. Except here at the airport, where people were crammed into every available spot.

She had seen pictures of Palo's beautiful house built on an American beach. She remembered that the house had ten bedrooms, nine bathrooms, a first-level powder room with a hand painted mural that scared everyone to death, numerous sitting areas and alcoves, a world-class gourmet kitchen designed by Kyle Merritt, the leading cable TV chef, a dining room for twenty-six, a massive game room, an exercise room with a continuous-motion lap pool simulating the waves of the ocean on the lower terrace, a sauna and a generous-sized hot tub, triple decks, a ground floor patio on the ocean side, and a southern-style palatial front porch with a circular drive on the front side. Not to mention an elevator, three under-house storage areas and two outside showers with hot water. Palo had said the pictures did not do it justice and that one day he hoped she could come for a visit.

Well, she was going for a visit now, wasn't she? She wondered for how long. How would a twenty-four-year-old dynamo of a woman, who rarely stopped talking, and could hardly sit still for ten minutes, live—all alone—in a house built for ten? She would be like a marble, rolling around in the Uffizi. But at least she would be warm, well fed, and safe from the Corona Virus.

She turned toward the entrance and saw her name on a poster board, "*Alyssa Peregrini.*"

The burly man with the smiling eyes saw her the moment she zeroed in on the sign and he quickly made his way over to her. "Ms. Peregrini?"

"Si. I mean yes."

He flashed her his I.D. card and she saw his picture and name beside the logo for Elite Transport, which was a Rolls Royce hood ornament embellished in gold leaf.

He took her rolling suitcase by the side strap and lifted it as if it weighed no more than a satchel.

"Please follow me."

He held out a disposable mask out to her. "Here, you should wear this."

Then he lifted a cloth that was resting under his chin, and placed it over his mouth and nose. She took a moment to shift her purse so she could put hers on. Wearing a facemask was what they were saying everyone should be doing on the last news show she had watched from her hotel room. But she'd had no idea where to get one. "Grazie. I mean thank you."

She was ushered out of the airport and into a limo. Her heavy suitcase was stowed in the trunk, easily lifted by Carl as if it was filled with only air. Which it definitely was not.

Inside that suitcase was all she owned on this side of the Atlantic. Winter clothing for the most part, for she had been warned about New York during the month of March. One had to be ready for anything, from a fine spring day at the park, to

465

a blustery snowstorm that could give you frostbite to your nose and toes if you were not properly dressed. Her suitcase contained selections to deal with whatever Mother Nature doled out. As such, it was not a piece of luggage she could easily lift. It had been hard enough to wrangle it through the busy airport despite the caster-type wheels.

Within moments, Carl had pulled away from the curb and they were exiting the airport and making their way out of the city through a dizzying array of highway overpasses and tunnels.

She looked out the window as the city she was still in awe of was left behind. The city where *Corona* was now running amok and shutting down enterprises that had never been closed before. Hotels, restaurants, stores, offices, government buildings, even TV and radio news stations and studios were closing—their news anchors, now harbingers of doom as they reported from their home living rooms.

The only entities that were fully operational and up and running at peak performance were the hospitals, testing labs, and nursing homes where the elderly were dying in record numbers. Along with firehouses, funeral homes, and morgues, where most people were now working double shifts.

The once bright and bustling city, always lit up—even late at night—was becoming dark and gloomy with the encroaching twilight and the threat of another winter storm. Alyssa took a moment to pray for the city that had hosted her for two active and fun-filled weeks.

The limo slipped into a tunnel filled with long tubes of light along the sides. She drew her coat over her shoulders, dropped her head to the seat back and fell asleep.

Chapter 64
Palo Saves the Day

Alyssa woke to the chiming of her cell phone, alerting her of an incoming text. She put her hand into the side of her travel purse, fished it out, and then lifted it to her face.

She was propped into the corner, her legs curled under her on the seat, her stocking feet tucked under her coat. Someone had removed her boots. She didn't remember taking them off. But there they were on the floorboard, completely unzipped; the tall supple knee-hi leather flopped over onto itself.

The puffy down-filled coat that had been on her shoulders was now bunched at her feet. The car was comfortably warm now; she was relaxed and toasty, despite the grey sky and the wind whipping the trees lining the highway.

She looked at the divider separating her and the driver named Carl. He had raised it to give her privacy. And he had also removed her boots. She was now certain of it. She smiled. And who said New Yorkers weren't courteous?

The text was from Palo. She tapped to open the text window.

Check your email was all it said. She closed the text app and opened her email program.

The driver says you are in Northern Virginia, so you have about six hours until you get to the beach house. There are no keys. The front door has a touchscreen deadbolt. You will need to enter a code for the deadlock to flip over. Then once inside you will need another code to disengage the alarm. 051609 is the code for the deadbolt. It's the day we all graduated from Stanford. Once inside, there's a panel to the left of the door to punch in the alarm code. It's just four numbers: 0516, but after you punch that in, you have to press STAY. I mean it. If you don't, the alarm company will call the polizia. When you leave to go anywhere, you punch in 0516 AWAY to arm it again. Pay attention when you are doing this. Do not be talking on the phone to one of your friends.

The driver has been paid, including a sizeable tip. I know how generous you are, but save whatever money you have left. You never know what might come up. There is a safe at the house with some money in it for household expenses, but I wasn't the last one there, so I don't know how much is in it. It's in a cabinet in the game room. Same six-digits plus a B opens it.

There is a drawer in the kitchen with a phone book and a list of local restaurants and grocery stores. Go online with either your phone or the computer in the game room to order food and whatever else you need using the company charge card you've been using in New York. Once you're settled, call me and we can go over the rest, but don't forget to mind the time difference. I'm not getting much sleep as it is with Trixie working double shifts at the hospital.

You'll be safe there at Sunset Beach. The people who live on the beach are kind. Although many will not be there now. Ask for help if you need it. Get some rest. You've had a rough couple of weeks doing that expo. I hate that you got stranded in the states, but happy you have a safe sanctuary, away from this COVID madness. Be safe. Ciao, Lyssa.

A few hours later, Carl pulled into a garishly lit gas station and stopped at a pump. In Italy, gas stations were called auto stops and the fuel was petro, but everything else was pretty much the same . . . except for the price per gallon instead of per liter, and the people. The people she had seen here in America were mostly heavier. Short or tall, they seemed less lean.

She supposed it was because they no longer walked as much here in the United States. Well, except for maybe in New York City. All she did in New York City was walk, walk, walk. She had taken a few day trips with friends to New Jersey and to

Long Island on trains or by car, as you could hardly get around anyplace outside of the big city without a car or a Lyft.

At home everyone walked everywhere—up hills, down hills, to the stores, to the restaurants, to visit *mamas* and papas and *zias* and *zios*, as well as friends or business associates.

She knew from the tours she led that many Americans struggled on the old stone staircases, tripped on the uneven pavements and cobbled streets, and complained if the parking lot was not on the same block as the place they were going to see.

She did not mind. She loved to walk. Which was good, as she loved pasta and bread as well.

At five-foot eight, she would be considered tall in America. Though some women she had seen were much taller. She didn't know by how much. The American feet and inches were hard for her to get used to; in Italy it was meters and centimeters. She was 1.73 meters or 173 centimeters. Her brother Palo, who, at six-foot-three, was 190 centimeters.

She was pretty sure she would not like knowing what she was in pounds. She was 65 kilograms. The number would be much higher in pounds, more than double she was sure, and that sounded very bad to her.

Carl got back inside the car and his voice came through the intercom. "Do you need to use the restroom or to get anything from the mini-mart?"

She didn't particularly like having the screen up while she was awake so she pushed the button and lowered it. "No, I am fine." She prided herself on having a young, tight bladder. She once rode with a friend from Sicily to Switzerland—seventeen hours—without ever having to stop to pee, despite drinking several *caffès* along the way. The last time she had used the facilities had been late in the afternoon when she'd left her hotel in New York for the airport.

"Would you like to stop for something to eat? There's a Huddle House diner a block away that my phone says is open all night. We'll be to Wilmington in about an hour. There may be a few more options there. But it's not like New York City here, there's not much open at 4 a.m."

"No, I am fine. But thank you. I just want to get settled. I have cereal bars and water with me."

He nodded. "I understand." He started the car and pulled away from the pump.

She looked around. During the drive she had noticed that the gas stations here were mostly within the cities and towns; the auto stops in Italy were usually situated on a hilltop or in a valley, set off by themselves, like oases along the highways. And they were huge facilities with enormous parking lots, and always very busy, even at night. This gas station was rather smallish and was next to a McDonald's and a place that sold metal sheds.

No one else appeared to be here. The parking lot and the store were completely deserted, except for the person watching from the checkout counter in the bright white lights that were a nimbus in the otherwise dark night.

At the intersection, where the traffic light blinked a steady attention–grabbing amber was one of the largest cemeteries she had ever seen. It seemed to go on forever as they drove by. The monuments were much smaller than one could expect in Italy. But there were so many more of them.

An overwhelming sense of loneliness descended. She knew very little about this country outside of New York. She knew about cowboys in Texas. Indians in Arizona, Eskimos in Alaska, hula girls in Hawaii, and that Disney had massive theme parks on both coasts. This wasn't her first trip to the Unites States; she'd come here with her family a few times as a young girl, and once to visit Palo in California when he was attending Stanford University. But she'd never been to Delaware, Maryland, Virginia, or North Carolina. States she knew they'd just driven through. She'd never been all-alone in a strange country. She'd had friends or clients, or family. Now she had no one—for who knew how long.

At the Expo, she had worked side-by-side with other

tour operators, many who crossed her path on a daily basis while leading tours in Italy, Germany, Switzerland, and Greece—the main places Palo's company led tour groups. At night, after closing up their booths, they would all band together or meet in small groups to have dinner and drinks and to sightsee. Everyone knew there was safely in numbers in such a big American city, but also, it was no fun to experience such a *bizzarro* city such as New York on one's own.

But here she was now, getting ready to experience North Carolina by herself. She would not know a single person in the entire state. Loneliness began to swamp her. Combined with her being exhausted, worrying about her mama's friends that were in *hospitales* dying from the virus, and missing her boyfriend, *Giancarlo*—who would know exactly what to do to take her mind off her troubles—she was desperate to go home. She did not want to be in here in America. She wanted to go home.

Tears slid down her cheeks. She bit back a sob and looked up in time to see Carl meet her shiny eyes in the rear view mirror. He shook his head at her dilemma, for surely Palo had filled him in.

He knew that she was a refugee in a strange land—an evacuee from one of the world's biggest cities. Carl reached back and handed her a small box of tissues, telling her to keep it when she tried to take only one.

She knew she needed to take her mind off her troubles. She did it in the only way she knew how—engaging with others.

"Do you live in the city?" she asked Carl.

"No, ma'am. I live in New Jersey. If you are a driver, you cannot afford to live in the city. Most of the city workers live in the suburbs."

"Suburbs?" she did not know that word.

"Outskirts. You may know the word as bario, maybe? No, sorry. That's Spanish. Towns on the periphery of a large city."

"Oh, *si. Una zona di periferia.* New Jersey is one I have heard of.

And so they talked. She learned about Carl and his family. He had a wife named Elsa and a son who was disabled with a spinal disease; their mixed breed Labrador named Junie that was a service dog and a much beloved pet; and Ralph the Mouth, their groaning monster compactor at the end of the hall that ate their trash and everyone else's in the building—at anytime, day or night, with many loud crunching sounds as it compacted and chewed up everyone's bottles and cans. He told her it sounded like a gunshot whenever it broke a large glass bottle or jar and made him cover his heart with his hand to make sure his heart was still beating.

He was fun to talk to and very entertaining when he talked about his son Carl, Jr.

"You should bring him to Italy one day. He would love seeing Pinocchio Park in the little town of Collodi and riding the funicular on the Island of Capri."

"That would be grand. But he spends most of his day in a wheelchair so it is difficult for him to get around. As much as he would like to ride on an airplane, I think a transatlantic flight would be too much for him. We are hoping to take him to Hershey Park in Pennsylvania in a few years though, maybe for his tenth birthday."

And as easy as that, Alyssa stopped feeling sorry for herself. She had so much to be thankful for. Many opportunities and places were open to her that would never be open for Carl Jr.

Carl saw through the rearview mirror that she had slipped into another funk and began regaling her with stories about his brother who was a bellhop for The Plaza Hotel. He told her all the weird requests he'd had over the years, the odd things he'd had to carry up to the rooms, and all the times someone wanted to be shown to the room Kevin McCallister had stayed in during *Home Alone 2*. Young girls often wanted to know where Eloise's suite was, as if she was still there. She wasn't, but the rooms had been kept the same for her and were often rented out for little girls' parties. Many people wanted their picture taken at the Oyster Bar that John Lennon and Yoko Ono frequented, often singing an off-key version of *Hey Jude* or *Imagine,* which Carl mimicked for her. And there was the occasional odd ball that wanted to know which room Truman Capote had stayed in. Alyssa laughed at all his stories, as they were very funny. Even the one about Truman Capote, even though she had no idea who he was.

Before she knew it, they were going over the Sunset Beach Bridge. The sun was just beginning to make its appearance on the horizon, giving the houses a backlit glow while the marshes were limned with burnished gold and many shades of green. It was beautiful, she thought as they climbed to the apex of the high bridge and then shot down to the long straight causeway unfurling in front of them.

There were beach houses to the right and what appeared to be an elegant inn to the left. Everywhere there was silence. No one was about. Security lights were beginning to flicker out as the sun rose when they reached the intersection by the pier and turned left onto Main Street. Alyssa unclipped her belt and slid to the right side of the car to look out at the oceanfront houses, wondering if she'd be able to spot her brother's house from the pictures she'd seen. But she hadn't been able to as it was still dark, until the moment Carl made the turn onto the circular drive and all the security lights came on and the house lit up like a mansion.

Here was the warm, welcoming beach retreat that her brother always said was his favorite place on earth. It was lovely and regal in an unpretentious way, although it did whisper money. Money that she was sure was well spent, as ten men would have had to agree on everything.

As a guide for a private touring company, she was used to staying in fabulous high-end resorts. This was different though, this was a private home—one her brother owned with his friends—and now her home for the unforeseeable future.

It didn't have Mama, or Palo, or Giancarlo. But it was nice—very, very nice.

Carl parked the car by the stairs, opened the trunk to get her suitcase, and then came around to open her door. Her boots were hard to zip. Her toes felt cramped. Staying still for so long had made her feet swell. She longed for a hot, relaxing bath.

She took great care, using the handrail and slowly walking up the steps as she admired the lush landscaping, the wide sweeping staircase and the impressive front doors with the stained glass sidelights. Inside, everything appeared dark—somehow expectant though—as if the house itself was always at the ready for one of the residents to show up.

Standing in front of the door, she punched in the code and heard the electronic click, clack, and clunk as the lock disengaged. She moved to the side as Carl reached out to open the door for her. The movement of the door opening turned on the foyer, hallway, and upper landing staircase lights.

There was a rush of feeling. Not of finding home precisely, but of discovering sanctuary. She heard beeping, and turned her head to see lights flashing and lighting up a numerical grid on a wall plate just inside the door. She punched in the code to disarm the alarm. Both she and Carl let out an audible sigh of relief.

Carl offered to take her suitcase to the upper level.

"I can manage it. I am not sure which bedroom I will take yet. There are some on each floor. Plus, there is an elevator so it will be no problem."

She reached into her coat pocket and pulled out a wad of bills. "Thank you for coming to my rescue. You can't know how much it meant to me to know there was someone waiting to take care of me during such a bad time."

"Keep your money. Your brother took good care of me. And it appears that he's taken good care of you, too. You enjoy this beautiful place in paradise." He covered her hand and pushed the money back into it.

"Do you need to use the facilities? Can I get you something to drink or eat? Would you like rest before you drive back?"

"No, I must get back. I have to help my wife with Carl

Jr. and then I have some executives I must pick up this evening to drive to Vermont."

"Geez, it never ends for you."

"It is good money while it lasts. The airlines will eventually slow down business and I will have too much time off then."

"Well thank you again. Take care of yourself. Who knows, maybe one day you will bring your family to Italy, and we'll get Carl Jr. on that funicular to the top of Capri."

He smiled at her, knowing full well that would never happen, but hopeful nonetheless. "That would be something for sure. If we get there, we'll be sure to look you up!"

He clasped her shoulder and reminded her to wear her mask anytime she went out in public. Then bid her to stay safe and went out the door, closing it firmly behind him.

She walked over and pressed the lock button on the keyboard and heard the deadbolt slide into its casing. Through the sidelight she saw Carl get into the car and drive off.

There had never been a time in her life when she felt as alone as she felt in that moment. She took a deep breath and turned to climb the steps as she began to order her day. Through the high skylights she saw that it was impossibly early, with only the barest hint of a sunrise developing around the edges of the sky. When she was able to reach the next level and see out the past the furniture to the windows that faced east, there was a purple glimmer of light on the horizon. There was no sudden emergence of the grand orb yet to come and light up the day, but with every passing second she stood anticipating it, the glimmer expanded until red, orange, and yellow joined the purple streaks. Dawn had arrived. It was glorious to watch. For a few moments, she pondered over the name Sunset Beach and wondered why this island was not called Sunrise Beach instead.

No longer tired, after having slept so much in the car and now being too antsy about what the future held to do anything but pace and fret, she decided she would tour the house. Then select a room and unpack. Maybe take a bath. Try to unwind. Talk herself into accepting this new and overwhelming challenge.

Then she would get out her laptop and post something so her friends would know she was safe . . . and where she was. She needed to call Palo, Mama, and Giancarlo.

Her stomach made gurgling noises. And she had to find something to eat.

First things first though—a bathroom. Her tight little youthful bladder was finally giving her some discomfort. She spied an open door down the hallway and walked down the hardwood flooring to what she suspected was a powder room. The light came on as her hand made contact with the rocker panel on the wall, just as she rounded the corner into the room. She screamed.

"Santa Madre di Dio!" Holy mother of God, she cried out as her hand went to her chest. It took a moment for her heartbeat to stop thundering in her chest.

Someone had painted a mural so lifelike, so real, that she was sure a leopard was in that small room, his eyes connecting with hers with every indication that she was going to be his dinner within a matter of seconds. This was the notorious painting that Palo was always telling her about. Joking about how it scared everyone the first time they saw it.

She finally caught her breath. She was surprised she hadn't pissed her pants. No way was she using this bathroom. She spun on her heel and left the room. Then closed the door firmly. In case the leopard was real. It really looked as if it could be. There was no way was her bedroom was going to be anywhere near that very realistic beast, lurking in the tall grass, waiting for a meal.

She grabbed her suitcase by the handle, pulled on it until it was fully extended, then rolled her it behind her as she made her way down the hallway toward the area where she suspected she'd find the elevator.

Chapter 65

Brent
Brent Decides to Leave New York City

Brent sat at his desk in his high-rise office in Manhattan. With a slight turn of his custom leather chair, he had a bird's-eye view of the city. It was seven in the evening and eerily dark when normally many offices would still be well lit.

The sound of copiers and fax machines would be humming as they spewed out copies of blue prints, both hand drawn and computer-designed sketches, specification pages, dimension adjustments, inspection and material lists, and price quotes. Instead, it had been nerve-wracking silent all day—every day this week in fact. Except for Saturday, the day the cleaners had come and turned over mostly empty trash containers into their hampers, vacuumed carpets hardly anyone had stepped on, and wiped down surfaces no one had touched.

In all the surrounding office buildings, it was the same. One office was lit out of fifty, if that. Ambient light coming from windows and reflecting onto neighboring buildings that lit up the sky, was now gone. If he looked up quickly, it almost seemed as if there was no building next to the one he was in. A second glance would show the meager light coming from security camera lights blinking red or LED readouts on terminals flashing green or blue. If you let your eyes adjust, you could make out glimmers of light reflecting off sleeping computer screens.

He was becomming sullen and uninspired working in an empty suite of offices. It was morosely quiet. You could easily imagine you were the last person left in a city that everyone had fled. Gone were the quick toot-toots of vying taxis, the blaring in-your-face laying on of the horn of a truck driver to a jaywalking pedestrian, and the constant underlying swish and hiss of tires of all types meeting wet pavement. The occasional siren still cleaved the air though, announcing yet another emergency vehicle rushing a COVID patient to the hospital. That sound never seemed to end for very long before another blared out. The sirens were totally unnecessary. There was no traffic that needed to be alerted to clear the way. He figured it must be habit on the part of the driver to flip the switch to make his mission known.

This wasn't his city anymore. It was otherworldly. Dystopian. He had to get out of here or he'd go crazy. He looked around and took in his office with fresh eyes. Everything could be moved, duplicated, or done without, in order for him to do his work. Most of his employees were working from home, why couldn't he? Or better yet, why not work from his home in North Carolina? As soon as that thought occurred to him, he felt his insides light up. Something came back to life inside him. Just like the power button on a laptop being pressed, it energized him.

Yeah . . . the more he thought about it, the better he liked the idea. He could move the special computers that held his architectural design programs: Autocad, Sketchup, Revit, 3D Studio Max, InDesign, V-Ray, and Photoshop . . . his mind kept exploring the options. Or . . . he did have multiple licenses for each, so he could easily load them onto different laptops. The job he was currently working on, with a deadline of late September, would not need all of the programs to be completed—just three of them.

He could lease printers, copiers, or simply buy a combination copier/fax machine that also scanned from his computer. He grabbed his pen and a notepad and began a list. He would need two monitors, a drafting table, paper, toner cartridges, drums, and his special ergonomic chair. He could pack up some things, order the rest, and have it delivered directly to *The Cockpit*, his Carolina home—the beach house he owned together with nine of his fraternity brothers from Stanford.

He made his way to the storage closet and started

grabbing boxes of supplies, piling them on the carpet in the long deserted hallway. He unlocked a tall security cabinet and took out two spare laptops. Then unplugged a laptop and the charger from the desk of a woman currently on maternity leave. Within an hour, he had everything he needed, piled neatly against the wall by the elevator.

His Lexus RX300 SUV was in the parking garage. It was not a full-sized SUV, but it was all he needed for driving in the city. It would hold everything he'd need for work that he couldn't lease or ship, plus his clothes and surfing equipment. The downstairs beach house storage rooms already held two of his better boards, but he'd treated himself to a new one this past Christmas and he'd been dying to try it out. Along with a new wet suit gifted to him by his parents that was super thin and fit like a second layer of skin, yet was touted to keep in body heat and even generate more.

Yeah! He'd go to the beach house. Get some work done on the new project. Surf until he exhausted himself so he could sleep. And fill himself up on food Kyle kept in the freezer. He'd take a case of his favorite wine, a case of Prosecco, and a case of Grey Goose for Bloody Marys.

The only thing that would be missing was a woman to rub up against, someone he could mercilessly tease to orgasms, and someone who would do the same to him with her tongue, her lips, and her warm hot mouth.

Julia, the woman he'd met on the beach over the Christmas holiday in Costa Rica, was supposed to fly in for Easter break, but clearly, that was not going to happen now.

COVID was settling a celibate life firmly in place for him and for many of his cohorts these days. Sex with a woman again seemed as unlikely to him as walking on the moon. Until this pandemic got sorted out, it would be hand jobs for him. There wasn't a condom designed that could protect you against this shit.

It was the first time he had felt envy on a large scale for

his married friends who had a partner in their beds to ease the burning yearnings. In this looming world of isolation, quite a few had steady companionship. A warm body to slide into at night to help ease the overwhelming fear settling in would be nice . . . but it wouldn't be worth the risk.

He imagined that waking up in a woman's arms, a woman you loved enough to marry, would make the joyless drudgery of facing each new day with its compounding bad news and dire warnings, tolerable—pleasant even. He had no idea, as he'd never fallen in love. Wasn't even sure he believed in it for himself.

The idea of being content during this crisis, of finding anything to bring joy, bloomed in his chest as he thought of being in his magnificent beach house at Sunset Beach. Yes, this was the thing to do. Go somewhere safe. Be in a place he loved. Feed his soul on the wonders of nature in a place he thought of as his sanctuary.

Chapter 66
Working From Home Requires a lot of Stuff

Brent walked around his office making sure he had everything he needed, then rifled through his desk drawers one last time before locking them.

He sat back in his chair, arched back as he threaded his fingers through the curling hairs on the back of his neck. The length reminded him that he'd missed his hair appointment in order to meet with a client last month. The stylist had rescheduled it for March 15th.

Now that shop, and every other one like it was shuttered. Talk about the ides of March. He puzzled things over. One manner of store closings in the city—take hair salons as an example. *Every* hair salon—throughout the entire city—all of them closing. The idea of that ever happening was insane.

But it had happened. They'd soaped up all the glass so no one could see in, barred the windows and doors, pulled down the chain gates, and keyed all the locks in all six deadbolts. Then put a crude sign on the door saying, *Closed Due to COVID-19.*

Well, it would have been enough to bewilder the masses, cause them to shake their unkempt heads, and put everyone except those favoring dreadlocks, into a nosedive of deep depression.

But to have *all* the stores and shops closed—Saks, Bergdorf's, Gucci, Macy's, Abercrombie, Armani, even the Apple Store—it was unfathomable, otherworldly. And it was for precisely this reason that he needed to leave the city and find another place to be.

He was fortunate to have an alternative world he could go to, one he could crawl into where he could pull the covers up over his head and hide out for a while. It would be a place to regroup, to get some work done, and to live in harmony with nature. His favorite beach beckoned. He would go.

He jumped up from his chair to go pack up his truck. Now that the idea had blossomed, he couldn't wait to get there.

As he loaded boxes from the office and carried suitcases from his apartment, he thanked Almighty God that he was not under contract to build a shopping mall right now. He had bid on one last year, and been sorely pissed when he'd lost the bid. Unanswered prayers he thought, just as the country singer had declared in his song. He smiled broadly.

The bid he had won instead, was for a hospital—a huge hospital on Long Island. No board in their right mind would put a hold on hospital constructio nright now. So that was the job he was currently working on—the job he would take to *The Cockpit* to complete.

He would be able to fully develop the plans there, while his employees, who were working from home, continued to send him their drawings, their worksheets and modifications, their material lists and cost estimates.

He couldn't help being excited about it. He had some wonderful ideas, some new concepts, and now some new must-have requirements to consider due to the virus. Many more sinks than were originally planned would be needed, storage areas for Personal Protective Equipment needed to be provided, more places for hospital staff to rest and regroup, and a morgue with more capacity . . . hmmm . . . maybe even an on-site crematorium?

Was that even doable? Would any hospital administrator even consider that idea? Was it too cross-purposed? Counter to their mission? Admitting defeat up front, before the patient even came through the front door seemed crass, yet it spoke of concierge options you could tick off. Gall bladder removal, check! Install four stents, check! Transfer to COVID unit, check! Cremation and ashes presented in a decorative urn, check! He crossed it off his mental checklist. There must be legal reasons they didn't have hospitals doing them now. Even so, who would want funeral directors picketing the site as they were building?

Surely, they would not cotton to the idea of losing a fair percentage of their business from such a cockeyed streamlined idea. Where was this odd train of thought coming from? He needed to get out of this city.

The last thing he remembered as he rode down the elevator for the fifth time with more boxes in his hands, was thinking about a woman's hot mouth on him.

Gads! He was so easily sidetracked these days. He knew he didn't have COVID, but he sure had the COVID madness everyone seemed to have these days: a stir-crazy loss of community feeling caused by social distancing, coupled with no one being able to see the facial expressions of the people they were interacting with.

Who knew how beneficial a smile quirked in your direction could be? Yet now, there was nary a smile nor an encouraging smirk to be had anywhere

It was a good time to get out of New York. To run off to an out of the way hideaway. To go to a place that would be experiencing spring within a few weeks—whereas, New Yorkers still had months of winter still ahead of them.

As he shoved boxes into the back of the SUV and then rearranged them multiple times until they were to his liking, he thought of the first time he'd visited Sunset Beach so many years ago. The barrier island he was running away to was so off the "beaten path" that road maps hadn't even shown a route to get to it until the late 80s. It was still a hidden gem to many. He nodded to himself as he fit an odd-shaped box into a tight space. If he was going to have to be isolated from the world, at least he could choose what part of it he wanted to hole up in. Satisfied with his thoughts and the amazing packing job he was doing, he pushed the button to close the rear hatch.

Now, about that woman problem . . .. He thought about the days when he and Chaz had routinely double-teamed with women, and the wild sexual abandonment they had all experienced as a threesome delivering every pleasure imaginable, and leaving three people sated in a heathen-exhausted bliss.

Overnight they'd both grown up when Chaz had lost his fiancé over their duplicity by insinuating Julia into a threesome when she was drunk. The lifestyle they had been living had lost its appeal like a thunderbolt for his friend Chaz, and he himself hadn't been able to get much satisfaction from the hedonistic lifestyle since.

He'd tried it a few more times, partnering with some guys he knew from his gym, but found he could never get the rhythm and trust he'd found with Chaz. They had been like brothers born to it. Of one mind when it came to the woman involved and seeing to her pleasure. Other men seemed to be into it strictly for their own pleasure. While he and Chaz had been all about the woman's pleasure—which made it a sporting event, sparking a friendly competition to outdo each other in the satisfaction arena.

They had made a good team, something he was never able to duplicate again. Eventually, he dropped out of that scene, abandoning it altogether. Plus it became too risky. One woman with two men no longer interested him, though he'd never part with the memories. Somehow, along the way, he'd grown up. He was no longer that greedy, misogynistic frat boy.

He still had longings though, strong sexual urges that needed to be satisfied. So he dated. But lately, he noticed his focus was on making a connection that was about more than hooking-up. A few times he'd gone as long as six months with one woman. But then one or the other would get a wandering eye.

There just didn't seem to be anything substantial he had in common with most women, to hold his interest—other than the sex.

Reviewing each case in his mind, as he carried his new surfboard and then his suitcases down from his apartment, he came to the conclusion that the women he had dated had been too polite, too agreeable, too complacent—too determined to get along and continue the mutually beneficial relationship rather than be passionate about an opinion or idea that the other might find objectionable or abhorrent, resulting in the end of reciprocal dispassionate harmony.

While wrangling a suitcase into the passenger front seat, he nodded to himself and even spoke out loud just to hear someone talk, "Yup, there had been no honesty in any relationship. No passionate debates. The placating nature of each woman, and to be honest, with myself as well, became a habituating scenario—each person gave up their true personality to force the connection to last." He finally realized he needed to use the power recliner to fit the case in. "There!" He slammed the door closed.

Then he continued his internal conversation, "Maybe we both wanted it to turn into something more permanent. I know that *all* of the women saw the need to form a permanent partnership. They all wanted to settle down, get married and have kids. Over and over it happened—exactly as if they were reading from a script. We were both actors playing parts with sex as the reward." He sighed audibly as if it pained him to realize just how shallow all his affairs had been.

"Then each time, over and over again, the day would come like a flip clock ticked off the date. Six months passed and they got restless for more—I wanted more, too. More fire, more sparkle, more passion. Something with intensity like Maureen O'Hara and John Wayne; Rhett and Scarlet; Ricky and Lucy; Kate and Petruchio like in *The Taming of the Shrew*. They only wanted an engagement ring."

He laughed and heard his laugher reverberate and come back to him from the high-up, cement garage ceilings. Realizing he was getting a bit punchy from all the hard work and should take a break, he nonetheless continued his diatribe out loud. "I wonder how Rhett and Lucy would have fared on a deserted island, or even better, Scarlet and Ricky." He had to chuckle at himself for even having such absurd thoughts. Hell, today there seemed to be more Rhett and Ricky couples as well as Scarlet and Lucy ones. He was getting really down on the idea of ever finding that special someone meant for him. Maybe she simply wasn't out there. Satisfied his suitcase was secure, he locked and closed the passenger door.

Throughout his musings he had completely filled his SUV. He reassessed the area and determined that his vehicle was now fully packed; everything he would need was inside. Despite being tired, he was excited to get on the road. He could sleep once he was ensconced in his safe sanctuary by the sea.

Chapter 67
Alyssa Gets to The Cockpit & Settles In

After finding an upper level bathroom, Alyssa washed her face and moisturized it, removing the last traces of the city, the airport and the effects of the recirculated air of the heated limousine. She went back to the kitchen where she had noticed an *Italiano* decanter with an *Evoo* metal tag decorating the counter. She poured some of the oil into the palm of her hand and used it to hydrate her skin. It smelled like home. Like being in San Gimignano, Sienna, or Lucca, one of the Tuscan hill towns she adored showing off to tourists.

She was beginning to feel refreshed, but knew that soon she'd be swamped with emotions and exhausted from her ordeal, so she took her time and wandered through the bedrooms on the upper level to find the one that best suited her. Every room boasted high-end furniture, two had custom Sleep Number beds with lifts, and a few had flat-screen TVs attached to walls. Most had alcoves with a desk for a laptop and a charging station. All had impressive art and designer touches.

She had a mystical princess-in-the-making feeling as she walked in and out of each room, trying to decide which one would be hers for however long her stay ended up being. Most were so audaciously male that she could almost smell the testosterone emanating from the walls. Those she didn't give a second thought. She needed something softer, and a little more welcoming.

She found it on the upper most level. Facing the ocean with a side view from a bay window that bumped out to show the neighboring beach access as well as the sea beyond, she almost fell to her knees. She looked all around her. My *Dio*, this was a princess room. She claimed it instantly with a fist to her heart as if genuflecting in one of her beloved *Duomos*.

She took it all in. Then, as her eyes roved around the room, she remembered. This was Alex's dead wife's furniture. Mallory had been her name. Palo had told her the whole story. She had died giving birth to twin girls a few years ago; her own family had sent flowers from Italy for her funeral. This had been Mallory's childhood furniture. French provincial, with the soft white and gold patina girls everywhere loved. The comforter was a fluffy white confection with eyelet lace trim, threaded through with lavender satin ribbons. It was perfect. The bed was double-sized with many coordinating pillows piled on top of it. All the other beds had been huge. Europeans, unused to so much space for sleeping, preferred smaller, more intimate beds.

When had everything become super-sized? She loved that the bed was only a full-sized one, not queenly or kingly, but full—princess-y. Full of everything life needed. People close, so they touched. So they knew someone else was alongside for the bad dreams that haunted, the night terrors that came from the horrors they'd seen or lived through. It was a bed where one could easily roll over in and find a comforting body to hold, to make love to.

She checked the phone in her pocket to see if Giancarlo had called. No, not yet. They had spoken many times while she had been in New York that first week, but not so much since. She replaced the phone in her pocket; spread her arms wide and spun around the room. This was lovely. Everything was clean, and crisp, and quaint. She even loved the floral impressionist art that reminded her of *The Artist's Garden at Giverny* by Monet. Stepping closer, she noted it was an original oil painting. One this size would have been costly. The frame alone had to have cost many hundreds of dollars. She took in the setting, the abundance of flowers in full bloom, the lush lawn, the pristine bench inviting a visitor to sit and take it all in. She would wake to this gorgeous scene every day and be comforted by this beautiful painting. It reminded her of so many gardens she'd walked through in Europe where everything was mature and slightly unkempt, yet so obviously lovingly tended.

This would be her room. She would honor Mallory's memory and sleep in her bed. Admire her art, and pretend she was a princess in this gold and white room with the canopy bed. It no longer held what she supposed had been a matching tester of frilled eyelet lace. But the intricately carved gilt headboard with its four tall, imperial posts signifying that royal, majestic nobles could have indeed once slept here was comforting. It was perfect. It was the only bedroom in the house that was at all feminine, so it would be hers. She wheeled her suitcase into the room, hefted it onto the bed and began unpacking.

She squealed her delight when the large drawers with the built-in dividers slid noiselessly out on smooth glides. This was not like her drawers at home that she had to shove and tug as they creaked and fought her to open or close.

There was no TV on the wall opposite the bed in this room as there had been in many of the others. Instead, there was a beautiful watercolor of meandering marshes with herons and egrets in the foreground. It was also in a gorgeous white and gold frame, triple matted with a gold-foil edge. The engraved gold metal description tag said Charleston, S.C. She knew Alex and Mallory had been married in Charleston, remembered that Palo had spent a whole week there as one of Alex's nine best men.

She much preferred the beautiful paintings to a television screen. She rarely watched TV in a bedroom anyway. Even when she was in a hotel, unless she needed an update on the news or weather, she hardly ever turned it on. Movies or favorite TV shows she watched in the living room with family or friends. Except at Giancarlo's flat. It seemed as soon as they finished making love, he was on his side, remote in hand, flipping through the stations looking for a soccer game.

She wished he were here; she could use a nice warm body hugging her close and helping to keep her mind off this COVID-19.

She carried her toiletry bag into the ensuite, unfolded it so all the compartments were accessible and hung it on the hook on the back of the door. She bent close to the mirror over the sinks and looked at her hair, her skin, and her eyebrows. She needed a facial, eyebrow waxing, and a conditioning treatment.

But she knew that none of the places where she could get those services were open now, not just here, but practically anywhere. She would have to order the supplies, have them delivered and do it herself. Or go vagabond and go without. It wasn't as if she had anyone to do her hair for or to put make-up on for. Her summer tan had faded. Maybe walking on the beach would restore it. Although Mama always said her fair skin was a lovely contrast to her dark shiny black hair. She had not been happy when Alyssa had put highlights in her hair last year. But they too, needed to be redone.

She went over to the door that led to a small private balcony,unlocked the door and went outside. It was chilly and the wind whipped her hair against her cheeks. Holding it back so she that could see, she took in the view. The ocean was very far away. She could just barely see the beach for the dunes were high and covered with vegetation. The sea grasses were blowing in one direction over all the swallows and swales. The terrain was undulating and creased like a sandbox trampled by kids and then left abandoned. There was a long wooden walkway leading over the dunes to the beach. She couldn't see where it ended as sections of it popped in and out of sight as it made its way to the sea.

Faraway, she could see a ship crossing the horizon with its nets hoisted, pointing toward the leaden sky, its keel lifting and falling into the churning dark waves. Looking off to the right, she could make out many long wooden walkways paralleling each other and then disappearing between other houses—nice houses, but not so grand as this one. The area between the walkways was thick with vegetation and marsh grasses, sea oats and vines. It was a wide expanse. She couldn't see where it ended in either direction. She doubted she had ever seen such long paths going to the sea.

This was nothing like what they had on the coasts in Italy.

Few beaches in Italy had dunes, covered or otherwise. And they had nowhere near this much sand. Streets were often edging the sand as roads snaked around and followed the coastline. The famous Lido, a seven-mile strip of sand along the coast of a barrier island, was one of the few places people could put out loungers and sunbathe.

She took in the pier with its weather-beaten building on the shore end and its wide wooden planks and rails leading out toward the horizon. It was one of the longest piers she had ever seen. Yet no people were on it. The beach, the pier, the walkways, they were all desolate. So much for being at the beach. She felt alone in the universe. Isolated, as if on another planet. Were there no people in the other houses? She saw no signs of life other than soaring seagulls, and once, a line of pelicans flew overhead.

On a better day, she would venture to the water, but not today, she thought, as she closed and locked the door, and then grabbed her phone from the dresser—still no call from Giancarlo.

She made her way downstairs to the kitchen. It was late evening in Italy; she would call Palo. Then she would forage into the freezers, check out the pantry, and make some food—maybe some linguine, and some nice big meatballs to go with it. She tapped the screen and found her brother's name under Favorites.

They talked for over an hour as he told her about the house, the local area, the ways to order food from the three grocery stores nearby, and the likelihood that there were few homeowners staying on the beach right now. He said that for most people, their beach houses were second homes—that many of the owners lived in Raleigh, Charlotte, or further inland during the off-season. He told her that the computer in the room with the pool table was Bookmarked for the house Amazon account. That she could go there, shop for what she needed, and that when checking out through the Cart, there was already a credit card on file and the delivery address preset.

"Do not change the name for the default address or your package will not get there. Brent is listed as the resident.

Tourists cannot get mail delivered to the beach houses, so you must always use Brent's name. Then your package will come straight to the front porch. Brent manages the bills so I will send money to him to pay for whatever you buy, but do not go crazy. Buy what you need, but not everything you want."

"I understand. I just need some toiletries, some cosmetics, a hoodie or jacket of some kind, some shoes so I can walk on the beach, and a few books to download to my Kindle."

"I want you to have what you need."

"I need my family."

"I know, piccola, I know. And I am very sorry you are stranded there. As soon as it is safe to fly again, we'll get you home."

"You know so may people, Palo. Can you not arrange for a private jet?"

"'Lyssa, I am well off, but I am not wealthy. It costs many thousands of euros in petrol to get a plane across the ocean, and for two pilots? Enough to buy a Citroën. So I think not. You are safer there anyway. The virus is very bad in some towns here. Hundreds of people are dying everyday in Lombardia. Rome is very vey bad."

"Oh Palo, that is very sad."

"I know. It is why you must stay there. Do something for me, why don't you? I need some articles for the websites. Write some blogs. That will fill your time."

"About what?"

"Anything. I don't care. Just not about the virus. People need distractions now, something to take their mind off the misery. Some how-to tips would be helpful. People need to know how to make masks. You know how to sew; maybe you can post something with a few pictures. Use things people can find around their homes as they cannot leave them to shop now."

"Okay. I will do that for you as you are doing so much for me. Palo, this place is amazing."

"I know."

She could hear the wistfulness in his voice. "I love it there. It is my favorite place in all the world. It's where I get to spend time with my friends, just relaxing . . . there is never work for me there. The time stands still for me at Sunset Beach. There is not a rush of things that I must do. It's also where I first kissed Trixie, and made her mine. "

"Aww, Palo. That is so sweet. Wait a minute, it wasn't in the room with the gold and white furniture, was it?"

He laughed. "No. That is Alex's room. Mine is the one with the sleigh bed that's adjustable. I am surprised you didn't take that room. It has a 65-inch flat screen."

"I do not watch much TV. You know that."

"Well you may want to keep up on the news. Things are changing everyday and the governments are mandating many new things. If you go out, which I do not want you to do, you must wear a mask and stay a safe distance from people. Two meters at least."

"I must wear a mask on the beach?"

"No. Just where there are other people nearby. Stay there at the house and take walks on the beach or around the island. Keep a mask in your pocket in case you see someone. And remember—"

"I know, I know. You need one less person to worry about."

"*Esattamente*. Exactly."

"*Ciao*."

"Ciao, *sorellina*."

She shut down her phone. Little sister. She sure felt little. Insignificant was more like it. Like the world was moving in so many directions, but here she was, stranded on an island. Literally.

Oh, well. On to those freezers she'd seen earlier. She'd take inventory of what was on hand and plan out some meals. But first, she needed some meatballs and pasta, with her Mama's homemade spaghetti sauce.

Chapter 68
Finally Packed Brent Leaves the City

He had finally finished loading the SUV. Since making the decision to get out of the city and work from the North Carolina beach house, he'd been a whirlwind of activity. Everything he'd need to have on hand to work on this project had been either ordered and shipped to the beach house or was in his truck. The SUV was jam-packed, but true to his obsessively well-ordered nature, things had been systematically loaded to allow for optimum utility of the available space. In other words, every inch had been used to its best advantage. His friend, Chaz, a renowned tiny homebuilder, would be proud of him.

He rechecked the freight elevator to make sure he hadn't missed anything, then took the elevator back to his apartment to use the restroom and to make sure everything was locked or turned off. He set the alarm and keyed the dead bolt. Then he rode the elevator back down to the garage, slid behind the driver's seat of his Lexus and pulled out of the garage into the meager predawn light of the sleeping city.

The city that never slept was having one bad dream after another—it was living out a nightmare. Every night on the news Governor Cuomo and Mayor de Blasio gave their dire updates. The many lives lost, the overrun hospitals, the new mandates because of it all, and the scientists foreshadowing an impending apocalypse if the people didn't get a handle on this pandemic. And over it all were the naysayers actually having the gall to call everything a hoax. As if political parties and hundreds of world leaders could globally agree on a plot to cause whole economies to collapse. Where did these idiots come from, Brent thought as he breezed through yet another traffic light without seeing so much as a garbage truck on the street.

Just as he came out of a tunnel, he heard the only sound

reverberating through the canyon of skyscrapers these days: the loud wail of a siren taking yet another victim to the hospital. Or if the news could be believed, to one of the shuttered stadiums that had been turned into a makeshift triage camp by the military. There, refrigerated tractor-trailers were lined up as places to store the bodies of victims that had succumbed to the virus.

This city had survived 9/11, but many were having doubts now if it was going to survive the pandemic and its resultant shut down. As one of the world's largest cities, it was daunting to see the apocalyptic effect this virus was having. Three hundred-year-old churches closed. Public schools, private academies, stately universities, all closed. And everywhere, skyscrapers devoid of lights, most probably didn't even allow night watchmen or cleaning crews inside. The streets were empty. It was eerily odd. And where had the homeless populations gone? He had never driven from one side of the city to another without seeing a panhandler, a street performer, or people living under a bridge. He had heard on the news that the city was putting them up in hotels. But that seemed too preposterous to be true. Who had that kind of money? Still . . . not a creature was stirring. Not even a mouse. As far as he was concerned, the city that never slept now appeared comatose.

Coming out of the Holland Tunnel and into the outskirts of the city just as the sun lifted from the horizon, he began to see a few other cars moving along the empty bridges and coming off the highway ramps. By the time he got onto the New Jersey Turnpike, there was a steady stream of cars and trucks leaving the city, most probably heading out of state.

Another oddity: there were no toll attendants. People without an EZ Pass attached to their windshield, or those who didn't have a bucketful of change in their console, were probably getting their tag photographed for a fine to be mailed out. Either that, or the city was forgiving the tolls. If that wasn't a sign of the seriousness of this epidemic to the city, he couldn't think of one better. The money being lost was incalculable. But no one seemed to care. Everyone was afraid—for themselves, for their families—for everything and everyone that mattered to them.

People all around him were likely attempting to find a safe haven far from the epicenter, while wittingly or unwittingly, becoming contagions ready to send the disease out in ripples like waves as they spoke, coughed, sneezed, sang out, or touched anything. The ashen-faced people he saw through the windows of their cars were likely already infected and were now taking the virus well beyond the city.

He could be one of them. But he didn't think so. It had been well over a week since he'd even seen another human face-to-face. Which was probably the reason he had developed this new habit of talking to himself. Still, once he got to the beach house, he knew he'd have to quarantine himself. But instead of dreading that thought, he relished it.

He anticipated months of connecting only by phone or computer—texts, calls, and emails. Other things he could ignore in favor of doing the work he loved with no interruptions. Weeks and weeks of little to think about, other than the beauty of the coast and the comfort of the spectacular beach house he had built, and his new hospital project. The office phones had answering machines with recorded messages; his personal voicemail said he had left the city to work remotely. His email said he was out of the office and unavailable for the next few weeks. If there was a true emergency, his assistant knew where he was and how to get in touch with him. But really, could there be a bigger emergency than what the city was experiencing right now? He thought not. Everything was dire now, for everyone. He was one of the lucky ones getting out.

He ran through the radio stations avoiding the news programs and searching for music instead, then he got to NPR. He trusted them to report things without bias so he listened to how the virus was affecting other countries. He heard the plight of India where thousands were stranded many miles from their homes as all forms of transportation had been shut down, leaving many who traveled extensively for their jobs, living on the streets in strange cities as homeless people.

The U.K. was just beginning to have outbreaks, and the talk was that no one high up in government was giving it any credence. Parties and concerts were still being hugely attended by millennials, who thought themselves immune. The entitled classes were not about to give up a single pleasure in deference to the health of their cities, towns, states, and countries. Some were completely resistant to any change in their lifestyle. In our own country, Florida was fighting lockdowns, trying to keep their spring break traditions in the face of waves of outbreaks.

China was being slammed as the evil purveyors of this dreaded disease as they too fought to contain it and look for a cure. Italy was being touted as by far the worst affected, as their daily death totals were in the thousands, wiping out whole villages as it ravaged the northern part of the country and eased into Germany and Austria. He thought of his friend Palo and said some prayers, as he knew he was likely in Florence seeing to the needs of his family. And Africa was a royal mess. They'd already had too many problems they couldn't handle. Now this.

He finally switched to Sirius and selected songs from the 90s. He had to focus away from the bad news, had to stop thinking about his investments, had to focus on the work he had to do. This new hospital he was working on would have to be built without any delays. It was his job to see to that. The community hospital had been urgently needed at the outset of this project, now it was imperative that his design sail through the necessary committees without a hitch. The members of which, were likely working from home and bemoaning anything that would delay construction of their long-planned hospital.

In Maryland, after gassing up and using the restroom, he looked for a place to get something to eat and discovered the only places open were McDonald's and Hardee's. But they were not open to go inside. It was drive-thru only. He ordered two Egg McMuffins, coffee and orange juice, promising himself he'd do better for lunch. He did not. In Roanoke Rapids, he had a choice of Taco Bell, KFC, Burger King, Hardee's, Popeye's, Wendy's, and McDonald's. He opted for a fish sandwich and a vanilla shake.

Getting back onto the highway, he mentally ran through the things Kyle had made for them during their last reunion in July. He knew that there were leftovers in individual containers stockpiled in both freezers for whoever could make it back to the beach house between reunions. He'd helped pack them up. There should be pasta in a thick meat sauce, tennis-ball sized meatballs made with beef, pork, and veal, a spicy shrimp scampi, Kyle's amazing version of shepherd's pie, Tuscan bean soup, sausage and egg breakfast casseroles, chicken piccata, barbequed ribs, boneless chicken wings, some leftover delivery pizza still in boxes, vegetable lasagna, a Cuban piccadilo concoction everyone had loved, Spanish rice with chorizo, minestrone, crab filled crepes, lobster bisque, ham with the best mac and cheese ever, and desserts—all kinds of cakes, tarts, pies, muffins, brownies, and cookies. All he had to do was get there and he'd have plenty of delicious food to eat. Not the stuff that was beginning to taste like cardboard.

He stopped in Leland at a gas station to use the facilities, and topped off his gas tank to patronize the station for being open and for letting him go inside to pee. Looking in the mirror at his reflection, his eyes bugged wide. He really should not have missed his hair appointment. The thick scruff of hair that he had to keep tucking behind his ears, that hung low on his neck, combined with the cold damp wind outside had given him a wild look. And to make matters worse, his poliosis was starting to show again—that weird shock of white over his left temple that made him look older and in his mind, sinister. His unwanted birthmark was edging its way out again as it always did, two weeks after he had it colored. Only this time, since he'd missed his appointment, it had been six weeks, and the darned thing was half an inch long.

His mom thought it dashing, always touching it and running her fingers through it to stroke it back, to place it where she preferred it, arching up and back over his left eyebrow. She referred to it as a Mallen streak because of some romance book she'd read in the 70s. All the men in that book had inherited the trait, and apparently, it had made them über sexy, because she always looked at his shock of bright white hair fondly, whereas he totally despised it. He had taken to dying it while he was in college, touching it up himself with shoe polish when he was too busy to bother with dying it. Now he had it professionally dyed, except that he hadn't, since early February.

Well, he thought, as he vigorously washed his hands and turned his head this way and that. All of his hair would grow out now and he'd become a shaggy mess as he sheltered in place and became a hermit. He kind of relished the idea. He smiled into the mirror. Yeah, he'd become a beach bum. He visualized himself running down the beach, long board in hand, scruffy unshaven cheeks, and wet strands of black hair amid the one white one slapping his face. Yeah, that was the ticket. He used his wet fingers to smooth back the thick tresses to give him a more proper businessman look. He wasn't at the beach yet.

He got back into the Lexus and buckled up. In less than an hour he'd be there. It would be time for dinner soon. The sun would be setting in an hour. It was overcast now, dark clouds were gathering and rain was threatening toward the west. If he was lucky, he'd make it before the downpour. If not, he'd unpack the truck tomorrow morning. Actually, that was a good plan either way, he thought as he pulled back onto Route 17. He was definitely getting tired.

He changed Sirius to a classical station playing piano concertos. The lilting, spirited notes instantly relaxed him. Yes, it was past time for some loud Rachmaninoff. He'd been on the road ten hours, with one more to go. At least, there was something to be said for no traffic on the roads.

Chapter 69
Alyssa finds Kyle's Meatballs in the Freezer

Alyssa found three containers of meatballs, each with six meatballs the size of bocce balls. They were showing signs of freezer burn so she took them all into the kitchen and rewrapped them individually, first with clear wrap and then with aluminium. She knew that in America, the shiny metal paper was called aluminum foil as they always made fun of her when she pronounced it al-u-min-ium.

But truly, decent-sized meatballs such as this would preserve much better if they were individually protected from the frost. With great care, she wrapped sixteen and then kept two out for dinner. The others, she rolled behind boxes of ice cream cones and éclair bars that were propped up along the top two shelves on the freezer door, figuring that the cardboard and the frozen ice cream itself would protect the meatballs even more from frost burn.

Before defrosting the two she had left out, she could tell that these were exceptional meatballs. She could see flecks of green spices and the cream-colored shavings of Parmesan Reggiano cheese, along with coarse ground pepper blended into the tri-colored meat. She knew it was Kyle's special blend as Palo had spoken of it often—a third pork sausage, a third something they called chuck, and a third ground Delmonico, all hand-blended with milk-sopped ducks of sourdough bread.

She put two of the prized meatballs in the refrigerator so they could defrost. Then she lined up the cans of tomatoes and searched for the other ingredients needed for Mama's sauce. She started some stone ground oatmeal from a canister she found in the pantry, because it would be a long time before the sauce was ready and she needed something for breakfast now. Her tummy was making loud grumbling noises.

She sat on a barstool at one of the high counters in the huge kitchen, feeling small and insignificant as she ate oatmeal blended with cinnamon sugar, dried cranberries, and walnut pieces, while making a grocery list for the Food Leopard on the mainland.

Palo said all she had to do was use the computer in the next room and she could select the brands she wanted and they would bring everything to the front door using a delivery service. She was going to make liberal use of the default charge card he'd told her about. She did not want to run out of milk, coffee creamer, fresh cheeses, breads, fruits, or vegetables. Oh, and chocolate. Palo said they usually had Godiva and Lindt Lindor Truffles in the pantry. It was not her favorite Sclitti hazelnut round, but it would have to do.

She checked all the closets in all the bathrooms, searched the pantries, investigated under the cabinets of the wet bar in the room where the pool table was, and dug through all the kitchen cupboards.

This was the most remarkably stocked house, she thought. She'd have enough wine and liquor to drink until the next decade, toiletries, lotions, and soaps galore, and even paper products, which she'd heard on the television in the kitchen while wrapping the meatballs, were in very high demand now. A man interviewed said he'd paid $10 for one roll of bathroom tissue. She felt guilty. At that price, this house had enough rolls to fund a nice investment account.

She downloaded the app to her phone to make it easier going about the house, after finally realizing that the local grocery store was Food Lion and not Food Leopard. Then she clicked on all the items she wished to have delivered and went over her grocery list one final time to make sure she had everything. She added a few bakery items that tempted her, and selected the delivery time, then chose her way of paying using Palo's credit card. She finalized the sale and received a confirmation. This was amazing!

All she had to do now was wait for the doorbell, allow

them to leave everything on the porch and then leave, before opening the door and hauling it all inside to put away after wiping it all down with the disinfectant wipes she found in the laundry area. She smiled and said out loud, "I like how they grocery shop in America!" The echo of her own voice coming back to her from the high ceiling startled her. It was too quiet in here.

Palo had told her there were docking systems with speakers throughout the house that were able to play music from mobile phones, but that he usually just told Alexa to play light jazz. She asked the Alexa canister on the serving bar to play Italian music and a woman's voice quickly agreed to play Italian favorites. The opening strands of *It's Amore* filled the kitchen.

She took the cans of tomato sauce to the fancy electric opener that took off the lids without leaving any sharp edges. Then she discovered the most amazing set of pots and pans in the butler's pantry. She only knew that it was called that because there was a fancy sign on a chain attached to the oversized door that said: *BUTLER'S PANTRY*.

She dumped the cans into the medium-sized super shiny pot, and started adding the ingredients to make the sauce. She would have to wait until the fresh mushrooms, onions, celery, carrots, garlic, and parsley got here, but for now, she added the evoo, found some vermouth in the bar, and perused the amazing custom spice shelves where each spice had its own hand painted ceramic canister. She knew the quality of the spices inside would be the finest one could find anywhere. She couldn't wait to taste this sauce. It would be like being at home, at Mama's table.

She needed some *origano*, as it was critical to the recipe even though only a pinch was needed, and knowing she'd never find it fresh this time of year, she flipped the clasp and sniffed the canister labeled "Oregano." Oh my. Under God's heaven, this was home. Tears came to her eyes. She held back a sob, although why, she didn't know, there was no one anywhere near enough to hear it. A wave of homesickness assailed her. Maybe if she could just talk to Giancarlo.

She picked up her phone and thumbed to his number again. It was almost noon here; it would be close to six in the evening where he was. He wouldn't be at work yet. Maybe not at all, as he was a bartender in a posh hotel where tourists stayed. Palo said the tourists were no longer coming and every place was closing. She touched his name on her list of favorites.

Then listened to it ring. And ring. And ring. It went to his voicemail. She listened to his jocular voice telling whoever called that he was out driving his Ferrari and to leave a message. He drove a Fiat. She debated leaving a message, but decided against it. Right now, her voice would have an acerbic quality to it, she was pretty sure of that. He'd call her back when he saw her missed calls.

She turned the sauce off to wait for the rest of the ingredients. Maybe she'd take a shower—or a bath. She loved soaking in a nice big tub of hot, fragrant water. In Italy, the tubs were typically short and narrow. She hadn't fit in the tub in her momma's house since her menses began. Like all the women in her family, the bloom of her hips kept her from enjoying a nice, long soak, as she had to turn on her side to fit into the tapered bathtub. Once, she'd needed Mama to come add some bath oil to the water to get her unstuck. Plus, there were always others waiting to use the bathroom. Here, she would be keeping no one waiting.

She walked down the hall, back to the bedroom with the en suite she had chosen as hers for her stay. She looked at the garden tub big enough for two. No oil would be needed to get her out of this tub. But it would take a lot of water to fill it. Conservation, always on her mind, she sunk her teeth into her bottom lip, debating.

Yes! She bent over and turned the tap to full on hot. Then she rummaged around under the sink for something bubbly. Nada.

She went back to the kitchen and grabbed the dishwashing liquid that sat beside the sink in its own custom ceramic holder. She would be Dawn-grease-cutting clean. She pumped a generous amount into a tall shot glass and ran back to pour it under the powerful stream of hot water.

While she waited for the tub to fill, she stood in front of the double sinks and stared into the huge gilt-framed vanity mirror. Her hair was messy, but nothing a brush couldn't tame if she'd wanted to tame it. She didn't. She wasn't going to bother with it now—maybe not tomorrow either. Due to this pandemic she might take a vacation from grooming it all together. Who would even know?

She dumped her bag of hair accessories onto the counter and selected a big strong clip that would hold her heavy hair up on top of her head. She'd wanted to cut it to the newer more modern styles, but her Mama had stomped her foot and said, "No! You do not cut your hair. Men like it long, and yours is thick and lustrous so men will like it even more. Stop trying to look like other women. I tell you, I know what men like: a little makeup, not too much so it gets on their shirts, lipstick that does not make them fear kissing you and having to wear it on their own lips, and hair they can run their fingers through and use to tug you where they want you. You trust me! Your mama knows. She was young and beautiful once, you know."

And she had been. She'd seen the pictures of her mama when she had been her age. Her blue-black hair had been her crowning glory. Her papa must have found his glory in it. Surely he had tugged her exactly where he wanted her many times—as he'd sired five sons and a daughter on her mama. Sadly, only she and Palo had gone full-term though.

Alyssa leaned in toward the mirror, he nose almost touching. She focused on eyes that were bloodshot. She fished for eye drops that were in her remedies bag and squeezed a generous amount into the dry eyes she typically had during the winter from furnaces running and drying out the air.

She looked at her face, tilting it this way and that. She wondered, did men think her pretty? Sexy? To her, she looked young, like a schoolgirl who should be carrying a tall stack of books in her arms. It was why she had added highlights to her dark hair, putting streaks of pale ash into her dark inky waves. It was a more sophisticated look she thought. Her mama had sniffed and said she'd ruined God's masterpiece.

She straightened up and quirked her lips into a smile. She thought her hair looked nice. She had a slightly angular face, squared off from the corners of her light brown eyes to where her jaw hinged, leading to a gently rounded chin. Deep dimples on her cheeks softened the harshness and gave her an impish look. She had always wondered if her shape was one of the most or least desired shapes for women's faces. When she had read an article on face shapes in a magazine one time, they said the most famous person with her face shape was Kathy Ireland. She did not know who she was at the time and had to Google her to see if she was as pretty as they were saying with that squared-off shape. And she was—devastatingly so. It had made her smile and perk up to know that a famous and very beautiful model had her exact same face shape. Kathy Ireland had been picked as the *Sports Illustrated* bathing suit model of the year thirteen consecutive times. So hers was a great face shape! Although, to be fair, it was probably not Ms. Ireland's face that had gotten her all those swimsuit magazine covers.

Alyssa had already known that her almond-shaped eyes were very much in demand with face models. Her eyes did not need an eyebrow pencil, eyeliner, or mascara to stand out. Her lashes were long and inky black on their own. She was lucky there. And her hazelnut colored eyes, typical for Mediterranean women, had a unique golden corona around the pupils. The combination made her look alert and spritely even when she was dead tired, which was a real bonus at the end of a day filled with dragging tourists all over the city of Florence.

She pouted her lips. They were nice and full, a natural soft rose color. She had a tendency to purse them, or to hold them to the side while biting on the inside of her cheek when she was fretting. She smiled at herself in the mirror and watched with vexation as her matching dimples materialized despite her wanting them to. Her father had loved her *fossettas*, her mother loved them, her brother loved them, and all her aunts and uncles loved to pinch the cheeks that housed them. She however, hated them. She thought they were another reason she looked too young for men to ask out.

But her straight white teeth were indeed lovely. They should be, it had cost her papa a fortune to fix the overbite caused by her thumb sucking until she was seven. He had gone to his grave paying for those protruding teeth as he had taken out a second mortgage to pay the orthodontist when she was a teenager. His life insurance had paid off both mortgages when he died so at least her mama had not had to walk to the bank every month with €40 to pay her old dental bill as her father had.

She pushed back from the mirror. She supposed that she was pretty enough, but probably not beautiful, not like Kathy Ireland, her new favorite celebrity. She looked over her shoulder at the tub. It was almost to the level she liked—enough to cover her thighs, her lush mound, and her full breasts. She liked her breasts well enough, but she hated the tight curls that were plentiful over her womanhood. It made a bikini wax necessary if she wished to wear a bikini swimsuit. And waxing was very painful. She often wore a conservative one-piece for that very reason.

She turned back to the tub and while it finished filling, she removed her clothes, letting them drop to the tiled floor. She shut down the tap and gingerly stepped into the tub. It was exactly as she liked it. Scalding hot. When she got out of the tub she liked to see her skin all pinked up.

It took her a few minutes until she was able to fully sit and relax against the back of the tub. Steam rose all around her, enveloping her like a warm cocoon. This was bliss. She dropped her head back, letting it fall and settle against the edge of the freestanding tub. She closed her eyes, and listened to the quiet. The silence and warmth encompassed her, entranced her. She drifted in and out of a hazy sleep as she enjoyed Dawn's "refreshing rain scent," the bouquet of the soft bubbles breaking with a feather light touch and soothing sound against her skin.

Chapter 70
Brent Arrives—a Virago & Boor Butt Heads

Her eyes popped open when she heard a door slam. She sat up, the water sloshing around her, some even splashing onto the tile floor before slowly settling. She thought from the loudness that the door closing with so much force had to have been the front door.

Her room, just to the left at the top of the stairs, with the bathroom being immediately to the left once inside the bedroom, would allow the sound to resonate up. She'd left both the bedroom and bathroom doors wide open, as she'd seen no reason to pull them to. She had a moment of regret that she hadn't rearmed the alarm. At least then she'd know that whoever had entered had access to the code.

Her breath hitched and she held it in as she waited for some other sound. Nothing. Convinced she had heard wrong or dreamt the sound, she began to relax back into the water. No. A loud thud reverberated up to her. Someone was definitely coming inside the house. And dropping things on the floor. Now, closing the door with another loud slam.

Did the Food Leopard delivery people have access to the house? Was it the housekeeper coming by? What should she do? She felt very vulnerable, sitting naked in the tub.

Then she heard voices.

"Are you sure that delivery is for this house?" she heard a man call out. Then after a pause the same person said, "Well, alright. Bring it up then. But I honestly don't think anyone is here now. Oh! Maybe my assistant placed the order. Of course! Just put it all in the foyer if you don't mind. I'm going to make another trip back to my car."

She heard a woman's voice call out, "Yes, sir!"

Then she heard the rustle of paper grocery bags being

unloaded onto the foyer tile—a lot of them.

She stood and grabbed the towel she'd left folded on the floor. *Madre di Dio, who was here?*

"The tip's already been paid, sir. No, that's too much. Okay, thank you. Let us know when you need anything else!"

Then the door closed with a solid slam. By then she had wrapped the towel around her and was walking down the hall to the top of the steps that led down to the foyer.

As she rounded the corner and looked down, a man with several messenger bags on his shoulders turned and looked up the stairs.

He saw her and stopped, his eyes wide as he stared up at her. It took a moment, but then he called up to her, "Who the hell are you?"

His voice was gruff. Impatience radiated from him as he let one bag drop down to the floor as if preparing for fight mode. His lips were pressed together in a tight line as if holding in more accusatory words.

His harsh condescending tone set her off. "And I would ask the same of you. Who the hell are you?"

She mocked him by using the same bad mannered tone. She could tell he wasn't taking it well when his eyes narrowed, his lips firmed, and he sneered up at her.

Then he stopped, dropped the other messenger bag and stood, hands on hips, taking in her dripping wet body covered in only a lilac colored bath towel. A slender arm was wrapped under her breasts, allowing for her ample cleavage to show over the edge of the towel. When she inhaled to stoke her anger, her breasts threatened to spill out over the top.

Brent's second assessment of the towel-clad woman at the top of the stairs was of mahogany colored curls piled high on a head tilted in bewilderment, brown eyes sparking with fiery glints, rosy lips, and breasts she was trying to keep confined. Generous, full breasts he was having trouble keeping his eyes off.

Each breath of her indignation threatened to expose a nipple. Her skin, above and below the towel was pink; he could smell something floral wafting off of her heated skin. Or quite possibly he was imagining that, as the distance between them was a whole staircase.

God, she was a young thing. And she would have normally been a welcome sight in such a state of disarray. But not right now. Not when he was this road weary and every bone in his body wanted to collapse. He wanted to be left alone. But whatever élan he held in reserve came to the forefront.

"Ladies first."

"I am Alyssa, Palo's sister."

"Oh. Is Palo here?" He was visibly cheered by this news.

"No."

Then she thought better of her answer. "Mmmm, maybe he is."

He arched an expressive brow her way.

She raised both of hers, her eyes wide with defiance. She didn't know who this man was. He could be anybody. But with all the stuff he'd piled by the door, she was betting that he belonged here—certainly more than she did.

His voice, full of confidence confirmed her thoughts. "I'm Brent Baldwin, one of the owners."

She took in a deep breath and let that thought settle as he blinked his eyes wide and watched her breasts heave from the action.

"Palo said I could stay here. I got stuck in New York when they closed the airport."

"I see."

His lips were pursed again. He was not happy about this turn of events. "I just left New York myself."

He took in a deep breath himself, then sighed like a bellows, letting every bit of air expel from his chest.

"We're supposed to email when someone is coming to use the house." His tone and expression was like that of a reprimanding and insolent adolescent.

A few long seconds passed and he sighed again, this time in a loud huff, as if he was conceding a hard fought chess match against a worthy opponent, and he was not at all happy about it.

More awkward seconds passed.

"But I guess I can't fault him. I didn't send out a message saying I was coming here either."

His conciliatory tone matched the resigned look on his face. This was a man fighting many emotions—none good.

There was complete silence for several moments as they stared at each other, neither daring to move as if holding their ground on this encampment battle.

"This changes everything," he finally ventured. "I had plans to be alone here, working."

"I had plans to be back in Italy with my family, my girlfriends, and my boyfriend. I guess neither one of us gets what we want."

She was a pragmatic person. The youngest in her family, although spoiled as she was, she rarely won in matters such as this. She had learned to accept things as they were and to just make the best of things. Take the top bunk. Eat the piece of pizza that had lost its cheese to the box. Give Mama the umbrella. Let Palo pick the dessert. Walk up the hill to take Sunday dinner to the priest instead of meeting her friends at the cinema. Yes, she wanted to be home. No, she could not be. She mentally stomped her foot. "I know this is your house, but it is my brother's as well. If I cannot go home, I have to stay here."

From where she stood, looking down at him, he was tall and athletic looking, with great gobs of thick coppery brown hair that had once been cropped short on the sides, but now the top went its own way and the cut had lost its shape and was all shaggy. A shock of white hair fanned back from his forehead. Another inch and he'd have a disaster up there.

As he watched her taking him in, and as if knowing how

unkempt he looked, he tunneled his fingers through his hair.

His week-old beard matched his hair, rakishly untrimmed, it appeared as an act of rebellion more than anything else. His assessing light blue eyes, bloodshot though they were, took her in while she studied the dimple in his chin that the scruffy beard had not yet obliterated.

His well-defined brows were a tad darker than the hair on his head. They, along with his chiseled features, gave him a prominent look of entitlement. There were two small creases between his brows as he frowned up at her.

He was a bit haggard from the trip, but he was still very handsome after what she knew had been a long drive. So . . . this was the playboy Chaz had hung out with during his college days. Palo had told her that back then, Chaz and Brent liked to share the same woman. Right now, he didn't look like he wanted to share anything—certainly not this house.

The sound of one of the bulging grocery bags crumpling in on itself and sending a can of tomatoes rolling off a step then clattering onto the tile floor broke the awkward silence.

"I uh, ordered some food."

"All this?" He frowned as he took in all the tall brown paper bags. There were 12 of them.

"Mmm. Yeah."

"So you expect to be here for a while?"

"I do. And you?" She tilted her head to the side and studied him. "You are the architect, yes?"

"Mmm hmm, yes to both," he said, pursing his lips again before picking up one of his bags by the long strap and then hoisting all the others back onto his shoulder in preparation for carrying them up the stairs.

He was clearly not happy about her being here—or seeing the disordered clutter in the foyer.

"I'll just go get d-dressed so I can s-start putting all this away," she said, her nerves finally giving in and making her stumble over her words.

He watched her turn away from the steps—took in the back of her thighs, knees, and shapely legs.

"You do that," he muttered as he made his way up the steps. At the landing he turned right. Down the hall, at the alcove on the left, he pressed the button for the elevator.

She remembered when the house was finished, that Palo had told her that Brent, as the architect, had what they all called *The Penthouse*. From the tour she'd taken earlier, she knew his bedroom was the on the top floor, all the way down on the right side of the house. It was a corner room that had long counters set up as workstations. It commanded views from two directions and had a sun deck with a raised platform so you could see out over the dunes. Furnished in a modern Scandinavian design, everything had clean lines and was sleek looking. She had brushed her fingers along the smooth surface of the built-in desk and bookshelves and had known the wood was of uncommon quality.

Let him go to his *penthouse*! The further away from her the better. Her room had a superior bathtub and that was what mattered to her. And, the fact that she had managed to select the farthest room in the house from his pleased her very much.

She stomped back up to her room then tossed out things from her suitcase until she found something that suited her mood. Pulling on paisley pajama bottoms and a soft, slouchy sweatshirt she went back down the hall and down the steps to where the bags of groceries stood waiting to be lugged up to the kitchen.

She would have used the elevator, but knowing that Brent was using it elevator for *his* things, she hauled each bag up the steps—clomp, clomp, clomping in her woven-leather mules until she had them all on top of the granite countertops.

She hitched her lips sideways into a self-deprecating smirk. She *had* bought an awful lot. As she worked to put everything away, while adding the ingredients she needed to the pot on the stove, she vowed to curb her need for gratification with food. This could be a long siege. She did not need to pack on pounds. She was a voluptuous 143, but even at 5'8" she could not afford to put on much weight and still fit into her clothes.

While the sauce simmered, she washed the vegetables and made a salad, then put it in the fridge to chill. All around her it was getting dark. Out of every window blackness was encroaching. When she walked to a front window and looked out, she saw a series of solar lights flickering both around the circular drive out front and across the street at a neighboring house. She stood watching until they all came on and stayed on. The light they cast out in a prism-like pattern was comforting and it gave her pause to remember her blessings. It was such a whimsical thing, but it cheered her immensely to see the soft fairy lights.

She walked to the back of the house to the glass doors and looked up for the moon, but the day had been cloudy and now the night continued to be more of the same. She returned to the kitchen and turned on every light she could find, just to make it cheery inside too.

She listened as Brent unloaded his vehicle. He was taking a lot of stuff into the big room on the main level that already held several boxes that had been delivered from a New York address that very afternoon. She hadn't known whom they were for, but now she did.

It appeared he was turning the room into a quasi-office/den. She supposed he planned to work down here, in this multi-purpose room while he was here. That sucked. She'd been developing her own plans for that room—doing her yoga regimen in the mornings in front of that huge TV, watching cooking shows in the afternoon in front of that huge TV, and bingeing on late night reruns of *The Big Bang Theory, Two and a Half Men*, and *The Golden Girls*, all of which she'd become pretty much addicted to during her weeks in New York.

When it became obvious that he wasn't going to stop his unpacking and setting up regimen, she poured herself some wine and cooked the meatballs.

He came into the kitchen half an hour later just as she had settled herself up at the counter, next to a beautiful imported ceramic plate bearing Kyle Merritt's signature. It rested atop a lovely woven placemat with the intricate cutlery Kyle had designed as well, placed on a folded paper towel.

She'd already brought out the salad, drained the pasta, and put one of the meatballs on the plate. She was coating it with a generous ladle-full of her Mama's sauce, while saying a quiet grace to herself as she prepared to dig in when Brent strolled in.

He took one look at her plate and stood stark still. "Is that one of Kyle's meatballs from the freezer?"

"Yes," she said, not breaking stride and shoving a bit of the meatball with a forkful of pasta into her mouth.

After she savored, chewed, and swallowed it, she added, "Palo said to help myself to whatever I found in the freezer."

"How long have you been here?" he asked still staring at her plate.

"Just got here this morning."

"So . . . I can assume that there are still more of his meatballs in the freezer?"

"Yes, I did not eat twenty gargantuan meatballs today. This is actually only my first one."

His condescending manner was starting to irk her. He acted as if he owned the place. Well, he did. But so did her brother. So she had every right to be here.

"Sorry. I've kind of had a hankering for one all day. It was probably the driving force to get me here tonight instead of tomorrow." He glanced over at the pot on the stove. "You make that sauce?"

"I did. It's my Mama's recipe."

"It smells wonderful."

"It is."

He gave her a sideways grin that made him look much younger, and less tired. "Are you going to make me beg?"

He walked around the counter to the other side, picked up the open bottle of wine and looked at the label. He nodded his approval. Then he went to the fridge, pulled out a bottle of Corona and twisted off the cap.

She watched as he lifted the bottle, threw back his head and chugged nearly half of it. The fingers wrapped around the bottle were long, slender, and capable looking. She couldn't help but think of him moving Chaz away from a lover and then taking over where Chaz had left off by pleasuring the woman with them. She could not help remembering the day Palo had told her stories about the two men—Palo was such a gossip—and she had kept pouring Chianti into his glass to keep him talking.

She wondered now what Palo had told Brent about her. Probably that she was good with numbers, sewed her own clothes unless they were cheaper to buy, and could hit a soccer ball off her head like a pro.

A long sigh followed after he had drained most of the bottle. His head settled after a few exaggerated turns and stretches of his neck. He looked like a different man. She guessed downing a good cold beer and knowing that your work for the day was finished could do that for anybody.

"Yeah, on your knees," she deadpanned. "You're a lousy host. If I could pack my bags and leave I would."

"I'm sorry," he said as he took the seat beside her. He folded his hands in front of him on the countertop and turned to look at her. "I just had these expectations."

He seemed revitalized. He'd brushed his wild hair and his eyes were no longer bloodshot. She focused on the odd shock of white hair emerging from his hairline. It was slightly off center. She could only imagine all the double takes and odd comments he'd had about it over the years. She thought it distinctive and a bit dashing. Now that she studied it, she could see the telltale darkness along the ends that told her he'd been dying it. He'd changed into jeans and was wearing a flannel shirt over a long t-shirt. He had lost that haggard look and was actually quite handsome now, and maybe somewhat approachable. She took a sip of her wine

"What expectations?" she asked.

"Being here all alone. Being able to walk around naked and scuzzy if I wanted to. Working as it suited me, day or night. Doing some surfing and kayaking with the rising or setting sun. Eating ALL of Kyle's leftover meatballs . . ."

She took another bite, purposefully, rolling it around on her tongue as she savored it, licking her lips to show her complete delight, and then murmuring her approval with a long drawn out sigh.

He watched her with desire. Not desire for her. Desire for the meatball of course. Well, maybe a bit of both.

"I think this virus has knocked all our expectations to the moon," she murmured.

He looked at her in a questioning manner.

"I was supposed to be back home in Italy by now. Eating dinner with my family, being with my boyfriend, going back to work tomorrow. My life is there, not here. I feel marooned."

"I couldn't stand the empty city any longer. I had to get out. I have a big project I'm working on—designing a huge hospital in an area that really needs one. And needs one now. I thought I'd be alone here to tackle it without interruptions, working through the night if I needed to, trying to move the construction date up. And on the way down here, I thought about Kyle's meatballs waiting in the freezer. After eating crappy fast food all day, all I wanted was one of Kyle's meatballs. Then for the last hour, that sauce you made has had me salivating for that too."

She looked over at him. "That's pretty good groveling." She nodded toward the pot on the stove. "Help yourself to the other meatball. It's already in the sauce. And there's a big bowl of salad already dressed in the fridge."

"Thanks. Sorry I was a jerk."

"Are you gonna stop?"

"Probably not," he said with a grin. "Nature of the beast."

"I have no problem with the rest of your expectations, except the naked one. Knock yourself out working, we're on separate floors, at opposite ends of the house, and I have ear buds if I need them."

She didn't bother telling him where she'd hidden the rest of the meatballs though. He'd never find them where she put them, on the freezer door behind all the cardboard boxes. She would go back and block the side view with a bag of frozen peas. She had to maintain some control. Holding the meatballs hostage could pay off for her later.

After taking the last sip of his beer, he got up and fixed himself a plate of the pasta topped it with the sauce, then the meatball, and a few fresh shavings of the Parmesan Reggiano that was in a prep bowl by the stove. He put the plate on the high counter and got the salad bowl from the fridge and filled a smaller bowl of it. Then he dug in.

"This. Is. Amazing," he said after a few bites, reverence and veneration in his voice.

"I know, right?" she said with a smile that was both welcoming and friendly.

They ate in silence and then he got up and went into the Butler's Pantry where there was an extra glassed-in chest freezer. He came out with two frozen plastic jars and put one in front of her. They were both containers of Taglianti Pistachio Gelato. He put the other jar beside his empty plate, went to the other side of the bar, opened the silverware drawer and slid a spoon across the counter to her. "I want it noted that I fixed dessert."

He retook his seat and they clicked spoons together as if toasting each other. And so the truce began.

Chapter 71
Brent Unpacks, Surfs, and Crashes

Despite being dog-tired, Brent stayed up most of the night unpacking both his personal effects and his office supplies and components. It was the way he rolled, always unpacking right away, never leaving things undone for the next day. Most of the people he'd worked with over the years said he was anal about working in an organized, precise environment, where everything had its place and was in it at all times, or was in his hand being used.

He assembled the drafting desk, the copier and fax cabinet, two lamp stands, and a worktable—things that he'd had overnighted and arranged to be hauled into the house by the housekeeper's husband.

When he'd built the house, he'd customized a desk and a long counter that were tucked into a niche so there were already had two ergonomic desk chairs in place that he could alternate between to keep his back from cramping up. One was adjusted for his morning back, the other for his late night back. It was a system that worked well for him.

After stocking all the supplies in the cabinet, replacing the tools in the storage area, and then breaking down and removing the trash to the recycling bins under the house, he felt he was ready to begin work in the morning.

Except that it was almost morning now, and work was the last thing he felt like doing. So was sleeping, though he should have been passed out by now. Yet he was energized in a way that only happened here, at Sunset Beach. Unwilling to waste another sunrise away from the ocean, he pulled out his new Christmas present wet suit from the hanger in the walk-in closet. His parents had done a lot of research and had bought the best. It was custom-fit to his measurements so it fit him like a second skin.

It was the last week of March and the air temperature was already 66 degrees. He could see the wind was blowing the muhly grass, but there was no rain due according to the weather app on his iPhone. So he and his Christmas-present-to-himself surfboard were going to be one this morning—at least until he got too tired to stand. Which was likely to happen sooner rather than later, as he hadn't gotten a good night's sleep since he'd started planning this escape from the city. He worked to get into the suit.

When he opened his bedroom door the rest of the house was quiet, so he was careful to tiptoe down the stairs to the ground floor, and from there to the under-house storage unit that housed the surfboards and kayaks, where he'd put his board last night.

He had to admit, he felt a rush that sent a pleasant shiver through his veins when he saw his long board, tucked onto a rack, waiting patiently for his return. Within minutes, he was on the beach access, making his way down the planks to the beach and praying he'd catch some decent waves to ride this morning.

Over and over again, he paddled out. Then rode the waves in. It was a high like no other to master getting up. Staying up. And gliding in on the path his board and the wave had teamed together to shoot through.

Not even an hour later, his body said uncle, and for once, he listened. Usually, he didn't. But his brain reminded him: You've been packing, schlepping boxes, not eating, driving with a single-minded purpose, and you still haven't slept. *Get off the board, dumb ass.*

He rode it in for the last time, grabbed it up, and dragged it behind him up the beach. Something he never did. He loved his boards too much to drag them through the sand. But he had to confess; he was beat. It was either drag it behind him or leave it behind. And that was unthinkable. The thought of sleep overcoming him and finally taking him to la la land was welcoming.

He looked up at the house as he walked up the access, this

time his board tucked under his arm and hugged close to his side. He saw movement on the back terrace. Alyssa was standing by the rail, coffee mug in hand. He couldn't see her expression as the cup was at her mouth, but he could see the rest of her.

She was standing tall in fleecy plaid pajama bottoms and a slouchy sweatshirt drooping off one shoulder. No bra strap showing. Generous tits. Long messy curls she kept lifting and running her fingers through. She was a gorgeous woman. He quickly checked himself. This was Palo's sister. Sisters were off limits. Always.

He lifted his free arm and waved. She waved back and gifted him with a beautiful, engaging smile. He remembered their clash-of-spoons truce from last night. She was actually a nice person. And a good cook, although the main ingredient, Kyle's world-class meatballs, had already provided the key element to the entree. Her mama's sauce had been stellar though.

He took an inordinate amount of time coming up into the main part of the house. Because of course, he first had to straighten out the storage rack—one of three—because all the guys loved surfing, kayaking, biking, bocce balling, volleyball, and corn hole. They also had a golf cart hogging a section that was cordoned off with cinderblocks, the battery temporarily removed and stored in a waterproof case. He and his frat boys loved their toys. Rutger had six jet skis stored at a local marina. Chaz often flew his business partner's plane into The Ocean Isle Beach Airport. And last week, he'd read in an email that Alex was getting big into drones on the west coast.

Satisfied that everything in the boy-toy world was straight and properly fit into its designated place, he peeled off his new, awesome wet suit. Since he was naked underneath, he took the elevator directly to the top floor. He carried his wet suit into the walk-in shower for a proper rinse then hung it to dry. After washing with his favorite Brickell Organic Spicy Citrus Hair, Face and Body Wash, his skin and scalp felt tingly all over. He dried off, wrapped a fresh towel around his lower half, downed half a bottle of cold water from the in-room mini-fridge, then made his way to the bed, where he nose dived. And crashed for sixteen hours. Life was good. Salt Life was better.

Chapter 72
Adapting to Lockdown

Oh, dear God, he was gorgeous. Even in the wet suit you could tell that his body was chiseled and honed. But then he unzipped it to a few inches below his navel and pulled his arms from the sleeves. Most people would look dorky with the long, formed sleeves slapping their thighs, but he was like . . . well . . . a god. Apollo maybe. She didn't know. Mythology was never her strong suit. Palo avoided sending her to Rome whenever possible for that very reason. She knew nothing of ancient Rome, or Greece for that matter—both places his tour groups frequented. It was why she was delegated to Florence or the hill towns of Tuscany. She simply could not get the gods right.

But Brent sure could. He was one. Only she didn't know which one. Was Aquaman a god?

She put down the binoculars when she thought there was a chance that he could see her standing in front of the glass door leading to an upper floor balcony. Instead, she went out onto the balcony to finish her coffee, and to sneak occasional glances at Brent's expansive chest and well-defined six-pack. The day had dawned sunny and fair. She stood in her pajama bottoms and Sherpa sweatshirt and rethought her misery of two days ago. This was a lovely place where she was now stranded. It was so different from yesterday's weather. Now she could see why Palo loved this house so. The view was breathtaking, and she didn't mean the one that included hunky Brent, although seeing him in the foreground was definitely a bonus.

Giancarlo still hadn't called, and each day it grated on her nerves a bit more. She missed sex. And she missed someone holding her afterward. She came from a family of cuddlers. Right now was a time that everyone needed someone to cling to; someone to tell them that everything was going to be all right.

Just do what they say, follow the rules, and all will be well. Except every day things got worse.

On the Internet she saw that Italy was leading in COVID deaths now. Everything was shutting down—transportation, hospitality, retail. Shops that had been open daily for centuries on the Ponte de Vecchio in Florence, and along the winding hill roads leading up through the tiny medieval villages of Collodi, Volterra, Cortona, and San Gimignano were now being shuttered. The inhabitants, squirreled away within the ancient walls of each town were now eerily focused on their television sets, watching the never-ending news updates that moment-by-moment were taking away their hope with their news reports showing footage of crowded hospitals and body bags being loaded onto trucks that were headed to mass gravesites or crematoriums.

Volunteers, looking for any way to help out, were delivering groceries to peoples' doors; pharmacies were delivering medicine through mail slots. One motorcyclist used his GoPro Camera mounted on his helmet to record his eerie errand of mercy delivering insulin. As he rode along the coast road working his way from Positano to Amalfi, he recorded the empty streets. During the entire trip he did not encounter another soul, either walking or in a vehicle—all the way down the winding, switch-backed road. No one was venturing out unless they had to go to the *hospitale* for help with the virus. Dogs were walked on sparse patches of lawn, just a few feet from their owner's door. Those who had cats kept them inside. There had been a few reports of dogs coming down with the virus, but nothing had been proven.

Mail was delivered without fanfare. A package or an envelope suddenly just appeared, either slipped through a slot in the door or left on the stoop by unseen carriers who hurried to get back in their vehicles, and then back to their own homes so they could get back in front of their flat screen TVs so they could learn how the world was coping with the pandemic.

Alyssa turned to go back inside the house. Enough

morose thinking she told herself. She had to be brave. Idly, she wondered whose room she had come into just for the sake of using their balcony to spy on Brent. After closing and locking the French doors to the little terrace, she faced back to the room to look for clues as to whose room this was.

On the nightstand was a thin playbill for South Pacific with some of the stage performers names circled with red ink. It was for The Brunswick Little Theater. The duvet cover was a paisley print done up in vivid shades of purple, almost neon in their bright hues. Cam. Definitely Cam—the up and coming performer and choreographer that everyone said was positively brilliant. He was based out of Wilmington, but was always flying to New York or L.A. to oversee auditions and rehearsals. Palo told her this past Christmas that Cam had a girlfriend who was a dancer.

His relationship had shocked his friends as they had all thought he was gay. It turned out he never had been, but like the consummate actor he was, he'd played the part for years—until the right girl had come along and stole his heart. Until then, even he hadn't known what was going on with his unresponsive libido. He was just as surprised as everyone else to find himself attracted to a girl—a rather young girl who had been in dire circumstances and in need of rescuing.

There was no one else this room would suit, she thought, tapping her fingers lightly against her lips. This was too easy. She wondered if she could guess the principal occupants of the other rooms. She knew that when the house was full, with both owners and guests that they all shifted to accommodate everyone. Palo had said that he hardly ever slept in the room he had designed, as he was usually the latecomer. But no one minded, as all the rooms were top-notch and loaded with amenities.

She went back to the kitchen for more coffee and heard the elevator opening up on the top floor. A few moments later she heard water being directed through the house and she knew that Brent was showering. Palo had once told her they had something in this house called instant hot water. He had explained that there were several heating stations throughout the house where propane was ignited and water was superheated by running through a fiery hot filament before being sent on its way to the many bathrooms. He had marveled that one could wash clothes and run the dishwasher while people in other parts of the house were showering.

It was one of those high-end luxury items that only the very wealthy in her country could afford. At home, she had to wait a long time for hot water to come from the boiler in the basement to the bathroom on the second floor, and there was not always enough hot water to satisfy her.

She took the blueberry oat bran muffins she'd made from the oven, sliced some fruit, and opened a container of limone yogurt—no, lemon. In America it was called lemon. She had to speak English here. People appreciated it when you took the time to learn their language instead of speaking your own and expecting them to understand you. In America you had to do that. Few people spoke Italian here. Most did not know a second language. In Europe many people spoke several languages, like her and Palo. She spoke Italian and English and was passable in German and French. Palo spoke those as well as Greek and Romansh, one of the four Swiss languages.

She sat alone at the counter eating her breakfast with a notepad at her elbow. Every once in a while, she would stop to write a line or two on topics she would write about for her brother's travel blogs. As no one was traveling now, she came up other ideas. People were living full time in their houses. She thought they needed some jokes, some cooking tips, ways to order products online and how to use them to color and cut their own hair.

After eating and cleaning up, and leaving a note beside the plate of muffins that they were anybody's, she went into the big room that had the television that took up nearly the whole wall. There was a laminated sheet next to five remotes that were color-coded with strips of labeling tape marking each function. It took many minutes, but she finally managed to find an American news show. She settled into a rocker recliner to learn about masks, social distancing, frequent hand washing, and wiping down shipments coming into the home. She had not done that with the groceries yesterday. She hoped she had not made either one of them sick.

The toilet paper shortages had her looking under each bathroom vanity again to do an inventory. The powder room on the first level, the one with the scary leopard mural, had 12 rolls, most of the others had 8 or 9, and a storage closet at the end of the hall had two 36-packs. She thought they would be okay for a while, as several bathrooms also had bidets.

Next, the news show had her running to check on hand sanitizer and disinfectant wipes. She found one canister of wipes under the sink in each bathroom but no hand sanitizer anywhere. Many pumps held liquid soap. That would have to do. It was important to wash your hands. Sanitizing them would not be necessary, especially as they would have very limited contact with other people.

In the storage closet she found big bottles of liquid hand soap to use to refill the pumps. So they had plenty of soap. A man named Dr. Faucci, from the TV news shows, said washing was one of the most important Ws, which were: Wear a mask, Wash your hands, and Wait six-feet away. She found a box of disposable gloves under the kitchen sink. She thought they had all the bases covered, as they said in America.

Going through all the bedrooms and bathrooms she found deodorant, boxes of tissues, cotton balls, cotton swabs, first–aid kits, and interestingly enough, a box of condoms in each nightstand drawer. She was surprised to find a few boxes of tampons and sanitary pads as well. Which got her to thinking again about which rooms belonged to each man.

She thought it might be fun to see if she could hunt for clues and figure out the occupant for each room. Although she knew that when the house was full, room assignments became first come, first served.

She remembered Palo's picture from the album of the finished house and his written stories related to that. Each man had decorated and furnished a room, even knowing that the rooms were not necessarily always going to be theirs to use. She knew the reunion weeks in July were crazy times when the men were often double bunked because of invited guests. And last year, three men had married, including Palo, and then two others had become engaged. Adding women into the mix was going to necessitate some changes for this coming year—if the Corona virus even allowed them to be here this July. And certainly more refurbishing would be needed for the babies that were already on their way. Alex's new wife, Emma was six months with child, and Deke's wife, Shaw, was due any day now.

In the game room she found a picture of the ten men who had gone to college together and then remained friends ten years later. They were posing on the back terrace after their first meal together at the beach house they had dubbed *The Cockpit*. She took the picture off the wall and slowly called out each man's name as she pointed down the rows.

She smiled as she finished naming them all, pleased she knew each one. It might be fun to match each man to the room they had furnished and decorated—the room thought of as theirs.

She had seen a copier in the alcove in the back of the room that served as a business center. It was one of those all-in-one machines, a fax, copier, and scanner. There was also a charging station, a desk with all kinds of office supplies—notepads, post-its, pens, pencils, sharpies, tape, scissors, shipping envelopes, and clips of all kinds. She carefully removed the photograph from the frame and made a color copy, then replaced it and rehung the picture on the wall. She took a pair of scissors from the drawer and used them to cut out each man's figure from the copy of the photograph. Then she took the paper doll men and went room hunting.

Chapter 73
Nice Detective Work!

She took Palo's picture, as well as Cam's, Brent's, and Alex's, and using some tacky mounting putty, she attached them to the doors of the rooms she had already deemed theirs. She looked at the other pictures and smiled. Kyle's and Chaz' would be easy. She took a quick zip in and out of the remaining rooms and promptly pronounced which ones were theirs. Kyle's had two restaurant scenes on the walls, both oils paintings of diners eating at outside cafes, one she suspected was his own restaurant in Portugal, and the other she recognized as being in Positano. The new Jeffrey Eisener Instant Pot cookbook on the nightstand went a long way to confirming her decision. Plus, after snooping through the drawers, she found some recipe cards in the top dresser drawer. She stuck Kyle's picture on the door and smiled. This was almost too easy.

She knew Chaz was a minimalist. She'd heard stories about his tiny houses and seen pictures of a tree house resort he'd built in Costa Rico. She hadn't been there, when he'd been building it, but Chaz had built a tree home for Palo at the villa, right after Papa had died. He had built it so that Palo would have his own personal space to mourn and a welcoming place to return to after the busy tours. Palo had shown her a catalogue of the custom furniture Chaz built for his homes. Every piece had clean lines with no fussiness anywhere. She had helped Palo select a few pieces to order for his new home.

She opened the door and walked into one of the bedrooms that faced the ocean. The surfaces were free of any decoration, all with recessed handles. There were built-in wall units, similar to what one would find in a high-end European hotel. Despite being luxurious, the bathroom with its amenities wasted no space.

Without any apologies, corner shelving held folded linens behind glass. The toilet housed a built-in bidet. An oversized single sink and its accompanying vanity led to a no-fuss walk-in shower. Tiled ledges all around held matching containers attached to the wall with *Shampoo, Conditioner,* and *Body Wash* engraved into them with no-fuss pump tops. Hooks and handgrips were in the appropriate places throughout the room, and small hampers and wastebaskets were hidden in niches. Everything was bright white—the marble tiles, the flooring, the rugs, the custom cabinetry, the countertop, even the towels and washcloths were white with no embellishments.

She opened a drawer in the vanity and took out a package of soap. She unwrapped it. Yup, the big bar of lemon-scented soap was white. She placed it in the white ceramic soap dish. On her way out of the room, she slapped the picture of Chaz on the door.

She had four pictures left in her hand—Dev, Rutger, Deke, and Sean. It was starting to get harder. Dev was an arms dealer, Rutger a sports enthusiast, Deke a celebrity lawyer, and Sean a financial lawyer specializing in the environment. She walked through the remaining rooms. "Aha!" she called out when she spotted the gun safe in the closet. It was almost too easy.

Brent stuck his head into the room. "Uh, can I help you find something?"

She walked past him and pressed her palm to the center of the door on her way out. "Nope. I found it."

"What were you looking for?"

"Clues."

"Clues? You're solving a mystery?"

"Mmmhmm. Almost done. Three more to go."

"Three more what?"

She held up the three pictures she had yet to match to a room. "I'm matching everyone's picture to their room."

"May I ask why?"

"Just something to do." She held her arm out indicating

the closed doors on the rest of the rooms on that level. "How've I done so far?"

He walked down the hall looking at the pictures she'd attached to each door, and then slowly sauntered back, his hands tucked into the front pockets of his chinos.

He looked different now that he was well rested, she thought. Still scruffy in the hair department, but a hunk in every other way. She couldn't help admiring his broad chest that stretched out his long sleeved dark blue Henley.

"Surprisingly accurate. Who's left?" he indicated the cut outs she still held in her hand.

"You can't help. I want to do the snooping and detecting all by myself. Besides, you already know who goes where."

He laughed. "Being the architect, I pretty much know where every single thing is in this house."

"I have Rutger, Deke and Sean left—two attorneys and a sports enthusiast. Rutger should be easy," she said as she turned to go down to the main level. "I just need to find some sports equipment, some smelly running shoes, maybe a poster of The Tour de France."

He laughed. "If that's all you know about the guy, you're not going to find his room."

"Oh?"

"Yeah. Oh. That's what you're going to say when you find his room. He doesn't do anything work related when he comes here. You'll find no jockstraps, tennis rackets, weights, not even running shoes. He takes a break from all that when he comes here."

"Huh," she huffed out, and then walked into the room at the end of the hall. The furniture was high-end, Scandinavian teak. Very sleek, very expensive. The bed was massive with tall, smooth, tapered posts reaching for the ceiling at each corner. The headboard had fancy metal scrollwork between the posts in a sunburst design. The puffy duvet that was soft as a cloud was a dark green color that complimented the pale sage walls. She ran her fingers along the dresser, picked up a small box in the center and lifted the lid. Inside were two enameled steel balls. She took them out and fingered them before carefully putting them back into the satin indention that held each one.

Leaning against the doorframe he smiled over at her, "Do you know what they are?"

"Very large marbles? Something you use to play a game?"

He threw back his head and laughed. It was so genuine, so gleeful, that she had to laugh with him.

"No, huh?"

"No."

"Well tell me."

"Not until you've picked the man who belongs to this room."

"I'm going to have to guess on this one. Deke, maybe? It has that California feel. And I know he has a lot of money."

"All of us have a lot of money."

"Who is the richest do you think?"

He tilted his head as if thinking. "Maybe me."

"Really?" she jerked her head back, truly shocked at that. "You don't *seem* as if that's true. At least not to me."

"I guess that's a good thing."

"Architecture, is it that profitable?"

"It can be. I do well with it. But most of my money comes from investing. A lot is old money, inherited stuff. But I'm proud to say; quite a bit is my own doing. I like to play around with tech stocks."

"Are you one of the ones losing money from this virus?"

"Some. But I'm diversified. I'm not worried. It always comes back. In fact, this is a good time to buy."

"Well, that's good. Geez, I sure wouldn't have picked you for the best fixed from all the others."

He looked at her, cocked his head, and raised an eyebrow, "Why not?" he seemed to be offended by this.

"Mmmm. You don't *act* rich like the others do. Palo says

you're the hard working one. That you never stop. I guess I think of the elite as living on yachts, going from one island to another."

He smiled and pushed off the doorframe. "Nope, no yacht. No plane. I have stock in companies that build them, but I don't have time to fritter away like that. Right now I'm into building medical centers. I'm designing a major hospital right now as a matter of fact."

"So you're like Bill Gates, doing humanitarian good works?"

"Well, I don't have *that* kind of money. At least not yet."

"So, not Deke's room? Sean's then?"

"Nope. Rutger's."

"Rutger's! Really?" She turned back to face the room and looked around. Took it all in again. "It does not look like the room of a man who's a sports jock."

"Rutger's many things. He's not just a jock. He's also an entrepreneur. And he's one more thing." He sauntered over and picked up the little box, flipped the lid up, and removed the two balls using only his knuckles. Then he moved them between his fingers like an expert in prestidigitation.

"Yeah, what are those things for?"

He took her hand, turned it over, and placed the balls in the center of her palm. "These are Ben Wa balls. They are inserted into a woman's vagina to give her pleasure. Rutger's a Dom." He wrapped his hand around hers to keep her from dropping them. Which she absolutely was trying to do.

"Careful, they're breakable. This particular set has been inside some very famous women. Rutger would not like it if you broke them."

She wrenched his hand away and tossed them onto the bed. "Ugh!" She wiped her hand down her pj pants.

He laughed. "They've been sanitized. Many times. Trust me, you'll get no germs from these." He walked over and picked them up, then put them back in the box and flipped the lid closed.

"I'm surprised Palo hasn't told you about Rutger."

"I am his sister. He tries to protect me from things like that. He would have never have told me anything sexual about any of you." That absolutely was *not* true. He had on many occasions gossiped about his friends to her. But she was not going to tell him that.

"I understand that. If I had a sister I would not have told her either."

"Rutger, is he like in those books about Anna and Christian?"

He pursed his lips and then nodded and said, "Maybe. A bit like that, but not all. I think he's getting tired of it all now though. It's not a lifestyle you do forever. It's a phase. You kind of outgrow it."

"You sound very knowledgeable about this. Have you had this phase as well?"

"I think we need to know each other better before we have this kind of conversation."

He plucked Rutger's picture from her hand, not the hand she was now rubbing against the hem of her sweatshirt to get whatever she imagined the Ben Wa balls had on them off. He stuck Rutger's image on the center panel of the door, as she had done for all the other doors. "C'mon. You have two more rooms to go. You have a fifty-fifty chance."

Chapter 74
Alyssa Matches Each Man to His Room

As they walked down the hall, Alyssa tried to remember any gossip about either Sean or Deke, and decided to fish for more from Brent. "So two lawyers out of ten guys. Is it typical to have one-in-five odds for producing lawyers at Stanford?"

"We actually had three, Cam has a law degree as well."

She turned her head to stare at him, "Really? How did he end up in show business then?"

"His last year in law school, he got talked into trying out for a community theater project—a fundraiser for one of his best mates who had leukemia—*Guys and Dolls.* He was a great dancer. He could really rock it on the dance floor at all the clubs we went to. He got hooked on theater after that. He went to L.A. for two years and worked on some dance shows, then some Broadway guy hired him to choreograph a show in New York, and the rest is history. He owns his own dance company in Wilmington now and directs, choreographs, and supplies talent for productions all over the world. The law degree helps with all the contractual stuff he has to do for his agency. Hmmm. You know what? Now that I think about it, he just might have more money than any of us."

"What happened to the guy who had leukemia?"

He stopped in front of one of the doors that didn't have a picture and just stared at her. "You're something, you know that? That whole story, and that's what you care about. That's nice."

He reached over and tucked a lock of hair that had come out of her messy bun behind her ear. "He died the following year. His name was Waverly. Cam named his agency after him, *The Waverly Talent Agency.*"

"That was a sweet thing to do, a great memorial to a friend." She ducked her head and smoothed errant the lock back into place, still feeling the thrill of his fingers where they had grazed her ear.

"Yeah, he's like that. So . . . back to the two remaining Stanford lawyers." He led her into the first room.

She looked around, noting everything, even opened the drawers and closets for clues."

"Did you open all my drawers, and closets too?"

"I didn't begin this game until after you were here. But I did go into your room when I was selecting one to use for myself."

"And what did you think of my room?"

"It's got some interesting posters. Skyscrapers and such."

"You mean like the Louvre Pyramid, The Sundrome, Waterfront Tower, Miho Museum?"

"Yeah, maybe?"

"They're all I.M. Pei's projects. He's my hero. I hope to achieve something functional, yet memorable with my upcoming hospital in Upstate New York that will be reminiscent of his Ronald Regan Medical Center."

"That wasn't how I knew it was your room."

He raised an eyebrow for her answer.

"Best view, slightly larger, secluded and off the beaten track."

"And how do you know I like those things?"

"Palo says you are 'starchy,' particular about things, and how do you say it in English? Not fond of froufrou things. Oh, and I saw several Architectural magazines on your nightstand."

"Well yes, I am detail oriented, so particular comes along with that. I like things streamlined, so definitely not froufrou-ish, by any means. 'Starchy?' I wonder what he meant by that? I am no more proper-minded than Alex, or Chaz, or Deke. Or even Palo. He has his high-minded side too."

"Is Sean proper-minded too?"

"Nice try, but you are not getting me to give you clues. So whose room is this?"

"I want to see the last one first."

They traipsed down the stairs and found the other room

that had yet to have a picture attached to its door. Alyssa walked in with Brent tagging along after her, his hands in his pockets, eyeing her rear end as she sashayed down the hall.

"Nice furniture." She ran her hand down the dresser, opened a few drawers. There was nothing inside. The nightstand had the same box of condoms as all the other rooms. "Did someone by a gross of these?" she asked as she checked the box to see if it had been opened. It hadn't. "They're in every room, the same kind, the same brand."

"It was Rutger's idea of a gag gift."

"Gag gift?" She asked with a puzzled expression on her face. Some English words she still could not translate.

"A gift for a joke," he supplied for her.

"But the joke would be on them, wouldn't it?"

"Why do you say that?" he asked.

"They are out of date by more than four years."

"Ah, true." It bothered him that she knew this. That someone or maybe many someones had worn condoms when having sex with her.

She walked over to the closet door and opened it. Then she walked inside. No clothes on any rods. She bent to check the lower shelves. Nothing, no shoes even. Almost all the men had left shoes of some kind. Brent followed and looked over her shoulder as she stooped to examine an empty gym bag. She stood, walked to the bedroom door and affixed Deke's picture to it as she declared, "This is Deke's room."

"Very good! It is indeed. How did you figure it out?"

"Two things, really. One, the box of condoms hasn't been opened in this room. In Sean's room several are missing—in fact, it's nearly empty. He lives close, in Wilmington. It would impress a woman largely to bring her out here for a weekend. Deke lives on the west coast, not quite so convenient. And then there's the gym bag in the closet."

"It's empty."

"Yes, but it has a sticker on it—an airline TSA sticker. The man flew here, ergo Deke. Sean's only an hour away by car."

"Very good, Miss Holmes. Your investigative skills are remarkable."

She bowed. "Thank you!"

"Whatever are you going to do to amuse yourself with the rest of the day?" he asked as they walked back to the center of the house and to the kitchen.

"I have several blogs I must do for Palo. And as it is a fair day, I think I will bundle up and see this amazing beach Palo has fallen in love with."

"Sounds like you've got a handle on things. I am going to finish unpacking and get to work. I.M. Pei died last spring, so the world is looking for a new architect to put on a pedestal. Plus, this hospital I'm designing is more urgently needed than ever with this virus affecting so many."

"Yes. I am worried about my family in Italy. It is very bad there."

"Palo is there. He will take care of everyone he loves. He is taking care of you, is he not?"

She smiled and grabbed her notebook off the counter, "Yes, he is. I have this wonderful house to live in, designed by a soon-to-be famous and much sought after architect."

She flung her arm out to indicate the French door refrigerator freezer and the commercial freezers beyond in the utility room. "We have food, we have Internet, and we have toilet paper. What more could we ask for?"

"Unexpired condoms?" he said jokingly. Then added, "And for you not to be the sister of one of my fraternity brothers."

She bit her lip and gave him an adorable crooked smile. "I have a boyfriend in Italy, Giancarlo. He doesn't answer his phone. I hope he is not sick with the virus. He is a bartender. It is possible he got sick from a customer. The hotel he works at has a lot of international clients, and many come from China this time of year. I am getting very worried about him."

"Maybe Palo can track him down for you."

"Maybe. He doesn't like Giancarlo very much though. I'll call him later; it's the middle of the night there now. I think I will take a long walk on the beach and then come back and make some soup. Do you like French Onion Soup?"

"I do. Especially with toasted bread and cheese on top."

"Then I will make some bread too, and later we can have a nice dinner."

"Much later. I have to get some work done today, I am behind schedule and need to get caught up."

"I have some work I need to do for Palo as well on the blog sites. You have a good day."

"Thank you, you too."

They both seemed hesitant to part, unsure of what to say . . . trying to be polite, but knowing they both had things they needed to accomplish today.

Alyssa turned and ran up the steps, eager to get to her room to prepare for her walk on the beach. She only had the one coat. It was the heavy, puffy, double insulated monstrosity she had used for walking the streets of New York City. It was a bit over the top for the beach, and way too bulky.

Her iPhone indicated it was 62 degrees now, going to 59, clear, but a bit blustery. No chance of rain, with the sun peeking out behind clouds. She decided to just add a heavy cable knit sweater to the sweatshirt she was wearing, and slipped off her pajama bottoms in favor of jeans over leggings to keep her legs warm.

She was always careful during the winter months to keep her legs warm; her thighs did not need another layer of insulating fat. She liked her legs the way they were so she always tried to wear tights or hose or leggings of some kind whenever she wore a dress or a skirt. The wind whipping around the corners or between the buildings in New York was brutally cold, cutting clear-to-the-bone. Hopefully, her walk on the beach would be invigorating, not abysmal from the weather.

Chapter 75
Alyssa Gets Acquainted with The Mailbox

She left the house by the back terrace, walking down the masonry steps and out to the back yard—which was little more than patio slates embedded in rocks with a fringe of turf around it and plumes of sea grass. She walked down a path to the hedge fence and the steps connecting to the walkway that led to the beach.

From the views out the back windows of the house, she had seen how long the walk way was, the length of two soccer fields at least, she thought. She looked both left and right as she made her way down to the sand, stopping to admire the bushes, palms, and feathery fronds on the swaying marsh grasses. Interspersed throughout were hardy succulents, some with sharp pointed deadly looking spines, some with long tendrils of vines wrapped around them, crisscrossing and trying to choke the intruders out.

Her European tours took her through some of the most beautiful gardens in the world, some centuries old, yet still maintained with impeccable care. This was a waste area and as such, it was primitive, yet beautiful in its own way. Nature's strategic garden, it provided layers upon layers of protection. Built up over the years, the mish mash of ground cover served to keep the sand in place, and it provided the marsh birds and wild animals food to eat and a place to live.

The raw, come-what-may landscape appealed to her wild side. She was not lazy, just reluctant when it came to gardening, so she liked it all the more for its haphazard design. The tiny purple, white, and yellow wildflowers that peeked out from under vines and meandered around clumps of sand brightened her day. While she couldn't make them grow, she adored flowers. Her mother's garden had many varieties in pots. She made Palo or some other man who was passing by move them from time to time so they could "catch the sun better." The plantings were lovely, her mama's pride and joy. And along with the imaginative benches, they created a tranquil sanctuary in a bustling compound.

She missed Mama and her peaceful little garden with the grotto of the Virgin Mary, surrounded by broken-dish tiles that were laid by her father many years ago.

She stepped down off the wooden steps and saw the wide expanse of the beach opening up in front of her, the ocean tumbling and crashing along the shoreline, and the fluffy white clouds amid a vivid blue sky. She forgot all about Italy and her family. This was breathtaking. She had never seen a wider beach. Had never seen one empty, as this one was. Looking to the left, she saw nothing but sand dunes and water. To the right it was the same, except for the pier jutting out into the water. Looking like weathered fence posts lined up atop black legs they marched into the sea. The pilings seemed to be fighting to stay in place while huge waves crashed into the creosote-coated poles that sank into the sand. She knew from thumbing through a history book she found on one of the bookshelves, that the 900-foot fishing pier had been built in 1960 and that it was an iconic part of beach life here on the island, drawing anglers from all over the area for generations.

Alyssa squinted and saw a dog being walked by a man wearing jeans and a flannel over shirt that was blowing open in the wind. One hand held the end of a leash; the other held a baseball cap to his head.

She watched as the man was pulled along by his very large, shaggy dog. They were a long way away but she could almost feel the joy when the man unclipped the leash and the dog bounded away and made a beeline for the waves crashing on the shore. The dog ran after a stick the man threw. As she walked steadily closer, she watched the process being repeated over and over again. The man threw the stick. The dog jumped into the ocean and retrieved it. Then the dog brought it back—all for a cursory pat on the head.

No way would she be doing all that running and swimming for a meager pat on the head. Then she saw the man take something from his billowing shirt pocket, bend and feed it to the dog. Well that was more like it. Then he clipped the leash back around the dog's neck and turned to leave.

Just as he was leaving the wet part of the sand, he reached into another pocket and pulled out what looked like a bread wrapper. He dumped the contents of the bag onto the sand and walked at a brisk pace up the beach, turning and smiling as a horde of sea gulls swooped down and began vying for the remnants of a loaf of bread. The dog barked frantically, the man smiled, and Alyssa laughed out loud.

She would not see another person on the beach that day. But this one man and his dog had cheered her immensely. She walked and walked, taking in the raw beauty of the beach. Used to walking six or seven miles on tour days—more for shopping trips into the cities or going on jaunts with friends, she kept up a brisk pace, taking it all in.

She walked under the very long and very high pier, looking up and seeing many placards at set intervals that she could not read clearly, but knew were some kind of history markers. She would have to come back to read them sometime when the pier was open.

She passed many accesses, counting them as she went until they ended with one labeled 40th Street. After that there were no more wooden accesses or street signs.

Soon there was a big sign marking the place as a reserve. Bird Island it was called. It spoke of a trail further down so she continued.

She saw a long straight line of huge boulders piled willy-nilly on top of each other, leading out to sea. It went for quite a long distance. She knew from all the seaports she had traveled to, that a ridge of rocks like this was a jetty or wharf of some kind—a place where the water needed to break for a channel. She had a goal now. To see what kind of harbor was on the other side. Something appeared in her line of vision as she looked over at the dune line and she stopped short.

Was that a post box she saw? She blinked and looked again. Yes, yes it was. Did someone live there? Were they were getting mail delivered at the edge of the ocean? How odd was that?

She had to satisfy her curiosity. This was unlike anything she'd ever seen on any seashore. She walked at an angle until she reached the mailbox mounted on a post. She had to struggle up a small rise to get to it, but then there were two welcoming benches.

She was a little tired, so after emptying the mailbox of its contents, she sat on a bench and went through all that she had found tucked inside it. Six crinkly notebooks, all uniquely different with pages brittle from salt water drying them out, many types of pens, an assortment of postcards and envelopes, a picture of a young couple on their wedding day, a baby rattle, some shells, a broken pair of sunglasses and a string of green, purple and gold balls she recognized as Mardi Gras beads, an American holiday Palo had told her about. He had been to New Orleans once for their very strange beginning of Lent event called Fat Tuesday. It had been celebrated just a few weeks ago, at the end of February if she was remembering correctly, as New York City celebrated it as well. It was the first time she had ever seen green beer and heard people in bars caterwauling a song about an Irish rose.

She had no idea how long she sat there reading the messages left in the little books. She didn't stop reading them until a dog bounded up and tried to join her on the bench.

"Sadie, down!"

The dog instantly removed her paws from the bench and sat on the sand. A woman dressed in a heavy quilt-puffed parka with a red scarf wrapped around her face walked up and said, "Sorry, she's rather starved for company these days. We haven't seen anyone out here for a long time. Of course it is a bit out of the way . . ."

"It is that," Alyssa said. Then she held up the pile of journals, she'd been balancing on her lap. "Although, it seems many people manage to find it."

"Indeed. Mind if I sit?"

Alyssa scooted over, not bothering to mention there was another bench just off to her left. She could use the company, and she suspected the other woman could too.

Her name was Charly, short for Charlotte, and she was British. She lived in Canada now as her husband had passed away. Her son and his wife and their four children lived in Toronto. They owned a second home here and were on an extended vacation while her son and daughter-in-law worked from their beach house. She was filling in for the role of their nanny, who had not deigned to come with them. She did not seem to be in any hurry to get back to her charges. Alyssa listened to her as she told stories of their many visits to Sunset Beach, the weddings they often saw performed on the beach, and how in the summer, there was often a line of people waiting to write in journals like the ones she had piled in her lap.

Alyssa listened to her run on and on about everything imaginable, berating her daughter-in-law for not being more hands-on with her children, extoling the virtues of her son, who cooked all their meals and ran the laundry machines, lamenting having sold her own sweet little home in Kent when her beloved Charles had died—never once asking her a question about her, where she was from or why she was there sitting on a bench staring at the ocean, tears streaming down her face as she thought of her mama, her brother, her friends, and Giancarlo . . . who still had not called.

A cell phone pinged and the woman pulled her phone from her coat pocket, read the text and stood up. "The brood is up from their naps, so it's back to work for me." She called to the dog that ran up from the beach where she had been poking her nose in crab holes.

Alyssa watched the woman shuffle away, completely dispirited by the thought of returning to a crowded beach house only to be lonely when she got there. She decided she never wanted to be that old woman—sad, bitter, overworked, and all alone.

She grabbed a pen, opened one of the journals and began writing. She made a list of all the things she was thankful for: a warm house, plenty of food, a lovely kitchen to prepare it in, unlimited hot water for long soaking baths, the many books that were loaded on her e-reader, plus many more on the custom built-in shelves, the hundreds of cable shows available on fourteen TVs (yes, she'd counted them), work she had to do for Palo, this beautiful beach to take walks on, stores of chocolate in the pantry, and even the sullen roommate with serious work on his mind and a body that made her sigh and work to catch her breath. She signed her name and added her city and country as she'd seen so many others do who had written on the previous pages.

She jumped up from the bench, a renewed vigor making her eager to return to the beach house and begin some worthwhile projects to fill the time before she could return home. She placed the pens and journals, cards, rattle, sunglasses, beads, shells, and the wedding picture back in the mailbox, closed the little door, tugged her sweater closer, and began the long walk home. It was growing dark, the sun quickly disappearing behind her as she took in the darkened beach houses lined up along the way. Some had security lights, but only ten appeared to have any activity going on inside them. She was slightly comforted to know that there were a few other people staying on the island, that she wasn't as alone as she had originally thought on arriving here. Still . . . it was pretty desolate.

She counted the accesses again. Stopped by the base of the pier to pray at the three wooden crosses. Marveled at the family of deer nibbling on scrub bushes in a washed out swale. Climbed up the steps then traipsed up the long wooden access that led to *her* house.

After hanging her heavy sweater up in the room off the foyer, she climbed the steps to the kitchen. Brent was drinking soup from a mug. She told him about meeting the woman at the mailbox. He listened intently, and then chided her for not "social distancing," and for not wearing a mask.

"That's what you got out of everything I just told you?"

"I got that you listened to a tired old woman droning on about her miserable life. But I am more concerned about you."

"Awww, that's sweet."

"Not really. You get sick—I get sick. I need you to respect that in the future." He picked up his mug again, drained the contents, put it in the sink and ran water in it. Then he mumbled, "Back to work," and ran up the stairs to the next level. She heard when he closed the door at the end of the hallway.

"When you get sick, I get sick," she mimicked. She went looking for fabric she could make some masks with. She'd seen something on TikTok about women from a church making masks for people who didn't have any. She could do that. She could sew.

An hour later she had ordered a mini-sewing machine, whimsical quilting scraps, rolls of elastic, spools of colorful thread, fabric shears and a complete sewing kit. Then she grabbed her laptop, warmed some red wine in a mug and threw an orange peel and a cinnamon stick into it. She settled into a comfy recliner in the big den to write a blog for Palo.

She had a perspective she wanted to share. She wanted people to know about this beach and its mailbox, and she wanted to encourage people to find ways to stay busy and to help others. This was not a time to brood and become depressed. This was a time to reach out, encourage, and be creative with life's challenges. She would make Palo proud. And she would stay out of that busy, rude man's way.

Chapter 76
Alyssa Helps Out, Watches Too Much News

Alyssa cut out fabric patterns, trimmed elastic to the required length, and wound matching thread through the bobbins of her new mini-sewing machine. For hours she made masks. So many that the stacks kept falling over. When she had filled the box that the machine had come in with carefully folded masks, she put in an order for food at the Food Leopard and when the lady came with her order, she gave her the box and asked her to please take it to a church that would distribute the masks to people who needed them.

The woman said that all the churches were closed right now. But that she herself would distribute them to anyone who needed them as she delivered groceries. She had tossed the box down from the steps to the woman whose name was Jan. During all this time they had been yelling at each other, one at the top of the masonry steps and one at the bottom—twelve risers between them for social distancing. Exceeding the prescribed six feet mostly because neither wanted to navigate the steps.

The woman caught the box and thanked her for her generosity and Alyssa promised she would make more for her to distribute.

Within a few days, an assembly line was established: Amazon would deliver the supplies Alyssa needed; Alyssa would spend several hours each day making masks; then the next day Jan would deliver groceries for Alyssa, and either Brent or Alyssa would toss down gallon-sized Zip-Lock bags filled with masks for Jan to catch.

Then the notes started coming. People thanking her for the beautiful masks she had made for them. The envelopes had to stay in a bag in the foyer for a day before Brent would let her read them. She had smirked behind his back at this the first time he had told her this new protocol that involved either wiping things down or leaving them to decontaminate overnight. They had argued over the ridiculousness of all this. But in the end he had won. She couldn't fault him for being overly cautious about protecting them both from this horrible virus. The numbers in the county were going up every day. The local hospital was having its first cases admitted and several assisted living places and nursing homes were having outbreaks that were causing them to go into lockdown. People were dying all over the country. New York and California had the most cases and the most fatalities. Every night on the news shows the numbers climbed higher and higher.

She had just closed the door after tossing down some bags to Jan when she heard Brent turn on the TV in the Big Room, as she called it. He often checked the news around lunchtime and then again in the late afternoon. It had become their custom to have a glass of wine together in the evening when the six-thirty national news came on before making dinner.

Something was happening. She could tell by the way the announcer was talking—high pitched and fast. She went in to listen.

Prince Charles of England had the virus. The Queen was in lockdown, and the Prime Minister had symptoms. Dignitaries and celebrities all over the world were coming down with the virus now. Sergio Rossi died from COVID complications in Cesena, Italy. He was one of Italy's most famous shoe designers. He was 84.

As far as she was concerned, his shoes were masterpieces. His espadrilles and heels were said to showcase a woman's femininity while embracing her feet in a comfortable caress. To her he was a genius, even though she could only afford to buy his shoes in consignment shops or during closeout sales. She cherished each carefully thought-out pair she owned. She still had her first pair—peach colored peau de soie sling backs that her father had bought her for her cousin's wedding when she had been one of the bridesmaids. She had been a teenager and her feet had grown some since then so they didn't fit anymore. But she kept them anyway as they were one of her father's last gifts to her. The news of Sergio's death from COVID impressed upon her how bad this virus was going to be, especially for the elderly.

The wife of Canada's Prime Minister, Sophie Grégoire Trudeau had tested positive for the virus and was now recovering from her bout with its flu-like symptoms. A press release said her fever had abated and that she was still self-isolating at home with her husband and their three children. There would be no public appearances until she tested negative for the virus at least twice. The Prime Minister's representative said his isolation would not interfere with his duties as head of the government. Citizens were getting worried as their leaders became infected and had to be quarantined.

People all over the world were trying to adjust to working from home as corporations, schools, and even churches shut down and began the process of communicating virtually. Whether holed up in grand houses, small apartments, quaint beach cottages, or hugely productive farms, everyone was dealing with shortages of the essentials. Alyssa felt guilty that she had so much here. Never in her life had she thought to feel grateful for toilet paper, hand sanitizer, or disinfecting wipes. Wine, yes, she was always grateful for good wine. Thankfully, the beer, wine, and liquor companies were ramping up distribution. It seemed that the country thought a good steady stupor was the best way to deal with this pandemic. Alcohol sales were up everywhere. It was how people were coping. She had watched some funny viral videos of women drinking wine.

One evening, Brent walked over to the bar and began the process of pouring himself a glass of wine. He was fastidious about preparing his wine. After wiping out a glass, he carefully poured the dark burgundy liquid from the open bottle she had left near the cheese board. The wine went through the cylinder attached to a stand that held the aerator. Holding the wine glass by cupping his open hand around the oversized bowl, he threaded his fingers around the stem, holding the glass as if it contained a precious life-giving elixir. Swirling it gently, he sauntered over and sat in one of the Stressless recliners that faced the TV. In Italy they had a name for men like him, but she dared not say it.

"What's new in the world of COVID?" he asked. It was ninety percent of the news coverage these days, usurped only by the presidential campaign and each candidate's faux pas of the day.

She ran down the highlights, including the news that mathematical models were in place in Wuhan, China that were based on social distancing measures, showing how the curve could be flattened and the virus eventually eliminated over time—maybe as early as 2023 if people masked up and kept six-feet apart. She wound up her spiel with how appreciative she was of all the supplies they had stockpiled, holding up her wine glass and adding, "I am especially thankful for this amazing stuff."

He nodded to her and lifted his own glass in salute. "Kyle knows wines, that's for sure. This is some very good 'stuff'. Makes the day slaving away worth it."

"How are things going with the hospital plans?"

"Okay. Right now it's revise, revise, revise. It will remain that way until everything is in place and it gets the special symbiotic-ness to it I'm looking for. It's a process. But it's coming together, bit by bit. Everything has to be separate, yet work together somehow. There has to be a flow to it. And at last, I finally found a way to add more sinks and sanitizing stations without massive infrastructure demands. Initially, I had a problem with the idea of recycling water used for hand washing. It just didn't seem hygienic enough. But I solved the problem. The key was reverse osmosis."

"I don't even know what that is," she said as she sipped her wine and admired the way his large hand caressed the large bowl of the wineglass. She thought she must be drinking too much, as she thought his thumb stroking the side of the glass was very sexy.

"It's a complicated principle. Boils down to this: pressure is used to force water through a semipermeable membrane. The membrane allows water molecules to pass through, while blocking up to 99 percent of its contaminants. A company that makes the tankless system will be able to provide essentially sanitized water for hand washing that won't take up a lot of space. In the model I've designed, the whole system will fit into the counter and cabinet space that was already allocated in each room where hand washing will be required. The bonus for me is that the current plan for all the plumbing does not have to be changed. *Huge* time saver."

He noticed that she was listening intently to what he was saying, as if this interested her. As if it mattered to her that he had spent three whole days researching nothing but this. Then she said something that floored him.

"That's amazing. What talent you must have to be able to come up with such a plan."

He blinked. What woman not involved in his field had ever given a second thought to his job or his ideas? Not even his mother would sit still long enough to hear an explanation of any facet of his work. Then she capped it off.

"Are you some kind of genius or something?"

He had to smile at her innocent praise of his relatively simple idea. "It was an *ingenious* idea, but no, I'm not an genius. Given the same challenge a lot of architects would have come up with a similar solution. But thanks. I needed that. Man does not live by wine alone."

They both turned back to the TV when an emergency tone and a newsflash came on the screen. A big storm was coming. Tornadoes were moving from the south into the outlying areas. They would not affect the coast, but the thunderstorm and high winds accompanying them would.

"Time to batten down the hatches."

She turned her head to the side and looked at him with

her brows quirked. "What does that mean? Batten and hatches?"

He smiled. It was not the first time he'd used an idiom that she did not understand. Not everything translated well.

"It's an old English phrase, it means to secure the hatch and tarpaulins to make a ship watertight for an upcoming storm. Colloquially, it means to prepare for the worst."

She jumped up. "I will prepare for a hurricane. Palo already told me how."

He laughed, "It's not hurricane season until June, May at the earliest. But just for kicks, how did he tell you to prepare for one?"

"Close all the windows and doors, bring in anything the wind could take away, check that the generator is working, and buy lots of food and wine."

He threw his head back and laughed.

She got an odd tingling sensation in her belly, followed by a warm feeling spreading throughout her limbs. She'd read a lot of Regency romances as a teenager and wondered if this was the swoony feeling the supremely sheltered women were always feeling when a handsome suitor approached them for a place on their dance card.

He stood and put out his hand for her to take. "Come with me. I'll show you just what we have to do."

Her hand in his, she followed him to a closet that had an access panel that he opened with a sequence of numbers. The small door popped open. He hadn't bothered releasing her hand and she marveled at how his large hand and long fingers engulfed hers like warm satin.

Using his other hand he gestured with a flourish. "See this series of switches?" he indicated a long row of silver toggles. "You can flip each one in turn, or throw this larger one, and the hurricane shutters will close over the windows, all over the house. Listen."

He threw the larger toggle and she turned her head at the whirring sound coming from the room beside the closet.

She slipped her hand from his and stepped out into the hallway and noticed the light coming from the powder room with the scary mural was fading as the room darkened. She stepped to the doorway of the small room and watched as a shield of light gray metal lowered over the window and settled into place just below the sill.

All over the house she heard shields lowering and clicking into place.

"That is how we prepare for a hurricane in *this* house," he murmured, his grin huge.

Her eyes were wide. "Amazing." Then she tilted her head and covered the little finger of one hand with the closed fist of the other. "Windows and doors—check! Now for the things the wind can blow away."

"The only furniture on the patio or decks this time of year is masonry. Everything else is stored at the end of the season." He mimicked her and wrapped his fist around the next finger, her ring finger, "Check!"

She smiled up at him.

"What's next?" he asked.

"Check that the generator is working."

"If the alarm is not going off the generator is working. It cycles through and shuts itself off after a quarter of an hour every Friday at eleven. It runs a system check and if anything is wrong a steady alarm will sound until someone shuts it off. No alarm? No problem." He smiled at her and said, "Check!"

She watched as he clasped her middle finger in his embrace along with the others.

"Next?" he asked.

"Buy lots of food and lots of wine."

"I think that's always been covered in this house. Since the day we all moved in, I have never been in this house when there wasn't food and alcohol stockpiled in great abundance." He covered her hand with both of his. "Check! We've ready for whatever Mother Nature throws our way."

She looked down at their clasped hands. Then quickly stepped away. "That's good. That's great. *Bellisimo!*"

"Yes. No worries. Tell Palo the same when he calls as he's sure to be checking the weather here."

The doorbell rang and Alyssa turned toward the door at the sound. "That will be the rest of the groceries being delivered by the Food Leopard."

"Lion."

She waved her hand at him, "Whatever." They'd already had this conversation several times, but she insisted on calling Food Lion Food Leopard because she said it trivialized the scary mural in the downstairs powder room.

"I'll help you put it away."

Her eyes went wide and she frantically shook her head no, for it wasn't Food Lion or Leopard, it was Walgreen's bringing her something she did not want him to see. "Oh, I can do it, it's just a few things I added to the order. Why don't you decant a bottle of that excellent Chianti for us?"

She said this knowing full well that she would have to find a way to pour her glass out or back into the bottle when he wasn't looking as her limit was one glass until she knew for sure. She added, "I'd better get dinner started. Look how late it's getting!"

She spun around and ran down the steps to get the bag that had been left at the door. They were no longer wiping things down as they had been assured that the items collected from the store shelves were by people wearing gloves, so she was able to grab the lone bag quickly and hide it in her room without him seeing where it had come from.

That night they had shrimp scampi and bruschetta made from canned tomatoes, as fresh tomatoes were not available at the store. She had been able to get away with drinking only a tiny bit of the Chianti. While Brent was checking the stock prices, she sloshed a fair amount of it from her glass into the sauce that was simmering on the stove.

After dinner they did the dishes together as he complimented her on the meal she had put together and the work she was doing for the local community by making masks for people who didn't have any. The federal government's now meager stockpile of supplies was going to the hospitals and nursing homes. Nationwide, there was a shortage of masks, and all over the country, people who had the materials and knew had to sew, were making them and either selling them or donating them.

Feeling a bit tired and a little on edge, Alyssa folded the laundry and then went to bed. Giancarlo had still not called.

Chapter 77
Alyssa Has News to Share, But Can't

The next morning she stood by the sink staring at the blue plus sign on the white plastic stick.

"Merde," she muttered. She counted up the weeks since she'd last been in Italy . . . with Giancarlo. Five. This was not good.

She took the stick with her and sat on the bed staring at it for a long time. She thought of Mama, and Palo, Trixie, and Giancarlo. With each she imagined their reaction. Then she shook her head as all those tumbling thoughts fled and she was forced to think about her reaction. How did *she* feel about this news?

After several minutes of letting her thoughts unravel and play out, she decided she was kind of happy about it. She loved the idea of having a baby. It was sooner than she would have liked, but she knew women who had waited too long and now could not have one at all. This changed things, but for the better she finally decided.

She and Giancarlo would get married; they would find a nice house outside the city, as even together they could not possibly afford one in a good neighborhood in Florence. Or maybe they would all stay at the villa. She would have their baby and they would be a happy family raising a beautiful little boy or girl with Giancarlo's dark, messy curls that she would be constantly combing with her fingers. Yes, this would be a good thing. They'd have one and then later maybe one more, as she did not want to get really fat like Mama had. So many pregnancies she'd had, but only two children had survived— Palo and her.

Mindful of the early hour in Italy, she decided to wait until late in the afternoon to call Giancarlo with her good news. They had only spoken twice since the day she had arrived in New York City, but that was because he was working as a bartender at night, and helping his family with their *Pharmacia*, using his Vespa to deliver needed medicine to people who were in lockdown, just like she and Brent were. She knew he was very busy, but this was news that could not wait. Giancarlo loved children. He was always stopping to kick a soccer ball back to the kids in the park when one when out of bounds and he often took his two nephews to the cinema on weekends. When it had been open. When they went to weddings or parties, he was always bouncing a *bambino* on his lap or teasing a toddler with a magic trick.

This was an unplanned event, but surely he would be thrilled. She knew that he loved her; he told her so all the time, calling her *amore mio* and crooning love songs when they went walking late at night over the bridges in *Firenze*.

Two days later when she was finally able to connect with him to share her news she was surprised to learn that her having a baby was not at all acceptable to him. In fact, he told her it could not happen. That she had to take care of this and as soon as possible. Then he told her the reason why.

He'd met a woman at the bar who owned a villa in Catatonia, left to her by her late husband. They'd hit it off spectacularly and she'd asked him to join her there, reasoning that if they had to be locked in their houses, for months at a time, they might as well be locked in together. The only reason he was not on his way south now to join this woman, was because he was waiting for his cousin to arrive from Impruneta to take over his delivery duties for his father.

He apologized that he was no longer in love with her. Adding that he simply could not be a father right now. Ending the call by telling her to find a doctor and to send him the bill at his new girlfriend's house, adding that he would text her the address when he arrived there.

The words that spewed from Alyssa's mouth after hearing

his curt declaration were disjointed and had four themes: what a despicable opportunist he was; how he was the lowest form of garbage, more vile than the dog shit people scraped off their shoes; that there was no place to go now even if she wanted to have the procedure done, and that she would never ever consider doing what he was telling her to do—her religion would not allow it, nor would her conscience.

She told him that she would have this baby and that her brother would see to it that he provided every single thing it needed or he would be the last person living in Sicily missing vital parts of his body. Reminding him that Sicily had long been known for mob violence.

Her lengthy, rapid-fire tirade was loud, in Italian, and rolling off her tongue at a volume that caused her words to reverberate throughout the house, sounding all at once as if someone was lyrically screeching, hollering in pain, and calling out unintelligible names as if castigating the vilest creature imaginable to the lowest realms on earth.

Brent did not need to know what the words were that she was spewing out to know that she was beyond furious. Separated by a staircase, two hallways and the walls of many rooms between them, Brent jumped up from his chair with his eyes wide and his ears straining for just one word that made sense to him—anything that would connect in his brain and be translated, so he would know what was going on.

He didn't even know who she was talking to. But she sure was yelling at someone. And it was the loudest, most discordant stream of Italian words he'd ever heard. He was only able to pick out two words he could interpret: *cazzo* and *Palo*. Both of which she had said over and over again. Palo had taught him *cazzo*. It was not a nice thing to call someone—the worst vernacular for a man's penis—dick, or maybe dickhead. He wasn't sure.

Then everything quieted down.

In stealth mode, he opened the door to his room and then started down the long hallway, each step measured and carefully placed. As he made it to the staircase, he heard her running through the lower part of the house. Then the back door that lead off the kitchen to the terrace was opened.

He was just in time to look out through the two-story window from the landing and see her run down the wooden beach access. His eyes followed her, watching as her hands swiped at what he could only imagine was a stream of tears running down her face. Her long hair flew out behind her as she ran. It was loose and he was surprised how long it was. She didn't slow her pace, running full out as if being chased until she was out of sight behind the dune line.

He debated going after her. He gathered that she had been on the phone with someone in Italy, and that whatever they had told her was news that had been devastating. He thought about calling Palo, although maybe Palo had been the bearer of the news that had sent her running.

He decided to wait. Whatever it was—the death of someone she loved, the horrible things that were happening in her beloved country, or possibly the news that she would have to be here with him for an even longer period of time than she'd previously thought—she needed time to process it.

He knew she longed to go home. That was no secret. His head tilted as he ran through each scenario. Then he smirked. There had been that word *cazzo* that she'd said over and over again. He knew she had a boyfriend. One who had been hard for her to get in touch with—she had told him that her boyfriend was not answering his phone. She had even asked him if someone's phone would still ring and go to voicemail if they had not paid the bill. He had told her no. That if someone hadn't paid the bill, the caller would receive a message about the number being out of service.

He shook his head back and forth and smirked again. Of course. A randy young man, single, in his prime, with his girlfriend on another continent. Of course he would be straying. It would not be unheard of for even the faithful to betray their sweetheart during this epidemic. His eyes opened wide. Why did the thought of her breaking up with some heathen lothario please him? He shook his head harder and walked back to his room. He was at a critical point with this project. He needed to give it his full attention. A broken hearted girl was the last thing he needed to focus on right now.

And, she was Palo's sister. So she was off limits. Boyfriend or no. He noted the time: 3:46. It would start getting dark soon. He'd be mindful of when she came back, make sure she was safely in for the night. Then get back to work. Italian women were known for their hot tempers. She was likely going down to The Mailbox. She talked about it a lot. The walk would be good for her; she'd blow off some steam, and come back, her cheerful demeanor back in place.

Only she didn't come back. Not for quite some time. It was full dark now, with only a tiny sliver of the moon rising over the ocean. He got up from the chair he'd been sitting in near the window. He was about to grab a flashlight and go looking for her when he saw her walking up the access, her head down, her legs dragging.

He met her at the terrace doors and opened up one side for her. She looked awful. Her hair was a knotted mess and it was clear she had been crying. Her face was puffy and her eyes were red, her nose too.

"You okay?"

"I will be."

"Anything I can help you with?"

"No. I'm just going to take a shower and go to bed."

'Okay. You know where I am if you need anything."

"Thanks."

"Seriously, if you need to talk . . ."

"I just need to be alone."

He watched her walk up the stairs to her room. Hmmm. He hated seeing her like this. If she wasn't better by tomorrow morning, maybe he'd call Palo.

He made a sandwich and took it, along with the open bottle of wine from the day before, up to his room to get some work done. But he found he couldn't concentrate. He wondered if she was heartbroken because her slime ball of a boyfriend had two-timed her. He'd never been heartbroken. He'd always been the one to call it quits when things got . . . weird. He'd never been in love with a woman. Lust? Oh yeah. Big time. But never more than a little infatuation mixed in with raging hormones. He couldn't imagine what she was going through, especially now when she was so far from home. She must feel pretty powerless he reasoned.

He'd get up early and make her a nice breakfast maybe that would help.

Chapter 78
Brent Tries to be Helpful

Alyssa got up to go to the bathroom. The clock on the nightstand said it was 9:28. She'd slept through the night. Mostly. In between crying jags. She decided she needed something to drink. Her throat was parched; probably from all the tears she'd shed. She was likely dehydrated. She opened her door to go down to the kitchen.

The smell of eggs frying in grease wafted up from the kitchen just as she got to the top of the stairs. Her stomached lurched. She realized quickly that she was going to be sick. She put her hand over her mouth and ran back to her room, just making it to the bathroom in time to kneel and slide up against the porcelain commode before retching her insides out.

She hadn't eaten since yesterday at lunchtime so there was little to come up. Still, her stomach heaved as if there was something that simply had to come up. Over and over she gave into the sensation as her stomach cramped, yet yielded nothing.

Finally it settled and she was able to get back into bed. When a low knock sounded on her door she moaned, "Yes?"

"I made you breakfast."

"Not hungry."

"Oh, you must be. You missed dinner last night. I made bacon and sunny side up fried eggs . . .," he said, trying to tempt her.

She groaned. "Please go away."

"You sure?"

"Yes! Go away!"

"Okay, okay."

At lunchtime he tried to bring her a bacon and egg

sandwich using the leftovers from the breakfast he'd cooked. She told him if he brought it into her room she'd throw the plate at him.

He called Palo at 2:20 in the afternoon when he heard her get up and use the bathroom then go right back to bed.

"I don't know what happened. She was fine until she got a phone call yesterday. She yelled and screamed in Italian at the caller and then ran out of the house and down to the beach."

"Which way?" Palo asked.

"West, I think. They way she usually does."

"She probably went to The Mailbox. She told me she writes in the journals. Why don't you get on your bike and ride down there and see if you can find something she wrote yesterday."

"That's a good idea."

"Might give you an idea what's wrong anyway. Maybe who she talked to, but I'm guessing it was Giancarlo. He's calling around town trying to find someone to help his father with medical deliveries for his pharmacy. They must have a lot of people needing medicine if he needs more help delivering it all."

"I'll call you when I get back, let you know what I found."

Brent grabbed his heavy parka, as it was only 48 degrees. Then he got his bike out of the storage area and rode it over the access and then down the beach to The Mailbox.

Once there he paged through the journal that was on top of the pile in the box. He had no trouble finding her letter. It was only two pages back as few people were making it down to the beach this far this time of the year. It had her signature in fancy script at the bottom. The entry was fairly long, almost the whole page. And it was in Italian.

He pulled his phone from his pocket and scrolled to his

recent calls and pressed the last one he'd dialed. Palo answered on the second ring.

"Yeah? You find something?"

"It's in Italian. I can't read it."

"Can you text me a picture so I can?"

"Sure. Hold on." He put the notebook on the closest bench, flipped to the camera, and drew back so he could get it all in with one shot. Then he sent it to Palo's phone.

"Just sent it."

A few seconds later Palo said, "Got it. Hold on while I read it."

A moment later, he heard Palo cussing. A long, low, vile string of words he couldn't begin to decipher.

"So what's up?"

"She's pregnant. I am going to *kill* Giancarlo!"

"Great, just great," Brent mumbled.

"He wants her to have an abortion. Is insisting on it actually. Only he doesn't understand, even if she wanted one, which I am pretty sure she doesn't, it's elective surgery and they're not doing that during COVID."

"Why doesn't he want his kid?"

"Because he has a new girlfriend. And he's leaving to go live with her in Sicily."

"Nice guy."

"I'm on my way to go see him now."

"Maybe you should calm down first."

"And give him time to get away? Not a chance! I'll call you later. See if you can get her to tell you the problem. I don't want her to know that we read her journal entry. She's scared to death right now. Try to get her to eat something. Dry toast, cereal, crackers."

"She's just going to bite my head off, but I'll try."

"She has no tolerance for being sick. She's going to hate being pregnant. Thanks for being there for her." Then the line went dead.

Giancarlo was in big trouble Brent thought, as he slipped

the notebook back into the box and got back on his bike. Geez. Pregnant. How were they going to manage her having a baby during this pandemic? No wonder she was so upset yesterday. And he'd made her greasy bacon and fried eggs. This was not how things were supposed to be going. He was supposed to be alone, in the house he built, working on the hospital he needed to get built, making great strides on the project and doing some surfing. Now he'd be nursemaid to a woman who was going to have a baby. Probably right there in the house. He shivered. And it was not from the cold.

Chapter 79
A Truce

The house was quiet when he entered through the terrace door. He removed his parka and washed up. Then he made a tray of food he considered to be close to a continental breakfast, and hopefully unobjectionable to a queasy stomach—a toasted sesame bagel with light butter, a few pieces of Emmental and Gruyere cheeses sliced thin, pear and apple slices and a pot of herbal tea.

He had hoped to find her asleep so he could leave it on her night table and be done with it. But when he tapped lightly on the door before toeing it open he heard her blow her nose before telling him to come in.

Sitting in the middle of the bed with the covers pulled over her lap she looked up at him, a questioning look on her face.

"I thought I'd fix you a bite to eat. Even if you're feeling under the weather, you still need to eat." He gently placed it on the bed beside her.

She snorted. "I am not under the weather. I am pregnant!" Then fresh tears cascaded down her face.

Well, so much for having to drag it out of her. He tried to look surprised by the news, "Geeeez! Are you sure?"

"Pretty sure," she pointed to a plastic stick lying across a hand towel on the dresser.

He'd seen something similar once, but thankfully, it had not had the evidence of inopportune timing.

"The blue plus sign means yes, and that's the second test," she barked at him.

"Hmmm." He walked over and stared down at it. "Well you don't seem happy about it."

She gave a half-hearted laugh. "No, I don't suppose that I am. My boyfriend broke up with me as I was telling him the news, demanding I get rid of it. I'm thousands of miles from my

566

home and family. My brother is going to be furious, like we really needed this right now. And I want my mother, although she is so religious that once I tell her there will be no option but keeping it."

Fresh tears flowed from her eyes and she used the cloth napkin he had so carefully folded and placed on the tray to swipe at them. "This is horrible! Nobody is going to want this baby except me!" she wailed.

"Well, you're the only one that matters. It's your baby. It's your decision."

She blew her nose into the dainty linen napkin, one of a set of 24 that had Kyle's signature logo. He cringed at the sight and handed her the box of tissues from the dresser. Kyle would have a fit if he saw her using one of his napkins to blow her nose.

"Well, it's the only decision that can be made right now any way. You saw the news show a few nights ago. No elective surgeries are being done. I doubt I can even get a doctor's appointment." She hiccupped and began crying in earnest, "I'm going to have to have this baby all alone, right here." She pointed her finger into the bed, digging it deep into the comforter. "On this bed! All by myself!"

He held back the shudder he felt building between his shoulder blades. This was not the time to imagine all that that would entail. Comically, he imagined him and Alex hauling the mattress out after the big event, trying to fold it in half to get it into the elevator.

Palo's words came back to him. The ones when he had thanked him for being there for her. He had no choice; he was going to have to step up to the plate. She was an ocean away from home. "I'm here," he whispered. "You won't be alone."

She looked up at him, tears pooling in her brown eyes, yellow-green flecks in the irises glinting from the wetness. Even with puffy, blotchy skin and red-rimmed eyes, she was still beautiful.

He repeated himself. "I'll be here. For whatever . . ."

rolling his hand in the direction of the bed to indicate the "right here," she had mentioned for the place where the end result would occur. Dear God, a baby. Here—in the beach house. He stifled a groan of defeat and defiance to this problem. What choice did he have? He could not fix this like he could a problem on a plan, by simply turning his pencil over to the eraser end, or using the mouse pad on his laptop.

She reached out her hand and took his, gripped it in hers. "Thank you, Brent. You can't know how much I appreciate that. It helps a lot." She pulled a wad of tissues from the box and swiped at her face.

Her problem was his problem now, and he had to be on board even though it terrified him. Remembering the words that Palo has translated, the words she had written in the journal, he knew that she was scared as well.

"Eat something," he said. "You'll feel better if you do." He nudged the tray closer to her hip.

"This was very nice of you." She picked up half of the bagel, dug her teeth into it and tore it, then chewed thoughtfully. Once she had swallowed, she looked up. "Oh God, I have to tell Palo. And mama. They are going to be so disappointed with me!"

He shrugged. "This isn't the first time this kind of thing has happened. They'll get over it. They both love you and they are only going to want what's best for you."

"Right now, that would be to *not* be having a baby."

"Well, that can't be helped now, can it?"

She sighed. "No. And even if it could, I wouldn't. I want to have it. It'll be mine. All mine. *My bambino*," she murmured, trying out the words for the first time. Her lips quirked to the side as if she had just been caught stealing a cookie from a cookie jar instead of discovering the consequences of dallying with a cheater.

As if reading his mind, she murmured, "*Imbroglione. Io sono stupido.*"

"You're not stupid. He's stupid. I know it's not the way you would have planned it, but we'll get through this. Everything will be fine."

He turned to leave. Before he could separate their hands, she squeezed his. "Thank you. I'm feeling better now just knowing you're here, and that you're willing to help."

Their eyes met and held. In those few seconds before he turned away, they searched each other's faces and through the connection of their eyes, they acknowledged their bond to be together in this.

"Good, I'm glad you're feeling better. Eat up, rest for a while, and then get back to making those masks. I know it makes you happy to feel you're helping out. Tonight you can call Palo. He'll be fine with the news. He'll love being an uncle. And your mama will be over the moon at the prospect of being a grandma."

She smiled at the thought. "I'll be down in a little while. After I take a shower. It does make me happy to have useful work to do."

"Give yourself some time if you need it. You don't have to call Palo or your mother today."

"True. Bad news can wait."

"It's *not* bad news."

"You don't know my family. Good Catholic girls don't do this."

He laughed. "I do know your family. And good Catholic girls do this all the time!"

She smiled at him. Then frowned. "But the papa of their bambino marries them."

He didn't want to say anything about that. For all he knew, Palo could be *convincing* Giancarlo to do the right thing this very minute. Instead he whispered, "You don't need him, his part's already done." He grinned wolfishly. "And you have plenty of family to take care of all the other parts. Drink the tea. It's peppermint. It'll settle your stomach."

He left the room, wondering if he'd made things better. She looked too young and innocent to be having this type of problem.

If Giancarlo had been anywhere close, he would have gone and bashed his face in himself. He didn't doubt that Palo was getting some satisfaction for himself right now.

Chapter 80
Yoga, Puzzles, & Neck Massages

The day progressed as he went back to work and she went back downstairs to make masks. And when it was time for them to have a drink and watch the news, he poured her some apple juice and they toasted the baby.

They did this each night, coming up with a new insanely ridiculous name each time. Gulf-wader Brown was so far his favorite name for a boy. Hypotenuse Brisket was the contribution for a girl's name that Alyssa adored.

Alyssa had been surprised that Palo had not been upset by the news at all. And Mama was unaccountably thrilled, just sorry not be there to help her.

Palo arranged for a female doctor in Wilmington to call her to introduce herself and to make sure Alyssa understood the things that were going to happen. She said she would come to the house once a month starting at the end of the first trimester, and then more often during the third trimester. She said she would send some pamphlets for her to read and some easy-to-use test kits, and that she was available day or night for any problems or questions she had. Alyssa suspected Palo was paying her a fortune for this personal attention, but she so appreciated it.

Dr. Ravena was very caring, and made her feel special, as if she hadn't done a bad thing, but instead, something completely acceptable and normal, not at all disgraceful. Her new doctor was so accepting of her situation that she felt no shame at all now. And knowing that she was not alone in this had relieved her anxiety considerably. She had Mama and Palo, and Brent and Dr. Ravena. Even though she didn't have Giancarlo, they would be enough. They would see her through this time of being with child while such a bad virus was spreading.

She and Brent developed a routine. He brought her a toasted bagel and some peppermint tea each morning to fend off morning sickness, and later in the day, he reminded her to take her prenatal vitamin once she had some substantial food in her tummy. She shopped Amazon and Etsy for baby items, building a registry so that her family and friends both stateside and in Italy could send her gifts when she was further along and they knew the sex of the baby.

Each morning she would do her yoga exercises in the workout room, doing mostly stretching poses to stay limber and using the bar to work on balance. She took brisk walks on the beach before settling in to make masks for the church ladies. She was also passing along cookies and brownies she had stockpiled in the freezer, as she could no longer eat them in the quantities she was used to.

In late afternoon she would grocery shop online and then begin the prep work for healthy nutritious dinners. After the sun started going down and Brent came down from the office, they would have a cocktail hour with cranberry or apple juice as her wine. After dinner they each indulged with a small bowl of Taglienti gelato while watching a movie. Sometimes they would play a game of Scrabble, Phase 10 or Gin.

They kept a card table set up in the corner where they had a 1,500-piece jigsaw puzzle of The Golden Gate Bridge. They would work on it when the mood hit, but neither was anxious to get much done on it after they'd struggled to complete the borders. San Francisco seemed so far way now. Even though they both had friends in California, it seemed like a different planet now. The disease was progressing so fast there that neither wanted a reminder of what was going on in L.A., San Diego, San Francisco, and in Palo Alto where Stanford University was.

All the owners of *The Cockpit*, the beach house where they were now in lockdown, had attended college there. Having bonded over their years together, and each having achieved major successes in their careers afterward, they decided at their tenth reunion to chip in and build the beach house on the barrier island of Sunset Beach.

Even though she missed being at home in Italy, she had to remember how blessed she was to have this wonderful house as a safe haven from COVID.

One evening in late May, after watching Dr. Faucci and President Trump vacillate over the success of different drugs being used to treat the virus, then the CDC Director expounding on the development of a vaccine, and then seeing an update across the country with graphs depicting the huge increases of people coming down with the virus, Brent developed a raging headache. Nothing seemed to help. He was miserable—and more than a touch grouchy.

Alyssa finally talked him into letting her use her skills in massage and aromatherapy to help alleviate the shooting pains at his temples. With her fingertips she gently rubbed his forehead with the lavender and peppermint essential oils she had made. Then she used a concoction she called Joy, which she had in a small roller ball bottle. In slow glides she smoothed it over his forehead and temples. Then she ran her fingers under the back of his head and massaged the oil deep into the skin of his neck, stopping to press and hold on pressure points. His head rested in her lap while his feet were propped on a pillow at the end of the sofa.

After a few minutes, she shifted her body to the side and gently lifted his head from the top of her thigh. She stretched his neck out and adjusted his position so that his head fell into the cradle of her crotch and she placed a small flax seed sack over each eyelid. Then she began working down the cords on the side of his neck to the tops of his shoulders.

Brent sighed with her efforts as she turned his head one way and then the other, stroking, pressing, and holding at critical points. Throaty groans that he had tried to hold back were forced out. Her hands were *a-maz-ing*.

His headache was all but gone now. However, an ache in his groin was beginning to make itself known. Her inner thighs were cradling the sides of his head, while the crown of his head was being pressed tight against her pelvis, resting right on her mons. All the while, her stroking him so sensually was doing incredible things to his penis.

When she noticed it, she laughed and took one of the lavender eye pillows from his eyes and dropped it on the long bulge tenting his khakis. He groaned and she watched as his penis jumped and almost dislodged the soft weighted sachet. She did the same with the other eye pillow. It was ricocheted off by a jerky spasm as his penis lifted impressively.

"Stop it," he hissed. "I swear to God, if you touch me there again, I will come in my pants."

She laughed, her delightful sound filling the cavernous room. It was as if they were a couple, entitled to coital benefits. He was sorry that was not the case.

Wickedly, he turned his head to the side and blew a gust of heated air right where he pictured her cleft to be and watched as her eyes went wide and she drew in a deep breath.

"Not so funny now, huh?"

She surprised him by grabbing up a throw pillow and brazenly covering his erection with it. Then she pressed it all around with both hands to seat the cushion where his penis was pulsing and throbbing for relief.

She watched his face contort as he groaned through parted lips. His body gave a violent jerk while his penis pulsed under her hand. Even through inches of padding and the heavy fabric she felt him come. Their eyes met and held as he spent into his khakis.

Her eyes sparkled with humor as she watched the depths of his eyes fall away from hers. His eyelids closed with the overwhelming pleasure and she felt his body shuddering from the release of tension.

Her fingers traced the skin and the dark stubble on his

jaw with tender strokes as if beckoning his eyes back to hers.

When his eyes fluttered open she touched the tip of his nose. "And that is how we get rid of a headache," she said.

"You've got a budding career there if you can figure out what to call it," he murmured.

"How much would you pay for this service?" Her smile was all knowing, her eyebrows quirked with chiding comicality. "Whatever's in my checkbook, it's yours."
She laughed and swatted his chest. "I am glad you are better."

"I am better by far! But now I need a shower." He eased himself off of her and then stood.

"You go. I will think of a name for my new company."

He smiled down at her. "Head-Away? Exced-drain? As-pour-in? Buff-her-in? All-leave?"

"How about Massage-onist?"

"That would not work. It's too close to misogynist which means woman hater."

"Oh, I did not know you Americans had such a word for that. You have too many words in your language."

He laughed as he went up the stairs, shaking his head as he called out, "You're good for me *Bella*." At the top of the stairs he turned and walked down the hall toward his room. "So good, it scares me," he muttered to himself.

Chapter 81
Facebook, Tik Tok, & Watching Videos

Alyssa bored easily. Her mama had always told her that idleness was not for her. When she was little, she counted buttons taken from old tin boxes, out loud . . . for hours. Or made a big salad for her papa for lunch by meticulously plucking the petals off of every dandelion she could find. Now she amused herself by watching videos of women drinking wine from grossly oversized wine glasses, someone playing hand puppet Pac Man with cars outside their apartment window, dog lovers knitting or crocheting hats for them and having Facebook fashion shows, or listening to cities around the world banging pots and pans together to thank first responders and hospital workers.

One night, she went out onto the terrace, and facing the ocean, she began to bang a wooden spoon on the bottom of one of Kyle's soup pots. A few minutes later she heard someone responding several houses down. Then another joined in. And another. It cheered her to know that they weren't alone, that there were other people isolating on the island as well.

The night the network news showed out-of-work Italian opera singers singing *Nessun Dorma* from their home balconies she ended up on a crying jag so severe that Brent had to get Palo on the phone so she could talk to both him and her mama before he could get her settled down.

The next morning, Brent marveled at her resilience. She was in the kitchen kneading bread while watching a woman on the small kitchen television doing the identical same thing. Everyone it seemed was going "Pioneer Woman" now. People who had never made so much as a canned biscuit, were now rolling out their own pizza dough, bread dough, and pretzel dough—until there was no yeast to be had at the stores. Then paper towels, napkins, disinfectant wipes, and even chicken parts became hard to get commodities as factory workers stayed home.

Then one morning he came down the stairs as if in a daze. As he poured coffee into a bowl full of cereal, then added two splashes of orange juice like it was creamer, he told her that the hospital project he had been working so hard on had been tabled for now.

The cost of building supplies had risen almost overnight. There was close to a thirty percent increase in materials and costs were still climbing. Some building supplies couldn't be had for any price. Rebar, steel frames, brick, sheetrock, electrical components . . . no one was producing anything. Factories were shutting down all over the country.

At first he was bothered by it—the fact that his hospital wouldn't be started anytime soon. He was a man who finished what he started. And he was just days from offering a completed plan. But now there was a nationwide shutdown.

He wasn't worried though. After fixing his coffee properly, he told Alyssa, "Being an architect is what I like to do, but it's not my only livelihood. The stock market still holds my interest. Even now, with everything going crazy, I like to play around with it. And right now, the market is remarkably strong. The hospital will be built when this is all over. Planning it out was just something I was doing . . . but now I'm not."

He let out a heavy sigh as if conceding a chess game where he hadn't seen the end coming until his opponent had knocked over his king.

"It might be time to load all the classics I haven't read on my Kindle and read them. I've been promising myself that I would do that for years. Or . . ." he looked over at her and winked. "Or you can entertain me. You up for a game of strip Scrabble?"

She laughed. "You must be kidding, you know thousands of words in English that I have never even heard of."

He wiggled his eyebrows. "Exactly my ploy. I'll turn up the heat so you don't get chilled," he waggled his fingers over at her. From her slipper-clad feet to her slouchy turtleneck sweater, she would be formidable due to her multiple layers. "That is, once you're sitting naked in your seat."

"I'm sorry about your hospital, but I am not getting naked to cheer you up. And also, I am very busy today."

She left him to go back to work on her projects. She took pictures and videos of some of the things she was working on and posted them online as a way to share how-to tips.

She made some humorous masks. One said, "Put your money where your mouth is," and had a facsimile of a dollar bill attached. She made another mask with a zipper where someone's mouth would be, saying, "Zip-it, it's a secret!" Then she made some masks with lips, sensuous lips that looked very kissable for both sexes. She had many requests for them and quickly filled the orders, donating everything she collected after postage to the local food pantries.

Using a coconut, she demonstrated how to do an at-home bikini wax. Apparently Palo had seen the video and sent a text asking, "And why would you need to do this now?"

In another blog, she says, "The freezer is your friend." Adding that, "There will be days when you absolutely won't want to cook. So, when making food, casseroles, stews and soups . . . always do a double batch. Then when you are having a bad day, depressed that you can't see your family, or just really weary of the whole COVID thing, at least you won't have to cook. She showed how to make individual packets using parchment paper so that the meals would freeze easily, take up less freezer space, and be able to be reheated in the microwave without having to be unwrapped.

She did a blog on touching up highlights with hair-dye markers. In another blog, she cut Brent's hair, showing how to layer it, feather it, and to use a trimmer to groom mustaches and beards. He'd only let her do it as he was planning on shaving all his facial hair off as soon as they were finished. That blog got the most hits. Both women and men, all over the world wanted to know if he was available—with or without facial hair.

She took videos of Brent surfing, when he was too far out for anyone to make out who he was. Because after the hair cutting video, she wouldn't have put it past her viewers to map out the coastline to try to figure out where he was living.

While Alyssa was blogging, face booking, tik-toking, ordering groceries, cooking, baking, arranging wildflowers, doing laundry, and remaking beds, Brent was working on house plans, reading architectural magazines and updates, shopping online, surfing, biking, or running on the beach. They fell into a pattern: breakfast together, a work activity for each, some exercise, lunch—usually a late one—followed by check-ins with family, friends, and doctors, and then walks on the beach before settling in for the night, as the temperatures were rising and the sun was setting later. They often found themselves holding hands on the way back, with Brent gently caressing her fingers with his.

There was the occasional break from the pattern though. One day, Brent saved a reckless teenager from drowning. On another day, Alyssa had her first driving lesson while Brent showed her around the area.

Meanwhile, they cooked together, they cleaned together, they did the dishes together, and they took even longer walks on the beach together. Occasionally Alyssa begged off, demanding a shorter walk when it was too chilly, sometimes just going down the access and then back.

To Brent, it seemed that Alyssa had boundless energy. Her mind was always coming up with new things to interest her . . . and to take her away from him. Up the stairs she'd go, or into the kitchen, or out onto the terrace.

Then he wouldn't see her again until he heard her

laughing in the TV room. He loved how she laughed out loud at *Progressive's Becoming Your Dad* commercials. She was still laughing long after the commercials were over. She delighted him. And it concerned him that this was so.

He had sat on the sofa across from her and watched her face crumple the night Kate Snow described her life in her Manhattan apartment with her husband as they both suffered the ravages of COVID. It broke his heart to see her so unhappy.

The following week he ordered flowers for her birthday from the local florist called Bloomer's, and he had a cake delivered from Purple Onion. Later that evening, they had watched the news and he had held her as she cried when Andrea Bocelli's concert *Music for Hope* was replayed from his Easter performance. He had sung in front of the empty cathedral in Milan, and the eerie ghostly emptiness of the huge square had torn her up big time. She was inconsolable, and again, it broke his heart to see her so unhappy.

He knew that she wanted to go home. He also knew that there was only one possibility of that happening. But he did not want to give her up yet. It was a given that he'd probably never see her again if she went home. Still . . . he made the call.

Chapter 82
A Very Sad Day

Then just barely into her eleventh week, she miscarried. It was early in the morning. The sun was not even up when the cramping began. In her sleep-fogged brain, she thought her period was starting so she made her way to the bathroom and sat on the toilet. Before she'd had time to register what was going on, she felt something slip out from inside her. She stared down between her legs and into the toilet at what had come out of her. There was no doubt what had happened.

The evidence of the baby that had been inside her could not be denied. She had lost her baby. Whether it was Gulf-wader Brown or Hypotenuse Brisket, it was too soon to tell. Just yesterday, she had made an appointment to go for a scan and blood work later this month.

She stood and stared down, her hand over her mouth, her tears dripping into the water. The finality was devastating. Sadness washed over her and made her knees week. She knelt on the floor and touched the flesh of the tiny baby. It was well-formed, the head taking up most of its size, but the arms and legs clearly evident in their folded up state. The water in the bowl was cold, but the little body still carried some warmth. Oh God, what was she supposed to do? Was she supposed to take it out? Bury it? Flush it? She had no idea.

She grabbed her phone and pressed the number that would call Brent. When he answered after the first ring, she simply said, "I just lost the baby."

A second later she heard him running through the house, heading for her room. She was still on the floor holding onto the rim of the toilet with both hands when he rushed in. He wore boxer-briefs that he had must have quickly put on as they weren't pulled up evenly.

He walked over to her, looking at her hands. Then he looked over her shoulder, and a sad sound of pain filled the room. Like a hurt animal keening he crumpled and then fell to a kneeling position beside her. One arm came up and gripped her shoulders and they stared down with tears filling their eyes. Then he slowly stood and lifted her into his arms and carried her to the bed. He placed her gently on the bed then laid down beside her and held her while she cried, his hands running over her head, her hair, her back. He cried too, but he tried not to make a sound doing it.

They stayed that way for a long time. Then he got up, found her phone and cscrolled to her doctor's number. She didn't answer so he left a message as directed. Within a few minutes the doctor called back and he told her what had happened.

She said how sorry she was, adding that she had been worried about this exact thing happening because of her mother's long history with first trimester miscarriages.

Palo had told both Alyssa's doctor and Brent that his mother had four miscarriages before carrying him to term. He had been concerned from the onset of Alyssa's pregnancy about her well-being.

The doctor asked a lot of questions that he tried to answer with Alyssa's help. Then she asked for a picture so she could see if the miscarriage could be confirmed complete, that no tissue or membranes were missing. The doctor told Brent that Alyssa would be all right given some time to heal emotionally. Physically, she might experience more cramping followed by bleeding similar to having a period. She cautioned him to call her back if it the bleeding was heavy or if it continued for more than a few weeks.

He asked what they should do with the body and was told that in normal times they would biopsy it, search for a reason, do some research for the future. But she said that wasn't something they could do now. She said she was very sorry. And that this would in no way impede her having another baby in the future.

And when asked, she said they could take care of the remains any way they saw fit. He said he would discuss it with her and thanked her for her help before hanging up. Then he went back to hold her and tell her everything that was said. There were more tears, more than he thought one could possibly have. She told him that she did not want to flush her baby, so he gently lifted it out and wrapped it up in a hand towel. He put it in her lap and she caressed every part of it while fresh tears streamed down her face. Then he folded the towel over it and took it from her. As he left the room he could hear her sobbing in great gulps. He knew that in the end, this purging of tears would be cathartic for her so he left her to it and carried the tiny bundle out of the room and down the hall to his room.

He found a small sturdy box and put the baby inside, then used a small square of bubble wrap packing to cushion the tiny bundle was still wrapped up in the hand towel. Then went to get dressed. He already knew where she'd want it taken.

It was low tide, so he rode his bike across the beach access and then all the way down to The Mailbox where he walked behind the dune line to bury the box. He found some heavy pieces of driftwood to mark the spot and to place around the area to keep any wild animals from digging up the box. The box had once held Belgium chocolates, now it held the remains of a very tiny Italian baby.

He sat on the bench and wrote in the journal asking God to take this sorrow from Alyssa and to heal her physically. Then he got back on the bike and rode back to *The Cockpit*. He had never felt lonelier in his whole life than he did on that early spring morning when the wind was whipping his sweater out behind him as he peddled up the beach. The sight of the house he had built was not as welcoming as it usually was. He didn't know when it would be again. He had been a part of that baby's life. Had wanted it as much as she had. He missed knowing it was inside her, developing. There seemed to be a hole in his heart where love for that little life had been growing as well. He looked to see if she was watching for his return. She wasn't.

He walked the bike up the access, clomped up the masonry

steps to the terrace, and propped it up beside the house. He'd put it away later. He needed to see how Alyssa was doing.

Her bed was empty. She had even made it. He called out for her. No answer. Then he looked through the entire house, calling out her name as he opened doors and searched each room and still didn't find her. He went outside. There was no sign of her. He wandered around the house, aimless, without a purpose. Seeing nothing of the fine finishing touches or well thought out décor. He jumped when he heard the first clap of thunder. Ran to the back door in time to see a jagged line pierce the sky before the heavens opened and rain fell like sharp knives.

He ran for the binoculars they kept handy in a utility room drawer then up to the window on the top level that had the best view of the beach. He saw a dark shadow in the distance, far off to the left, walking along the shoreline, coming from the east, opposite of where he'd just been. She rarely walked in that direction. But he was sure it was her as he watched the wind whip her hair around her head.

She was out there, with no shelter. It didn't even look as if she had a coat on. He ran for his raincoat and grabbed her parka as well. Then he flew down the steps and out the door that led to the terrace level.

Rain fell across the wooden planks of the beach access so hard he could hear them resounding from the noise and feel the vibration coming up through his Nikes. He didn't stop running until he got to her, now huddled into a tight ball on the beach, her head against the wet sand, her hands protecting it from the pelting, stinging rain. He had never run faster in his life.

He covered her with her coat and then stripped off his and added that one on top, too. Then he pulled her up, and with her tucked into his side he walked her back. When they reached the access, he lifted her into his arms and carried her up to the house, stopping at the outside shower. She was shivering, she was crying, and she was his. Some how he knew this. Knew it like a revelation as lightning lit up the sky over the ocean.

Chapter 83
Hot Water Outside Shower—Best Idea Ever

Not for the first time, he gave himself a mental pat on the back for having the foresight to have hot water running to the outside showers. In retrospect, it was probably the best single thing he'd added to the original plans.

Right now, he was grateful he'd gone to the trouble of installing a special Noritz on-demand system. Knowing that the beach house would be used year round by several of the men who were avid surfers and distance swimmers like himself, it seemed a no-brainer, but it had been a hard to sell to the others.

If there was anything he appreciated more after catching the waves for an hour during the winter months, it was having a nice hot shower as soon as he got his wet suit stripped off. The added benefit was that sand and water were not tracked into the elevator, and from there, all through the house. No matter how fine sand was, and Sunset's was one of the most pulverized beach sands there was, it still acted like sandpaper on marble, tile, and hardwood flooring.

As an added luxury, he'd bought and paid for a towel warmer, so that after his shower he could wrap himself in the divine warmth of a toasty plush towel.

Every man who had stayed at the beach house during the off season, had emailed him that what was once thought of the most over-the-top and frivolous item on the building budget was now the most appreciated extravagance he'd ever had to talk them into. Right now, it was a godsend. Alyssa's body was very cold—too cold. Her skin was waxy looking—pale and leeched of color

Tossing the wet coats aside, he adjusted the temperature coming from the high-pressure rainfall showerhead. When it

585

was a soft warm flow, he aimed it at the cedar bench and sat with her in his lap as the water ran over them. The resulting mist created by the water hitting the cold air, caressed their faces and warmed the air all around them. Soon, they were cocooned in a warm, wet fog.

He held her in his arms and softly rocked her, knowing that his world was also being rocked in a very permanent way in that moment. He suddenly wanted to be committed to this woman in a way he had never been committed to anything else in his entire life.

School, sports, even work had been a lark—something to do to keep from being bored. But this, this woman in his arms? She was his purpose now. Everything from this moment on would be about her first.

The stories about Tristan and Isolde, Romeo and Juliet, Paris and Helen, Jack and Rose, Edward and Vivian, Rick and Ilsa, Sally and Harry, Sam and Molly, Baby and Johnny, Tony and Maria, Navarre and Isabeau—the total dedication they had to each other made sense now.

How had this happened? And how was he going to tell Palo?

He looked down into the face of the woman he held in his arms. She looked back at him, her eyes no longer wet from tears but from the mist all around them. God, she was beautiful, with her dark eyes glistening, her long lashes fluttering to keep the mist out, and her full lips parted in wonder. Something had shifted for them in these moments and they both knew it.

"Are you warm enough?" he asked, and she nodded.

"We should get you out of these wet clothes," again she simply nodded.

"It hurts that I lost the baby," she said, and he watched as tears threatened again. "So bad."

"I know. But there will be others one day."

"I wanted this one."

"I know you did."

"I must've done something wrong."

"No, you didn't. These things just happen. It's nothing you did so don't beat yourself up over it. C'mon, we need to get you out of these wet clothes and into something warm. Let me help you get this stuff off you," he indicated the soggy fleece sweatshirt that was heavy with water and plastered to her.

She curled her fingers around the hem and he helped her drag the sodden weight up and over her head. Under it, she wore a bra with satin covered cups that were fully stretched to accommodate her full breasts. It was also soaked though but not heavy with excess water. Drops of water ran down her chest and into the hollow between her breasts from the loose tendrils of her hair that were glued to her shoulders now that the sweatshirt was off.

He stood her up and worked to peel the damp stretch denim off her hips, then pulled it down her legs. Her legs were clammy with the cold, but he was heating up, his insides firing up like a stoked locomotive at the sight of her exposed body. She was beginning to shiver again. He watched as her skin began pebbling with goose bumps. As soon as he got her stretchy jeans off, he stood her under the shower again. Her color started coming back as soon as she was under the spray. When her skin was pink, he turned off the water and folded her into one of the warmed oversized towels he had taken from the resin towel locker.

He quickly stripped his clothes off and wrapped a towel around his midriff. Then he lifted her into his arms and carried her to the elevator.

The whole way up he held her tight to his body; her face snuggled into his chest. He refused to take her to her room, knowing that if she went to her bedroom she'd remain there for the night. He wanted her with him, in the room they often ate in, where they watched TV and talked late into the night. He did not want her alone tonight. And he didn't want to be alone and without her.

"I need a shower."

"You're clean enough. Right now you need some warm clothes and something warm to drink." He placed her on the long sofa in the corner he now thought of as hers.

"Strip off your bra and panties off while I run upstairs and get you some warm pajamas. Then I'll warm up that fabulous soup you made, the fuzzy pasta."

She laughed. "Pasta e Fagioli."

It was close to noon now, so he picked up the remote and clicked on the channel for the local news coming out of Wilmington, before running up to her room.

He had only been in this room a few times before today. Mostly to talk to Alex about golf plans or dinner plans when he'd been in residence. But it never failed to remind him of Alex's first wife who had died giving birth to twin girls. Alex was now happily married to a local Shallotte girl with an infant son in addition to the two girls. But there was always a twinge of sadness for Melody upon entering this room and seeing her childhood white and gold-gilded French Provincial furniture.

As he walked past the floor Cheval mirror he saw his reflection and stopped. Dear God, his hair. The wind and rain on the beach, then the outside shower had done a job on it. It was sticking up at weird angles. He ran his fingers through it. There would be no taming this without a good shampooing. Instead, he went into the en suite, stuck his head under the faucet and let the hot water rinse out what it could. Thankfully, Alyssa had been keeping it somewhat short he mused, as he grabbed a towel from the rack and rubbed it dry.

He was assailed by her smell in the towel and in this room. A clean lemony scent with a touch of lavender and rosemary, it evoked Italy. The few times he'd been there it had been all about the history and architecture, the pizza and the wine, and World Cup Soccer. But he remembered the smells in the shops, in the old houses, in the galleries and museums; even musty from old paper and canvas they always evoked a touch of lemon and rosemary. He spotted her perfume bottle on the vanity and picked it up. Ubiquitous in all the Italian shops, he recognized the tall frosted bottle of Villa Floriani Limoncello Satin Body Spray.

When had he *ever* cared about a woman's fragrance? What was happening to him?

He put the bottle down, noted the tidy bathroom, and hung the towel on the hook on the back of the door. Then he marched to the dresser and opened drawers until he found a soft fleecy pair of drawstring lounging pants with a matching top. On impulse, he grabbed her hairbrush from the dresser. He realized he knew her in ways he had quietly absorbed, bit-by-bit, day-by-day. She would want to brush her hair smooth. She would want to look nice, just as she always did.

He fast-walked down the hall then ran down the steps. And saw her snuggled under a cloud-soft bamboo throw she had vacillated about ordering from Amazon for weeks until he had finally ordered it for her himself.

She was unbelievably sexy looking, and soft hearted in her concern as she watched the news in a way that bespoke compassion and a deep sense of caring.

This wasn't a whim. This wasn't a relationship he could walk away from. This was like Alex and Emma, Deke and Shaw, Chaz and Mags. This was a grand, larger-than-life love. Palo would have to understand that and forgive him. And maybe he would, as he too, was committed in the same manner to Trixie.

She looked over at him, tears brimming her eyes. "Tom Hanks and his wife got COVID in Australia. They are quarantined at home now. She says it is awful, that they are so sick. If they don't survive, this is so very bad . . .."

Tears freely flowed, as she swiped at them with a tissue. And just like that, her own worries and sadness about losing the baby were gone, and she was latched onto someone else's problem, someone's else's hurt and distress. This was the woman he had fallen in love with. It had stealthily crawled over him and seeped into every pore. It was as if he'd been dipped into a vat of petroleum with a live electrode charge running through it. He was energized in a way that he had never been before.

He bubbled with joy and could not seem to keep his mind from straying to thoughts of her. Every single moment seemed consumed with what she was doing, thinking, desiring? And was it the same for her as it was for him? His life's work now would be to secure her to him, to make sure she felt the same way about him as he felt about her.

"They are quarantined in the hospital there. She says she is so sick she can hardly stand and she has lost her sense of smell and taste. They don't know how they got it, but she said she's been sanitizing everything in sight like crazy, but they still got it. So sad, so very sad for them."

He came over, sat on the edge of the sofa, and gathered her into his arms and gently rocked her. "They'll be okay, nothing bad can happen to Forrest Gump that he can't overcome. And Rita Wilson has survived devastating breast cancer; she'll come out on top of this. Don't you worry." He kissed the wet tendrils of hair curling at her temple, then pulled back and stared down into her teary face. "You know you can't get this upset about every single person who comes down with this, a lot more people are going to get it. You are going to have to stop watching the news if this keeps bothering you so badly."

"It's just so sad."

He pulled her closer and wrapped his arms tightly around her. "I know. But don't worry; we're going to be okay. And so are Tom and Rita. Now let's get you dressed in some warm pjs and fill you up with some fussy soup."

She laughed. "Fagioli."

"How can something spelled like Fag-ee-o-lee, be pronounced fazool? And don't get me started on bruschetta."

"The French are worse; au jus, croissant, crudités, vichyssoise," she muttered in defense of her Italian heritage.

"Actually, I think Spain is worse, with Quinoa," he said.

"Or maybe the Greeks with Gyro."

He laughed and stood, dropping her clothes on her chest. "Get dressed while I ladle up the *fazooool*. Then if you're a good girl, I'll brush your hair out for you."

"And what if I'm a bad girl?" she said giving him a smirk.

"Then I'll spank you with the back of the brush," he whispered. And the meaning was clear that it might be something he'd really consider doing.

"Ohhh, dangerous territory . . ." she said more to herself than to him as he left the room. "Dangerous indeed." But the thought of being bent over his knee kind of excited her.

She grabbed her pjs and went down the hall to the leopard bathroom and put them on. Then she finger combed her hair. The rain had frizzed and curled it, making a huge halo around her head. She took the ribbon from a tiny vase of rosemary she'd put on the vanity earlier in the week, then gathered her mass of hair and tied it behind her head. Turning her head this way and that, she murmured, "Better, but not good."

She missed her salon in Italy. They always knew what to do to tame her wild hair. The wind blown salty grit, along with the rain, and something indefinable in the beach air, always managed to muck up her long tresses. Maybe she should cut it, she thought. Then laughed out loud as she remembered, the celebrities on TV and their homegrown haircuts.

"What are you laughing about?" he asked as she came out of the bathroom dressed in her adorable plaid pants and oversized top that had POWERED BY CANDY in bright pink and teal puffy lettering on the front.

"Those home haircuts this morning on the news show."

"I saw a few. They were pretty awful, weren't they? Speaking of which," he said as he carried their bowls on a tray, "mine could stand another trim. You game to give it a go again?"

"Sure. I'm actually getting pretty good at it."

"Good, then I'll try my hand at doing yours if you like."

"No way! Thanks, but no thanks. I'll never forget the hair cut Palo gave me. Took months to grow it out."

"Well, can I brush it out for you after lunch?"

"Sure. After I shower and shampoo it."

"Deal."

She sat down in front of her bowl. "Smells like you burnt it."

"Nah, just the toast."

"Ah, more bread for the gulls in the morning."

"Yeah, I need to find the right setting for that thing."

"You just need to watch it. You get distracted."

"Says the girl who burns oatmeal."

"Yeah that was a disaster. I got totally wrapped up in that news show about the balcony singers in Napoli."

"Palo says it's a nice tribute that they're doing all over Italy now."

She shrugged. "It's just sad, is what it is."

He looked up and saw the tear coursing down her cheek. "Homesick, again?"

"Always. I miss my mom. So much has happened. When I told her about the baby, she was so happy. And now I have to tell her I lost it. And Palo too."

He reached over and gripped her hand. "Tomorrow's soon enough. Just take it easy today and try to relax. It's been a long day for you already and it's just past noon."

"Thank you for being there for me through it all."

"My pleasure. Now eat your fuzzy soup."

The news show switched to the local virus numbers, higher now mostly due to nursing homes and assisted living centers. They watched as the county numbers climbed; as the mandates were reiterated over and over again, as Dr. Fauci updated the nation, as Dr. Mandy Cohen admonished North Carolinians for not wearing masks or social distancing, as President Trump tried to restore calm and encourage the nation while worrying about protecting investors and the stock markets.

They were touting these as unprecedented times. But they really weren't. If there was one thing Alyssa knew about, it was history. And in Europe, they had been through these types of epidemics many times, over many centuries. She knew the devastation that could come if the virus could not be stopped.

Chapter 84
Wine is Life, Love is in the Air

She felt immeasurably better after a hot meal and snuggling in the cloud-soft throw courtesy of Brent. During the news program she'd even laughed a few times at some of the videos people submitted to show how they were filling their days by amusing themselves and their families. She'd seen most of them before as she followed social media rather closely. The hand covered by a sock acting as Pac-Man in a window as it "gobbled" up cars passing by on the street had her in hysterics with tears rolling down her cheeks again. But this time they were happy ones. She loved that video and was never tired of seeing it.

It felt good to laugh. She pulled her laptop from the side table and selected the collection of videos she had put in her Favorites file. It was women drinking wine with noisy children in the back ground, one woman with a huge wine glass that held a whole bottle all at once, women helping their kids with intricate math problems, then slipping around the corner for a gulp of wine before coming back to stare cross-eyed at a new algebraic equation. Alyssa cracked up over a mother, who, when she looked down from her dinner preparations to her toddler pulling on her sweater, only saw very expressive eyes and a completely white head. Then she saw the empty flour canister. Alyssas hysterical laughter made Brent chuckle out loud while he was in the kitchen cleaning up after lunch.

"You have to admire that women's poise," she called out to him. "She just reached across the counter, grabbed her husband's wine glass from his hand, and drained it."

She clicked on video after video and laughed until she had to pee. In the bathroom she noticed that she had sort of stopped bleeding. Time to move on she told herself. Lots of women went through this. Her mama had been through it many times. She would survive it and she would count her blessings. This would have been a horrible time to bring a child into the world. And if she was to be honest with herself, though she really wanted a baby, she really wanted a baby who had a father who wanted to be there for his child. Like hers had been there for her. She thought of the baby cradle he'd make for her, the doll houses, tree houses, puppet show stages, scene sets for plays, and even the hope chest she had yet to begin filling. It was still in her papa's workshop under an old blanket. Yes, maybe this had been a good thing. She would have welcomed this baby, loved it . . . but God knew best. He always did. She believed that.

She came down the staircase after having had a long shower and a short nap. She smiled when Brent held a glass of red wine out to her. "Here, you can drink now. You can emulate your new friends on those videos."

She smiled and took the glass from him. "Grazie. I am realizing that I am the fortunate one. I do not have to spend the evening cleaning up a hundred-pound bag of puppy kibble used as mortar bombs by twin boys, or marker marks all over the bathroom walls by budding young artists who were supposed to be taking a bath, or a light blue linen sofa that had a economy-sized jar of peanut butter smeared all over it."

"The flour girl was pretty adorable though, she looked very much like a miniature ghost."

"She was probably the easiest to clean up."

"Yeah, but not the walk-in pantry she was in when she pulled it off the shelf and it overturned onto her head. Five pounds of flour makes a huge mess."

She took a sip of her wine. "I noticed there was never a video of wine being spilt."

He laughed, "They keep that under lock and key. Or the kids know there would be hell to pay if they wasted their momma's wine."

"In Italy, wine is life. Everyone respects it, even the

children. They know not to disturb the vines, to stay away from the vats and presses, and not to touch the bottles or corks."

"The beer, wine, and alcohol industry is reaping the rewards of COVID. I read that home brewing is causing shortages of key ingredients."

"I think it's cheating if you don't grow the grapes yourself, that is the essence of wine."

"Well, not everybody has five acres to devote to that."

He walked her into the TV room and she settled on the couch while he chose a recliner.

"Then they should make beer. Or gin. Or tequila."

"Tequila requires farming for worms."

She laughed. "Palo makes his own Kahlua, Grappa and Limoncello for Christmas presents."

"I know. I am a recipient of his gifts. His Limoncello is the best I've ever had."

"His secret is Everclear."

"Ahhh, that explains its potency. We should make some," he said.

"It is hard to get sugar some days. And if I put in an order for twenty lemons, I will probably only get two, but I will try."

"Shame the liquor store doesn't deliver. I doubt there's a bottle of Everclear around here," he said as he sipped. "It would be a fun project though."

"I will start collecting lemons and sugar."

"I will put my mask on and brave the liquor store."

"I will find some kitschy bottles."

"Kitschy?" he asked.

"Whimsical glass things we can use to put the Limoncello in—for gifts. We can send them to our friends."

"I think that is an excellent idea!"

"Well, especially now that I can drink some of it," she said with a small laugh.

But he knew she was still grieving over losing the baby. She was hiding it well, but she was still hurting. He wished she had a woman to talk to, someone who would understand.

In the kitchen, Alyssa had just finished putting their gelato bowls in the dishwasher, when Brent came up behind her and wrapped his arms around her middle. He ran his lips from the bottom of her neck up to her ear and felt her shiver. Then he gathered his courage and whispered, "I'm afraid I'm falling for you Aly."

She spun inside the circle of his arms then reached up to wrap her hands around his neck, her lips in a pout, "Afraid?"

"Well . . . there is Palo to take into consideration."

"He will not be pleased?"

"No." It was unequivocal. As if he knew it like he knew his mother's name.

"Why not?" This seemed to surprise her. "He likes you."

"He likes me as a *friend*. Not as a suitor for *you*, his sister."

"Why not?" Her puzzled expression, with her mouth quirked to the side and her teeth sunk into the side of her bottom lip was adorable. He wanted to run his longue along the inside of her lip and feel the soft underside. He wanted to do . . . oh, so many things. The image of Palo with steam coming out of his ears floated front and center in his mind.

"I am much older than you, for one. And he's seen me . . ."

"Seen you what?" with her fingertips she stroked the hair on the nape of his neck, toying with the curls she found there.

It did things to him. Nice things.

"Well, when you're in college, you don't much care about privacy when the opportunity for sex comes along. We've all seen each other uh, *in flagrante delicto*."

"Ewww."

He smiled down at her. "You asked. Any way, I told him I wouldn't."

"Wouldn't what?" her finger was teasing his ear now, circling the inner and outer rim, caressing the lobe. He felt himself go fully hard.

"Wouldn't do this. Ever."

"This?" she asked as she met his eyes and ran her hand alongside his jaw.

"This," he breathed as he surrendered to the lust coursing through him and pulled her body close to his, her back up against the countertop. His lips covered hers. Soft lips met and opened as their breaths mingled for the first time. He leaned in to let his tongue have its way between her parted lips, exploring her mouth and relishing every answering quake he felt from her body's reaction to his kiss.

He let everything fall away. He didn't think about his work, COVID, Palo, or the impropriety of their ten-year age difference. He just felt the woman in his arms. Tasted her sweetness. Reveled in her unique smell. And grew impossibly hard.

He pulled away, saw that she was dazed, and went back for another. That glazed look in her eyes, that surrendering to the passion between them fueled yet another kiss—deeper this time, the kind that emptied out everything else and made room for wild passion to come in.

He pulled back and gave her a crooked smile. It was comical how she mimicked him.

"What's so funny?"

"You. Afraid of Palo. He would do nothing to harm you. He is a kind man to everyone."

"You don't know him like I do."

She tilted her head to the side in a questioning manner. He could see she was running things through her head. Her hand covered her mouth. The thought that had just occurred to her was evident on her face, "Giancarlo?"

He didn't say anything.

"Did he do something to Giancarlo?"

That she was concerned for the welfare of that schmuck brought heat to his face as his hands clenched in anger behind her back.

"He only made sure he stayed to help his father with his business instead of leaving." He did not mention how Palo had achieved that.

She smiled, and then laughed. "I should have known that Palo would do something. I am glad that Giancarlo is not hurt. And I am glad he is not the man for me anymore. Can we do more kissing now?"

He laughed as well. She pleased him immensely. He bent and obliged her with several deep kisses then pulled back to look at her kiss-swollen lips. From her glazed expression, he knew she was worked up, that she wouldn't fight him if he carried her to his bed. But he wanted more than a tumble.

Besides, he knew she wasn't ready yet—her body needed to heal. And what kind of schmuck made love to a woman on the day she'd miscarried another man's baby?

But she wasn't giving up. She teased his lips with her fingertips.

Her shy smile undid him. She was so young. He kept forcing himself to remember that she had just lost a baby. And they had to address that.

"You know that I was going to help you get ready for the baby. Be with you when it came. I'm very sorry he or she didn't make it. I truly am. But next time . . . I want it to be my baby inside you."

There. He'd said it—what he'd been thinking for weeks. He leaned his forehead against hers. "Alyssa, I'm so gone on you . . . I can't even tell you. I've never felt this way before. My mind doesn't know what to think. But I can tell you this for sure, when it's time for you to have a baby, I want to be the one to give it to you."

Her eyes blinked wide as she tried to take it all in.

"This is not the time to tell you all this, and I am probably light years ahead of any feelings that you might be developing for me, but I need you to know I'm not just horny. That this is about more than that." He waved his fingers between them indicating that the *this* he was referring to, was how they were now getting along.

He wrapped her head between his hands, threaded his fingers into her hair and tugged her head back until their eyes met and held. "Tell me you feel this, too. Maybe not as strongly as I do, but that you feel something for me other than friendship."

Slowly she nodded her head. Her light brown eyes with the dancing irises met his and he felt buoyed with the thought that she too, was in this strange but wonderful eddy of emotions with him—that they were rushing to the same place . . . feeling the same passion.

She smiled up at him and coyly nodded, "What I feel, is this," she quipped, as she thrust her hips so that her belly connected with his pelvis, and the hard-on he sported now leapt to nestle in the notch at her hip. He smiled back at her and then returned her thrust once. Twice. Then he groaned with frustration and pulled away.

"I *don't* just want sex with you. I want you to be sure you have feelings for me, like the ones I have for you."

"Oh, I have feelings. I'm just not all that ready to accept that they are real."

He quirked a brow at her and looked puzzled. "And why is that?"

She lifted her brows and shrugged. "I just had a man I thought I was in love with dump me—the man whose baby I was carrying. A man who did not want that baby to have a life. He wanted me to get rid of it. He would probably be doing cartwheels now if he knew what happened this morning. He also told me that he loved me. That he was *loco* for me. So . . . I have to be the sane one here. I have the most to lose. Again."

"I would never . . ."

She covered his lips with her fingertips. "Let's just go

slow and take our time. I will come to trust my feelings again, and yours as well." She touched her heart with her fist. "But I don't trust myself right now. It's too new. Too much has happened. You might have noticed that I am highly emotional. I want to trust you, like I trusted Giancarlo . . . but that did not work out." She patted his chest. "So, let's go slow."

"I agree. That's the smart thing to do."

He bent and lifted her up to the counter. Met her eyes with his and quirked a smile. "How slow?"

She returned his smile. "We can still play. Do things . . . one does not have to be in love to have sex."

He nodded. "That is true. In fact, most people who have sex are not. I have had a lot of sex over the years. And not once have I been in love. That is not something I will ever be able to say again."

She grinned. Like a woman who knew she was in the catbird seat, she knew she was the one in control. "I think some cuddling on the couch would be nice . . . more of those devastating kisses would also be nice . . . a little fondle here or there might even be welcome," she murmured as her hand dipped down and found the long length of him and gently squeezed. "But we will have to stop . . . because we must right now."

He groaned and pulled her close, his lips sunk into the side of her neck. "You are killing me. But we'll do it your way until you can catch up to where I am."

She nodded. "How about watching some more episodes of *Schitt's Creek* with a chai latte and an almond biscotti?" she asked.

"You know, if you ever wanted to go into business making that stuff, you'd make a killing."

"Nah, in Italy every girl learns to make it with her mama. Biscotti is in big jars in every home. No one ever has to buy it."

"I'm thinking I just might not let you go home."

She raised her finger and waggled it front of his face. "So you can see, we cannot be in love. I am Italian. You are

American. We only live together here, in this house because of the COVID."

He pulled her off the counter, wrapping her legs around his waist. "Then maybe I will make the most of my time and not be in love. Just hungry . . . for you."

"And my biscotti."

He laughed as he carried her around the kitchen to the big jar on the pantry shelf. "Yes, you and your biscotti. And your fuzzy soup."

She grabbed the jar and he carried her and it into the TV room and softly settled her onto the sofa. "I'll fire up the Keurig and make the lattes. You fire up Netflix."

"Maybe later, I'll light your fire," she teased as she grabbed for the remote.

"That fuse is already lit and burning, and you know it."

She made an exploding gesture with the hand that wasn't working the remote and winked at him.

He groaned, then shook his head as he made his way back to the kitchen. He would welcome that explosion when it came. But for certain, it would not be happening tonight.

Chapter 85
The Beaches Re-open—Yay Salt Life!

It was mid-May before The Town of Sunset Beach began to re-open the beaches. At the online town meetings, residents protested the closure of the beach strands. They wanted a place to exercise, to walk their dogs and to ride their bikes. They thought it the perfect place to gather in beach chairs in big circles with ample room for social distancing. They wanted to howl at the full moon on the mild seasonal nights.

Bowing to pressure from both the islanders, who were returning in droves from the cities—more like running from them—and mainland residents who wanted access to the beach as a place to recreate and to safely get out of their houses, they removed the tapes that were blocking off the accesses. The yellow tape on the beach access that led from *The Cockpit* had not been a problem for them, for it had only been attached at the street. The beach house was too far east on Main Street to be of concern to anyone.

There had been no occupied houses near them during the cold winter months, so it hadn't mattered. Even if there had been tape leading down to the beach, Brent would have simply tossed his board over to the sand and then vaulted over the yellow tape. If someone had seen him running or biking or surfing, no one living on the island would have reported it. And even if they had, it was likely that the gendarmes when alerted would not have been inclined to rush off in pursuit of the homeowner culprit. It just wasn't that way here.

Yes, all the local parks and playgrounds had been closed and roped off, as well as the roads leading to them barricaded. But it had been cold and the area had been in lockdown, so a lot of people weren't even aware of the restrictions. But now it was warming up, the sun was coming back, and people were desperate to go someplace where they could get some fresh air and get away from the staleness of their homes. It was springtime after all; time to get back outside and into nature again.

The Town finally relented and began opening things up, but not without rules and stipulations, and signage. Lots of signage—sometimes, laughable signage.

Masks were still required, social distancing was crucial, and accesses were marked as one-way, designating alternating walkways as the ones to be used to go to the beach and the others, the ones to use to return from the beach. These signs were all but ignored—causing harsh recriminations between the people who obeyed the signs and the people who did not.

It was a bit confusing and people were often caught going the wrong way without knowing it. Some people were nice about it and didn't make a big deal over it, moving aside to accommodate them. But some were not so nice and had to make it known that they had the right-of-way, "Hey, read the signs, you idiot! You're going wrong way!"

Even in paradise, patience was wearing thin. The tiniest things could be the catalyst toward resentment. Yes, being at the beach was nice. But not everyone wanted to share.

But once on the beach, laughter and good cheer could be found again. People brought their evening cocktails in soft coolers, had fancy waterproof totes for snacks, and often had a plastic plate of some yummy appetizer that they'd pass around to share. Some went so far as to erect collapsible side tables to hold their beverages, their sound bars, and their cell phones.

The main entertainment would be the rising moon. The understudies were the stars and Venus and Jupiter popping out— along with a few high-flying kites fighting against the tug from the ground.

More often than not, the whine of a remotely controlled RC Tumbler, running over the sand and then flipping crazily over itself multiple times, could be heard from the dune line, where the teenagers preferred to hang out. Their parents opted for the stability of the firmly packed sand for their makeshift outside living rooms.

It was nice seeing all the clusters of people spread out in wide arcs of low-rise chairs. Chatting away, catching up on events, and discussing the news of the day, they were freed from their stylish cages.

There was hardly anyone who couldn't give you the daily count for cases of COVID that had mounted up in the county. For a few it was personal, as they knew someone who had contracted the disease. For most, it was something they were watching people experience all over the country, while they stayed safe, living a relatively unchanged life in a resort atmosphere. Unchanged except for the lack of paper products, cleaning solutions, certain toiletries, limited versions of small batch liquors, and of course, chicken parts.

Life was good at the beach. Few were sick. The weather turning mild buoyed everyone's spirits. But all over the country, teachers were dealing with a technology few understood, with only a handful being proficient enough to successfully teach online, as hospitals and staff were quickly becoming overwhelmed. Zoom became to the way to teach, to conduct business, and for clubs to meet.

As more and more people were forced to work from homes, realtors were inundated with people wanting to relocate. Without childcare, some wanted to surround themselves with family to help out with those duties. The mantra became: *If you didn't need to live in the cities, then why do it?*

Others saw an opportunity to improve their lot, to get out of their overpriced city dwellings and find their dream home, whether it be in the country, the mountains, or on the coast—masses were on the move.

With summer just around the corner, a house on the beach became the ideal for many families, whether working or retired, homebuyers came in droves from all over country. Developers all over the coast were scrambling to meet the demand. For Sale signs on land that had been on the market for years were pulled up. Huge tracts were cleared. Every day there was a smoldering pile of debris on a cleared lot where trees had been clear-cut to make way for houses.

Then suddenly, there were severe shortages. Developers and Do-it-yourselfers who were taking the time being stuck at home to do home improvement projects were causing a run on building materials. Overnight building materials were in high demand. Over several weeks prices soared. Factories and lumberyards had all but shut down to protect their employees, so less of each commodity was being made, while more was now being demanded. It was the perfect storm. A housing shortage loomed, reminiscent of the one the country had experienced after World War II when the men who had been fighting the war returned home.

But even as the price for building supplies soared, people still wanted out of the cities. They snapped up any available housing the day it came on the market, often having bidding wars to the seller's delight.

Some families opted for the RVing lifestyle to get them safely out of the cities and on the road to places where they could easily practice safe distancing. RVing was becoming the preferred way to travel great distances while still keeping the family safe.

Cam, who had a fifth wheel RV stored at Willow Tree Campground in Longs, SC, had recently emailed everyone that he and Tamara were planning on taking it down south to visit her grandmother who was now all alone and living in an old rundown bayou bungalow with no way to get provisions. They were going to settle her affairs down there and hopefully move her back to Wilmington, at least until the virus was no longer a threat. No one could tell from the tone of the email whether this meant that Cam and Tammy were an item now, or if Cam was just being Cam, and helping someone out.

And many people were remortgaging their home to get

cash out so they could live on a boat, buy an RV, or build a cabin in the woods. Since building supplies were scarce everywhere, using refurbished or repurposed materials was becoming hugely popular. It was a heyday for any handyman with a skillset for building and a can-do attitude.

For Sunset Beach, all this meant that the price for real estate rose even higher. It drew out the people who were sitting on property and waiting for the right time to sell it. The right time was definitely now.

In New Hanover County, where Wilmington was located, there were often less than 100 homes on the market under $400,000. In Brunswick County, where Leland, Southport, Holden Beach, Ocean Isle Beach, and Sunset Beach were located, homes were bought and settled, usually with cash, inside of a month—many with no inspection required. Countywide, it was unusual for a home or a lot to stay on the market for over a week.

And now that summer was coming, and COVID was still rampant in the cities, people wanted to flee to someplace safe. For many, the beach was the number one place to go.

The island of Sunset Beach, pretty much built out when sewer lines were installed in 2012, making it unnecessary for lots to perk, there were few lots available to build on. Homeowners on the island, most of whom contracted to rent their beach houses out during the summer season, only came to stay for a few weeks during the spring to get their houses spruced up and ready to rent. Now, they were staying longer—some even opting to forego the lucrative summer rental season altogether.

The prevailing thought was, if one could work from anywhere, why not live at the beach? So the coast was the place to be. And Sunset Beach was as perfect a beach as any place on earth.

The workforce no longer needed to stay in Charlotte, Greenville, Raleigh, or Rockingham. And so they didn't. Once the strands were re-opened everyone got into their cars, drove to the beaches, and filled the beach houses.

For Brent and Alyssa, used to being isolated with no sounds of traffic on the roads, doors continually opening and closing with people calling out to one another, or loud talking on the accesses—most people arguing about the direction others should be going—it was a whole new world.

Chapter 86
Cutthroat Scrabble & the Word Pahoehoe

What started as a fun game of Scrabble, soon became cutthroat when Brent learned just how smart Alyssa was. As they played he discovered that just because English wasn't her first language, it didn't mean she didn't know the language well—very well.

The game ended with him collapsing from laughter with tears leaking from his eyes, when after a long struggle with her tiles, Alyssa finally played. Her word was PAHOEHOE. She had connected to the P he had put down for STROP. Which he had thought she would challenge him on, but she hadn't.

"Pa-hoe-hoe? What kind of word is that?"

After letting him laugh himself silly, she handed him the dictionary.

"No way."

Good-naturedly, he took the book from her and thumbed to the Ps.

The look on his face when his finger ran down the page and found the word there was priceless. It was her turn to laugh. And she did—long and loud.

"How the hell could you possibly know that word?"

She smiled over at him. "Easy. I live in a country where there are volcanoes. I am a tour guide, so I take people to them. I have to tell them all about them and lava fields are everywhere."

He read the definition: "Hardened lava with a smooth surface."

"In Italy, we have eleven fields of volcanoes. Maybe you've heard of them? Mount Sabatini? Mount Amiata? Mount Cavo? Or maybe Mount Vesuvius or Mount Etna?

They make souvenir jewelry out of *pahoehoe* all over the world. It is also called lava flow or lava stone."

He grinned over at her. "You win. The word itself is sixteen points *and* you landed on a triple letter space for an H, *and* a double word space. You beat me by 8 points. Claim your prize, Woman!"

She smiled over at him, a coy expression and big grin on her face. "I know what I want."

"Oh you do, do you?" he asked, as he crawled over the sofa to get to her.

"Yeah. What you promised when I was better. I am all better now."

He put his hand behind her neck and drew her over to him. "You're sure?" His eyes met hers, questioning that this was true.

"I'm sure."

He stood, took her by the hand, and pulled her up until she was standing. Then he lifted her into his arms. "Your room or mine? And can we take the elevator up, or must I carry you all the way up the stairs?"

"Mine. And the elevator is fine. Actually, even the sofa is fine."

He turned and looked down at the leather sofa. "You know, I believe this is a virgin sofa. We should do something about that."

"We should."

He held her in his arms over the sofa and began lowering her. When she was six inches away from the cushions, he removed his hands and dropped her. She bounced and laughed as he fished in his pocket for his wallet, flipped it open and removed a condom from behind his emergency one hundred dollar bill.

He had told her that he'd wanted to be the one to give her a baby someday. But this was not the time. Not when COVID was raging—not when he wasn't sure of her feelings for him.

He bent and kissed her as he began taking off his shirt. "I

hope you are not shy. I'm an architect, so I am stimulated by the visual. I can *envision* things, but I like to see them in the *flesh*."

"I bet you say that to all your women."

He put his knuckled finger to his chin as if thinking. "Mmm no."

"You've never said that before?"

"Nope."

"Well . . . that's probably because they're all anxious drop their panties and strip for you."

His knuckle still in place, he deadpanned, "Yes."

She laughed, then grinned and reached for his waistband. "I, too, am stimulated by the visual."

He laughed and lowered himself down to her, covering her body with his as he tossed his shirt aside.

Minutes later, after he had stripped her of her lounging pajamas and put her in the position he wanted, she had to agree; he was getting the full visual of her—and a very wicked one. She looked up at him and tried to read his facial expression. It was one of heavy desire. His eyes were focused between her legs—on her pudenda. Her knees were bent, with her hands where he had placed them, on her knees caps, pulling them apart and up toward her chest. She was wide open for his scandalous scrutiny of her womanhood.

"So hot, so very fucking hot," he murmured as his thumb stroked her slick labial lips. Holding himself over her with one arm propped near her shoulder, his eyes traveled from her generous breasts—the nipples long and hard and shiny from his many wet kisses and the deliciously torturous tugs of his lips and teeth—to her luscious, beckoning vulva with the well-manicured mons. She was perfection. His cock was hard and heavy, aching to be inside her. He let his thumb tease her clit, smiled down at her when she whimpered.

She moved a hand away from her knee and gripped his penis. Hard. It had been throbbing and jouncing, lifting toward the place it wanted to go. It was now the neediest thing on the planet.

"Aargh!"

"You sound like a pirate, she teased," as she carried the moisture she found at the tip down its length with her palm.

He sucked in a loud hiss of air. "It's definitely time to do some plundering before you get me off with you hand."

He moved to the side to get the condom he'd put on the coffee table. She watched with entranced eyes as he took it from the package and rolled it down his long, thick, hard cock. He turned back to her, his eyes smoldering.

"Do you see your target?" she quipped.

He laughed. "Yes."

His voice grew reverent. "So sexy you are. I love how you are so spirited and free with your gorgeous body."

He positioned his arms above her shoulders on the sofa and leaned in, kissed her passionately on the mouth, his sheathed cock grazing her thigh with the effort. He ended the kiss. Leaned back up and looked into her face.

"I want you to watch me enter you." He grabbed a pillow and shoved it behind her back so that she could see between them. They both watched as he placed the tip at her opening and slowly entered her.

He looked into her face and their eyes met before dropping to where they were joined and he was inching in. She was aching with want, needing him inside her. All the way inside her.

He was craving being inside her more than life. The want was both unbearable and exquisite.

Not able to reach him from this position, she could only watch as his shoulders tensed and his face grimaced with the need for restraint. Then he closed his eyes tight and plunged deep. She was shoved back again the arm of the sofa, the pillow he'd placed behind her cushioning her back from the force of his thrust. Both of them groaned, his more guttural, hers more of a whimper.

As she continued to hold herself as he'd instructed, he watched it all. Saw her breasts bounce and his penis enter and retreat from her. It was decadent and depraved, but unbelievably hot. He fought to keep from coming.

"What do you need?" he hissed out.

"My legs around you," she whispered back.

"Then do it. Do it now."

She removed her hands from her knees and lifted her legs up and over his hips—locked them behind his back and arched up and into him. Her hands, freed from holding herself open for him, caressed his chest, explored his pecs, rubbed the coarse fanned out hair, and toyed with his flat nipples. Low moans told her he liked that, so she did more, caressing his nipples between her thumbs and forefingers and gently tugging.

When he pressed into her, holding himself steady and then grinding, her hands left his chest so that she could grip his butt cheeks and hold him to her. He saw her eyes close tight in concentration while her mouth gaped open in awe. He watched as the sensation of bliss crossed over her face. He was so hard and so deep inside her that he could feel everything. The heat, the trembling, the convulsions, then the eruption . . . the total letting-go release that overcame her. Of course her loud, "Aaaahh, aaaah, aaaah," followed by a long low keening would have been a dead giveaway regardless.

He finished hard after hearing her come, gasping for breath as he plunged into her, over and over again, the violence of his body's reaction to her orgasm somehow making him race toward completing his.

When it came, he felt as if his mind left his body, careened around the universe, fell into a psychedelic cataclysm, then rejoined his body as it spasmed and shook, and he ejaculated as if emptying his soul into her core.

He collapsed on top of her, turning in the last second, to pull her off the side and not give her his full weight.

Neither said anything for a long while, both lost to their thoughts.

He finally broke the silence. Strands of her hair were stuck to his mouth so he huffed to blow it away from his lips. "That was amazing," he breathed out.

"Yeah." She sounded sad somehow.

He looked down and into her face, "You okay?"

"Mmmhmm. Yeah. We're kind of perfect together aren't we? Like a pirate and a wench having a fight to the finish. Only we both won."

He laughed. "I like your analogy. Now that you mention it, I do feel kind of shipwrecked."

"I feel . . . um . . . completed. Whole but yet, not wholesome."

He laughed again, so hard it forced him out of her. He grabbed between them as he slid from her, securing the condom. "Definitely, not wholesome."

He sat up and chuckled again. "Although experiencing earthshattering orgasms is supposed to be very healthy for the body."

He got up and walked to the powder room to dispose of the condom.

She admired his fine ass as he moved down the hall toward the "leopard room." He had a few of her nail marks on both cheeks.

When he got back she had put all her clothes back on so he did the same. Then they snuggled together at one end of the couch; her covering them both with her favorite throw. Within moments, they were both asleep.

An hour later, as Brent held her sleeping form under his outstretched arm, lightly stroking her arm, he heard the electronic lock on the front door click open. Then bags being dropped onto the tile foyer.

Rutger and Pauline were here. He had a moment of regret. He liked their life here, his and Alyssa's—alone, them getting to know each other . . . each falling in something he was slowly defining as love. But he wanted to make her happy.

And she wanted to go home. He wrote a mental note to himself: Google pahoehoe jewelry and find her something nice that would remind her of her time here at *The Cockpit*.

Chapter 87
Surprise! Rutger & Pauline Show Up

Brent gently shook Alyssa to wake her from her nap. Their amorous lovemaking, after their highly competitive Scrabble game, had wiped them both out. He had known that Rutger and Pauline were heading this way from California, but he hadn't known when they would arrive. Once darkness had settled in, he had figured they wouldn't get here until the next day. Now that he heard Rutger let himself in and trudge up the steps, he was revived. He always loved seeing his frat boys. You never knew what you'd get with Rutger, but you were always in for something fun and outrageous.

Rutger knew that Brent and Alyssa were in residence, but damn! It smelled as if Kyle was here now, too. While lifting both his and Pauline's suitcases over the threshold, he'd caught the aroma of something heavenly, and as he'd climbed the steps, he'd called out, "Kyle? When did you get here? Whatever that is, it smells delicious."

Several steps behind him, a very tired Pauline followed, lugging a flight bag. "Mmmm, yeah. It sure does," she moaned. "I'm famished."

Brent tapped Alyssa on her cheek, trying to wake her. He was thankful they had put their clothes back on before falling asleep on the sofa. "Wake up Babe, Rutger and Pauline are here. I think the aroma of your meatball stew from dinner lured them here."

The pot of meatball stew that Alyssa had made for dinner was cooling on the counter and waiting to be put way. The robust aroma from it simmering all afternoon was evident throughout the house. Smells from the kitchen tended to funnel up and down the staircases and over the years acted as a silent dinner bell when everyone was in residence. Both Rutger and Pauline were salivating by the time they made it up the steps.

Alyssa's eyelids fluttered open. "Rutger? Rutger's here?"

"Yes, and Pauline, too. They just flew into the Ocean Isle Beach Airport. They're on their way to Europe."

"Europe!"

He saw the light in her eyes, and he registered how quickly her thoughts made the connection to Italy being in Europe—where her mama and her brother were. In that moment, he knew he could not deny her this passage home.

"Yes, they are going to Europe—Switzerland and Germany, I think. And they said they *might, just might* be able to help get you home. We'll have to see. Italy is still not safe. And most of Europe isn't either."

She had nodded as if she understood his words. But from the light in her eyes, he knew that the only word she had truly focused on was *home*.

Although now that Alyssa was fully awake, and she had a moment to   think about it and process her feelings, it occurred to her, that yes she missed Mama, and yes she missed Palo. But she no longer missed Giancarlo. Not a whit. So was Italy truly her *home* now?

Brent made his way to the landing with Alyssa following behind him, calling out, "Rutger! Pauline! We're so glad you made it here safely!"

Rutger looked up and took in the two of them in their matching t-shirts and lounging pants, "Who is that stunning woman? And why do your pajamas match?"

Brent smiled down at him. Rutger knew Alyssa was in residence, but he hadn't seen her in many years. "This is Alyssa. Palo's sister."

Brent hesitated. In their many texts, he'd told Rutger that

his relationship with Alyssa was evolving into more than just friendship. But now, after having had sex with her, he realized that there would be no way to hide how they felt about each other. After tonight's stupendous lovemaking, they would both certainly want more of the same. So they might as well come clean now.

He took Alyssa's hand and pulled her over so she was standing in front of him. He bent his body so that his chin rested on her shoulder and he wrapped his arms around her waist while pulling her close. "We've . . . mmmm . . . kind of become a couple. But please don't let on to Palo. We are not quite ready to tackle that issue yet."

Rutger barked out a laugh. "Never would I have figured *you* as the one to break the code of honor between the brotherhood and their sisters." He stood there smiling; yet shaking his head. "Trust me, I won't say a thing to Palo. He's got enough to worry about right now."

He turned to address Alyssa. "Alyssa, great to see you again! We met once, when you were a teenager. The first time I went to Italy. You had braces then, I believe."

Alyssa frowned down at him. "Not my favorite years. I hated those things."

"I remember. But look at you now. You have a gorgeous smile . . . among other things," he said, his eyebrows raised as he looked knowingly at Brent and winked.

Pauline had made to the top of the staircase. While Rutger had gallantly carried all the bags, except for the flight bag Pauline had on her shoulder and her oversized purse, she appeared to be the weariest from the climb. Rutger quickly made the introductions and then Brent helped Rutger get their luggage to the elevator and then to their room.

Alyssa called out to Rutger and Pauline that she would get some dinner ready for them and they both called out grunts of appreciation.

"This is a lot of stuff, Bro, you staying for a while?" Brent asked.

"Just a day or two. Pauline's going to be flying us over the pond on Tuesday. We both have business to take care of. Hers in Switzerland and mine in Germany."

"Nice that you guys have your own plane."

"Yeah. We'd never have considered flying otherwise. It's too risky right now."

Pauline nodded. "Everything's bonkers right now. There's hardly any ground help. We had a real hard time finding a place to refuel."

"Well, get your stuff sorted. Alyssa made Pasta Primavera ala Dom DeLuise as she calls it, and what you smell is her meatball stew. Really good stuff, and there's plenty of both."

"The stew smells wonderful," Pauline said, "and thank you. We're famished."

Come down when you're ready and we'll have a cocktail first."

"Now, you're talkin' my language," Rutger said. "A bottle of Kyle's special vintage red would be much appreciated right now."

"You're very lucky we saved some then," Brent laughed. "We've been here since mid-March. It's been tempting not to drink a bottle every single night."

"This is not a bad place to be holed up in," Rutger said, smiling as he looked around, the familiarity of his room warming him. "It's always good to come *home*," he murmured and he leaned over to give Brent a big hug.

"See you in a few," Brent said as he closed the door behind him. From the looks they were giving each other, he sensed Pauline and Rutger would appreciate a few moments alone to acclimate. The word traveling through the frat boy grapevine was that he was thinking about proposing. He wondered if Rutger was waiting until they were in Germany with his family to pop the question. He figured that might be the case.

On the way down the stairs, he smiled at the thought.

They were a great couple. He remembered the day Rutger had met Pauline.

Sean had been the "chauffeur" Rutger had consigned to accompany him when Rutger had picked Pauline up from the Ocean isle Beach Airport. She had flown in from California to meet him that day—a blind date that started with an email letter—except that they were both celebrities with social media pages, and they'd shared quite a few emails before agreeing to meet, so they already knew quite a bit about each other.

Sean, and the frat boys who had been home at the time, had the pleasure of seeing Pauline topless that day as Rutger began her introduction to the D/s lifestyle. After introducing her to his friends, who had been hanging out in the kitchen, Rutger had taken her out onto the terrace where he'd fed her a meal prepared by Kyle.

They'd all watched from a discreet distance as Rutger offered Pauline world-class delicacies by hand as she knelt on a cushion beside his chair while he enjoyed getting to know his new sub. Brent remembered thinking at the time, how hot Pauline looked, kneeling at Rutger's feet, topless, and taking food so daintily from his fingertips with her lips.

Brent made a mental note to make sure he filled Alyssa in about that day. She already knew that Rutger and Pauline were a couple, and that they frequented BD/sm clubs where Rutger often did demonstrations, some including Pauline. But she might not know how their "first date" had played out right here at *The Cockpit.*

When Brent walked into the kitchen he saw Alyssa at the stove, stirring the grilled vegetables into the roasted garlic sauce she had made. The meatball stew was being warmed up in the Insta-Pot. She looked so beautiful with her hair piled on top of her head and clipped in place. It was a look he loved, messy yet elegant as wispy tendrils escaped to frame her beautiful face.

He stood behind her and pulled her in close to his body, one hand pressing on her lower belly and the other stroking along the inside of her arm while she stirred and turned over the mushrooms and eggplant, squash, tomatoes and onions.

"Smells heavenly," he murmured against her ear.

She turned and looked up at him. "Yeah, it does. I remember Papa making this during the summer, so many fresh vegetables from his garden. And momma beside him, making cavatappi on the gigantic cutting board he'd made for her as a wedding gift. She still uses it to this day."

Brent reached around her and snagged a piece of asparagus from a canapé platter, dipping the tip into a puddle of vinaigrette, then tilting his head and dropping it into his mouth. "Mmmm, that dressing is amazing." He gave her hip a squeeze. "You're a damn fine cook, I'll say that."

"Momma and Papa made it look so easy and they seemed to have so much fun together making dinner that we all, just kind of learned by their example. Papa always wanted to experiment and try new things, while Momma wanted to stick with traditional family recipes. Somehow it all worked out. Nobody ever went hungry at the Peregrini Casa." She placed the wooden hand-carved spoon in its ceramic spoon holder beside the stove.

"Well, I am happy to be the recipient of all their hard work. Hey, I need to talk to you about Rutger and Pauline. Theirs was a very unique relationship . . . right from the very beginning."

"I already know all about their first date. Palo told me. He said Rutger brought her here from the airport topless, and then fed her like his pet, kneeling beside him out on the terrace. He said they have a *Shades of Grey* thing going on. That she likes him to be in control of her, in a sexual way."

He chuckled and stroked her neck. "Boy, you and Palo sure are close."

"Well, my dad died when I was a young teenager. Palo thought it was his duty to *inform* me of things going on in the world so that I would be prepared for anything that came up."

"But *Fifty Shades of Grey*? That's pretty out there for a teenager."

"He actually gave me the books, said to read them. He said if someone came on to me in that manner, he wanted me to know what I was in for, so that I'd know how to handle myself. He has always said, the more informed you are, the better decisions you can make. If you're curious and you don't know what things are about, yet you want to . . . well, then, that's when it's easy to make the wrong decisions."

He turned her to face him as he stared into her light sienna-colored eyes with the light green glints around the black pupils. His hand cupped her cheek. "Did you ever . . . did you want . . .?" he seemed unnerved that she might be more adventurous along those lines than he was.

She chuckled and placed her hand over his where it caressed the side of her face. "No worries there. I found the books interesting, but I like the softer side of lovemaking."

She lifted her other hand and ran her fingers through a lock of his hair to sweep it back. Sometimes he had deep furrows created by his fingers digging into his thick hair and parting it unevenly. That was when his black hair that contrasted so vividly with his white streak blended the white in odd ways into the inky black—like it was shot through with white threads. She liked his white streak to stand out on its own as an emphatic accent, not to be interspersed as thin white hairs. He called it his poliosis, and preferred it would not be there at all, so he tried to keep it dyed. She had dyed it for him several times with a home kit she ordered online, but his hair grew so fast it that made its reappearance in only days, so she had finally convinced him to let it grow natural.

Her voice grew raspy. "I like how you were soft and tender as you somehow knew I needed you to be at first—then you went hard and fierce when I was a little frantic at the end."

He smiled down at her and lightly kissed her on the nose, murmuring. "I liked it when you were frantic for me."

Then he pulled back and looked down into her face, raising his eyebrows and forcing her to be honest with his eyes on hers. "You sure you don't need more . . . uh . . . manhandling?"

She smiled and sighed. "We were perfect together tonight. I *hope* there will be more opportunities for pleasure between us."

"If I have any say in the matter, there will be."

"I would like to experience your mouth on me . . . down there." The mischievous gleam of her eyes dropped down to indicate the area she was referring to. "And I want to put my mouth on you . . . there." She focused her eyes on the buttoned-up opening of his pajama bottoms.

He groaned.

"We will be perfect together again. I know it. Trust me, your *brutal* tongue lashing will be all the rough treatment I require," she said in a husky whisper.

His eyes widened and he ran his fingers through his hair again. He did it so often, she was sure he wasn't even aware of it. "The brutality will have to be on your end. Until I learn all your secrets, you can use my hair to tug me wherever you want me."

"Aahh. Then it's good thing it is growing out so fast." She smiled and dropped her hand so that she could cup him. In seconds he was hard and pressing against her hand.

They heard the hum of the elevator bringing Rutger and Pauline down.

"This will have to wait until later," she said as she gave his balls a gentle caress.

His eyes closed and his head went back. She snapped the waistband of his pants to take him out of his reverie. "I have to serve dinner to now. You can help me clean up the dishes afterward."

Chapter 88
It's Nice to Have Some Company

After Alyssa had made a salad and both entrees were ready, she set two place settings and Brent texted Rutger that dinner was ready. Rutger and Pauline settled themselves at the high counter and Brent and Alyssa kept them company while they cleaned up the kitchen.

"So what do you guys do all day? I've only been here during the summer months, when it's been warm and sunny." Rutger said.

"Well . . ." Brent began. "Let's see. Alyssa cooks and cleans, and does laundry. She makes masks she donates to the community, she listens to Podcasts, watches Tik Tok videos, she cuts my hair, and sometimes she dyes my poliosis, she orders groceries from Food Lion, and a gazillion things from Amazon. She gathers those pretty little orange flowers that are close to the dunes and floats them in bowls, sends me to Food Lion to the pick up lanes to get stuff loaded into the back of my SUV. Then I drag forty bags into the elevator and help her put things away.

"Meanwhile, I do the house finances and tend to things around the house that need fixing. And even though my project has been delayed, I still continue to do a little work on it most days. I surf, ride my bike, read.

"Together we play board games and do puzzles. We have Zoom meetings with family and friends. In the mornings, we watch the deer . . . the coyotes . . . the birds and the bats—sometimes the sunrise—almost always the sunsets. She likes to take long walks on the beach. She goes down to the Mailbox and writes in the journals. I run from here to one end of the island and back. One day we toured the whole island on bikes and then raced over the bridge. She really likes the Drifter Kyle keeps here for Amy. We keep busy. It's a big house, and there's a lot to do if you're stuck in it and have to maintain things."

He did not mention that they also liked to play pool in the game room where he would come up behind her and notch his erection into the crack of her ass when she was bent over the table. Or when he would watch her from the opposite side of the table when she bent low to make a shot and the vee of her t-shirt would gape open and reveal the upper swells of her breasts. Encased in a peach, pink, or flesh-toned demi-lace bra it was all he could do not to climb up onto the table and take her right then. Talk about a boner, he thought, as just the thought was causing him to adjust himself on the sly.

"Well, thanks for all you do to keep on top of things. Both of you," Rutger said as he speared some romaine and a cherry tomato from his salad bowl with his fork. "Good dressing," he murmured. Pauline nodded in agreement, her mouth too full to talk.

The men talked about the other frat boys, both trying to get an update on the news each had heard. Rutger had recently spoken with Cam so he shared their conversation.

"Cam went to Willow Tree to get his fifth-wheel last week. He and Tamara decided they needed to go to Ozark, Missouri to get her *grammy*. She's living in an old farmhouse in a defunct mining town with no way to get food or medicine during this COVID mess. She milks her cows and takes care of chickens, so at least she has milk and eggs. She chops wood to stay warm and to cook food. Her closest neighbor is four miles away, but they sold everything and left a month ago. It's a hard life for a woman in her seventies. So they plan on bringing her back to Wilmington to live with them. She has some health issues that need to be attended to according to Cam. I think he was hinting at some heart issues."

"Wow, he's doing a lot for a woman he picked up in a strip joint in Myrtle Beach," said Brent.

"You probably don't know the whole story. Tamara was

talked into moving to Myrtle Beach by her sleazy boyfriend, who unbeknownst to her, got her a job stripping at a men's club.

"You know how bored Cam gets with the jaunts we make him accompany us on when we go down to Myrtle Beach? After a while, Cam leaves the group and starts wandering around backstage—checking things out and snooping around the dressing rooms.

"He happens to be outside a dressing room when both the owner and her boyfriend are threatening the young girl. They tell her that if she refuses to strip for the crowd, she's out on the street. She starts crying. It does not go over well with Cam to hear her a woman in distress.

"A few minutes later, when she's shoved onto the stage, she dances her little heart out to the music, but doesn't take her clothes off. The boyfriend jumps up on the stage and rips her shirt off and pulls her bra down exposing her tits."

"Oh, I remember now," said Brent. "Cam hops up on the stage, wraps her up in his sport coat and runs out of the club with her. Then he hijacks somebody's limo and gets out of Dodge right before the boyfriend and the owner of the club run out and give chase."

"Yup. He ended up taking her to Wilmington, and he stayed there with her the whole first week of our reunion. He gave her a job dancing for one of his shows. He's told everyone that she is one of the best dancer's he's ever worked with. Tamara went on to do more shows, and last year, he helped her get set up in her own place. By then, he was madly in love with her."

"What? I thought he was gay!"

"Everybody thought that. Turns out he was just a late bloomer—a very late bloomer, according to him. There were rumors once that his dipstick didn't register very high on the testosterone scale. That testosterone never oozed from any pore might have been true once. But now . . . he's all male and primed for action."

"So now what?"

"He's hoping that RVing with her all the way to Missouri and back will kindle something between them."

"Wow. I thought he fell for that guy at Stanford, the one he was always hanging out with," Brent said. "The one who died from cancer that he named his company after."

"No, they were just good friends. Cam says he was just doing what everyone expected him to do. From his mannerisms everyone thought he was gay. So he tried to be gay. He said he tried dating a few men, but that it never felt right. He went to a few clubs and danced with guys, but he said he could not get past the hand holding and flirting stage. It felt weird, not something he was in to."

"But then he met Tamara . . ." Brent prompted.

"Yup," said Rutger. "He says she was *it* for him. He knew it that first night. Now . . . all he has to do is get her on board."

"She's not lesbian is she?"

"I don't think so. Anyway, taking this driving trip over to Missouri in a pickup truck and camping in an RV will keep them in close quarters, so that should help decide things."

Rutger used a piece of bread to sop up the last bit of sauce from his bowl. "Alyssa, this primavera is amazing stuff. You seem to have inherited your mama's touch with vegetables and pasta."

Pauline nodded, and mumbled through her last mouthful of stew, "And the meatballs! My God, they're fabulous." She pantomimed shoving the ones that were left in the serving bowl into her mouth. And they all laughed.

Rutger smiled over at her and put his hand over hers where it rested on the countertop. "Normally, she would ask you about dessert, but it's late and we're both full. Do you mind if we take the rest of this bottle and head up to bed? We're bushed." His hand was already gripping the neck of the bottle. Only a fool would have denied this athletic hulk of man the wine that remained in the bottle.

"Help yourself. Remember, it's not ours. Kyle bought it

for the house. It's for everybody."

"He's a generous soul, who definitely knows wine," Rutger said as he stood and moved to clear his dishes.

Alyssa stopped him, with a hand on his arm. "We'll take care of cleaning up. You guys get settled. We'll see you in the morning. I'll make fresh cinnamon buns."

Rutger patted his tummy. "Coming here always makes me need to re-notch my belt."

"If you feel like it, we can walk on the beach in the morning," Brent said to Rutger, "catch up a bit more."

"Sure. Despite being exhausted now, I'm usually up with the sun."

Pauline thanked Alyssa and they hugged each other. Brent and Rutger fist-bumped. "Later Bro," they said in unison.

Chapter 89
Quiet, Considerate Love Making

Like a well-oiled machine, Alyssa and Brent had the kitchen cleaned up and everything put away within minutes.

"So . . . shall we see who pulls who's hair?" Brent asked.

Alyssa laughed out loud, then quickly covered her mouth with her hand. She wasn't used to having to curb her enthusiasm, as they were not used to anyone else being here.

She poked her finger into the middle of his chest. "Whatever we do, we must be *quiet*," she whispered.

He tilted his head and looked at her with eyebrows raised. "I doubt you can do that. I've heard you . . . mmm . . . express your pleasure."

She smiled and leaned up to kiss him on the lips. "Well, forget it then," she said as she turned to make her way up the stairs.

"Wait, wait, wait. I have an idea."

She turned back and looked him up and down, "I'm listening."

Brent took her by the hand and led her up to her room. His room was too close to Rutger's for his plan to work. But her room . . . with the door closed . . . might just be ticket . . . to sexual oblivion.

Once he had them ensconced in her bedroom, with the door closed, he took her hand and led her into the en suite. He closed that door as well.

Then he lifted her up onto the onto the granite countertop and began tugging her lounging pants down.

"So . . . you have decided that I will be the one pulling your hair," she murmured. Then added, "Even so, I do not remember giving you permission to pull mine should things ever be reversed."

He gave her a devilish smile, "You think there is a chance that our places will not be reversed?"

She shrugged. Then smiled. "Maybe yes, maybe no," she said with a waggle of her hand.

"Well . . . ladies first of course."

"I am so ready to taste you." He picked up her hand and brought it to his mouth. He kissed the back of it, then turned it over and kissed her palm. "My appetizer," he whispered.

She waggled her eyebrows. "In Italy they call that *aperitivo* or piccolo antipasto."

"Trust me, there will be nothing little about what I've got in store for you later."

He pushed her so her back was up against the mirror, then stripped off her lounging pants and her panties. He stood, took her face in his hands and kissed her. His lips parted hers and his tongue delved in to dance with hers. They both groaned.

They each took their turn fencing with their tongues and savoring every part of the other's mouth. Then he pulled away, found the padded vanity stool she'd ordered from Wayfair that she'd asked him to put together.

"I knew when I assembled this that it would come in handy one day." He pulled the small bench up to the counter and made himself comfortable, his legs under the opening. Then he wrapped his hands around her ass and slid her toward him. He found her already wet and slick.

His tongue teased her lips to get her to open to him before his mouth got to work devouring her. He was like a starving wolf consuming her, lapping at her, and then demolishing her with his lips, tongue, and even the drag of his teeth.

All the while he listened for telltale signs . . . her breathing hitching, her soft moans, her repeated "aaah, ahhh, ahhhs." When he felt her fingers delving into his hair, he used firm lips to clamp around her swollen clit while he lightly sucked and flicked the little nub with his tongue.

He just managed to get the washcloth he'd placed on his knee up to her mouth in time. He heard her keen into the terrycloth muffler for a very long time, before she let out a slow hiss. He moved his hand and allowed the cloth to fall from her lips to the floor.

He'd never seen anything like it. This woman had come for what he thought was a full minute. His sense of pride puffed. Something else had also puffed—substantially.

He was long and hard, pushing his own lounging pants into a tent. The tip making a wet spot. He stood and yanked on the drawstring letting his pants droop, grabbing a condom from the pocket before he let them fall to the floor. He ripped open the wrapper and rolled it on, then pulled her off the vanity and onto his cock, wrapping her legs behind him. Then he leaned her against the nearest wall and began grinding in small circles.

He bent his knees to lower himself enough so that he could lift her by her bottom and get deeper inside her. With the fingers of each hand digging into her butt cheeks, he pressed her to him until he could rub her soft cleft along his thick ridge, and he could stroke her where he needed her and hopefully, where she might need him.

"Mmmm," she moaned, "You could take me right here. Bang me hard against this wall."

"Except that they are right down the hall . . ."

"Nothing they haven't seen or heard before."

He pulled back and looked into her face, shocked at her suggestion. "Are you saying you want to be watched or listened to?"

She covered his lips with her fingers. "I am not saying anything. Except that I want you now. Hard. Firm. Fast."

He hiked her further up, wrapping her legs even tighter around his waist and causing them both to moan. Then he walked his legs between hers to get them as close as they could possibly be to each other where they were joined.

Holding her up against the wall with his body shoved into hers, he reached down and grabbed the edges of her baggy sweatshirt and pulled it up over her head and off.

He pulled first the straps, then the cups of her bra down. The sight of her full breasts affected him as it had before; his penis jumped and throbbed, his stomach muscles tightened, and a hot drumming pulse sped through his veins. His hands cupped the firm mounds; his thumbs flicked the hard tips. Her moan, coupled with her eyes closing and her head lolling to the side, satisfied his ego.

"Can never get enough of these," he huffed as his hands pressed against the undersides lifting them, so his mouth could kiss, lap, and gently latch on. He tugged on the tips with his teeth and lips until the crests were dark, swollen, and the nipples long and hard.

He bent his knees so he could press up into her and thrust harder. He withdrew some of his length, but she was having none of that and gripped his hips hard. He felt her centering him, making his pelvis press more firmly into her, sending the hard ridge of him where she needed him most. She arched her body so she could feel his probing hardness against that most sensitive spot.

Then she joined him in a series of frantic thrusts. With ragged breaths, they tried not to bang up against the wall. She keened his name and came with him as he growled and lightly bit into the side of her neck. This time there was no muffler for either of them. Her keens turned to whimpers, while his growls turned to vile curse words.

After a few moments of being nearly comatose, he managed to carry her to the bed. He collapsed on top of her, with the leg of his soft flannels still wrapped around one ankle.

"Why do you chase me to the finish like that?" he was finally able to ask, his lips just below her ear, still attached to her neck, his breath raspy.

"I can't wait to hear the sounds you make when you

come," she teased. "It's like a roar and a grunt and a deep sigh all tangled together. Then lots of cursing."

He smiled at that. He twirled a lock of her hair around his finger as he looked down into her flushed face. "I wonder . . . are you used to lovers who don't take their time with you? So much so that you have to take what you want?"

"I've only had three. But yes, compared to you, they were far faster about . . ." she gestured with her hand circling, "the ending thing. What is it you Americans call that? The big 'O'? At least the first several times anyway, then it gets better. If they were not in a hurry to leave, the second time was always much better for me."

"It generally takes time to learn what a woman likes. With men it's easy to figure out pretty quickly what pleases them. They don't keep it a secret. With women . . . it does take some finessing. But you're different."

"How? How I am I different?" She stroked her fingers down his back, letting her nails lightly scratch his corded muscles.

"You're eager, playful—earthier."

"Earthier? What does that mean?"

"Hmmm. Lusty? Not prim. Not proper. But into it."

"Oh, I am definitely into it. You do things no one's ever done. Magical things."

"Oh yeah? Like what?"

"Mmmm . . . well, I like the way you roll your hips. And when you grind down and grip my ass, holding me tight to you, you give me time to get my head into it."

"Your head into it?"

"Yeah. I think women need to think about what's going on. Interpret it in a way that defines the meaning or the emotion."

"Such as?" His face was scrunched in confusion.

"Like when you grip me and hold us immobile for a few seconds. I imagine you're thinking, 'I need her close, as close as she can be to me.' That's a hot thought. It triggers something that tingles inside and it makes me get even wetter down there. I can actually feel myself gushing a bit when I have thoughts like that." She waved her hand over the rumpled bedcovering to where they were still joined.

"What does this do for you? What do you think I am trying to tell you right now?" he asked, as he pushed into her and she felt him jerking, his erection probing and delving deep inside her.

"I think you are telling me you have recovered. That you would like a second helping."

He smiled down at her and kissed the tip of her nose. "That must be a universal language then? This want I have for you in such an obvious way. It must be a sign that we must reapply our efforts. Me to satisfy you, before ineptly sating myself inside you."

"Why ineptly?" she asked.

"Because you already wrung me out the first time."

"So no roar? So grunt, no sigh?"

"I'll see what I can do."

He took her lips with his and closed his eyes, savoring her taste, delighting in her mouth as his tongue chased hers. He sighed.

"That's out of order," she whispered as she leaned back. He flipped them over so that now he was under her. He managed to kick off the pant leg. He wrapped his hands around her hips and sat her up, lifting her and lowering her until they had set an easy sensual pace. Their eyes met and held the whole time.

After several deep plunges and hard thrusts, he sped up, meeting her glide for glide as his thrusts became more frenzied. He backed off when he felt he was close to coming and held her to him as he came up off the bed to meet her downward slides.

Then he let her take over, to put him where she needed him. She sat up tall, leaned back, and changed the angle. He heard her groan—felt it when her channel slicked with more moisture. He reached down and used his thumb to tease her clit.

With his other hand he pinched a nipple. She gasped, threw her head back and he felt her come . . . watched her shatter.

Her eyes were closed to the ecstasy, her hands forced open and frozen in place at her sides as if anything moving would detract from the pleasure. She was like a beautiful open-mouthed statue, her neck thrown back, part of her long hair escaping her hair clip and cascading down her back, her breasts jutting out, the nipples hard peaks. Nothing moved on the outside. But on the inside, he felt every tremor as her vagina contracted and released in a spasmodic rhythm while her clit throbbed with a steady thumping pulse under his thumb. It was glorious to watch. Commanding to have caused it all to happen.

He could not say how long it took for her body to begin to soften and to collapse in on itself. But when she fell forward onto his chest and he felt her tears of release, her body melting into his in utter replete happiness, he knew the moment he fell in love with her.

Complete, and with total abandon, he tumbled and fell. With no care whatsoever that he was still inside her, well on his way to his own satisfaction, he joined the ranks of the love-struck.

She raised her head, opened her eyes and smiled. He was toast.

After a few quiet moments, where he could hear the sound of a gull screeching as it flew over the house, she breathed out, "That was a-maz-ing! I feel all jiggly and loose inside."

"I kinda do, too," he mumbled, as he tucked an errant curl behind her ear.

The revelation of his intense feelings for her had taken the edge off his erection and made him soft. He felt himself slide out of her.

"Oh no!" she cried, "I forgot all about you."

"I am completely satisfied to stay just like this."

She started working her way down his body. "Well, you do that. I've got this."

And before he knew what she was up to she had done away with the condom and wrapped her lips around him, and was drawing him into her warm mouth.

Her stared up at the tray ceiling, remembering the day he had installed the fan right above his head as well as all the others in the house. He would never have imagined in that day, that he would fall in love with a woman from Italy, in what was technically Alex's bedroom, in his beloved beach house, during a pandemic, with one of his fraternity brother's sisters, who was now between his legs, her soft hair caressing his thighs while she sucked him off.

He closed his eyes, hissed softly between his teeth, grunted, barked out a growl, and then roared. When she crawled up over him to settle snuggled into his side, his arm wrapped around her, and he sighed. Life was good . . . at the beach . . . in this beach house . . . with Alyssa in his arms.

Chapter 90
Are They the Classic Cabin Trope?

He had forgotten that Rutger and Pauline were in the house until Alyssa had untangled herself from him and hopped out of bed. They had slept with her in the crook of his arm, her legs thrown over his. He had to massage his shoulder to get it working again. Still . . . it had been nice, waking up with her there.

"I have to get up! Rutger and Pauline are going to want breakfast!"

They had probably been doing something along the same lines that they had been doing last night—maybe with chains or blindfolds—so they were likely still sleeping themselves.

"You don't have to serve them. They are not guests. This is his house too. He knows where everything is and he can make them breakfast. Come back to bed." He gestured with a crooked finger as he sat propped up against a pillow while she rummaged through the dresser for something to wear.

She stared at him with googly eyes. "You do not know what it means to be Italian. Come, get up," she came over and tugged on his arm. Not able to budge him so much as an inch as he quirked a brow at her.

"*We* must fix breakfast. It's the right thing to do. Also, I am excited to do it. We never have guests!"

"I told you, he is not a guest. He owns this house, too."

"I know that. But they are traveling. And I want to do this for them. And I am Italian. I have no choice in the matter. I would dishonor Mama if I did not prepare food for them. Now come. You only need to help with cutting up fruit and the bread toasting."

Reluctantly he shoved off the sheet, showing off muscular

thighs and legs covered with dark hair. "Okay, okay. I suppose breakfast with friends will be something to look forward to. We've been the only ones here for a long time now."

"Yes! I need a girlfriend to talk to!"

"Well, don't delve too deeply into their relationship. I have no idea how temporary this may be with them."

"He seems smitten."

He looked over at her as he pulled his lounging pants on. "Smitten? How does one look smitten?"

"He smiles a lot, and looks at her like she's a delicious tiramisu with candied violettas on the side. He looks hungry for her." She waggled her eyebrows. "You are looking a bit smitten as well . . . what is your favorite dessert?"

"Lemon meringue pie," he said without having to think about it.

"Ah," she smacked his arm as she walked by. "You like it tart. *And* sweet. I can be like that."

He smiled as he swatted her butt. "You are like that. Deliciously tart sweet. And *very* sexy."

She bent over, ruffled her hair up, and then caught it all up in a scrunchie she pulled from her wrist as she walked down the hall in front of him.

"What are we having?"

"I took a breakfast casserole I made last month out of the freezer last night. It is my mama's recipe. It will go well with some fresh fruit. You start the coffee. And we must have mimosas! Do we have any more of that buono La Marca Prosecco? It will be perfect, I think."

She turned to go down the steps and he followed.

"A case was delivered last week. Your brother has been very generous. He must miss you."

"I must call him tomorrow. It's been a few days since I have talked with him."

"Are you going to tell him about us?"

She looked over her shoulder at him. "What do you think?

I am not sure . . ." She was clearly conflicted by the look on her face.

"I vote no. Not ready for that showdown yet."

"*Pollo. Avere paura.*"

"You know I don't know what that means . . ." his voice always lowered when he was chastising her for speaking in her native tongue. Although he didn't really mind it—the way she spoke the language was lyrical and he could just imagine her talented tongue curling inside her mouth as she formed the words.

"*Pollo* means chicken. *Avere paura* means you have fear."

"Yes, I have fear. Who wouldn't? He's what 6-4? I'm 5-9 1/2. And you know he's not going to be happy about this."

"He was not so happy about Giancarlo either."

"No big brother wants anyone screwing his sister."

"In Italy we call it *fottere.*"

They were on the bottom step now. He wrapped his fingers around the back of her neck and bent to kiss her cheek, "Well, if he saw what you were doing last night, he'd wring my neck like a little *pollo.*"

She threw her head back and laughed. He felt his body flush with pleasure. What was this woman doing to him? Making him deliriously happy, that's what, he told himself.

Once in the kitchen, they started pulling things from the refrigerator. The counter was covered with green bags filled with fruit, as they both began working on their project.

"Seriously, *will* he be angry, do you think?" she asked.

Brent chuckled. "Oh yeah."

She thought about that as she put the casserole on the counter and preheated the oven, then pulled out a fruit platter. "Why do you say that? I know that he likes you."

"It's not the same when it's your sister."

Rutger walked into the room, wearing a smile and loud plaid pajama pants with a long sleeved black t-shirt that read: ZOMBIES EAT BRAINS, YOU'RE SAFE.

"No, no it's not," he added, joining the conversation. "Sisters are off limits." He opened the fridge, took out a bottle of water and chugged it. Wiping his lips on the sleeve of his shirt, he pointed the empty bottle at Brent. "You in BIG trouble, Kemosabe."

Then he elbowed Brent in the shoulder, "However . . . he should know what is likely to happen when two people are thrown together during a crisis."

Pauline came into the kitchen, saw that they were preparing breakfast and offered to help. Having spent time on the steps re-tying the laces on her running shoes, she joined the conversation, "Actually . . . what you're talking about . . . two people hooking up after a sustained time together alone, is very common. It even has its own trope."

"Trope?" asked Alyssa, "I am not familiar with that word."

"Well, I'm not sure what it used to mean, but its colloquial definition has its roots in literature and rhetorical devices. It means it's a very popular theme in romance novels."

Alyssa looked over at Rutger, "Isn't she a bit too classy for you? Colloquial? Rhetorical? I still don't know what she means."

Rutger smiled and pulled Pauline in close to his chest. "I like my girls ridiculously smart. I hit the jackpot with her. Sometimes I even listen and nod when I don't know what the hell she's talking about."

Pauline laughed and touched Alyssa on the arm, "Okay, try this explanation. There are themes romance stories are built around—a way for people to meet, and then the reason for them to keep connecting during the story. Some popular hooks are The Billionaire's Baby, where a woman unknowing sleeps with a billionaire and then three months later discovers she's pregnant with his baby and that he's a billionaire, and often she happens to be the type of girl who wants a simple life—to live off the grid or something—while he jet sets around the world. As we all know, opposites attract.

"One of my favorite tropes or themes is the Blind Date

scenario. And I adore the Secretary and Her Boss books. There are over a hundred story plotlines in the romance genre—Friends to Lovers, Girl Next Door, Holiday Romance, Marriage of Convenience, Identical Twin Swap, and Wedding Date. A trope you're probably familiar with is The Beauty and the Beast story.

The one Rutger is referring to is a pretty popular storyline called The Cabin Trope or The Stuck Together Trope. It's about forced proximity, where the hero and heroine are trapped in a snowed-in cabin during a blizzard and forced to be together day and night. Whether they're enemies or acquaintances or complete strangers, let the drama begin! Ostensibly, their motive will be to get out of the situation at hand. But, as time progresses, they get to know one another and they begin to like what they see. And so . . ." she pointed between Alyssa and Brent, "they begin to enjoy each others' company . . . as they let the rest of the world begin to fade away."

She took a sip of the mimosa Brent handed her before continuing; "Sandra Brown wrote one that's pretty much a classic now, *Send No Flowers*. But in my opinion the best one ever was Judith McNaught's *Perfect*. The movie with Claudette Colbert and Clark Gable, *It Happened One Night*, was also a classic cabin trope. My, this is really good."

Alyssa blinked, having tried to take all this in. She looked over to Brent and smiled, "So, we're a trope."

He smiled back and lifted his glass to her. "And we'll be a famous one when Palo discovers it and pummels me to death."

"Well, I have a theory," Rutger offered.

"Well, let's hear it. I don't know if you can top Pauline's though."

"So . . . let's say you are living confined, cabin-ed up such as you are," he waved his champagne glass around to encompass their surroundings, which were clearly not cabin-like in any way.

"Palo knows this. He likes you both, and would want you to be helpmates to each other during these trying times. He's a smart man; he knows how these things of forced proximity can go. He loves Alyssa and thinks she is a good woman who could use a good man in her life. He loves Brent and knows that he is a good man. What better way for them to meet and get to know each other than to be holed up in his beautiful beach house? So even though he didn't plan this, his brain thinks . . . *hmmm, this could work. Two people I love finding each other. I* think he would be happy about this." He gestured with his glass again to encompass them both.

"Ahhh . . . he didn't arrange it, but maybe if he could have . . . he would have . . .," Pauline said, then added, "I like that!"

Alyssa and Brent looked at each other. Brent was the first to speak.

"Well, he *does* like me. I think I am his favorite frat boy."

"He does like you, but *Kyle* is everyone's favorite frat boy."

"Good point. Gotta go with the food and wine procurer."

But then Rutger had to throw a wrench in, "Although he has seen you in ménage situations, on many occasions. That could be strike against you."

"What is this ménage?" Alyssa asked.

"Oops. That was thoughtless of me," Rutger looked abashed. He actually flushed with color at the gaff.

Pauline, taking the awkward situation in hand, wrapped her arm around Alyssa's shoulders and pulled her out of the room and into the family room.

"Good going, Bro," Brent said with a snide look, brows raised in Rutgers direction when they were out of earshot.

"Sorry. Pauline and I have such an open relationship, I just didn't think before the words came out. I was picturing you and Chaz with those volleyball twins on the coach's pool table."

Brent snapped his head back and his eyes closed tight at the memory. "Yeah, not our finest moment."

"Leaving used condoms in all the leather-fringed pockets for his wife to clean up capped it. We could have used you two in our last game instead of you guys being off the team.

We lost you know."

"Don't remind me," he sighed deeply, the air coming out in slow, pained exhale. "I'd better go talk to Alyssa."

"Pauline can handle it, she has a special way about her. I've seen her handle truly despondent runners who couldn't finish a race, ones who got badly hurt, and ones who lost their sponsors over stupid comments they made. From the beginning, she insisted we share our pasts with each other. She said we'd get it all out then go forward from there, not regretting anything and not letting it define who we were together."

"So define what you are together. This is serious?"

"Yeah. This is it for me. I ain't ever lettin' this woman go."

"Wow. That was pretty fast, for you. I thought you'd be riding out this dominant gig for those huge fees for a lot longer than this."

"Yeah. But when you know, you know. And I know. She's it."

"Hmm," Brent said as he poured out mimosas for them. Then he checked the casserole for doneness. It was perfect, and the timer was about to go off for the all the bread he'd toasted.

"Breakfast is ready!" he called out. Then sotto voce, he leaned Rutgers's way and asked, "This sudden trip to Europe have an ulterior purpose then, other than business?"

"Mmm, yeah. I have to see my grandmother in Switzerland."

"She ill?"

"No, but she always told me that she wanted me to give her engagement ring to my bride when the time came."

The timer went off and Brent pulled everything out from the oven.

"It's that serious then?"

They could hear the girls getting up and returning from the family room.

"We'll talk later, but yeah. I'm ready. And I want to start a family. This virus has made me realize what really matters, and it's not work. It's family."

Brent nodded. He realized he hadn't seen his parents since Christmas. He missed them even though he talked to them several times a week and even Face-timed with them on the occasions when his father was home from golfing and his mom was home from playing tennis. A few times when they had other family visiting they had Zoom parties, where he could watch someone blow out candles on a birthday cake and wish them well.

"Don't say anything to Alyssa. You know how girls talk. I want this to be a surprise. I'm going to show her my hometown from a hot air balloon and then pop the question. The Zugspitze in the background should make it memorable."

"Just don't drop the ring in the snow below, *that* would make it memorable."

"Had to put that awful thought in my mind, didn't you?"

Brent chuckled as he took the bowl of fruit Alyssa had prepared from the refrigerator and placed it on the counter. Alyssa came around the island just then to test the casserole to make sure it was done.

"Perfetto!" she proclaimed and they all found seats at the high counter.

When they were all seated, Rutger took Pauline's hand, kissed the back of it, then blessed the food for them. "Lord, thank you for this food prepared by loving hands, our safe trip here to be with friends, and the promise of a better tomorrow for all our loved ones all over the world. In Jesus name we pray." And they all said, "Amen."

Brent took Alyssa's hand under the countertop, and squeezed it tight. Then he added, "And thank you for divine providence and our very own cabin trope right here at *The Cockpit.*"

They all laughed and chowed down on the wonderful breakfast and then they all agreed that they'd stay up late and play a game of Mille Borne.

Chapter 91
Both Brent & Rutger are Mooney-eyed

Early the next morning, just as the sun was beginning to rise over the ocean, Brent and Rutger took a walk along the beach, heading toward Tubbs Inlet and Ocean Isle. Rutger and Pauline were planning on leaving the next day to fly to Myrtle Beach International Airport for a larger plane, and then from there, on to Frankfurt.

They continued to update each other on what they knew about the other Cockpit owners, their wives, and their families. Then Brent told Rutger about leaving New York, driving to *The Cockpit*, and finding it occupied by Palo's beautiful sister, later discovering that she was pregnant by reading her message in a Kindred Spirit notebook, and then having to have Palo translate it for him. He told him about helping her through the horror of her miscarriage, and then the teasing and fun ribbing that had lead up to their making love that first time . . . and later him realizing that he was falling in love with her.

"It's odd how that happens," Rutger said, his hands in the pockets of his chinos as he walked alongside Brent in the hard-packed sand at the water's edge.

"It happened to me at a park not far from her condo near Coronado. She was running late due to the bad weather in Chicago, and the heavy air traffic expected in San Diego, so I decided to walk to the park and do a few laps around the track. My foot has healed just fine, but it still needs strengthening, so I try to walk both forward and backward for a mile or two whenever I can, to stretch out the ankle.

"Well here I am, going into the park and this man and woman are on the path in front of me, walking toward me. He's got his arm possessively hooked in hers and his other hand sealing the connection. It was a very possessive hold, tender but assertive. I noticed it tighten as I approached. Then I noticed her. She was beautiful—exotic looking with lots of long dark hair, and dazzling green eyes. And she was pregnant, very much so. She wore some kind of stretchy yellow top that was stretched to its limits by her huge tits and swollen belly. It was practically see-thru because the fabric had been pulled so thin. I could clearly define every curve, every swell. I could see her dark nipples that were the size of half dollars, the nipples as long and as hard as pencil erasers. I mean really, she might as well have been wearing nothing.

"But it was the look on the man's face that jolted me. He was unabashedly proud. He gave me a slight nod and smiled as he continued to parade her by me. And I knew, I knew exactly what he was feeling—what he was saying. *This is mine. I own this. You can look at it. You can admire it. But you cannot have it. It is mine. All mine.*

"I remember I almost stumbled as they passed me. It was the way I had felt every time I had taken Pauline to a sex club and displayed her for other men to see. My cock got poker-hard watching other men look at her while we acted out scenes in all the different club salons. I watched the glints in their eyes as they studied her while I fingered her. All the while, she lay naked, her passion building on a velvet-covered Victorian settee because she trusted me. She knew that even while I was displaying her, I was protecting her. Under a fancy crystal chandelier that sent tiny rainbow prisms over the walls of the room, she would climax as they watched my fingers move between her legs, drawing up moisture from her slit and circling her clit with the pad of my thumb over and over until she came.

"I recall the feeling I had when she was on all fours on a bed in a mirrored room as I slammed into her ass while a line of men stood not ten feet away watching, as her tits bounced and I pinched them. They watched as she came and then I came, often showing evidence of spent passion by spilling my jizz all over her back.

"I *had* that feeling. That proud, boastful feeling of showing off what I owned. What belonged to me, that no other man could have—the woman who would do my bidding, no matter what I asked of her—no matter who was around to see. She was submissive to me—completely submissive to a man just as she had secretly longed to be so for so many years. And that man was me. I was proud—exactly as this man was. We were both proud of the woman on our arm—his very pregnant with his child, and displaying her fertile womanhood out in public, and confirming for all to see that he was virile; that she was doing his bidding, and that he owned her. She was his possession.

"In that moment, I knew I loved Pauline like this man loved his woman. And I also knew that I no longer had the desire or the need to show her off. Unless she needs it for herself in the future, I am perfectly fine keeping her all to myself. So, making her mine by proclaiming to the world that I want her beside me for all time is now paramount. I want her as my wife and the mother of my children, if we are so blessed."

There was silence for a few moments as they walked and Brent took in Rutgers's proclamation and the intensity he saw in the set of his jaw.

"Wow, you're all grown up! Welcome to the world of the strait-laced." He smacked Rutger's arm. "You're a fuddy-duddy old man now!"

"Well . . . I want to be somebody's 'old man' now, and that's saying something."

"I think it's great! I love that you're so happy."

Rutgers smiled over at him, a sheepish grin on his face, "Really, you don't think I'm crazy or stupid, or just mooney-eyed over a woman?"

"Oh yeah, I think all that. But it fits, you know. I can see that you're happy. And you two are perfect together."

"Yeah. Yeah, we are."

"Then go find that ring and seal the deal." He put out

his hand.

Rutger reached out and shook Brent's outstretched hand and pulled him into a hug.

"Best man?" he asked as they pulled apart.

"You bet! Anywhere. Anytime."

"I love you, Bro."

"What 'til the guys hear about this."

"Yeah, quite a few were there when I met her."

"Y-y-yeah . . . topless in the *Cockpit's* kitchen."

Rutger smiled, and then huffed out a laugh. "I don't think I'll have any trouble getting Kyle on board to cater the wedding. He *really* liked her tits as I recall."

"He did. He's mentioned them quite a few times—every time her name is mentioned in fact."

"Well, he'll have to get over it. She's mine."

They had reached the inlet and turned to walk back, now they were within sight of the beach house. They could see the two women they loved on the terrace off the kitchen, waving at them.

They waved back and increased their pace. "We're gonna be pussy whipped," said Brent.

Rutger grinned broadly, and said, "Yeah. I'm looking forward to it."

Chapter 92
Alyssa is the Perfect Hostess

Having taken some time on her own to walk on the beach and look out at the ocean, Alyssa ran many things through her mind. The dunes, now resplendent with glorious color as the sun was up and shining on the sea grass, were so beautiful it made her heart ache.

She pressed her fingertips to her lips and watched as the sun rose in infinitesimal increments, knowing that in Italy, it would soon be setting. If she returned to live in Italy, she'd miss Brent. And if she was honest with her herself, she had to admit that she'd miss him with more of an ache in her heart than she now held for her family. So instead of being here and pining for Mama and Palo, she'd be there pining for Brent.

Maybe she could go home for a visit and then come back. Would Brent want her to come back? She hated the uncertainty of her life right now. COVID was making it hard to plan things out. And she was one who liked to plan things from beginning to end. There was no such thing as each new day being a blank page . . . in her book. In her book, each day already had something written on it, often many things were written on it.

But from the moment when she had stood all alone, in a busy New York City airport, one that was filling with up with people just like her who were all learning that their plans and lives had just been changed in ways that they could never have imagined, she had had one goal on her mind: to get back home to her family—to her life—to her home. Now she was concerned about one very scary thing. That she did not know her own mind anymore. Yes, COVID had taught her that there were some things that she could not control. But had it also shown her that maybe she had tried to control too much? Yes . . . maybe she had.

She turned back to the ocean, saw the morning walkers collecting their things and beginning to walk up the beach. It was moving toward mid-morning. She had noticed a daily pattern on the beach since the weather had turned nice. Now was the time for the dog walkers and bike riders, and parents and grandparents pushing strollers. Soon, there would be a lunchtime crowd, then an early afternoon one, then late-afternoon people who would bring food and drinks and stay through the dinner hour, then it would be evening and photographers would gather to capture the sunset, then dusk would filter in and people would trickle away. All would be social distancing, walking many feet apart, or sitting in large circles. Then full dark would settle in and the strand would be desolate, with only a few sparse stragglers remaining. Some would have telescopes, others flashlights for ghost crabbing. Another night of sheltering in place would be ahead of them. Everyone was still sheltering in place—out of an abundance of caution—the latest catchwords.

She walked back up the access to *The Cockpit's* backyard, waved up to Pauline who was standing outside on the deck off her bedroom. It would soon be time to serve lunch. And she had offered to do Pauline and Rutger's laundry for them as the hotels they'd been staying at had closed all their laundry facilities. She was happy to help in any way she could. They were good people. She forced herself to walk with a more uplifted gait.

Distracted as she was with everything going on, she could not ignore years of training from Palo and ingrained behavior learned from Mama. She was helpful. She was a good friend. She was a good host. Even though *The Cockpit* was not her house, she felt she was Palo's ambassador. Although, in this case—maybe the maid. But she really did not mind.

Chapter 93
Alyssa Gets to go Home

When Rutger and Brent got back to the beach house and had climbed the back stairs to the terrace, it was clearly obvious by Alyssa's huge grin and the fact that she was close to jumping up and down without leaving the floor that she had news.

"Guess what?" she asked as she leapt into Brent's arms and hugged him around the neck. Looking over her shoulder he could see she had kicked up one of her claw-footed bear slippers and now the pink shaggy fur was catching the breeze.

He pulled back and smiled down at her.

"What?" There was no telling what had set her off. It could be something as simple as a perfect banana with no blemish that peeled like a charm, or something as complicated as a sixteen-step soufflé turning out nice and tall and sitting on the counter waiting for them to devour it.

"Pauline said I could go with them to Europe, that they would drop me off in Italy at the Florence Airport! I can go home!"

He blinked and stood stock-still. The fact that she could go home had been on his mind. The *would* she go home if she could, had been too. He had been the one to call Rutger in the first place . . . to maybe suggest it. But they were still in the middle of a pandemic. They were supposed to be stuck here together for a long time, at least until a vaccine was developed and approved.

That she would leave him and go home to Italy felt like the worst idea ever. He didn't know what to say. Especially in light of her buoyant bouncing as her ursine-clad feet hit the floor of the terrace and she bounced on her toes. Clearly, the thought of her leaving him had brought not a moment of dismay into her charming little curly-haired head.

He said the only word he could form, "Home?" Even to him his voice sounded foreign. As if he'd never said that exact word.

Her eyes met his and she stopped bouncing. The implications piling up and falling over like dominoes toppling and running through her mind as if everything was just now occurring to her, was evident by the wide-eyed fear that had replaced the insane giddiness of just a moment before.

He took in a deep breath, somewhat appeased that she had at least realized the ramifications of this new plan. She would be leaving him—possibly forever.

In front of him and to the side, he could see Pauline and Rutger tense up. Rutger gave Pauline a look that clearly said, *we should have talked this over . . ..*

"That's great! I am happy for you," he managed to choke out.

He saw Alyssa's eyes fill with tears. Clearly she was torn. He rubbed his hands along her forearms, trying to send some comfort as his eyes searched hers.

He knew what he had to say. His tongue tripped as he forced the words out, "You go home, to your mama and Palo. I know you miss them."

His words were generous, but the hurt in his eyes dissipated all her former happiness. She was crying now, her hands breaking free from his so that she could cover her face. She fell into his chest and sobbed. His arms wrapped around her and he gently began stroking her back. As if he was the one who had to hold them steady, while his own heart was breaking.

Rutger led Pauline away and he heard them open the door and go inside the house.

Her bawling was wetting his shirt. Yet he could have stood there forever holding her like this if the alternative was to let her go.

"It's okay," he murmured. "I knew you'd have to go home

to Italy someday. I just didn't think it would be now." Although he had been to one to arrange it, hadn't he? He could have kicked himself.

He took a handkerchief from his pocket and lifted her chin so he could see her face. He began to gently wipe the tears from her cheeks. He smiled at her. "I thought we had all the time in the world, here in *The Cockpit*, safe and protected from the virus . . . being together, just you and I." Fifteen minutes ago he would have added, falling in love. But now didn't seem to be the time to declare his feelings. She obviously didn't feel as he did.

Chapter 94
Doing Laundry as Part of Touring

Brent stood watching Alyssa sort and flip clothes into the machines, pop in a detergent pod, close the doors, press a series of buttons, and then turn to rapidly fold what she'd taken from the dryer.

"Wow, you look like you do laundry for a living."

She frowned, "Well . . . I kind of do."

He quirked a brow as if questioning that.

"Our tour clients expect the hotels to do their laundry. Hardly any of them actually *do* laundry on site, as there just isn't room for the machines or the availability of extra water or electricity in most places. I get the concierge to collect the clothes for me, and then I take them to an automat and do it for them. At no charge of course, per Palo's orders."

Brent smiled, "It's why he gets the big bucks for his tours. Customer service is everything in that business."

"Don't I know it."

"You miss doing the tours, don't you?"

She thought for a moment before answering. "I miss being out and about. And I miss meeting all the people and hearing all their stories about their lives back home."

"How are your videos going?"

She smiled over at him. "Good. Except Palo asked about the last one in a text. In the last video I recommended using a sugar-based paste wax instead of the cold strips for a bikini waxing and buying a small slow cooker if you can't afford a specialty wax melting pot. He commented: "And why do you need to do this now?"

Brent laughed. "Uh oh."

"I am getting a lot of hits now. That one got a lot of

responses. But people seem to like the cooking and sewing ones the best."

"I saw the one you did on Your Freezer is Your Friend, about making double batches of casseroles and soups. You're becoming quite the influencer. You seem to have a solid list of followers."

"I wouldn't think you'd have time to watch them."

"Well . . . the hospital *is* off the table right now."

"Oh yeah."

She turned from where she'd been matching socks on the counter, her face all lit up. She put her hands on his chest and took a deep breath. "Can't you go with us?"

"I can't live in Italy. My work is here. In New York, when all of this mess is over."

"No, I mean can't you go with *me*, and then come back?"

He thought for a minute. "Maybe. It would be up to Pauline if she can fit me in. But it could only be a short visit for me—maybe a week or two. I can't stay much longer than that; I have to be ready as soon as we can start building. We're looking at early June for groundbreaking now. You will want to stay there once you get back as I know it's your home, and then I will have to leave *you*. I don't know which would be worse, you leaving me or me leaving you. If I went with you, would you come back with me?"

His face had gone from open and friendly to closed and pensive as he waited for her answer, his teeth sunk into the side of his bottom lip, waiting for her answer.

"I think I might like coming back, if that would be something you would want me to do."

"More than anything in the world," he whispered as he reached for her and wrapped his arms around her. He repeated it into her ear. "More than anything in the world."

Chapter 95
Maestro Stuck in Adagio

He helped her take the laundry upstairs. In the elevator, he asked, "So there *is* a chance you won't want to stay in Italy? Even though that's where your job is."

"I only want to see my family. And there is no job right now to be worried about. Everything is shut down. As long as there is no commercial flying there are no tourists. But I don't want to give you up. I want to be with you." Her eyes were glistening with unshed tears, but she managed a small smile. "You said that day that you'd give me a baby. Did you mean it?"

He tilted his head to the side, studying her. "What are you saying, or asking, exactly?"

"In Italy it is the man who orchestrates a love affair, right now you are a *maestro* stuck in *adagio*. We have passed the crescendo, if you want me to come back, you should declare yourself."

He grinned broadly, "I am a slow conductor, eh?"

"A little more *allegretto* would be nice," she gave him a tentative smile.

"Okay. How about I join you on this trip? Then we come back. In the meantime, we can work on this baby if that is what you want. The thought of you leaving, and never coming back has pushed me into *Allegro*."

Her eyes went wide. "You are serious? A baby? You and me together?"

He nodded and smiled down at her as he twirled a lock of her hair around his finger. In that moment, he knew he would give her as many babies as she wanted just to keep her.

"Let's go upstairs and pack. The sooner we get there, the sooner we can come back and begin our project."

She flashed him her biggest smile. "I am already packed. My suitcase is on the landing."

His face fell. "You *were* leaving me then." The low monotone of his voice conveyed his utter disappointment. It had been her aim to just walk away and leave him—after all they had been to each other.

She put a hand on each side of his face, cupped his jaw, and then scratched his two-day beard with her fingernails. "I did not pack all of my things."

She looked down at her feet. "I was even planning on leaving Yogi and Boo Boo here for when I returned."

He put his hands over hers and together they both looked down at her slipper-covered feet. "Well, if you were willing to leave Yogi and Boo Boo, then I suppose you *did* mean to come back here."

"Well, not necessarily here—but to you. Wherever you are, that is where I want to be—that is, if you want me to be there."

He took both of her hands in his and kissed along her fingertips, then turned them over to adoringly cover her wrists with his lips. "I will always want you to be there—whether it's here or in New York. Never leave me, Alyssa I couldn't stand it."

He took her hand in his and together they left the elevator and walked down the hall. They left the hamper of clean clothes on the floor by the door that still had Rutger's picture attached to it.

They took the stairs back down to the kitchen. "What time is this flight supposed to be?" he asked. At the landing he looked down and saw her suitcase in the foyer. Only her carryon he noted, not the big, big case.

"Pauline said a Lyft was coming tomorrow at noon to take them to Myrtle Beach Airport where a bigger plane would be waiting. She's decided to leave her plane here at the Ocean Isle airport for the return to San Diego. She said she doesn't want to take hers across the *Pond* with the lack of ground crew workers. Hers only holds enough petrol to get to London, not Germany or Italy." She poured them each a glass of iced tea and they each fixed theirs to their liking. Hers with sugar and lemon, his with some stevia. She took some chocolate chip cookies she'd made from the pantry and they each ate two.

He looked at his watch. It was mid-afternoon. "We have plenty of time."

"Time for what?" she asked as she walked down the hall, her drink in hand. She grabbed the newel at the bottom of the stairs and looked back at him. She saw he had followed her so she started climbing the steps up toward her room. He continued to follow.

"Our little project," he said, his eyebrows doing a Groucho Marx imitation when she turned to look at him.

She laughed and the sound enchanted him. He would have to man up and tell her how much he loved her, and then put a ring on her finger before the baby came. It had already been a crazy year, and it was getting even crazier by the minute. But the thought of securing her to him forever made him happier than he could ever remember being.

Pauline came down the hall carrying a flight bag on her shoulder and pulling a suitcase just as they made it to the top of the stairs. "So I assume he's coming?" she asked.

"I will be soon," he quipped.

She put her bag down and put her hand on her hip. "I mean to Italy?"

"Yes," he said simply.

"You have your passport?"

"Yes."

"Good. I hate when I have to do a smuggling act. Rutger said he'd get the checklist and do the house check while you pack."

"Good. How long are we going to be gone?"

"Nine days. Pack extra masks and sanitizer, and some folded up TP. Most places are out of it and the last two planes I leased didn't even have any in the bathrooms."

Pauline worked the wheels of her suitcase around them as Alyssa started toward her room.

He leaned toward her and whispered, "How'd you know I'd be going?"

"Are you kidding? You wear it all over your face. You're stone in love with her."

Brent stepped back and blanched. "It's that obvious?"

Pauline laughed. "Well, I've only met you one other time. But I don't remember you being all lit up from the inside out. And the way your eyes follow her whenever she leaves the room, it's like a watching a border collie herding sheep."

"Nice," he said, clearly not meaning it and taking it for an insult rather then the compliment intended.

"Yeah, well the way I understand it, you'd better have a game plan by the time you get to her mama's house. Unless you plan on sleeping with Palo in the tree house, while Trixie sleeps with Alyssa all next week."

"I'll come up with something."

She patted him on the arm. "Love's like being in a tidal pool. One minute you're fine, the next minute you're swept into a current you have no chance of fighting. Welcome to the club."

She eased around him, "Really nice house you built here."

He stood staring after her as she effortlessly moved around him and down the staircase. She placed her luggage next to Alyssa's. He could hardly reconcile her to the shy, topless woman he'd met here last July when Rutger had brought her to *The Cockpit* and displayed her to five of his best friends. Rutger's hands had gripped hers behind her back to keep her from covering herself when she was introduced to Kyle and she instantly recognized him as the world famous chef she adored. She had flushed a deep red from the tops of her breasts up to her hairline. She had been lovely—the scene sexy as all get out.

She had been a new submissive then, as Rutger had required her to be. But this woman, who was going to command her own jetliner and fly them to Europe, was anything but submissive right now. She was confidant, assertive, and completely in charge. Despite him knowing that she had the mighty warrior Rutger wrapped around her little finger, he knew she would remain obedient to Rutger, even after Rutger got down on one knee and proposed.

Love was crazy--and so very different for each person. He was a goner though, just as Rutger was. Here he was, getting ready to walk into a bedroom, and for the very first time ever, with the idea of impregnating a woman. When he stopped to ask himself why, he was honest. He loved her and he wanted to give her what she wanted more than anything else. And what was it that *he* wanted? He just wanted her. Oh, he would love being a daddy to a cute little ballerina or tiny little surfer dude. But his main purpose was to keep her—to make her happy. This was the way he thought he could do that.

When he walked into her bedroom and saw her splayed naked on the king-sized bed, her hair a riot of curls tumbled around her pillow, her arms spread wide beside her head, with one foot bent and positioned alongside the opposite knee, teasing him with a glimpse of her femininity, and showing him how readily accessible she was, he was humbled. The only things she was still wearing were Yogi and Boo Boo.

This beautiful, sweet, funny woman wanted to have his baby. He looked at his watch and calculated everything he had to do before it was time to help her with dinner. He was an organized person, and a fast packer. He figured he had an hour to do his damnedest. He kicked the door closed with the heel of his sneaker, and began removing his clothes.

She got on her knees and crawled over to the edge of the bed and unzipped his chinos while he unbuttoned his Henley. Before his shirt hit the floor his penis was in her mouth. He let her play for a while, then pulled out of her mouth and climbed up onto the bed. He tugged her into place and placed his lips on her. She was already slick and needy. He had decided they would come together this time. This would just be a little primer.

He grabbed his cock, pinched the tip, and tugged hard to make him be able to last longer. He could have come now just from looking at her.

He licked and kissed, and sucked on her, learning what pleased her from the different noises she made and from her body arching toward his. When she began trembling, he moved up and covered her body with his.

When he entered her they both sighed. It was bliss. They enjoyed a moment to acclimate their bodies, to absorb the pleasure and feel each nuance of their bodies joining. Then complete and total abandonment followed.

He thrust hard into her as she welcomed each stabbing plunge, arching up to meet him with equal fervor, her arms wrapped under his to grip his shoulders for leverage. When he was close, he shoved his fingers between them and stroked her clit with his thumb. She keened . . . he grunted . . . she whimpered . . . he roared, and then they held as tight to each other as their gripping hands on each others hips could, as wave after wave coursed through them.

He felt her shudder, tremble and heard her moan, "Brr-eee—nnt!" She felt his body go rigid, felt the pulsing deep inside her core, and heard his low groan.

Had she never been with a man before she would have worried, because he sounded as if he was in horrible pain. She knew that he was not.

He stayed on top of her feeling the aftershocks for a long time. Then like a love-sotted doofus, he willed every drop of semen to find its way through her channel; beseeched every single sperm to seek out and finagle its way into an egg. He had never felt so manly before—or so essential. So determined to give this woman what she desired so fervently. In a usually closed off corner of his mind he thought of his mother. And how it would please her to no end to have a grandbaby to dote on. He was at a time in his life that he could please everyone, including himself, if he welcomed a son or daughter into his lineage.

He fell off to the side after a few moments, or maybe he'd slept and she'd pushed him off. He wasn't certain. But they managed to make love again a few minutes later. While still on their sides, whispering naughty things, and caressing every body part that they could reach while still joined—and always kissing, nibbling, or licking on something—her neck, his chest, her ears, his chest, anything they could get to without uncoupling. She came hard when he reached down between them and stroked her clit with his middle finger while tugging gently on her nipples with his teeth and lips. He came when she stroked his balls and rimmed his puckered back opening with a tentative finger. He felt he had broken apart and every cell had collided with some part of the cosmos. He was surprised he was still intact, and in human form, when moments later, he opened his eyes to her smiling, mischievous face. After taking a few seconds to regroup, he asked, "Where did you learn that?"

"You don't want to know."

"No, you're right. I don't."

They slept. The iPhone he'd set before walking into the room earlier went off and they both opened their eyes and smiled at each other.

Like a total idiot, and the worst singer ever, Brent softly sang the opening lines from Buddy Holly's *Maybe Baby*: "Maybe baby, I'll have you. Maybe Baby, you'll be true. Maybe Baby, I'll have you for me." He kissed her on the nose. "Maybe we made a baby. When can we find out?"

She laughed. "Well, what used to take months can take only days now, but still 9, 10, or 11 at the earliest . . . it depends. But that's the soonest, I think. I have never been pregnant before this last time, but I have been worried about it once or twice before. I've only taken two tests before this last one. There was no baby either time."

"There may not be this time either. But, I'll tell you what.

I'll make the supreme sacrifice. I will keep on trying." He held his right hand up, the three middle fingers hooked in front by his thumb and baby finger. "Scout's honor. On my honor I will do my duty. And I was an Eagle Scout; we take our pledges seriously."

She laughed and scruffed up his hair.

They got up to shower, dress, make the bed, and for him—to pack.

Where normally, on the last night of a beach stay, everyone would go out for dinner, with COVID, there was no such thing as going out to dinner now. But there was delivery. So Rutger offered to order pizza as the local pizza chains were still delivering.

But Alyssa refused to let Rutger and Pauline eat inferior pizza. She said she would make a pizza. And she did. Everything from scratch, even the sauce—a pepperoni and Italian sausage with mozzarella and Parmesan Reggiano cheese on dough she let rise, kneaded, tossed, and then threw high into the air. She amazed them all with her cooking and baking skills.

"Kyle better watch out," Rutger said between bites. "He could lose his standing as Top Chef around here with you around. They were careful about the amount of wine they consumed as they all had enough experience with flying and drinking to know high altitudes and alcohol didn't bode well for the body, skin, eyes, and general mindset. And Pauline of course, didn't have any.

Chapter 96
Sex with a View

The next morning, while Brent and Alyssa were in their room having their second "baby making session," Rutger and Pauline were in their room. They had made the bed, showered and dressed. Now Pauline stood in front of the French doors that led to the balcony. She admired the view of the dunes, often catching the barest glimpse of the head of someone likely walking their dog near the water's edge.

Their room was on the main level. It didn't have the vast, high-up views of the dunes and the beach like those on the next level did, but from their vantage point, they could still see all the way to the ocean.

The foreground of beach was hard to see in some places because the swallow of the dunes was so broad, and the abundant grasses and bushes that comprised the swallow were so tall. But the view from the shoreline to the shrimp boats out in the distance was unobstructed and they could see the glints from the morning rays of sunshine on the water.

Still, from this far away, it was hard to see anyone on the beach clearly without binoculars or field glasses. It was not possible for someone on the beach to make out the two of them inside the room without some optical help either.

But that was not likely what Pauline was thinking about. Having been naked and exposed in varying poses in many salons all over the world, where many men and women were in attendance, she was no longer shy about her body. She was likely to be sad about leaving *The Cockpit* and Sunset Beach—just as he was.

Rutger came from behind and wrapped his arms around her waist. She often wore athletic clothes when flying as she found them both comfortable and convenient for quick bathroom breaks and for allowing her to be agile in her clothing so she could step over the piles of sports equipment they often ferried back and forth for the various marathons and competitions. Although this plane was a small business jet, it would have plenty of room to maneuver around in.

Rutger's hands caressed her tummy over the smooth material and then they found their way under the stretchy waistband. He caressed her lower belly, wondering exactly where her uterus was. If he gave her a baby one day, where would it begin to grow after traversing the birth canal and journeying through a fallopian tube—exactly where would it grow for nine months? He was not conscious of how his probing actions were so very different from his usual *let's turn her* on actions.

"You planning on doing a gynecological exam?' she asked.

"Mmmm, maybe."

"What *are* you doing?"

"Trying to figure out where things are."

"You should know where every inch of me is by now. You've either kissed it, licked it, shown it off, or covered it with marshmallow fluff or chocolate syrup."

He chuckled. "Yeah," he said, remembering her reaction when he'd unpacked his sex toy bag and produced a jumbo jar of hip-o-lite on their first trip.

He changed his tactics and reached under her sports top and lifted the bra band over her tits, displaying her for anyone who happened to be on the beach or on a boat out on the ocean—with a pair of high-powered binoculars. Neither of them would have cared.

With one hand passively spanning her midriff, and the other toying with her nipples, he began alternately French kissing and blowing hot air into her ear.

No one could see, he knew they were too far away, but still, he gave her every impression that they could. Her body was so beautiful that they mostly definitely would look. She was some pretty hot stuff without her clothes on. He told her this all the time. It was one of the jobs of a Dom to continually build up his sub by telling her how desirable she was—not just to him—but also to everyone who saw her.

His words of flattery, now crooned into her ear were setting them both on fire. "Your sweet tits are amazing, the nipples the tastiest I have ever sucked Fluff off of."

She smelled good, too—spicy and flowery all at once. He could never get enough of her essential essence. Blended with her trademark rose scent, it made him lightheaded and content, in a way that no other woman ever had. He was able to totally relax with her. She inspired him with her many great ideas. Because he loved her so much, she made him desperate to please her, to seek out her pleasure before his. Her coming, always made him come even harder. Since humiliation was her kink, and he'd had to learn what it took to please her, he basked in what he'd accomplished. But from the very beginning, it had been her willingness to obey him and her desire to please him in all ways that had made them the perfect couple. Now the words to shame her came to him easily, as his ultimate aim was to gratify her, and to feel her come apart in his arms.

"There's a surfer walking up to the dune line. He stops and drops his surfboard when he spots you framed in the window. His smile is huge, his eyes bright with delight at seeing you half naked, your head thrown back as passion washes over you. He's admiring you, his eyes taking in every bit of exposed skin. He's taking in these sweet beauties and imagining his fingers tugging on your tight, long nipples. Licking them, lightly biting them, drawing them into his mouth and sucking on them, hard—the way you like."

She moaned and slumped forward. He had to pull her back into his groin to keep her from bashing her head into the glass. Her body was pressed into his hardness. He began stroking his cock along the crack of her ass.

Inching her out of her workout capris and pulling them down until he could cup her sex and slide a finger inside her, he groaned from finding her so damned ready. Oh she was wet, so wet. He'd never known a woman who could get this slick with just his fingers—or just his words.

"He's picturing you on all fours, your beautiful ass accepting his long, thick prick while his fingers work your pussy."

She moaned and moved into his hand forcing his fingers deeper.

"He's putting his hand down into his swim trunks now, gripping his member and jerking off at the sight of you."

Rutger stripped her clothes off until she was naked against the glass. Then he lowered his zipper, bent his knees, and rubbed his penis between her legs and along her slit, coating himself with her moisture. He positioned the tip at her tight puckered opening. He slowly forced his way in, just the tiniest bit. That's all she really needed sometimes, just the naughtiness of him being there, while his fingers did the magic, stroking and tapping on her clit.

"Oooh," she cried as he used the glass to support him so he could press his fingers more firmly against her slick hairless mons, while his penis was wedged further up into her ass. She cried out and hissed, as she slumped against the glass, threatening to dislodge him where he was impaling her. He noted that there was too much friction, not enough glide, so he withdrew. Using a small Grab and Go packet he took from his pants pocket, he applied a generous amount of virgin coconut oil on the tip of his penis and along the hard length. Then flexing his knees again and pushing down on her lower back, he reentered her. For all of ten seconds he withdrew in increments and then shoved back in a bit further. Then he came inside her ass like it was the first time. It always felt like the first time with her.

He knew that she needed that ultimate shame of a man coming in her dark, secret place, before she herself could come.

It had been the hardest thing for him to relearn—to come before his sub did. Yet it worked every time. He felt her vagina clench around him. The middle finger of one hand was still toying with her clit. His other hand was gripping her hip to keep her from falling to the floor between his spread legs. Her knees tended to give out just when she needed them the most, so he was always firmly supporting her body with his.

As orgasms went, this was the pinnacle—the peak lovers strived to reach and then fall headlong into. Very nearly achieving nirvana together, with both pleasuring each other and taking them to the ultimate height and breadth of sensation one could attain, they were made one.

He steadied his stance so he could hold her just as they were for as long as possible. One hand was cupping her womanhood, the other gripping under her breast and strolling the nipple, his penis still buried deep in her ass, both of them staring out to sea . . . each coming out of their own fantasy of the event. Hers, he knew, was being watched. His, was completely owning a woman, every part of her, so much so that she would do anything he said—at any time—in front of anyone. This was how they were. And he thought they were perfect together . . . a master and his sex slave. A man and a woman so in tune with each other, with their bodies . . . and now, with their hearts.

He realized he was at an all-time highpoint in his life with this woman. The love he had for her washed over him as she quaked with the late spasms running through her body. Using his inborn strength, he drew them both up until they were standing again, her back to his front.

"Rutger, Rutger, Rutger," she whispered, her head thrown back and tucked into the side of his neck. He could feel her lips moving and the breath leaving her body as she mouthed the words over and over again.

He smiled and continued the narrative he had started at their onset, "The man came in his hand, while I came deep inside you," he whispered back. "We are both so in love with you."

She smiled and looked up at him. Their eyes met. "This girl is in love with you both. You make a really good team."

He smiled. "I like this fake exhibitionism. I get to get you off without really showing you off."

"I thought you liked showing me off."

"I did," he said.

"Did?" she asked, confusion on her face.

He separated from her, and then walked her backward until he was able to sit in the oversized leather chair by the window. He pulled her onto his lap and wrapped his arms around her. Then he told her about the man and woman he had seen in the park and how it had affected him, ending with, "So, I think I don't want to share you anymore—that I just want you all to myself. How do you feel about that?"

She looked up into his face, registering the seriousness of his expression, the certainty in his eyes.

"Well, I'm fine with that. But I thought you were into it, that I pleased you by letting you show me off."

"Oh you did, you absolutely did. But things change in a relationship. You're not just a sub doing my bidding any more. You're my woman. You are mine. And I want you to be *all* mine." He ran a finger down her nose, took in her own serious expression. "Is that okay?"

She gave him a happy grin. "Well, of course that's okay. I live to please you. If it pleases you to keep me all to yourself, then I've done my job."

"Your job?"

"Yes. The job of a sub is to please her master in all things. I will continue to do whatever pleases you. And I am one lucky sub, because that's exactly what gets me off . . . making you happy. Whether I'm naked in front of others or just naked in front you, I'm the luckiest sub in the world because I love you, and I know that you will take care of me."

He held her jaw and kissed her deeply. "And I always will."

He stood with her still in the circle of his arms. "I'm going to wash you now and then watch while you get dressed again. That will have to do for me until we get settled in Germany. You've got a plane to fly and I think I've held up the pilot long enough."

She laughed. "That's one of the things I like about flying my own plane. Everything's to my schedule."

"I have to admit, it's a great perk to have a pilot as my submissive." In his mind, he substituted the word fiancé. He could not wait to get his grandmother's ring and put it on her finger.

He walked her into the walk-in shower, then took her hand and kissed the back of it while stroking her ring finger. Soon—soon, she would be his wife—and his submissive for all time. Although, he was beginning to think he was outgrowing the D/s kink in favor of a more traditional relationship. He hoped Pauline wouldn't miss the lifestyle when they began backing off.

After soaping her up, he took the rain head off the wall and rinsed her thoroughly, taking care not to get her hair wet, as he knew she had already washed and styled it. When she stepped out, he hurriedly washed himself so he could get out to towel her dry. He would never tire of doing things for her.

She might be his sub, and therefore submissive to his needs, but he was her Dom and his needs were to take care of her. For as long as he lived, he would cherish her. And make sure he fulfilled every sexual need she had.

And just now, they had both agreed that no one would be watching anymore. He squared his shoulders. It was ludicrous, but now he felt like an adult. He was leaving his old ways behind so he could become a proper husband. He liked the feeling.

They were all on the bottom landing at noon when the Lyft driver pulled around the circle drive. While he got out of the car and loaded the luggage, Brent went over the checklist with

Rutger a final time.

Satisfied everything was locked, secured, timers set, and all appliances and water connections turned off, they masked up and piled into the SUV limo and headed to the Myrtle Beach Airport.

Alyssa was excited about seeing her family. Pauline was excited about the new plane she would be flying, and Rutger was excited about presenting his grandmother's ring to the sub he was so madly in love with. Brent was excited about seeing Alyssa happy at home, possibly with his child. He kept chiding her that maybe there would five passengers onboard the plane. Brent was also eager to see his good friend Palo, who it seemed from his most recent calls, could use some cheering up.

Chapter 97
Being Flown to Germany

The long plane trip to Germany, the train trip into Florence, and the hired car ride to Impruneta to Alyssa's family villa, were all tiresome but uneventful. Pauline was a dedicated and intent pilot, rarely speaking except to point out something or to ask Rutger to get her something. Twice she put the plane on autopilot to use the restroom, leaving Rutger in charge. He didn't have his pilot's license, but Pauline had been teaching him how to use the controls for quite some time. She felt safe going to the potty with autopilot on.

In the airports and in the train and bus stations, Brent became increasingly annoyed at all the people wearing their masks improperly. He was constantly pointing out each person who was wearing their mask under their nose by jabbing his finger into a friend's side and saying in a loud, carrying voice, "Wearing a mask under your nose is like putting a condom over your balls instead of your penis!"

Of course, he was purposefully, saying this loud enough for the violator to hear him. It was interesting watching the reactions he got. Most just pulled their masks up, but not without smirking at him first. A few told him to mind his own business and called out a couple of choice curse words. Some ignored him. One, actually thanked him saying, "I hadn't thought about it like that."

She laughed each time at his exasperation as he saw yet another "improperly worn condom," as he called it. It was so like Brent to notice these things, and she had a feeling that it was also so *unlike* him to comment on it to strangers. But that showed that he cared. And of course, she already knew that he was a stickler for the rules.

That was how Brent knew she loved him. She didn't have

to say it, but she showed it in so many caring ways. He would have loved to hear her say it though, or have her show him some affection in public. But that wasn't likely as he was discovering that she was shy around strangers. He'd had no way of knowing that until now.

It was something that surprised him initially, knowing that her job was to deal with people from all over the world. When he asked her about it, she explained it away, saying, "I meet them all by email weeks before they arrive, and we become, how you say . . . pen pals. We are very good friends when we finally meet. Then I lead them on many tours and I am their *best* friend."

It had been a long, tiring trip, but finally they were getting out of the private car and collecting their bags after the last leg of their journey. In a few minutes it would be time to tell Palo that he was sleeping with his sister. He was not looking forward to that chummy talk. But it sure wouldn't be now, as everyone was running out of the stone farm house's heavy double doors and latching on to Alyssa, her mama hugging her tight to her chest and then her brother lifting her by her underarms and holding her high in the air and spinning her around in tiny circles while he grinned up at her. Then it was her mama's turn again. She patted Alyssa's cheeks and stroked her hair, swiping at her nose with a lace handkerchief as her eyes filled with tears that spilled down her wrinkled face. Then all her relatives joined in and the workers sidled up to greet her. Everyone was speaking rapid-fire Italian and crying, except for Palo and Trixie, who were standing off to the side, her smiling, and him beaming with joy.

Clearly, this woman that he loved was loved by many others. He wasn't jealous, but he did experience a possessiveness that surprised him. He had never understood people who tattooed their skin with the names of their lovers, but now he wanted his name inked on her in a prominent place where everyone would see it.

Hmmmm, he thought. This must be what the wedding band was all about, a form of branding. He vowed right then and there that he would find the widest wedding band possible that would fit her little finger. Dear God, he was going to propose marriage to this woman. She had managed to thoroughly bewitch him.

Was he put out about that? Concerned it was too soon? Hell no! He was anxious to bind her to him—to show the world that this beautiful, spirited woman was his. Then a thought occurred to him. Would she *want* to be just his? For all time? It scared him that she might say no, that now that she was home, she might want to stay here.

Chapter 98
Brent's First Morning at the Villa

On the morning after they arrived at *Villa Stelle Cadente*—the country house of the shooting stars—Brent, unable to sleep, answered a knock on the kitchen door. A stone pathway led around the house to the back where there was a large terrace for entertaining. The kitchen was on the backside of the house and that seemed to be the door everyone went in and out of. In the short time he'd been there he'd noted that no one came through the ornate front door at the end of a large double arched entranceway, which was a shame as the inlaid stonework was amazing. The front entrance had been built with materials that were meant to last for centuries, yet it never seemed to have any traffic, whereas the hand-hewn wooden kitchen flooring was showing the abuse it took instead. During daylight hours, someone was constantly going in or out.

He sighed at the perfidy of homeowners. What had no doubt once been the grand entrance to a magnificent estate, with a large bailey capable of handling the hooves of horses with little damage, was no longer even being used. Instead, for the sake of convenience, the homeowners were allowing major scaring and deep gouging in the wood planking and cracks in the tile work of its ancient kitchen by letting it become the everyday thoroughfare instead. Brent was in a bad mood, seeing Palo's family home deteriorating by senseless neglect, and he was very tired. So when he opened the door to a tall man holding a bouquet of flowers, reeking of too much cologne, who had a lot of black hair that was being forced to stand on end with overdone hair gel, he was not at all receptive.

The man faltered, not recognizing Brent. Unable to place him, he took a breath and called out in a booming voice, "I hear

Alyssa is home. I am the baby's father. I am Giancarlo." He shoved his hand forward as if to shake Brent's.

Through no conscious effort on his part, Brent's fist connected with the man's jaw. Then he slammed the door shut before the man fell to the ground, the flowers arcing high into the air.

Brent hadn't understood what the man had said as it had all been in Italian. When he'd picked out the words *bambino* and the name *Giancarlo* his fist had flew out and struck the man's face. Like a spring, wound too tight then triggered, he couldn't have stopped it. He wouldn't have wanted to even if he could have.

Palo had just come down a small staircase built into the corner, ducking his head at the last second to avoid rapping his head on a beam at the bottom. It appeared to be a well-practiced move. "Who was that?"

"A no-count lowlife."

"Giancarlo, then."

"I don't want him to see her. Ever."

Palo squinted his eyes in confusion as he looked at him askance.

"Noted. I'll take care of it." He took his phone from his back pocket, turned away, and rattled off a series of commands in rapid-fire Italian. Replacing his phone, he turned back and said simply, "Done."

Trixie clomped down the narrow, steeply curved steps, taking them one at a time. There was no need for her to duck her head. Despite her tall heels, she cleared the beam by several inches.

When she made it to the bottom she turned and saw them staring at her. "What? You never saw a woman come down a staircase?"

They both laughed. Palo took her by the elbow, leaned in and gave her a kiss. "I suppose if I had to come down those steps in those platform shoes, I'd be making more racket than that."

"Speaking of racket, did I hear the kitchen door slam?"

"You did," Palo said and gave her another kiss. Then he broke off and said. "Go out the front door. The back one's got an issue right now."

"Everything in this house has an issue," Trixie said, "How has your mom managed to live here all these years?"

"She's not one to complain. Thank the Lord for that." Palo took her by the arm and led her through the house to the front door.

Chapter 99
Someone's Panties Found in the Orchard

The week they stayed at the villa, Alyssa kept busy. She worked on her blog, spent time cooking with her mom, and walked the grounds of the villa with Brent, showing him everything her father and grandfather had built and all the vineyards, orchards, and fields of vegetables they had planted.

One night after dinner, Brent found her in a utility room off the garage doing the household laundry. There were two commercial washers and dryers on the back wall and she was busy filling them.

He leaned on the doorframe watching Alyssa sort and flip clothes into machines, press buttons, and tip detergent at the speed of light. He also admired her butt as she bent over the baskets to retrieve more items.

"Wow, you *do* have a system for doing laundry."

She turned to him and frowned, "Well . . . I kind of have to."

He quirked a brow as if questioning that comment.

"It's expected that I will do the laundry when I'm at home. Always has been."

Hands in his pockets, he sauntered over to her. "So, here I am, your Prince Charming, to take you away from all this." He moved his hand in a circle indicating the little cinderblock room.

"Unless you had your own valet as a stowaway on the plane and then traveling with us in the transport van, there is no taking me away from this chore. Mama wears three outfits a day, Palo at least two, and don't get me started on Trixie's filthy scrubs. They require two pre-soaks."

"Who does this when you are not here?"

"I do not know. I only know that whoever there are, they

disappear when I show up. There was a big pile waiting for me."

He wrapped her up in his arms. "I'll help you. And then tonight, we'll both sleep naked to save laundry.'

She ran her finger down alongside his chin. "You know I cannot sleep in your bed in my Mama's house."

"Okay, I'll sleep in yours."

"Palo will not allow that."

"What if we call a priest to marry us while we're here?"

She pushed against his chest with both hands and stepped back to look up into his face. Her eyes were wide, her brows lifted in perfect crescents. "Really? You would do that?"

"Of course. To sleep with you . . . I would climb every mountain, ford every stream, folll-low ev'ry rainbow—"

"Until you fiiind your dreaaaam!" she finished for him.

Palo, now standing in the doorway, chuckled, "We're singing songs from *The Sound of Music* now?

Alyssa spun around, "Palo! Brent wants to have a priest marry us while we're here!"

"While you're here? Were you planning on leaving with him?"

Except for the sound of a dryer running there was complete silence in the room.

"I thought you understood. We love each other."

Palo looked over at Brent, one eyebrow lifted in defiance. "So now you are stealing my sister away from us? Is that it?"

"What can I say, Palo? We fell in love. Just as you and Trixie did."

"Mama will not like this."

"Neither of you liked Giancarlo . . ." Alyssa said in a hushed voice.

"Yeah, well . . . he wasn't moving you to America."

"I love Brent. I want to be where he is. His job is in New York, so he has to go back there."

Palo walked over and pulled her into his arms. He was so tall, and she so petite, that their height difference was comical.

"I know you do," he whispered. "I have known it for quite some time actually. You never were able to hide things from me."

"So, can you get a priest to come to the house, what with the COVID?"

Palo sighed long and deep. "I believe the priest who married Trixie and me would do the honors here at the house. But there can be no guests. We cannot take a chance with Mama."

She smiled up at him. "I understand. Thank you, Palo."

Palo looked over at Brent, his uplifted brows expressing the fact that he had many unanswered questions.

Brent walked over and offered his hand to Palo. "I do love her Palo. More than I ever thought I could love anyone or anything. She is my everything. I promise, I will take good care of her. She will want for nothing."

"I do not want you to spoil her. Papa and Mama had a good marriage because they had to work hard for everything they had. I want that for her as well. Things that come easy fall by the wayside easy. Promise me you won't spoil her."

Brent laughed as Palo reached for his hand. "Do you know your sister? She never stops. She is always doing something for others . . . helping someone . . . making food or masks or quilts or something for some organization."

"Well . . . keep her that way. I do not want her back if she has lost her lovable heart."

"Trust me, you will not get her back. She is mine."

"Well then, you two go tell Mama. I will call the church and beg the priest."

"I am happy to make a contribution . . ." Brent said.

"That was a given. Ally, after you talk to Mama, call your friend at the courthouse. You'll need a license."

She stood on her tiptoes and kissed Palo's cheek. "Thank you."

After Palo left to call the priest, and Alyssa and Brent had spoken to Mama, Alyssa tried to coax Brent to follow her into the orchard for what she called some "alone time" away from

Mama's watchful eyes.

"Can't right now," he said as he walked up behind her, pulled her hair to the side and kissed her on the side of her neck. "I'll have to catch you another time. But, tag. You're it. You'll have to find me later, maybe steal into my room."

"Why not now?" she asked with a pout.

"Your brother just texted, he's waiting for me at the tree house."

"What for?"

"He wants to know if there's any way a room can be added to it?"

"Why?"

"It seems they will be in need of a nursery soon."

Her mouth gaped open and her eyes widened. Then she began screaming, "Yaaaayyy! I'm going to be an aunt!"

He had to cover her mouth to stop her. "Shhh, they don't want anyone to know yet. I shouldn't even have told you. You know how things can go . . . they want to wait before telling Mama."

She nodded; she did know how things could go. "You have your meeting. I will go find some gelato and go to the orchard by myself."

He swatted her on the butt as she turned to leave, "I'll expect to see you later . . . naked, in my bed. But be quiet. There is nothing wrong with your Mama's hearing."

"I know. I never could get away with anything around here."

He looked at this watch. "You know, I don't trust you to be quiet. You never come quietly. I'll tell you what, meet me in the orchard by that gnarly old tree you showed me in half an hour."

"You're on."

Thirty minutes later she was moaning into his neck, "I hate these clothes between us. If not for them, you'd be in me by now."

He inserted his thumb into the elastic waistband of her spandex capris. Dragged them down to the tops of her thighs. Pushed hard against her hips so she'd stay up against the bark of the tree while he used both hands at her hip to tear her panties off. Then he lifted her onto his impossibly hard penis and impaled her.

She felt his jeans fall to his ankles as he entered her. Heard his long satisfied groan as he seated himself fully inside her. "This is as tight as a cork in a bottle," he whispered into her ear causing her to shiver.

"Feels so good," she hissed. "Don't leave."

He flexed his knees and was able to lower her onto him, taking himself deeper inside her. "Yes, yes," she groaned, "stay just like that."

"I can't stay like this. It's a squat with dead weight on my pelvis and knees. But feel this, I promise it will be light-years better than good when I'm finished with you."

He began bouncing her up and down, lifting her and then dropping her onto his penis, shoving tightly into her as his hands gripped tight on her ass where she was propped up against the tree.

He felt her vagina clench, then pulse, and was just able to get his mouth over hers in time to swallow her scream. He followed her out into the universe, his jaw hard as he clenched it to keep from shouting when his climax came over him.

Shuddering and still vulnerable from the passion spilling from him, he managed to keep them upright, but just barely.

The next morning Palo tossed Brent a paper bag that hit him square in the face as he said, "I found these in the orchard this morning." He didn't have to ask what was in the bag.

They had searched in the dark but could not find the panties he had torn from her and tossed aside.

"It is a good thing you are getting married, or I would be beating you up right about now."

Brent opened the bag and looked inside. Yup. Peach-colored and torn at the side. "It's a good thing we're getting married period. I tell you, Palo, she caught me off guard. I didn't mean to fall for her. But I fell hard. I cannot live without that woman in my life."

Palo nodded. "I know the feeling. I have to check the olive press. Come with me and we can discuss the plans you drew for me."

"Sure. Give me a tour of the homestead. I would love to see how you manage all this and the tour business too."

"I have a lot help—good help. But now you're taking away my best tour guide."

"Well . . . you're not doing any tours now. The airlines are nowhere near close to being up and running again."

"By the time they are, she'll be pregnant."

"God willing."

"Mama had four miscarriages before delivering me. Be careful with her and watch her closely. She's already had one."

"Trust me. The moment I know she's with child, she'll have a team of doctors. I will take care of her, Palo."

"See that you do."

"She is my life. You have no worries there."

Chapter 100
Married & Stateside

They were married two days later, and back home at *The Cockpit* a week later. Every day they walked on the beach. Toward the end of the summer season they were able to watch a turtle nest "boil." There were not many nests this year.

And every day, they worked on making a baby—some days, more than once. Brent's hospital project was set for groundbreaking in a few weeks so they were planning to move back to his New York apartment so he could be on hand to oversee the project.

The day they were packing up Brent's SUV for the trip back, Alyssa took her COVID calendar off the wall. It was where she kept track of the things she hoped to accomplish each day. It was also where she charted her periods. Hers was late—significantly. She was surprised it hadn't occurred to her that it hadn't come. But then they'd been busy packing.

She had an extra test in her old bathroom, saved from the twin pack she'd ordered when she'd needed one before. Once married and back at the beach house, they had taken advantage of Brent's superior space, huge tiled-in shower, spectacular beach view and magic number bed. Every once in a while, she went down the hall and took a hot bubble bath in her "old" bathtub. She walked there now to retrieve the test.

It was too late in the day to take it now. But tomorrow before driving back to New York, they would know if there was the essence of one more person making the trip.

Brent had so much on his mind these days, what with the hospital, and the move, and his parents nagging him to plan a proper wedding reception for his family and friends to attend. They were thinking 500 guests. Brent was thinking 30. Due to

COVID they hadn't gone forward with any plans yet, but even when they could, he doubted that he and his mother would come to an agreement on anything about the reception where they would repeat their vows.

Thankfully, Alyssa was happy to stay out of it. In her mind they were already married. She was not eager to stand in front of a brunch of strangers and repeat her vows. She didn't want the fuss. But she promised that whatever was decided between the two of them, that she'd show up in something white and eat cake.

The cake was of more concern to her than anything else. It had to be a white chocolate cake with buttercream icing, with absolutely no fondant anywhere. It had to be the lightest textured white cake imaginable with only the barest hint of chocolate throughout, with a sweet raspberry coulis sandwiched between the iced layers as filling. Whenever the wedding cake was mentioned, she recited the same exact thing. It was her idea of the perfect cake. And always, she offered to make it, "Let me make it, please. I do not want anyone to be disappointed. Least of all me," she would add with a grin. She was hoping Brent and his mother could agree on less than fifty guests so the cake could be the size of a large bakery cake, and not some huge triple-tiered monstrosity. But so far, they hadn't managed to agree on anything.

Throughout the day, she noticed that she had to go to the bathroom a bit more than usual, so she was excited to take the test the next morning. She did not want to worry Brent or give him any reason to be sad for the trip, so she waited until he left for his final run on the beach before retrieving the kit and going back to the new bathroom to take it. The other bathroom still had such bad memories attached to it.

While preparing the test and then peeing on it, she prayed for a positive result. Then she went back to their bedroom, made the bed, and stared out at the ocean until the timer on her phone went off.

Taking a deep breath, she went back into the bathroom and gasped when she saw the blue line. Oh my, no more wine for her, she thought as she wrapped the test stick in a baggie to save as a memento, and stuck it between the clothing in her suitcase. Then she took a shower and got dressed. While in the shower, she decided how she would tell Brent. She was giddy with excitement, but she would not share the news until they were back in New York.

Chapter 101
The Move Back to NY and Alyssa's News

When they arrived at the door to his apartment a little after ten that night, and Brent had opened the door for them, Alyssa released the handle on her wheeled suitcase and placed her purse on the carpet in the hall instead of walking inside. "Tradition says a new bride should be carried over the threshold of her new home by her new husband for good luck."

Brent set down the bags he had been carrying. "Well then, we must garner all the good luck we can, my beautiful new bride." He bent and easily lifted her up and into his arms. As he was carrying her inside, she asked, "Do I feel heavier?"

And of course, as any good husband should, he said, "No, no, of course not."

"Well, I *should* feel heavier, for you are carrying two people now."

He looked down at her face, his brows drawing together in confusion, then his eyes popped wide open as her meaning dawned on him.

She laughed and said, "I am pregnant!"

He stumbled in through the door and nearly dropped her. He managed to get her to an armchair in the living room, where he plopped her down sideways.

His open hand smacked his forehead and his fingers raked through his hair as he tried to process the news. "Whoa, you need to slow down. We just got married for God sake," he huffed out as he ran the fingers of both hands through his hair again, making it stand on end.

"Okaaay," she said as she righted herself in the chair and blew hair out of her face. "I will slow down. How is eight months from now looking for you on your calendar?" This was her snippy voice and it rarely boded well when she used it.

He pressed his lips together then took his phone from his pocket and pretended to scroll up, down, and sideways as if checking his calendar. "That is perfect! Absolutely perfect! I will block off that day. Let's do the wedding that day, too."

She sat up straighter and sent him a wicked smile. She loved it when he got angry at her, as he rarely ever did. But it meant that soon he would be contrite, then sorry, then very amorous. "Perfect! I will only need a big white sheet to wear, you know, one of those sized-for-a-king things. And since I will be so fat, what difference will one piece of cake make? Or six or even eight?"

He drew in a deep cleansing breath, then smiled over at her. "A baby," he whispered. He said it with so much reverence that she knew the gist of their conversation was truly sinking in.

He walked over to where she sat and knelt, his hand on her knee. His eyes were moist now, his face soft and relaxed. His small smile grew into a huge one. "I'm going to be a father. It could be a son."

"It could be a daughter."

"Which do you want?" he asked.

"I do not care."

He thought for a moment. "Neither do I. We will love either."

She covered his hand with hers. "We will."

"I'm sorry that I did not take the news well initially. I have a lot on my mind. I suddenly have a wife. And many projects starting in just a few weeks. I am also very tired from the trip. And now I have to plan for a son.

"Daughter," she countered.

"When will we know?"

"Maybe in two months? I am not so sure."

"We are technically still on our honeymoon. Can we still. . ." he waved his hand between the two of them.

"Yes, until maybe the last month or so."

"Did you tell me this tonight so I would have to empty the truck by myself?"

She laughed. "No. I can help."

"Oh no you can't. I forbid it."

He eyes went wide and she sat up straighter. "Forbid?"

He knew he had made a grave error in his choice of words. "That was the wrong word."

He took a moment to regroup, "How's this? In light of your previous experience, and also your mama's history, how about you let me carry everything upstairs?"

She quirked a brow as if thinking. They both knew they had just established the pecking order. He was the boss of her where her health was concerned. Yet she would have an equal say in any decisions concerning both of them, and that of their child. She was pleased that he was willing to go to any length to safeguard the health of their child.

"I can use the freight elevator. You can push the button to hold it for me. And after I collapse on the living room floor you can fix dinner."

"You have food here?"

"Well, there may be a few things in the freezer, but what I meant was you can order carry-in."

"Deal."

"There is something wrong with this fight," he said.

"Oh?"

"Yes. Our fights are supposed end with sex."

She had to laugh at that. That was exactly what she had thought as well. "We might be too tired after moving everything up. You especially."

"You know what? It's a secure building and there's an attendant in the parking garage. I'm not going to worry about unloading the truck until tomorrow."

"Okay. I'll 'fix' dinner. Where's your carry-out file?" She knew her husband. She knew he had to have one.

"It's in the kitchen drawer by the refrigerator. It's labeled

Local Restaurants. Call Tandori Kitchen, they take forever. That way we can finish our fight. You know . . . end a fight the way it's supposed to end. In bed."

"Okay. I will need my overnight bag though, it's got my toothbrush, hairbrush, makeup remover . . . that kind of thing."

"Yeah, I'll need mine too. And I'll also get our laptops, make sure the truck is locked and put a fifty in the attendant's hand."

"What do you want from Tandori Kitchen?" she asked as she perused the menu.

"Whatever takes the longest to make. I want to see if I can wave at the baby with my tongue first."

She blinked at that statement as she heard the apartment door close. Then laughed.

She found her purse, took out her phone and requested a whole Tandori chicken done in the traditional manner in a kiln, knowing it would take at least 30 minutes to marinate, 45 to cook, and 20 to deliver.

That would give him plenty of time to "wave" at their baby.

The next day, after they had settled in, he found her a doctor, and called his parents to give his mother permission to begin planning the reception. Alyssa had already started designing a nursery on her laptop. Unbeknownst to him, she had used her phone to learn about all the newest baby products and had even picked some things out to put in her "cart" while Brent had been driving them back from North Carolina.

The following week, Brent called his team back to work and they broke ground for his hospital two months later. Then there was the biggest wedding reception Alyssa had ever been to—and it was hers! She made the cake in the chef's kitchen of his parent's country club where the event was held. No other place was open yet due to COVID. The tables were widely spaced and everyone was masked. There was music, but no dancing. She only had four pieces of cake, not the six she had told him she'd have.

Brent started working on plans for a house in the suburbs after the Christmas holiday was over. Just as spring began to turn into summer, Alyssa delivered a healthy baby boy.

Zoom videos weren't cutting it for Mama, so as soon as it was safe to fly, they took little Lucca to Italy. It was the beginning of many transcontinental flights back and forth for the little family, who welcomed a little girl two years later. Brent designed a villa on property Mama gifted them that was just a short bike ride from *Villa Stelle Cadente*. The family spent their summers in Italy at the villa, and often had frat boys and their families there as guests.

Chapter 102

Cam & Tammy
RVing to Ozark to get Grammy

COVID shut down pretty much all of Wilmington—for sure, the world of entertainment, in and around the city—the studios, the theaters, every stage of every kind. Whether it was ballet, opera, live theater, the symphony, concerts . . . everything was cancelled. Thalian Hall, The Wilson Center, Greenfield Lake Amphitheater, Amuzu, and Brunswick Little Theater—all were locked up.

All of Cam's ventures and venues were shuttered. Every project was aborted, even though most were nearing completion. They had been gearing up for the summer season. All the actors, musicians, dancers, sound people, filming crews, lighting crews, props, makeup and wardrobe crews were now under quarantine. And had been for several months. It didn't appear as if life was coming back to normal anytime soon.

But that was okay with Cam. Sure, he missed the work—it was his life. And he loved it. But COVID had given him an opportunity he would not have otherwise had—a chance to spend time with Tammy—away from others who monopolized her time.

Since he had basically kidnapped her from that strip club in Myrtle Beach, it had been a whirlwind. He'd seen that she had talent when she'd done a little dancing during the stripping episode. Afterward, when he saw that she showed real promise as a dancer, he'd seen to it that she had the best training from renowned dancers, actors, and voice instructors. She'd wowed the crowd during her first musical. Now she was a star. He'd made her one.

And while she was flitting all over the place and making every show she was in a hit, he was no longer in her circle on a daily basis. He had set her up with a place to live. But now she could afford her own apartment. He'd shown her the city. Now she knew it better than most. He had taught her enough that she could handle life on her own. And she was doing very well with that. Except for the business end. He didn't trust anyone not to take advantage of a young, aspiring actress and dancer—especially someone from as remote a place as Ozark, Missouri. He'd introduced her to his friends and colleagues, mostly singers and dancers, and they'd taken her under their wings and accepted her into their circle.

He'd found little opportunity to spend large amounts of time with her. Because he was in a position of mentor, agent, business manager, lead choreographer, and often her producer, she was his subordinate and subject to his approval and support. So he was walking a fine line here, being her friend, confidant, co-worker, and boss—and wanna-be boyfriend.

Sure, they still went out to dinner once or twice a week, or grabbed a bite here and there for lunch. But because of propriety issues, there just hadn't been the necessary time to be playful in a dreamy romantic way. He was entertaining, a great tour guide, very adept at teaching her to be more sophisticated without having her lose that special homemade charm—but he was miserable at making her fall in love with him. He was stone in love with her. Had been from that very first night. But this was a *Tammy and the Bachelor* scenario that desperately needed some ratcheting up.

He thought back to the night he had met her. So much had happened to him that night. He'd found out he wasn't gay and that girls did it for him—and this one in particular. That night he'd had a boner he'd had to hide from her and that he'd had a Dickens' of a time getting rid of later. And he'd learned he had the best frat boys ever.

He'd ditched them on the first night of their two-week

reunion and all they'd been concerned about was how was he, was he safe, and damn, all of them had thought for sure that he was gay. He'd thought so himself. Except that that hadn't worked out for him either. He'd gone from not hitting it off with girls, to not hitting it off with men, until he began to think of himself as asexual. Since neither sex had ever turned him on, he began to get frustrated and anxious about his future prospects. Would he never have a mate, or come home to a family with adorable show biz-minded kids?

COVID became the catalyst for him to spend some quality one-on-one time with Tammy when she came to his riverfront loft apartment to talk to him one evening. He opened the door to a tearful young woman, trying to dab at her eyes while keeping her facemask in place.

He immediately drew her under his arm and led her into the living room. "Oh no it is your grandmother?"

"Yes," she sobbed. "She's all alone. She can't get any food delivered. There's no one coming to chop wood for her anymore. And she needs it to keep the house warm and to cook. And the well's froze up again." She waved a piece of paper at him that she took from her pocket. "I just got this in the mail."

He sat her down on the sofa and took the letter from her. Then paced the room as he read it.

Tamara

I needs yore help Hole town is leevin Ain't got no food no mor not for Maybell and others nor chickens niehter I's not broke but there es no way to get anyting here to the farm can you come hom

Grammy

"Who are Maybell and others?"

"Her milking cows. She had twenty, but she's only got three now. She sells milk and eggs to the locals. But with COVID, I doubt that anyone is going out to the farm to buy any."

"Well, let's go," he said. "How soon can you get packed?"

"How are we going to get there? I checked, I can't get a flight."

"I have an RV stored at Willow Tree Campground. It's about an hour and a half from here. We'll go get it and then we'll drive to Springfield. That's where you're from, right?"

"It's a little city just outside there. It's called Ozark."

"You go back to your place and pack what you need and I'll get some stuff together here and call the campground to get the RV ready. We can be on the road by three or four o'clock."

"You would do that? Drop everything and leave right now?"

She was still swiping at her eyes, her eyeliner and mascara horribly ruined. But she still looked beautiful to him.

"Well, of course! Anything that concerns you concerns me."

"Well, thank you! This means a lot. I just don't know what to do. I only knew to come here."

He wrapped an arm around her shoulder and walked her to the door. "You did that right thing. Don't worry; we're going to take care of her. Just hurry and get some clothes together—warm ones. I'll gather up some food. Anything else we'll need is already in the RV."

"Okay, I'll go pack. I wish I could call her, but she doesn't have a phone." She started cry again.

"It'll be okay," he said as he drew her close and shoulder hugged her. "Once we're on the road, I'll call the local authorities in the town where she lives. Surely, someone there can help out until we can get there."

"I checked my phone. It's been snowing real hard there."

"It'll be okay. I have a 4-wheel drive truck. We'll get there. Just go pack. I'll be over in an hour to get you."

"Okay."

She leaned over, and standing on her tiptoes she reached up to kiss him on the cheek. "Thank you. I don't know what I'd do without you."

He squeezed her hand. "Hopefully, you won't ever have to find out."

Three hours later, Cam's fifth–wheel camper, a monstrous Outback, was hooked up to his heavy-duty F350 extended cab pickup truck. He set the navigation system to Ozark, Missouri and they were on their way, heading west. The trip would be a little over a thousand miles—16 hours with no stops. It would take them 2-3 days to get there, depending on the weather and the availability of gas.

He looked over at her as they drove along Old Buck Creek Road to Camp Swamp Road toward Highway 9. The huge leather passenger seat dwarfed her. Her elbow was resting on the console and she was gnawing at the cuticle on her thumb. She looked scared and anxious, rocking back and forth a bit as if trying to urge the truck to go faster, when he was already ten miles over the limit.

But he was excited and up for the challenge of this road trip. This little adventure to her hometown might just be the thing to bring them closer—get them to know one another better. Out on the road, away from the city and their jobs they could be themselves, not a big time producer and one of his dancers. Whether staying in RV campgrounds or dry camping in the wilderness, they would get a chance to interact with each other as equal partners sharing a common goal—to get *Grammy*.

Although, he had a secondary agenda—or in his mind, maybe it was the primary one, and Grammy was the ancillary one. Regardless, he was going to see if he could get Tammy to fall in love with him.

He had a lot more ahead of him than just driving and setting up and tearing down campsites. He had to do it all with grace and humor, and look rakish and sexy while he was at it.

Meanwhile he had to distract her or he'd be in love with a woman with no left thumb. "So tell me about Ozark, how many people live there?"

"About 2,200, give or take. But I understand that a lot of old timers and their families are pullin' out now. An old mining town is not the place everyone wants to be right now. They're using COVID as an excuse to walk away from the rural farms and the towns that are all shutdown to go the larger cities on the east coast."

"Hmmm. Ironically, just where we're leaving."

"I'm worried she won't come back with us."

"Well, it's her home. It's all she's known."

"Yeah. But it's a hard life. Always has been for her. And now that she's all on her own . . . she's not going to be able to manage. It's a lot of work milking cows and caring for chickens. And now that no one is coming out to get milk or eggs . . . she's going to be broke soon if she isn't already." She started crying again.

"Tell me about the good times. What was it like growing up and having all those women in your family teaching you to dance?"

She turned her head to face him and smiled. "It was grand. We had such a good time. I loved it all."

"Then tell about it. I want to hear the good stuff."

She talked for an hour steady, making him laugh while she laughed. Then she fell asleep, her head on the headrest as if she was just looking out the window. By maneuvering the electric side mirror he was able to see her lids resting on smooth cheeks, the lashes catching the shadows of the passing trees as the sun glinted through the window on its way down behind a thick forest of pines and loblollies.

It would be hours before they had to stop, as his tank was full. He turned on some soft jazz and settled into the drive.

The story of Cam & Tammy is next.

My husband and I lost our RV in the tornado that took three lives and devastated our local community of Ocean Ridge Plantation in February of 2020. It's been hard to do the research for this story without it. But we hope to get another one soon so I can give Cam the happily-ever-after he deserves.

Look for updates on my website:
www.jacquelinedegroot.com

The Kindred Spirit Mailbox and How it Came to Be

Once upon a time, there was a woman named Claudia who loved walking the tide line of Sunset Beach. She was young and beautiful and resembled a young Ava Gardner. She lived in Hope Mills, NC, which is near Fayetteville, and worked as a kindergarten teacher. She was single, but hopeful of finding a husband and having children one day. It was a great joy for her to be able to travel to the beach on weekends. She was an artist and a musician and a happy-go-lucky, free-spirited woman who loved nature and thought everyone a kind soul. She wore a Carnaby Street-styled hat to protect her head from the sun and had a canoe named *Moses* she hid in the marshes to use when she visited the beach. She was adventurous and was once known to have climbed the extremely tall crane left empty on weekends when workers were installing the huge rocks for the jetty at the Little River Inlet, a few hundred yards past the mailbox. She sat at the top of the crane and took panoramic pictures—one by one, for a 360 panoramic view. Frank Nesmith kept the roll of pictures curled in a coil at the bottom of a tin bucket until he died a few years ago.

For many years Claudia had a daydream while walking the tideline—she saw a rural mailbox shimmering in a sandbar. She called the dream a "mirage," as she could never reach the mailbox stuck in the sand. It would disappear before she got to it. She continued to wonder why she saw the mailbox mirage. Finally, in her thirties, she gathered a mailbox mounted on a post, along with a posthole digger, and she trekked down to the beach to the east end of Sunset Beach toward Tubbs Inlet, and a sandbar she had admired and stared at fairly often.

Later, when she had difficulty getting the mailbox to remain embedded in the sand, she turned and there was Frank Nesmith. Another Kindred Spirit. A man who she would come to love and a man who would help her fulfill the purpose of her mirage—to secure Bird Island as the beautiful coastal reserve it is today, and will be, for future generations.

* Note: This is not the location where The Mailbox is currently located, just where it was for its first years. It is now on the west end, about an hour's walk past the 40th Street Access. It's actually in SC.

Chicken Bog!

A southern recipe that will warm your innards during the bleak mid-winter, or anytime, really. It is so good that there is a Chicken Bog Festival in Loris, NC where cooks vie for the honor of being selected for the Best Bog. Seriously, check it out—Loris Bog-off Festival. This recipe is from my good friend Jeff Carter, who did make it during the melancholies of winter, and it was the only thing we looked forward to while slogging our way toward spring. He made it outside over a propane burner in a cast iron Dutch oven hung on a tripod, so it is highly adaptable to camping.

1 gallon of water
1 yellow onion diced
1 whole chicken cup up
2 lbs. kielbasa sausage—sliced about _" thick
4 cups yellow rice mix—we use Mahatma

Boil water. Add chicken pieces. Cook for one hour. Remove the chicken to a cutting board and let cool. Meanwhile, brown the kielbasa slices (Jeff omitted the browning part so you can too, but we like it browned better). After the chicken has cooled a bit, debone and remove the skin, then return the meat to the pot (Jeff's fingers were so calloused from being a carpenter that he was able to do this right over the pot). Add the sliced kielbasa (Jeff sliced the sausage over the pot as well, with a very sharp hunting knife, occasionally snagging a piece with his teeth). Add the rice package and cook until the rice is done. Salt and pepper as needed. Mmmm, good!